THE DARK LORD'S GUIDE TO HONEYMOONING (AND OTHER ACTS OF TYRANNY)

ALSO BY
TIFFANY HUNT

Guides to Villainy and Love:

The Dark Lord's Guide to Dating (and Other War Crimes)

GUIDES TO VILLAINY AND LOVE

BOOK TWO

THE DARK LORD'S GUIDE TO HONEYMOONING

(AND OTHER ACTS OF TYRANNY)

TIFFANY HUNT

SCARLETT PRESS

SIMON & SCHUSTER

London New York Amsterdam/Antwerp Sydney/Melbourne Toronto New Delhi

First published in Great Britain in 2026 by Scarlett Press,
an imprint of Simon & Schuster UK Ltd

Cover designed by Greg Stadnyk

1 3 5 7 9 10 8 6 4 2

Simon & Schuster UK Ltd
7th Floor, 199 Bishopsgate,
London EC2M 3TY

www.simonandschuster.co.uk
www.simonandschuster.com.au
www.simonandschuster.co.in

The authorised representative in the EEA is Simon & Schuster Netherlands BV, Herculesplein 96, 3584 AA Utrecht, Netherlands. info@simonandschuster.nl

Simon & Schuster Australia, Sydney
Simon & Schuster India, New Delhi

A CIP catalogue record for this book
is available from the British Library.

PB ISBN 978-1-3985-5905-9
eBook ISBN 978-1-3985-5912-7

Printed and Bound in the UK using 100% Renewable Electricity
at CPI Group (UK) Ltd

FSC www.fsc.org
MIX
Paper | Supporting responsible forestry
FSC® C013604

For those who bloomed in the dark—
sharp-tongued, softhearted, and
"unmanageable."
You were never too much.
They were just too little.

1

March into Enemy Territory

(It's Not Conquest If You Don't Enjoy It)

Kazimir

The first sign that things weren't going to plan was the lack of screaming.

I surveyed the abandoned village with mounting irritation. This wasn't how conquering was supposed to go. The buildings stood empty, doors creaking on their hinges, no livestock to scatter. Some structures had been torched down to blackened husks, while others had merely been toppled.

"Not exactly the glorious conquest I'd envisioned." I guided my horse into the village square, where even the well had been destroyed. The ring of stones had been broken and tossed in, with a stench that suggested something had been left down there to rot. "Years of plotting my dramatic entrance into Solandris, and there's no one here to tremble."

Arabella rode up beside me, sunlight catching the golden braid draped over her shoulder and warming her fair, freckled complexion. She looked perfect, and far too amused for my liking.

"What did you expect?" she asked. "Peasants lining the streets to welcome their new overlord with confetti?"

"Not confetti. Terror, Arabella. Widespread, trembling terror." I gestured at the empty windows. “I wanted shrieking, tears, maybe fainting. At minimum, some panicked fleeing would have been nice.”

The empty villages were a minor disappointment in an otherwise perfectly executed opening move. Auremar’s border defenses would tell me everything I needed to know. Response times. Magical capabilities. Weak points in their formations. And if I happened to claim a strategic foothold in the process, well, that was just efficient multitasking.

I surveyed the empty square one more time, as if willing villagers to materialize just so I could terrorize them properly.

“Poor villain.” Arabella’s hazel eyes sparkled with mischief. “All dressed up for conquest with no one to conquer.”

I tried to scowl, but she was the single person allowed to laugh at me without risking dismemberment.

I had gone disgustingly soft.

“They’ve robbed me of the full villainous experience.” I sighed. “I’ll have to put it in the official complaints ledger.”

Behind us, my army marched in formation. War-hardened mercenaries, elite guard, and local forces made up the bulk, with a smattering of new recruits called into service. Weapons gleamed under the autumn sun and banners snapped in the wind. Shadow warriors drifted among the trees that flanked the road.

Thanks to the Heirloom’s newly stabilized power, and my magical bond with Arabella, summoning them no longer left me exhausted. The region’s magic no longer sent jolts of agony through my runes.

The Heirloom was now a constant thrum of power even from its secure location back at Skyspire. My bond with Arabella hummed alongside the connection, her magic intertwined with mine in ways that made us both more powerful. The sensation was intoxicating, like standing at the edge of a cliff with wings spread, knowing I could soar or destroy with equal ease.

Some might call it premature to launch an invasion before mastering the Heirloom of Dominion. Those people were cowards who’d never held a kingdom by the throat.

Yes, the artifact's full power remained frustratingly out of reach. Our attempts to channel the ley lines still ended in nosebleeds and unconsciousness more often than world-shaking displays of dominion. But that was Griffin's problem to solve. Despite his tendency to accidentally animate furniture, the enchanter was brilliant when he focused.

Besides, I'd never been the type to sit idle while my weapons were being sharpened. The Heirloom would be ready when it was ready.

Four weeks had passed since the Hero's Guild dared enter Skyspire's walls. Since Sims fell and Arabella risked everything to mend the Heirloom. Four weeks of rebuilding, rearming, and preparing for the war that was no longer a distant threat but a certainty barreling toward us.

Now we were here on Solandris's doorstep, claiming the Arvoryn Pass that cut through the mountains separating my lands from Auremar's. Tomorrow, we would take his northernmost outpost. Tonight, we'd camp just beyond this village, giving the troops rest before battle.

Auremar was gathering his own forces, pulling in allies. Given enough time, he could amass an enormous army and try to intercept me before I reached the capital of Sunspire.

I was going to crush him before he got the chance.

"You're smiling," Arabella noted as we passed a scorched barn. "Care to share, Your Supreme Darkness?"

"I could, but it's too filthy for a public setting."

She snorted. "Since when has that stopped you?"

Before I could retort, Thorne rode up and addressed me in his gravelly voice. "My lord, the scouts say the next three villages are also deserted."

Right. Scouts. Military strategy. I tried to focus on our next moves—pushing deeper into Solandris, forcing King Auremar's hand. My runes hummed with power, hungry for conquest. "Any sign of the Hero's Guild?"

"None."

That didn't shock me. After Arabella and I crushed their invasion, the remaining Hero's Guild had retreated with their tails between their legs and Auremar's forces on their heels.

"This feels too convenient," Arabella said, studying the empty buildings with narrowed eyes. "All these villages, abandoned? No resistance at all?"

"It's not a trap." I gestured to the shadow warriors gliding through the ruins, double-checking everything. "It's a strategic retreat. Auremar doesn't want to leave us any resources. No food, no shelter, no civilians to conscript. He's pulling everything back to defend what matters."

"The Golden Rose Fields," she murmured.

"And the palace." I nodded. "He's starting to believe he can't stop us in open terrain, not with the magic at our disposal. He knows something's changed and his borders no longer hinder me. So he's concentrating his forces where his own magic is strongest. Classic defensive strategy when you're outmatched. He won't sit there for long, though."

"Still." She frowned at a collapsed storefront. "I don't like it."

"You don't have to like it. You just have to trust that I know what I'm doing." I flashed her a grin. "Besides, when have I ever led you astray?"

"Do you want the list chronologically or by severity?"

A strangled yelp made me twist in the saddle. Griffin, my jittery yet brilliant enchanter, was locked in a battle of wills with his mount. A sturdy mule that seemed determined to walk sideways rather than forward. Griffin's unnaturally long limbs flailed wildly, his straw-like hair sticking up in a permanent state of electrocution that no amount of combing could tame.

"Griffin," I called, unable to hide my exasperation. "Did you never learn basic horsemanship?"

"My lord," he gasped, adjusting his new spectacles. "I'm convinced it's possessed by a minor demon."

"If that were true, it would be more cooperative." I eyed the stone tablet clutched to his chest. "And why did you bring that blasted thing out here?"

Since Sims's death, Griffin had appointed himself keeper of the Doom Scroll—a misnomer, as it was actually a stone tablet roughly the size of a dinner platter, covered in shifting lines of glowing text.

"I thought it might be useful," Griffin insisted, nearly dropping it as the mule lurched. "The tablet shows troop movements, magical disturbances, weather patterns."

"No weather reports. Tell me something useful or put it away."

A shadow passed overhead. Massive, dark wings that made my chest seize unpleasantly. But when I looked up, it was only Nyx soaring above the village. Her scales caught the light in a way that made her look . . .

"Is it my imagination, or is your dragon pink?"

Arabella raised a hand to shield her eyes from the sun, though I caught her glance at me from the corner of her eye. "It's more of a rosy shimmer over her black scales. I think she's going through a phase. She's been very moody lately, and yesterday she refused to eat unless I hand-fed her."

I snorted. "And you indulged this behavior?"

"Says the warlord who changed our route because his wife mentioned she'd never seen Dead Man's Falls."

"That was tactical." I lied. "The Falls offered superior vantage points."

Arabella's knowing smile made heat rise to my face. I cleared my throat. "How much longer until she's large enough to carry you?"

The thought that Arabella might use the dragon to flee had long since evaporated. She was bound to me, in magic and in heart.

"A few more weeks, perhaps?" Arabella looked up at Nyx with unmistakable affection. "Her wingspan has nearly doubled since the Guild attack. The beast master thinks the exposure to all the magic at Skyspire has accelerated her growth."

Arabella began using a ridiculous baby voice to praise Nyx as "the best, cleverest dragon." Nyx preened at the flattery, executing a showy spiral that made several soldiers duck.

I couldn't look away.

I was besotted, completely and utterly obsessed with my wife, and I no longer bothered to hide it. Even a minor hint of her attention had me feeling like the most powerful man in the world. Not because of the armies at my back, but because she was at my side.

And soon, she'd be able to fly into battle. The vision of my brilliant, ruthless wife swooping down to obliterate our foes sent such an immediate surge of desire through me that I shifted in my saddle.

Arabella was still fussing over Nyx, who was now turning somersaults in midair.

A savage chill ran down my spine like shards of ice sliding between my vertebrae. I stifled a gasp, clenching my fists until my leather gloves creaked under the pressure. Rage followed the pain, so vicious and foreign it made me dizzy.

For an instant, I had the insane impulse to make Nyx drop from the sky. This wasn't the familiar possessive jealousy I'd felt before. This was darker. Hungry. Wrong.

The fury vanished as quickly as it came, leaving me feeling odd. What the hell was that?

Thorne's voice broke through my confusion. "My lord, are you well?"

"Fine." I unclenched my hands. "Just deciding which one of Auremar's nobles to hang first."

Thorne nodded, accepting this as perfectly reasonable.

Moments later, a rider galloped toward us from the road ahead. Thorne moved to intercept, exchanging brief words before returning. "Scouts report Lord Sebastian of the Northern Peaks is fleeing this way, pursued by about thirty Solandrian soldiers."

Griffin let out a squeak and promptly toppled off his mule. He wheezed from the ground, the Doom Scroll clutched to his chest. "Lord Sebastian? Here?"

I raised an eyebrow. "You know him personally?"

Griffin coughed and then grimaced in pain. "His scones are legendary, and his treatise on nonviolent conflict resolution was quite revolutionary. Though I heard his poetry is dreadful."

I turned back to Thorne. "The name is familiar."

"He was on the list," Thorne said simply.

Ah, yes. The man who'd invited the Bone Witches to a solstice ball.

"I wonder why they're chasing Sebastian," Arabella said.

I turned to her, brow furrowed. "You know him?"

She looked equally surprised by my question. "Of course I do. But how do *you* know him?"

An awkward silence fell, broken only by Griffin's pained groans as he tried to untangle his long legs. Thorne waited patiently, his gaze fixed on the road ahead as if the fate of this scone-loving lord was just another Tuesday.

"He was . . . considered," I said carefully. "As a prospect."

"What prospect?" Arabella's eyes widened before a slow, wicked smile crossed her face. "Sebastian was on your kidnapping shortlist?"

"Griffin suggested him," I said quickly. "When we were exploring options."

The enchanter was now attempting to haul himself back onto his mule, trembling with what seemed to be a mixture of hero worship and a craving for baked goods. "I merely pointed out his qualifications! Heroic bloodline, significant magical potential, excellent culinary skills."

"Griffin," I snapped. He flinched. "I believe the local forest is brimming with giant spiders and glowing moss. Perhaps you should inspect those phenomena firsthand."

The enchanter's face went from pale to a sickly green. "No, my lord. The safety of the group is . . . highly preferable."

Arabella looked from Griffin to me, fighting a smile. "You would have hated Sebastian." She lowered her voice. "He snores."

I made a strangled sound of surprise. How did she know such an intimate detail? Red hazed my vision, my mood twisting from warm contentment to murderous craving. I'd have Thorne save Lord Sebastian from the soldiers just so I could kill him myself.

I was silently listing creative means of execution when I caught the glimmer of mischief in Arabella's eyes.

I shot her the darkest scowl I could muster. "Not funny. A joke like that could get someone killed."

"But your murder face is my favorite face." She leaned in closer and gave me a heated look. "Well, second favorite."

Thorne cleared his throat, reminding me we still had a choice to make.

Still smiling, Arabella turned to him. "Bring Lord Sebastian here safely."

I glowered at them both for good measure. "And deal with the soldiers pursuing him. I want the commanding officer brought back for a chat."

Thorne issued a quick salute and led several riders ahead. Nyx screeched as she dove after them.

"Nyx, come back!" Arabella yelled, but the dragon only flicked her tail at us and kept going.

I watched them vanish around a bend. "That dragon has about as much respect for authority as you do. Maybe she'll learn to follow orders before she has to carry you into battle."

Arabella arched a brow. "Having second thoughts, my lord? I hear Sebastian is wonderfully obedient." She nudged her mare closer, sliding a gloved hand up my thigh. "But where's the fun in a partner who never argues back?"

I placed my hand over hers. "So," I asked, voice low. "How *do* you know Lord Sebastian of the Northern Peaks?"

2

Collect Strays and Fugitives

(Your Wife Has a Soft Spot)

Kazimir

Sebastian was the only noble who was ever truly kind to me." Arabella's gaze tracked the bend where Thorne and his men had vanished.

My jaw tightened. "Kind."

"Yes, Kaz. Kind. It's this strange concept where someone treats you well without expecting anything in return." She threw me a sidelong glance. "You might try it sometime."

"I'm the Dark Lord. I don't offer *kindness*. I offer a fortress of fear and shadow so impenetrable that you can afford to be kind within its walls." I let my voice drop to a rumble. "You're welcome."

She let out a laugh that made several soldiers glance our way before hurrying to look busy. "Sebastian and I grew up together, in a sense. His father brought him to court every summer, and we'd escape the tedium of state dinners to explore the palace gardens."

Nyx's triumphant roar echoed from somewhere ahead, followed by a cluster of very human screams. "Ah. At last, the terror I'd been missing."

Pity I wasn't there to savor it firsthand, but my intervention wasn't necessary. I refused to leave Arabella until we were certain this wasn't some elaborate trap. Paranoid villains kept their wives alive.

"So you were childhood friends," I pressed, unwilling to let the subject go.

"We were. Though as we grew older, we saw less of each other. His father sent him to the Academy when he was fourteen." She shrugged. "After that, it was mostly formal events. The last time I saw him was three years ago at a midsummer ball. One dance, some polite conversation, nothing more."

I measured her words. "Just pleasantries?"

Her eyes narrowed. "If you're asking whether he tried to court me, the answer is no. Sebastian was always proper to a fault." Mischief sparked in her expression. "Unlike some people who kidnap women from their carriages."

"A remarkably efficient courtship method."

"A tactical disaster that somehow worked out in your favor."

I laughed and dismounted. "The best villainous schemes always are."

I extended my hand—a gesture that was hers to refuse. She never did. Arabella placed her hand in mine and descended with deliberate slowness, pressing against me until I could feel her heat through leather and linen. I caught her waist, holding her suspended against my body. I was acutely aware that we had an audience but absolutely refused to care.

I brushed my thumb against her hip. "We'll never get to that outpost if you keep looking at me like that."

Her answering smile quelled the jealous beast stirring in my gut. Whatever history she shared with Sebastian, her future was forged with me. "Try to behave, my lord." Her lips brushed my ear. "It'd be a shame to incinerate him before the introductions."

I snorted and set her down as Thorne's party returned.

Thorne rode at the front, his scarred face grim. Behind him rode a man I recognized from description alone, though the reality was more . . . aesthetically irritating than I'd anticipated.

Lord Sebastian of the Northern Peaks rode a lathered white stallion, his fine riding clothes splattered with mud. Even disheveled, he was annoyingly handsome—tall and broad-shouldered, with golden blond hair that fell to his shoulders, partially tied back. His features were classically aristocratic—high cheekbones, strong jaw, and eyes of such startling violet that I immediately suspected magical enhancement.

I already hated him on principle.

Despite his finery, Sebastian looked ready to collapse. His face was ashen, and he swayed in the saddle like a drunk at closing time.

"Apologies, my lord." Thorne dismounted. "We couldn't take prisoners as instructed."

"Why not?"

"The dragon got to them first." A muscle twitched below Thorne's left eye. "All of them."

I pinched the bridge of my nose. Nyx—Arabella's dragon, Arabella's gift, Arabella's chaos incarnate—had once again decided my orders were merely suggestions. Between the dragon and her mistress, I was beginning to wonder who truly ruled Skyspire.

It was definitely me. Probably. Mostly.

I scowled at Arabella. "Your dragon ate my prisoners."

She shrugged with one shoulder. "Next time I'll ask her to chew more slowly so you can at least get their names."

Sebastian tried to dismount but slipped. Before he hit the ground, a thick vine burst from the undergrowth and coiled around his waist, lowering him gently.

"Thank you," Sebastian murmured to the vine, patting it absently. "Very considerate."

The vine swayed in what looked like acknowledgment before releasing him and wriggling back into the forest shadows.

I stared. "Did you just thank a *plant*?"

He brushed dirt off his sleeves. "It would be rude not to." His eyes widened as he seemed to remember he stood in front of the Terror of the Western Realms, not hosting a garden party. "My lord."

Arabella cleared her throat—hiding a laugh, most likely. "Someone fetch him water!"

Griffin scrambled to oblige. "I'll do it!" His voice cracked. He tried a quick dismount but got his boot stuck in the stirrup. The mule, sensing weakness, shuffled sideways, dragging Griffin with it.

"Blessed fucking bollocks of the seven saints!" Griffin dangled halfway to the ground, contorted like a pretzel. "Son of a plague-riddled whore's unholy pustule!" He yanked at his trapped foot. "May your entrails be used as skipping ropes for demon children, you rot-brained, shit-spewing, corpse-fucking cesspool of a—"

The stunned silence that fell over the company finally registered. Griffin froze, his face turning the color of a ripe tomato.

I leaned toward Arabella. "I didn't know he had it in him."

"I'm taking notes," she whispered back.

Griffin continued his battle with the stirrup, though his curses had been reduced to mortified mumbling. Meanwhile, a young soldier handed Sebastian a waterskin. The nobleman accepted it with trembling hands, gulping greedily. When he lowered it, his gaze met mine, and I was struck again by the uncanny color of his eyes—not a vain magical enhancement at all, but a marker of his heroic bloodline, just like Arabella's abilities.

"Lord Sebastian!" Arabella approached him with outstretched hands. "It's been too long."

"Lady Eve—" He caught himself. "Lady Blackrose. You look well." His tight smile flickered between us.

"And you look terrible." Her tone was kind despite the blunt words. She gestured to me. "May I present my husband, Lord Kazimir Blackrose?"

I stepped forward, letting him see exactly what I was—a warlord who had claimed this woman and would soon claim all of Solandris. I let my dominion magic ripple outward. Shadows crawled along the ground, and a cold wind stirred the leaves overhead.

"Lord Sebastian," I said, my voice threaded with power.

To his credit, the man didn't flinch. After visible internal struggle, he squared his shoulders and bowed formally. "Dark Lord Blackrose. I've heard much about you."

"All of it is true."

Sebastian swallowed. I resisted the urge to glance at Arabella, already knowing the look I'd find on her face. She'd asked—quite reasonably—for me to behave. And I was, naturally, doing nothing of the sort.

But in my defense, I was being *remarkably* restrained.

Griffin finally freed himself with a triumphant "Aha!" He stumbled forward, hair wilder than usual, face flushed. He fidgeted with his spectacles while casting furtive glances at Sebastian.

"Griffin is our court enchanter," Arabella said.

A strange, soft smile crossed Sebastian's face. "We've met, actually."

I blinked in surprise. "You have?"

Griffin looked like he might spontaneously combust. "At the Conclave of Arcane Tinkerers. Three years ago. Though I never imagined you would remember."

Sebastian gave a polite nod. "To the contrary. Your demonstration of weather manipulation was quite memorable."

"I thought you'd only heard about his scones," I said, eyeing my enchanter suspiciously.

Griffin turned a shade of red I'd previously only seen on battlefield wounds. "I . . . that is . . . I should really go look for that glowing moss you mentioned, my lord. Vital research. Extremely time-sensitive."

Before anyone could stop him, Griffin bolted into the forest.

I sighed. "Thorne, go after him before he gets lost or eaten by something."

Thorne's long-suffering nod conveyed his deep and abiding resignation to his fate. He followed Griffin into the trees. I made a mental note to give Thorne a raise. Or at least stop hitting him with eyeballs when he didn't show up to meetings.

Arabella studied Sebastian's pale complexion with concern. "Perhaps we should rest and have something to eat."

I signaled the attendants, who hurried to set up a field tent. Sebastian watched with the dazed expression of someone who couldn't quite believe where he'd ended up.

A shriek announced Nyx's return. The dragon soared overhead, looking insufferably pleased with herself. Fresh gore dripped from her scales and teeth, and something metallic dangled from one claw. She landed with a flourish of wings that nearly toppled the half-erected tent. Attendants scattered, cursing as they fought to hold the canvas.

The dragon pranced toward us and dropped a piece of Solandrian armor at Arabella's feet like a cat presenting a dead mouse. Nyx then turned her attention to the bloody mass between her teeth. With a sickening *crack*, she bit down. The object snapped in two—a human femur, I noted with clinical detachment.

Nyx dropped the pieces and began gnawing one end. The sound of crunching bone echoed in the sudden silence.

Arabella winced.

Sebastian stared, color draining from his already pale face. "That's—a dragon?"

"A shadow dragon." Arabella's voice was overly bright. "She's still young."

"Why is she pink?"

"We're still figuring that out, actually."

Sebastian couldn't look away from the carnage. "Excellent source of calcium for the soil, I suppose. Just . . . a terrible way to procure it."

I found myself oddly delighted by Nyx's timing and decided to forgive her. Nothing said "welcome to the villain's camp" like a dragon devouring human remains.

The tent was finally secured, and servants arranged a simple meal inside. Before entering, I stepped directly into Sebastian's path. The shadows at my feet darkened, and I let just enough power leak through to make the air crackle.

"You're not here to save my wife, are you?"

His violet eyes met mine without flinching, then shifted to Arabella. "Does she need saving?"

"No," she said firmly. "I don't."

Sebastian studied her face, then nodded. "Then I'm not here to save anyone but myself, Dark Lord."

I held his gaze a moment longer, searching for deceit. Finding none, I stepped aside and let him pass.

Inside, we settled around a low table set with bread, cheese, and wine. Sebastian fell upon it like a starving man. Arabella sat beside me, her knee occasionally brushing mine under the table. Outside, Nyx's continued bone-crunching provided a macabre backdrop to our conversation. Every so often, she would let out a contented growl and fly off, presumably to retrieve another course from the buffet she'd left strewn across the landscape. Each time she cracked another skull, Sebastian flinched hard enough to rattle the dishes.

"So," I said as a servant poured wine for Arabella, "why were Auremar's soldiers chasing Solandris's most famous baker?"

Sebastian set down his bread. "The king declared me 'royal property' due to my bloodline."

"Property?" Arabella frowned.

He nodded. "That was the exact wording in the decree—'All persons of heroic descent are hereby designated property of the crown and must submit to royal authority for the greater good of Solandris.'"

I leaned back, swirling my wine. "Do you know why?"

"No, but I wasn't eager to stick around and find out." He ran a hand through his hair. "I only got wind of it hours before they came for me, and fled here. Though I didn't expect you to be so close."

"Straight to the Dark Lord of the Western Realms?" I asked, unable to keep the surprise from my voice.

"Everyone knows what happened to the Hero's Guild when they attacked Skyspire. Ironically, it seemed like the safest place to be."

I stared at him. In all my years as a warlord, no one had ever sought me out for protection without offering something substantial in return—usually their soul, metaphorically speaking. Certainly not a man with heroic lineage, the very sort of person who should have been organizing resistance against me.

"We'll give you sanctuary," Arabella declared before I could respond.

I shot her a look, which she pointedly ignored. The thought of this noble, scone-baking paragon of virtue hanging around my fortress made me grind my teeth.

"Thank you." Relief flooded Sebastian's voice. "I had hoped, but I wasn't certain." He cleared his throat. "Your hospitality is most appreciated, Lady Blackrose."

"Arabella, please." Her smile was warm and genuine. "We've known each other too long for formalities."

Something in my chest tightened at the easy familiarity between them. The way she softened when she looked at him. The shared history I wasn't part of. I knew it was irrational. Arabella was *mine*, bound to me by magic and choice and a frankly obscene number of orgasms. But rationality had never been my strong suit when it came to her.

"We're preparing for war," I pointed out, my voice dangerously mild. "We don't have time to babysit Solandris's favorite pastry chef."

Arabella gave me a warning look. I ignored it just as she had ignored mine.

Sebastian pretended not to notice our silent battle of wills. "I understand your reluctance, Lord Blackrose. But I assure you I won't be in the way. And I may have information that could be useful."

I folded my arms. "Such as?"

"Auremar has been . . . changing." He fixed his violet eyes on me, then Arabella. "The court whispers that he spends hours locked in the ancient chambers beneath the palace, consulting with practitioners of forbidden arts."

That caught my attention, but I kept my expression neutral. Sebastian didn't need to know we already suspected something along those lines. "What kind of forbidden arts?"

"Blood magic, primarily."

Arabella and I exchanged glances.

"And you believe this is connected to his sudden interest in collecting people with heroic bloodlines?" I asked.

Sebastian nodded. "It must be."

Cold, quiet rage settled over me. It all pointed to the same madness

Atticus Evenfall had spoken of—a dark power behind the king's throne. If Auremar wanted heroic blood for something big, it threatened more than just Sebastian's life.

It threatened Arabella.

My chair creaked under my grip as I imagined the king's hands on her. Then his perfectly coiffed head on a spike. His palace reduced to rubble. His bloodline ended with prejudice and fire.

I'd accidentally thwarted his plans once. The second time would be intentional, thorough, and deeply satisfying.

My gaze flickered to Arabella, who was watching Sebastian with a thoughtful frown. I reminded myself she was no longer a pawn in her father's games or a prize for a decrepit king. She was the Dark Lady at my side, capable of leveling armies and looking devastatingly beautiful while doing it.

Auremar would never touch her.

If he tried, I'd make what happened to the Hero's Guild look like a pleasant afternoon tea.

"I came with nothing but the clothes on my back and my horse," Sebastian continued. "No provisions or wealth. I can offer only my gratitude and whatever services you deem valuable." He hesitated. "Though I should warn you, my skills run more to diplomatic negotiations and pastry than warfare."

Skyspire had become my sanctuary with Arabella. *Our* sanctuary. I'd grown accustomed to having her entirely to myself, with no competition for her attention save my advisors and the dragon. The thought of sharing that space with someone from her past, someone who knew her before she became my wife, was unexpectedly galling.

But she had taken Sebastian under her protection, and despite my overwhelming desire to feed him to Nyx, I would honor that.

"Fine," I conceded. "But try anything suspicious and you'll discover firsthand why my enemies don't live long enough to spread rumors."

"Understood." Sebastian inclined his head. "Thank you, Lord Blackrose. I won't forget this kindness."

My eye twitched. I considered housing Lord Sebastian in my trophy room, where he would be surrounded by the gentle clinking of enemy skulls in the evening breeze. "It's not kindness. It's strategy. If Auremar wants you badly enough to send troops, I want to know why."

A loud crunch from outside made Sebastian jump. A fresh slurping noise followed, wet and enthusiastic.

"Is the dragon always like this?" he asked weakly.

"No." I smiled with dark cheerfulness. "Usually she's much worse."

Arabella nudged my leg under the table. Hard. "Nyx's appetite has increased dramatically in recent weeks."

"I see." Sebastian was clearly trying not to listen to the dragon's feasting. "And will she accompany us to Skyspire?"

"Of course," Arabella and I said at the same time.

Alarm flashed across Sebastian's face before he smoothed it into a polite smile. "Wonderful. I've always found dragons fascinating."

"They find heroic bloodlines delicious." I paused for effect. "Something in the marrow, or so I've heard."

"Kazimir," Arabella warned.

I shrugged innocently. "Just sharing scientific facts."

Lord Sebastian might not be easily frightened away, but I had an entire citadel at my disposal. Surely I could make him uncomfortable enough to leave voluntarily.

And if not, well, accidents happened at Skyspire all the time.

Sebastian glanced between us, a calculating intelligence in his eyes. "You two seem well matched."

"We are." I draped my arm possessively across the back of Arabella's chair. "Perfectly matched, in fact."

"Against all odds," Arabella added drily, though she was smiling.

Sebastian's gaze lingered on her. "I'm glad to see you happy, Arabella. It's been too long since we spoke."

"Almost as if her father deliberately kept her isolated," I commented. "Strange, that."

"Not strange at all," Sebastian replied, surprising me with his frankness.

"Lord Evenfall's treatment of Lady Arabella was well-known among the nobility, though few dared speak of it openly. My father tried to intervene once, after an incident. Lord Evenfall threatened to dissolve all trade agreements with the Northern Peaks in retaliation."

Arabella stiffened. Through our bond, I felt a flicker of resentment. Not at Sebastian, but at the reminder of how the world had stood by and watched.

I brushed my thumb over her shoulder in support. "What incident?"

Sebastian looked to Arabella, a question in his eyes. I watched her for the cascade of emotions—anger, shame, bitterness.

But there was nothing. Instead, a faint line appeared between her brows. She nodded slightly, giving permission.

"When we were fifteen," Sebastian began carefully, "my family hosted an Autumnal Equinox celebration. Arabella attended with her father. During the festivities, I found her locked in a root cellar. She'd been there for hours because she'd spoken to a young man without her father's permission."

I felt Arabella's confusion spike. A cold, hollow sensation followed by a wave of secondhand humiliation and a slow-burning rage that mirrored my own. Her face, however, remained a carefully controlled mask.

She glanced at me with an almost imperceptible shake of her head. She didn't remember.

But the memory wasn't just lost to time. It was stolen. Plucked from her mind by Auremar's mages, with her father's blessing, just like the memory of her mother's murder. Atticus had let them do it. Let them carve away pieces of his own daughter's life, one humiliation at a time, until only the acceptable parts remained.

Until she was the perfect, obedient prize for a king.

My shadows darkened the corners of the tent. The urge to go straight back to Skyspire and personally eviscerate Atticus Evenfall was so strong it was a physical ache in my bones. I wanted to carve my displeasure into his flesh. Slowly. Artistically.

"How convenient," I said, my voice deadly soft, "that Evenfall is currently enjoying my hospitality in Skyspire's dungeons."

Sebastian's eyes widened. "You have Lord Evenfall?"

"He sold his daughter to King Auremar," I said flatly. "Among other crimes. Some of which you apparently know."

"I see." Sebastian's expression was carefully neutral, but I caught a brief flash of satisfaction in his eyes. "How unfortunate for him."

I couldn't help reassessing Sebastian then. Perhaps he wasn't entirely worthless. Anyone who took pleasure in Atticus Evenfall's suffering had at least one redeeming quality.

I rose from my seat and turned to Arabella, who was still processing Sebastian's revelation with that distant look in her eyes. "We should rejoin the army. Lord Sebastian will return with us to Skyspire after our business is finished here." I fixed him with a cold stare. "I trust you'll find our accommodations adequate."

"I'm sure they'll exceed my expectations, Dark Lord." He stood and bowed with perfect courtly grace.

I narrowed my eyes. This would be more difficult than I'd anticipated. Lord Sebastian wasn't easily intimidated, and worse, he seemed genuinely fond of Arabella without being inappropriately familiar. It made him harder to hate than I'd hoped.

But that wouldn't stop me trying.

"Am I going to regret this?" I asked her as Sebastian left the tent. Disconcertingly, rows of tiny flowers sprang up in his wake, as if the earth itself wanted to celebrate his presence.

Her gaze was distant, but then she turned to me with that characteristic gleam of mischief in her eyes. "I've had to put up with two of your ex-lovers." The word landed with the delicacy of a thrown axe. "The stabby Viscountess and the Syndicate's Chair of Whispers. I think I'm owed one scone baker."

"They weren't lovers," I said quickly.

She narrowed her eyes. "What?"

A muscle in my jaw tightened. This was treacherous ground, the kind that led to conversations about feelings and vulnerability and other terrifying concepts. I settled for a shrug, a gesture that felt entirely inadequate. "I didn't love them."

And I do you.

The words were heavy on my tongue, desperate to escape. I clamped my jaw shut to keep them from pouring out.

Arabella's breath hitched. The air thickened, charged with the sudden, terrifying weight of a truth neither of us was ready to voice. Her gaze flickered away first. "Right." Her voice was a little too bright. "I should check on Nyx."

She slipped outside. I followed, frustrated and edgy. My first instinct was to burn something—the forest, Auremar's palace, Sebastian's gentle, pitying face. My second, more practical instinct, was to regain control. We had corpses to deal with, soldiers to regroup, and a war to launch.

As if summoned by my thoughts, Thorne emerged from the forest with Griffin in tow. Griffin perked up at the sight of Sebastian, then immediately tripped over his own feet.

Arabella moved to help him, the picture of grace. But I could feel the tremor of her anger through our bond, the icy sorrow of a stolen past pressing against her ribs.

Auremar's soldiers were dead, reduced to dragon snacks. But their king had reached back through time and hurt Arabella all over again, right here in front of me, and I couldn't do a damn thing about it except plot increasingly elaborate revenge.

For over a decade, I'd dreamed of my army poised on the border of Solandris. This should have been a glorious march toward my destiny. Instead, I felt a chill across my skin, as if every moving shadow might hide some new threat to the woman whose memories were now weapons against her.

"My lord," Thorne said, his voice a low rumble at my side. "Shall we make camp?"

My eyes locked on Arabella. She was now engaged in conversation with Sebastian, while Griffin hovered nearby looking like an overeager, singed scarecrow with moss in his hair. She was smiling at something Sebastian said, a polite curve of her lips that made the possessive monster in my chest roar with irrational jealousy.

But I caught the way she rubbed her arms, a small gesture of discomfort she probably didn't realize she was making.

I couldn't undo the damage her father had inflicted. Couldn't restore the memories Auremar's mages had carved away. But I could keep her moving, give her space to process without the stench of dead soldiers as a backdrop.

"No." I turned to Thorne. "We're finding a different place to camp."

Arabella's head snapped up, her smile vanishing. She strode toward me, her brow furrowed. "Leaving? Kazimir, we just got here. The army—"

"Will follow," I cut in. "The situation has changed." I finally met her eyes, letting her see the granite resolve there. "The dead bodies will stink by morning."

She narrowed her eyes, no doubt her truth-sense telling her that I was hiding something.

I knew, intellectually, that this change of plans was absurd. Arabella was no fragile flower. She had faced down the Hero's Guild, unleashed devastating magic, and stared into the abyss of her own past without flinching. She could handle herself better than most of my generals.

But parts of her mind had been cut away like unwanted weeds, and that would rattle anybody. Even a Dark Lady.

I wanted to return to Skyspire now, if only to peel the skin from Atticus Evenfall and mail it to his king. But we had a war to start first.

I turned back to Thorne, making the decision final. "We'll advance as far as we can go tonight. Then I'll scout the vantage point myself."

"Kaz?" Arabella asked quietly.

"I don't want any more surprises." I gestured vaguely toward our new guest, who was now being enthusiastically questioned by Griffin about his heroic lineage. "Griffin, you're riding with us. You too, Scone Lord."

Sebastian flinched at the nickname but wisely kept his mouth shut. Griffin, on the other hand, looked like he'd just been handed a basket of enchanted kittens.

I sighed. This was going to be a long campaign.

3

Ignore the Ominous Portents

(They're Probably Nothing)

Arabella

Our new campsite was a disaster.

I picked my way through the maze of half-erected tents, dodging ropes and stakes. The entire army had been forced to make camp in near-total darkness to maintain secrecy. The evening air carried the mingled scents of damp earth, sweat, and dinner. Occasional curses punctuated the night as someone stubbed a toe or knocked over equipment. No one truly complained, however. Every single soldier followed Kazimir of their own volition, and every one knew of his wrath. The companies were well-oiled machines of terror.

For the remainder of the journey, I'd coached Griffin on riding to spare him further humiliation with the mule. Results were mixed.

Now, the enchanter was hovering near Lord Sebastian's tent, wringing his hands and occasionally smoothing down his disastrous hair. The man was a magical genius and a social catastrophe, and tonight, he was a spectacle.

"What are you doing?" I asked.

He jumped, spinning around so fast he nearly lost his balance. "Lady

Blackrose! I was just . . . going to find Lord Blackrose . . . I'm making progress on the, uh . . ."

My truth-sense tingled behind my eyes. The man was such an abysmal liar.

"I'm sure," I said drily. "Go to bed, Griffin. You can talk to Lord Sebastian tomorrow."

He flushed a blotchy red that was visible even in the darkness. "Right. Of course. Bed. Excellent idea." He scurried away, tripping over a tent stake and nearly face-planting in the dirt before righting himself and disappearing into the darkness.

I suppressed a smirk. Sebastian was a relic of a life I'd thankfully escaped—a kind, hopelessly earnest boy who had grown into a kind, hopelessly earnest man. A perfect, harmless piece of bait to dangle in front of Kazimir, if only to watch my Dark Lord's jaw tighten in that particularly delicious way.

Just as I turned to leave, a snore ripped from Sebastian's tent, loud enough to stir a nearby horse. It sounded less like a man sleeping and more like a bear choking on a badger.

Ah, yes. *That* I remembered. He'd produced the exact same noise once, face down on his dessert at a dreadfully dull banquet when we were children.

I walked on, silently thanking all the gods that ever lived that Kaz didn't snore. The Dark Lord had many terrifying qualities, but at least I could sleep without feeling like I was bedding down next to a drowning bear.

A low, gurgling groan echoed from the shadows nearby, followed by a pathetic-sounding burp. Nyx was sprawled dramatically across a patch of flattened grass, looking less like a terror of the skies and more like a child who'd eaten too much cake at a birthday party.

A very, very bloody birthday party.

"Serves you right," I murmured, stroking her snout. She leaned into my touch with a soft whine, her stomach making another unhappy noise. "I don't feel sorry for the soldiers, but perhaps you'll remember this lesson next time. Metal doesn't digest well."

She gave a small, smoky sigh that smelled of burnt hair. Then she burped again, and a distinctly human-shaped tooth clattered to the ground.

"Charming," I muttered, though my mind had already drifted back to Sebastian's arrival and the disturbing gaps it had revealed in my own history.

The cellar incident happened when I was fifteen—a full year after my mother died protecting me. A year after they'd altered my memories and locked me in the tower for the first time. And yet, even after all that, I'd still had enough spirit left to defy my father. The thought should have made me proud, but instead it filled me with a cold, creeping dread.

How many times had they done this? How many memories had they stolen? My mother had died when I was fourteen, but I'd been made to believe she'd died from an illness when I was eight. Six years of my life with her, just . . . gone. And if they could erase that, what else had they taken?

What else had they done?

Kazimir thought some of those suppression runes in the tower were too old to have just been for me. Had my mother been locked there too, her own power suppressed the same way mine would be?

A bitter taste filled my mouth. It was a grim sort of irony that Kazimir and I were both navigating our own peculiar brands of amnesia. He'd woken from the Heirloom's activation with no recollection of the cataclysmic vision he'd experienced. He didn't remember the ancient, malevolent Shadow King screaming for vengeance from behind my husband's storm gray eyes. He didn't remember the crushing weight of centuries of rage and imprisonment that I'd glimpsed through our bond, a darkness so profound it had nearly swallowed him whole.

I'd seen it. I'd seen the entity wearing Kaz's face, twisting his features into a mask of hate.

And I hadn't told him.

Part of me insisted it was for his own good. He was already battling the ghosts of his past; he didn't need to know he was also the vessel for a slumbering evil with a penchant for world domination. The other, more honest part of me was simply a coward. How do you tell the man you—you're falling for that he might be possessed by a cosmic evil?

I hoped my own missing memories didn't conceal a similar secret. Though if I did have an ancient entity living inside me, I prayed it was at least one with a decent sense of humor and a less homicidal agenda.

I finally found Kazimir near the edge of camp, a black-clad silhouette under the gloom of the trees. The heavy cloak he was shrugging into was one I recognized—the same midnight wool he'd worn the day he'd snatched me from my carriage, its hem and collar stitched with runes that shimmered faintly in the moonlight. Once, he'd told me it looked "suitably dramatic." I would die before admitting he was right.

He moved like a dark god, all six-feet-plus of arrogant Dark Lord wrapped in barely leashed power. That insufferable confidence came from knowing he could destroy anyone in his path, and it showed in the way he carried himself.

Sharp planes and wicked beauty defined his face: high cheekbones and an aristocratic nose paired with a mouth that had no business looking so kissable when it regularly issued death threats.

He was a kidnapper. A villain. A warlord who'd upended my entire world and usually made me want to wipe that arrogant smirk off his face.

But damn it all, when he was close, I forgot every sensible reason I'd had to run.

Sensing my presence, he turned. The look in his eyes when they found me was a wave of possessive heat that washed over me and settled deep in my bones. It chased away the chill of the missing memories, the lingering horror of my father's sins, and the weight of the secrets I was keeping. In Kaz's gaze, I wasn't a broken thing with pieces missing. I was his. Seen. *Wanted.*

"What are you thinking about?" he asked.

I offered a small, crooked smile. "Wondering if you're ever going to get a new cloak."

A corner of his mouth tugged upward. He didn't push for the real answer, and a quiet sort of gratitude bloomed in my chest. He knew today had been a shock. He was giving me the space to process it. It was one of the things about him that constantly surprised me—this undercurrent of quiet respect that ran beneath the violence and the dominion magic.

"Where have you been, anyway?" he asked, adjusting the drape of the cloak over his shoulders.

"Playing chaperone. I had to shoo Griffin away from Sebastian's tent before he serenaded him."

Kazimir's expression darkened. "He's going to be a problem."

"Griffin or Sebastian?"

"Both." His gaze narrowed. "Have you considered that your dear Lord Sebastian might be a spy?"

"Would you have let him into our camp if you thought he was?"

"Maybe," he said, and the infuriating thing was, my truth-sense didn't so much as tingle. He was just that devious. "The enemy you see is less dangerous than one you don't."

"He's not a spy, Kaz," I said, rolling my eyes. "He's just a man who's very good at baking. And apparently, smart enough to seek protection from the only person who could help him, no matter how intimidating that man looks in a cloak."

Kazimir flashed me a devilish smile. "I'm taking the northern ridge," he said, changing the subject. "Getting the lay of the land." He wasn't using a portal, conserving his magic for the inevitable battle tomorrow. Instead, he would ride part of the way and climb the rest.

"I'm coming with you," I announced.

He stared at me as if I'd suggested we take up knitting. "Absolutely not."

"I'm not asking for permission." I crossed my arms. "You're not leaving me here with a lovesick enchanter and a scone-baking nobleman while you go have all the fun."

He let out an exasperated sigh, sending a plume of white into the air. "It'll be cold," he said finally. "And there's a steep climb at the end."

"I'll manage."

His gaze turned stormy. The unspoken fear for my safety was so loud in our bond it was practically screaming. He was being ridiculous. And a little bit sweet, in a terrifying, Dark Lord sort of way.

I took a step closer. "Admit that you want me to go with you."

His jaw tightened, but the reply, when it came, wasn't the sarcastic retort I expected. It was quiet, the words cutting through the air with a raw conviction. "I always want you with me."

Another awkward beat stretched between us. We'd been having a lot of those lately.

Kaz looked away first, his shoulders stiffening. The warmth in our bond shuttered as his walls slammed back into place. "Though a night of peace and quiet does have its appeal."

Bastard. I decided to aim for his pride, a target I knew I could hit from a mile away. "Worried you can't protect me as well as your army can?"

His head snapped back toward me, eyes flashing silver. "*Our* army. And the fuck I can't."

"Then it's settled."

He muttered a curse under his breath, but instead of calling for my horse, he swung himself onto his own black warhorse. Then with one smooth, powerful motion, he leaned down and lifted me onto the saddle in front of him.

The world tilted, then I was settled against the hard planes of his chest, his arms a cage of warmth and strength around me. He adjusted his cloak so it enveloped us both, a private world of shared heat and the familiar scent of winter storms and steel.

I leaned back against him. It felt right. Safe. I didn't think I would ever get tired of being in his arms.

"I've commissioned proper armor for you," he said as we left camp. "Not just leathers, either. Something more substantial for when you go into battle."

"You mean the armor I have for tomorrow isn't good enough?"

"It's decent, but you deserve something befitting the Dark Lady, with better protection."

I smiled into the darkness. "All right. Talk, Dark Lord."

"About what?"

"Don't play dumb. It doesn't suit you." I shifted, turning my head to look at him. "Your sudden change of plans. Abruptly deciding to march us for hours in the dark. You said it was because the bodies would stink, but that's not the real reason."

He was silent for a long moment, the only sound the soft thud of hooves on the dirt path. "I don't like surprises," he finally said.

"You live for surprises," I countered. "You thrive on chaos. You practically generate it as a byproduct of breathing."

"Nyx ate my prisoners," he grumbled.

"Try again." I waited.

He sighed, the sound long and heavy. "Auremar has spies everywhere. Now soldiers. Even if they were only chasing Sebastian, I didn't want you exposed."

"I'm not a child, Kazimir. I can handle myself."

"I know," he said roughly. His arms tightened around me. "But it was what Sebastian said about finding you in that cellar. They hurt you. Over and over again. And I can't do a damn thing to stop it because it already happened."

His anger was a low-burning fire I could feel through our bond. It wasn't just a warlord's fury; it was something far more personal.

The conversation had turned, as I'd known it would, to my stolen memories. I hadn't been ready to talk about them before, not since interrogating my father. The revelation had been too raw, the betrayal too vast. But now, after a few weeks, the shock had curdled into a cold, simmering rage. And a burning curiosity.

"What was so dangerous about a fourteen-year-old girl that they had to erase parts of her?" I mused aloud.

"Some memories are better left buried," Kazimir said, his tone grim.

"How many have you buried?" I asked, the question slipping out before I could stop it.

He stiffened against me and fell quiet. I gave him space to decide if he wanted to continue, just as he had for me.

"I remember every excruciating detail," he finally said. "Every cut, every betrayal, every lesson in pain. I couldn't forget if I tried."

There was truth in his voice, the raw, unvarnished agony of a past he couldn't escape no matter how much power he accumulated. I knew the broad strokes—the mother who carved runes into his bones, the father he'd beheaded at seventeen. But the details were shadows he kept locked away. He'd promised to tell me more one day, a day when the telling wouldn't break him. I'd accepted it. But now that I'd seen the Shadow King behind his eyes, I wasn't sure waiting was the right choice.

"What happened to your mother?" I asked quietly.

"I don't know. She abandoned me, and I had . . . a rough patch. By the time I thought to look for her to exact some vengeance, I couldn't find her. After some digging, I heard a rumor that she'd been killed crossing the Eastern Sea, but I never got confirmation."

I waited for him to elaborate. When he didn't, I turned my attention to the forest. The night was crisp and bright, with enough moonlight filtering through the trees for us to see the ground ahead as it steepened. We reached the base of the ridge and dismounted. The rest of the way was a steep climb over loose rock and thorny brush. I was proud of how easily I kept pace with him, my muscles burning in a satisfying way. All our training sessions—the sparring, the dodging of shadow bolts—were paying off.

"You're slow," he teased as I scrambled up a particularly steep incline.

"I'm saving my energy," I shot back, breathless. "For when I have to carry you back down after you trip in the dark and sprain your ankle."

He chuckled, a low, dark sound that echoed in the quiet night. He reached the top of the outcropping first and turned, offering me his hand. I took it, and he pulled me up the last few feet.

We stood on a narrow ledge of rock overlooking the vast, sleeping expanse of northern Solandris. The air was thin and cold, biting at my cheeks. Below us, the land was a tapestry of shadow and silver, bathed in the light of a thousand distant stars.

"There." Kazimir pointed to a cluster of dark shapes nestled in a fold of the hills. "That's the outpost. We'll take it before dawn."

It looked like a child's toy from this height. "When did you start thinking of the army as *ours*?"

"Around the time you started setting things on fire," Kazimir replied with a smirk. "Are you ready for tomorrow?"

"I'm not sure. It's one thing to fight off sanctimonious invaders in your own home. It's another to march into theirs and go looking for a fight."

"It's all the same when you're in the thick of it," he said dismissively. "Stick with me or Thorne. Watch, and learn."

I bristled at his arrogance. "Are you trying to keep me out of the battle?"

His gaze snapped back to me, and the corner of his mouth twitched. "I know better than to try," he said, his voice dropping. "You're the Dark Lady of Skyspire. I'd never force you to stay back like some helpless damsel, mostly because you'd probably set me on fire again, and I'm rather fond of this cloak."

For all his worry and possessiveness, he would never take my agency from me. We both knew it would infuriate me, and he was right—I would absolutely set him on fire. "Besides," he continued, "what better way to learn than to observe a master?"

"Your modesty is truly inspiring." We were silent a while longer, breathing in the cold air. "I wish we could just use the ley lines," I said finally. "We have the Heirloom. We'd sweep through Solandris in days instead of this slow march."

Kazimir's jaw tightened. "You think I haven't considered it? That I don't want to end this quickly?"

The truth was, we'd both been eager to test the Heirloom's full potential after that first activation. The raw magic flowing through us had been intoxicating, the entire world bending to our combined will. But our first attempts at wielding it had been . . . educational.

Three days after the activation, we'd tried channeling the ley lines to reinforce the citadel's defenses. What should have been a simple strengthening spell had instead torn a crater in the courtyard and left Kazimir unconscious for several minutes.

The second attempt, a week later, had been more modest—using the Heirloom to scry on Auremar's movements. We'd managed it, but the effort had left us both bleeding from our noses, our minds feeling like they'd been scraped raw.

Since then, Griffin had been poring over ancient texts, running resonance tests, filling notebooks with calculations about ley line harmonics. He'd been muttering about "sympathetic frequencies" and "blood-key calibration" for days. It was why he'd come with us instead of staying at Skyspire. Kaz wanted him close in case he had a breakthrough.

In the meantime, we had benefited from the Heirloom's power—we just couldn't bend reality with it yet.

"What about one of your personal portals directly into Sunspire Palace?" I mused. "Kill Auremar, claim the throne, and we could be back at Skyspire in time for dinner."

"I've considered it, but it wouldn't stop the war." He shook his head. "No, the conflict has to be fought and won decisively for this to work."

I nodded. That made sense—Auremar's death would create a power vacuum, but not peace. "So we do this the hard way."

He was silent a moment before he said, "And there's you to consider."

I stiffened. "I'm not fragile."

"No, but you're also inexperienced. Your power is immense, Arabella, but you've had it fully unleashed for less than six months. The Heirloom amplifies everything—including mistakes."

He was right, and I hated it. My magic came to me instinctively, but I was still learning control. Just last week, I'd accidentally summoned a flock of shadow ravens that had terrorized the gardeners.

I sighed. "So we're stuck with conventional warfare."

"Well, it won't be *too* conventional." He smirked and pulled me closer. "We'll master the Heirloom, but not in the middle of a campaign where one wrong move could obliterate our own army."

I turned to face him.

"Feeling better?" he asked quietly, his eyes on my face.

I nodded, the anger and confusion of the day finally receding, replaced by the sharp, clear reality of the here and now. Of him.

His thumb traced the line of my jaw, sending shivers down my spine. "Good."

His mouth crashed against mine, searing in the cold night air. The sweep of his tongue past my lips drew me open for him, and I tasted that particular darkness that was uniquely Kazimir. When his hand fisted in my hair, the sharp pull dragged a gasp from my throat. He swallowed the sound, his other arm locking around my waist to haul me flush against him.

I sank my teeth into his lower lip—hard—and the growl that vibrated through his chest reverberated through mine where we were pressed together. His fingers dug into my hip, anchoring me in place as he reclaimed control of the kiss. My pulse hammered. Heat pooled low in my belly despite the freezing wind that whipped around us.

Rough stone scraped through my shirt as he pinned me against it. The press of his thigh between mine wrenched a sound from me that I couldn't contain. He kissed me until my lips went numb, then sensitive, then almost painful. My lungs burned for air, but the need for oxygen paled against the need for *this*—for *him*. My hands twisted in his cloak as my legs trembled beneath me. Only his weight kept me upright, kept me tethered to the earth when every nerve in my body was threatening to ignite.

When we finally broke apart, we were both breathing like we'd run up the entire ridge.

"I would very much like to get you back to our tent," I murmured, my voice husky.

A wicked glint appeared in his eyes. "Why wait?" His lips and tongue traced a fiery path down my neck. "We could have some fun right here."

He was always pushing, always testing the boundaries, a recurring, delicious theme in our strange life together. He brought one hand to the base of my throat, his touch light, and asked the question that had become a game between us. "Tell me a fantasy."

I opened my mouth to reply, a suitably scandalous suggestion already forming on my tongue, but he suddenly went still. His head snapped up, his gaze fixed on the distant, northern horizon.

"What is it?" I asked, following his line of sight.

The sky was clear, a vast, dark canvas pricked with diamond-bright stars. I squinted, searching for whatever had caught his attention, but saw nothing unusual. No movement, no shadows, no threat that I could discern.

"Kaz?" I pressed, unease creeping up my spine.

He blinked, and the intensity in his expression shuttered. "It's nothing." His voice was too casual, too controlled.

"You're lying."

He turned back to me, his hands settling on my waist with deliberate gentleness. "It's late." He pressed a kiss to my forehead. "Let's get back."

The abrupt shift from heated passion to this careful distance set every instinct screaming. Whatever he'd seen had rattled him badly enough that he was retreating behind his walls again. I let him guide me back down the ridge, but my gaze kept drifting to the northern sky.

Stars. Mountains. Nothing more.

So why did his shoulders remain tense the entire journey back? And why did his grip on my hand feel less like affection and more like he was afraid I might disappear?

4

Process Existential Dread Through Carnal Distraction

(It's Basically Therapy)

Kazimir

The camp sprawled before us in the moonlight. My blackout orders had been followed to the letter—not a single torch or lantern pierced the darkness.

I guided the horse through the maze of tents, my mind still snagged on what I'd seen from the ridge. Dark wings, impossibly vast, stretching across the northern sky. Not a cloud formation. Not a trick of the light. Something ancient and wrong that made the runes in my bones ache with recognition.

Then I'd blinked and it was gone.

I forced my mind away from those impossible wings, focusing instead on the immediate, the tangible. Arabella's warmth against my chest. The subtle shift of her hips with each step of the horse. Her scent mixing with leather and night air. My body responded to the distraction eagerly—too eagerly.

By the time we reached camp, my cock was hard and my hands itched to confirm she was real, solid, here.

"You're brooding," she said, her voice cutting through the darkness.

"I don't brood. I strategize."

She snorted softly. "You're strategizing very intensely about something that was supposedly nothing." She turned her head, and I caught the flash of her smile in the moonlight. "It's very attractive, if that helps."

What helped was the way her ass pressed back against me. What helped was knowing that in a few minutes, I'd have her alone in our tent, and I could work out this restless energy in a much more satisfying way.

Our tent was pitched at the center of camp. I dismounted first, then lifted her down. My hands lingered on her waist, thumbs brushing the strip of skin where her shirt had ridden up. She shivered.

"Sleep," I said firmly. "You need rest before tomorrow."

"I'm not tired." She stepped closer, her fingers finding the edge of my cloak. "Besides, you're the one who looks like he needs to work off some tension."

She wasn't wrong. The vision of those wings had left me wound tight as a crossbow string. Add to that the appearance of Lord Sebastian—with his perfectly earnest face and his history of sharing dances with my wife—and I was one provocation away from setting something on fire.

I held the flap open for Arabella, then followed her inside.

The space was spartanly furnished—a large bedroll, our packs, a small chest. But it smelled like magic, like us, and that was enough to make my blood heat.

"Help me with these," she said, already working at the laces of her tunic.

I moved behind her, my fingers replacing hers. But instead of loosening the ties, I pulled her back against me, my mouth finding that spot where her neck met her shoulder. She melted into me with a soft sigh.

"Kaz . . ."

I nipped at her skin. "I thought you weren't tired."

"I'm not." She pressed her ass back against my cock, and I bit back a groan. "But if you keep doing that, we're never going to get these clothes off."

And that was something I really wanted. We broke apart long enough to deal with clothing, but even that simple task became complicated. Her fingers kept finding bare skin instead of buckles. My mouth kept returning to her throat when I should have been unlacing her shirt. We were making enough noise to wake half the camp, fumbling and cursing softly as we fought with stubborn fastenings.

"Fuck this," I growled, giving up on finesse.

I spun her around and pushed her onto the bedroll, following her down until she was on her hands and knees. My hand fisted in her hair, pulling her head back just enough to expose the elegant line of her throat.

"Good?" I growled against her ear.

"Yes." The word came out breathless, needy, perfect.

I yanked her leggings down over her hips with zero ceremony. She was already wet—I couldn't see it in the darkness but I could smell her arousal, feel the slickness against my fingers when I touched her. It made my cock throb painfully against my own clothes.

I freed myself with one hand, keeping the other tangled in her hair. No preamble, no teasing—I notched myself at her entrance and thrust home.

She cried out, the sound muffled by a pillow as I pushed her face down into it. Her cunt clenched around me, hot and perfect and *mine.* I set a punishing pace, each thrust driving her into the pillow.

This wasn't tender. This was claiming. Taking.

Her whole body trembled as I pounded into her. Every thrust drove deeper, harder, chasing away the memory of those phantom wings and the gnawing certainty that something was coming for us. For her.

The sounds of our coupling filled the tent. My thrusts grew erratic as I chased my release, driving deeper, harder. She was moaning into the pillow.

I pulled her hair harder, forcing her to arch her back. The new angle let me hit that spot inside her that made her whole body seize. My foot knocked against something as I adjusted position, sending it toppling with a tremendous crash.

I didn't care. Let the whole fucking army know I was taking my wife.

But Arabella tensed beneath me, embarrassment flooding through our bond.

"Stop thinking," I commanded, punctuating the words with a particularly deep thrust.

She shook her head, fighting to keep quiet even as her body trembled on the edge. The conflict between her need for release and her determination to maintain some dignity in the middle of an army camp was holding her back.

Fine. If she needed permission to let go, I'd give it to her.

With a thought and a flick of my fingers, I cast a silencing ward around the tent. The magic shimmered into place, cutting us off from the outside world.

I bent low so I could speak into her ear. "Now scream for me."

I thrust inside her a few more times, angling my cock just how I knew she liked it. Her body shuddered beneath me. Without the fear of being overheard, she let out a satisfying cry as she came.

The sound pushed me over the edge. I buried myself to the hilt and came hard, filling her with pulse after pulse of my release. Stars exploded behind my eyes. My runes sang with power. For a moment, nothing existed except her and this and us.

For a moment, we stayed like that, breathing hard. My whole body tingled and I didn't want it to end. If someone had told me a few months ago that I'd rather stay buried inside my wife than conquer Solandris, I would have laughed in their face and had them executed for wasting my time.

"You could have cast that spell from the beginning," Arabella said once she caught her breath.

"Where's the fun in that?"

She pushed herself up on shaky arms and looked at me over her shoulder. Even in the darkness, I could feel the heat of her stare. "We've been trying to be quiet for weeks. In our own chambers. In our own fortress."

I smirked, still buried inside her. "I've never made it a secret that I like people to know how thoroughly I satisfy my wife."

She clenched around me deliberately, and my cock twitched with interest despite having just come. "Arrogant bastard."

I pulled out slowly, feeling my seed drip from her. It sent a fresh wave of possessive satisfaction through me. *Mine. Marked. Claimed.*

We cleaned up in comfortable silence, though I noticed her movements were a bit unsteady. Good. I wanted her to feel me tomorrow while she rode into battle. A reminder of who she belonged to.

As we settled onto the bedroll, she curled into my side, her head on my chest. I traced a finger over her bare shoulder and then down to her breast.

"Kaz, what did you really see on the ridge?"

I tensed, but forced myself to relax. "Nothing that matters tonight."

She didn't press, though I felt her disbelief. Instead, she traced one of the scars on my chest, following the runic pattern carved there. Her touch was gentle, almost reverent. It made something uncomfortable twist in my chest.

"I've been thinking," I said, changing the subject before she could ask more questions I didn't want to answer. "About that fantasy you never got to share earlier."

She stilled. "Oh?"

"I've found something for us to work on." I kept my voice casual, though my cock was already showing interest again. Overachiever.

"Such as?"

"Intimacy with an audience."

Her breath caught. Through our bond, I felt a spike of arousal mixed with embarrassment. Interesting. Very interesting.

"What makes you think I'd be interested in that?" she asked, but her voice had gone husky.

"Call it intuition. Or maybe it's the way your heart is racing right now." I pulled her closer. "We've had sex all over Skyspire, often with a chance of getting caught. This would just be . . . more intentional."

"That's not quite the same thing." She buried her face against my chest and quietly laughed.

I pressed a kiss to the top of her head. "Sleep now. We'll discuss the details later."

"You can't just drop that on me and expect me to sleep."

"I can and I do." I waved a hand, removing the silencing ward. The sounds of the camp filtered back in—distant voices, the crackle of dying fires, the stamp of horses. "You'll need your strength tomorrow. For the battle and . . . other things."

She muttered something that sounded suspiciously like a threat against my manhood, but her breathing was already evening out as she relaxed into sleep.

I lay awake longer, staring into the darkness. The vision of those wings haunted me, a shadow at the edge of my consciousness that I felt like I should recognize but couldn't quite grasp. My runes burned with warning, but I didn't know what was coming.

Only that it was.

5

Watch Your Wife Bloom
(into a Beautiful, Bloodthirsty Monster)

Kazimir

The sky was still black when we reached the low hill overlooking the outpost. I dismounted and turned to Thorne. "After the battle, I need you to organize collection teams."

His brow furrowed. "Supplies? Weapons?"

"Bones." I kept my voice casual. "From the fallen Solandrians. I want them gathered, cataloged, and transported back to the citadel. Intact specimens preferred, but fragments will do."

Thorne's expression didn't change, but I caught the slight pause before he nodded. "Understood, my lord. Any specific bones?"

"All of them." I turned back to survey the outpost below. "Well, as many as you can reasonably collect without spending all night playing gravedigger."

"Right." Another pause. "Should I ask?"

"You could." I smiled. "But I won't tell you."

It wasn't the strangest request I'd made in his years of employment—that honor probably went to the time I'd needed seventeen gallons of rendered pig fat and a condemned priest—but it ranked in the top ten. Still, Thorne simply pulled out a small notebook and made a notation.

"Bone collection teams," he muttered, writing. "I'll have them standing by."

"Excellent." I gestured to the valley below. "Now, shall we discuss the outpost?"

The walls were high enough to discourage bandits, not high enough to stop me. Torches guttered along the ramparts, and I could make out the silhouettes of guards walking their rounds.

They had no idea death waited just beyond their sight.

"Two hundred men," Thorne rumbled. "Give or take."

"And the wards?" Arabella asked as she led her horse up beside mine.

I waved a dismissive hand. "Standard defensive enchantments. Nothing sophisticated—just basic alarm spells and a few protective barriers. They'll have a mage or two stationed here, maybe three given how close we are to the border." I smiled into the darkness. "But here's the beautiful irony: Solandris's natural resistance to me has made them complacent. Their mages are trained to reinforce that resistance, not to actually defend against a proper assault."

"And that resistance no longer works on you." The smile in Arabella's voice was unmistakable.

"Thanks to you." I glanced at her, letting my appreciation show. After we'd activated the Heirloom, her bloodline magic neutralized Solandris's effect on my power.

Thorne grunted. "The mages?"

"Will be too busy trying to figure out why their defensive spells aren't stopping me to mount any real counterattack. By the time they realize something's wrong, it'll be too late."

After all these years of being held at bay by their damned Golden Roses and sanctimonious king, I was finally here. Finally ready to carve my name into their precious kingdom.

Arabella shifted beside me. Even dressed for war, she was devastating. She'd braided her hair back for battle, wearing light armor from the armory. She'd grumbled about it again this morning, but I'd insisted. My wife wasn't yet battle-hardened and going into a conflict without protection was folly.

Behind us, our forces waited in perfect silence. Not the massive army I'd eventually need to take the capital of Sunspire, but more than enough for this. Shadow warriors crouched between my human soldiers, their forms fully opaque. The fighters I'd brought were veterans, handpicked for this first strike, with the bulk remaining at the pass, awaiting orders to march.

My runes sang for violence. It had been too long since I'd let loose and painted a battlefield with terror.

"Watch and learn," I repeated to Arabella, though I knew she'd do more than watch. My wife was no passive observer—she'd want her own taste of conquest before the sun rose.

I closed my eyes and drew in a breath of predawn air. The outpost below had three main defensive positions: the gate, the eastern tower, and the barracks. Traditional siege tactics would have us bombard the walls, maybe attempt to scale them under cover of archer fire.

Boring. Predictable. Not my style.

I whispered into the wind, letting my dominion magic seep into the words and send them toward the main gate. The spell was delicate—not a hammer blow but a needle. Their minds were soft, pliable things, full of homesickness and boredom.

For a heartbeat, nothing happened.

Then the screaming started.

A guard stumbled back from his post, sword drawn, eyes wide with terror. He had just seen his companion's face melt and re-form into something from his deepest nightmares. He swung his sword in a wild arc, catching his fellow soldier across the throat. Blood sprayed in the torchlight as more guards rushed to help, only to fall victim to the same illusions.

"What did you—" Arabella started.

"Watch."

More screams erupted along the wall as my illusions took hold. Guards turned on one another with savage desperation, seeing demons where their brothers stood. One man threw himself from the ramparts rather than face whatever horror my magic showed him. Another curled into a ball, sobbing for his mother while his comrades tore one another apart around him.

Beside me, Arabella was gaping.

I smirked. "Learn."

The infection spread. My dominion magic jumped from mind to mind like a plague, each guard's terror feeding the next. Within minutes, the eastern wall was a charnel house of self-inflicted carnage.

With the gate guards busy murdering one another, I turned my attention to the rest of the outpost. "Now," I commanded.

Our forces surged forward like a black tide. Shadow warriors flowed over the walls while my human soldiers charged the gates—gates now conveniently undefended, their guards too busy dying at their own hands.

I vaulted onto my horse and rode toward the carnage, Arabella beside me. Through our bond, I felt her excitement spike, tinged with something darker. She was learning to love this—the power, the chaos, the absolute dominion over life and death.

And I had never been more in awe of her.

The gates hung open, one guard still twitching in a pool of his own blood while another cowered in the corner, whimpering about the eyes in the walls. I rode past without a second glance. The courtyard beyond was pure chaos—soldiers half-dressed, stumbling over one another, swinging at shadows and friends alike.

A robed figure stumbled from the tower, hands weaving defensive wards. The mage's face was pale with confusion and fear. "The barriers! How—"

I didn't let him finish. A tendril of shadow lashed out, wrapping around his throat and lifting him off the ground. His hands clawed uselessly at the darkness as I rode closer.

"Surprise," I said pleasantly, watching his eyes bulge with the realization that everything he'd been taught about Solandris's protection was a lie.

I released the spell. He dropped like a stone, gasping. Before he could recover, one of my shadow warriors descended on him, blade finding flesh with brutal efficiency.

A captain tried to rally the soldiers. "Form ranks! It's just illusions, you fools! Form—"

My blade took his head before he could finish. Blood sprayed across my face, hot and metallic. The familiar rush of battle sang through my veins, better than wine, better than anything except being buried inside my wife.

I spun, catching a desperate sword thrust on my blade. The soldier's eyes were clear—one of the few who'd resisted my initial spell. I drove my sword through his chest and watched the light fade from his eyes.

Around us, the battle raged. My forces cut through the confused defenders like a scythe through wheat. Some Solandrians tried to mount a defense, forming small pockets of resistance, but they were scattered and terrified.

We dismounted and sent our horses back through the gates.

I kept one eye on Arabella as we fought. A Solandrian soldier charged her, sword raised. I started forward, but she didn't need me. She sidestepped, graceful as water, and drove her dagger up under his chin. The man dropped, and she was already moving to the next target.

Thorne shadowed her as ordered while her magic flared in controlled bursts. Light and shadow danced around her hands—the duality of her power more pronounced with each passing day.

Pride swelled in my chest. My wife, my Dark Lady, baptized in blood and thriving.

I turned back to my own killing, sword moving in practiced arcs. Each death fed the hunger in my runes, the carved magic pulsing with satisfaction. This was what I was made for—not council meetings or diplomatic dinners, but this. The honest simplicity of conquest.

A crossbow bolt whistled past my ear. I turned, annoyed at the interruption, and found a cluster of archers on the western wall. With a gesture, I sent phantom flames racing up the stone. The fire wasn't real but their minds couldn't tell the difference. They fled, screaming about being burned alive, leaving their positions undefended.

"Behind you!" Arabella's voice cut through the din.

I spun, shadows already coiling around my fist, but she was there first. Her dagger took the attacking soldier in the kidney, dropping him with brutal efficiency. Our eyes met across his falling body, and the heat in her gaze had nothing to do with battle fury.

Well. Almost nothing.

"I had him," I said.

"I know." She smiled, fierce and beautiful. Blood was splattered across her face. "But I wanted him more."

Fuck. We were definitely going to have to discuss this new bloodthirsty streak of hers. Preferably while naked.

More soldiers poured from the barracks, these ones more organized. Someone had managed to rally them—probably a veteran sergeant who'd seen enough battle to recognize illusion from reality. They formed a defensive line, shields locked, spears bristling.

Behind them, three robed mages emerged, hands crackling with defensive magic.

I grinned. Finally, some proper resistance.

"The Dark Lord!" one of them shouted, voice cracking with panic. "Focus the wards on him! Channel the kingdom's—"

But nothing happened. I watched the confusion ripple across their faces as they realized their advantage had been stripped away.

"Looking for something?" I called across the courtyard.

The lead mage's face went white. He tried again, pouring more power into the spell, but I could feel his magic sliding off me. No resistance. No weakening. Nothing.

I charged them head-on. At the last second, I opened a portal and reappeared behind their line. My sword opened throats before they could turn. Blood painted the courtyard stones, and still my runes sang for more.

The battle raged on. I fell into the rhythm of it—cast, kill, move, repeat—though not so much that I lost sight of Arabella. My magic painted nightmares across the outpost. Soldiers saw their dead mothers crawling from the ground. The walls seemed to breathe and pulse like writhing flesh. The very air whispered threats and promises of worse to come.

This was what I was made for. This moment, this power, this absolute dominion over lesser minds.

And this was just a drop of blood before the hemorrhage. Soon all of Solandris would know what it meant to stand against the Dark Lord Kazimir Blackrose.

6

Watch, Learn, and Set Something on Fire
(Preferably the Enemy)

Arabella

Blood ran hot down my arm as I yanked my shadow dagger from the soldier's throat. The construct dissolved into wisps of darkness between my fingers, leaving nothing but the metallic tang of death on the air and a body at my feet. My chest heaved as I gulped for breath. The leather armor Kazimir had insisted I wear—clearly designed for someone with fewer curves and more height—pinched uncomfortably under my arms.

Dawn barely touched the sky, painting it a sickly gray pink above the chaos of battle. Screams and the clash of steel echoed across the outpost's courtyard, punctuated by the occasional crack of magic. The air shimmered with sorcery thick enough to taste.

I'd never killed so many people in a single morning. Or so many people at all.

I flexed my fingers, calling another dagger into existence. The shadows coalesced eagerly, responding to my will with a hunger that still surprised me. Dark magic was supposed to be difficult, draining. For me, it felt like breathing, each exhale manifesting as deadly shadow constructs.

"Lady Blackrose!" Thorne's voice cut through the din. "On your left!"

I whirled, throwing up a shield of light on instinct. An arrow shattered against it. Two archers had taken position on the ramparts, bows trained on me.

I reached for my magic again, but this time called on my bloodline—the power of the First Hero that flowed through my veins. Golden light bloomed between my palms, warm and alive. I shaped it with my thoughts, my will, my rage. Three birds of prey formed from the light, their wings beating with silent fury as they launched toward the archers.

The men barely had time to nock another arrow before my constructs tore into them. One screamed as talons of pure energy ripped across his face before bursting into flames. The other toppled backward off the wall, his bow clattering uselessly to the stones below.

Watch and learn, indeed.

I could feel Kazimir's approval through our bond, a warm pulse of satisfaction that mingled with my own sense of accomplishment. I could also feel the vast reservoir of his power. He was somewhere on the other side of the outpost, surrounded by a whirlwind of shadow and blood. I could feed my power into his if needed, amplifying his already formidable strength. But so far, he hadn't drawn on our connection. He hadn't needed to. The Dark Lord was in his element, and his magic flowed freely.

My body still hummed with the memory of Kazimir's hands on me last night, the way he'd pressed me into the pillow and made me come so forcefully that even now, in the middle of battle, I felt the heat of his body inside mine and wanted nothing more than to have it again.

A grunt of pain nearby snapped me back to my immediate surroundings. One of Kaz's mercenaries was down, clutching a bloody leg. I darted over and pressed my hand over his wound. "Hold still."

Life magic flowed from me, warm and golden, knitting tissues and sealing veins. The bleeding stopped. The soldier looked at me, his eyes wide with a mixture of gratitude and pure, unadulterated fear. Most of the army still viewed me as a terrifying, unpredictable sorceress. They weren't entirely wrong.

"Get back to the line," I ordered.

I pushed myself up just as a new wave of Solandrian soldiers charged through a shattered gate, their faces grim, their swords raised. Five of them, all converging on me.

"The Dark Lady!" one of them spat when he saw me. "Traitor to Solandris!"

At least they'd stopped trying to save me.

I threw up a shield, a shimmering dome of force that cracked under the first blow. I was powerful, yes. But I wasn't yet a seasoned warrior. My magic was raw and mostly untrained, fueled more by instinct than technique. And my inexperience was beginning to show.

The lead soldier circled left, barking orders. "Flank her! She can't hold that shield forever!"

A cold tingle pricked behind my eyes. A lie. He was trying to draw my attention while the real attack came from—

I spun right just as another soldier lunged from my blind spot. My truth-sense had caught his deception before my eyes could. I let him think his feint had worked, then at the last second dropped my shield entirely and rolled beneath his strike. As I came up, I drove a shadow dagger into his exposed side.

I hastily re-formed my shield and swung around.

A third soldier circled, looking for an opening. The others hung back now, eyes narrowed, assessing. These weren't the panicked, confused men who'd fallen to Kaz's illusions. These were trained fighters who'd regrouped and adapted.

I gritted my teeth and pushed more power into my shield, feeling it wrap completely around my body. With my free hand, I began to form another shadow dagger, but the strain of maintaining both light and dark magic simultaneously made my vision swim. Kazimir made it look so easy, juggling multiple spells as effortlessly as breathing.

Another sword crashed against my shield. I staggered back a step. The shield flickered, threatening to collapse.

Panic, cold and sharp, pricked at me. I was trying to hold the shield with one hand while desperately trying to form a new set of shadow daggers with the other. My magic felt sluggish, my focus splintering.

One of the soldiers, a burly man with a snarling, piggish face, grinned as he saw my shield waver. He raised his sword for a final, shattering blow.

This was it. This was how I was going to die. Well, at least I'd go down fighting.

Then a shadow fell over us.

Kazimir didn't even seem rushed. He was simply *there*, a dark storm of controlled violence. His face was spattered with blood, his eyes glowing with silver light. He looked like a god of war—beautiful and terrible and utterly merciless.

His eyes locked onto the soldier whose sword was poised to break through my shield. He didn't raise a hand. He didn't draw a weapon. He just spoke a single, guttural word in a language I didn't recognize.

The effect was instantaneous and horrifying.

The pig-faced soldier gasped, his eyes bulging. He dropped his sword and clawed at his own throat, his face turning a mottled purple. He made choking, gurgling sounds as smelly black water began to pour from his mouth, nose, and ears. His companions stared in horror as he collapsed, his body spasming on the dry, dusty ground.

Kazimir's gaze swept over the remaining soldiers. Another muttered syllable sent them choking too. They fell one by one, thrashing uselessly until they were still. Drowned on dry land.

He hadn't raised a finger.

He turned to me, his face a thunderous mask. The air around him crackled with residual magic, the runes on his neck glowing with a faint, malevolent light beneath his grime-streaked skin. There was no "I told you so" in his eyes, though. No chiding for my recklessness. There was only a cold, possessive fury that anyone had dared to get that close to me. That anyone had even *thought* about harming what was his.

To everyone else, he was the Scourge of Azroth, a terrifying warlord executing his enemies with casual, brutal efficiency.

To me, standing there covered in sweat, grime, and blood, his dark hair plastered to his forehead and his eyes burning with protective rage, he was the most breathtakingly attractive thing I had ever seen.

The adrenaline of the fight, the proximity to death, my own surging power all coalesced into a single, undeniable thought.

Invading a kingdom was excellent foreplay.

The ghost of a smirk played on my lips. He noticed it, of course. He noticed everything. His own expression softened almost imperceptibly, the raging storm in his eyes calming to a low, possessive simmer.

"Well?" he asked, his voice a low rumble that vibrated through me in places completely inappropriate for a battlefield. He gestured dismissively at the dead men at our feet. "Did you learn anything?"

He was still pissed. Royally pissed that I'd nearly been skewered.

"I learned that drowning people with magic is remarkably efficient." I tried for snark, but my voice was still a little shaky. The battle raged around us, but everyone was giving the villains a wide berth. "And that you have a flair for the dramatic, but that's not really new."

"Your shield failed. We're increasing your training." It wasn't a suggestion.

I rolled my eyes, affecting a weary sigh. "Kaz, you already have me fighting animated wooden constructs two nights a week, we spar with actual swords every other day, and I practice my own magic until I see spots. What's next? Sleep deprivation? Blindfolds? Fighting with one hand tied behind my back?"

A dangerous, wicked glint entered his eyes. He stepped closer, crowding me against a barricade, his body a solid wall of heat and power. His lips brushed my ear as he leaned in.

"Now that you mention it . . ." His voice dropped to a sinful whisper. "I've been thinking about blindfolds. And restraints. Though not for combat training."

A shiver of pure, unadulterated lust crawled straight down my spine and settled between my thighs. Gods, we were both terrible people—flirting in the middle of a massacre we'd orchestrated.

"I had it under control," I lied.

"Of course you did." His lips moved to my neck, teeth grazing just below my ear. "But I was getting bored over there."

The heat of his breath against my skin made my knees weak. The inappropriateness of it all—standing amidst death and destruction while wanting nothing more than to tear his clothes off—was its own kind of intoxication.

Before I could reply, he straightened, his public mask of the cold, aloof Dark Lord snapping back into place. He grabbed my arm, his grip firm but not painful.

"Come on." He began scanning the battlefield. "Let's go find someone else to kill."

He started dragging me along with him, deeper into the beautiful, bloody chaos he'd created.

The battlefield thinned as we advanced. Kazimir slipped between shadows, his magic reaching out to crush throats and snap bones. I followed in his wake, my own power flickering between golden light and consuming darkness as I dispatched those who thought me the easier target.

We were unstoppable. Untouchable. A perfect union of destruction.

"That commander—the one with the silver pauldrons," I called, pointing to a man barking orders atop another makeshift barricade.

Kazimir's eyes narrowed. "Shall we divide his attention?"

I grinned, already understanding the strategy. We'd practiced this maneuver in the training room countless times, but never unleashed it in battle. I circled left while Kaz moved right.

The commander spotted me first—the smaller target, the presumed weaker link. His sword raised as he shouted commands to his remaining men. Three broke formation, charging toward me.

I let my shadow daggers dissolve, instead calling forth the inverted healing magic I'd been perfecting. Gold light tinged with black swirled around my hands as I reached for the approaching soldiers. The first man's momentum carried him straight into my outstretched palm. His skin withered on contact, aging decades in seconds as I siphoned his life force. He collapsed, a desiccated husk.

The others faltered, their faces masks of horror. That moment of hesitation was all Kazimir needed.

He materialized behind the commander in a swirl of darkness, one hand gripping the man's throat. "Your men are dead," he said simply. "Your outpost is fallen. Do you yield?"

The commander's face contorted with hatred. "Death before surrender," he spat.

Kazimir's expression darkened. "As you wish."

I felt the surge of power through our bond as Kaz ended the man's life. One by one, the remaining soldiers dropped their weapons, finally breaking under the weight of inevitable defeat. Victory was ours—swift, brutal, complete.

An eerie quiet settled over the outpost, broken only by the groans of the dying and the crackle of a few lingering phantom fires Kazimir had yet to extinguish. His mercenaries moved through the courtyard dispatching the wounded soldiers.

Kazimir stood in the center of the carnage, a statue carved from shadow and fury. The silver light had faded from his eyes, leaving them the color of a storm-tossed sea. He turned his head, his gaze finding mine—possessive, hungry, and just a little bit proud. I felt myself flush under his scrutiny, my body responding to the unspoken promise in his eyes. Victory made him voracious, and I was more than ready to reap the rewards of our conquest.

Then the world tore apart.

It wasn't a sound. It was the *absence* of sound, a pressure that sucked the air from my lungs and replaced it with something burning and foul. A dissonant chord shrieked through my body, a vibration that ran up through the soles of my boots and into the marrow of my bones.

The Heirloom seared my mind.

Dozens of voices screamed at once—not in my ears, but inside my skull. A chorus of pure, undiluted terror, the sound of souls being ripped from their mortal tethers. I saw it. A vision, stark and blinding. A flash of a golden field drenched in blood, of lives harvested like wheat, their essences siphoned into a gaping, black wound in the fabric of reality.

I staggered, my hand flying to my mouth as nausea crashed over me. The world spun, the courtyard dissolving into a smear of gray stone and crimson stains.

A scream ripped through the silence—raw, agonized, and terrifyingly close.

It was Kazimir.

I forced my eyes open, my vision swimming back into focus just in time to see him collapse. He dropped to his knees. The runes carved into his skin blazed with blinding, white-hot light, searing through his clothing and armor. His back arched, his body convulsing in agony so profound it stole his breath.

He clawed at the glowing runes, his jaw clenched so tight I heard his teeth grind. All his control, his impeccable, terrifying dominion, shattered into a million pieces.

No. Not again. I lurched toward him and fell beside him.

There we were. The conquering Dark Lord and his Lady, brought low in the heart of our first victory.

I could only do one thing. My hands were shaking so violently that instead of merely touching him, I draped my body over his and tried to help with his pain.

7

Retreat Under a Poisoned Sky

(and Other Tactical Necessities)

Kazimir

There are levels to pain, a connoisseurship one acquires with enough practice. The clean bite of a well-honed blade is a sharp, honest agony. A broken bone is a throbbing nuisance. Magical exhaustion feels like having one's soul wrung out like a damp dishrag.

This, however, was a new vintage, and it was fucking foul.

It was a symphony of agony conducted by a mad god, and my own bones were the orchestra.

One moment, I was savoring the sublime, blood-soaked afterglow of a flawless victory, my eyes drinking in the sight of Arabella—fierce, beautiful, and terrifying. The next, the universe folded in on itself. The runes carved into my flesh and bone—the very foundation of my power—blazed with the heat of a failed star. Every sigil screamed in protest, as if my mother's knife were at it again, digging for fresh bone to brand.

I distantly registered the battlefield. Scattered bodies, the air thick with the metallic tang of blood and conquest. Standard stuff. But the view was quickly obscured by a shimmering veil of agony as my knees decided, without consulting me, to buckle and meet the dirt.

A scream tore itself from my throat—a raw, ragged sound that stripped away every scrap of the Dark Lord's carefully constructed terror, leaving only the primal agony beneath.

Amaryska's face swam before my eyes. I was nine. Strapped to a stone altar in my mother's workshop—a room that perpetually smelled of incense and my own blood. Her version of a nursery.

"Hold still, boy." My mother's voice, clinical and dispassionate. The blade in her hand, etched with its own glowing runes, caught the candlelight. "Power requires sacrifice, my darling," she whispered as the blade bit deep, "and you are going to be so very powerful."

Unconventional parenting, to be sure.

The knife bit deep, scraping against bone. I hadn't screamed then. I'd learned early that screaming only made it last longer.

When she was finally finished, she wiped my blood from her hands onto her gray robes stitched in red.

"There," she said, her voice flush with the satisfaction of a job well done. "The foundation is laid. When these heal, we can move on to the more advanced sigils." As she unstrapped me, she whispered, "One day, you'll see this as the greatest gift I ever gave you."

I was on my hands and knees, my body slick with a cold sweat. My stomach heaved in a violent, gut-wrenching spasm. I managed to turn my head just in time to vomit a thin, bitter bile onto the stones. Weakness, absolute and terrifying, washed over me. My magic, my very essence, felt tattered. Violated. As if some celestial parasite had sunk its fangs into the core of my being and was attempting to drain me dry.

Fuck. *Fuck.* This was not part of the plan. Public displays of catastrophic, debilitating weakness were generally frowned upon in the Dark Lord business. Bad for morale. Terrible for my reputation.

Through the shrieking static in my skull, a single, anchoring presence cut through—Arabella.

She lay across me, her hands on my back. A wave of her clean, offensively bright magic washed over me. It felt like cool water on a burn, soothing the worst of the fire but not extinguishing it. Her touch was hesitant, her own shock crackling through our bond, but she was *real.*

And just as quickly as it had begun, the searing agony vanished, leaving behind a hollow, aching void and a weakness that made my limbs feel like they were filled with wet sand. The light from my runes dimmed, their glow fading back beneath my skin.

I lay there breathing hard. Arabella shifted so that she was beside me instead of on top of me, her hands trembling.

Shit. We were in the middle of a conquered enemy outpost, surrounded by my men, who were currently busy slitting the throats of the survivors. They couldn't see this. They couldn't see their invincible leader laid low, puking like a green recruit after his first battle.

Control. That was the first and only instinct. *Seize it, wield it, fake it if you have to.*

I forced myself to straighten. My head swam, and for a terrifying second, the world tilted sideways. I gritted my teeth, planting a hand on the ground to steady myself. Arabella's hand stayed on my back.

Thorne hurried over, his face a mask of concern.

"My lord?" he ventured, his eyes flicking from me to Arabella and back again.

I drew a breath. It felt like inhaling shards of glass. "Secure the outpost," I managed to rasp. "Hold this position. Send scouts south but engage no one. Await my orders."

Thorne's eyes widened slightly at the clipped, urgent commands, but he simply nodded, his jaw tight.

"And Thorne," I added, channeling every scrap of menace I had left, "the official story is that I was overcome by the sheer brilliance of my own victory. Anyone who suggests an alternative version will be used for target practice."

He swallowed. "Understood, my lord." He turned and began barking orders.

Excellent. Now for the hard part.

Getting the hell out of here.

My only priority was removing Arabella from whatever this was. Back to Skyspire. Back to the controlled environment of my fortress where I could figure out what fuckery was afoot without an audience.

I turned to Arabella. "Skyspire."

She nodded, her eyes full of questions. "Can you manage a portal?"

Usually, a portal was as simple as breathing for me, but now . . . "We're about to find out."

I closed my eyes, focusing my will, what was left of it. I reached for the familiar threads of spatial magic, the power to bend and tear the fabric of reality. I pictured the Inner Sanctum, the cold, dark stone of my private workroom. I pulled.

The air in front of us began to shimmer and fracture. A hairline crack of pure darkness appeared, as thin as a spider's thread. But the portal wasn't obeying. Instead of a smooth, silent tear, it shrieked—a high, keening wail like tortured metal. It flickered, spitting sparks of corrupted energy, unstable and malevolent. It felt like I was trying to open a door while a ten-ton behemoth was holding it shut on the other side.

Black spots danced in my vision. The weakness intensified, threatening to drag me back down to the unforgiving stone.

"Kazimir!"

Arabella's voice was sharp, cutting through my faltering concentration. Her hand closed around my forearm, her grip strong.

And then she pushed.

It wasn't a physical shove. It was a deluge. A torrent of her magic, bright and clean and an utterly offensive shade of heroic gold, poured into me. It wasn't the slow, symbiotic exchange we'd grown accustomed to through the Heirloom. This was a desperate, full-force intervention. Her untainted, heroic power slammed into the corrupted, struggling dregs of my own.

With a final, guttural roar, I shoved the last of my energy into the spell. The portal snapped open, revealing the familiar stone of my workroom. I hooked an arm around Arabella's waist and hauled us through.

We collapsed onto the floor as the portal slammed shut behind us with a deafening crack of thunder. The backlash left us gasping, a tangled heap of exhausted Dark Lord and dangerously competent Dark Lady.

Silence. Utter, profound silence, broken only by the sound of our ragged breathing. The air in here was still and cold, smelling of ancient stone, ozone, and the faint, alchemical tang of my various ongoing experiments. A stark contrast to the iron-scented chaos we'd just left.

For a long moment, we just lay there, tangled together on the floor, the raw, visceral power of our escape leaving us both shaking and drained.

My first coherent thought, after the roaring in my ears subsided, was for Arabella. I pushed myself up onto one elbow. My gaze raked over her, a frantic, clinical assessment. No visible wounds. No blood—that was hers, anyway. Her face was pale, her eyes wide with shock, but she was breathing. She was whole.

"Are you all right?" I managed, my voice hoarse.

She pushed herself up, her hair a wild storm around her face. "Fine. Just . . . drained." Her eyes fixed on me with worried intensity. "You're not, though. What in the nine hells was that?"

"I don't know." The admission cost me. I was the Dark Lord. I was supposed to have answers. I was supposed to be in control.

I frowned, my fingers instinctively tracing the burning runes beneath my skin. The sensation was familiar—that prickling awareness that came when magic shifted in unexpected ways. But this was different. The usual hum of power that connected us to the earth's veins felt tainted. Like drinking clear water only to find mud on your tongue.

"Something's wrong with the ley lines," I said, the realization crystallizing as I spoke. "Something's wrong with—"

I stopped, the words dying in my throat.

The ley lines were the foundation of all magic in the Western Realms. They were what made the Heirloom of Dominion so powerful, what gave it the ability to dominate entire kingdoms.

I shook my head, my mind already working, analyzing, compartmentalizing the visceral horror of the memory. The burning runes. My mother's voice. That was old news. The corruption, however—the alien presence in my magic, in my Heirloom—that was new.

And I do not appreciate new things I haven't personally approved.

I levered myself into a sitting position, my back against the leg of a heavy oak table littered with alchemical glassware. I ran a hand through my sweat-damp hair and let my head fall back against the table leg with a dull thud.

"What. The. Fuck," I said angrily. "Is wrong with my Heirloom?"

8

Share Your Villain Origin Story

(and Make It Emotionally Devastating)

Kazimir

The door to my workroom burst open with a bang that made my already throbbing head pulse with fresh agony. Vex stood in the doorway, her silver hair a wild storm around her face, eyes wide.

"What in the hell—" she began, then stopped abruptly as she took in the scene before her.

Me, sitting on the cold stone floor, looking like I'd just lost a bar fight with a minor deity. Arabella, tangled beside me, looking similarly disheveled but with an added, infuriating dusting of heroic concern. And air that still sizzled with the ghost of our chaotic portal.

Vex's gaze flicked between us. Her eyes—today a shade of stormy gray that mirrored the churning chaos in my own mind—narrowed. "My lord. My lady." Her voice was deceptively calm, but I could feel the thrum of her agitation through the very stones of the citadel. "Judging by the magical signature that just rattled the teeth of every sentient being in a five-mile radius, and your current . . . floor-based strategy meeting, I'm going to assume the invasion is not going precisely to plan."

"An astute observation, as always, Vex," I said, my voice still a rasp. I let my head thump back against the table leg again. It was a nice, solid, grounding sensation. "Make a note: Invading Solandris is marginally more inconvenient than anticipated."

Vex stepped fully into the room, closing the door behind her with a soft click. She moved with that eerie grace of hers, crossing the stone floor to crouch beside us. "What happened?"

I waved her away, already pushing myself to my feet. My muscles were jelly; my bones felt brittle. But I'd be damned if I'd stay sprawled on the floor like some defeated novice. "The usual." I gestured vaguely. "A general sense that the universe is conspiring against my meticulously laid plans."

Arabella swayed as she rose, and I steadied her with a hand on her elbow. "We think there's something wrong with the Heirloom."

Vex's eyebrows shot up toward her hairline. "Again?"

"I need you to handle things," I said, not giving her a chance to ask more questions. "The army will be expecting orders, which are to hold position until we return in a day or two. Tell Thorne to leave the management to the generals and get his ass back here with Griffin so we can figure out what happened. In the meantime, double the patrols around Skyspire or below. No one in or out without my direct approval."

"And what will you be doing while I'm managing your empire?" Vex asked as she made for the door.

"Fixing this temporary setback."

She nodded, accepting the vague answer with the ease of someone accustomed to filling in the blanks herself. "Understood."

It was only after she'd left that I remembered. "Shit. Sebastian."

Arabella raised an eyebrow. "What about him?"

"Forgot to tell Vex we have a stray hero holed up in our war camp." I ran a hand through my hair, which was sticky with sweat and blood. "He'll be fine. Thorne can handle one pompous, golden-haired refugee."

Arabella snorted.

"Come on." I led her out of the workroom, through the cold stone corridors of the lower levels, and up the winding stairs to our private tower. The guards we passed snapped to attention, their faces impassive.

As we climbed, I felt her magic wash over me—a healing current, subtle but persistent. The ache in my bones eased slightly, and the worst of the dizziness receded.

I glanced back at her. "Thanks."

She smiled, a small, tired quirk of her lips. "Can't have the Dark Lord falling down the stairs. Bad for the brand."

"Indeed."

Our chambers were at the apex of the citadel, a sprawling suite with panoramic views of the distant jagged peaks and the endless sky. But I bypassed the sitting area, the bed, and the bathing chamber. My destination was a small, unassuming door tucked away in an alcove near the fireplace, hidden behind a tapestry.

I pressed my palm against the wood. The dozen or so wards I'd layered over it flared to life, shimmering in waves of color before recognizing me and dissolving. Finally, a small, sharp protrusion lifted out of the door. A quick sting, a drop of blood absorbed into the wood, and the door swung open silently to reveal a small curved room. The walls were bare stone, and the space was sparsely furnished with a couple of armchairs and a single pedestal of polished black obsidian.

And upon that pedestal, nestled on a cushion of velvet, sat the Heirloom of Dominion.

It looked deceptively simple—a circlet of gold, delicate yet sturdy, etched with intricate patterns that resembled the flow of ley lines across the land. Inside the band, a faint rose motif of thorns chasing thorns twined around, barely visible unless you held it up to the light. The air in the warded chamber was heavy with contained power, as usual, but the Heirloom gave off a low, discordant hum like an instrument horribly out of tune.

I stared at the circlet, my jaw tight. Ten years of searching, scheming, and slaughtering for this one, stupidly elegant piece of gold. Ten years of believing it was the key to absolute, unquestionable power. And now?

"It wasn't supposed to be like this."

Arabella stood beside me, her arms crossed over her chest. "You thought you'd put on the magic hat and the whole world would just kneel?" Her words were playful, but the delivery held weight. She was invested in this too.

"That was the general premise, yes."

I took the Heirloom from its pedestal. It was cool to the touch, but the moment my fingers closed around it, that discordant hum intensified, vibrating up my arm, through the runes in my bones.

Before Arabella could protest, I lifted the circlet and placed it on my head.

The world didn't go black this time. I didn't collapse. But the effect was no less unsettling.

The power was there, a surge of raw, untamed energy flooding my senses. A promise of the dominion I'd craved for so long. But it was muddy. Beneath the surge of power was a cold, alien undercurrent that made the hairs on my arms stand on end.

And there was something else.

A flicker of movement at the edge of my vision. A sliver of shadow deeper than the ambient darkness of the room, coalescing and then vanishing when I tried to focus on it. A whisper, formless and subvocal, slid into the back of my mind, a sibilant hiss that wasn't a word but felt like a command.

. . . mine . . .

I felt as if something hungry were watching me, looking out at the world through a crack in the wall of my own mind. Cold dread lanced through me. I ripped the Heirloom off my head and tossed it back onto the pedestal.

"Fuck."

"What is it?" Arabella asked. "It felt ugly and twisted."

Of course, she would have seen most of it through our bond. I forced myself to meet her gaze. "It feels like power," I said slowly, "but corrupted. It's different than before—when I first placed it on my head, it was just raw potential. Overwhelming, yes, but pure. Now there's something else underneath." I flexed my fingers, trying to shake off the phantom sensation of a foreign presence.

Her worried concern was written plainly across her face. "I'm fine," I snapped, turning away from both the artifact and her penetrating gaze.

"You don't look 'fine,'" she pressed. "You look like you were about to be sick again. What's going on? What's so important about conquering that gods-forsaken kingdom that you're willing to risk . . . this?" She gestured vaguely at me, at the Heirloom, at the entire mess we were in. "Why Solandris? Why are you so obsessed?"

I whirled on her. "Why not Solandris? It's rich, it controls key trade routes, its resources would strengthen my position against the Syndicate, and it's ruled by a self-righteous hypocrite who deserves to be brought to his knees. Are those not reasons enough?"

"There are other rich kingdoms. Other strategic locations." She shook her head. "This is personal to you for some reason. Why, Kazimir?"

Her hazel eyes pinned me, her truth-sense stripping away my deflections, wanting honesty. And something inside me, some long-locked door in the dungeon of my soul, creaked open.

I sighed heavily and ran a hand over my face, feeling the rough scrape of my stubble. Why Solandris? It was a question I hadn't allowed myself to fully articulate in years.

The fight drained out of me, replaced by the weight of memory. I leaned back against the cold stone wall. "It's complicated."

"I have time," she said softly, moving closer until she was standing just a breath away. She didn't touch me, but her presence was an invitation. *Talk to me.*

And for some insane reason, I wanted to.

"You know I killed my father." I watched her face, saw the flicker of acknowledgment. "He was a mercenary warlord. A brute named Vargus who called his own lands Azroth, a petty but brutal fiefdom on the eastern coast. He wasn't my father in any meaningful sense of the word. He was my progenitor. A biological necessity."

I paused. The memories were still so vivid I could taste rust coating my tongue, feel old blood slicking my palms. "My mother, Amaryska, was a powerful sorceress. But when Vargus's army landed on her small island in the eastern sea—or the Shattered Sea as many call it—the population was easily overwhelmed. The mercenaries took what they wanted from the island. He took what he wanted from her. And the result was me."

Arabella's breath hitched. She knew about my mother carving the runes into my bones, but not the circumstances of my conception. I saw the horror dawn in her eyes, quickly followed by a wave of emotion. It wasn't pity. Pity, I could have handled. Pity, I could have sneered at. This was something that felt dangerously close to understanding.

I blew out a frustrated breath and sank into a chair.

"Amaryska raised me as a weapon." The words came more easily now, a torrent held back for too long. "A tool for her revenge. The runes in my bones, the training, the constant lessons in warfare and sorcery . . . it was all to forge me into something that could one day slit his throat. She saw the potential in my magic, in my ambition. So she nurtured it. She was a brilliant, ruthless teacher. And a monstrous mother."

I pushed out of the chair and began to pace again. "I slaughtered my first battalion for her when I was fifteen. At seventeen, I led a rebellion against my father, finding allies among the rebels Vargus had crushed. It wasn't difficult. His own people could barely stomach him. I walked into his hall during a feast, with his own commanders at my back, and beheaded him at his own table. That's how I became the Scourge of Azroth."

The memory was as clear as yesterday. The look of shocked disbelief on Vargus's face. The spray of blood. The satisfying thud of his head hitting the floor. It was a triumphant moment.

"And your mother?" Arabella asked quietly. "You said she abandoned you."

I gave a short, bitter laugh. "Once her revenge was complete, she vanished. Her weapon had served its purpose. She didn't need me anymore."

Arabella remained silent, letting me gather my thoughts. I hesitated at the next part. The nightmare that stalked the edges of my mind in the darkest hours, the thing I'd spent sixteen years trying to bury so deep it could never claw its way back to the surface.

The demon.

Even thinking the word made my skin crawl, made the scars on my chest burn with phantom pain. "The commanders who had backed me, my supposed allies . . . they saw a seventeen-year-old boy who had just toppled a warlord. A threat. So they sold me."

"*Sold* you?" she whispered.

I met her gaze, and for a moment, the Chamber of Accords materialized around me. I saw Zaraiah's venomous smile, heard her taunt. *Has your new wife heard stories of that incident?* I remembered the hot spike of fear, the cold rage at having my deepest wound exposed. I'd shut Arabella out then, viciously. Because Zaraiah had wielded the story as a weapon, and I refused to let it hit its mark.

But this was different. Arabella wasn't wielding anything but a request for the truth. A truth she had earned a hundred times over when she bound herself to the Heirloom, when she fought for my home as if it were her own. She'd seen me at my most powerful and my most pathetic, and she was still here. To keep this from her now wasn't guarding a weakness. It was insulting her strength.

"When Zaraiah mentioned this," I said, forcing the words out, "I refused to speak of it. She wanted to use it as a dagger. For you, it's just a fact. Another ugly stone in the foundation." I took a breath. "They sold me to a demon."

Arabella's breath hitched. A flash of understanding—and something fiercely protective—lit her eyes as the pieces clicked into place. Zaraiah's comment about my *fascination with demonic anatomy.* The memory of my fury in the Chamber of Accords, the splintering chair, the thorns thick with poison. Arabella's expression wasn't one of horror at the revelation, but of recognition at the weight of my confession. She knew what it cost me to say those words aloud to her now.

"That's what she was talking about," Arabella murmured, her quiet way of telling me she understood.

"Yes." The memory was a room in my mind I kept locked. The seduction, the slaughter, the sheer, messy trauma of it all—I still wasn't going to give her every detail. But I could give her the shape of the thing. "I escaped," I said simply. "I came back, raised my own army, and took Azroth for myself, along with its strategic port city on the coast. I killed every last one of the men who betrayed me. Slowly."

I stopped in front of Arabella. Her expression wasn't pity. It was a cold, hard fury that mirrored my own. "I spent the next few years building my power. Taking what I wanted. Proving that I was beholden to no one. I took Skyspire. I took the kingdoms on the eastern coast, one by one. I clawed my way into the Syndicate's good graces by loaning out my mercenaries to them—for a fee, of course—until I became so indispensable to them they had to offer me a chair. I built an empire on a foundation of fear and control, because it's the only foundation that holds."

My gaze fell on the Heirloom again. "Then I came for Solandris."

"Why?" she pressed. "Because it was next on the map?"

"Because it was wealthy and strategically vital. But it stopped me." I clenched my jaw. "A kingdom of sanctimonious flower-worshippers and their vaunted heroes. I marched my forces to its borders, my magic at its peak, and I was thrown back. Not with armies. Not with steel. With its magic. Some inherent property of the land, of its ley lines, that blunted my own power. It made my runes ache. It weakened my shadows. It was the first time in years that something had not just resisted my will, but actively repelled it. And I . . ." I trailed off, searching for the word.

"You hated it," Arabella supplied, her voice a soft whisper.

I nodded. "To lose is one thing. To be denied, to be told there's a power I cannot have, a place I cannot conquer, is unacceptable. Solandris isn't just a kingdom to me, Arabella. It's an insult. It's the one damn thing in this world that has ever said 'no' to me and made it stick. I want to remake it. I want to crack it open and own the power that denied me. I want to grind their Golden Roses and their self-righteous history into the dust. Because I can. Because I should have been able to years ago."

The confession left me breathless. My heart hammered against my ribs hard enough to hurt. I'd never told anyone the whole story like that. The only other person who knew all of it was Vex. I'd laid out the ugliest parts of myself, the blood and betrayal and ambition that had forged me, and Arabella was just . . . watching me. I braced myself for the recoil, the judgment, the fear.

Instead, she stepped forward and wrapped her arms around my waist, pressing her cheek against my chest, over my heart.

The unexpected affection sent a jolt through me. My entire body went rigid. Affection was a language I was not fluent in, even with her. My first instinct was to pull away, to reestablish the distance, the control.

But her arms were warm around me. She smelled of the intoxicating scents of battle and magic. I could feel the steady beat of her heart against my ribs, out of step with my own but somehow stronger. Beating out a slower tempo that reverberated through every part of me in an invitation, willing my heart to follow hers.

Something in my chest cracked open.

Slowly, I let my own arms come up to encircle her. I rested my chin on the top of her head, her golden hair soft against my skin, and for the first time in what felt like a lifetime, I just breathed.

It was terrifying.

And the best thing I'd ever felt.

We stood like that for a long moment, the silent, warded room a world away from the battles and betrayals outside. Finally, she stirred, pulling back just enough to look up at me.

"All right," she said. "My turn."

I blinked. "For what?"

"To try the magic hat."

9

Start with Brilliance, End with Screaming

(The Villain's Journey)

Kazimir

Arabella made the suggestion as if it were the most obvious thing in the world. She pulled away completely, turning to face the Heirloom. "You said it yourself, the land of Solandris resisted you. But it's *my* land. My blood. The First Hero's blood runs in my veins. He's the one who forged it, if all accounts are true. Maybe it's not just about amplification. Maybe it needs a specific key to turn the lock. And time is more critical now than ever, right? We need to return to Solandris."

It was logical. It was brilliant. It was absolutely terrifying. The thought of that corrupted power touching Arabella—she was connected to it more than I was. If she wore the Heirloom now, what would happen?

"It's too dangerous."

"More dangerous than you going back in there alone and getting your mind scrambled?" Her perfect eyebrow arched in challenge. "You can guide me. I can be your eyes. We do it together. Anyway, it's not like I haven't worn it before."

Her logic was infuriatingly sound. And the stubborn set of her jaw told me she wasn't asking for permission. She was telling me what was going to happen. Godsdamn, I lov—cherished that about her.

I let out a long, slow breath. "Fine," I ground out. "Try it. But if you feel anything wrong, you take it off immediately. Understood?"

She rolled her eyes. "Yes, Daddy."

I scowled at her. "You don't have a daddy kink."

Her lips turned up wryly. "No, because my father is a bastard too, though not—" Arabella sighed and left the rest unsaid. She didn't need to compare our fathers, though I felt much angrier at the way she'd been treated than any ill treatment I'd ever received at the hands of my mother.

She approached the pedestal, lifted the circlet, examined it briefly, took a deep breath, and settled it onto her head.

For a second, nothing happened.

And then, she gasped. Her eyes went wide, not with pain, but with awe. "Kaz," she whispered. "I can feel them again."

I placed my hands on her shoulders, focusing her. "Good. Find the lines that run beneath Solandris. Show me."

I closed my eyes, opening my mind to our bond, letting her act as the conduit to the Heirloom. The world dissolved, and the vision she was seeing flooded my mind.

It was breathtaking. A glowing web of pure energy, veins of golden light crisscrossing the continent, pulsing with the lifeblood of the realm. I saw the smaller lines converging on Skyspire, feeding our fortress, and spreading out in every direction.

And then I saw Solandris.

And the breath caught in my throat.

The ley lines there weren't gold, but a dead, necrotic black, like veins filled with poisoned blood. The infection was centered around the capital of Sunspire but already spreading, tendrils of darkness creeping outward, poisoning the magic of the land.

I cursed. "That's what happened on the battlefield. We were too close to the corrupted lines. My magic tried to connect with them through the

Heirloom, and . . ." I trailed off, remembering the searing pain, the feeling of something alien invading my power.

"It's spreading," Arabella said, her voice tight with concern. "And our magic is connected to each other through the Heirloom. That's why we felt it." She told me briefly of the screams she heard, as if dozens of lives were abruptly ended. "Does it have something to do with Auremar?"

I was still holding her, still watching the black ley lines. "Most likely. Sebastian told us Auremar rounded up the heroic bloodlines, didn't he? He must have gotten what he needed."

Arabella shuddered. "So they're all dead? Every remaining descendant of the First Hero?"

I squeezed her shoulders. "We can't know that yet. But it's a safe bet that Auremar had to find a lot of them"—my jaw tightened in anger—"to equal one of you."

Her voice was hollow. "And since he couldn't get me, he . . ."

"That's my assumption, yes." My own voice sounded distant, as if it belonged to someone else. I felt the vision of the ley lines fade as Arabella's focus faltered, but I didn't need to see it anymore. The image was burned into my mind. I released her shoulders and took a step back.

I was *this close.* The outpost was ours, the army positioned, Solandris's border defenses crumbling. And now—

Without the Heirloom's full might, pushing deeper into Solandris would be suicide. I'd be stretching my resources against the kingdom's full strength if they were allowed to rally. We needed to fix this and return within days. *Days.* Not weeks. Not months.

But even as I thought it, I knew. This wasn't a loose connection or a misaligned rune. This was rot. Corruption. Poison spreading through the very foundation of the power I'd spent a decade hunting.

The victory at the outpost now felt hollow. Our grand first step into conquering the kingdom had landed on rotten ground. The ultimate prize, the power I had clawed and killed for, was nothing more than a festering disease.

I had been too late.

The absurdity of the failure was so immense, so spectacular, that I started to laugh. It started as a low, incredulous chuckle that scraped my throat raw. Ten years of planning, of bloodshed, of relentless ambition, only to discover that sanctimonious bastard Auremar had poisoned the well with his incompetence.

It was like conquering a brothel only to discover it was a leper colony.

The laugh grew louder, sharper, tipping over the edge from bitter amusement into something unhinged. It was the sound of a man's carefully constructed world cracking down the middle.

And just as quickly as it began, the laughter stopped. The air in the small chamber crackled, growing heavy and cold.

My magic erupted without conscious thought—a shockwave of dominion energy that shattered the closest chair and part of the wall behind it. Splinters of wood and fragments of stone rained down around us.

It wasn't enough. My fist clenched, and the next chair didn't explode, it merely unraveled as my dominion magic unmade it. It collapsed in on itself and then disappeared.

"I spent a DECADE!" My voice cracked, a ragged edge to it that I'd never allowed anyone but Arabella to hear. "Tracking down every scroll, sacrificing everyone who stood in my way. I built an entire bloody EMPIRE for this moment! IT WAS MINE!"

I seized a jagged shard of the chair and hurled it across the room.

"Kaz!" Arabella's voice barely penetrated the roaring in my ears.

My magic surged again. The obsidian pedestal cracked with a sound like breaking bones, a spiderweb of fractures racing across its surface before it collapsed into a pile of glittering black shards. The air temperature plummeted so rapidly that frost crystallized on the walls.

I kicked the remains, my composure fractured beyond recognition. "Do you know what it's like to build your entire identity around a single purpose, only to have it rendered meaningless? What it's like to claw your way up from nothing, to earn every ounce of power with blood and pain?" The room darkened until the angry glow of my runes was the only source of light. "I'm going to peel Auremar's skin from his body. And then I'm going to make him watch as I use it to bind the grimoire that details exactly how I'll unmake his precious kingdom."

I whirled toward the door, my magic crackling around me. Every fiber of my being demanded violence—blood and screams to drown out the howling failure in my mind.

"Kaz." Arabella's voice sliced through my rage.

I froze, one hand already on the door, fingers digging into the wood. My gaze snapped to her, the rage momentarily suspended as I registered the shimmering barrier between us—a translucent shield she'd cast to protect herself from the destruction I'd unleashed.

Shame cut through my fury. But it was the look on her face that truly arrested me. It wasn't fear. It was a deep, quiet hurt that I didn't have the first clue how to decipher. I had just laid my soul bare, my ambition, my entire reason for being, and in response, she looked wounded.

I reeled in my shadows, feeling like I was failing a test I hadn't been given. "I would never—" I began, the words catching in my throat.

"I know." She let out a small breath. The shield dissolved into sparkling motes of light. "But the chamber is rather small for your magnificent wrath, and I wasn't keen on picking splinters out of my skin all evening."

Her attempt at humor didn't quite mask the hurt in her eyes.

"Besides," she added, gesturing with her chin, "I was protecting the Heirloom."

My gaze followed the gesture, and with a jolt of alarm, I remembered with dawning horror that the godsdamned thing was still on her head.

The Heirloom was now a direct conduit to that magical plague. Using it wasn't just dangerous; it was an invitation for that corruption to flow directly into the bearer. Into us. *Into my wife.*

Rage, hot and sharp, mingled with a cold, terrifying dread. "Take it off," I said, my voice dangerously quiet. "Arabella. Take it off now."

She tried to. Her hands flew to her head, scrabbling at the golden band. A look of panic flashed across her face.

“I can’t,” she choked out, her fingers sliding uselessly off the smooth metal. “Kaz, it’s . . . it’s stuck.”

I grabbed it to help. The Heirloom of Dominion flared with a blinding golden light. The metal burned my fingertips, searing hot as if fresh from a forge. I tried to wrench it free, but it clung to her as though fused to her skin.

“It’s burning!” Arabella cried out. “Kaz, get it off me!”

I gripped the circlet more firmly, ignoring the scorching pain that lanced through my palms. The runes carved into my bones flared in response, muting the waves of agony up my arms.

“Hold still,” I commanded, though my voice betrayed more fear than authority.

Arabella cried out as I pulled harder. “Hurry,” she gasped between ragged breaths. “It feels like it’s melting into me.”

The golden light intensified, becoming so bright I could barely look at her. The metal began to liquefy beneath my grip. Not loosening. Transforming. Sinking into her flesh like molten gold. She screamed. Then, with an audible *shimmer*, the circlet vanished. Her screams turned to whimpers, then silence as her eyes rolled back.

“Arabella!” Terror clawed through my chest as she slumped forward into my arms. I cradled her limp form against me, my heart hammering with a panic I hadn’t felt since I was a child facing my mother’s knife.

The Heirloom had sunk into her flesh as if it were nothing more than a mirage, leaving only the faint, gilded outline of a crown tattooed across her forehead.

10

Merge with a Magical Artifact

(and Other Unexpected Relationship Milestones)

Arabella

Consciousness returned slowly. The first thing I noticed was warmth—not the searing burn from before, but something pleasant like sunshine on bare skin. The second was Kazimir's arms around me, his voice a low, urgent murmur above my head.

"—bella. Arabella, please. Open your eyes."

I blinked them open to find his face inches from mine, storm gray eyes wild with barely controlled panic.

Relief crashed over his features so violently that for a moment I thought he might cry. Instead, he crushed me against his chest, one hand cradling the back of my head.

"Don't," he said roughly, "*ever* do that again."

"I'll try to avoid having magical artifacts burn my skull in the future," I said against his blood-soaked clothes.

He pulled me back and stared at me for a long moment, then helped me stand. The searing agony that had consumed me moments ago had vanished completely, replaced by a strange, humming vitality that coursed through my veins. Not even the faintest echo of pain remained—only a peculiar sense of expansion, as if my skin could barely contain whatever new power now resided within me.

"What the hell just happened?" I traced my forehead where the Heirloom had been. Instead of metal, I felt only warm skin with a faint, pleasant tingle, as if someone had drawn the circlet's shape with warm honey.

Kazimir gaped at me, his earlier panic shifting to bewilderment. "The Heirloom. It melted into you. There's a mark—" He traced the air above my forehead, not quite touching. "Like a golden tattoo, but barely visible."

"But why would it do that?" I asked, still feeling my forehead. "Why would an ancient artifact designed to control ley lines suddenly decide to melt into me?"

Kazimir shook his head, genuine confusion darkening his features. "I have no idea. Nothing in the texts mentioned anything like this."

A chill ran through me as I remembered the vision of darkness coiling inside him, the Shadow King's presence that he seemed completely unaware of. Could that be why? Was the Heirloom somehow responding to the darkness within him by seeking refuge in me instead? The thought formed a knot in my throat, but I swallowed it down. Now wasn't the time to voice such concerns—not when I barely understood what had happened.

My mouth quirked up despite the sick twist in my stomach. "For someone who just had their life's ambition literally absorbed into his wife's head, you're taking this remarkably well."

He gestured vaguely at the destroyed room. "I've already had my tantrum for the day. There's nothing left here to destroy."

"I can still feel it." I looked up as if I could see my own forehead. "It's merged with me somehow. I can sense the ley lines, but they're fainter now."

Kazimir's fingers hovered just above my skin, and I felt the familiar electric tingle of his magic brushing against mine. "Can you control it? Sever the connection?"

I concentrated, trying to push the Heirloom away. Nothing happened.

Then I tried a different approach—not pushing it away, but closing a door in my mind.

To my surprise, it worked. The awareness of the magical currents faded to a background hum. "I can block it out. Not remove it, but I can choose not to listen."

His shoulders relaxed fractionally. "Good. Very good." He ran a hand down his face. "We need to research this. If the Heirloom is connected to those corrupted ley lines, and now it's connected to you . . ."

The implication was clear—the corruption could flow into me.

"We'll figure it out," I said with more confidence than I felt.

He took my arms and turned me around as if he could figure out a solution just by staring at my head. "I suppose we don't have much choice. It's not as if we can pry it out of your skull."

"That's the spirit," I said drily.

When I faced him again, genuine worry flickered behind his eyes. "Are you certain you're all right? That thing is powerful, and now it's woven into you."

I grinned. "On the bright side, we'll never misplace it."

Kazimir shot me a wry look. The tension slowly dissipated, replaced by bone-deep exhaustion. The battle, the chaotic portal jump, the emotional eruption, and now this—it had all taken its toll.

"You know," he said slowly, voice taking on that sardonic edge I recognized as his coping mechanism, "I nearly got myself killed for that artifact on multiple occasions. And now it's decided to take up permanent residence in your head. The universe must have it out for me."

"Maybe it's doing you a favor." I gestured to the destruction around us. Water from melting frost was running along cracks in the floor. "Since you've redecorated, I suppose we're done here?"

His lips twitched. "In my defense, discovering that your decade-long quest for power has been sabotaged by a sanctimonious flower king is rather irritating."

As we moved back into our main chambers, I couldn't help reflecting on what had just happened. Not the Heirloom merging with me—though that was certainly worth a minor existential crisis—but Kazimir's reaction to the corruption of the ley lines.

His rage hadn't surprised me. And I'd never once feared he would harm me. What hurt was how he'd seemed to dismiss what we'd found together. In his tirade about his decade-long quest, there had been no acknowledgment of us.

Of me.

If the Heirloom proved worthless, perhaps finding me hadn't been worth it. No—that wasn't quite right. What I really wanted, what made my chest ache, was for him to say that regardless of the Heirloom and his plans for conquest—*I* had been worth it. That kidnapping me, marrying me, opening himself to me had value beyond strategic advantage.

I wanted to matter more than his ambitions.

But he hadn't said that. In his fury over Auremar's interference, there had been no mention of what we'd built together, no acknowledgment that perhaps his decade-long quest had transformed into something more meaningful than mere dominion.

Weeks ago, when the Heirloom was cracked and useless, I'd asked if he regretted kidnapping me. He'd said no.

I knew Kaz had meant it, but today he'd experienced a life-altering setback. Naturally, I had questions.

Like would he regret marrying me if I couldn't help him conquer Solandris? If the Heirloom was now bound to me and useless to him? And another darker thought—what if I was partly to blame?

The setting sun filtered through storm clouds, casting our bedchamber in bruised purple and angry red—a fitting reflection of our mess. The day had ended far differently than it had begun.

Kazimir immediately began stripping off his battle-stained clothes. I followed suit, every muscle aching from the fight and subsequent magical chaos.

I shed the last of my armor, standing in just my thin, stained undershirt and leggings. "I feel like I've been dragged behind a horse across the entire Western Realms."

"You look it too."

I shot him a glare. "Such flattery, my lord. It's a wonder I resisted your charms for so long."

I regretted the words immediately, but his smile widened into something genuine. The tension between us eased. This was familiar territory—the banter, the teasing.

Kaz gestured to the bathing chamber. "Ladies first."

I appreciated the solo bath offer. After a battle, the idea of soaking in each other's blood and grime seemed revolting.

Once in the bathing chamber, I paused at the ornate mirror, curious. There—a faint shimmer around my forehead, like sun shining on gold. The outline of the circlet was barely perceptible, but unmistakable once you knew to look for it.

Well. That was a problem.

If Kaz and I could see it, so could anyone else who bothered to look closely. We'd need to figure out how to conceal it before I left our chambers.

I scrubbed off the worst before filling the tub, then sank into hot water with a groan of pure pleasure. But my thoughts wouldn't stop racing. For the first time, I felt grim satisfaction. Maybe this wasn't a disaster. Maybe it was a safeguard.

If the Heirloom was part of me, that shadowy entity from the vision couldn't use it through Kazimir. Or so I hoped.

As long as I kept the ley line corruption from leaking into me.

Later, while Kaz bathed, I combed out my hair and threw on a silk nightdress. Too restless to sit still but too exhausted for anything else, I did the only sensible thing and flung myself dramatically onto the bed.

I heard the bathroom door open. The bed dipped as he sat beside me.

"Planning to sleep in that position?"

"I'm contemplating the mysteries of the universe," I replied without opening my eyes.

"If you figure them out, let me know."

I cracked one eye open. He was gloriously naked, hair still damp, water droplets clinging to skin. His scars stood out starkly, a roadmap of old pain and power.

The lean muscles of his torso caught the lamplight, each defined ridge and hollow carved by years of warfare and training. He really was beautiful to look at, and I never squandered an opportunity. Broad shoulders tapering to a narrow waist. The subtle flex of muscle beneath skin that looked both battle-hardened and touchable. Powerful, corded thighs with strength even at rest. And nearly every bit of him covered in scars.

Everything about Kazimir radiated controlled power—from the casual way he held himself to the unconscious grace in his fingers splayed against the sheets. Even sitting still, there was something predatory about him, all coiled energy and barely leashed violence.

I could barely handle how unfairly attractive he was, but he was all mine.

Even when he came to bed soaking wet. "You're dripping on the sheets."

"Perhaps you should do something about it."

I rolled my eyes but sat up, reaching for his towel. "Turn around."

He obliged. I began drying his hair, fingers working through damp strands. He made a sound of contentment.

"Why does the Heirloom need dominion magic to work?" I asked. "If Soriven created it, did he also wield dominion magic?"

Kazimir groaned and ran a hand down his face. "Gods, Arabella, I don't know. I've spent years trying to decipher that thrice-damned trinket, and now it seems utterly pointless. It's a corrupted, useless piece of—"

"It's fused to my head." I gave his back a light shove. "So I'd say it's still rather relevant."

A muscle worked in his jaw. "Fine. From what I've pieced together, Soriven didn't wield dominion magic. He was a light mage—what your people would call a 'hero.' But he understood that light and shadow must exist in balance. The Heirloom was designed to channel both."

I frowned. "But if it needs dominion magic to work properly, and Soriven couldn't provide that . . ."

"Then he must have had help. Someone with dominion magic who worked alongside him. The historical records are frustratingly vague."

I slid around to face him, my hand on his shoulder. "Do you think that's why the Heirloom bonded with me? Because I have both types of magic?"

"It's possible. Your bloodline gives you an affinity for light magic, but you've also embraced the shadows. You're a bridge between the two."

I flopped back against the pillows, suddenly too tired for more revelations. "What happens now?"

Kazimir was silent for a moment. "We'll need to make a decision soon—return to Solandris with whatever we've got, or officially retreat and regroup." His jaw tightened. "I'm not ready to retreat."

"How much time do we have?"

The mattress shifted as Kazimir stretched out beside me, his bare skin warm through my thin silk. "I'd say we have a little time to kill before Griffin gets back." He trailed a finger over my stomach. "The trick is to adapt."

I rolled onto my side, and his hand came to rest on my hip. "Is that what you're doing now? Adapting to the fact that your precious artifact is now melted to my forehead?"

Something flickered in his eyes—a shadow of earlier rage, quickly suppressed. "It was never about the artifact itself. It was about what it could help me achieve."

"And now?"

He was silent for a long moment. Then he traced the Heirloom's outline on my forehead, his touch featherlight. "Now, I trust that it's exactly where it needs to be."

The simple statement stole my breath. Trust. From Kazimir Blackrose, who trusted no one, who built his empire on fear and control. Trust was the most precious gift he could offer.

The knot in my chest loosened. "I was worried. When you were raging about your decade-long quest . . . it was like I didn't exist. And if I hadn't fought you so hard in the beginning, if we'd activated the Heirloom sooner, maybe Auremar wouldn't have had time to corrupt the ley lines."

Kazimir's expression softened. "I wouldn't trade what we have now for anything—not one argument, not one battle of wills, not one night of you telling me to go fuck myself." I snorted. "Not even for having activated the Heirloom before Auremar could interfere."

It wasn't a declaration of love. But from Kazimir, it was as close as I'd ever heard. It was enough for now.

I leaned forward and pressed my lips to his. His hand slid to my neck, fingers tangling in my hair as he pulled me closer.

When we broke apart, he smirked. "Besides, now that the Heirloom has decided to take up permanent residence in your skull, I suppose I'll have to keep you around."

"You're stuck with me, Dark Lord."

He shifted to prop himself against the headboard, looking down at me with a smug expression as if to say it was the other way around. He ran a finger down my jawline.

I sat up to face him. "Why didn't you force me? When you first brought me here?"

Kazimir's hand stilled, his eyes searching mine. "What?"

"After you kidnapped me," I hurried to explain. "You needed me to activate the Heirloom. You could have forced me. Plenty of men with less power have done worse, for no reason at all." I swallowed hard. "Obviously, I'm glad you didn't. But . . . was it because of what your father did to your mother?"

His expression darkened. "I'd never cross that line, no matter what. Not ever."

The raw honesty made my heart ache. For all his darkness, all the blood on his hands, there were some evils even the Dark Lord wouldn't commit.

"Thank you," I whispered.

His answering smile was small but genuine. "Don't thank me for basic decency, Arabella. It sets the bar rather low."

I laughed. "Fair enough." I straddled his hips. My nightdress rode up my thighs, and I felt his immediate response to our new position.

Kazimir's hands settled on my waist, thumbs tracing circles on my hipbones. "Why do you insist on wearing these things to bed? I'm just going to take it off."

I rocked my hips over his erection. "Maybe I like you taking it off."

His eyes darkened with desire. In one swift motion, he hooked his fingers in the neckline and tore. The silk ripped clean down the middle.

"Kaz!" I yelped, more surprised than upset.

"I'll buy you a new one." He pushed the torn fabric off my shoulders. "Maybe I'll rip that one too." His hands gripped my hips, pulling me flush against him. "Now ride me."

11

Confess Everything but Love

(Your Body Will Do the Talking)

Arabella

The command sent a pulse of heat straight to my core. This was Kazimir at his most dominant, his most possessive, and gods help me, I loved it. I loved the way he took control, the way he demanded exactly what he wanted. Gods knew I fought him on everything else, but in this, there was a freedom in surrender. I loved the fire in his eyes when he looked at me like I was the only thing in the world that mattered.

I reached between us, wrapping my fingers around his thick, hard length. He hissed in pleasure as I stroked him once, twice, before positioning him at my entrance. I was already wet, ready for him, my body responding to his touch with embarrassing eagerness.

I sank down onto him slowly, savoring the delicious stretch, the feeling of fullness as he filled me completely.

His hands clenched on my hips, his knuckles white. "Gods, Arabella," he breathed, his eyes squeezed shut. "I will never, ever tire of this. Of you."

"Look at me," I whispered.

Kaz's eyes snapped open, blazing with silver light. He watched me as I began to rock against him, his gaze intense, possessive. It was a claiming but I didn't know who was claiming who. His hands roamed over my body—cupping my breasts, tracing the curve of my waist, sliding down to where we were joined.

I bent to place an open-mouthed kiss on his collarbone, tracing a scar with my tongue. Kaz shuddered and ran his hand through my hair. "I've never . . ."

I pulled back to look at him, waiting.

He put his hands on either side of my face and held my gaze.

"What?" I whispered.

"I've never felt as close to anyone as I feel to you."

I understood. Neither had I. I'd never allowed someone to look at me the way he did and enjoy it. Never allowed someone to know the shape of me and grant me the same privilege. Being open with him still frightened me, but now the fear was accompanied by a thrill.

Unsure what to say back, I leaned in to kiss Kazimir's mouth. Sliding my tongue along his lower lip, tasting him as I rocked against his body.

"You feel so fucking good," he rasped, his hips beginning to buck up to meet me. "So tight around me. Tell me you love it, Arabella. Tell me you love feeling me inside you."

"I love it," I whimpered, my pace quickening. The friction was exquisite, building a frantic, coiling heat deep in my belly. My world narrowed to the stretch of him inside me, the sight of his face contorted in a mask of raw pleasure, the sound of his low, guttural groans.

"Faster," he commanded.

I obeyed, increasing the pace until I was riding him in earnest, my breath coming in short, sharp gasps. The world narrowed to just the pleasure and the intensity of his gaze as he watched me chase my release.

"Kaz," I moaned. My climax shimmered on the horizon, close, so close. My thighs trembled.

His thumb found my clit, circling it with just the right pressure. "That's it," he coached. "Take what you want. Fuck me until you've taken all of me."

His dirty talk was a current that dragged me under. My breath came in ragged gasps.

"Kaz . . . I'm—"

"I know," he hissed, his hands sliding from my hips to grasp my ass, pulling me down harder onto his cock with each thrust.

That was all it took. The knot in my core tightened, tightened, and then exploded. A cry tore from my throat as waves of pleasure crashed over me. My body felt weightless, my vision blurring at the edges.

But he wasn't done.

As I was still cresting, lost in the throes of my climax, he wrapped his powerful arms around my waist. "Oh, no you don't," he grunted, and then he surged up, thrusting into me with a force that stole the air from my lungs and sent a secondary, shocking wave of bliss through me. *Oh!*

A strangled cry ripped from my throat. The wave crashed, a violent, shattering explosion of pleasure that sent stars bursting behind my eyelids. My body convulsed around him, my muscles clenching and unclenching.

"Still coming?" he asked roughly. He thrust up again, driving me back down onto him at the same time.

"Yes," I managed, my voice breaking.

"Again," he demanded, and thrust again. Harder. Deeper. "Again. Again. Again."

Three brutal, punishing thrusts that sent me spiraling, my orgasm shattering and re-forming into something even more intense, my entire body shaking with the force of it.

Kazimir buried himself deep inside me one last time. His body went rigid, and a harsh groan ripped from his throat as he came with a shuddering, violent intensity that mirrored my own. He held me tight against him, his face buried in my neck, his breath coming in harsh pants.

We collapsed against the headboard, a tangle of sweat-slicked limbs and shuddering breaths. I slumped forward, my head resting on his chest, my body limp and boneless. I could feel the frantic beat of his heart against my cheek.

We lay there for a long time, the only sound the crackle of the fire and our own ragged breathing. Eventually, his hand came up to stroke my hair.

"Better than conquering a kingdom," he murmured. His arms were still wrapped around me, holding me tight, as if he was afraid I might just vanish into the ether.

"Mm," I agreed languidly, smiling against his skin.

I shouldn't have been surprised, but each time with him somehow took me to levels of bliss I didn't know existed, with or without magic. Kazimir was insatiable, his stamina bordering on supernatural. A war god. A sex god. Was there anything he couldn't do?

Well, yes. Be vulnerable. He was still struggling with that.

Then again, so was I.

A shadow fell across the tower, darkening the room momentarily. Kazimir tensed beneath me, his eyes narrowing as he glanced toward the window.

"It's just Nyx," I said, feeling the flicker of her excitement to be home through our bond. "She's back."

Kazimir relaxed slightly, though his expression remained wary. "The others will be following soon, then."

I nodded. Thorne and the rest of our party would be returning to Skyspire, bringing with them news of the outpost and, presumably, our new guest, Sebastian. The thought of dealing with all of that—the reports, the strategies, the political maneuvering—was exhausting.

"I don't want to deal with any of them today," Kazimir grumbled, echoing my thoughts. "Not after everything else."

I smiled, trailing my fingers down his abdomen, feeling his body stir with renewed interest beneath me. "Maybe I can persuade you to stay in bed a little longer."

His eyes darkened with desire, and he flipped us over until the length of his body pinned mine to the bed. "If you insist, my lady."

12

Never Skip Dinner

(or Your Villain Will Get Hangry)

Kazimir

My stomach growled with such violence that Arabella lifted her head from my chest to stare at me.

"Was that you or an earthquake?" she asked.

"When did you last eat?" I countered, running my fingers through her hair. The shimmer of the Heirloom caught the firelight for a moment before disappearing beneath the strands.

She frowned, considering. "This morning? No, wait. Last night?"

"Exactly." I sat up, pulling her with me. "We need food before I start considering which of my minions looks most appetizing."

"Griffin's probably stringy." She stretched against me, all languid satisfaction and bare skin, and my body stirred with interest despite my exhaustion. "All that nervous energy."

"Thorne would be tough as leather." I swung my legs over the side of the bed, hunting for clothing. "Vex would probably poison me out of spite."

"Sebastian would taste like cinnamon rolls."

I shot her a dark look. "Arabella."

She grinned wickedly.

We dressed reluctantly. Arabella's hair was a wild tangle down her back, and she kept fidgeting with it.

"What are you doing?" I asked.

"Trying to figure out how to hide this." She gestured vaguely at her head, where the Heirloom had merged with her. "The shimmer shows through if the light hits it right."

She finally settled on a deep side part, letting her hair fall forward to shadow that side of her face. "I might have to cut bangs if this is permanent."

"Don't you dare." I liked her hair exactly as it was—long enough to wrap around my fist, golden enough to catch the firelight when she rode me.

"Possessive about my hair now too?" she teased.

I pulled her against me for another kiss. "About everything concerning you."

We finally made it out of our tower, heading down toward the small kitchen in the Inner Sanctum. The sun had long since set, and the corridors of Skyspire were lit by the orblights. Maybe we could still avoid everyone at least until morning.

"Finally emerged, have you?" Vex's voice came from directly behind us.

I didn't jump. I absolutely did *not* jump. But Arabella's hand tightened on mine, which meant she'd been startled too.

"How'd you do that?" Arabella asked, turning to face my steward.

Vex's purple hair caught the orblight as she smiled. "Practice." She looked us up and down with an expression that suggested she knew exactly what we'd been doing. "Late dinner is being served in the private dining room, if you're interested in actual food rather than whatever you've been sustaining yourselves on."

"Vex—" I started, irritation flaring.

"Thorne's back," Vex interrupted smoothly. "With Griffin. And your guest." Her eyes narrowed at me. "The one no one thought to inform me about."

"It was sudden," I said, not bothering to sound apologetic. "Lord Sebastian is under our protection for the time being."

"Wait. *Lord*?" Vex scowled.

"Yes, why?"

She huffed irritably. "I didn't prepare the right rooms for him, then."

I scowled right back at her. "It doesn't matter where he sleeps, does it? He's lucky to get anything that's not in the dungeon. Just give him a cot and access to a bath. I'm sure he'll—"

Arabella and Vex pinned me with the same look. A look that said Sebastian's accommodations absolutely *did* matter, and obviously I was a brutish warlord with no regard for decorum or the respect owed to a minor lord. Never mind that he was an enemy who was likely plotting my demise and was lucky his accommodations weren't six feet underground.

I was about to remind *them* that the warlord in question was paying the bills and feeding them exotic food when Vex spoke first.

"I'll get the servants to prepare new chambers while we eat."

"You invited him to dinner? Send up a tray of bread and water—"

Another glare.

I glared back.

Somehow in the last few weeks, Arabella and Vex had reached a point in their relationship where they agreed with each other over me. I didn't know when or how it happened. I didn't even know Arabella had a relationship with Vex, and this new development suggested a burgeoning friendship.

Before I could unleash my bubbling fury, Vex abruptly excused herself and vanished back into the shadows.

"She's good at that," Arabella observed. "I could learn a thing or two from her."

I huffed. "Since when did you become friends?"

Arabella looked at me like I'd sprouted horns out of my ears. "Is it a problem?"

A flash of possessiveness, hot and violent, surged through me. Mine. She was mine. No one else's. Ever.

I swallowed hard. "It's a problem when my steward and my wife present a united front against me."

Arabella's chin lifted, her gaze as steady as my own. "I'll form friendships with whomever I please, Kazimir. Or do you intend to approve my companions like you do your military appointments?" The challenge in her voice was unmistakable, a sharp edge honed by a lifetime of fighting for every scrap of autonomy.

"I'm not the type to share," I growled.

"So you've mentioned on multiple occasions." She stopped walking, forcing me to halt as well. "My having friends doesn't diminish what we have, Kazimir. Unless you're truly that insecure."

I stepped closer, shadows curling at my fingertips. "Insecure? I've conquered kingdoms."

"And yet one friendship threatens you." Her magic flared, golden light crackling against my darkness until the nearest orblight shattered in a shower of sparks.

Before I could retort, she shrugged. "Besides, I'm surprised you don't see it—Vex is a badass exactly like you."

I frowned, thrown off balance by the unexpected turn. *I* was a badass. Arabella was a badass. Vex was too, certainly, but she didn't look it with her slight frame and color-shifting hair. Though I supposed that was part of what made her dangerous.

"Explain."

"She's ruthlessly practical," Arabella said, as if it were the most obvious thing in the world. "She anticipates needs before they're spoken, she doesn't suffer fools, and she moves through this citadel like a shadow with a purpose. Her loyalty isn't blind obedience; it's to the stability and power of your rule." She paused, her eyes locking onto mine. "The only difference is that her domain is logistics and secrets, and yours is conquest and chaos."

I blinked. The comparison was accurate, irritatingly so. On seeing my expression, Arabella smirked.

But what really coiled in my gut wasn't insecurity—it was raw possessiveness. I commanded armies, orchestrated alliances, moved people like chess pieces. Arabella was the queen on my board, and now she was forging connections in *my* fortress with *my* steward.

The idea that Vex could earn Arabella's trust so easily, without my orchestration, grated against every instinct I had. It wasn't a threat to my power. It was a crack in my absolute dominion, a reminder that my wife didn't revolve entirely around my will.

I found I very much disliked it.

Arabella was looking down the corridor reluctantly. "I suppose we can't avoid them forever."

I was in a mood to try, but we had things to accomplish.

The short walk to the dining room took us through a section still bearing scars from the Hero's Guild attack. Piles of stone waited to be cleared, and scaffolding covered one wall where the stone had been blasted away. The sight of it made my blood simmer—not just at the damage, but at my own failure to prevent it.

Construction sounds echoed even at this late hour—Vex had the repairs running continuously.

"Part of the new wards," I said as we approached a team of rune carvers inscribing glyphs into a freshly repaired wall. The defensive wards had been temperamental since the attack, refusing to stabilize properly after whatever the Hero's Guild's magic had done to them. So I was starting from scratch.

Arabella asked questions about them, and for a moment, I forgot about our other problems and enjoyed her curiosity. Her insatiable appetite for knowledge rivaled my own.

" . . . layers upon layers of protection that will make even the gods think twice," I said as we moved on. No one would ever breach my citadel again.

Through one of the damaged outer walls, another keep was visible across the chasm—a half-ruined structure on its own isolated island. I'd warded it so heavily that even looking at it too long made most people's eyes water.

Arabella's gaze followed mine to the crumbling keep. Her eyes narrowed, then widened as if seeing through a veil for the first time. "How have I never noticed—"

“The Old Keep.” My voice dropped low enough that the workers couldn’t overhear. “When I first took Skyspire, that whole area resisted renovation. Workers had accidents. Tools shattered. The building itself seemed to reject any attempt to alter it.” I shrugged. “I gave up trying to change it, but it turned out to be exceptional at containing dangerous items. It’s a magical vault, of sorts, and why I keep it heavily warded.”

Her lips parted, no doubt to ask what kinds of things, but my stomach chose that moment to voice another complaint with a sound that could have woken the dead.

13

Share Your Table with a Hero

(Without Strangling Him, Somehow)

Kazimir

The private dining room was one of the few spaces that had escaped damage during the attack. It was considerably smaller than the Great Hall, with a table that could only seat six people comfortably. A roaring fire in the large hearth completed the intimate setting.

We'd barely entered when the door opened again, admitting Thorne with Griffin and Sebastian trailing behind. A guard hovered at the doorway—Sebastian hadn't been allowed to navigate the Inner Sanctum alone.

"My lord," Thorne said with a nod. "My lady."

"Lady Blackrose," Sebastian said with a deep bow that was both excessive and graceful. "I don't know how to thank you for your extraordinary kindness. And Lord Blackrose—" He turned to me with another bow. "Offering sanctuary to someone who has no claim on your mercy is . . . unexpected, given your reputation."

I glowered at him, about to remind him that I hadn't offered him anything.

"You're welcome, Sebastian," Arabella said, clearly fighting a smile. "Any enemy of Auremar's is a friend of ours."

Friend. I didn't like that word. Ally, perhaps. Useful asset, certainly. But friend? No.

"Thank you," Sebastian said warmly. I noticed his gaze had drifted to the black roses. He frowned slightly, then seemed to forcibly drag his attention back to us.

Beside him, Griffin was practically vibrating with excitement, looking at Sebastian like he was some kind of hero. Which, technically, I supposed he was. How nauseating.

As people found their seats, Sebastian's eyes kept flicking to the roses, his brow furrowing. He opened his mouth as if to say something, then closed it again, shaking his head slightly.

Thorne caught my attention. "A word?"

I let him pull me aside. Griffin was already stammering at Sebastian about the architectural integrity of the dining room's vaulted ceiling, though Sebastian seemed distracted, his violet eyes darting to the centerpiece again.

"The aftermath was handled," Thorne said, his voice low. "Most of our forces were still dealing with the bodies when you left. The few enemies who witnessed anything are no longer witnesses."

"Good." The last thing I needed was word spreading about my moment of weakness. My enemies would pounce on any sign of vulnerability.

"All in all, morale is high, my lord. The victory was decisive. The outpost is secured, and our forces are ready to move on your command. It was a perfectly executed campaign."

I resisted the urge to grumble about how it was hardly a campaign when everything had gone to shit before we'd even properly begun.

Thorne paused.

"What?" I prompted.

"Some of the shadow constructs you left behind are apparently still wandering around, terrifying the remaining servants in the outpost."

"They'll dissipate eventually." Probably. My control over them had been growing stronger lately, but I hadn't actually tested them at such a distance. I could recall them of course, but couldn't be bothered just now.

"When are you returning?" Thorne asked.

I shook my head. "A few days, at most. We'll know more after I speak to Griffin." I refused to acknowledge a full retreat might be necessary. There was still time to reach Sunspire and take it before Auremar could muster his full forces. "The bone collection?"

"Proceeding as ordered," Thorne said. "They're being gathered and cleaned. Should be ready for transport within the day."

We returned to the table just as Vex entered. Sebastian immediately stood, nearly knocking over his chair in his haste.

Vex's eyes narrowed slightly when she saw him. "I was moving his rooms," she said, taking her seat with precise movements that meant she was irritated. "Lord Sebastian will be quite comfortable now."

Sebastian's violet eyes fixed on her with obvious interest. "I hope you didn't go to too much trouble, Lady . . . ?"

"Vex," she said simply. "I'm Lord Blackrose's steward."

"A steward of remarkable grace and skill, I'd venture to say," Sebastian said, and then his eyes widened in horror. "To manage such a fortress each day." He clamped his mouth shut, his face flushing.

Everyone stared.

Thorne blinked slowly. "Did you just rhyme?"

Sebastian looked like he wanted the floor to swallow him. "My most sincere apologies. It's an unfortunate lingering effect from an incident."

"The Bone Witch incident," Griffin breathed, his eyes going wide. "You still rhyme?"

"Only when I'm particularly stressed or . . ." Sebastian glanced around the table. "It's most inconvenient."

"You invited Bone Witches to a winter solstice ball," I said flatly. "And you're surprised there were consequences?"

"I'd hoped that fostering understanding between disparate magical communities might—" Sebastian stopped, pressing his lips together as if physically preventing another rhyme from escaping.

"It could have been worse," Vex said, picking up her knife. "I once tracked down a Bone Witch who cursed one of our suppliers."

Sebastian swallowed. "And what happened?" He seemed to have forgotten to rhyme in his eagerness to change the subject.

Vex grinned. "She speaks only in limericks now." She twirled the knife between her fingers. "The witch, I mean. Not the supplier."

"See?" Arabella whispered to me. "Badass."

The food arrived—roasted fowl with vegetables, fresh bread, wine from my private reserve. Sebastian's eyes widened slightly at the spread, though he kept glancing at the roses with increasing agitation. "I didn't expect such a—" He paused delicately. "That is to say, your hospitality exceeds all reasonable expectations."

"You'll find most villains are quite civilized," I said, tearing into the bread. "Until we're not."

Throughout the first course, Sebastian kept shooting worried glances at the black roses, occasionally tilting his head as if listening. Finally, he actually shook his finger at them sternly.

"Is there a problem with the flowers?" Vex asked abruptly.

Sebastian froze. "I—that is . . . they're quite—" He sighed in defeat. "They're being terribly gossipy, if you must know."

Griffin dropped his fork. "The roses are *talking* to you?"

"All plants talk," Sebastian said defensively. "These are just particularly chatty. And rather inappropriate, if I'm being honest. The things they're saying about—" He cut himself off, face reddening.

"What?" Arabella leaned forward, fascinated.

Sebastian looked supremely uncomfortable. "I'd rather not repeat it in polite company. Or any company. Ever."

Griffin looked at his precious roses with betrayal. "They're gossiping and I can't hear them."

"They're only magically enhanced to sample blood," I said slowly. "But you're telling me they've developed personalities?"

"Oh, they're quite opinionated," Sebastian said miserably. "That one"—he pointed to a rose on the left—"keeps making highly inappropriate suggestions about what you and Lady Blackrose were doing before dinner."

Arabella choked on her wine.

"Trust me, the roses aren't breaking any news," Thorne muttered into his wineglass.

Vex shot him a look. "Lord Sebastian, you'll have to forgive the roses. And Lord and Lady Blackrose. They're still very much in their honeymoon phase."

Sebastian blinked, clearly uncertain how to respond to that. "I . . . see. How lovely for them?"

Griffin nodded earnestly. "It's been quite educational, actually. The structural reinforcement spells I've had to add to certain chambers—"

"Griffin," I said dangerously.

"—are completely confidential and I'll never speak of them again," Griffin finished in a squeak.

I was ready to strangle him. How the hell did *these* roses know anything? Especially not activities in a bedroom they hadn't even been inside. It wasn't so much about the obvious—everyone already knew Arabella and I were insatiable. It was the principle.

Today, bedroom gossip. Tomorrow, war plans and weaknesses.

At least the only plant-whisperer I knew was a pacifist Scone Lord, and he wasn't going anywhere without my permission.

"And that one"—Sebastian pointed to another rose as if desperate to latch on to another subject—"is critiquing everyone's table manners. Rather harshly, I might add."

"I can't help with the dribbling," Thorne rumbled. "You try eating after you've taken a boot to the face!"

"Did you lose a tooth in the battle?" Arabella asked with concern.

"Nearly," Thorne said, touching his jaw gingerly. "A bit tender, too."

"I can fix that," Arabella said, already rising from her seat.

"Would be grateful, my lady. I didn't have time to seek out a healer." Thorne pushed back from the table with a scrape of his chair.

They excused themselves, Arabella's hand already glowing faintly with healing magic.

I returned my attention to the roses. "This is absurd."

"I do apologize," Sebastian said. "I've been trying to ignore them, but they're remarkably persistent. It's like having a table full of maiden aunts who've had too much sherry."

Griffin, apparently unable to contain himself any longer, burst out, "Lord Sebastian, do you remember my atmospheric harmonizer at the Conclave?"

Sebastian's face lit up. "The snow machine! Of course I remember. Brilliant concept, even if the execution was a bit chilly."

Griffin went scarlet. "You saved everyone with those mountain flowers. The way they just sprouted from the stone—"

"I sense a story," Arabella said as she and Thorne returned to their seats. Thorne was working his jaw with satisfaction.

"I was presenting." Griffin's words tumbled over one another. "A device to create controlled weather patterns for agricultural purposes. But the third rune was misaligned, and instead of a gentle spring shower, it created a flash-freezing blizzard inside the conference hall."

"Chaos everywhere," Sebastian added with a fond smile. "Alchemists scrambling to protect their volatile concoctions, papers flying, half-finished automatons short-circuiting."

"And you just walked toward it," Griffin said, his voice full of awe. "Everyone else was running away, but you walked right up to my disaster and fixed it with flowers."

"A simple biomantic cultivation," Sebastian said. "Hardly worth mentioning."

"Simple," I repeated drily. Who did he think he was fooling? Creating life from stone wasn't simple. It required significant power and precise control. Sebastian was deliberately downplaying his abilities.

"And then you gave me a scone," Griffin continued, still staring at Sebastian like he'd hung the moon. "In the middle of all that chaos, you pulled out a scone and said my device was brilliant."

"It *was* brilliant," Sebastian insisted. "Just needed a bit of fine-tuning."

Vex leaned forward slightly. "You carry scones to magical disasters?"

"I carry scones everywhere," Sebastian said, studying her intently. "You never know when someone might need one."

Vex blinked. For the first time since I'd known her, she seemed at a loss for words.

Sebastian winced suddenly, glancing at the roses. "I beg your pardon, but might we possibly remove the centerpiece? They're becoming quite insistent."

"What are they saying now?" Arabella asked, clearly entertained.

Sebastian's face went scarlet. "They're . . . offering commentary on Lord Blackrose's shadow constructs. Apparently, they find them 'melodramatic.' And they're making wagers about who at this table will—" He stopped abruptly. "I really cannot repeat it."

I waved my hand, and shadows engulfed the vase, transporting it to another room. "Better?"

"Infinitely. My deepest gratitude." Sebastian sagged with relief.

I scowled. The only reason I'd granted his request was because I could not have villainous secrets just handed over to the Scone Lord.

The conversation continued through dinner. Despite being surrounded by people who could kill him in a dozen creative ways, Sebastian maintained his excessive politeness, thanking the servants profusely for each course, complimenting the seasoning with unnecessary detail, and somehow making Griffin actually speak in complete sentences.

It was infuriating how comfortable he was.

"The citadel is remarkable," Sebastian said over dessert—a tart that he immediately asked the recipe for. "I'd love to see more of it."

"No," I said flatly.

Griffin opened his mouth, probably to volunteer, but I cut him off with a look. "You'll be in your laboratory. Working on the only thing that matters right now."

Griffin deflated slightly but nodded.

"I can show Lord Sebastian the non-sensitive areas," Vex said. "A brief tour while Griffin focuses on his research. We can't have our guest accidentally stumbling into something unfortunate."

The unspoken threat hung in the air: better a controlled tour than Sebastian exploring on his own. I wondered if locking him in his chambers would be considered better than the dungeon. Surely Arabella and Vex couldn't object to that.

Arabella looked ready to volunteer to join them, and I quickly cut in, "Fine. But nowhere restricted. And always under escort."

"Of course," Sebastian agreed easily. "I would expect nothing less from a strategist of your caliber."

Was he always this exhaustingly polite, or was this some elaborate form of mockery?

A guard was summoned to escort him back to his quarters, but Vex stood instead. "I'll take him. I need to ensure the guest quarters are properly warded anyway."

"And Vex," I added darkly. "Remove any plants from his vicinity."

"What kind of magic does he actually have?" I asked Arabella once they were gone.

She shrugged. "He was never particularly powerful that I knew of. Just good at small things. Growing flowers, making plants bloom out of season. Though apparently also conducting full conversations with bloodsucking roses."

"That save at the Conclave was seamless," Griffin added. "The precision required to create that exact temperature gradient, in that exact pattern, without any preparation . . ." He sighed. "It was masterful."

Interesting. Very interesting. And deeply annoying.

Vex returned just as Thorne was pouring another round of wine.

"Did the pretty lord find his rooms acceptable?" Thorne asked with a smirk.

"He thanked me seventeen times in the span of a five-minute walk," Vex said. "And apologized for his footsteps being too loud."

"He makes excellent scones," Arabella offered. "The best I've ever had. I wouldn't be surprised if there's magic involved somehow."

"His baking is magical?" I asked, unable to keep the sarcasm from my voice. Because of course it was. Fucking heroes. I motioned for Thorne to pass me the wine and emptied the bottle into my glass. I was going to need something stronger if this conversation continued.

"Don't underestimate good pastry," Arabella was saying seriously. "Everything he makes tastes like happiness."

"Happiness," I repeated flatly.

"You know what I mean. That warm, comfortable feeling you get from good food."

"My grandmother always said you could judge a person by their bread," Thorne added thoughtfully.

Yes—I needed something stronger. I motioned for the servant in the corner to bring whiskey.

"Sebastian's scones are amazing," Griffin was saying. "They suggest someone with patience, precision, and an understanding of transformation."

I took the whole bottle of whiskey, too. "They're just scones," I muttered, pouring three fingers and knocking it back quickly. Sebastian's presence in the citadel wasn't going to be good for my health. I was already drinking too much. Good thing my runes dampened the worst of alcohol's effects, though that particular perk seemed counterproductive tonight.

"Have you ever had a proper scone?" Arabella asked me. "I mean a really good one? Flaky but not dry, sweet but not cloying, with that perfect crumb that—"

"Enough about the fucking scones," I snapped, and the candles flickered.

The others exchanged glances that suggested they'd be continuing this conversation later. Without me.

"Fine," Arabella said, giving me a patient look. "Let's discuss why Auremar is murdering everyone with heroic blood."

All eyes snapped to her. No one else had heard this yet.

"Sacrificing them for what?" Thorne asked.

"Power, probably. Or to fuel something." I glanced at Arabella, who was absently touching her temple where the Heirloom had merged. "The point is, he's rounded up most of the heroic bloodlines in Solandris, and we have good reason to believe he just sacrificed them."

"That's why he wanted Sebastian as property," Griffin said, his eyes widening. "Not just for political leverage, but for—"

"Ritual purposes," Vex finished grimly.

"The outpost was embarrassingly easy to take," I continued. "My shadow constructs are stronger than ever—I can summon more each day without strain. If not for this setback, we'd already be marching on the capital."

"Once we control the ley lines, none of Auremar's schemes will matter," Vex said.

"Except we can't control them while they're corrupted," I corrected.

I told Vex, Thorne, and Griffin what we'd discovered about the ley lines, leaving out the detail that the Heirloom was currently residing in my wife's skull.

When I finished, Griffin was practically bouncing in his seat. "The magical theory alone is fascinating! To corrupt an entire network of ley lines would require—"

"It would require murdering dozens of people with heroic blood," Arabella said flatly. "Maybe hundreds."

The table went quiet.

I drummed my fingers against the table. "The fool doesn't even know what he's doing."

"What do you mean?" Arabella asked.

"Auremar." I practically spat the name. "He's trying to siphon power from Solandris—from the Shadow King's prison, if our intelligence is true. But he's an idiot playing with forces beyond his comprehension." My jaw clenched. "He thinks he can control it, draw from it like a well, but instead he's poisoning the entire network."

"You think it's accidental?" Vex's silver eyes narrowed. "The corruption?"

"Of course it's accidental," I snapped. "Auremar's many things—a tyrant, a murderer, a hypocrite—but he's not suicidal. Corrupting the ley lines undermines his own kingdom's defenses. No, this is pure incompetence. He's reached for power and grabbed a viper instead."

My hand tightened around my empty glass. The thought of that golden-crowned fool bumbling his way into continental catastrophe made my blood burn. I forced my fingers to relax before the glass shattered.

"He's probably been at it for years," I continued, reaching for the decanter. "Slowly bleeding whatever's down there, not realizing he's letting something else seep out. Something that's rotting the ley lines from within."

"But what could be powerful enough to—" Griffin started.

"I don't know." I took a long pull from my glass, letting the spirit burn away the bitter edge of my ignorance. "But whatever it is, Auremar's incompetence has turned it into our problem."

"So this isn't just about conquest anymore," Thorne said slowly. "If Auremar's corrupting the ley lines—"

"The damage could spread," Vex finished. "To neighboring kingdoms. To the entire continent's magical ecosystem."

"We have plenty of work to do." I drained the rest of my whiskey. "Our priority now is clear. We need to figure out how to fix the ley lines. Everything else—Auremar, the invasion, even Sebastian's mysterious baking magic—comes second.

"Griffin, tomorrow I want a full update on your Heirloom research. Everything you've compiled so far. We'll use that as our starting point." I set down my glass with finality. "Then you can start looking into purification rituals."

"I'll keep the army ready," Thorne said. "When you want to move, we'll be prepared."

They all looked at me expectantly, waiting for dismissal or further orders. My advisors. The people I trusted most in the world.

"Tomorrow," I said. "Tonight, we rest. We've all earned it."

They filed out one by one, Griffin still muttering about magical theory, Thorne heading to check on the night watch, Vex disappearing into whatever shadow she emerged from.

As everyone filed out, Arabella lingered, sliding her arms around my waist from behind. "What are you thinking?"

The ley lines. Auremar. A hero who baked magical scones and made my people like him. "No one is that genuinely nice."

She huffed a laugh. "Not everyone has to be a villain."

"Those people are boring," I said, turning in her arms. "And they don't get to have you."

"No," she agreed, going up on her toes to kiss me. "They don't. Did you actually eat anything at dinner, or were you too busy glaring at Sebastian?"

"I didn't get dessert."

The look in Arabella's eyes shifted from teasing to wanting. I pushed her backward until the heavy oak table pressed into her thighs and trapped her there, my body pressed to hers. Mine.

Just as her breath hitched, the doors creaked open. A servant entered, tray in hand, to clear the remnants of our meal.

"Out," I snapped, not bothering to look at him.

With a flick of my wrist, shadows slammed the doors shut, the bolt sliding home with a heavy thud.

"That was rude," Arabella said, but her hands were already sliding up my chest.

"I'm the Dark Lord. I'm allowed to be rude when someone interrupts my dessert."

14

Attempt a Magical Extraction

(Without Exploding Your Wife's Head)

Arabella

"Try it again."

My words came out through gritted teeth. My scalp prickled where Kazimir's fingers traced another pattern, his dominion magic pulsing against the Heirloom like someone playing an off-key lute directly on my brain.

His hand stilled. "This isn't working." That particular edge had crept into his voice—the one that meant something was about three seconds from being set on fire. "Nothing's changed."

We stood in Griffin's main laboratory in the North Tower, surrounded by the organized chaos of his experiments. It was actually quite impressive when you weren't worried about it exploding. Three levels of workspace connected by a spiral staircase that moved on its own but occasionally got confused and deposited people on the wrong floor. Glass vials lined the walls in rainbow gradients, some bubbling ominously despite having no heat source. Shelves crammed with containers stretched from floor to ceiling. Some held perfectly ordinary herbs. Others contained things that pulsed with their own light or occasionally tapped against their containers as if testing for weaknesses.

A half-assembled contraption that looked like a metal spider crossed with a pipe organ dominated one corner. Another held what appeared to be a collection of preserved eyeballs that tracked our movements with disturbing focus.

Any blank spaces on the walls were covered in chalk equations that rewrote themselves as Griffin's theories evolved.

I'd avoided this tower for good reason. The last time I'd visited, Griffin had accidentally animated all the furniture, and I'd spent an hour being chased by an overly affectionate ottoman.

I rubbed my temples, trying to ease the building pressure. We'd been trying to remove the Heirloom all morning. "Maybe if you used less brute force and more finesse."

Kazimir stepped back, his jaw tight. "Maybe if you hadn't put the damned thing on in the first place."

"Oh, I'm sorry." I dropped my hands. "Next time an ancient artifact of unimaginable power wants to disappear into my skull, I'll tell it to ask your permission first."

"That's not—" He stopped. His jaw clenched so hard I could see the muscle jump. "You know that's not what I meant."

"Do I? Because it sounds like you're blaming me for trying to help."

His eyes flashed dangerously. "I don't merge with random magical artifacts."

"No." I crossed my arms. "You just invade kingdoms on a whim and wonder why things go sideways."

The air between us crackled. Not with magic—with the familiar friction of two stubborn people who didn't back down.

But fighting with Kazimir wouldn't get the Heirloom out of my head. I took a deep breath. Then another. The familiar scent of sulfur and burnt herbs that permeated the lab helped ground me.

His posture shifted, some of the rigid tension easing from his shoulders. He studied me with that intense focus that usually preceded either brilliant strategy or spectacular violence. "Maybe we're approaching this wrong. The

Heirloom merged with you when the ley lines were corrupted. Perhaps it's protecting itself."

"Maybe." I closed my eyes, searching inward for that golden shimmer that now lived beneath my skin. *Leave. Get out. Vacate the premises. Find a new home.*

Nothing.

Please?

Still nothing.

I'll melt you down and turn you into earrings.

The Heirloom pulsed once, almost like it was laughing at me.

I opened my eyes to find Kazimir watching me expectantly. "Anything?"

"It thinks I'm funny."

His lips twitched. "At least someone does."

I glared at him, but some of the tension eased from my shoulders. My gaze snagged on a collection of failed experiments, with jars labeled with dates and cryptic notes like "Do not feed after midnight" and "Achieved sentience—had to put it down."

"Why does Griffin have so many eyeballs?" I nodded toward the collection that was still watching us.

"Failed scrying experiments. They're mostly harmless. Don't make direct eye contact with the green one."

A screech from outside made us both turn. Nyx's massive head appeared at the window, her silver eyes fixed on me with an intensity that was somewhat weakened by the shimmering pink blaze forming along her snout.

"No." I crossed to the window, keeping my voice firm. "You're not allowed in here. Griffin's familiars, remember?"

She screeched again, talons scraping against the stone in clear protest.

"I don't care if it looked delicious. Stay out. You can barely fit through the window anyway."

Her head tilted. That look—the one that said she could fit anywhere she wanted to, thank you very much—was unmistakable.

"Don't even think about it. I'll find you later, I promise."

She huffed, sending a small puff of purple flame through the window that singed a stack of papers on the nearest desk.

"Nyx!"

She flew off with what could only be described as a teenage sulk, her tail whipping past the window hard enough to rattle the glassware on the nearby shelf.

"Our little arsonist is becoming more defiant every day." I turned back to Kazimir. "And she's just a dragon. Can you imagine adding a child to the mix? They'd burn down the citadel before they could walk."

"At least that's one disaster we don't have to worry about."

"Thank the gods." I meant it.

We'd talked about it after the attack on Skyspire, when the healers had been fussing over both of us. Neither of us had experienced anything resembling a healthy childhood—his mother had carved runes into his bones, my father had locked me in a tower. We'd be terrible parents, and we both knew it.

I'd been drinking a yearly prevention potion since my father had allowed me out of my tower, but Kazimir had gone further. Years ago, before he'd even claimed Skyspire, he'd undergone some sort of dark magical procedure to ensure he'd never father children. The details were vague and probably horrifying, but the result was permanent.

I wasn't upset about it. If anything, I was relieved. We had enough problems without adding a tiny Dark Lord or Lady to the mix. Besides, we'd probably be starting wars and dodging assassination attempts for the foreseeable future. Hardly the environment for raising a child.

I pushed thoughts of hypothetical offspring aside. "Let me look at the ley lines again. Maybe I can see something different today."

I closed my eyes and reached for the Heirloom's power. It responded eagerly. The world exploded into ribbons of golden light, all twisted together in an endless web.

I focused on Solandris, following the lines toward the Golden Rose Fields. Unfortunately, the corruption was worse and showed no sign of fixing itself.

Before I could say anything, footsteps thundered up the stairs. The door burst open, and Griffin practically fell through it, Vex and Sebastian right behind him.

Griffin's face was pale, his glasses askew, and his hands were shaking.

"My lord. My lady." He gasped for breath. "I have news. Bad news. Very bad news."

15

Maintain Dungeon Security

(Unless Your Staff Decides Otherwise)

Kazimir

Griffin stood in the laboratory doorway like a man awaiting execution. His gangly frame trembled, those ridiculous amber eyes wide behind his askew glasses. Behind him, Vex maintained her usual composure, though the slight twitch in her left eye told me whatever Griffin had done was spectacularly bad. Sebastian hovered near the back, looking distinctly uncomfortable.

"Speak," I commanded, my voice deceptively calm. The kind of calm that preceded someone losing vital organs.

"My lord," Griffin began, wringing his hands. "I was—that is, Vex was showing Lord Sebastian around the citadel, as planned."

"The non-sensitive areas," Vex clarified, which immediately told me they'd gone somewhere they shouldn't have.

"Yes! Absolutely non-sensitive!" Griffin's voice cracked. "Just the . . . the dungeons."

"The dungeons," I repeated. The temperature in the room plummeted. One of his preserved experiments frosted over.

"Just the Necromantic Wing, my lord!" Griffin hastened to add, as if that made it better. "I was retrieving samples from the storage vaults. For the purification research. The texts suggested that understanding how death magic interacts with corrupted life essence might give us insight into reversing the ley line contamination. And I ran into them during their tour of the lower levels—"

My shadows darkened with my impatience.

"We started talking about magical theory." Griffin's words tumbling out faster now. "The interaction between life magic and death magic, the theoretical applications of biomantic principles in necromantic spaces—it was fascinating, really, and Lord Sebastian had such insightful questions about the containment matrices—"

"Griffin." Arabella's voice cut through his rambling. "What did you do?"

He paled further, which I hadn't thought possible. "I—I wanted to demonstrate a simple reanimation principle. Just a small spell! A tiny manipulation of the death essence in Cell Block Seven—"

"Cell Block Seven," I said slowly, "where we keep the high-security prisoners."

"It was supposed to be contained to the empty cell! But the spell, um, sort of cascaded."

The runes in my bones began to burn, responding to my rising fury. "Define 'cascaded.'"

Griffin opened his mouth, closed it, opened it again. No sound emerged.

With a sigh that suggested she'd rather be literally anywhere else, Vex stepped forward. "Sir Darian Lightbringer escaped his cell, my lord."

The silence that followed could have frozen hell.

"I assume," I said, each word precise and lethal, "that you immediately recaptured him and returned him to his cell."

Griffin squeaked like a dying mouse.

"No, my lord," Vex said, meeting my gaze steadily. "The spell somehow created a connection between two separate parts of the prison system. Lightbringer, who has apparently gone quite mad from his withdrawal, managed to grab Lord Evenfall during the chaos."

Arabella gasped.

"They both escaped through one of the Tempest Cages," Vex continued.

The Tempest Cages—those delightful iron spheres suspended beneath the floating isle that housed the dungeons, dangling over the void on enchanted chains. They swayed perpetually in the storms below, a special torment for prisoners I particularly despised.

Arabella shook her head. "I don't even understand how that happened. How did they get from their respective cells down to the Tempest Cages?"

"The magical specifics are still unclear," Vex admitted, her jaw tight. "But the general sequence is this: Griffin's spell created a feedback loop through the containment runes. The Silent Sentinels glitched—their animation briefly confused by conflicting signals. The cells opened themselves, and there was a few minutes of chaos. But most of the prisoners headed upward to escape, and we apprehended them without any trouble."

Vex sighed. "But in his addled state, Lightbringer stumbled through the corridors during the chaos and encountered Lord Evenfall. They headed for what they thought was an exit—the chain-hauled lift."

"But the lift took them *down*," I said slowly, understanding dawning.

"The undead operator was glitching from the necromantic surge," Vex confirmed. "By the time they realized their error, they'd reached the Tempest Cage platform. When they tried to retreat, the cascading spell hit the enchanted chains. The nearest cage released and plummeted with them inside."

"Then they should be very dead," I said, grasping for that one silver lining.

"They should be," Vex agreed. "But as you know, some of the defensive wards have been temperamental since the Guild's attack. Instead of falling to their deaths, they sort of . . ." She made a floating gesture with her hand. "Bounced. Downward. Slowly."

"Are you saying they *floated*?" Arabella's voice rose an octave.

"Like dandelion seeds on a breeze," Sebastian offered helpfully, then immediately looked like he regretted speaking.

My gaze snapped to him. Of course. The mysterious Lord Sebastian, who just happened to arrive seeking sanctuary, who just happened to be touring the dungeons, who just happened to be present when my prisoners escaped.

"You," I snarled, shadows coiling around my feet. "You're a spy."

"Kaz—" Arabella started, but I was already moving.

"First you show up at precisely the right moment, then you ingratiate yourself with my staff, and now—coincidentally—two valuable prisoners escape while you're touring the fucking dungeons?"

Sebastian backed up, hands raised, and he almost fell out the door. "Lord Blackrose, I assure you—"

"Your assurances mean nothing." My shadows reached for him, ready to pin him to the wall and extract the truth.

Arabella stepped between us, her hand on my chest. "Let me."

She turned to Sebastian, her hazel eyes sharp. "Did you have anything to do with their escape?"

"No, my lady," Sebastian said immediately. "I had no notion this would happen—not even a fraction." He winced.

Arabella studied him for a long moment, that subtle tension around her eyes that meant she was using her truth-sense. Then she nodded. "He's telling the truth."

"Actually," Vex interjected, "Lord Sebastian prevented it from being worse. When Griffin's spell began cascading through the other wings, Sebastian used his magic to seal them."

"Vines and roots," Griffin added eagerly, apparently forgetting he was still in mortal danger. "It was brilliant! The biomantic energy created a natural barrier against the necromantic overflow—"

"Griffin," I said very quietly, "stop talking before I feed you to the void beasts."

He made a strangled sound and fell silent.

"Where are they now?" Arabella demanded.

"I've already informed Thorne," Vex said. "He's taken a team to retrieve them. Assuming they survived the landing."

"Oh, they survived," I muttered. "Because nothing in my life is ever that simple."

“My lord,” Griffin ventured, “I’m terribly sorry—”

“Sorry?” I turned on him. “You released a Hero’s Guild knight-commander who knows our defenses and a vindictive noble who sold his own daughter. You compromised our security, endangered our operations, and demonstrated a level of incompetence that makes me question why I haven’t already turned you into a decorative wall hanging.”

“My lord,” Sebastian spoke up, “if I may—the fault is partly mine. I encouraged his demonstration. I was genuinely curious about the theoretical applications—”

“Of course you were,” I snarled. “How convenient that your curiosity led to chaos.”

“Kaz, he’s trying to help,” Arabella said.

“Help? This is help?” I gestured wildly at the general catastrophe. “Your father is loose, and Lightbringer is on his way to Auremar to tell him everything he knows. And all because these idiots decided to play show-and-tell in my fucking dungeons!”

“To be fair,” Griffin said weakly, “the spell matrix was theoretically sound—”

“Griffin,” Vex and Arabella said in unison.

He closed his mouth with a snap.

I pressed my palms against my eyes, trying to ward off the headache building behind them. The runes in my bones throbbed in rhythm with my pulse, each beat sending fresh waves of pain through my body. First the corrupted ley lines, then the Heirloom fusing with Arabella, now this.

I turned to tell Arabella that Thorne had likely already found them, but she was gone. I stared at the empty space where my wife had been standing, then at the still-swinging door.

“Shit,” I muttered, and ran after her.

Behind me, I heard Griffin’s tentative voice: “So . . . am I fired?”

“Not yet,” Vex replied. “But I’d start practicing your groveling. You’ll need it when they get back.”

16

Find What You've Lost
(or Kill It, Whatever Works)

Arabella

"Where the hell are you going?" Kazimir's voice chased me down the corridor as I practically sprinted toward our chambers.

"After them, obviously. We can't leave it up to anybody else." I didn't slow down, though my hands trembled as I reached for the door. "But I need to change first. Can't exactly hunt down escapees in a dress."

"You could," he said, catching up to me. "You'd look magnificent doing it."

"Flattery won't distract me from the fact that my father just escaped from your supposedly inescapable dungeons." I threw open our chamber door hard enough that it bounced off the wall.

My father. Free. The thought sent ice through my veins before I buried it under anger. I'd spent weeks pretending he didn't exist, that he was just another prisoner in Kaz's dungeons. But fathers don't become strangers just because you wish them to. And apparently, don't stop being trouble just because you leave them to rot after saving their worthless lives.

"Is Griffin still alive?" I yanked open my wardrobe.

"Barely." Kazimir leaned against the bed, watching me tear through my clothes. "Along with Sebastian and Vex, though I'm reconsidering all three."

I pulled out my new leathers—the latest ones Kaz had commissioned for me, reinforced with protective enchantments and flexible enough for light combat. They'd just arrived, and I was looking forward to trying them out. Instead of blue like the last ones, these were black with silver buckles that were enchanted so they didn't catch the light. Stealth leathers. "Going soft on me? The terrifying Dark Lord I married would have already mounted their heads on pikes."

"Must be your terrible influence." His tone was dry, but I caught affection beneath it. "I didn't used to keep prisoners long enough for them to escape. They were either immediately useful or already dead."

The word "prisoners" made my stomach twist. That's what my father was now. What I'd made him. Just like he'd made me one.

"And what was Griffin thinking?" I pulled off my dress. My fingers fumbled with the clasps on the leathers, and I had to try twice before getting them open. "Showing off necromancy to Sebastian of all people?"

"Hero worship," Kazimir snorted. "Literally, in this case."

I paused, halfway into my leather pants. "That man could probably make friends with a basilisk."

"Don't give him ideas."

I struggled with a particularly stubborn buckle, cursing under my breath.

"Need assistance?" Kaz pushed off from the bed. "Or is your intention to let our escapees go free?"

"I can dress myself, thank you very much." But my fingers slipped again. "Fuck."

He crossed the room and batted my hands away with surprising gentleness. His fingers replaced mine at the buckle.

"Arms up," he murmured, his breath ghosting across my collarbone as he worked the stubborn leather into place.

I obeyed, watching his face. The concentration there, the care in each movement made my pulse quicken. I blinked, and he was done.

"There." His hands lingered at my waist, thumbs tracing the edge of the leather. "Ready to hunt?"

A few minutes later, Kaz's portal spat us out into ankle-deep swamp water. The smell hit next—rot, stagnant water, and something metallic.

"Delightful," I muttered, pulling my foot free from the mud with a wet squelch.

Above the twisted trees, the storm clouds beneath Skyspire churned endlessly, occasionally lit by flashes of lightning that revealed nothing but clouds and dark floating rock.

Kazimir raised his hand, and shadows peeled away from him. They formed into sleek wolves, ravens, and serpents before dispersing into the murk. The display sent an involuntary shiver down my spine, equal parts fear and something considerably less appropriate for our current situation.

"What exactly lives down here?" I asked, turning in a circle to look at the gnarled trees and clinging fog.

"The magic from Skyspire affects everything below. Mutates it. Makes it unpredictable."

A branch cracked somewhere to our left, and I instinctively summoned a shadow blade into my hand. The reminder of my power was comforting. Not like the helplessness that kept trying to claw its way up my throat.

Kaz turned to the south. "Stay alert. I don't want you eaten by an overgrown deer with fangs."

"You say the sweetest things." We picked our way through the swamp, following what might have been a path if you squinted and had a generous definition of the word. "How do you even know where they landed?"

"Educated guess based on the Tempest Cage positions and wind patterns." He gestured ahead where the trees thinned slightly. "They should have bounced somewhere near the old emergency ascension system."

"The one the Hero's Guild used to attack us? We still don't know who told them about it." The thought had been gnawing at me since the attack. "Who the spy was—or is."

Better to think about spies than about my father and the last time I'd seen him—during that interrogation weeks ago. I'd walked away from that room and hadn't looked back. Hadn't visited. Hadn't even asked Kazimir what he'd done with him beyond "put him in a cell."

Like my father had done to me.

"All these weeks later, and we've still not heard from Pip," Kazimir said, ducking under a low-hanging branch that dripped something viscous and green. "He's the only one unaccounted for."

I picked my way through the muck, remembering those frantic days after the attack. "We questioned everyone who survived." A beetle with too many legs scuttled across the water away from me. "Every servant, every guard, every kitchen boy who could still draw breath."

And I'd used my truth-sense on all of them.

The memory of those exhausting interrogations made my head ache. Hours upon hours of sitting across from terrified staff members, feeling for that telltale prickle behind my eyes that would signal a lie. None of them was the spy. They were all genuinely shocked by the attack, genuinely loyal—or at least, genuinely more afraid of the Dark Lord than the Hero's Guild.

Which is why Kazimir decided to question the dead. He'd suggested it so casually, as if raising corpses for interrogation was as mundane as checking the weather.

I suppressed a shudder. The Necromantic Wing of the dungeons had reeked of death magic and preserving salts as Kazimir worked his necromancy on the fallen. One by one, he'd animated the bodies of those who'd died defending Skyspire—or attacking it. Their slack faces and clouded eyes had haunted my dreams that night.

"You questioned everyone except Sims," I said.

"His loyalty was never in doubt." Kazimir's jaw tightened. "He died protecting the citadel. Protecting us."

The dead had shambled forward at his command, their voices hollow echoes of what they'd been in life. Each one had denied being the spy or knowing who it was. Watching them speak, I'd felt nothing. No prickle of deception or cold tingle of lies. Just an unsettling blankness where my truth-sense usually resided.

"I still don't know if my magic even works on the undead," I admitted, stepping carefully around a puddle that reflected too many colors to be natural water. "For all we know, every corpse you raised could have been lying through their rotting teeth."

"Regardless, Pip is still our likely culprit."

"You really think that nervous kid was a spy?"

"Everyone's a spy until proven otherwise."

The swamp gave way to slightly firmer ground, though "firm" was relative when everything squelched. We emerged into a small clearing dominated by the twisted metal remains of what had been an elegant magical lift system. Now it looked like a giant had used it for target practice, all bent beams and shattered crystal matrices.

"I always imagined a great black void down here," I admitted, eyeing the wreckage and thinking about how my father must have felt, plummeting through the air. I imagined his terrified face and almost smiled. "You know, befitting the whole 'Terror of the Western Realms' aesthetic. Speaking of which, where do you keep the void beasts?"

Kazimir's laugh was dark and amused. "Void beasts?"

"You're always threatening to feed people to them."

"Ah." He stepped over a puddle that bubbled ominously. "Arabella, my darling wife, the void beasts aren't real."

I blinked. "What?"

"They're a euphemism. A colorful way of saying 'I'm going to kill you and dispose of your body in a creative manner.'"

"You're joking." I turned to look at his face.

He still wore that amused smirk. "No."

"But—" I stared at him. "Everyone's terrified of them!"

"Exactly. The threat of being fed to mysterious, unknowable horrors is far more effective than simply saying 'I'll throw you off the battlements or separate your head from your body.'" Kazimir shook his head in mock-disgust.

"Though I'm disappointed you didn't figure it out sooner. I thought you'd appreciate the theatrical misdirection."

"So what do you do for minor infractions?" I asked, resuming our trudge through the swamp. "Since you're apparently not feeding servants to mythical creatures?"

"All villains worth their salt know that it would be terribly inefficient to keep replacing servants." He stepped over a fallen log. "For minor infractions, I usually go with public humiliation, wage garnishment, or making them clean blood off the dungeon walls—that stone doesn't stay polished on its own."

We continued deeper into the swamp, with no sign of our escapees. The shadows Kazimir had sent ahead occasionally returned, whispering reports in that strange guttural language of his.

I'd never asked, but since we were sharing more these days . . .

"Why do you need to talk to your constructs?" I asked after another reported and then left. "I can hear what mine say in my head. And for that matter, what language is that? I've heard you speak it a few times now."

Kazimir didn't look at me, his gaze still fixed on the treacherous path ahead. "It's the tongue of the island I grew up on with my mother. It's what my shadows respond to." He hesitated for a fraction of a second. "And I don't *need* to speak it aloud. But conversing with them in my head doesn't come as naturally to me as it does to you."

I exhaled in relief. At least it wasn't related to the Shadow King—just a piece of Kazimir's past he could name and understand.

Then I stopped dead. "Are you telling me there's a type of shadow magic that I'm better at than you?"

A muscle twitched in his jaw. "Don't look so smug."

"I am absolutely going to look smug." A wide, triumphant grin spread across my face. "The great and terrible Kazimir Blackrose has to mumble sweet nothings to his shadow puppets, while I can hold entire silent conversations with mine. I am a prodigy."

"They aren't puppets," he growled, though there was no real heat behind it. "And you aren't a prodigy."

"Admit it. You're impressed. Maybe even a little turned on."

His smirk was a slow, crooked smile. "I'm always a little turned on when it comes to you, or hadn't you noticed?"

Before I could come up with a suitably flippant reply, a guttural snarl ripped through the air. A creature burst from the overgrown reeds to our right. It might have been a boar once, but now it was a lurching horror of knotted muscle and overlapping tusks, with patches of sickly green crystal growing out of its hide.

It charged.

I didn't even have to think. I threw out a hand, and a wall of thick, tar-like shadow erupted from the ground, slick and impassable. The beast hit it with a wet smack and stumbled, its hooves sliding in the mud. In that split second of confusion, a spear of solidified darkness launched from Kazimir's side and buried itself in the creature's thick skull. It dropped without another sound.

Just as the adrenaline began to fade, more rustling came from the trees. Two more of the mutated boars emerged, followed by a pack of skeletal, six-legged wolves with glowing red eyes and a fluttering of overgrown bats above.

"The welcoming party," Kazimir muttered, shadows coiling around him. "I thought we would have encountered them before now."

This time, I stepped forward and let my power surge. The shadows at my feet swelled, growing into monstrous parodies of the creatures before us. A towering wolf of living darkness, its teeth impossibly long and sharp, rose beside me. Shadowy serpents bigger than trees uncoiled from the ground, their eyeless heads weaving through the air. I didn't send them to attack. I just let them exist—a silent, overwhelming promise of annihilation.

The mutated creatures skidded to a halt. They stared at my horrors, then at each other, a primal intelligence warring with their aggression. After a tense moment, the lead boar snorted, backed away, and the entire nightmarish menagerie melted back into the swamp.

My constructs dissolved into ordinary shadows.

"They'll just come back," Kazimir noted drily.

I shrugged, wiping a splash of mud from my cheek. "There was no reason to kill them. They're just defending their territory."

He shot me an incredulous look. "You have no trouble killing your enemies in battle, but you spare the rabid swamp beasts?"

"I'm complicated," I shot back, "or hadn't you noticed?"

Shaking his head once again, he stepped around the dead boar. "I suppose the mutant beasts are good security for the swamp. With any luck, they've already devoured Evenfall and Lightbringer."

My stomach twisted. How would I feel if something had already happened to my father?

"So what's the plan when we find them?" I asked, sidestepping something smelly and purple. "Assuming they're even together."

"Kill them."

"Kaz—"

"What?"

"My father knows things. About what happened when my mother died, about Auremar's plans—" The words tumbled out, desperate justification for something I hadn't even decided yet.

"Your father is a lying sack of shit."

I ducked under a low-hanging branch. "And Lightbringer could be leverage."

"I'm not in the mood to entertain Lightbringer any longer." Kazimir stopped walking and turned to face me, his expression one of barely contained irritation. "You want to keep the man who led an assault on our home as a pet?"

"I want to be smart about this. You're the one always going on about thinking three moves ahead."

His jaw tightened. "That's different."

"How?"

He took a step closer, shadows darkening the path. "Because I'm not emotionally compromised by familial connections to manipulative bastards."

My hands clenched at my sides. "That's rich coming from the man who literally beheaded his father at dinner."

"Exactly my point." Kazimir's eyes flashed silver. "I didn't keep Vargus around to chat about his motivations."

"Well *I* want my memories back." The admission burst out of me, raw and desperate. All those blank spaces in my mind, all those stolen moments with my mother—they haunted me more than any tower ever could.

"Congratulations." He leaned down until we were nearly nose to nose, his voice dropping to a lethal whisper. "Now your father's free to create new traumatic memories for you."

We glared at each other, magic crackling between us. His shadows writhed. My own power hummed beneath my skin, ready to match him if necessary. The swamp around us had gone silent—even the insects were smart enough to avoid two powerful mages having a domestic dispute.

But underneath my anger, some part of me listened. *Emotionally compromised.* Was that what I was?

"You think I'm being weak?" My voice cracked. "If that's what this is about, I locked him in a cell just like he locked me in a tower."

Kazimir's expression shifted, some of the anger bleeding away. "Arabella—"

"This is Griffin's fault," I said, needing to deflect before he could finish that thought. "He thinks 'oops' is an acceptable response to catastrophic failure—"

"Griffin's an idiot," Kaz allowed, letting me change the subject. "But he's *my* idiot. Your"—he bit the word out—"*friend* is the one who encouraged him."

"Sebastian was curious! It's not his fault Griffin has the impulse control of a toddler with fire magic!"

A scream cut through our argument. High, terrified, and definitely human.

We looked at each other.

"Apparently, your father's found something worse than us," Kaz said.

Another scream, this one cut short. My heart hammered against my ribs. Despite everything, despite the tower and the lies and the stolen memories, hearing him scream still made something in my chest twist.

"We should probably hurry," I said.

"Probably." But neither of us moved, both caught in that strange space between our fight and whatever came next. Kaz's hand found mine. A third scream, followed by maniacal laughter, reminded me that I didn't want the decision taken away from me. My father's fate, whatever it may be, needed to remain in my hands.

I sighed. "Let's save my horrible father from whatever's trying to eat him."

"The romance never ends with us, does it?"

We started toward the screaming, hands still linked. Kazimir's strong presence grounded me, reminded me that I wasn't that helpless girl in the tower anymore. I had power now. I had choices.

"Next time," Kazimir muttered, "we're executing prisoners immediately."

The screaming got louder. We walked faster, then ran toward the sound, splashing through puddles and leaping over roots. The screams were accompanied by another voice—harsh, demanding, slightly unhinged.

We burst through a wall of hanging moss into another clearing where Sir Darian Lightbringer had my father pinned against a tree. The knight-commander looked even worse than when I'd last seen him—his hair wild, eyes bloodshot and desperate, hands wrapped around my father's throat.

"I know you have it!" Lightbringer was screaming. "Give me some!"

My father's face was turning an alarming shade of purple.

For a moment, I froze. There he was—Lord Atticus Evenfall, the man who'd controlled my entire life. Now he was the one gasping for air, helpless and terrified. The girl he'd locked in a tower would have found poetic justice in it. Would have wanted to watch.

That girl was still in there, I realized. Still angry. Still helpless. Still checking the tower door, hoping today would be different.

But now I had power.

"Enough," I called out, stepping into the clearing.

Lightbringer spun, dropping my father, who crumpled into the mud. The knight's eyes were wide and frantic. Whatever Auremar had been giving him, the withdrawal had driven him past madness.

"You," he spat. "Corrupted bitch. You should be—"

Kazimir's shadows surged forward, but I held up a hand. "Mine."

Lightbringer laughed. "You think you can take me, little girl? I'm a knight-commander of the—"

"You know," I said conversationally, stalking toward him, "I didn't get a proper chance to fight you before."

He lunged at me with his bare hands. I sidestepped easily, letting him stumble past. He spun, swinging wildly. I ducked under his arm and drove my knee into his stomach. He doubled over, wheezing.

"The great Sir Darian Lightbringer," I mused, conjuring a shadow spear. "Terror of dark mages everywhere. Reduced to attacking old men in swamps. Pity you're not even fit to fight me now."

"Whore—" he gasped.

I heaved the spear through his shoulder. He screamed, stumbling back against a slime-covered cypress, his hand flying to where the bolt of shadow jutted from his flesh.

Before he could recover, more shadows surged from the ground at my command—thick, coiling serpents of solid darkness. They hissed silently as they wrapped around his limbs, constricting with crushing force. With a flick of my wrist, they lifted him, kicking and sputtering, until he dangled a foot above the swampy ground, utterly helpless.

My boots made soft sucking sounds in the mud as I approached him. The fear scenting the air was thick and intoxicating. I could see it in the whites of his eyes, could feel his panic as a frantic, hammering drumbeat against my own senses. I had been right—this wasn't a fight at all.

But that didn't stop me from savoring every second of this. This was control. This was power. This was everything I'd never had in that tower.

No more helpless girl. No more locked doors. No more waiting for someone else to decide my fate.

"You look unwell, Commander." Sheer terror contorted his features. I glanced over at my father, who was trying to melt into the bark of a nearby tree. This performance was for him, too. A clear, final lesson on who was in charge now.

"Is it the withdrawal?" I continued, circling Lightbringer. "Does it hurt? That gnawing emptiness where Auremar's little gift used to be?"

"Go to hell, witch," he spat, though it lacked conviction.

"Your insults aren't very clever." I stopped in front of him and created a new toy—a delicate, razor-sharp stiletto. "Auremar promised you strength. He promised you power. But the truth is, he just made you a better slave."

Lightbringer mustered another glare, and the lie he still clung to—that his mission was righteous—pricked behind my eyes.

"You're going to die here," I told him, tracing his jaw with the stiletto, not quite touching his skin. "I can make it a clean cut. Or"—I let the blade dip, and a single drop of his blood welled up where it touched—"it can be very, very slow. I am the Mistress of the Healing Arts, you know. I know precisely how much a body can endure before it breaks. I could keep you alive for days."

His eyes widened, the last vestiges of his knightly bravado shattering. This was the terror I wanted to see. The kind Kazimir inspired. The kind that meant no one would ever lock me away again.

"Tell me who the spy in Skyspire is," I ordered. "Who told the Hero's Guild about the emergency ascension platforms?"

A low, guttural noise caught in his throat. "No," he panted. "I don't know."

I waited for the telltale cold prickle of my truth-sense. Instead, I felt nothing. Sir Darian genuinely didn't know who our spy was. Not anymore, at least.

Well, that was disappointing.

I studied his glazed eyes more carefully, noting the way they struggled to focus, how his pupils contracted and dilated erratically. The magical substance Auremar had been feeding his knights wasn't just creating dependency. The withdrawal had carved holes in his mind, selective amnesia that conveniently protected Auremar's secrets even as it destroyed his pawns.

"Worthless," I sighed, letting the stiletto dissolve. This was a waste of time.

"You're a monster," Lightbringer rasped. Blood trickled from the corner of his mouth.

"Took you long enough to figure it out." I smiled coldly. "Goodbye, Sir Darian."

I didn't bother with another weapon. I simply closed my fist, and the shadow serpents constricted, crushing the air—and life—from him in one final, brutal snap of breaking bone.

Killing Lightbringer was easy. He'd invaded my home and killed my friend. He'd nearly gotten Kaz killed.

"I warned you," I said quietly as he collapsed. "I told you what would happen if you came for us again."

Lightbringer tried to speak, blood bubbling from his lips, but whatever he wanted to say died with him.

I turned to find my father staring at me like he'd never seen me before. Covered in mud, bleeding from scratches, he looked nothing like the man who'd locked me in a tower. He looked small. Pathetic.

"Well," Kazimir said, sounding amused. "I guess you changed your mind about keeping our knight-commander alive?"

I swiped mud from my cheek. "He annoyed me."

"And him?" Kaz jerked his chin toward my father.

I considered it. Really considered it. It would be so easy. One gesture, one thought, and I'd never have to think about him again. Never have to wonder if keeping him alive made me weak or strong or just as cruel as he'd been.

But my hands wouldn't move. The shadows wouldn't rise.

I'd thought power would make me feel safe from him. But standing there, covered in mud and blood, I remembered the fourteen-year-old girl isolated from everything and everyone. The girl with stolen memories and a dead mother and a father who'd let it happen.

"No," I said finally, the word scraping my throat. "He still has information we need."

It was a lie, and we both knew it. I wasn't keeping him alive for information. I was keeping him alive because I wasn't ready.

Kazimir sighed, but there was understanding in it. "Fine. But if he escapes again, I'm feeding him to the void beasts." He stalked toward my father, and his entire demeanor shifted. Shadows wrapped around the tree, and his voice became steel. "Did you hear that, Evenfall? The void beasts are particularly hungry this time of year. Nothing but bones left when they're done. Sometimes not even that."

My father pressed himself harder against the tree. He knew now—had seen what I'd become, what I was capable of. The daughter he'd locked in a tower could have killed him but didn't.

I hoped he lay awake tonight wondering what I had in store for him instead of death.

17

Play Their Game

(When Refusal Means Death by Creative Cursing)

Kazimir

Evenfall wouldn't stop blubbering.

The entire journey back to Skyspire, the man alternated between sniveling gratitude for our timely rescue and incoherent ramblings about how Lightbringer had "gone mad" and tried to kill him. As if I gave a single, solitary fuck about his traumatic swamp adventure.

"Please, I can be useful!" he begged as I shoved him back into a cell. "I know things—"

"You've been saying that for the past hour." I slammed the cell door with a satisfying clang. "The only reason you're still breathing is because my wife finds you marginally more valuable alive than dead."

"Arabella—she wouldn't—"

"Your daughter," I said, letting ice creep into my voice, "just executed a knight-commander without blinking. I'd reconsider your assumptions about what she would or wouldn't do."

The memory of it sent a hot rush of desire through me. Watching her crush the life from a man who'd threatened her family, her power flaring bright and ruthless—it was the most exquisite thing I'd ever seen.

Her situation with her father, on the other hand, was going to take more time. She was still processing. And until she dealt with her past, I'd keep putting Evenfall back in his cell.

"You should have let me kill him," I'd said to Arabella as we prepared to leave the swamp. For emphasis, I'd pushed Evenfall face-first into a foul-smelling puddle.

She'd given me a hard look, but it wasn't condemnation. "Information first. Then you can have what's left."

"Promise?"

The barest twitch at the corner of her mouth was all the answer I needed. That, more than any words, told me we were fine.

The dungeons, however, were not. Griffin's little reanimation project had been catastrophic. Containment wards were shredded. The binding matrices that kept prisoners from tapping into their magic were completely fried. At least it explained how Lightbringer had gotten as far as he had. I spent the rest of the day and most of the night rebuilding the entire security infrastructure from scratch. By the time dawn bled through the grimy high windows, the runes on my bones ached with a deep, grinding pain, and a spectacular headache was pounding behind my eyes.

Griffin, at least, had the decency to look properly terrified when I finally cornered him.

"My lord, I'm s-so sorry, I didn't mean—"

"Shut up." I leaned in close. "You're confined to your laboratory until further notice. No leaving except for meals and sleep. You will focus entirely on the Heirloom research, and you will report your progress to me twice a day."

"But my—my other experiments—"

"Can wait. Or rot. I don't care." The shadows at my feet darkened. "The only thing you should be thinking about is how to make the Heirloom work without killing us. Do you understand?"

He swallowed hard. "Yes, my lord."

"Good. Because if another disaster happens while you're supposed to be solving our most critical problem, there won't be enough of you left to reanimate."

And because I was still furious, I pointed to the stack of ward anchors that needed reinscription. "And after that, you're going to carve every single one of these. By hand. No magic. And if you make even one mistake, I'll have you start over from the beginning."

His face went white. "But that will take—"

"Weeks? Months?" I let him feel the cold fury I'd been holding back since I'd returned with Evenfall. "Yes."

That seemed to break him. He just nodded, his throat working. The thought of that tedious, mind-numbing labor was the worst punishment I could think of for someone like Griffin. It was almost cruel enough to satisfy me.

Almost.

I was crossing the bridge from the dungeons to the Great Hall when Vex caught up to me, her once-again silver hair catching the morning light. At this point, I was so used to the frequent changes that I barely registered them.

"We've found something for your houseguest to do," she said without preamble.

"Please tell me you've thrown Sebastian off a lightning bridge."

"Baking."

I stopped walking. "Vex."

"He's in the main kitchens." She had a thoughtful look on her face. "The staff is fascinated."

My voice rose. "He could be poisoning the entire citadel."

"He's still under guard, though he doesn't seem to notice," she replied, amused.

"He goes nowhere but the kitchens and his chamber without my express permission," I growled. "And see that he doesn't poison anyone. Accidentally or otherwise."

"Yes, my lord."

We reached the Inner Sanctum's courtyard to find Arabella pacing, her expression thunderous. Nyx was perched on a high pile of rubble from the reconstruction, pointedly facing away from her. The dragon's scales shimmered with an even deeper rosy hue than before, the pink tint spreading across her obsidian hide like a sunrise bleeding through storm clouds. Even her wing membranes had taken on a faint blush, giving her the appearance of some exotic jewel.

"She's sulking," Arabella said when she saw me. "Apparently, she was trying to warn me about the escape while we were in the North Tower, but I sent her away. Now she won't come down."

"Have you tried apologizing?"

She narrowed her eyes. "What would you know about apologizing?"

"You're right," I said with a smirk. "It's a useless strategy."

Arabella opened her mouth, likely to tell me exactly how useless I was, but was cut off by a flash of blue-green smoke. The haze coalesced into a heart-shaped crystalline vial that hovered between us, pulsing with a sickly light. A viscous liquid swirled inside—sometimes fuchsia, sometimes gold, never settling.

"That's . . . new," Arabella said, reaching for it.

I caught her wrist. "It's from the Syndicate—the Alchemist."

"How can you tell? And why not just send a letter?"

"Presentation." My eyes narrowed on the shimmering alchemical compounds coating the vial. "The Alchemist finds simple correspondence boring. Likely when they sent the letter about your father, they didn't have time to send something more dramatic."

I motioned for Arabella to take it. We all knew what this was about. The moment her fingers brushed the glass, the vial dissolved. The liquid didn't fall; it hung in the air, forming glowing, molten script.

Dearest Lady Blackrose,

How delightful that your father yet breathes! The possibilities are simply thrilling. As you'll recall, you now owe me a debt for the information regarding your father's planned assassination. I have decided how you shall repay it.

You and your fascinating husband will meet me at the God Spire in three days' time. Bring the item—you know the one. Or perhaps you don't? How wonderfully uncertain!

Should you fail to appear, or attempt any silly heroics, the consequences will be of such that even your new power cannot mitigate.

With anticipatory delight,

The Alchemist

The words hung in the air for a moment longer, then melted away into smoke that smelled of sulfur.

Vex whistled low. "The Alchemist's getting bold."

"By every rune etched into my bones," I snarled, "I'm going to flay them alive and use their entrails to spell out 'Fuck Around and Find Out' across the battlements." I clenched my fists. "Or perhaps as garland for the winter solstice. I haven't decided which would be more satisfying."

"What's the God Spire?" Arabella asked.

My headache intensified. "The Syndicate's main stronghold in the Lawless Expanse. To the east across the Shattered Sea."

"That's not ideal timing," Arabella said, her hand rising toward her head as if to touch the Heirloom that was still fused there. "Can we refuse?"

"Not without consequences," Vex said. "Debts to the Alchemist are magically binding. Refusal triggers a cascade of curses designed to be instructive."

"The kind that make death seem preferable," I finished. "Their curses tend to involve painful, grotesque transformations that can't be reversed."

Arabella sighed. "So we go. Despite the Heirloom situation and the corrupted ley lines, not to mention a waiting invasion."

"It's a trap," Vex stated flatly.

"Obviously." I took a deep breath to focus my anger into something productive. "Three days isn't enough time to sail there, and even if it were, I don't want to mess with pirates or sea monsters."

"Can't you just open a portal, or . . ." Arabella made a vague gesture I'd come to recognize as her shorthand for "do something impossibly magical."

"Not to the God Spire. The entire Expanse is shielded against that kind of entry." I paused. "And anyway, it might be too far for a personal portal, even for me. But sailing won't be necessary." I turned to Vex. "Contact Captain Brecca with urgent instructions to be prepared to leave first thing tomorrow from Azroth's Claw."

"Who's Brecca?" Arabella asked.

"My ship's captain."

She frowned. "But you just said you didn't want to sail."

"I did." A crooked smile curved my lips. "Some things are more entertaining as a surprise."

Vex cleared her throat. "And what of Lord Sebastian?"

I considered it. Leaving him here unsupervised was a risk. Taking him into the heart of the Syndicate was another. But I preferred the risks I could watch. "He comes with us," I decided. "I want him where I can see him."

"Very well." Vex nodded and departed to begin the preparations.

Arabella waited until she was out of earshot, then turned back to me. "So we're really doing this? Traveling across the sea to meet with a maniacal alchemist while I have a world-altering artifact fused to my skull?"

"The Alchemist knows about the Heirloom." I gestured to the golden circlet. "I'd bet all my titles that's the 'item' they referred to. And they know we can't refuse. Which means they also know we're in a position of weakness. The retreat from Solandris, the corruption, the fact that we're scrambling for answers—the Alchemist has impeccable timing. This summons isn't just about collecting a debt. It's about forcing us to show our hand when we're most vulnerable."

"So what do we do?"

"We go. We play their game. And we get back here as quickly as possible to deal with the real problem."

Above us, Nyx gave a mournful, theatrical cry as she took off into the sky. Apparently, our lack of attention had offended her.

Three days to prepare for walking into the heart of Syndicate power, wearing an artifact that could reshape reality. All to pay a debt to one of the most unstable entities in existence.

What could possibly go wrong?

I mentally began listing disasters—it was a very long list.

18

Bond over Baked Goods

(and Avoid Thinking About Tomorrow)

Arabella

The vast main kitchen of Skyspire sprawled across its own floating island, connected to the Great Hall by a reinforced lightning bridge wide enough to transport feast supplies.

I paused at the threshold, taking in the sheer scale of the operation. Dozens of cooks hustled amid the din of shouted orders and clattering pots. At the chamber's heart, a series of interconnected hearths roared with enchanted flames that never smoked, their heat perfectly controlled by glowing runes carved into the stone surrounds. Roasted meat and fresh bread warred with the sharp tang of spices.

I rarely ventured here. But the promise of Sebastian's scones had drawn me in, along with a desperate need to think about anything other than my father rotting in the dungeons.

I kept waiting to feel some clarity about Lord Evenfall's fate. Death seemed too merciful for someone who'd locked me in a tower, calling it love while he paraded suitors past me like I was a prized cow. But if not death, then what? Let the Dark Lord have him?

Kaz would be pleased, but it would simply be a way of passing on the decision I should be making.

"Move it, or I'll use your bones for stock!" a woman's voice boomed across the cavernous space.

I startled, but the words weren't meant for me. The command had come from Marna, who ran the kitchens with the same iron fist Kazimir used to rule his territories, and woe to anyone who disrupted her domain.

Which made the sight before me all the more surprising.

Sebastian stood at his own dedicated workstation—prime real estate in Marna's kingdom—removing a tray of golden scones from the oven and placing them on a cooling rack. It was hard to miss the tall, golden-haired nobleman with his sleeves rolled up to reveal forearms dusted with flour. He looked like he'd stepped out of a fairy tale and into a villain's lair.

He'd changed since we'd found him in the forest. Gone were the bloodstained traveling clothes, replaced by loose dark trousers and a simple linen shirt in charcoal gray—practical Skyspire attire that looked strange on someone who'd probably spent his entire life in Solandrian pastels. The darker colors made his violet eyes stand out even more, and I made a mental note to thank Vex. Sebastian had arrived with nothing but the clothes on his back, yet somehow she'd already equipped him with an entire wardrobe.

She perched on a nearby stool, the tips of her black hair faded into silver, watching him work with an expression of mild amusement. And Griffin . . .

Griffin wasn't supposed to be here at all.

As I approached the group, I resisted the urge to check that the glamor hiding the Heirloom's outline was still in place. The spell Kazimir had taught me this morning was holding, but I wasn't convinced I'd mastered it yet.

I sat down next to Griffin. "Aren't you supposed to be working on our problem?"

He jumped at my voice, nearly dropping the Doom Scroll balanced on his knee. "Lady Blackrose! I—that is—I'm on break? A very legitimate, authorized break. Please don't tell Lord Blackrose."

"Griffin's counting this as a meal," Vex confirmed, though her tone suggested she found this as dubious as I did. "I'm supervising."

"Like I'm a child who can't be trusted near sharp objects," Griffin added miserably.

"Marna's rules, not mine," Vex said with finality.

I shook my head. "Relax, Griffin. I'm not here to police your punishment."

"Oh good." His shoulders sagged with relief. "Because Sebastian promised me first taste of the new batch, and I've been waiting for *ages*."

Sebastian glanced up from his work. "Arabella! Perfect timing. These will be ready in just a moment."

Something about the familiar way he smiled triggered a strange flutter in my chest. Not attraction—that particular ship had never even left port—but a recognition that felt significant somehow, yet I couldn't grasp why. Like it should attach to a memory but didn't.

I blinked, disoriented.

"Are you all right?" Sebastian asked.

"Fine," I said quickly, forcing a smile. "Just hungry."

Marna chose that moment to materialize at Sebastian's elbow, making all of us jump. She was a broad-shouldered woman with arms like a blacksmith's and a voice that could make rag dolls stand up straight. Her dark hair was pulled back in a severe bun, and her weathered face bore the scowl of someone who'd spent decades managing chaos through sheer force of will. She peered at the scones with a critical eye.

"Hmm," she said finally. "Acceptable."

From Marna, that was practically a declaration of love.

Sebastian beamed like she'd just crowned him emperor. "Thank you! I was worried about the oven temperature—"

"Don't let it go to your head, boy." But there was something almost fond in her gruffness. Until she turned her gaze on Griffin, who winced reflexively. "No explosions in my kitchen, enchanter."

She stomped away, bellowing at a cook who'd committed the sin of letting a sauce reduce too far.

Griffin was frowning. "Last time I was here, Marna threw a ladle at my head."

"You deserved it," Vex and I said at the same time.

"Griffin's been explaining the Doom Scroll to me," Sebastian interrupted, saving Griffin from further humiliation. "Fascinating device."

Griffin's entire face lit up. "You really think so? Most people find it morbid."

"Morbid?" Sebastian wiped his hands on a cloth. "It's brilliant. Though I wonder if you've considered adding a happiness index as a counterbalance? Might provide interesting comparative data."

Griffin practically melted at the suggestion, and I had to admire Sebastian's technique. He'd always been good at making people feel seen.

"Lord Sebastian," Vex said, drawing his attention. "I've been instructed to inform you that you'll be accompanying Lord and Lady Blackrose to the God Spire tomorrow morning."

Sebastian's eyebrows rose. "Tomorrow *morning*?"

"Portal opens at dawn," Vex confirmed.

"Right." Sebastian's movements became more purposeful, his earlier leisurely pace abandoned. "Then I should finish these quickly. Can't leave Marna's kitchen in disarray—she'd hunt me down across the realms."

Griffin made a strangled sound. "I've *always* wanted to go to the God Spire. The Academia of Malice is there—the only university dedicated to studying villainy from an academic perspective."

"You're not going," Vex said firmly.

Sebastian, with the diplomatic grace of someone trained in courtly politics, said, "Griffin, I'm sure your research is important, if you need to stay here."

It was perfectly calibrated to make Griffin feel important without undermining Kazimir's punishment. Griffin shot Sebastian a grateful look, and then the enchanter pushed his spectacles up on his nose and his eyes brightened like he'd had an epiphany.

I waited for an outburst but was distracted when Sebastian handed me a plate with a flower-shaped scone, still steaming, along with a small pot of clotted cream. I took a bite and nearly moaned. It was perfect—light, crumbly, with just the right balance of butter and sweetness from the blueberries. And the cream was obviously enhanced with something magical that transcended traditional baking. "Sebastian, this is perfect."

"Thank you, my lady," he said with a grin.

Two passing kitchen maids saw his smile and collided with the grace of startled chickens, their faces flushing crimson as they stammered apologies—not to each other, but to the air in front of them, their eyes still fixed on Sebastian like he'd just conjured the sun. The rest of us pretended not to notice as they fled, whispering furiously about "those eyes" and "the whole package."

"Are you coming to the God Spire, Vex?" Sebastian asked, turning those violet eyes on her.

"Someone has to keep Skyspire from falling out of the sky," she said with a wry smile. "With all the reconstruction and Lord Blackrose leaving, I'm needed here."

"A pity." Sebastian arranged more scones on plates. "Though Griffin tells me you're the one who actually keeps this place running, so it makes sense."

"Flattery will get you extra jam," Vex said drily, "but it won't change my responsibilities."

Sebastian laughed. "Worth a try. Though Griffin's been quite vocal about your competence."

"When he's not terrified of her," I added teasingly, but Griffin was staring thoughtfully into space and didn't hear me.

"A healthy fear of Vex is a sign of intelligence." Sebastian passed her a plate with a scone. "Anyone who isn't at least a little intimidated by someone who can manage Kazimir Blackrose's citadel is either brave or foolish."

Vex took a bite of the scone and made an appreciative sound. "Your magic—it's not just life force manipulation, is it? There's something else in this."

Sebastian's hands stilled for a moment. "You can taste it?"

"I can sense it," Vex corrected. "The enhancement. It's subtle, but it's there."

"Biomantic cultivation," Sebastian said. "I sense life and purpose in organic things. The yeast in this dough is alive—I can coax it to rise perfectly. Those herbs drying? Their cells are dying, but they still have intent, a reason for being. I can keep them potent, prevent spoilage. The preserved meats are further gone—I can tell if they're safe, but I can't change them. It's like . . . living things sing to me. Dying things with purpose hum. True death is just silence."

She brushed a crumb off her face. "That must be overwhelming."

The Doom Scroll suddenly flared with red text, drawing Griffin's attention. "Oh, that's not good."

"What?" I moved closer, trying to read the moving script.

"Magical disturbances near Solandris. A merchant's entire cargo of silk spontaneously transformed into angry butterflies. That's . . . actually kind of amusing. But this—" He pointed to another line. "Three mages in Sunspire fell into comas while attempting a simple scrying. And here, a ley line intersection near the border just collapsed."

My blood ran cold. These weren't random events.

"That's unusual," Sebastian said, frowning. "What would cause something like that?"

"Griffin, you should inform Lord Blackrose immediately," I said, perhaps too quickly. Sebastian didn't know about the corruption of the ley lines.

Griffin started to protest—clearly wanting to stay for the scones—but Sebastian was already wrapping one in a clean cloth. "Blueberry," he said, pressing it into Griffin's hands. "Still warm."

"My hero." Griffin looked like he might cry.

Sebastian chuckled good-naturedly. "Good luck with your research."

Griffin practically floated out of the kitchen.

Vex stood. "I better make sure he actually delivers that message—it's too important for him to get distracted." She paused to look back. "Sebastian, save me one of the lemon ones?"

"Already set aside," he assured her.

As their footsteps faded, the background noise of cooks and clattering pans seemed to recede, leaving Sebastian and me in an odd bubble of quiet.

The Heirloom pulsed warm against my forehead, hidden beneath the glamor. If the ley lines were deteriorating this quickly, we didn't have time for the Alchemist's games. But refusing to go to the God Spire wasn't an option. The warning about my father had saved his worthless life, and now I owed a debt I couldn't refuse to pay.

It would have been simpler if I'd just let Auremar's assassins have him and ignored the Alchemist's warning.

But then I'd never have learned the truth about my mother.

"Arabella?" Sebastian's voice pulled me back.

"Just thinking about the trip," I said, finishing my scone. "The timing is unfortunate."

"Most things involving the Syndicate are." He began covering the remaining scones. "Though I'm curious to see the God Spire. I've only heard stories."

"What about your father?" I asked. "Aren't you worried Auremar will retaliate against him for your sudden departure?"

Sebastian shook his head. "He's in no danger from Auremar."

"How can you be certain?"

"The heroic bloodline came through my mother's side," he explained, his voice softening at the mention of her. "She's been gone for years now. Without her connection, my father is just another minor lord from the Northern Peaks—hardly worth Auremar's attention or wrath."

I frowned. "Still, your father must have some political value. Auremar doesn't strike me as the type to let potential leverage slip away unused."

"Oh, my father has survived far stickier situations than an angry king." The affection in his voice was unmistakable as he began wiping down the workstation. "Most of the court thinks he's a simple, practical man—too straightforward for intrigue. They underestimate him constantly. It's his greatest asset."

"He taught you well, then."

Sebastian glanced up, surprised. "What do you mean?"

"The way you let people underestimate you," I said. "The polite, harmless nobleman routine. You're more like him than you might think."

His expression shifted—something between pleasure and melancholy crossing his features. "I suppose I am," he said quietly. "Though he'd be horrified to know where his lessons have landed me."

"In the Dark Lord's fortress, covered in flour and making scones?"

Sebastian's laugh was soft but genuine. "Not exactly the diplomatic triumph he'd envisioned for his son." His gaze turned assessing.

"What?" I asked, hoping the glamor hadn't slipped.

He shrugged. "You look different."

"Oh," I said, relieved. "It's been years since you last saw me properly."

"That's not what I mean." He set down his cloth and turned to face me fully. For a moment, something raw and complicated flickered in those violet eyes—a look that made my chest tighten inexplicably. "You look . . . settled. Like you've found where you belong."

"I have," I said simply.

"Good." His voice was almost wistful. "That's . . . good."

He held my gaze for another heartbeat, and I had the strangest sensation of standing at the edge of a precipice, looking down at something I'd lost but couldn't remember losing. Then he blinked, and the moment shattered.

"Another scone?" he asked, his cheerful mask sliding back into place. "I made extra."

"No," I said, standing too quickly. "I should go. Packing to do."

"I should finish up here and do the same." He turned back to his cleaning. "Are you certain Lord Blackrose wants me along? I'd hate to be an imposition."

I studied him more closely. Was he trying to avoid going? Or was this about something else?

"Kazimir wants you where he can watch you," I said.

Sebastian huffed. "He doesn't trust easily, does he?"

"Few people do. Don't you want to go?"

He shrugged. "I admit Griffin's description of the Academia sounds interesting."

"Then it's settled."

As I headed for the door, I couldn't resist one last glance back. Sebastian was standing perfectly still, staring off into nothing.

A young cook—broad-shouldered, elbows deep in dough—caught Sebastian's eye from across the room. The man's gaze lingered, his smile warm and inviting as he paused mid-knead to watch Sebastian remove his apron.

Sebastian offered a polite nod, his expression pleasant but distant as he hung his apron on a hook. The cook's smile faltered, and he returned to his dough with slightly more force than necessary.

I left before I could examine why the sight of Sebastian forcing cheerfulness made something in me simultaneously relieved and strangely bereft.

It was the same feeling of reaching for a memory that wasn't there.

19

Plan a Honeymoon

(to a Stronghold of Villains)

Kazimir

"Absolutely not."

Sebastian stood in my war room with flour still dusting his nose, looking far too comfortable for someone who'd been in my fortress less than a week. His guard hovered outside the door, wisely keeping his distance.

"My lord, I understand the journey is necessary for you and Lady Blackrose," Sebastian said, his tone measured and polite. "But surely my presence isn't required? I could remain here, assist Vex with—"

"You're coming with us to the God Spire or you're leaving altogether. Through a window if necessary."

"That seems unnecessarily dramatic," he muttered. "Though I suppose defenestration is rather traditional for Dark Lords."

It was the first hint of sass I'd detected from Sebastian. Either he'd already been spending too much time with Arabella, or he was unnecessarily comfortable here.

I stepped closer, letting shadows gather around my feet. "I have other options at my disposal, if you don't like either of those."

Sebastian's jaw tightened. A tiny crack appeared in the floorboards near his feet, and a single thorny vine pushed through, twisting anxiously before he stepped on it.

"Sebastian." Arabella sat on the war table, legs swinging. Her hazel eyes were concerned. "What's really going on?"

He was silent for a moment, and another hairline crack appeared in the stone, this time sprouting a nervous cluster of white flowers that bloomed and died in the span of a breath.

"Nothing changed," he said finally, clasping his hands behind his back. "I simply thought I might be more useful here. The kitchens, the gardens—"

Arabella's expression shifted, that subtle tightening around her eyes that told me her truth-sense had just activated. But instead of calling him out on the lie, she simply studied him.

"What's it going to be, Scone Lord?" I growled. "Leave our protection or go with us to the God Spire?"

I did have a third option—the dungeons. But they were still chaotic, and Arabella would never agree.

Sebastian exhaled slowly, violet eyes meeting mine. "I'll accompany you to the God Spire."

Damn it.

"Let me be crystal clear. We're going to a place where your particular brand of well-intentioned chaos will be a catastrophic liability. Therefore, you will remain in whatever quarters you are assigned unless you have been given permission to leave, and you will touch nothing. If you so much as step a toe out of line, I will have you chained to your bedpost for the duration of the trip." I leaned in, crowding his space until he had to crane his neck to look at me. "Or I'll kill you. It will very much depend on my mood."

To Sebastian's credit, he didn't flinch. He just held my gaze and nodded. "Yes, my lord."

The door burst open before I could elaborate on the various ways I could make his life miserable. Griffin stumbled in, his burnt-straw hair even more disheveled than usual, carrying an armload of scrolls that immediately scattered across the floor.

"My lord! Terrible news! Well, not terrible exactly, more inconvenient, though I suppose it depends on your perspective—"

"Griffin." My voice could have frozen fire. "You have five seconds to explain why you're not working."

"The research!" He scrambled to collect his scrolls, knocking over an ink pot in the process. Black liquid spread across my battle maps. "I've been analyzing the data from your last . . . collaborative session, and I believe we're on the verge of a breakthrough, but—"

He paused, his face doing something complicated. His eyes darted to Sebastian, then away, then back to me with an expression that screamed, "Please don't ask me to elaborate in front of company."

"But?" I prompted, my patience thinning.

"But we can't afford delays in communication. Not now." He fumbled with the Doom Scroll, nearly dropping it as he tried to pick up his papers. "The magical disturbances near Sunspire are escalating. Three more incidents just this evening."

I saw where he was going with his babbling but decided to hear him out.

"And," Griffin continued, gaining momentum now, "if you'll recall, on the way to the northern outpost, we needed to conduct experiments in the field. Real-time adjustments based on your combined magical output. The God Spire trip could take weeks. If something happens while you're there, and I'm here—"

"You'd be unable to provide support," I finished.

"Precisely!" He brightened, then immediately looked nervous again.

Sebastian, who'd been watching this exchange with obvious curiosity, opened his mouth as if to ask a question. No one bothered to enlighten him.

"So you're telling me," I said, each word dripping with irritation, "that you have to come with us to the God Spire."

Griffin's face lit up. "Oh, can I? That would be wonderful! I've never been across the Shattered Sea before. Well, there was that time with the exploding portal, but that doesn't really count since we ended up in that cave with the sentient mushrooms—"

"Griffin."

"Yes, my lord?"

The urge to strangle him was so strong I had to clench my fists. Griffin, my disaster-prone enchanter, at the Syndicate's headquarters, where a single misplaced spell could start a war. "Pack light. If you bring anything that explodes, combusts, or develops sentience during the journey, I'm throwing you overboard."

"Oh, but—"

"Overboard, Griffin."

He gulped. "Got it. And don't worry, my lord, I've already delegated the ward carving to my third assistant. He's terribly slow, but very meticulous. It will only set us back a few more weeks."

"You're finishing those ward anchors when we get back. All of them."

His face fell slightly, but the excitement of the trip clearly outweighed his disappointment. "Yes, my lord. I'll just . . . go pack my travel-sized alchemical kit!" He backed toward the door, tripped over his own feet, caught himself on the doorframe, and disappeared down the corridor.

I was beginning to feel less like a Dark Lord and more like a beleaguered chaperone on a field trip from hell. "He's a disaster waiting to happen." I turned to Thorne, who'd been standing silently in the corner. "You're coming, obviously."

"Wouldn't miss it." His gravelly voice held dark amusement. "Someone needs to keep you from murdering the entire Syndicate."

"That's what Arabella's for."

"I'm more likely to help," she said cheerfully.

I rubbed my temples. The headache from reconstructing the dungeon wards hadn't fully faded. The final and most crucial preparation was ensuring I could maintain control of Skyspire from afar. Auremar was quiet, but that only made him more dangerous. Vex would remain in charge, the only one I trusted to execute my will without question. "We need communication with Skyspire while we're gone. If Auremar makes a move—"

"Already handled." Vex entered the war room carrying a small ebony box. "I found the shadow-linked scrying crystals."

She opened the box, revealing two crystals that absorbed the light and pulsed with a darkness that made my runes ache pleasantly.

Arabella peered into the box. "How do they work?"

"Messages travel through the shadow realm," I said. "Undetectable, unblockable."

Vex nodded and handed me one of the paired crystals. "If there's a crisis, you'll know about it within a few seconds."

"Define 'crisis,'" Arabella said.

"Full-scale invasion, magical catastrophe level seven or higher, or an unfortunate or untimely death."

I nodded and tucked the crystal into an inside pocket of my jacket. "I'm leaving three constructs of myself, in the off chance we've picked up another spy or assassins try to get in. Two will be doing my usual brooding routine in my study or walking the battlements here, and the third will go to the army at the outpost. Auremar won't know I'm gone unless he's bold enough to attack directly—and if he is, we'll know about it in under an hour."

Vex's expression was perfectly neutral. "Yes, my lord." She paused. "Lord Sebastian provided some surprisingly useful defensive formations. Purely protective, but nearly impregnable for short-term sieges."

I looked at Sebastian with new suspicion. "You gave my steward military advice?"

"Defensive only," he said quickly. "I don't do offensive strategy. But I'm very good at not dying."

"That remains to be seen."

As Vex left, Arabella hopped off the table, her boots hitting the floor with a decisive thud. "You know what this is?"

"A clusterfuck?"

"A honeymoon." Her smile was wicked as she moved closer. "You never did take me on one."

"Most honeymoons don't involve potentially hostile magical entities and binding debts . . . or so many people."

"Most honeymoons are boring." She traced a finger along my chest, right over where my runes were carved. "Unless you're saying you can't handle a little excitement?"

Sebastian made a strangled noise. "My lord?"

"You're still here," I said without looking at him. "Why?"

He practically ran from the room, his escort hurrying to catch up.

I stared at Arabella for a long moment, feeling something shift in my chest as her words sank in. Not just lust—though there was plenty of that—but deep admiration.

"A honeymoon," I repeated slowly, the idea taking shape in my mind. "Arabella, that's brilliant."

Her eyebrows rose. "Don't sound so surprised."

"No, listen." I stepped closer, lowering my voice even though we were alone. "If we present this as a honeymoon trip, we control the narrative. We're not responding to a summons—we're simply taking our overdue wedding tour. A short getaway after a decisive victory in northern Solandris."

She smiled. I began pacing. "In the Syndicate, debt is leverage. If it becomes common knowledge that I'm beholden to the Alchemist—"

"The other chairs would use it against you," she finished. "They'd start speculating what information was valuable enough for the mighty Chair of Dominion to go into debt."

My shadows curled with pleasure at how quickly she grasped the implications. "But a honeymoon—"

"Gives us the perfect misdirection." Her smile turned predatory. "And when they ask about that massive surge of power from Skyspire during the Guild attack—"

"We blame it on our explosive marital bliss." I couldn't help but laugh. "Heroic bloodline, dominion magic . . . things get intense when we're together. I'll send word ahead to prepare for my bride. No one else needs to know about the Alchemist. We meet them under a social pretext, conduct our business privately, and get back to the Western Realms before Auremar realizes we're gone."

Arabella's eyes gleamed. "Plus, no one questions newlyweds wanting privacy. We'll have freedom to move about the Spire unencumbered."

I reached for her then, unable to resist. My hand slid from her waist to cup the curve of her ass through her gown. I pulled her flush against me, letting her feel the effect her words had. "Do you have any idea how attractive you are right now?"

"Because of my face or my devious mind?" She tilted her head, challenge in her voice.

"Both." My voice dropped lower as I trailed my fingers up her spine.

"Just try to remember it's a cover story, my lord," she whispered, her fingers tangling in my hair. "We have an alchemist to see and not a lot of time before we need to be back here, dealing with a mad king."

Thorne cleared his throat. Loudly.

"You heard the lady, Thorne," I said, still holding Arabella's gaze. "We're going on our honeymoon. Prepare accordingly."

Thorne escaped while we were distracted, probably to warn the others that we were in one of our moods. The ones where we couldn't seem to stop orbiting each other, trading barbs that were really just foreplay.

"We should finish packing," Arabella said finally, though she didn't move away. "This is stupid, isn't it? Walking into the Syndicate's stronghold with the Heirloom literally fused to my head?"

I pulled back enough to meet her eyes. "Probably."

She studied me with those hazel eyes that saw too much. "You want to know what the Alchemist knows. About the Heirloom. About us. About what's coming."

She wasn't wrong. The Syndicate had been suspiciously quiet since their last visit. No threats, no demands, just waiting. It made my skin crawl. And if the Alchemist could give us a heads-up, it would make the trip worth it.

Arabella placed a kiss on my lips. "Just promise me that if this goes badly—and it probably will because our plans always go sideways—we handle it together. No heroic sacrifices. No sending me away for my own good."

The thought of anyone trying to take her from me made my runes burn hot enough that she flinched.

"Sorry," I said, forcing the rage down. "I promise." I meant it with every rune carved into my bones. I sat in a chair and pulled her into my lap. "Anyone who tries to separate us will discover exactly why I'm called the Terror of the Western Realms."

She smiled. "Your ego needs its own cabin on the ship."

"Lord Blackrose?" Griffin's voice drifted from the corridor. "Should I pack the emergency explosion containment kit? Just in case?"

I closed my eyes. "Are you planning to bring something that might explode?"

"Um—"

"Overboard, Griffin."

His footsteps retreated, followed immediately by a crash and creative cursing.

"We're all going to die," I muttered.

"But at least it won't be boring," Arabella agreed cheerfully.

Nothing with her ever was.

By the time we'd finally finished the travel preparations late that night, I was ready to burn the whole citadel to the ground for a moment of peace. Griffin tried to smuggle three separate "definitely not explosive" devices into his luggage, Sebastian kept sprouting thorny vines and rhyming, and Thorne had threatened to tie them both to the outside of the ship.

The exhaustion hit me all at once as Arabella and I climbed the stairs to our chambers. Between the invasion attempt, rebuilding the dungeon wards, and now this impromptu journey, I'd had three days of almost no sleep. My runes ached with a deep, bone-weary pain that no amount of posturing could hide.

"I swear to every dark god that ever existed, I'm going to set something on fire," I muttered, already unbuttoning my coat.

Arabella wrapped an arm around my waist. I wasn't sure if the gesture was for her benefit or mine. "You already set three things on fire today."

"Those were demonstrations of what happens when people won't stop asking me stupid questions," I growled, my hand landing on the heavy door to our rooms. "We have less than three days to prepare for what's obviously a trap, and I'm fielding inquiries about whether we need to bring extra pillows."

Arabella leaned against the door, a tired smile gracing her freckled face. "I need a bath." She began pulling her hair from its braid. "And then I need you to do unspeakable things to me so I can stop thinking about tomorrow."

"I can manage that."

She glanced up at me, one eyebrow raised. "You look ready to collapse."

"I'm never too tired for unspeakable things."

She laughed, shaking her golden hair free. "Liar. But I'm up for a quickie if you are."

"Quick can be good." I was already loosening the laces of her dress. "Very good, if done right."

Her hands moved to my belt. "Yeah?"

I unlocked the heavy door with renewed enthusiasm.

Only to be greeted with a blast of freezing air.

The large gothic window stood wide open, autumn wind howling through the room. The fire in the hearth guttered and sparked. Papers from the desk swirled in miniature cyclones across the floor.

But that wasn't what made me reach for my magic.

Arabella wrinkled her nose. "What is that *smell*? Did the servants forget to collect our swamp clothes?"

"No," I said, my gaze fixed on our bed. "That's not it."

A human arm was lying on the sheets—pale and bloated, with a greenish tinge creeping along the mottled flesh. The dirty sleeve clung wetly to the skin, and the whole thing ended in a ragged, torn mess where it had been severed—or more accurately, *worried off* by teeth rather than cleanly cut.

The fingers were artfully arranged in an obscene gesture.

"Is that . . ." Arabella moved closer, her voice far too calm for the situation. "That's Lightbringer's sleeve."

"Seems like it." The bedding was ruined, but at least there wasn't much blood. "But I distinctly remember leaving his body to rot in the swamp, not bringing it home as a trophy for your case."

"Oh, for fuck's sake," Arabella groaned, rushing to the open window. *"Nyx!"*

A rumbling purr echoed from somewhere above us. The dragon. I stared at the severed arm. At our violated bed. Then at the open window framing a stormy sky.

"Why?" I managed to choke out.

"She's still angry I didn't listen when she tried to warn us about the escape."

"How did she even get in here? The window's too small."

"She's been getting into smaller and smaller spaces these days. It's how she gets to Griffin's familiars. But it might also be shadow-walking." Arabella's voice held a note of wonder. "I've been reading about shadow dragon development. When they reach a certain age, they can slip between shadows, existing in both the material plane and the shadow realm. Usually, it doesn't manifest this early. Mature shadow dragons use it as a pathway." She gestured around the room. "They step into one shadow and emerge from another, regardless of distance."

I glanced at the dark corners of our chamber. "She could be here right now?"

"She's not. I can feel her sulking on top of the tower."

I glared at the arm in disgust. With a sharp gesture and a pulse of magic, I vanished the entire mess—the arm, the sheets, the bedding, even the pillows. The mattress underneath was thankfully unsoiled. "That was our best bedding."

"You have twelve sets exactly like it."

"Had. Now I have eleven." I flicked my wrist, and the window slammed shut, the latch clicking into place.

Arabella shivered. "I'm freezing."

Another gesture, and the fire roared back to life, flooding the room with warmth. I pulled her down onto the bare mattress, rolling so she was beneath me. "I can warm you just fine."

"Mmm." Her hands slipped under my shirt, and I flinched as her cold fingers trailed over my abdomen. "Nyx can't come to the God Spire."

I pulled back slightly. "Obviously not. We'd be inviting a war if she decided to pull a stunt like this on the Alchemist."

"She won't understand that."

I groaned, dropping my forehead to rest against hers. "Do you want me to tell her?"

Arabella laughed. "You can't intimidate a dragon into good behavior."

"Watch me."

"Kaz."

"Fine." I trailed kisses down her neck, feeling a surge of satisfaction when she squirmed beneath me. "What do you suggest?"

"We give her a job. Make her feel important. Maybe patrol duty while we're gone?"

I nipped at her collarbone. "You want to leave a vindictive teenage dragon in charge of something?"

"With Vex supervising, obviously."

It wasn't the worst idea. Nyx was protective of Skyspire now that she considered it her territory. And Vex had a way with difficult personalities. She managed me, after all.

"I'll consider it," I said finally.

"Good." Arabella's hands pulled at the hem of my shirt. "Now, where were we?"

"I was about to prove that quick can be very, very good."

Her breathing hitched as my mouth moved lower, tasting the skin just above the neckline of her dress. “Kaz, what if the Alchemist wants something we can’t give?”

“Then we get creative,” I said, my voice muffled against her skin. “We lie, we cheat, we burn the whole Spire down if we have to.”

“Oh. Well in that case—” Her thought was cut off by a sharp gasp as my hand slid up her thigh and found the right spot.

20

Make a Dramatic Exit

(Featuring Purple Flames and Public Panic)

Arabella

At first light, we stepped out of the portal nexus into an open courtyard on top of a hill. Salt air and smoke filled my lungs, and I saw the white stone buildings and gray tiled roofs of Azroth's Claw. The city where Kaz had beheaded his father at that infamous dinner table.

As I took it in, Kazimir's mouth curved in that particular smile he reserved for things he'd conquered. "You should see it at night. The harbor lights look like fallen stars."

The city was everything Solandris wasn't—raw, violent, beautiful. Where my homeland suffocated under golden perfection, this place breathed chaos. Ships of all sizes bobbed in the water, their flags bright splashes of color against the cream sails and deep blue sea. The entire city clung to the cliffs overlooking the harbor.

Controlling this port gave Kaz enormous leverage over the Western Realms. Nothing moved between the Shattered Sea and the inland kingdoms without his say-so, including Syndicate trade, unless it was willing to go far to the south of the continent.

"It's different than I imagined," I said softly.

Kazimir came to stand beside me, his shoulder brushing mine. "What did you imagine? Blood in the streets? Public executions?"

"No. Just . . . less alive." I gestured toward the bustling marketplace visible in the distance. "It looks thriving."

"It is. I make sure of it." There was a note of pride in his voice. "The port trade has tripled since I took control."

"From your father."

His expression darkened momentarily. "Yes."

I wanted to ask what it felt like to return to the place where he'd become the Scourge of Azroth. But this wasn't the time, not with an audience.

"Can we stop? Just for an hour?" I knew we couldn't, but I wanted to walk those twisting streets, taste the foreign spices I could smell even from here, maybe burn down a corrupt merchant's stall or two.

"Soon." Kaz's gloved hand found mine. "When this business with the Alchemist is done, I'll show you every shadow and secret. The night markets where they sell poisons alongside pastries. The cliff gardens where my father's witches grew their most dangerous plants."

I squeezed his hand. "I'd love that."

Griffin hovered nearby. "Did you know that most portal networks have a 0.03 percent chance of depositing you in the wrong century? I once ended up—"

"Griffin," Kazimir's voice cut through the enchanter's rambling. "Not now."

Behind us, Sebastian made a sound like a dying cat. "The boat, the boat, we'll miss the boat! My stomach wishes to revolt!"

"You're getting worse!" Griffin pushed his spectacles high onto his nose. "That's interesting. Yesterday you managed most conversations normally. What's wrong?"

Thorne's laugh sounded like gravel in a meat grinder. "Stress."

"This isn't the time for jest—I barely got dressed—I mean—" Sebastian groaned. The dark circles under his eyes suggested he'd been up all night.

"Sunset. Harvest. Damn the bone witch to darkest rest!"

Kaz's shadows darkened the path at our feet. "I can already tell this is a mistake."

"Sorry," Sebastian muttered. "I didn't want to be tardy."

Thorne just shook his head and continued down the path toward the docks, probably questioning every life choice that had led him to babysitting this particular circus.

I caught Sebastian staring back at the horizon as though he could see Skyspire from here.

Sebastian's hesitation yesterday had bothered me. But what if it had something to do with Vex? He'd asked if she was coming, after all.

The alternative—that it had anything to do with *me*—was uncomfortably close to that precipice feeling I'd gotten in the kitchen. Better to believe he'd wanted to stay behind for a silver-haired reason than examine why his wistful look had made my chest tight.

I leaned in to Kaz and lowered my voice. "Do you think there's something between Sebastian and Vex?"

He scowled. "I've had other things on my mind. Their secretive looks haven't been a priority."

I grabbed his arm. "There've been secretive looks?"

He squeezed his eyes shut. "No. I don't know. I don't *want* to know, Arabella."

"You're not interested in what happens to your oldest friend?"

He scoffed. "I'm interested in what happens to her, as in I don't want to see Vex killed when one of Griffin's experiments runs amok, nor would I want to see her fall off the battlements—unless I throw her myself. But I'm not interested in her relationship status or who is dating who or turning the citadel into the main setting for a long romance scroll with spin-offs."

"Well, we don't always get what we want." I looped my arm in his as we continued walking, ignoring another scowl. "Just because you found a companion who tolerates all your eccentricities doesn't mean that others don't deserve a chance at that kind of happiness, if that's what they want." A pause. "And I'm surprised you know what a spin-off is."

"Thank Griffin and his stories from the Enchanted Isles," Kaz muttered. Then he sighed. "Any interest Sebastian may have in Vex is likely one-sided. I'm not even sure Vex experiences attraction."

"That you've seen anyway." I'd never heard her talk about it, though I hadn't known her long enough to be privy to that kind of personal information. "Come on," I said, tugging Kaz forward. "Let's see this ship you've been mysteriously vague about."

He'd refused to give details this morning, just kept saying I'd appreciate the surprise. As we descended toward the harbor, weaving between merchants and sailors who gave our party a wide berth, I tried to guess which vessel was ours. The sleek warship with black sails? The triple-masted merchant vessel bristling with weapons?

"There." Kaz pointed to . . . nothing. Just empty air between two piers.

"Very funny."

"Wait for it."

If we hadn't been in such a hurry, I would have thought Kazimir was pulling some elaborate prank, though it wasn't really his style. A few seconds passed with nothing happening, and then—

"Holy shit."

A ship was descending from the clouds overhead. The hull was dark wood that absorbed the morning light breaking over the sea. Its twin masts were rigged with dark sails that snapped in the wind, plus some smaller third mast I didn't understand the purpose of but assumed made it faster. As it docked, large chains descended from the hull and tethered it with a sizzle of magic. The whole thing bobbed gently about ten feet above the water. Crew jumped over the side to meet us.

"It flies." It was the only thing I could say.

Kaz's face was set in his Dark Lord mask, but a hint of humor flashed in his eyes. "The *Sky Serpent.* Fastest vessel in any realm, capable of sailing sea or sky." His voice held pure masculine pride. "I took it from a pirate lord who thought he could blockade my harbor. He was wrong."

"High. Sky. Fly. I think I'd rather die."

We turned. Sebastian stood behind us, his face pale, one hand pressed to his stomach. I frowned. Perhaps bringing him was a bad idea. It was seeming more likely that his reluctance to go to the God Spire had more to do with seasickness than blossoming love.

Griffin, on the other hand, was practically vibrating with excitement. "Please tell me you'll let me examine the propulsion runes!"

"You'll sit quietly and touch nothing," Kaz said flatly.

Griffin backed up until he was standing beside his definitely-not-explosive luggage.

A small crowd had gathered to watch our departure. The dockworkers and sailors had bowed as we passed, though I caught several of them stealing glances at me. The Dark Lord's mysterious bride, come to see their city at last. I couldn't wait to return for a proper introduction.

We boarded via a gangplank that materialized from thin air, and I immediately fell in love. The deck was smooth wood embedded with crystals that glowed blue, the railings carved with protective wards that hummed against my palm.

A woman with sun-bronzed skin and dark hair braided down her back met us at the gangplank—the captain by her insignia. Beside her stood a tall, broad-shouldered woman with deep brown skin and dozens of braids pulled into a thick tail.

"Lord Blackrose." The captain's nod was curt, professional. "I would have brought the *Sky Serpent* to Skyspire if I'd known you needed her."

"It was sudden," Kaz replied. "This gave you time to prepare." His gaze swept the assembled crew. "Captain Brecca, get us underway."

"Aye, my lord." She turned to her crew without missing a beat. "Stations! Prepare for ascension!" Her first officer was already moving, barking orders that sent sailors scrambling to their posts.

The entire crew—perhaps fifteen souls in total—dispersed in a blur of movement, with only a few curious stares cast my way.

I wanted to explore, but we headed for the cabin first. It was at the stern, behind a door marked with the Blackrose crest. I'd just caught a glimpse of a small but cozy, darkly appointed space when a roar split the air. The ship lurched, tilting at an angle that sent me stumbling into Kaz's chest. Outside, someone screamed.

We burst onto the deck to find half the port in chaos. Sailors dove into the water. Merchants abandoned their stalls. And above us, wings spread wide, Nyx circled like an avenging dark angel.

"I told her to stay!" I shouted over the panic.

"Clearly, she didn't listen!" Kaz was already raising his hands, prepared to defend the ship. Nyx, misinterpreting his stance as a challenge, let out another roar and released a stream of purple fire that caught the edge of a sail. The canvas caught fire instantly.

Captain Brecca was already shouting orders, her first officer directing crew members with buckets toward the flames.

Kaz snarled a word that made my ears ring, and water rose from the harbor in a massive spout. It doused the burning sails, but not before embers rained down on us. The remaining water flooded the deck, instantly soaking everyone and everything.

"Nyx!" I reached for our bond, flooding it with command. *Land. Now.*

She folded her wings and dropped like a stone, hitting the deck hard enough to almost shake us off our feet. Her silver eyes fixed on mine, defiant and furious.

"We discussed this!" I stopped. Took a breath. Kaz was still putting out spot fires, swearing creatively in three languages. "You were supposed to stay with Vex."

Nyx lashed her tail, fixed her stare on the main mast, and opened her mouth.

"Don't you dare!" I commanded.

"She's bluffing," Kaz said, finally getting the last flame under control. His coat was singed, his hair drenched.

Nyx breathed a small jet of fire at the mast, which started smoking.

"Shit." He raised a hand to douse that, too.

"Like dealing with a wild child, really," Sebastian offered, then winced.

I forced myself to relax my posture and stopped in front of Nyx, meeting her eyes. She looked at me and I saw the hurt, the fear that I was leaving her behind.

My throat tightened. "Oh, sweet girl. I wasn't abandoning you."

She puffed out a smoky breath.

"If you stay, you'll have to behave. No burning things. No eating people. No shadow-walking into private rooms."

Nyx uncurled slightly, her tail swishing with tentative hope.

"And you listen to me. Actually listen, not pretend to listen while plotting mayhem."

She perked up immediately, nearly knocking Griffin overboard with an enthusiastic tail wag.

It was the best I'd get. I looked at Kaz, who was examining the damaged sails with the expression of someone calculating exactly how many people he'd need to kill to feel better.

"We can't leave her," I told him. "She'll follow anyway and probably burn half the coast doing it."

"The Syndicate—"

"Will have to deal with it." I brushed soot off my cloak. "Besides, showing up with a dragon sends a message."

"What message? That we can't control our pets?"

"That we're too powerful to need to."

He considered this. "I hate when you make sense."

"I know." I reached up to wipe a smudge of ash from his cheek.

Kazimir approached Nyx, who lowered her head to his level in what could almost be described as contrition. But her eyes glittered with mischief.

"Listen carefully," he said, his voice low and dangerous. "You will not breathe fire on my ship again. You will not disrupt my crew. You will obey Arabella without question. And when we reach the God Spire, you will remain hidden unless we call for you. Break any of these rules, and I will personally ensure you spend the rest of your very long life eating nothing but the blandest fish in the deepest, darkest cave I can find. Are. We. Clear?"

Nyx blinked her silver eyes slowly, then deliberately exhaled a small puff of smoke directly into Kazimir's face.

He didn't even flinch. "I'll take that as a yes."

I bit my lip to keep from laughing.

Behind us, Sebastian had found a bucket to be sick in—we weren't even flying yet—while Griffin rattled off calculations about weight distribution and magical resonance. Nyx preened, smug as any cat who'd gotten the cream.

Or dragon who'd gotten her way through arson.

"Excuse me, Lord Blackrose?" Griffin asked. "Should I reinforce the hull's protective matrix to account for dragon-adjacent thermal fluctuations?"

Kazimir closed his eyes, looking like he was praying for patience. "Yes, Griffin. Do that. Do it quietly. Do it without exploding anything."

"Of course! I'll just need some silver wire, a focusing crystal, and—oh, is that a perpetual motion engine? How fascinating!" He was already wandering toward the stern, where several important-looking mechanical components were housed.

"Thorne," Kazimir said without opening his eyes.

"On it." The security chief was already following Griffin, one hand hovering near the enchanter's collar like he was ready to physically restrain him from touching anything vital.

The ship lurched beneath our feet as the anchor chains retracted with a thunderous clank. Nyx, still looking entirely too pleased with herself, settled at the bow like some bizarre figurehead, wings tucked against her sides.

"Prepare for ascension!" Captain Brecca called again. She hadn't batted an eye at the dragon staying on board. Apparently, serving the Dark Lord meant adapting to chaos.

The crystals embedded in the deck flared to life, pulsing with blue white power that spread through intricate rune patterns carved into the wood. The ship trembled, and I instinctively grabbed the railing as we began to rise.

"The harmonics are incredible," Griffin whispered. His gangly form was sprawled on the deck, ear pressed to the wood, long fingers splayed as if trying to absorb the magic through his skin. "It's like the ship is *singing*. The resonance frequency must be calibrated to the fifth harmonic of—"

"Griffin," Kazimir snapped.

The enchanter scrambled to his feet, adjusting his glasses which had gone askew. "I'm merely observing. The way the crystals channel ambient magical energy through the—"

"Quietly," Kaz said.

Griffin nodded enthusiastically, then immediately began muttering calculations under his breath, his amber eyes wide with delight as he scurried to the nearest crystal to examine it more closely.

The *Sky Serpent* rose higher, and my stomach dropped as the harbor shrank beneath us. The ships looked like children's toys, the people mere specks. The city of Azroth's Claw was a gleaming crescent around the natural harbor. From this height, I could see the fortifications that ringed the outer edges.

"It's beautiful," I said, leaning into Kaz as we watched the city fall away.

Sebastian staggered to the railing beside us, his face a concerning shade of green. "The ground . . . so far." He swallowed hard, clutching the wood like it was the only thing keeping him from floating away.

"You're not even rhyming anymore," I observed. "Progress."

He shot me a miserable look. "The terror has temporarily overwhelmed the curse." A small, purple flower bloomed from the wooden railing where his fingers gripped it. "Though apparently not my magic."

The ship leveled out as we cleared the coastal cliffs, the sea stretching endlessly before us.

"We'll maintain this height until nightfall," Kazimir explained. His hair whipped around his face in the high-altitude winds. "Then descend to just above the waves. It's safer to travel low when crossing at night."

"Safer from what?" I asked.

He shrugged. "Sky pirates. Sudden thunderstorms. Creatures that hunt in the upper atmosphere."

"There are creatures that hunt this high up?" Sebastian squeaked, somehow going even paler.

"Only the ones with a taste for noble flesh," Kaz deadpanned.

Sebastian made a strangled noise and slid down to sit on the deck, a small patch of moss instantly sprouting beneath him for a cushion.

I elbowed Kaz in the ribs. "Stop terrorizing him."

"He'll be fine," he murmured, but there was amusement in his eyes.

The wind picked up as we gained speed, the ship cutting through clouds like a knife. Salt spray still somehow reached us, mingling with the cold air to create a bracing chill. Below, the coastline receded. The landscape transformed into the treacherous beauty of the Shattered Sea—named for the hundreds of tiny islands scattered across the shallow waters and its violent history. Their hidden reefs and unpredictable currents made the passage deadly for any vessel that didn't know the routes. Kazimir had told me the fragmented geography had made it a difficult place for anyone who tried to live within it or conquer it, with centuries of raids and bloodshed.

Griffin had convinced one of the crew members to explain the propulsion system to him and was now taking frantic notes, his spindly form quivering with excitement.

"I've never seen him this happy," I remarked.

"Wait until he realizes I won't let him dismantle anything," Kaz replied drily.

Nyx let out a contented rumble from her perch, her silver eyes half-closed in pleasure as the wind rushed over her scales.

I leaned against the railing and felt a strange sense of freedom. "For what it's worth," I said, "this is already the best honeymoon ever."

He wrapped an arm around me and kissed my temple. "I aim to please."

Sebastian groaned from somewhere behind us. "Flying. Dying. Someone please stop me from crying."

"I could knock him unconscious," Thorne offered.

"Please," Sebastian whimpered, and Kaz said, "Do it."

"Wait—" I started, but was too late to suggest a less painful option like giving Sebastian a tonic.

As Thorne's fist met Sebastian's temple with a meaty thud, I decided this was definitely the strangest honeymoon in the history of honeymoons. Which, knowing us, meant it was perfect.

21

Play Drinking Games with Pickled Organs

(May Cause Vomiting, Flowers, and Philosophy)

Arabella

The next day, I emerged from our cabin feeling deliciously used and more than a little smug. Kaz and I had defiled every surface of our quarters.

The wind that had been so fierce yesterday had gentled to a pleasant breeze. The *Sky Serpent* sliced through fluffy clouds, leaving wisps of white trailing from her creaking hull. Below, the sea sparkled, broken by craggy islands and the occasional pod of something that might have been dolphins . . . if dolphins had tentacles. Nyx glided to the north of us, stretching her pink wings and hunting.

I'd spent yesterday afternoon exploring every inch of this magnificent vessel while Sebastian recovered from Thorne's tender ministrations and Griffin pestered Captain Brecca. The cargo hold alone was a treasure trove of bizarre artifacts and supplies, though Griffin had been firmly banned from examining any of them after he'd accidentally activated a navigational compass that began pointing exclusively toward him. Brecca had been less than amused when her entire bridge crew spent an hour trying to figure out why all their instruments were tracking Griffin's movements through the ship.

Kazimir emerged from below deck, his hair still damp from washing. He wore a simple black tunic and trousers today, though he somehow managed to make even casual clothing look intimidating. He caught my eye and smiled that private smile that made my insides flutter.

"You look pleased with yourself," he said, coming to stand beside me.

"I am." I leaned into him, lowering my voice. "Though I might need a healing salve if we're going to continue at last night's pace."

His laugh was low and wicked. "I'll be gentler tonight."

"Don't you dare."

Thorne lounged against the mainmast, somehow managing to look both relaxed and ready to murder anyone who breathed wrong. Beyond making sure Griffin and Sebastian behaved themselves, he had little to do now that we were in the sky.

Griffin had commandeered a corner of the deck where he'd spread out his research notebooks, muttering calculations.

And Sebastian sat cross-legged near the port railing, a cup of tea steaming in his hands as he watched the clouds drift by. He looked better than yesterday—less green, more his usual pleasant self—though I noticed small flowers had sprouted from the deck.

"We should play a game," I announced.

Everyone turned to look at me.

"A game," Kazimir repeated flatly.

"Yes. You know, fun? Entertainment? That thing normal people do when they're not plotting world domination?"

He smirked. "I'm familiar with the concept, but we're fresh out of eyeballs."

Griffin's head popped up from his notes. "Oh! Yesterday when I was categorizing the cargo manifest—which you said I could do as long as I didn't touch anything—I found the most peculiar collection of pickled organs!" He beamed. "Hearts, livers, a badly preserved pancreas—they're just sitting in the hold. No labels, no preservation spells beyond the basic anti-rot enchantments."

Sebastian carefully set down his teacup. "Why would anyone pickle organs?"

"Emergency rations," Thorne suggested.

"Spell components," Griffin offered.

"Intimidation," Kazimir added.

I grinned. "Game supplies."

They all stared at me.

"We could play cornhole. But with organs."

"That's . . ." Sebastian paused, clearly trying to find a polite way to say "insane." " . . . creative."

"It's brilliant." I was already heading for the stairs to the hold. "Griffin, show me these jars."

Twenty minutes later, we'd hauled up six large glass containers filled with murky brine and an assortment of preserved body parts. The crew gave us a wide berth, though I caught several of them placing bets on what exactly we were planning.

Sebastian peered into a jar containing what was definitely a human brain. "This is disgusting."

"This is *amazing*," Griffin said, scrambling out of the hold after me, his gangly limbs unfolding like a spider emerging from a drain.

Kazimir's expression darkened. "Griffin. Back to your research."

Griffin's enthusiasm deflated like a punctured soap bubble. "But my lord, I was just—"

"The artifact won't fix itself."

I glanced at Griffin's face—the bloodshot eyes behind his smudged glasses, the way his shoulders hunched with exhaustion.

I touched Kazimir's arm lightly, leaning in to murmur, "He was up all night working. Look at him."

Kazimir's jaw tightened, but he studied Griffin more carefully. "Then he should be sleeping."

"I'm too keyed up to sleep!" Griffin protested, having heard that part perfectly well. His voice cracked slightly. "My mind is racing with resonance patterns and harmonic frequencies and the way the energy signature keeps shifting when—"

"Fine." Kazimir cut him off with a raised hand. "You can play. So you don't make any disastrous mistakes while your brain is mushy."

Griffin brightened immediately.

"However," Kazimir continued, his tone brooking no argument, "you're sleeping tonight. Actual sleep. Even if Thorne has to knock you upside the head like he did Sebastian."

"That won't be necessary, my lord!" Griffin squeaked.

I rolled up my sleeves. "Thorne, help me set up targets."

We commandeered two crates from the cargo and cut rough holes in the tops, spacing them about twenty paces apart on the deck. The ship's gentle sway would add an extra challenge, as would the wind.

Kazimir disappeared below deck and returned with two bottles of something that smelled strong enough to dissolve iron. "If we're doing this, we're doing it properly. Miss a throw, take a drink."

"That seems unwise," Griffin said.

"That's the point," I said, using tongs to fish out a liver. It squelched wetly in my grip. "Oh, that's horrible. Perfect."

"I'll keep score," Captain Brecca offered, abandoning her charts with the barely contained glee of someone who'd seen a lot of weird shit in her career but nothing quite like this. "Haven't seen entertainment this twisted since the Pirate King's birthday bash. That ended with three deaths and a marriage proposal."

"Just keeping score?" I asked. "Not playing?"

"Can't drink on duty." She pulled out a small notebook. "But I'll take side bets on who vomits first."

"My money's on the pretty lord," Thorne said, nodding at Sebastian. He hadn't bothered to lower his voice, but Sebastian didn't seem bothered by the assessment.

We divided into teams through the simple expedient of Kazimir claiming me before anyone else could speak. That left Sebastian, Griffin, and Thorne to sort themselves out.

"I'll take Griffin," Sebastian said, surprising everyone.

"Really?" Griffin's voice cracked slightly.

"You've got good hand-eye coordination from all that delicate enchantment work," Sebastian reasoned. "Also, Thorne scares me."

Thorne shrugged. "So I'm alone?"

"You could wait for Nyx to return from hunting," I suggested.

"I'll manage."

The first round was educational. The organs had vastly different aerodynamics—brains threw straight but splattered on impact, hearts were dense but had an unfortunate tendency to bounce, and the mystery organs (we'd given up trying to identify some of them) flew in completely unpredictable arcs.

Sebastian's first throw, a kidney, went wide by three feet and slapped wetly against the deck.

"Drink," Brecca called cheerfully.

Sebastian took a careful sip and immediately coughed. "What is this?"

"Pirate moonshine," Kazimir said.

My throw landed dead center with a satisfying splat. "Ha!"

"Beginner's luck," Thorne said, then landed his own organ—possibly a gallbladder—right through the hole.

Griffin stepped up, holding what was definitely not a human heart. It had too many chambers and a suspicious number of valves. He squinted at the target, adjusted his glasses, then threw with surprising accuracy.

"Yes!" He did a little dance that involved a lot of flailing limbs.

Kazimir's throw was perfect, because of course it was. The liver sailed through the air and through the hole without even touching the sides.

"Show-off," I muttered.

"You love it."

I did.

The second round, after everyone had taken a few drinks, got interesting.

"So Griffin," I said, fishing out something purple and squishy, "how'd you end up working for the Dark Lord anyway?"

Griffin missed his throw entirely, the organ sailing over the side of the ship. He took a large gulp of moonshine. "Would you believe it was an accident?"

"Yes," everyone said simultaneously.

"I was trying to summon a minor demon for my thesis project at the Academy in Valmont—Solandris wouldn't admit me. It was a small thing, just needed it to answer some questions about infernal energy conversion rates." He hiccuped. "Accidentally opened a portal to Lord Blackrose's bathroom instead."

I nearly dropped my organ. "His bathroom?"

"He was in the bath," Griffin added helpfully.

Kazimir's expression could have lit Griffin on fire all by itself. "We agreed never to speak of this."

"You said *you'd* never speak of it, my lord," Griffin corrected. The moonshine was making him bold. "I made no such promise. Anyway, instead of killing me—which would have been reasonable—he offered me a job."

"Why?" Sebastian asked, his head swiveling to look at Kaz. He almost lost his balance.

"Because anyone who could accidentally breach my wards was either a genius or cosmically lucky." Kazimir shrugged. "Either way, it's damn useful."

"It was luck," Griffin admitted. "Definitely luck. I transposed two runes and created an entirely new summoning matrix. Haven't been able to replicate it since."

Thorne snorted. "That explains so much."

Griffin adjusted his glasses. "But I'd had trouble with employment before that. And it was a wonder Lord Blackrose kept me on after my second disaster."

"What was that?" Sebastian asked.

"I was attempting to create a self-sustaining weather system for agricultural purposes—a permanent rain cloud that would follow farmers around—when Lord Blackrose happened to be passing through the village."

"I was there to collect taxes," Kazimir clarified, landing another perfect shot. The man's aim was irritatingly good, even with pirate moonshine. "Instead, I found a village drowning under three feet of pink snow that smelled like roses and turned anything it touched temporarily invisible."

"A simple pigmentation error," Griffin said defensively.

"The villagers chased him with pitchforks once they could find him again," Kaz continued. "After that, I started making Griffin experiment in the North Tower under heavy wards."

Griffin hiccuped again. "'Twas a promotion."

I turned to Thorne as he prepared his next throw. "What about you?"

He landed another perfect throw before answering. "Lord Blackrose killed my previous employer. Offered me double pay and better benefits. I said yes."

"Benefits?" the captain asked.

"Combat bonuses," Thorne said seriously. "Magical healing."

Brecca looked seriously offended, as if these benefits hadn't been part of *her* employment package. Kazimir noticed and said, "You have first refusal on any salvage rights. Thorne gets healing spells."

Brecca's irritation vanished, replaced by a satisfied smirk. She raised her notebook in a salute.

Sebastian suddenly laughed. "The Dark Lord provides better employee benefits than the royal court of Solandris." The moonshine was definitely working. He'd progressed from careful sips to generous swallows, and his aim was suffering accordingly. Another organ went wide, this one sticking to the mainmast with a wet thwack.

"The flowers are getting bigger," Griffin observed, pointing to the small garden that had sprouted around Sebastian's feet.

Sebastian swayed. "When I was eight, I accidentally turned my father's entire study into a greenhouse during a particularly tense lesson on trade negotiations."

"The same kinds of flowers?" I asked, lining up my next throw.

"Varies by emotion." He touched a blue bloom—a tiny morning glory—and it disappeared.

"That's adorable," I said, then immediately felt bad when he looked mortified. "I mean it's sweet!"

"Arabella finds everything adorable," Kazimir said. "Yesterday she called my shadow warriors 'cute little murder puppets.'"

"They are, though. The way they prowl around all menacing." I mimicked their stalking motion, nearly dropping my organ.

"You're drunk," he observed.

"You're pretty," I shot back.

Captain Brecca made a note in her book. "Three to one odds on Lady Blackrose initiating public displays of affection within the hour."

"I'll take that action," Thorne said.

We'd been playing for a while when I finally asked the question I'd been wondering about. "Sebastian, why didn't you ever write? After . . . everything?"

He missed his throw so badly the organ went backward. After his requisite drink, he said quietly, "Your father told me you were sick. Said the healers recommended no visitors, no letters, nothing that might upset you."

"That bastard."

"I should have known better. Should have tried harder." He looked at me with those earnest violet eyes. "I'm sorry, Bella."

I hadn't heard that nickname in years. "It's not your fault."

Kazimir's hand found mine, squeezing gently. Through our bond, I felt his rage at my father simmering just below the surface.

"Next round," Brecca announced. "Score's tied, somehow, despite Lord Sebastian's complete inability to aim."

"The ship keeps moving!" Sebastian protested.

"The ship's been steady as stone for the last hour," Thorne pointed out.

We'd moved on to the mystery organs now, things that defied identification and probably belonged to creatures that had too many legs.

"I wish Vex were here," I said, watching Griffin attempt to calculate the perfect throwing angle while swaying dangerously. "She'd destroy all of you at this."

"Vex doesn't play games," Kazimir said, then added, "unless it's eyeball golf."

"She played cards with me last week."

He turned to stare at me. "She what?"

"Beat me six hands out of seven, too." I landed another throw, though it was getting harder to aim with the moonshine making everything fuzzy. "Why is that weird?"

"Vex doesn't do things for fun," Thorne said. "She works, she organizes, she occasionally threatens people with elaborate death scenarios, but she doesn't play."

"Maybe she just needed someone to ask," Sebastian suggested, then immediately looked like he regretted speaking.

"Or maybe," Griffin said, glasses now completely askew, "she's been replaced by a doppelganger! We should test her when we return. I have a kit for that."

"You do?" I swayed on my feet and landed against Kaz's solid chest. He wrapped an arm around my waist to keep me steady.

"I have kits for everything. Detecting poison, identifying cursed objects, determining if your reflection has gained sentience—"

"That last one can't be real," Sebastian interrupted.

"Happened twice at the Academy," Griffin said solemnly. "Poor Marcus is still negotiating visitation rights with his mirror self."

I must have been more drunk than I thought because Griffin's statement made perfect sense.

By the fourth round, we'd abandoned any pretense of proper scoring. Sebastian had given up entirely and was lying on his back, making the flowers around him grow into increasingly elaborate patterns. Thorne was throwing with his eyes closed just to make it fair. Griffin had started drunkenly narrating each throw like it was a dramatic battle.

"An' the gall—gallblabber soarsh through the air!" he announced, completely wrong about the organ's identity. "Will it fin' dish target? The crowd holdsh ish breath! The very fate of the—the realm hangsh . . . in th' balance!"

It landed three feet short with a sad splat.

"The realm is doomed," Thorne deadpanned.

I was leaning heavily against Kazimir, who despite drinking as much as the rest of us, seemed frustratingly unaffected.

"How are you still sober?" I demanded.

"Practice," he said, then proved he wasn't entirely unaffected by pressing a kiss to my temple. "Also, my runes."

"Cheater."

"I want it on record," Sebastian said from the deck, "that this is the strangest thing I've ever done."

"Including the Bone Witch incident?" I asked.

"That was an accident. This is on purpose. This is us actively choosing to throw pickled organs around while drinking something that might be poison."

Griffin hiccuped thoughtfully. "Technic-cal-ly, the Bone Witch cursh was also a choice. Jush . . . sheveral bad choishes shtacked on top of each other."

"I thought it was rather mild, as curses go," Sebastian continued, missing his throw by a spectacular margin. "But Auremar was furious. Called it an attack on the dignity of the crown."

"The dignity of his crown was compromised long before anyone started rhyming," Kazimir muttered, landing another perfect shot.

"At least rhyming has artistic merit," I added, trying to fish out something that might have been a liver. I gave up trying to use the tongs and thrust my whole arm into the jar.

Sebastian took another drink, and vines curled around him. "You know what's funny? The curse made people more honest. Hard to lie when you have to make it rhyme."

"Poetry ash truth," Griffin mused, swaying backward so far I thought he would fall. "Thatssssh profound."

"So what you're saying," Thorne said slowly, "is that we're all cursed right now. By moonshine. Into throwing organs and telling the truth."

We all stopped to consider this.

"Are we the organsh?" Griffin asked, squinting at the jar where I was still trying to grasp the slippery liver. "Meta-metaphorically shpeaking. Are we all jush . . . pickled thingsh being thrown at arbi-arbitrary targetsh by forshes beyond our control?"

"That's dark," Sebastian said as my hand finally closed around my organ.

"No, no, he's onto something." I pointed at Griffin with my liver, the pickle juices running down my arm and onto the deck. "We're all preserved in our own jars of trauma and bad decisions, and life just keeps throwing us at holes we can't quite reach."

"Some of us reach the holes," Thorne said.

"Because you're already dead inside," I said with the certainty of superior logic. "Preserved. Like these organs."

"I need to lie down," Sebastian announced. He was already lying down.

"The real question," Kazimir said, his lips twitching as he fought to keep a straight face, "is whether we're aiming for the holes, or if the holes are aiming for us."

There was a long, contemplative silence broken only by the sound of snapping sails and Sebastian's flowers aggressively sprouting.

"I hate all of you," Griffin finally said, words slurring together. "You've ruined organsh *and* philoshphy for me."

"We should do this more often," I announced. "Spending time together without trying to conquer anything. Just being people. Weird people throwing organs around, but still."

"To weird people," Sebastian said, raising his cup.

"T'organ throw-wing," Griffin added.

"To not dying at the God Spire," Thorne contributed.

"To family," I said, then immediately worried I'd overstepped.

But Kazimir raised his cup. "To family."

We drank, and Sebastian immediately turned green.

"Side of the ship!" Brecca barked.

He made it, barely.

"Called it," Thorne said.

"Thatsh cheatin'," Griffin protested. "He vomitsh all the time."

As they bickered and Sebastian groaned, I looked at our ridiculous group and felt a warmth that had nothing to do with the moonshine. We'd need to descend soon, according to Brecca, to avoid the night predators. And we needed food and rest.

"Last round," I announced. "Winner takes all."

"Takes all what?" Sebastian asked weakly, returning from the railing.

"Pride. Glory. The last pickled brain."

We lined up for our final throws. The wind had picked up, adding an extra challenge. Or maybe we were all just too drunk to stand straight.

Griffin went first, his throw wild but enthusiastic. "For sh-ience!"

The organ arced high, sailing well past the target—and Nyx materialized from the clouds like a pink-scaled arrow. She snatched it midair with a triumphant screech, her jaws snapping shut around the pickled prize.

"Nyx, no!" I called, but she was already winging away. "You don't even know what that is!"

She ignored me completely.

"Automatic disqualification," Thorne said. He went next, landing another perfect throw because apparently being drunk didn't affect his ability to hit things. "For professionalism."

Sebastian somehow managed his first successful throw of the entire game. "For not embarrassing myself further!"

We all cheered.

Kazimir stepped up, the last brain in one hand, his other arm still holding me around the waist. "For my wife," he said, then threw it with perfect accuracy.

I stood on my tiptoes to place a kiss on his cheek. "How sweet, Lord Blackrose." Kaz caught me as I lost my balance.

Captain Brecca tallied the final score. "Thorne wins, somehow, despite being a team of one."

"D'mand a recount," Griffin said, stumbling over to the target. "M' lasht throw went through the hole. It jush . . . went through sho fasht you couldn' see it."

"The dragon ate it," Thorne pointed out.

"Welllll"—Griffin hiccuped—"thash a hole isn tit?"

As they argued, I leaned into Kazimir's side, watching the sun sink toward the horizon. The ship began its nightly descent, dropping below the cloud cover to skim just above the waves. The temperature rose, and the air became heavier with salt and moisture.

Tomorrow we'd reach the God Spire. Tomorrow we'd have to be Lord and Lady Blackrose, powerful and terrifying.

But today, we'd thrown organs at boxes and gotten drunk on possibly poison, and it had been perfect.

"Thank you," I said quietly. "For being ridiculous with me."

Kaz turned me in his arms, studying my face. "I've conquered kingdoms, Arabella. Destroyed armies. Built an empire on fear and power." His thumb traced my cheek. "But this—being ridiculous with you—might be the best thing I've ever done."

"You *are* drunk," I accused, but my heart was racing.

"Possibly. Doesn't make it less true."

Behind us, Sebastian had started singing something about flowers and regret while Griffin tried to harmonize. Thorne was collecting his winnings from Brecca, who was trying not to laugh and mostly failing. Then they began arguing over their bet on what constituted PDA between me and Kaz.

"We should probably send everyone to dinner before they fall overboard," I said.

A distant, pitiful screech echoed across the water. I looked up to see Nyx hovering unsteadily about fifty yards off the port bow. The dragon's body convulsed with a wet, rattling heave—the kind of sound that starts deep in the belly and promises disaster. Her wings stuttered mid-beat, her entire body lurching sideways as she banked hard toward the ship.

"No," I breathed, frozen in place as the calamity hurtled toward us.

"Move!" Brecca shouted at Sebastian.

But he was too drunk and too slow. Nyx swooped low over the deck and projectile-vomited the pickled organ—along with the seafood she'd eaten today—directly onto Sebastian's head.

The splatter was *spectacular.*

Sebastian stood frozen as a piece of something unidentifiable slid down his face. The flowers around his feet immediately wilted and died.

Kazimir's laugh was the kind of deep, genuine sound I'd never heard from him before. He actually bent forward, one hand pressed to his stomach, tears forming at the corners of his eyes.

"That's—" He couldn't even finish the sentence. "That's the best thing I've ever seen."

"Called it," Thorne said. "The dragon vomits second. Directly onto the pretty lord. That's got to be worth bonus points."

"I'll allow it," Brecca said, making a note and pulling her shirt up over her nose. "But the deckhands are going to demand hazard pay to clean that up."

Nyx landed on the bow, looking simultaneously miserable and smug.

Sebastian made a small, defeated sound and swayed toward the stairs.

"Stop right there," Brecca commanded, her captain's voice cutting through Kaz's continued laughter. "You're not tracking that smell through my ship."

He froze mid-step. "I beg your pardon?"

"Strip. Now. Throw the clothes overboard." She pointed at the railing. "Everything. I don't care if you're a lord or a king—that stench isn't going below deck."

"Here?" Sebastian's voice cracked. "In front of everyone?"

"Would you prefer to still be inside the clothes when they get tossed over the side?" Brecca asked sweetly.

Sebastian looked around desperately for support. Griffin was too busy trying not to fall over. Thorne was grinning. I was clinging to Kazimir, who was still shaking with laughter.

With a sound of pure defeat, Sebastian began unlacing his tunic.

"I can burn them!" Griffin offered, having found a mast to hug for support. At least, that's what I thought he said. It came out more like "Ickenburndem." He gave a dramatic hand flourish. "Been wurrr-king on a new 'cineration shpell—"

"NO!" everyone shouted in unison.

22

Behold Cosmic Horror
(While Accepting Mysterious Delays)

Arabella

The Lawless Expanse stretched beneath us like a festering wound on the world's surface. Where Solandris had golden fields and Kazimir's territories boasted dramatic mountain ranges and forests, this place was a patchwork of scorched earth, toxic swamps, and settlements that sprouted like mushrooms after rain—quick to grow, quicker to die. The air itself felt thick with competing magics that made my skin prickle and the Heirloom pulse against my skull.

"I'm dying." Sebastian moaned from where he'd collapsed against a coil of rope. His normally perfect long hair was frizzy from repeated washings to remove the vomit, and the flowers that had bloomed so cheerfully yesterday now drooped pathetically around him. "This is it. This is how I meet my end. Not in glorious battle, not saving innocents, but because I threw pickled organs while drinking pirate moonshine."

Griffin sat beside him, his long limbs folded like a grasshopper's, looking equally miserable. His glasses were askew, and he kept wincing at the morning light. "The theoretical applications of organ aerodynamics seemed so important last night."

"You tried to write a thesis proposal on the back of a navigation chart after dinner," Thorne reminded him. He stood at the rail, irritatingly unaffected by last night's festivities. "The captain had to pry it from your hands."

"It was groundbreaking work," Griffin mumbled. "I think my brain is trying to escape through my eye sockets."

I took pity on them. "Would you like me to fix that?"

Sebastian's head snapped up so fast he immediately regretted it, groaning and clutching his temples. "You can cure hangovers?"

"Of course." I moved toward him, flexing my fingers. "It's a simple enough spell." I'd healed Kaz and myself last night before bed.

The golden light that poured from my hands made them both flinch, but within seconds, their expressions shifted from misery to wonder. Sebastian's eyes cleared, the green tinge leaving his complexion. Griffin straightened, adjusting his glasses properly for the first time this morning.

"Oh," Sebastian breathed. "Oh, that's magnificent."

"I could kiss you," Griffin said, then immediately turned crimson. "I mean—not actually—that would be inappropriate—Lord Blackrose would murder me—"

"Yes, I would," Kazimir said as he came up behind me, though his tone was more amused than threatening. The incident with Nyx last night had put him in a fantastic mood.

But this morning, he'd returned to his full Dark Lord persona—long black coat billowing dramatically despite the lack of wind, shadows curling at his feet, expression carved from stone and a flash of silver in his stormy irises. Yesterday's playful husband had been packed away with the pickled organs. But I knew better. I could see the slight quirk at the corner of his mouth, the way his eyes softened when they landed on me.

This version of him—dangerous and commanding—was just as attractive as the one who'd gotten semi-drunk and thrown organs at boxes.

"There," Kazimir said, pointing ahead. "The God Spire."

It wasn't a tower in any conventional sense. It was a spine. A massive, glistening black spine that plunged down from the heavens like a stake driven through the mountain's heart.

As the *Sky Serpent* approached, I saw more details. The corpse was inverted with its head buried somewhere in the stone below while its grotesque pelvic girdle crowned the summit.

The closer we got, the more wrong it became. Multiple empty hip sockets served as balconies and docking ports. Each vertebra was the size of a small fortress with windows dotting the spine at irregular intervals. Great ribs curved out of the spine, supporting even more platforms and buildings. Bridges of bone and metal connected different sections, and I could see figures moving across them—some humanoid, others decidedly not.

And the whole thing crackled with an eerie, purple-green light that seemed to originate from deep within the bones themselves.

"What in the nine hells?" I whispered.

"The corpse of a forgotten god," Kazimir said matter-of-factly. "Slain in a primordial war, or so the story goes. The Syndicate built their headquarters inside and around it."

I couldn't tear my eyes away from the grotesque, magnificent structure. "It's . . ."

"Practical." He shrugged. "Divine corpses are nearly impenetrable by conventional magic. Perfect for housing secrets."

A deep, resonant sound rolled across the landscape—something between a groan and a sigh.

Sebastian was gaping. "It's breathing?"

"Yes," Kaz confirmed. "About once every hour. The resonating chimes inside the god's corpse mimic deep, unsettling breaths. Some say it's just the wind through the hollow chambers. Others believe the god isn't quite as dead as advertised."

"Power like that doesn't just disappear," Griffin said, though he looked unsettled.

Kazimir glanced around our little group, but his gaze landed on Sebastian and stayed there. "The Spire has a way of inviting trouble, so no wandering off and accidentally joining a cult or signing away your soul."

"That happens here?" I asked.

"Friday is recruitment day," Thorne rumbled. "Though most new acolytes are dead by Monday. They really should think about changing those initiations."

I couldn't tell if he was joking.

The *Sky Serpent* began its descent toward a dock that jutted from what might have been a shoulder blade. Other vessels were moored there—sleek black ships with red sails, floating platforms powered by bound spirits that wailed softly in the wind, and something that looked like it was made entirely of tentacles.

Nyx launched from the bow with a shriek that echoed off the god's bones. Heads turned on the docks below. A few figures scrambled backward.

I watched her spiral upward, pink-tinged wings catching an updraft. She was a fearsome creature in her own right—she'd be fine.

"Remember," Kazimir announced, gathering us all near the helm. "The God Spire operates under different rules than Skyspire. First and foremost, we do not display our full power here."

Sebastian raised his hand. "Wouldn't a show of strength be beneficial?"

"The Syndicate values equilibrium above all," Kazimir said. "No single member can be allowed to outstrip the others too dramatically. And it controls more than most people realize," Kazimir continued, though he was speaking primarily to Sebastian now. The rest of us were already well-versed in this particular lesson. "They have shadow governments on both sides of the sea, puppet kings who don't even know they're dancing on strings. Every major trade route, every significant assassination, every war that's mysteriously ended or begun—the Syndicate has a hand in it."

"Controlling them means controlling the world," I said quietly.

He looked down at me with a smirk. "First Solandris, *then* the Syndicate. Taking them on now would be like fighting a hydra while standing in a snake pit during an earthquake."

"How do they manage such vast and varied interests?" Sebastian asked.

"Debt." Kazimir's smile was sharp. "Every kingdom needs something eventually. Loans for wars. Magical artifacts for succession crises. Discreet elimination of rivals. The Syndicate provides, and then they own you."

"But not you," I offered.

"No, never me." He adjusted his coat, and I noticed he'd added several subtle touches since this morning—a pin bearing the Syndicate's seal, rings on specific fingers, a particular fold to his collar that probably meant something to those who knew how to read it. "I spent years making myself indispensable to them. Every member of the Syndicate ended up owing me something, and when the previous Chair of Dominion had an unfortunate accident—"

"That you caused?" I asked.

"That I may have facilitated," he corrected, "I called in every debt at once. Told them they could either repay me in gold—which would have bankrupted half of them—or give me the vacant Chair of Dominion."

Sebastian shook his head. "They must have hated that."

"They still do. But they need me more than they hate me." He gestured to the Spire. "The Syndicate is built on mutual benefit and mutual blackmail. Everyone has leverage on everyone else. It's the only way to keep this many villains from murdering one another."

The ship touched down with barely a bump and the chains began to lower. Captain Brecca was already barking orders to her crew, preparing to resupply while we conducted our business.

Kaz addressed everyone again. "We're going to be exactly as powerful as they expect us to be. No more, no less."

We all turned toward the gangplank, where a figure waited for us at the dock.

The Alchemist hadn't changed since their visit to Skyspire weeks ago, but seeing them here, in a hostile environment, hit differently. Their robes shifted through colors—purple to green to gold to black, never settling, never still. The mask covering the upper half of their face gleamed with symbols. Their smile, the only visible part of their face, was knowing and amused.

Everything about them seemed designed to prevent an accurate assessment, which in a sinister place like the God Spire, meant they were a truly dangerous enemy.

"Showtime," I whispered, straightening my shoulders and adopting what I hoped was an intimidating expression.

We descended the gangplank, Kazimir leading with me at his side, followed by Thorne, Griffin, and Sebastian. The Alchemist watched our approach, their gloved hands constantly in motion, fingers twitching and gesturing as if casting spells or manipulating unseen energies.

"Lord and Lady Blackrose," the Alchemist said once we'd disembarked. Their voice had that same musical quality I remembered, neither male nor female. Their gaze shifted to our companions. "Ah, and you've brought entertainment. How thoughtful."

Sebastian stiffened, and I felt a surge of protectiveness. "They're our associates," I corrected. "Not entertainment."

"Of course, of course." The Alchemist waved a dismissive hand. "Forgive my poor attempt at humor. I know who they are, of course. Master Griffin, good to see you again. And Lord Sebastian of the Northern Peaks. I do so admire a man who can survive both Auremar's court and Lord Blackrose's company." At Sebastian's look of surprise, the Alchemist continued, "No need for alarm. It made sense that you would flee to the one couple that could ensure your safety. I hope they request a favor from you in return someday."

At this, Sebastian cast an unsettled look at me. I shook my head. "Lord Sebastian is enjoying our hospitality." I gave the Alchemist a cold smile. "We don't charge for helping a friend."

I could practically feel Kaz's grumble beside me.

The Alchemist wasn't fazed. "Information is a gift, Lady Blackrose. And I do so enjoy giving. But we can speak of it tomorrow at our meeting, if you wish."

Kazimir's eyes narrowed. "Our arrangement was for today."

"Was it?" The Alchemist's fingers danced in the air, tracing patterns that left faint, glowing trails. "How careless of me. But I heard you were turning this into a honeymoon trip, so it won't be a waste." They winked—or at least, I thought they did. It was hard to tell with the mask. "Why not enjoy yourselves until tomorrow? The God Spire has many delights to offer newlyweds."

"We're on a schedule," Kazimir said, his voice dropping to a dangerous register.

"And I'm afraid my schedule has changed," the Alchemist replied, their tone remaining light despite the obvious tension. "Something about a plague of sentient, militant beetles in the lower markets. It's Friday, you know."

"Friday is recruitment day," Thorne muttered.

"Precisely. Can't have the beetles eating the potential cultists. It'd be bad for business." The Alchemist's robes shifted to deep crimson. "Tomorrow morning, then? Unless you'd prefer to wait longer?"

I placed a hand on Kaz's arm, feeling the rigid tension in his muscles. "Tomorrow is fine," I said smoothly. "It gives us time to explore."

The Alchemist's smile widened. "Excellent! I recommend the Gilded Gallows for tonight. It's quite the experience for first-time visitors."

Kazimir scoffed, then seemed to remember our cover story and slid his arm possessively around my waist. The ruse wasn't strictly needed for the Alchemist, who knew our purpose here better than we did, but others would be watching. "I have other plans for my wife."

"I'm sure you do, but maybe you'll make an exception." The Alchemist's eyes gleamed behind their mask. "Until tomorrow, then."

With a final glittering smile, they glided away, their color-shifting robes rippling around them.

"They're playing games," Kazimir growled, his grip on my waist tightening. "The Alchemist never does anything without multiple layers of purpose."

"At least we have time to rest and prepare," I pointed out. "And I wouldn't mind seeing more of this place."

Kazimir looked down at me, his expression softening slightly. "You would find the corpse of a dead god fascinating, wouldn't you?"

"Absolutely." I grinned. "How often does one get to explore something like this?"

He sighed, but the corner of his mouth twitched upward.

As we collected our belongings and prepared to enter the Spire proper, I noticed Kazimir scanning our surroundings. His eyes missed nothing—the positions of the guards, the movement patterns of the strange creatures that scuttled along the walls, the subtle magical wards that shimmered in the doorways.

"You don't believe their excuse for a moment, do you?" I asked quietly.

"Not a single word," he confirmed. "The Alchemist is up to something. They always are."

"A trap?"

He considered this, then shook his head slightly. "No, not yet. If they wanted us dead or captured, there are more efficient ways. This feels more like positioning. Moving pieces on a board before making their play."

"And what's our countermove?"

A cold smile touched his lips. "We explore, we observe, we gather information. And we prepare for whatever they have planned tomorrow."

"And if it's a trap?"

Kazimir's eyes met mine, hard as steel but with that flicker of warmth he reserved only for me. "Then we spring it, survive it, and get back to the war in Solandris as quickly as possible. I didn't come this far to be outmaneuvered by someone who can't even decide what color robes to wear."

I laughed despite myself, and he pulled me closer as we approached the massive, vertebra-shaped entrance to the God Spire. The structure seemed to inhale as we crossed the threshold, and the air around us resonated with that unsettling, breathing sound.

Behind us, Sebastian groaned. "You're both insane. Absolutely insane. Why do I follow you? I can't explain."

23

Choose Your Battles Wisely

(She'll Win with the Tower Argument Every Time)

Kazimir

The sheer ostentation of the God Spire never failed to impress me, even after all these years. Where Skyspire was built on practicality—a fortress designed to intimidate and protect in equal measure—the Spire was pure theater. Every corridor curved like a spine. Every doorway resembled a gaping maw. Even the floor tiles pulsed with that purple-green light, as if we were walking on the nerves of something still alive.

I led our little party toward the central channel of the Spire, what would have been the spinal cord in a living creature. Arabella walked beside me, her eyes wide as she took in the grotesque magnificence of the place. She'd adapted to the Spire's horror with remarkable speed, treating the breathing corpse of a god like a tourist attraction rather than an abomination. It was one of the many things I lo—appreciated about her. Sebastian looked like he might be sick again, and Griffin kept stopping to examine architectural details that would probably inspire some new disaster back at Skyspire.

He paused to study a pulsing vein of light in the wall.

"The last person who tried to take a sample ended up with their fingers fused together," I said.

Griffin snatched his hand back.

We passed a series of shops and establishments built into the smaller chambers of the vertebrae. The Syndicate had turned the god's corpse into a bustling hub of commerce, though what they sold here would make most kingdoms declare war on sight. Soul fragments glistened in jars. Cursed artifacts hummed behind glass. One shop advertised "Custom Nightmares—Delivered While Your Enemy Sleeps!"

"This place is something," Arabella murmured, leaning closer to me.

"'Something' is certainly one word for it," I agreed, placing a hand at the small of her back. The gesture was possessive, but also protective. The Spire attracted the worst of the worst, and while I had no doubt Arabella could handle herself, I didn't want to test it unnecessarily.

We reached the central lift—a platform suspended by chains running down the length of the spine. A hulking figure stood guard, its body wider than its height, skin like cracked stone. A golem of sorts, not a person, though I'd never been able to determine exactly what magic animated it. The Syndicate kept some secrets even from their own.

"Lord Blackrose," it rumbled in a voice like stones grinding together. "Your quarters are prepared."

The lift carried us upward through the hollow core of the Spire. Sebastian pressed himself against the back railing, clearly uncomfortable with the height. Griffin, in contrast, leaned precariously over the edge, watching the floors rush by with childlike fascination.

"If you fall," I said without looking at him, "I'm not saving you."

Griffin straightened immediately.

As we rose, a strange whisper brushed against my thoughts—not words exactly, but a sensation of recognition. As if the dead god's bones were greeting an old friend.

I inhaled slowly. The lack of sleep was taking its toll on me.

The lift slowed as we reached the upper levels of the Spire. Here, the chambers were larger and more luxurious. A single large vertebra housed a different Chair of the Syndicate or their most valued associates. My apartment occupied the third from the top.

The doors opened onto a short hallway ending in a massive door, which like the rest of the floor was protected with wards that would make most mages weep. I pressed my palm against the center, letting the magic recognize me.

"Welcome back, Lord Blackrose," the door said in a deep voice. "Shall I incinerate the unauthorized visitors?"

"They're guests," I said before Sebastian could bolt. "Full access for the duration of our stay."

"Acknowledged. Please note: The kitchen poltergeist has been acting up again."

"Of course it has." I pushed the door open. "Welcome to our home away from home."

I'd forgotten how impressive the apartment was, honestly. When you own a floating fortress made of lightning bridges and shadow magic, your standards for intimidating architecture tend to skew a bit high. But even I had to admit that my quarters in the God Spire had a certain macabre elegance.

The central atrium soared upward through the entire vertebra, revealing multiple levels connected by a spiraling staircase carved from a single massive bone. Dark wood furniture created a warm environment against the black bone walls, and everything was draped in rich fabrics of midnight blue and silver. Witchlights drifted lazily through the space, casting a soft glow over the polished floors. Archways led off to various chambers—dining room, library, guest quarters, and my private suite.

"This is incredible," Arabella breathed, immediately drawn to the tall windows. The view was admittedly spectacular, if you enjoyed looking at a wasteland dotted with the occasional explosion or monster attack.

"You keep this place fully staffed?" she asked, noting the fresh flowers, the polished surfaces, the distinct lack of dust.

As if to answer her question, a line of staff appeared from a side door.

"I make regular trips to the Spire for Syndicate business. It's more practical to maintain a permanent residence than to arrange accommodations each time."

What I didn't say, but knew she would understand, was that the staff were also my eyes and ears within the Spire. They reported everything they saw and heard, providing invaluable intelligence on the other Syndicate members' activities.

A door at the far end of the chamber opened, and a tall, thin man emerged. His shoulder-length gray hair was tied back, and he wore the standard servant's uniform but with throwing knives strapped to his thighs.

"Lord Blackrose," he said, bowing. "Lady Blackrose. Welcome to the Spire. I am Marlowe, the head of staff at the apartment."

"Marlowe's managed this residence for five years," I explained to Arabella. "He ensures everything runs smoothly in my absence."

"I've prepared your rooms as instructed, my lord," he said.

I turned to our companions. "Thorne, you know where your quarters are. Griffin, Sebastian—Marlowe will show you to yours."

Marlowe gestured for Griffin and Sebastian to follow him. "This way, gentlemen."

As they moved toward the staircase, Griffin hefted his satchel higher, trying to look casual and failing miserably. The bag clinked.

"Griffin." My voice was dangerously soft. "What's in the bag?"

He clutched it protectively. "Just some personal items. Books."

"They clink." I took a step toward him, and he backed up until he hit the door.

"Metallic books?"

I held out my hand. "Show me."

With the air of a condemned man, Griffin opened his satchel. Inside, nestled between actual books, was a device that looked like an octopus mated with a clock. Gears protruded at odd angles, tentacle-like tubes connected various components, and the whole thing hummed with barely contained energy.

"Is that going to explode?" I asked with forced calm.

"No!" Griffin said quickly. "Well, not *explode* exactly. More of a controlled implosion that creates a localized temporal bubble—"

"I specifically ordered you not to bring anything that could explode," I reminded him, my voice dropping to a register that made even Thorne stand a little straighter. "Did I not make myself clear?"

"You did, my lord, but—"

"But you decided my direct order was more of a suggestion?"

Griffin clutched his bag tighter, and his mouth began opening and closing as my shadows curled around his neck. They weren't touching him, not yet, but for the thousandth time since I'd hired the enchanter, I was seriously considering it.

To family, Arabella had toasted. But my experience with family was they were always trying to kill you in one way or another. Griffin was no exception. In fact, he proved the rule.

My shadows curled tighter, and for a split second, I wanted to *squeeze*. Not just threaten—actually crush the life from him. Watch his eyes bulge, hear the wet snap of—

I reined the shadows back sharply, my jaw clenching. What the hell was wrong with me?

"I—I didn't think—" he stammered.

"No, you didn't." I plucked the device from his hands. "Thorne."

My security chief stepped up, having watched the entire exchange with his usual stoicism.

"Lock this in the warded safe until we leave," I ordered. "If Griffin asks for it before I give permission, break one of his fingers."

Griffin made a strangled sound. "It's perfectly safe. I've tested it exten—"

A sharp look from me silenced him. "The last time you said something was 'perfectly safe,' a suit of armor developed a bloodthirsty personality and beheaded three servants before I got there."

Oblivious to the drama unfolding below, Sebastian's voice drifted down the stairs in a cry of delight. "Is this a fully stocked kitchen?"

"Yes, my lord," came Marlowe's response.

"This is perfect!" Sebastian's excitement was palpable even from a distance. Sebastian appeared at the railing, his face bright with joy—though his smile wavered when his gaze landed not on me, but on Griffin's face. "Griffin, would you like to help?"

There was a pause, then Griffin's hesitant voice: "I'm not particularly skilled in the culinary arts."

"Nonsense! Everyone can bake. I'll give you something simple that can't possibly explode."

"You'd be surprised," I muttered.

Arabella squeezed my arm. "It might keep Griffin out of trouble."

"Doubtful, but one can hope." I turned to Thorne. "Keep one eye on them as you go about your other duties. I'll deal with his insubordination more thoroughly later."

Thorne nodded, his expression stoic as ever. "I'll ensure they remain within acceptable parameters of chaos, my lord."

With that settled, I led Arabella up the spiral staircase, past the kitchen where Griffin's gaze was fixed on Sebastian with rapt attention.

Our suite was the largest in the apartment, dominated by a bed that could comfortably sleep six and windows that offered an even more impressive view. The bathroom alone was the size of most inn rooms, featuring a tub carved from a single piece of black marble.

"This is where you stay when you visit?" Arabella asked, running her hand along the silk bedding.

"When I must." I ran a hand through my hair. "I prefer Skyspire but business sometimes requires a presence here."

Arabella moved to the windows, gazing out at the strange landscape below. "It's beautiful, in a terrifying sort of way."

"The Syndicate appreciates luxury just as I do," I explained, watching her. "Power without comfort is just work."

She turned, a mischievous smile playing at her lips. "Speaking of luxury, tell me about this Gilded Gallows place the Alchemist mentioned."

I groaned. "It's a waste of space. A playground for villains with more gold than sense."

"But what *is* it?" She perched on the edge of the bed, looking up at me expectantly.

"A nightclub," I said, removing my coat and draping it over a chair. "Music, dancing, overpriced drinks, the occasional ritual sacrifice—though that's usually restricted to the VIP section."

"I've never been to a nightclub before," she admitted, curiosity bright in her eyes. "What's it like?"

I sat beside her, loosening the collar of my shirt. "You remember how the overt hedonism of our wedding feast threw you off balance? The Gilded Gallows is significantly less . . . tasteful."

"I've grown since then," she protested. "I'm not the same sheltered noblewoman you kidnapped."

"Clearly not." I reached out to brush a strand of hair from her face, and then lingered with my hand moving to her neck. "You're the Dark Lady of Skyspire now. Mistress of the Healing Arts." I brushed my thumb over her lower lip, watching it part. "Scourge of pickled organs."

She laughed, leaning into my touch. "Exactly. We're the most powerful people here. What's the worst that could happen?"

"Now you're just inviting trouble."

"—and there's no reason not to experience something new." She took my hand, her expression turning serious. "I spent my entire life locked in a tower, Kaz. Everything was controlled, measured, restricted. Now I have the chance to see things I've never seen before, do things I've never done."

I studied her face, saw the determination there. My instinct was to refuse, but the way she was looking at me—eager and excited and alive—made my arguments crumble. Denying her this small adventure felt wrong. Like I'd be no better than her father, keeping her caged for my own comfort.

Anyway, Arabella's freedom wasn't mine to give, but hers to take. Ironically, the closer we became, the more I had to remind myself of that simple truth.

"When you put it like that . . ." I sighed.

She grinned, knowing she'd used the one argument that would win every time, and straddled my lap with her arms around my neck. "I promise to be on my best behavior."

I rested my hands on her hips. "Your best behavior still involves setting things on fire."

She laughed, and the sound should have warmed me. It *did* warm me. But underneath that pleasant feeling, a possessive fury so intense it made my teeth ache. It was completely involuntary, and completely out of place for the situation.

I brushed it off with a smirk. "You should know, membership requires a crime."

She pulled back. "What?"

"To enter the Gilded Gallows, you need to have committed a crime. It's their way of admitting only the right sort of clientele."

She considered this for a moment. "Does killing the knight-commander of the Hero's Guild count?"

"Absolutely."

"Then I'm qualified." She leaned forward, pressing a quick kiss to my lips. "What's your crime of entry?"

I smirked. "You know I have plenty."

24

Attend a Social Gathering
(and Try Not to Lose Your Staff)

Kazimir

The kitchen had become a war zone of flour and honey. Griffin stood at the central counter, his gangly frame dusted white from head to toe, while Sebastian moved around him with the efficiency of someone who knew what they were doing.

"We're heading to the Gilded Gallows," I announced from the doorway.

Both men looked up. Griffin's face brightened with curiosity, while Sebastian's expression grew wary.

"The nightclub?" Griffin asked, abandoning whatever sticky mess he'd been attempting to shape. "I've heard fascinating things about their acoustic enchantments. Apparently, they use resonance crystals to—"

"To make the music loud enough to drown out screaming," I finished drily. "It's not an academic exercise, Griffin."

"Screaming?" Sebastian paused in wiping his hands on a towel, but he wasn't looking at me.

I turned to see Arabella as she entered, and nearly swallowed my tongue.

Her dress clung to every curve of her body, cut low enough in front to make my mouth go dry. A slit ran up one side, revealing a tantalizing glimpse of thigh with each step. Her golden hair was swept up, exposing the elegant line of her neck.

"Where'd you get that?" I asked roughly.

She smiled, doing a small turn. "I packed it when we decided this was our honeymoon. Never had a reason to wear it before, but I hoped there'd be an occasion for something special."

"Special" was one word for it. "Devastating" was another. The dress made her look dangerous in a way that had nothing to do with magic and everything to do with the kind of feminine power that brought kingdoms to their knees.

"You look . . ." I paused, searching for words that wouldn't sound like complete capitulation to my baser instincts. "Illegal in several kingdoms."

Her smile widened. "Thank you. You don't look terrible yourself."

I'd chosen black as usual—a silk shirt open at the collar and dark trousers that wouldn't show bloodstains. Standard villain attire, really, but the way Arabella was looking at me suggested she approved.

I resisted the sudden desire to whisk her back to the bedroom. Instead, I glowered at Sebastian, who was looking at Arabella with his mouth open. As my shadows darkened the corners of the kitchen, the fire in the hearth guttered and nearly went out.

Sebastian caught my gaze and turned beet red before looking carefully at the sugar he was supposedly measuring. He had to squint now that the room was so dark. "Why do you want to go to a place that has screaming?"

Still glaring at him, I was about to suggest he learn how much fun it could be when Arabella intervened.

"Surrounded by criminals, villains, and monsters, all trying to one-up each other with their evil accomplishments?" Her smile turned wicked. "It sounds like fun."

"You have a strange definition of fun," Sebastian muttered, but there was fondness in his voice rather than judgment.

"You're welcome to join us," Arabella offered.

I resisted the urge to grind my teeth. The last thing I needed was to babysit Griffin in a den of vice or watch Sebastian have a moral crisis every time someone committed a minor atrocity. And if his reaction to my wife's dress was any indication, I'd already have my hands full murdering anyone who looked her way.

Griffin perked up. "That sounds—"

"Terrible," Sebastian interrupted firmly. "We have . . . baking to finish. Important baking. Very time-sensitive."

I caught the meaningful look that passed between them, something weighted with unspoken conversation. It was odd, actually, but I didn't want to get into it now.

Arabella gestured to the explosion of flour that was centered on and around Griffin. "What happened here?"

"The poltergeist," he said solemnly. "I've been trying to negotiate with it using a series of respectful hand gestures, but I may have accidentally signed something offensive. The flour was its rebuttal."

"Ah," she replied. Because what else did you say to that? She looked around the room but found no supernatural creatures in sight.

"Thorne?" I called as Griffin began explaining why he was using hand gestures when he could just talk to the poltergeist, even though no one had asked.

My security chief appeared from the direction of his quarters, already dressed for an evening out—which for Thorne meant the same black leather he always wore, but with slightly more knives visible.

"Not interested in the nightclub scene, my lord," he said before I could ask. "Thought I might hit the markets. Some of the vendors here carry unique imports that could be useful at Skyspire."

I didn't ask what kind of imports. Thorne's shopping habits were his own business, and I'd learned long ago that ignorance was sometimes bliss when it came to my staff's recreational hobbies.

After delivering my standard warning of trusting no one and avoiding dark corners, I led Arabella from the apartment, cutting off Griffin's treatise on the different types of poltergeists and their communication preferences. For a moment, I almost felt sorry for Sebastian, then was promptly horrified at the uninvited thought. I replaced the emotion with petty glee, wondering when the nobleman would have enough of the chaos and leave.

My hand strayed low on Arabella's back, feeling her body through the thin silk of her dress. Then lower to squeeze her ass as we waited for the lift. I dragged her against me until her body molded into mine.

"Let's stay in," I murmured against her ear, "I have better entertainment in mind."

She laughed, pushing me back gently. "Later. I want to see this nightclub first."

The walk to the Gilded Gallows took us deeper into the Spire's commercial district. The shops here catered to a more specialized clientele than those near the entrance. Poison vendors displayed their wares in glowing vials. A tailor advertised "Cloaks of Dramatic Entrance" and "Capes That Billow Ominously in Still Air." And yet another establishment claimed to sell "Authentic Villain Lairs—Assembly Required."

The Gallows itself occupied an entire vertebra near the middle of the Spire. The entrance was a massive archway carved to resemble a gaping maw, complete with stone teeth and a tongue that served as a red carpet. It was actually squishy when you walked on it. Music poured from the opening—not the refined melodies of court entertainment, but something primal and driving that seemed to bypass the ears and go straight to the blood.

A line of hopeful patrons stretched from the entrance, each trying to look more menacing than the last.

"I didn't realize we'd have to wait." Arabella was eyeing the queue.

I almost laughed. "We don't."

The line of waiting villains parted before us, some bowing, others simply pressing themselves against the wall to avoid catching my attention. I kept my expression deliberately cold, my gaze sweeping over them with obvious disdain.

A bouncer hulked beside the entrance. His skin was the color of gray stone, but with his hooves, tail, and horns, he looked like the sculpture of a minotaur come to life—which was exactly what he was.

He was also completely naked.

"Name and crime," he grunted, not looking up from a scroll.

Arabella was trying to look anywhere but at the huge swinging dick between his thighs. It nearly touched the floor.

"Lord Kazimir Blackrose," I said.

The bouncer's eyes widened slightly as he looked at us for the first time. "Chair of Dominion. My apologies."

"And my wife, Lady Arabella Blackrose," I added. "Slayer of Sir Darian Lightbringer, Knight-Commander of the Hero's Guild."

The minotaur-thing looked impressed. "Welcome to the Gallows, my lady."

We made a wide berth to avoid touching his . . . member . . . and entered.

Inside, the Gallows lived up to its reputation for excess. The main floor was a writhing mass of bodies and magic, with a sunken dance floor and opulent gold and silver furnishings draped in black velvet. The air was thick with smoke that alternated colors between purple, green, and blue. Around the edges, booths and tables offered some semblance of privacy, though "privacy" was a relative term in a place where voyeurism was considered a mild vice.

The clientele was exactly what you'd expect from a villain's nightclub. Demons with long tails and horns chatted with corrupt nobles over cocktails. A group of reformed cultists had taken over one corner, their ritual scarification gleaming in the strobing lights as they danced with abandon. A pair of necromancers argued at the bar, their animated corpse servants standing stiffly behind them. In one booth, a wraith was consuming the life force of a willing victim, who writhed in ecstasy as they faded.

And everyone else was staring at us.

I was accustomed to being the center of attention everywhere I went. But the way they were looking at Arabella—with a mixture of curiosity, desire, and calculation—made my jaw clench. I let my expression settle into the kind of cold fury that had made armies turn and flee, and was gratified to see several patrons suddenly find their drinks fascinating.

The crowd parted as we moved through it, my glare carving a path forward. Arabella took it all in with wide eyes, her grip on my arm tightening when a particularly bold demon leered at her. With a flick of my wrist, shadows coalesced around the creature's neck, severing its head cleanly. The body crumpled as the head rolled across the floor before both dissolved into sulfurous smoke. The message was clear—and the path before us suddenly much wider.

"Cementing your reputation?" Arabella observed.

"Just giving a demonstration of what I'll do to anyone else who looks at you the wrong way," I replied, not even attempting to hide my bad temper. The demon wouldn't be dead, unfortunately, but it wouldn't be able to return until it was summoned again.

We made our way to a raised platform on the far side of the room. Unlike the other VIP sections, which were merely elevated above the main floor, mine was elevated and also separated by a barrier of shadows. The bouncer—a construct of bone and metal—recognized me immediately and stepped aside.

Inside, plush seating surrounded a table laden with bottles of rare spirits. The shadows provided a one-way view; we could see out, but no one could see in unless I allowed it.

"This is yours?" Arabella asked, settling onto one of the couches.

"One of the perks of being a chair," I explained, pouring us each a glass of bloodred liquor. "Each member has their own space."

A server appeared—a faun with delicate, spiraling horns that caught the light like polished bronze. Her lower half was covered in russet fur that matched her wild curls, and ended in hooves. She wore only a simple black vest that left little to the imagination, adorned with pins that I recognized as awards from various criminal enterprises.

"Welcome to the Gilded Gallows, Lord and Lady Blackrose," she said with a bow that managed to be both respectful and suggestive. "What can I bring you this evening?"

Arabella leaned forward, her eyes bright with curiosity. "What would you recommend? I'm in the mood for something I've never tried before."

The faun smiled. "First time at the Gallows deserves something special." She tapped a hoof thoughtfully. "I have just the thing. I'll be back shortly, my lady."

She vanished into the crowd. I settled back into the plush seating and pulled Arabella against my side. My fingers trailed on the bare thigh revealed by her slit. From here, we had an excellent view of the entire club, and I could keep an eye on all the entrances and exits.

Our meeting with the Alchemist wasn't until tomorrow, but I wouldn't put it past them to stage some kind of preliminary test or observation. They were notoriously fond of games.

"This is incredible," Arabella breathed, her eyes wide as she took in the spectacle below us.

On the main dance floor, the usual mix of grinding bodies and questionable life choices was in full swing. But the Gallows prided itself on offering entertainment that went beyond simple debauchery.

On a raised dais to our left, an orgy was in progress—a writhing mass of limbs from at least six different species. A pair of shapeshifters kept changing forms mid-thrust to appreciative applause. Presiding over this carnal chaos was a succubus, her wings unfurled over the spectacle as she whispered instructions that sent ripples of pleasure through the assembly.

My face hardened into a scowl. "Not a fan of performance art?" Arabella teased.

"Not a fan of demons," I replied flatly, and hated the look of sympathy she gave me. Instead, I looked at something else.

To our right, a group of vampires had claimed another platform. They passed a human woman between them with the casual elegance of sharing a fine wine. She arched and cried out in ecstasy each time fangs pierced her skin, her face flushed with pleasure.

"Is she actually choosing that?" Arabella whispered, watching the woman arch as fangs pierced her neck. "Or is she under some kind of thrall?"

I shook my head. "She's likely paying them. Vampire bites are quite the luxury experience these days. Why give them away for free when they can get paid for eating?"

Arabella shuddered and looked away, but I noticed she kept glancing back at the vampires, more fascinated with them than the crescendoing cries coming from the orgy participants.

In a corner booth lit by candlelight, a circle of ancient witches sat knitting, their wrinkled faces serene beneath wispy gray hair. At first glance, they looked like harmless grandmothers, with the kind of maternal faces that suggested fresh-baked cookies and bedtime stories.

Then I noticed *what* they were knitting.

A man levitated upside down above their table, suspended from the ceiling by invisible threads. His impossibly long, dark hair hung toward the table in silky strands, and the witches were incorporating it into their work—pulling, weaving, creating an elaborate tapestry. The man's face was serene, almost blissful, as if he were in the deepest, most peaceful sleep of his life.

"What's happening there?" Arabella asked, leaning forward.

I opened my mouth to explain, then closed it. Studied the scene more carefully, watched as one witch paused to stroke the floating man's cheek. He sighed in his trance, a smile ghosting across his lips.

"I—" An unfamiliar sensation crept over me. "I actually don't know."

She turned to me with exaggerated shock. "The great Lord Blackrose admits ignorance? Should I summon a scribe to document this historic moment?"

"Very funny," I said drily. "There are still plenty of terrible things I know far too much about."

She watched the scene with renewed interest. "He looks happy, though. Maybe it's not sinister at all."

"In a place called the Gilded Gallows, I'd bet against 'not sinister,'" I replied. "But you're right—he doesn't appear to be suffering."

Near the back of the club, a minor demon summoning was underway—probably someone trying to impress their date by calling up a lesser imp to mix cocktails. That rarely turned out well. Already the bouncers were moving in that direction with the weary efficiency of people who dealt with this sort of thing nightly.

The server returned with drinks that sparkled.

Arabella sipped hers cautiously, then smiled. "Sweet and refreshing. What is it?"

"Liquid moonlight with a touch of distilled rebellion," the server explained proudly. "A house specialty to get you started."

A commotion near the entrance drew our attention. A group of fae nobles swept in, their stances arrogant as they surveyed the club with predatory smiles. Their glamors flickered occasionally, revealing glimpses of needle-sharp teeth, hollow eyes, and bark-like skin.

Nearly every woman in the club turned to watch them, expressions ranging from curiosity to naked desire.

I huffed in disgust. "Fae."

"Not a fan of them, either?" Arabella asked. We watched as one particularly tall fae with translucent wings caught the eye of a young human woman and beckoned her with a finger.

"They've cultivated a reputation as immortal sex gods," I said, swirling my drink. "But all that fairy wine secretly does things to their bodies. That's why they always target the younger humans. Easier to impress when you have no basis for comparison."

Arabella's lips quirked. "The wings are compensating for something, then?"

I nearly choked on my drink. "Let's just say there's a reason they rely so heavily on glamor and enchantment."

"And here I thought they were just naturally irresistible," she said, watching as the fae led their admirers to a private alcove.

"Nothing natural about it," I muttered. "Just centuries of good marketing and magical coercion."

"It works. When I was a teenager, I used to daydream about a fae lord rescuing me from my tower." Arabella turned a wicked grin toward me. "But I'm happier with how things turned out."

I gave her a flat stare and said in a low voice. "*Please* stop setting the bar so low, Arabella."

She laughed and leaned forward to get a better view at a fight that had broken out near the bar. The combatants were using enchanted chairs as weapons, and the other patrons cheered them on.

I found myself relaxing slightly despite the chaos. Arabella's delight was infectious, and her lack of moral outrage was refreshing. She wasn't trying to change anything or save anyone—she was simply observing, learning, experiencing.

It occurred to me that this was what I'd been missing in my previous entanglements. Not just acceptance of who I was, but genuine enjoyment of the world I inhabited. Arabella didn't just tolerate my darkness—she found it fascinating. And I found myself wanting to show her more of it, to watch her eyes light up with that particular blend of curiosity and wickedness that was becoming increasingly addictive.

"I still think we should have pressed Griffin and Sebastian to come tonight," she said after a while. "Griffin especially. He seems like he could use some loosening up."

"Sebastian would be clutching his pearls and Griffin can barely contain his chaos when he's trying to be *careful*."

"But that's exactly why he needs this. He's so worried about disappointing you that he's tied himself in knots. A little debauchery might do him good."

I snorted. "Considering his antics at our wedding, I'm guessing Griffin knows how to debauch himself just fine."

As if summoned by my words, a familiar gangly figure appeared on the edge of the dance floor.

"Son of a—" I cut myself off, recognizing the distinctive silhouette. "Griffin."

Arabella followed my gaze and burst into laughter. "Oh my gods, look at him go."

Griffin was indeed going. His long limbs flailed in a dance style that reminded me of a scarecrow in a windstorm, his wild hair still caked in flour that shook out all over the floor. He'd shed his outer robe and was down to a shirt and trousers, both of which were clinging to his lean frame. But it was his partner that made the scene truly surreal.

He was dancing with an imp—about three feet tall, with purple skin and tiny horns. It was keeping pace with Griffin's erratic movements with the kind of gleeful abandon that suggested either genuine enjoyment or complete insanity.

They were drawing considerable attention.

"I wonder what Griffin's crime was," Arabella mused with a grin.

"Oh, he has plenty, most of them accidental."

I dropped the shadow barrier just enough to catch Griffin's eye. When he saw us, he grinned and waved, then said something to his partner before making his way to our section. He climbed the stairs to the VIP area, giving the bone and metal construct a wary look, but the construct let him pass at my nod.

He arrived slightly out of breath, his hair sticking up and his shirt translucent with sweat. "Lord Blackrose! Lady Blackrose!"

"I thought you were baking with Sebastian," I said, not bothering to hide my irritation.

"We finished!" Griffin's grin was infectious—or would have been, if I were susceptible to such things. "The scones were amazing, if I do say so myself. We needed something to do, and Lady Blackrose was very convincing in her argument that we should experience the local culture."

"And where is Sebastian?" I asked, scanning the crowd for the blond nobleman.

Griffin's expression grew vague. "He's . . . We got separated at the entrance."

"Oh." Arabella put a hand to her mouth. "I should have anticipated that."

Griffin fidgeted with his sleeve. "Well, the bouncer asked for our names and crimes. I told him I was responsible for the Great Rust Spore incident. You know, when I released a magically engineered fungus that dissolved the ceremonial armor of the entire Royal Guard an hour before the King's Jubilee Parade?"

"Griffin." I remembered the incident. It had been an early, unauthorized test of a metal-eating agent meant for siege warfare. I'd been furious at his recklessness and secretly delighted by the chaos it caused in Auremar's court.

"Right. So Sebastian actually surprised me by claiming he had a crime too! Something about 'unauthorized diplomacy' and the 'Rhyming Curse incident.' But the bouncer didn't believe him at first. Then I told him we were with the Chair of Dominion, and we were allowed inside." Griffin lowered his voice. "But then Sebastian couldn't, um, he couldn't bring himself to walk past the naked minotaur."

Arabella pressed her lips together but shook with laughter.

A cold weight settled in my stomach. Sebastian, the man who couldn't bring himself to harm a mutated swamp creature, loose in a place where murder was considered a recreational activity. "So you let him wander off alone?"

Griffin finally seemed to register my tone. His excitement dimmed. "He said he'd be fine. He's very capable, my lord. Very resourceful."

Griffin had the common sense of a lemming with a death wish, but at least he had some experience with the darker side of magic. Sebastian, however, had a complete inability to recognize danger until it was gnawing on his leg.

Although if Sebastian *did* get himself killed, it would solve several problems. I wouldn't have to worry about taking him back to Skyspire or dealing with whatever political complications his presence might create. And Arabella would be sad, but she'd get over it eventually.

Before I could decide whether to send a shadow warrior to track down Sebastian or simply write him off as an acceptable loss, our server appeared again. This time she carried a tray with two goblets filled with wine so dark it was black.

"Compliments of the house," she said, setting the goblets before us. "Twilight Wine, for the honored guests."

The wine was a specialty of the Gallows—fermented with certain herbs that heightened sensation and lowered inhibitions. Not dangerous, exactly, but definitely potent.

Arabella reached for one of the goblets, but I caught her wrist. She shot me a withering look. "I was going to check it."

"Apologies, my lady." The corner of my mouth twitched, and I released her.

She passed her hand over both goblets. Her truth-sense was different from my ability to detect poison, but it would reveal any malicious intent behind the gift.

"No poison, no compulsions," she said after a moment. "No hidden agendas. Just wine and enhancement."

I felt a surge of pride. She was learning to think like a villain, to question gifts and check for traps. It was a necessary skill in our world, and one that might keep her alive.

"What about Sebastian?" Arabella asked. "We can't leave him to wander the Spire on his own. He stress-flowers."

"He's a grown man," I said, though I already knew I'd lost this argument.

Arabella gave me that particular look that meant I was about to be forced into doing something decent. I sighed. She would never forgive me if something happened to him while we sat here drinking.

I turned to Griffin, who was still swaying slightly to the music. "You let him wander off, you get to retrieve him. And then you take him straight back to the apartment, where you're going to resume your research."

Griffin's face cycled through three distinct emotions in rapid succession—resigned acceptance, visible dismay, and then a peculiar brightness that made his amber eyes go wide behind his spectacles. "Yes, my lord—oh! I love this song!"

It didn't sound like the music had changed at all, but Griffin pushed out onto the dance floor and moved toward the door with a series of enthusiastic twitches that made more flour puff out from his hair and settle on the people near him like a dusting of snow.

Arabella settled back against me. "Griffin wasn't even that disappointed. I think he has a crush on Sebastian." She lifted her goblet of Twilight Wine.

I tried to picture Griffin attempting courtship through a series of catastrophically failed magical demonstrations, each one more disastrous than the last. Sebastian would probably find it charming.

Shaking my head, I took my goblet and pulled her closer. "Be careful with this."

Arabella raised an eyebrow.

"My runes burn through most poisons and spirits before they can affect me," I explained. "But this stuff is enchanted to bypass physical resilience and interact directly with your magic. It's intense."

"Good intense or bad intense?" she asked, her curiosity piqued.

"That depends entirely on your company."

She smiled and raised her goblet in a toast. "To new experiences."

"To new experiences," I agreed, and we drank.

25

Recognize an Old Enemy
(and Become a New One to Your Wife)

Kazimir

The Twilight Wine hit my tongue like ice and turned it numb before warming into a fiery burn as it slid down my throat. The effect was immediate. Every nerve ending seemed to come alive, making me hyperaware of Arabella's presence beside me. The silk of her dress against my hand, the subtle scent of her perfume, the way her lips glistened where the wine had touched them.

I watched Arabella's eyes widen as it hit her, her pupils dilating. "Oh," she breathed. "That's . . . that's . . . *fuck*."

I knew exactly what she was feeling. The wine amplified everything—especially desire. Even the brush of fabric against skin became an erotic experience. I shifted in my seat, suddenly acutely aware of the weight of my clothes, the texture of the couch beneath me, and most of all, the heat radiating from Arabella.

She turned to me, her eyes dark with want. "Is it always like this?"

"Yes." My voice was rough. "That's why it's so popular."

She moved closer, her hand finding my thigh. "No wonder."

The touch sent a jolt through me, far more powerful than it should have been. I caught her wrist, but instead of pulling her hand away, I guided it higher. "You said you wanted to try something different," I murmured against her ear, feeling her shiver in response. "The shadows are still partially down."

Her voice was husky, filled with want and excitement. "Here?"

"If you want." I let my hand trail down her side, feeling the way she arched into the touch.

Take her, a voice whispered in the back of my mind. *Show them all who she belongs to.*

The thought sent a spike of arousal through me, followed immediately by an inexplicable flash of anger. The voice felt foreign and intrusive, but the wine made it difficult to focus on why.

I pushed the stray thought aside. I was a villain. I didn't see anything wrong with claiming my bride in front of an audience, especially one that appreciated such displays. And if the way Arabella was pressing against me was any indication, she was amenable to the idea.

"We can stop anytime," I murmured. She nodded.

I pulled her onto my lap to straddle me. My hands found her waist, then slid lower, bunching the silk gown as I explored the smooth skin of her thighs.

I let my fingers drift higher, toward the heat I could feel radiating from her core. "Just think—anyone could see."

She glanced around the booth, taking in the shadows and the strategic positioning that would hide most of what we were doing. Below us, the orgy was still in full swing, and several other couples had found their own dark corners.

"You know," she breathed against my ear, her voice thick with the wine's influence and lust, "after our wedding, when you threatened to claim me in front of your entire court . . ." She paused, pressing closer, and I felt her heart racing against my chest. "I couldn't stop thinking about it."

My hands stilled on her thighs. "Is that so?"

"I hated how much I wanted it." Her admission came out in a rush, her cheeks flushing deeper. "The idea of everyone knowing exactly who I belong to."

In all our time together, through every battle of wills and moment of passion, she'd never admitted to belonging to anyone—least of all me. She'd fought that notion with teeth and claws, and now here she was, straddling my lap in a den of villains, offering it freely.

"Say it again," I commanded.

Her eyes met mine, pupils blown wide. "I belong to you, Kazimir Blackrose."

The thrill that shot through me was equal parts triumph and humility. This magnificent creature, this woman who could bring me to my knees with a look, was choosing to be mine.

"And I," I said, sliding my hand higher under her dress, "belong to you."

Her hands curled into my hair as she whispered, "What's mine, stays mine."

"What's mine stays mine," I echoed.

She gasped as my fingers found the edge of her silk undergarments, already soaked through. The Twilight Wine made every sensation electric, and I could feel her trembling as I traced lazy patterns against the fabric.

"So wet for me already," I murmured, pushing the silk aside. "And I've barely touched you."

"The wine—" she started, but I cut her off by sliding three fingers into her in one rough thrust.

"Not the wine," I corrected, curling my fingers to hit that spot that made her back arch. "This is all you."

My thumb found her clit, working it in tight circles as I fucked her with my fingers. The wine amplified everything—I could feel every flutter of her inner walls, every pulse of her desire. She was so responsive, so perfect, grinding down against my hand with abandon.

"Kaz," she moaned, burying her face in my neck. "Oh gods, I'm already—"

She came with shocking suddenness, her whole body going taut as she clenched around my fingers. The sound she made—a long, broken groan muffled against my throat—nearly undid me.

I laughed, dark and rough, continuing to work her through it even as she whimpered from oversensitivity. "That's it. Let them all hear you. Think about all those people out there realizing exactly what I'm doing to you in here."

She shuddered, drenching my fingers further. "Too much," she gasped, her hands fisting in my shirt. "Kaz, please—"

"Please what?" I asked, adding a fourth finger and watching her eyes roll back. "Please stop? Or please don't stop?"

"I don't—fuck—I don't know," she babbled, caught between pushing into my touch and trying to escape it. The wine made everything too intense, too good, and I used that mercilessly, drawing out her pleasure until she was begging.

Only when she was trembling uncontrollably from another orgasm, tears of euphoria gathering in her eyes, did I ease my fingers out of her. She slumped against me, panting hard.

"I haven't even touched you yet," she complained weakly, and I could feel her lips curve into a smile against my neck. She turned her head to lay it on my shoulder as she sucked in breaths. "But I'm utterly exhausted."

"Oh, I fully intend to let you return the favor," I promised, shifting so she could feel exactly how hard I was beneath her.

She suddenly went rigid. "Kaz," she said, but this time her voice was sharp with alarm rather than desire.

"What?" I sat up, alert.

"There." She pointed toward the far side of the dance floor, where the crowd was thickest. "I think I saw Pip."

The name hit me like a bucket of ice water, cutting through the wine's effects with brutal efficiency. Pip. The missing servant from Skyspire. The one who'd vanished during the Hero's Guild attack. The person I suspected of helping our enemies breach the citadel. After all these weeks, the little bastard had finally surfaced.

I scanned the crowd, looking for the familiar figure—young, brown hair, nervous demeanor. "Are you certain?" I asked, shifting Arabella off me.

"I think so. It was just a glimpse." She shook her head. "But he was moving toward the back exit."

I was going to get answers, even if I had to tear them from his mind piece by bloody piece. I conjured three shadow warriors with a thought, their forms materializing from the darkness around our booth. "Stay with Lady Blackrose," I ordered them. "If anyone approaches her, kill them. If she's threatened in any way, burn the place down."

"Kaz, wait—" Arabella started.

"Stay here." Raw, irrational terror spiked through me. I needed her safe. "If it's an ambush, I don't want you caught in it."

The look she gave me could have frozen hellfire. "What happened to doing everything together?"

She's weak. She'll slow you down. The traitor will escape because of her.

The thought slithered through my mind, both foreign and familiar. My jaw clenched as pure, undiluted rage flooded through me, replacing the fear. Pip had betrayed us. Helped enemies into MY fortress. Nearly gotten Arabella killed. The fury was so intense it made my vision blur at the edges.

With a sharp gesture, I sealed the shadow barrier around us. "This is different," I said coldly. "This is about Skyspire's security. My failure. My responsibility."

"Your—" She stood, wobbling slightly from the aftereffects of her orgasms. "Kaz, we talked about this. You promised—"

She questions you? Show her what happens to those who defy the Dark Lord.

I blinked. Where was that voice coming from? It felt wrong, like wearing someone else's clothes. But the anger—the anger at Pip, at the betrayal, at everything—that was definitely mine. Wasn't it?

"You will stay here," I commanded, my voice carrying the weight of dominion magic. I watched her flinch as my power pressed against her, though we both knew it wouldn't work.

"You just tried to compel me," she said, her voice dangerously quiet. "Like I'm one of your subjects. Like I'm—"

Property. She's yours. Make her understand that.

I shook my head, trying to clear it. These thoughts—they came in whispers, sliding between my own fury like smoke through cracks. Something was wrong. This wasn't how I—

"I'm trying to protect you," I snarled, the rage making my control slip.

"Stop." Her magic flared, golden light pushing against my shadows. "Listen to yourself. This isn't you talking."

She's trying to control you. Manipulate you. Just like everyone else.

I leaned in, but she didn't give an inch. "Maybe this is exactly who I am," I hissed. "The Dark Lord doesn't need anyone's permission or help to handle his own domain."

Arabella glared at me, and the fact that she didn't have a witty comment or barbed accusation to hurl was worse than if she'd slapped me. Then I saw the tears of fury gathering in the corners of her eyes, and I would have preferred that she had. She could have knocked me across the nightclub with her power, but she turned the full force of her fury on me without lifting a hand.

For a moment, the whispers went silent. In that silence, I saw myself clearly—standing here, trying to dominate the one person who'd chosen to stand beside me.

I'd never made Arabella cry before, as far as I knew, and the soul-crushing guilt made me want to fall to my knees and beg her forgiveness.

But then Pip's face flashed in my mind, and the rage returned tenfold.

He's ESCAPING.

"I don't have time for this," I said, turning toward the barrier. "Stay or go, I don't care. But I'm catching that traitor."

The rational part of me—what was left of it—screamed to stop, to turn around, to fix this. But the fury, the whispers, the *need* to catch Pip and make him pay—

I dropped the barrier and vaulted over the railing of the VIP section, landing on the main floor and causing a mild panic as people scrambled to get out of my way. But with every step, even through the rage and the wine and those revolting whispers, one thought kept breaking through:

What have I done?

26

Recognize You're Not Yourself

(But Have No Idea Who You Are)

Kazimir

The closed alley outside the Gilded Gallows reeked of piss and sulfur, a charming combination that perfectly matched my mood. I stalked through the narrow passages between buildings, shadows rippling at my command as they searched every corner, every hidden doorway, every possible escape route.

Nothing. Not a trace of that traitorous little weasel.

"Find him," I snarled at more shadow constructs, and they dispersed to search the God Spire's labyrinthine underbelly. The rational part of my mind—what little remained through the haze of rage—knew this was futile. If Pip had been here at all, he'd have a dozen escape routes planned. The boy might have been nervous and twitchy, but he wasn't stupid.

I stood there, breathing hard, trying to master the rage still burning through me. Pip. The little weasel had been right there, practically under my nose, and I'd let him slip away.

Because of her. Because she distracted you.

No. That wasn't fair. Arabella had spotted him in the first place. If not for her, I wouldn't have known he was here at all.

The whisper slithered through my thoughts again, and I shook my head. These intrusive thoughts were getting worse. They felt like mine but . . . not. Like looking at my reflection in warped glass.

A man's panicked yelling cut through my thoughts. I froze, listening. It came again, followed by the sound of something crashing.

Not my problem. I had a traitor to find.

But the yelling had come from nearby—just around the corner. And it was followed by a very familiar voice saying, "I really must insist." A pause. "That you cease and desist."

Sebastian. What the hell was he doing in a dark corner of the Spire by himself? Spending time with Griffin was clearly having a detrimental effect on his survival instincts.

For that matter, where was my chaotic enchanter?

I rounded the corner to find the pretty lordling backed against a wall, surrounded by five thugs who looked like they'd graduated from the Generic Henchman Academy with honors in Looking Menacing and minors in Poor Life Choices. Three goblins with rusty knives, a half ogre whose breath I could smell from twenty feet away, and judging by the way he was swaying, a very drunk necromancer.

They weren't particularly intimidating as far as villains went—more the type to pick pockets than slit throats—but they had Sebastian outnumbered and cornered.

The interesting part was the plants. Massive, thorny vines had erupted from every crack in the alley floor, creating a verdant cage around Sebastian. They twisted and writhed with his fear, some as thick as my arm, all radiating a distinctive golden-green glow of magic.

"Look at the pretty magic," one of the goblins cackled, poking at a vine with his knife. "Bet his coin purse is as pretty as he is."

My already foul mood darkened further.

Sebastian, to his credit, maintained his insufferably polite demeanor even as more vines sprouted around his feet. "I'm certain this is all a misunderstanding. Perhaps we could discuss this over tea? It'll be nicer, I guarantee."

"We don't want your tea, princeling," the necromancer slurred. "Your purse and whatever else you're carrying, for starters. And then maybe we'll see what else you've got to offer."

The implication was clear, and Sebastian's face went pale. "There's been a mistake—I'm not a prince, you see." The vines grew thicker, thornier. Any competent magic user would have sent them lashing out, turned the alley into a killing field of nature's fury. Instead, Sebastian just stood there looking mildly distressed.

I could have walked away. Should have, probably. Let natural selection take its course. Sebastian had chosen to wander off alone in one of the most dangerous districts in the known realms. These were the consequences.

But Arabella would never forgive me if I let her childhood friend get murdered.

Besides, a more rational voice pointed out, *you need something to hit, and these idiots are volunteering.*

"Villains," I said, stepping out of the shadows. All five would-be muggers spun toward me, and I had the satisfaction of watching the color drain from their faces.

"That," I gestured lazily toward Sebastian, "is my wife's pet. And while I personally find him about as useful as a chocolate teapot, she's rather fond of him."

"Lord Blackrose," the half ogre stammered. "We didn't—this isn't—"

The goblins scattered, their self-preservation instincts overriding their greed. The necromancer attempted to shadow-walk away but was too drunk to manage it properly and ended up face-first in a puddle.

The half ogre was too stupid to run.

The shadows at my feet stretched, solidifying into razor sharp tendrils that shot toward all five would-be muggers. They screamed. Within seconds, all were suspended in the air, the darkness wrapped around their throats.

"Please," the necromancer choked out. "We didn't mean—"

"I've had a very trying evening," I interrupted. "And you've just made it worse."

I tightened the shadows, watching with detached satisfaction as their faces turned purple. The rage that had been burning through me found an outlet in their fear and pain. It would be so easy to keep squeezing until their necks snapped—

"Lord Blackrose!"

Sebastian's voice broke through my thoughts. I turned to find him still pressed against the wall, surrounded by enough vegetation to count as a small forest. The vines had grown even thicker, some sporting flowers.

"Please," he said quietly. "Don't kill them."

I raised an eyebrow.

He swallowed. "They don't deserve to die."

I stared at him incredulously. "Are you serious?"

"I'm afraid I am." He straightened his jacket, which had been rumpled in the scuffle. "Violence only begets more violence. I prefer to find peaceful solutions."

The sheer absurdity of his statement cut through my rage. Here he was, cornered in a dark alley by men who clearly meant him harm, and he was advocating for mercy. It was ridiculous. Naive. Utterly heroic.

And somehow, the absurdity of it helped clear my head.

I let out a harsh laugh. "Fine." I turned back to the dangling villains. "You heard him. He's feeling merciful."

I, however, was not. What happened next was quick, efficient, and thoroughly satisfying. By the time I was done, all five were unconscious, bones were broken, and at least two would need magical healing to walk properly again.

I turned back to Sebastian, who had sputtered and rhymed in protest the entire time. "There—not dead. But they might wish they were. You can dismiss those now," I said irritably at the vines still writhing around him.

"I . . . yes. Of course." He closed his eyes, taking a deep breath, and the vines began to slowly retract. "I thought you weren't going to hurt them."

I smiled coldly. "You said you didn't want them dead. I obliged."

Sebastian looked at the villains at my feet, then back at me. "You are correct. Thank you for the assistance, Lord Blackrose."

"You had enough power there to level half the district," I snapped. "Why didn't you use it?"

He blinked at me, genuinely puzzled. "For what?"

"To defend yourself, you imbecile. Those vines could have torn them apart."

"Oh." He looked down at the retreating vegetation with surprise, as if seeing it for the first time. "I suppose they could have. That never occurred to me."

I stared at him.

"Violence isn't really my forte." He brushed dirt off his coat. "Besides, they were just desperate people trying to make a living."

"They were going to rob you. Possibly worse."

"Yes, well." He shifted uncomfortably. "It wouldn't be the first time."

The casual way he said it made something twist in my chest. Not sympathy—I didn't do sympathy—but a kind of frustrated disbelief. Here was someone with enough magical power to make even me take notice, and he just . . . allowed people to hurt him.

"If you don't have the sense to protect yourself," I said coldly, "perhaps I should have let them have their way with you after all."

The words were cruel, calculated to cut, but instead of flinching, Sebastian tilted his head and studied me with those unsettling violet eyes. "You're upset."

"I'm always upset. It's part of my charm."

"No, this is different." A small vine crept up the wall beside him, flowering with tiny white blooms. "You're not yourself."

The fact that he was worried about me, of all things, made the simmering rage flare white hot. In response, the blooming vine shot forward, wrapping around my wrist with surprising strength.

"What the—" I yanked my arm, but the vine held fast. "Release me!"

"I'm sorry!" Sebastian looked mortified. "It's not intentional—they respond to my emotions—"

I snarled, and shadows erupted from my hand. The vine didn't just wither—it combusted, creating a smoking hole in the bone wall that went deep enough to see the chamber beyond.

Sebastian jerked back but didn't flee. "Lord Blackrose," he said, and I wanted to hit him just for the sympathy in his voice. But he plowed on, oblivious to the danger. "Would you like to talk about what's troubling you?"

"What's troubling me," I said, my voice dropping to subzero temperatures, "is that I'm wasting time babysitting an idiot who's too precious to defend himself when I should be hunting down a traitor. What's troubling me is that I specifically told everyone to stay out of trouble, and yet here you are, alone, nearly getting yourself violated by street thugs because you lack the basic survival instincts the gods gave a particularly stupid moth. The only reason you're still breathing is because my wife has a baffling soft spot for you."

Sebastian flinched and went blessedly silent.

"Get back to the apartment," I ordered. "And if you deviate by so much as a single step, I'll let the next villains keep you."

He hesitated.

"Go!" I roared. Shadows erupted behind me, forming into massive wings.

The Scone Lord scrambled away, nearly tripping over an unconscious thug in his haste. I watched until he turned the corner, heading in the right direction, then sent a shadow warrior to follow him. Just to make sure he actually made it back. For Arabella's sake.

The rage was still there, simmering beneath my skin. But Sebastian's words echoed in my mind. *You're not yourself.*

I thought of Arabella's face when I'd tried to compel her. The tears in her eyes. The way she'd said, "This isn't you talking."

But if it wasn't me, then who the fuck was it? There was no one else to take the blame for my bad behavior.

The hunt for Pip resumed, but my focus was shattered. Every shadow I sent out searching came back empty. Every lead turned into nothing. The wine's effects were shifting from heightened senses to a pounding headache, and those whispers kept sliding through my thoughts.

By the time I gave up and returned to our apartment, dawn was already breaking over the God Spire. I'd spent the entire night hunting ghosts and fighting my own mind, the Twilight Wine ensuring every moment was torture without Arabella there to . . . to . . .

I was going to murder the Alchemist. Slowly. Creatively. With extreme prejudice.

27

Submit to Romantic Treatments

(Despite Wanting to Murder Each Other)

Arabella

"The venom creates a tingling sensation that opens your pores while simultaneously dissolving the top three layers of dead skin." The spa attendant held up a jar of purple liquid containing a particularly angry jellyfish. She wore the spa's uniform—a flowing black robe with silver embroidery that made her look like she was officiating a cult ritual rather than explaining beauty treatments. "It's completely safe when administered properly."

I stared at the translucent creature pushing against the glass. Its tentacles glowed with green light that screamed, "I will kill you painfully and without remorse."

"Define 'safe,'" I said.

"Well, the fatality rate is under ten percent." The attendant's smile never wavered. "And those are mostly due to allergic reactions. Or improper handling. Or that one incident with the siren who tried to make friends with it."

"Fascinating," I said, taking an instinctive step away from the jar. "But I think I'll pass on having deadly toxins rubbed into my face today."

The attendant nodded. "As you wish, my lady. Perhaps you'd prefer our volcanic hot stone massage? The stones are harvested from active volcanoes and blessed by fire elementals."

"That sounds—" Less immediately lethal? "—lovely."

Beside me, Kazimir stood like a statue, his face a mask of rigid control. He hadn't spoken more than three words to me all morning, and those had been "Get dressed. Now." He'd barely looked at me since the disaster at the Gilded Gallows, and I'd been too furious to attempt conversation.

The Twilight Wine had worn off hours ago, leaving me with nothing but a headache and the crystal-clear memory of him trying to compel me to stay put while he chased after Pip. Unfortunately, the wine didn't cause hallucinations. What I'd seen had been real.

And what I'd seen was my husband attempting to use his power to control me, just like every other man in my life had tried to do.

The worst part? When I'd looked into Kaz's eyes at the Gilded Gallows, I'd seen someone else looking back. Someone who'd wanted to hurt me.

And I'd known it wasn't Kazimir.

I'd spent the night alone in our suite, alternating between rage and hurt, waiting for him to return so I could properly eviscerate him. But dawn had come, and he'd still been gone. When he finally appeared, disheveled and hollow-eyed, the Alchemist's message had arrived immediately after, summoning us to the spa.

So here we were, trapped in a bizarre wellness center with a woman who thought deadly venom made an excellent beauty product, pretending everything was fine. The only thing keeping me from setting something on fire was the knowledge that the Alchemist would use any perceived weakness against us.

Speaking of . . .

"When will the Alchemist be joining us?" I asked the attendant.

"Oh, not until after your treatments! They're getting their weekly acid peel. Takes about three hours to properly dissolve the old face and grow a new one. In the meantime, we have many options for our honeymoon package—"

"Honeymoon package?" Kazimir's voice could have frozen lava.

The attendant's smile somehow grew wider. "The Alchemist insisted on our most romantic couple's experience! They said you two lovebirds deserved the full treatment after your whirlwind journey."

I felt my husband's magic spike dangerously. Before he could do something we'd regret—like turn the attendant into a jellyfish for his very own—I grabbed his arm. His muscles were rigid under my touch.

"How thoughtful of them," I said with my most glittering smile.

Three hours. Three hours of pretending everything was fine while my husband and I could barely stand to be in the same room.

The attendant's smile grew strained as she glanced between us. "Wonderful! If you'll follow me, I'll show you to our volcanic therapy room."

She led us through the Villainous Corporate Retreat & Spa, a labyrinth of black marble and obsidian that occupied an entire level of the God Spire. The decor was exactly what you'd expect from a high-end resort catering exclusively to villains: elegant, opulent, and just a touch macabre. Crystal chandeliers shaped like human rib cages. Plush velvet lounges the color of fresh blood. Fountains powered by the wails of tortured souls.

I had to admit it was impressive. Under different circumstances, I might have enjoyed it.

We passed a room where a group of necromancers in fluffy black robes were getting pedicures from tiny undead beetles. In another chamber, a demon lord floated in a pool of what appeared to be liquid gold, his many eyes closed in bliss.

"Here we are!" The attendant stopped before a set of double doors made from volcanic glass. "Your private therapy suite."

She pushed open the doors to reveal a dimly lit room dominated by two massage tables. The air was heavy with the scent of sulfur and exotic incense. In the center of the room, a pit of glowing coals radiated heat, and arranged neatly beside it were rows of black stones that glowed with inner fire.

"Please disrobe and lie face down on the tables," the attendant said. "Your therapists will be with you shortly."

Kazimir's only response was a grunt that might have been agreement or might have been a warning that he was about to murder everyone in the vicinity. Hard to tell.

I sighed. This was going to be a long day.

She left, closing the doors behind her with a soft click. The silence that descended was suffocating.

I went behind my screen and started undressing, hyperaware of every rustle of fabric. On the other side of the room, I heard Kazimir not moving at all.

"Are you going to just stand there?" I asked as I took a silk robe from its hook.

"Yes. No one touches me except you."

I shoved down the complicated feelings his confession stirred up and poked my head around the screen. "We need to present a united front. You know that."

"I'm aware," he snapped. Then he let out a tense breath. "We're wasting valuable time. Let's just come back in three hours to meet with the Alchemist."

"They'll know something's wrong if we don't participate." I headed toward one of the massage tables. "So if we're stuck here, we might as well make the best of it."

The heat from the coals warmed my skin as I removed my robe, leaving only my undergarments. I could feel Kazimir's eyes on me, a tangible weight that sent a shiver down my spine.

Damn him. Even furious, I still wanted him.

I lay face down on the massage table, arranging a soft black towel over my lower half. "Are you going to join me, or are you going to stand there brooding the entire time?"

"I'll pass," he said stiffly.

"Suit yourself."

Two attendants entered—different from the jellyfish enthusiast, thankfully. They were identical, with skin that shimmered and eyes that reflected light like a cat's. Without speaking, they moved to the pit of coals and began selecting stones with metal tongs.

One approached my table while the other stood awkwardly looking at Kazimir.

"My husband will be observing today," I said smoothly.

The attendant nodded and the other set to work, placing hot stones along my spine. The heat sank into my muscles, and I couldn't help the small sigh that escaped me. It felt divine, the tension of the past twelve hours beginning to melt away.

Until Kazimir spoke.

"You're doing it wrong."

The attendant froze, a stone hovering inches above my shoulder blade.

"The stones should follow the meridian lines," he said coldly, "not the spine."

I turned my head to look at him. "Since when are you an expert on hot stone massage?"

"Since I studied with the fire monks of the Ashen Wastes." He approached the table, radiating power and irritation. "Leave us," he commanded the attendants. "I'll handle this myself."

They practically fled the room, the door closing behind them with a thud that echoed in the sudden silence. Kazimir selected one of the stones.

I propped myself up on my elbows, ready to give him a piece of my mind, but then he placed the stone on my shoulder, and . . . oh.

Oh.

The pressure was perfect, the heat radiating through layers of tension I hadn't even realized I was carrying. He added another stone, then another, each placement deliberate and precise. When his hands touched my back, I nearly jumped off the table. Not from fear or anger, but from the electricity that shot through me at the contact.

"I didn't know you studied with monks," I said, my voice embarrassingly breathy.

His hands moved to my lower back, fingers pressing into knots of muscle with expert precision. "When I was looking for the artifact. The fire monks believe that true mastery of the self begins with understanding the body's energy pathways. Mostly, it's about the way the body channels magic."

His touch was impersonal, clinical almost, but devastatingly effective. Each press of his fingers sent waves of pleasure-pain through my body, releasing tension and replacing it with a warm, liquid sensation. His dominion magic hummed faintly through his touch, not compelling but soothing, like a warm current flowing through my muscles. Hands worked lower, finding every ache, every pain, every spot that made me melt into the table.

This was Kazimir without words—taking care of me the only way he knew how when everything else between us was fractured.

We lapsed into silence, the only sound the occasional hiss from the coals and my own involuntary sighs as he worked magic with his hands. Despite everything, my body was responding to his touch. Desire pooled between my thighs, and I resisted the urge to squirm. I'd known Kaz was good at this—he'd given me massages before—but with all the heightened emotions between us, every touch felt like fire. I pressed my face into the table to muffle the completely inappropriate sound that wanted to escape.

This was not fair. We were fighting.

He must have sensed the change in my breathing, because his hands slowed, becoming less clinical and more exploratory. His fingers traced the curve of my spine, lingering at the sensitive spot at the base of my neck.

"Arabella," he said, his voice rough.

"Don't." I cut him off, suddenly unable to bear whatever he was about to say. I wasn't ready to talk about it, to hear his excuses or justifications. Not when the wound was still so raw. "Just . . . don't."

I sat up abruptly, clutching the towel to my body, and slid off the table. "What's next on this ridiculous spa itinerary?"

Kazimir's expression shuttered, all traces of vulnerability vanishing. "How should I know?"

A quick glance around the room revealed a small card on a side table. I picked it up, scanning the elegant script. "Looks like we have a mud bath next, followed by the hot springs and a salt scrub." I looked up at him with a sweetly venomous smile. "Doesn't that sound delightful?"

His glare could have curdled milk. "I'll pass on that, too."

"Oh, no you won't." I grabbed my robe and slipped it on. "I'm not having you stand there glaring at me while I try to relax. You can either participate or get out."

"Those aren't the only options."

"They are if you want to maintain our cover." I yanked the sash tight around my waist. "The Spire expects us to be on our honeymoon. What kind of newlywed husband refuses to join his bride in a mud bath?"

His jaw worked, a muscle ticking in his cheek. "Fine."

"Great." I headed for the door, not bothering to check if he was following. "Let's go roll in some cursed bog essence."

The mud bath was located in a cavernous room dominated by a large pool of black scented mud. The attendant—yet another cult robe–wearing enthusiast—explained the mud was harvested from the shores of the Lake of Eternal Torment and contained rare minerals that drew toxins from the body.

"It also exfoliates!" she added brightly.

Kazimir looked like he was contemplating murder, but he dutifully removed his clothes once the attendant left. I absolutely did not watch. I definitely didn't notice the faint violet glow from the scars on his chest, or how the mud barely rippled when he lowered himself into it.

"Are you going to sulk the entire time?" I asked as we settled on opposite sides of the pool. The mud was surprisingly warm and tingled against my skin in a not-unpleasant way.

"Probably."

We glared at each other across the pool of mud. I was aware of how ridiculous we must look—two powerful sorcerers having a marital spat while covered in magical mud—but I couldn't bring myself to care.

"Are there any other Syndicate members in residence?" I asked, changing the subject before I said something I'd regret.

Kazimir seemed relieved at the shift. "Not currently, but that means nothing. The Alchemist plays every angle." He shifted in the mud, grimacing. "This feels like being slowly digested."

"That's probably what's happening." I sighed, sinking deeper into the pool. The mud made a soft *glorp* as I shifted position. "Griffin and Sebastian made it back okay last night."

"I'm aware." Kazimir's voice was flat.

I counted to five, reminding myself that we were supposed to be maintaining appearances. "Griffin had a bump on his head. I healed it this morning."

That got a reaction—Kazimir's eyes snapped to mine. "What happened?"

"Some amateur tried a demon summoning outside the Gallows. Griffin attempted to help." I examined my mud-covered fingernails with exaggerated interest. "Apparently, his advice was correct, but the summoner didn't listen. There was an explosion."

"Of course there was." Kaz shook his head. "Was Sebastian with him?"

"They ran into each other afterward. Sebastian seemed fine—a bit embarrassed about something, but fine." I paused. "Why?"

"Just making sure Griffin followed orders." I didn't even need my truth-sense to detect that lie but was too annoyed to push for an explanation.

The mud bath was followed by a visit to the hot springs—a series of pools carved into the bones of the Spire. We sat in separate pools, steam rising between us, pretending the other didn't exist while being excruciatingly aware of every movement.

Kazimir remained stoic throughout, participating in each treatment with the enthusiasm of a man facing execution. But his shadows kept twitching at the edges of my vision, and sometimes I would catch a dark expression on his face that went beyond murderous and into more volatile territory. The salt scrub that followed—performed by sentient loofahs—at least had the benefit of making him wince when they attacked a particularly sensitive spot.

Small victories.

The final treatment was the most awkward—a steam room where we were expected to sit naked and sweat out more "toxins." I peered down at my pruned fingers, then at the steam rising around us. After the mud digestion, the volcanic rocks, and the enchanted loofah assault, I was fairly certain if there were any toxins left, they were hiding in some very stubborn corners of my anatomy.

Before leaving, the attendant assured us the steam was infused with rare herbs that promoted "marital harmony and fertility," which made Kazimir's scowl deepen to previously uncharted depths.

We sat on opposite benches, carefully not looking at each other. The heat was intense, making it difficult to breathe, let alone maintain my anger. I closed my eyes, trying to focus on the sensation rather than the naked man sitting across from me. But that only made me more aware of the sound of his breathing. I felt his gaze on me, dark and hungry and full of things he wasn't saying.

So much for a honeymoon.

Even though I knew our "honeymoon" was a cover story for our real purpose here, I'd still hoped to enjoy myself a little more than I had so far. The God Spire was fascinating, full of wonders and curiosities I'd never seen before. Under different circumstances, exploring it with Kazimir might have been fun.

The door swung open, letting in a blast of cooler air as an attendant announced that our time was up and the Alchemist was waiting for us.

The dining chamber was a small, elegant room with a table set for three. The Alchemist was already seated. Their customary mask was in place over their eyes, but the skin below was a brilliant shade of pink. Kazimir stepped inside first, putting himself slightly between me and the Alchemist. I noted the protective gesture with a complicated twist of emotion.

"Ah, the happy couple," they said as we entered. "You look positively radiant, Lady Blackrose."

"Thank you," I said, slipping reluctantly into the role of adoring wife as Kazimir pulled out my chair.

Kazimir's hand lingered on my shoulder as he took his own seat, a possessive gesture that wasn't entirely for show. Even when we were fighting, there was an undeniable connection between us, a fierce protectiveness that went both ways.

The Alchemist glanced over Kazimir. "Lord Blackrose, your aura is positively crackling with negative energy. Was the massage not long enough?"

"We're here to discuss business," Kaz said flatly.

"And we shall." The Alchemist's fingers tapped a rhythm against the table. They seemed to decide to let the matter drop. "After we've eaten. One should never speak of important matters while hungry—it leads to poor decisions."

The meal was light but exquisite—delicate pastries filled with what the Alchemist assured us was "ethically sourced" dragon meat (which I declined because Nyx would never forgive me), a salad of rare herbs, and wine that changed color with each sip.

Throughout the meal, Kazimir and I played our parts, exchanging small touches and meaningful glances. If anything, we might have overdone it, my hand resting on his thigh under the table, his arm draped possessively across the back of my chair.

"So refreshing, don't you think?" The Alchemist settled into their chair with a contented sigh. "Nothing like a good spa day to wash away one's troubles."

"Indeed," I agreed, taking Kazimir's hand. His fingers interlaced with mine automatically, the gesture so natural it hurt.

"Though one wonders," he added, his thumb stroking across my knuckles, "why you insisted on meeting here rather than somewhere more conventional."

"Conventional is so boring." The Alchemist selected a sugar-dusted pastry in the shape of a tiny dragon. "How was your evening at the Gilded Gallows?"

Kazimir's eyes narrowed slightly. "I suspect you already know the answer to that."

"Oh? Did you run into someone you knew?" They bit into the pastry, sending a puff of powdered sugar into the air. The innocent act might have been more convincing if they weren't literally twinkling with suppressed glee.

"Enough games," Kazimir growled. "State your business so we can conclude this farce."

The Alchemist set down their pastry, and suddenly all playfulness vanished from their expression. The shift was so dramatic it felt like the air itself grew heavier.

"Very well," they said, their musical voice dropping to something more serious. "Let's discuss why you're really here, shall we?"

They leaned forward, their ever-shifting robes settling into a deep, midnight blue. "I know you have the Heirloom of Dominion."

28

Sit Through a Lecture

(The World Is Ending, But First: Mythology)

Kazimir

The silence that followed the Alchemist's declaration was absolute. Even the ambient sounds of the Spire seemed to pause, as if the dead god was holding its breath.

I leaned back in my chair, affecting disinterest while calculating exactly how quickly I could smother the life from their body. The Alchemist had significant magic, and I wasn't even sure of all their skills, but that wouldn't stop me from trying. "That's a fascinating theory."

"Theory?" The Alchemist's mask caught the light as they tilted their head. "Oh, Lord Blackrose. We're past theories now. The magical signature from Skyspire these past few weeks has been distinctive. Like watching fireworks spell out 'We Have the Heirloom' in forty-foot letters."

Arabella's hand tightened on mine under the table. Through our bond, I felt her pulse quicken, but outwardly she remained perfectly composed.

"I must say, the fact that you and Lady Blackrose managed to activate it at all is quite impressive."

Kill them, a voice whispered in my head, cold and ancient. *They know too much.*

I forced the thought down, though my shadows stirred restlessly at the edges of the room. "Let's say, hypothetically, that I possessed such an artifact," I said. "What would stop me from simply killing you now? If I had the Heirloom, I could level this entire Spire with a thought."

The Alchemist nodded, seemingly delighted by the threat. "Oh, absolutely. The power you and Lady Blackrose have managed to harness together is genuinely impressive. That magical bond of yours—" They gestured between us with their fork. "Quite remarkable. I've never seen anything quite like it."

"You're stalling," I observed.

"I'm offering context." They set down their utensils and folded their hands. "Before you decide to murder me and potentially collapse the God Spire onto the heads of several hundred villains—which would be dramatic but inconvenient—perhaps you'd like to satisfy your curiosity?"

"Perhaps," I conceded, "I might be persuaded to hear what you have to say before deciding whether to kill you."

"Wonderful!" The Alchemist stood, their robes shifting from midnight blue to deep purple. "This room is secure from all forms of surveillance, magical or otherwise. But if you'd be more comfortable, we could relocate to the sitting area? I find threatening conversations go better with tea."

They didn't wait for an answer, simply gliding toward a set of plush couches arranged around a low table near the window. With a wave of their hand, a tea service materialized—delicate porcelain painted with scenes of battles between gods and monsters.

Arabella and I exchanged a look. Her truth-sense wasn't triggering any warnings, and my own instincts—beneath the constant whisper to *kill, destroy, dominate*—suggested the Alchemist wasn't planning an immediate betrayal.

We followed.

The Alchemist poured tea. "Sugar? Honey? Essence of tormented souls?"

"Get to the point," I said, not touching the offered cup.

"Very well." They settled back into their seat, mask glinting. "What do you know of the First People?"

The words triggered something in me—a strange sense of déjà vu, as if I'd heard this before in a dream I couldn't quite remember.

"Mythical beings said to have created magic," Arabella answered before I could speak. "The ancestors of the fae."

"Not mythical," the Alchemist corrected. "And not the ancestors of the fae, though that's a common misconception. The First People were something else."

This is pointless. Kill them.

I gritted my teeth against the intrusive thought. "What does this have to do with the Heirloom?"

"Everything. Before humans, before the kingdoms and empires you know, there were the First People," the Alchemist began, their musical voice taking on an almost hypnotic quality. "They weren't gods, but they were close. Magic as we know it originated with them."

The Alchemist sipped their tea thoughtfully. "They created the ley lines from their magic, as tools. A network of power that would sustain magic throughout the realm so that their servants—humans, fae, and other beings—could harness it themselves. But even then, the First People were few, and as millennia passed, they began to fade. Most chose to merge with the ley lines themselves ten thousand years ago or more, becoming one with the magic they had created." The Alchemist's voice softened. "But a precious few lingered, walking among the younger races as their numbers dwindled to nothing."

Arabella leaned forward slightly, but I tried to maintain a facade of disinterest.

"For thousands of years, these last First People watched civilizations rise and fall," the Alchemist continued. "They became myths, then legends, then forgotten entirely. By the time the Shadow King rose to power two millennia ago, perhaps only one remained—a being so ancient that even the fae considered them eternal. This last guardian of the old world had watched humanity for millennia without interference, even as the Shadow King's evil spread across the land."

The Alchemist was silent for a moment. "But then, despite everything—despite the laws of their kind, despite the vast gulf between their natures—they fell in love with a human. From that impossible union came Soriven, born precisely when the world needed him most."

"The First Hero," Arabella murmured.

"Indeed. Half-human, half-something far greater. Soriven inherited the First People's connection to the ley lines and his father's mortality, along with humanity's ambition and fear." The Alchemist's fingers drummed against their teacup.

That uncomfortable feeling intensified. I *knew* this. Somehow, in my bones, I knew exactly what the Alchemist would say next, but it was leading somewhere I didn't want to go.

"Soriven created the Heirloom of Dominion," I said, the words coming unbidden.

"Yes, but do you know why?"

"To stop the Shadow King," Arabella said quietly.

I glanced at her, surprised. Had she known that all along?

The Alchemist nodded. "By the time Soriven reached his full power, the Shadow King had ruled for nearly three centuries. Soriven knew conventional weapons and magic wouldn't be enough to break such entrenched dominion. So he created a weapon specifically designed to channel and control the ley lines, giving the wielder ultimate power to combat and contain the Shadow King. But the Heirloom's very nature demanded a price—it was forged from the Shadow King's own essence and bound with Soriven's First People magic, two opposing forces that could only work in harmony through genuine union."

"The dual requirement." Arabella was looking at me. "Dominion magic and heroic blood."

"Yes." The Alchemist sounded pleased. "The Heirloom requires both the power to dominate and the will to protect. One without the other renders it inert."

Lies, the voice hissed. *Soriven was a thief, a usurper—*

"And the marriage requirement?" Arabella asked. "If Soriven wielded the Heirloom alone . . ." She trailed off, but I knew exactly where her thoughts were going.

It was the same question that had plagued me since the Heirloom first refused to respond to my touch. I'd spent years searching for it, certain that my dominion magic would be enough. When it remained dead in my hands, I'd been forced to dig deeper, eventually uncovering the marriage requirement that had led me to kidnap Arabella in the first place. But even after everything—the wedding, the consummation, successfully activating it—we still didn't understand why Soriven hadn't needed a partner.

"Did Soriven somehow wield both dominion and heroic magic?" I asked, though the theory felt incomplete even as I voiced it.

"Ah, now that's where Soriven's half-human nature becomes crucial," the Alchemist said. "Being half–First People, Soriven could naturally channel both protective and dominion magic within himself—yes, he could wield dominion magic that he'd learned mostly from spying on the Shadow King. His dual heritage allowed him to hold opposing forces in balance. But full humans?" They shook their head. "While we can learn various forms of magic—as Lady Blackrose demonstrates beautifully—we cannot serve as a sole conduit for the Heirloom's opposing forces. The artifact channels the raw essence of both the Shadow King and the First People. That level of primordial power, held in opposition within one human body, would tear us apart."

"So the marriage requirement—" I began.

"—is the only way for humans to wield the Heirloom," the Alchemist finished. "One person channels dominion, one channels protection. The marriage bond, when consummated, creates a magical bridge between two souls. It's the only way beings like us can replicate what Soriven could do naturally."

The Alchemist's tale supplied several missing pieces to our puzzle. I didn't show it, but I was relieved. Imagine the embarrassment if I'd gone through all that trouble—the abduction, the negotiations, the bone-and-hair wedding rings—only to discover I could have wielded the damned thing myself with the right meditation technique.

The thought should have been amusing, but it twisted something uncomfortable in my chest. Arabella and I had barely spoken since the Gilded Gallows. Since I'd thrown her past trauma in her face like I was just another common villain.

I pushed the feeling down. Vulnerability was a luxury I couldn't afford with the Alchemist watching us so closely.

"Fascinating history lesson," I said gruffly. "But I fail to see—"

"Patience, Lord Blackrose." The Alchemist held up a hand. "You see, my family has been Weavers since the First Hero's time—guardians of the ley lines. One Weaver in each generation, sworn to protect the magic and watch for signs of the Shadow King's return." Their lips quirked. "The other members have no idea, of course, but there's always been a Weaver in the Syndicate since its inception—it's the perfect position to monitor magical anomalies across the realm."

Now that was unexpected. Even the voice in my head seemed to pause in its murderous suggestions. "So it was your people who put that three-headed chimera in front of the Heirloom," I said. "The one I killed."

"Yes." The Alchemist showed no sign of anger or resentment. "When the chimera was killed and the Heirloom went missing, I was concerned, as you can imagine. Soon after, when Skyspire began emitting unusual magical signatures, I knew where it had gone."

I stood abruptly, shadows coiling around my feet. "This is all very interesting, but you haven't given me a single reason not to end this conversation with violence."

The Alchemist tilted their head. "Tell me, have you noticed anything unusual in Solandris lately? Beyond its typical resistance to your advances, I mean. Any corruption in the magical fields? Difficulty accessing the ley lines?"

Arabella and I exchanged another glance. I finally reached for my teacup.

"I'll take your silence as confirmation." The Alchemist leaned forward.

"Let me explain a piece of the story that most people don't understand. The First People created the ley lines like a vast spider's web, connecting all magic across the realms. When Soriven imprisoned the Shadow King, he didn't build a cage—he wrapped him in that very web, layer upon layer of magical silk, until the Shadow King was completely cocooned at its heart."

They traced patterns in the air, and faint lines of light appeared, forming an intricate web of ley lines that reminded me of Griffin's cartography apparatus. "The prison isn't a room with walls and a door," they continued. "It's a cocoon suspended in the magical plane of the web. The Golden Rose Fields of Solandris? They're where seven primary strands anchor the web to physical reality. As long as those anchor points remain strong, the cocoon holds."

The light-web flickered, its strands dimming. "But Auremar has been poisoning those anchor points for years—harvesting the roses incorrectly, spilling blood where there should be renewal. The strands grew brittle. The cocoon began to fray." The Alchemist's fingers clenched, and the web dissolved. "Five days ago, King Auremar did the unthinkable. He completed a great sacrifice—hundreds of those with heroic blood. Anyone connected to the ley lines felt the disturbance."

The teacup in my hand cracked. I set it down carefully, controlling the urge to shatter it completely. We'd suspected the sacrifice, but hearing it confirmed didn't make the information more welcome.

"The kings of Solandris were supposed to be guardians of the prison," Arabella said, her voice tight with anger. "That's why my bloodline was important."

The Alchemist nodded. "Originally, yes. The kings of Solandris were descendants of the First Hero, tasked with maintaining the prison. Over time, the line has thinned, diluted. As you may already know, Auremar barely has a drop of heroic blood, if any. By rights"—they looked at Arabella—"you should be closer in line for the throne of Solandris than you are, if not a princess."

Arabella's jaw tightened. "I have no interest in that throne."

"We know the ley lines need purification," I said, cutting off that line of discussion. "If you hadn't dragged us here for mud baths and lectures, we could be working on that problem."

The Alchemist's smile was sad. "Lord Blackrose, the ley lines beneath Solandris aren't just corrupted. Through his meddling, Auremar has *released* the Shadow King from his prison—but not into our world. Into the web itself."

They paused while Arabella and I digested that information. My hand clenched. "How?"

The Alchemist's voice dropped. "In his greed for power, Auremar let the prison threads fray. The sacrifice was the final blow—it caused enough damage for the Shadow King to seep into the exposed ley lines. Now he's spreading through them, taking them over, searching for a way to manifest physically again."

The Alchemist's fingers drummed against their knee. "Within a year, probably less, every ley line in the realm will be his—and beyond our use."

Arabella glanced at me. "Just as we took Solandris's northern outpost, Auremar was releasing the Shadow King into the ley lines."

The Alchemist nodded. "That's my conclusion as well, based on the timing."

I stood and paced away. The Shadow King had stolen what should have been mine. All that planning, all that conquest, and another villain had slipped in and stolen my prize out from under me. The headache that had been building behind my eyes flared into blinding pain, and for a moment, I could have sworn I heard laughter—cold, ancient, and triumphant—echoing in the recesses of my mind.

I gripped the back of a chair, my knuckles white. "So what does this mean?" I demanded, forcing the voice back. "How do we stop it?"

"There are only two ways to fix the ley lines now." The Alchemist held up one finger. "First, you could unweave the prison itself. Let the Shadow King manifest physically so he's no longer inhabiting the ley lines. Of course, then you'd have an ancient god of tyranny walking the earth again, so perhaps not ideal. Given that it took the full might of Soriven and the Heirloom to imprison him the first time, I don't recommend this approach."

"And the second?" Arabella asked.

"That's where things get interesting." The Alchemist moved toward the door, their robes shifting to a deep silver. "And why I needed you both here, at the Spire, rather than anywhere else."

29

Receive Your Assignment
(While Standing on a God's Pelvis)

Arabella

The Alchemist didn't wait for us to agree. They simply turned on their heel and glided toward the door. "Come along. What I need to show you isn't something one discusses over tea."

I glanced at Kazimir. His jaw was tight, shadows coiling restlessly around his feet—a sure sign he was contemplating violence. Through our bond, I felt his frustration mixing with something else. Fear? No, not quite. More like . . . recognition. As if some part of him already knew what the Alchemist had just revealed.

"We could still kill them," he murmured, low enough that only I could hear.

"We could." I rose from my seat. "But then we'd never know how to fix the ley lines. And you hate not knowing things almost as much as you hate being manipulated."

His lips twitched—not quite a smile, but close. "You know me too well."

"Not well enough, apparently." The words came out sharp, and I saw him flinch, but I couldn't bring myself to feel guilty about it.

The Alchemist led us through corridors I hadn't seen before, past doors marked with symbols that made my eyes water to look at directly. Other villains passed us in the halls—a vampire countess dragging a sack of bones, a merchant whose skin gleamed like molten gold—but they all gave us a wide berth.

"Nothing says 'trustworthy' like secret passages in a villain's lair," Kazimir drawled.

The Alchemist laughed, the sound musical and strangely genuine. "You're one to talk, Lord Blackrose. I've heard rumors about the hidden chambers at Skyspire."

"Just rumors," Kazimir said smoothly.

As we walked, I thought about everything we'd just learned, but some things were more confusing than ever.

That vision at the end of the Heirloom activation had been as real as the stone beneath my feet. The Shadow King's consciousness, ancient and malevolent, wrapped around Kazimir like he *was* the darkness itself. Not a memory. Not an echo. Something that had felt utterly, terrifyingly *present.*

The vision had shown me shards—pieces of the Shadow King that had escaped during the binding. I'd watched them flee into the world, seeking vessels, seeking *hosts.*

But how could the Shadow King be escaping his prison *now* if pieces of him had been loose in the world all along? What did it mean that he was living in the ley lines from beneath Solandris while simultaneously . . . what? Growing? Awakening? Inside my husband?

None of it made sense. And the not-knowing gnawed at me.

I glanced at Kazimir. His jaw was set, shadows trailing behind us.

He didn't remember the vision. Every day I kept silent felt like another stone added to the wall between us, but what was I supposed to do? Blurt it out in front of the Alchemist?

No. This was a conversation for when we were truly alone. If it was a conversation we should have at all—and I still wasn't convinced of that.

In the meantime, we continued walking through villain-infested corridors with a Weaver who already knew too many of our secrets.

"Where exactly are we going?" Kazimir demanded after the third turn down a narrow passage.

The Alchemist's mask caught the light from the wall sconces. "We're almost there."

"There" turned out to be a heavy door at the top of a long spiral staircase. The Alchemist pushed it open, and we emerged onto a landing platform and into the howling wind. "This platform is reserved for the chairs and their flying beasts. It's rarely used these days, as most of us prefer more conventional transportation."

I cast a glance at Kaz, who shrugged. He hadn't known about it either.

The platform jutted out from the Spire like a tongue, with nothing but open air on three sides. We were at the topmost point of the Spire—the god's massive pelvic girdle. I automatically scanned the skies for any sign of Nyx, but saw only churning clouds and the occasional lightning flash in the distance.

The view down was dizzying. The spine plunged directly below us, a chain of glowing vertebrae disappearing into the churning clouds. A steady, low hum vibrated up through the soles of my boots—the chimes from the rib cage far below.

A particularly vicious gust of wind nearly knocked me sideways. Before I could steady myself, Kazimir's magic wrapped around us in a barrier of shadow and will that cut the wind to a gentle breeze.

"Thank you," I said stiffly.

He didn't respond, but I felt his satisfaction through our bond. Smug bastard.

The Alchemist moved to the edge of the platform, their robes somehow unaffected by the wind even before Kaz's spell. "Beautiful, isn't it? In a horrifying, existential-dread-inducing sort of way."

"You didn't bring us here for the view," Kazimir said.

"No." The Alchemist turned to face us. "I brought you here because what I'm about to propose requires you to understand the scope of the problem. And the solution."

"Get to the point," Kazimir growled.

The Alchemist sighed. "Very well. If the Shadow King is allowed to fully infect the ley lines, most of the magic in the world will be lost, and he will have already won. As I said, there are two ways to purify the ley lines now that the Shadow King's corruption has begun to spread. Freeing him completely is obviously out of the question. Which leaves us with option two."

They began to pace along the edge of the platform. "First, you must temporarily reroute part of the ley lines to cut them off from the infection. It will be a stopgap measure only—the ley lines are too ancient and can never truly be separated. But it would buy time for the next part."

"Which is?" I prompted when they paused for dramatic effect.

"To truly purify the ley lines, you must round up the remaining people of heroic bloodline and keep them from Auremar." The Alchemist's voice took on an urgent quality. "Only then can you perform a ritual to force the Shadow King back into his prison."

I felt Kazimir's anger spike through our bond. "That's two tasks," I pointed out, trying to keep things civil. "Saving the ley lines and gathering heroes."

The Alchemist's laugh was musical and slightly unhinged. "No, my dear. Rounding up the heroes *is* the task. I'm simply micromanaging. You can't complete that job if all the ley lines are corrupted before you begin."

"It seems like an awfully big task for one piece of information," Kazimir said. I knew that tone. It usually preceded someone losing a limb.

"What can I say?" The Alchemist spread their hands. "I am also a villain. Did you expect charity?"

A dozen questions crowded my mind, but I started with the most practical. "Why can't we just kill Auremar and stop him that way? It would be easier than finding every person with heroic bloodline scattered across the Western Realms."

"An excellent question." The Alchemist moved closer, and I caught a whiff of their surprisingly floral scent. "If you simply blast King Auremar off the map—which I'm certain you're both capable of—you might damage the carefully balanced magic containing the Shadow King. We don't know the full scope of Auremar's meddling. The prison is already weakened; a sudden, violent magical discharge near its center could shatter it completely. The realm would go from dealing with one mortal tyrant to facing an ancient, unstoppable one."

"So what exactly are you proposing?" I pressed. "How are we supposed to help?"

"The Heirloom cannot only draw power from the ley lines, but also act on them directly. Shape them. Redirect them. Since you have the Heirloom and are now its guardians"—their mask tilted as they studied my face, and I had the uncomfortable feeling they could see right through my glamor to the Heirloom—"and I do hope you'll trust me with the full story one day—rerouting the ley lines falls to you."

"How?" Kazimir's question was sharp, impatient.

The Alchemist walked to the edge of the platform, looking out over the expanse below. "There's a reason I asked you here specifically. Do you know why the Syndicate chose this location for its headquarters?"

"Because villains have a flair for the dramatic?" I suggested.

"Yes," they conceded with a slight nod. "But primarily because of what lies beneath us."

"The nexus," Kazimir said, his voice tight.

"Indeed." The Alchemist turned to face us. "One of the greatest nexuses of ley lines in the Eastern Realm. The very reason this god died here, in fact. It was drawn to the power, consumed too much of it, and . . ." They made an expansive gesture. "Well, you can see the result."

I moved closer to the edge, peering down at the chaotic landscape below. "You want us to isolate this nexus from the 'diseased' portion."

"Precisely!" The Alchemist clapped their hands together. "Using the Heirloom, you can save a huge chunk of the network of ley lines. It will give you enough power to work with while you complete the larger task. Lord Blackrose has his runes to maintain his magic, and you have your innate bloodline, but there's no doubt access to pure ley lines will make you both exponentially stronger."

I processed this information, turning it over in my mind like a puzzle piece that didn't quite fit. Something was missing. I folded my arms. "And where exactly are we supposed to find these heroic bloodlines? Auremar's been hunting them down and sacrificing them, remember?"

"Not all of them," the Alchemist said. "Many have gone into hiding. Others don't even know what they are. You'll need to find them and, er, *convince* them to help—and bring them to the nexus in Solandris."

The task would be enormous. "And what about the inhabited ley lines themselves? Won't the Shadow King continue to spread while we're running around kidnapping heroes?"

"Most certainly. That's why we need to start with the nexus beneath the Spire," the Alchemist explained. "To temporarily prevent him from getting this far while you use these ley lines for your magic."

"Do you know what makes me so powerful?" I asked suddenly. "My bloodline, I mean. Why my magic resonates so strongly with Kazimir's?"

The Alchemist went very still. For the first time since we'd met them, they seemed caught off guard.

"No," they said after a moment.

Cold pricked behind my eyes, sharp and undeniable—my truth-sense. "You're lying." I stepped forward, ignoring Kazimir's warning touch on my arm. "Why won't you tell me?"

The Alchemist's shoulders sagged slightly. "Would it make any difference if I did?"

"Yes."

"Then I won't tell you." They held up a hand before I could protest. "Because I am uncertain, and *that* is the truth. I have theories. Suspicions. But nothing concrete enough to share. Speaking them aloud might do more harm than good."

My truth-sense confirmed it—they genuinely believed withholding the information was better. But that didn't make it any less frustrating.

"Theories about what?" I pressed.

The Alchemist turned back to look at the dead god. "About why your blood sings with power that should have faded generations ago. About why the Heirloom responds to you in ways it shouldn't. About why King Auremar was so desperate to obtain you specifically, when there are others with heroic bloodline he could have claimed more easily."

I nodded. "Tell me."

"When you've saved the nexus and begun gathering the others, perhaps I'll share my theories, assuming we're both still alive at that point." The Alchemist's voice was gentle but firm. "Consider it motivation."

I wanted to scream. Or set something on fire. Preferably the Alchemist.

But before I could act on either impulse, they turned and headed back toward the door. "Shall we discuss the specifics of the ritual? I assume you'll want to attempt it soon. Time is, after all, of the essence. And the Shadow King is spreading faster through the web every day."

I looked at Kazimir, seeing my own frustration reflected in his gray eyes. What choice did we have? The world was ending, one ley line at a time.

And apparently, we were the only ones who could stop it.

The Alchemist left us on the platform, assuming we would follow. As soon as we were alone, Kaz's shoulders sagged slightly, as if he'd been holding himself rigid through sheer force of will.

"Kaz?" I touched his arm, concerned.

He shook his head. "I'm fine. Just . . . processing."

But he wasn't fine. I could feel it through our bond—something dark and cold slithering beneath his stoic exterior.

"We haven't been able to manipulate the ley lines," I said finally. "Not really. Every time we've tried with the Heirloom, it's been—"

"Resistant," he finished, his jaw tight. "I know."

"So how are we supposed to reroute an entire nexus when we can barely get the Heirloom to respond to simple commands?"

Kazimir placed a hand on the door. "The Alchemist claims they have a ritual. One specifically designed for this task."

"And you trust them?"

"No." He met my eyes, and I saw the same helpless frustration I felt reflected back at me. "If we do nothing, the ley lines are gone forever. If we try and fail—"

"We might make it worse," I finished softly.

He was quiet for a moment. "There's still the matter of performing this ritual without revealing that the Heirloom is currently fused to your skull."

I glanced toward the door. "I think they already know."

Kazimir's eyes narrowed. "What makes you say that?"

"The way they looked at me when they mentioned the Heirloom. That comment about hoping we'd trust them with the full story 'one day.'" I touched my temple reflexively. "They're too clever not to have figured it out."

"Brilliant." Kazimir's tone was dry. "So we're attempting a dangerous ritual with someone who knows our greatest secret and who we have absolutely no reason to trust."

"When you put it that way, it sounds like a terrible idea."

"It *is* a terrible idea." His expression was grim. "But we don't have a choice, do we?"

I sighed. "On the bright side, we can tell Griffin we know what happened to the ley lines."

30

Say the Wrong Thing Repeatedly

(It's a Special Talent)

Kazimir

We'd spent the rest of the day listening to the Alchemist drone on about ley line theory, ritual components, and the precise magical frequencies required to isolate a nexus. Under normal circumstances, I'd have found it fascinating.

Today, I'd barely heard a word.

The whispers had started again—faint at first, like the hiss of wind through dead leaves, but growing steadily louder as the day wore on. An insistent scratching at the back of my skull.

As we walked back to our apartment, Arabella and I maintained a careful distance from each other. We hadn't spoken a word about last night. We'd been perfectly civil in front of the Alchemist—the picture of Dark Lord and lady, united in purpose if not in heart.

But now, alone in the corridor, each step echoed too loudly, each breath felt too shallow. Arabella walked beside me, close enough to touch but miles away in every way that mattered.

I should apologize. I knew that. Last night at the Gilded Gallows, I'd crossed a line. The Twilight Wine had heightened my senses, my desire, my possessiveness—but it hadn't robbed me of my faculties. I'd known exactly what I was doing when I tried to compel Arabella to stay behind while I pursued Pip.

She defies you. She will always defy you.

The whisper slithered through my mind, cold and venomous. I shook my head, trying to dislodge it.

At our apartment, Arabella headed straight for our suite. I followed her inside, steeling myself for the conversation we needed to have.

Before I could utter a word, Arabella strode to the balcony's double doors and flung them open. Cold wind rushed in, carrying the scent of ozone and distant rain. For one wild moment, I thought she might be planning to throw me off the balcony.

Then Nyx swooped down from the darkening sky, her massive form barely fitting through the doorway. The shadow dragon's liquid silver eyes fixed on me with unmistakable hostility as it lumbered past me, heading straight for our bedroom.

"What's she doing?" I asked, the first words I'd spoken directly to Arabella in hours.

"Going to bed," Arabella replied, her voice neutral. Too neutral.

I followed her into the bedroom just in time to see Nyx sprawl across our bed—our very large bed, but not large enough for a dragon and two people. The beast stretched luxuriously, her wings unfurling to touch the walls before settling back against her sides. Her bulk took up nearly the entire surface, leaving room for maybe one small person to squeeze in beside her.

The message couldn't have been clearer if Arabella had painted it on the wall in blood.

"Off," I commanded, pointing to the floor.

Nyx opened one silver eye, regarded me with reptilian disdain, then closed it again. A low growl rumbled from her throat as she sank deeper into the pillows, her claws shredding the silk with deliberate malice. The same silk sheets I'd been hoping, in my more optimistic fantasies, to share only with Arabella tonight.

The beast mocks you, as does its mistress.

I rubbed the runes along my collarbone as a wave of frustration washed through me. Everything felt louder than usual—my still-lingering headache from a day spent planning a complicated ley line ritual, the rustle of Nyx's wings, the faint rush of blood in my ears. If I closed my eyes, the new swirl of half words in my skull threatened to drown out my own thoughts. I tried to focus on the sound of my breathing.

"Arabella, about last night—"

She turned to face me, arms crossed. The soft glow from the enchanted lamps caught in her golden hair, creating a halo effect that belied the steel in her gaze. "Don't say it unless you actually mean it."

I did mean it. Mostly. The part of me that wasn't still seething with frustration, that wasn't being needled by the dark whispers, genuinely regretted my actions.

"I shouldn't have tried to compel you," I said, the words coming out stiffer than I'd intended. "It was . . . inappropriate."

Arabella's eyebrows rose. *"Inappropriate?"*

"What would you prefer I call it?" I snapped, then immediately regretted it. This wasn't going well.

"I'd prefer you understand what you did," she hissed. "You were ready to rip Pip apart for betraying Skyspire, but you don't see how you betrayed me?"

I ran a hand through my hair, tugging at the roots in frustration. "It's not the same thing."

"Isn't it?" She stepped closer, her hazel eyes flashing. "You used your power against me, Kaz."

Arabella's resistance to my dominion magic was one of the first things that had intrigued me about her. Trying to use my compulsion on her was a low, dirty trick I hadn't attempted since the day we'd met. It was a fundamental violation of the strange, unspoken terms of our truce, our partnership, our . . . whatever this was.

The whisper grew louder. I pressed my fingers to my temples, trying to focus. A corner of my thoughts insisted I should just double down, push her to forgive me, reclaim the upper hand.

Another, darker voice whispered that she was the one who should be begging me. The violent hiss of that second voice startled me.

"I was trying to protect you," I said, the excuse sounding hollow even to my own ears.

"From a sixteen-year-old boy who might not even have been there?" She yanked the braid loose from her hair with enough force to make me wince. "Or were you protecting your ego from the possibility that Pip got away?"

"Fine," I conceded. "I wanted to catch him. He betrayed us, Arabella. He let the Hero's Guild into our home. Sims *died* because of him."

"And I wanted to help you catch him!" She took a step toward me and pointed her finger at my chest. "But instead of treating me like a partner, you tried to force me to stay behind like a child."

I had no good answer for that. She was right. In that moment of rage and fear—fear that Pip would escape, fear that Arabella might be hurt—I had reached for the easiest solution. Control. Dominance. The very things I'd sworn I wouldn't use against her.

How dare she question you.

"Kazimir, you commanded your shadow warriors to watch over me like I was some prized jewel."

"You are prized," I snapped, voice rising despite myself. The shadowy voice inside my head hissed encouragement. "Don't you get that? Why do you think I'm with you?"

"Why *are* you with me?" she asked.

The question caught me off guard. "Why am I—"

"Why are you with *me*, Kaz, and not some vapid princess?"

I blinked, momentarily thrown. I thought back to that day months ago when I'd chosen her from a stack of candidates. A simple sketch had captured something in her expression—mischief dancing at the corners of her mouth, intelligence burning in her eyes. The reports of her setting suitors on fire had sealed the deal.

She'd defied me from the moment we met, and I'd never been so enchanted.

Tell her she is nothing but a tool for your power.

"I like you," I said, ignoring the whisper. "And you're sexy."

I knew that was the wrong answer even as my stupid mouth supplied it. The temperature in the room dropped ten degrees. Not literally—though with our combined magical potential, that was always a possibility—but emotionally. Arabella's face went carefully blank, a sure sign I'd fucked up royally.

"That's it?" she asked, her voice deceptively light. "You kidnapped me, married me, and bound our lives together because I'm *likable* and *sexy*?"

Put that way, it did sound rather thin.

"What do you want me to say, Arabella?" I spread my hands. The dragon was now emitting a low, threatening rumble. "That I was drawn to your defiance? Your strength? The way you never back down, even when facing a Dark Lord who could snap your neck with a thought?"

"I want you to tell me the truth," she said. "All of it."

The truth. Such a simple request, and yet so impossible to fulfill. How could I tell her that from the moment I saw her, something in me recognized her? That when she stood before me on that road, refusing to cower, I felt as if I'd been waiting my entire life for someone who would look at me and see not just the monster, but the man?

Weakness. This is weakness. She makes you weak.

"You're my wife," I said, the word feeling inadequate for what she had become to me.

She stepped into my space, glaring up at me. "Do you feel anything for me at all?"

"Of course I do!" I roared. "Do you think I'd let just anyone see me collapse in a heap of agony? Or tell them my deepest secrets? I've killed men for looking at their reflections in my polished boots, Arabella. You have turned my entire world upside down, and you're asking me if I *feel* something?"

"Then what is it?" she demanded, tears welling in her eyes, which only made me angrier. "What is it you feel? Say it!"

I reached for her, but she stepped back.

The words she wanted—needed—to hear lodged in my throat. Those three words. The ones I'd never said to anyone, not even my mother. Especially not my mother, whose idea of "love" involved carving runes into her son's bones.

Love is a lie. A trick. A weapon to be used against you. The whisper was almost a shout now, the voice disturbingly familiar. I pressed my palms against my eyes, trying to block it out.

"You can't say it either," I pointed out, deflecting.

"I fed my life force into your precious artifact!" Her voice cracked. "I literally poured pieces of my soul into that crown to save you. If that's not—" She stopped herself. "What more proof do you need?"

"Words," I snarled, closing the distance between us and lowering my voice. "Just three simple words that you seem as incapable of saying as I am. They don't matter."

The moment the sentence left my mouth, I knew I'd made a catastrophic error. Arabella went very, very still. Then, without a word, she walked to the wardrobe, pulled out my cloak, and threw it at my chest.

"Get out," she said quietly.

"Arabella—"

"Get. Out." Her magic flared, the air around her crackling with power. "If the words don't matter, then neither does this conversation."

Kill her, the voice screamed. *Kill her kill her KILL HER—*

I grabbed the cloak, my hands shaking with the effort of not listening to the violent urges. Maybe distance was exactly what I needed right now. Before I did something truly unforgivable.

"Fine," I said, slinging the cloak around my shoulders. "Enjoy your night with the lizard."

I left without looking back, closing the door with deliberate softness when what I wanted was to blast it off its hinges.

The apartment had other bedrooms, of course. But I'd be damned if I'd wake Marlowe to make up another bed, or let anyone know that the fearsome Dark Lord had been kicked out of his own bedchamber by his wife, who preferred to sleep with a pink dragon.

Lightning flickered occasionally beyond the tall windows, illuminating the bizarre outlines of bone archways. This was the God Spire. I, Kazimir Blackrose, Chair of Dominion, was not supposed to skulk on a sofa like a cast-off dog.

Fitting, though, muttered that hateful whisper in my head. *So weak. Why do we grovel? She should kneel.*

"Shut. Up," I whispered fiercely into the empty hallway. Excellent. Now I was scolding the voices in my head. My runes ached with the effort of fighting them.

After some frustrated wandering, I found myself in the small library, trying to lose myself in texts about agricultural magic and theoretical mathematics—anything unrelated to my current disaster of a life. But the words swam before my eyes, rearranging themselves into accusations.

Why are you with ME, Kaz?

Because you're brilliant. Because you match me in ways no one else ever has. Because when you smile, it feels like sunlight breaking through storm clouds, and I don't even care how cliche that sounds.

Because I would burn the world to keep you safe, but I have no idea how to repair what I've broken between us.

Three little words. Was it really so difficult?

Yes, it was. Because the last time I'd heard those words, they'd been followed by the bite of a knife against my skin, the searing pain of magic being carved into my bones.

I love you, my son. This will make you strong.

I pressed my palms against my eyes until I saw stars. My mother's voice—*her exact cadence*—echoing up from whatever pit I'd buried it in, dragged to the surface by the same restless thing clawing at my skull all evening. The smell of blood and burning flesh as she carved each rune. Her soft humming as she worked, as if mutilating her child was no different from embroidering a tapestry.

The night passed in a haze of restless pacing, failed attempts at reading, and the constant, maddening whispers. By the time dawn broke, I was exhausted, my temper frayed to the breaking point.

The smell of cooking food drew me to the kitchen. I was utterly unsurprised to see Sebastian standing at the stove, expertly flipping the most perfect pancakes I'd ever seen. Griffin sat at the table, watching with undisguised admiration. Thorne leaned against the counter, a mug of something steaming in his massive hands.

They all looked up when I entered, then quickly looked away again. It was painfully obvious they knew about the fight. They'd probably heard the shouting. Villains have excellent hearing.

"Good morning, Lord Blackrose," Sebastian said, his voice carefully neutral. "I hope you don't mind. I thought I'd prepare breakfast to thank you for your assistance the other night."

I grunted in acknowledgment, pouring myself a cup of tea. I'd almost forgotten about the incident outside the Gallows. It felt like a lifetime ago, not two nights past.

"These pancakes are incredible," Griffin said around a mouthful. "How did you get them so light?"

Sebastian smiled. "Family secret."

I tuned out their conversation, focusing on my tea. The kitchen door opened, and Arabella walked in, her hair damp from a bath. Our eyes met briefly before she looked away, her expression carefully blank.

"Morning," she said to the room at large.

Sebastian's face lit up. "I've made breakfast to thank your husband for saving my life the other night. Those ruffians would have done far worse if he hadn't intervened."

Arabella's head snapped up. "What ruffians?"

Sebastian looked between us, suddenly uncertain. A hint of color rose in his cheeks. "Five of them cornered me outside the Gallows. Lord Blackrose intervened. Even spared their lives when I asked, though I think he broke most of their bones first. I would have told you when I returned, but you seemed preoccupied."

The silence that followed could have been bottled and sold as a weapon.

I watched the information sink in—Arabella's expression hardened, her eyes flashing with renewed anger. So I'd spared the thugs at Sebastian's request, but had tried to compel *her*? The comparison wasn't fair—the situations were entirely different—but I could see how it looked to her.

Without a word, she turned on her heel and swept out of the kitchen.

"Did I say something wrong?" Sebastian asked, frowning.

I ignored him and followed Arabella into the hallway, catching up to her in three long strides. "Arabella, wait."

She kept walking.

"Would you just stop and listen?" I reached for her arm, then thought better of it, letting my hand fall back to my side. "I'm trying to apologize."

She whirled to face me, her eyes blazing. "Are you? Because it sounds like you're trying to justify what you did."

"I'm not," I insisted, though part of me—the part being needled by the whispers—wanted to do exactly that. "I was wrong. I shouldn't have tried to compel you. It was a breach of trust, and I'm sorry."

The words were right, but my tone was all wrong—stiff, formal, lacking the genuine remorse I actually felt beneath the whispers' influence. Arabella could tell.

"You don't mean that," she said quietly. "Not really."

Before I could respond, she turned and left.

I watched her go, frustration building in my chest. "Shouldn't we be having angry hate sex right now?" I called after her, the words escaping before I could stop them.

Arabella raised her hand in a rude gesture before disappearing down the stairs.

A small squeak drew my attention to the corner, where Thorne stood frozen, a look of absolute horror on his face. He turned and practically ran in the opposite direction, no doubt wishing he'd never witnessed this particular marital spat.

Somewhere behind my temples, that gruesome voice rumbled: *Let her go. Let them all go. You need no one.*

I pressed both palms to my forehead. "Thorne!"

He stopped mid-flight, shoulders hunching. When he turned back, his expression was carefully neutral—the look of someone trying very hard not to think about what he'd just overheard.

"My lord?" His voice came out slightly strangled.

"The boy. Pip." I stalked toward him. "Any sign of him?"

Thorne's relief at the subject change was palpable. "Nothing yet, my lord. The shadow warriors are sweeping every level like you ordered, and Spire security is checking every room, closet, and crawlspace." He paused, jaw tightening. "We've also been monitoring all departures, as per your command that no one leaves until their transports are thoroughly inspected."

"And?" I could already tell from his expression that this hadn't gone smoothly.

"There have been . . . grumbles, my lord. Complaints about overreach, delays in important business." Thorne's mouth twisted. "A few tried to leave anyway. The Merchant Prince of the Southern Isles was particularly vocal about his 'diplomatic immunity.'"

"Was he now?" A cold smile curved my lips. "And how did that work out for him?"

"He's currently enjoying the hospitality of the Spire's holding cells while his ship is being *very* thoroughly searched." Thorne's own grim satisfaction showed through. "The shadow warriors found three separate smuggling compartments, though no sign of our missing servant."

I nodded slowly, processing this. As Chair of Dominion, I had the authority to lock down the entire Spire—but that didn't mean the other powerful entities here had to like it. Every hour that passed with no answers would erode my position further, give my enemies more ammunition.

I shoved the thought away. "Keep searching. If Pip is still in the Spire, I want him found."

Thorne bowed and departed with considerably more haste than dignity, leaving me alone in the corridor with nothing but my spiraling thoughts and that damned voice in my head.

I let out a final, near-feral snarl, and stormed off in the opposite direction from Arabella, my cloak billowing behind me. At least I could always count on a good dramatic exit, even if everything else in my life was going to hell.

31

Make Decisions While Angry

(Your Best Ideas Happen This Way)

Arabella

I stormed out of the apartment, my feet carrying me faster than my thoughts could catch up. The God Spire's corridors were mercifully empty at this hour. Most villains, it seemed, weren't morning people. I passed a few bleary-eyed servants and one vampire who hissed at me before realizing who I was and scurrying away.

I slowed down. My fingers trailed along the smooth, polished bone of the walls as I walked, feeling the faint hum of ancient magic beneath my touch. I had no destination in mind. All I knew was that I needed to be away from Kazimir and his half-hearted apologies. Away from the memory of his voice asking if we should be having "angry hate sex" right now. Of all the idiotic, insensitive, completely *Kazimir* things to say.

Men. Dark lords. Whatever.

The worst part was that some traitorous piece of me had briefly considered it. Angry sex with Kazimir was . . . well, memorable, to say the least. But no. I had standards, and apparently, I needed to remind myself of them more often.

The Heirloom pushed against my skull. It seemed to sense my agitation, sending cool waves of energy down my spine. I paused at a window overlooking the impossible architecture of the Spire. Little creatures that resembled winged mice had built a nest on the outside window ledge, their tiny claws scratching against the bone as they wove together bits of stolen silk and parchment.

"Stupid, arrogant, emotionally stunted villain," I muttered.

A passing goblin in a tailored suit gave me a wide berth, clearly assuming I was talking to him. I ignored him, too consumed by my own thoughts.

The truth was, beneath my anger, I understood Kazimir better than I wanted to admit. His childhood had been a nightmare of abuse disguised as love. His mother had carved runes into his bones while telling him it was necessary. His father had been a tyrant that Kaz had disposed of himself. Of course he'd be wary of admitting feelings, of making himself vulnerable.

But understanding didn't erase the hurt. It didn't change the fact that he'd tried to compel me.

And it didn't change the fact that some childish, wounded part of me needed to hear the words from him.

Our ritual with the Alchemist wasn't scheduled until later. I had hours to kill, and spending them anywhere near Kazimir seemed like a recipe for disaster—or at least property damage.

What I needed was a distraction. Something productive to do with all this restless energy. To help me regain control over at least one aspect of my life. I could explore the Spire, perhaps visit the infamous Academia of Malice that Griffin had mentioned. Since he no longer had urgent Heirloom research, he was taking Sebastian with him there today. But I didn't want to be around people I knew.

I could go shopping in the bizarre marketplace I'd glimpsed on our arrival. I could find a quiet corner and practice my shadow magic.

Or . . .

Two nights ago, on our way to the Gilded Gallows, we'd passed a small shop that looked different from the others. The sign had caught my attention—a simple wooden board with a painted eye, half-closed, and the words "Mnemosyne's Memories" beneath it.

A memory mage.

For weeks, I'd been haunted by the knowledge that pieces of my past had been stolen from me. That somewhere in my mind lurked the truth about what had happened the night my mother died trying to protect me. That night had ended with me locked in a tower for a year.

What if I could get those memories back?

I hesitated, knowing what Kazimir would say if I told him my plan. He'd insist on coming with me. He'd hover, protective and possessive, questioning the mage's every move. Or worse, he'd try to forbid it entirely, citing the dangers of memory magic.

And he'd be right, a small voice in my head pointed out. Memory magic was notoriously unpredictable, especially when undoing the work of other mages.

But I was tired of pieces of myself being locked away, controlled by others. First my father, then Auremar, and now, in a different way, Kazimir.

Decision made, I turned and headed for the nearest lift that would take me down to the lower levels where the shops were located.

The lift was a strange contraption—a cage of bone and metal that descended through the Spire, offering glimpses of various levels as it passed. I counted fifteen floors before the doors opened onto an enormous, bustling marketplace.

The central atrium of the God Spire was a marvel of twisted architecture. What had once been the rib cage of some enormous entity now formed a cathedral like space, with bone arches soaring hundreds of feet overhead. Tiered galleries had been carved into the ribs themselves, connected by spiraling staircases and swaying rope bridges, each level crammed with shops, stalls, and businesses. The central space below remained open, a vast gathering place for the Spire's eclectic inhabitants.

Unlike the upper levels with their polished elegance, this area had a grittier feel. Vendors hawked everything from enchanted trinkets to questionable potions. The air smelled of incense, exotic spices, and something metallic that I chose not to identify.

I wound my way through the first sections, past stalls selling cursed jewelry and bottled nightmares. A vendor tried to interest me in "genuine demon tears," but I brushed past without stopping. I didn't spare much thought for wandering alone through the Spire's underbelly. Let someone try something. I'd been itching for a fight.

It took me nearly an hour of searching, backtracking, and asking careful questions before I found the shop again. Mnemosyne's Memories was tucked between a shop for a soul launderer and another called "Ethical Necromancy Services," which seemed like an oxymoron. The contrast was striking—while its neighbors boasted flashy displays and aggressive advertising, the memory mage's establishment was understated, almost serene. The windows were frosted glass etched with delicate patterns of intertwining vines, offering no glimpse of the interior. And the wooden door contained beautiful carvings of more vines, flowers, and potion bottles.

It was . . . cozy.

For a moment, I hesitated again. Was I really going to do this? Without telling Kazimir? I pushed the thought away. Yes, he'd taught me shadow magic, helped me understand the darker aspects of my power. But this wasn't about combat or necromancy or any of the skills he'd shared. This was about my own mind, my own history.

He'd try to stop me, I was certain of it. He'd list all the ways it could go wrong, all the dangers of tampering with locked memories. And the worst part was, he'd probably be right. But this was something I needed to do, with or without his support.

Besides, I was still furious with him, and imagining the hypothetical argument with my husband only made me more determined.

With a deep breath, I pushed open the door and stepped inside.

The interior of the shop was nothing like I'd expected. Instead of the dark, incense-heavy atmosphere typical of magical establishments in the God Spire, Mnemosyne's Memories was bright and airy. Tall windows along the back wall—windows I was certain weren't visible from the outside—let in streams of sunlight that illuminated the space. Shelves lined the walls, filled with books, plants, and small, curious objects that shimmered with inner light.

From a doorway at the back of the shop emerged a woman who seemed as out of place in the Spire as a butterfly in a nest of hornets.

She was middle-aged, with laugh lines around her eyes and silver streaking her dark hair, which was pulled back in a simple braid. Her clothing was practical—loose linen pants and a flowing shirt, cinched at the waist with a blue sash embroidered with silver symbols. But it was her smile that caught me off guard—open, genuine, lacking the predatory edge that characterized most interactions in this place.

"Welcome," she said, her voice warm and slightly accented. "I am Mnemosyne. How may I assist you today?"

I stepped farther into the shop. Despite the pleasant atmosphere, my instincts were on high alert. Nothing in the God Spire was as benign as it appeared.

"I'm interested in recovering some memories," I said vaguely. "Ones that may have been deliberately suppressed or erased."

Mnemosyne's expression didn't change, but something in her eyes sharpened. "I see. Please, have a seat." She gestured to a small seating area near the windows, where comfortable chairs surrounded a low table. "Would you care for tea?"

I nodded, taking a seat while keeping my back to the wall and a clear view of both the door and the woman.

Mnemosyne busied herself with a small kettle that heated instantly at her touch. As she prepared the tea, she spoke without looking at me. "Suppressed memories are delicate things, Lady Blackrose. Like butterflies with damaged wings—handle them too roughly, and they crumble to dust."

I stiffened. "You know who I am."

She smiled, bringing over a tray with two steaming cups. "The Dark Lady is not easily mistaken for anyone else. Besides, news travels quickly in the Spire. Your arrival with Lord Blackrose has been the subject of much speculation."

I should have been prepared for this. Our arrival had hardly been a secret—we'd said it was our honeymoon, after all. I accepted the offered cup, inhaling the fragrant steam. It smelled of mint and something wild and unfamiliar.

"It's mountain thyme," Mnemosyne said, noting my curiosity. "Good for clarity of thought."

After checking for poison or other enchantment, I took a cautious sip. It tasted pleasant enough, though I doubted its efficacy for my particular problem. "I need to recover specific memories," I said, setting down the cup. "Memories from when I was a child. They were locked away by powerful mages."

"May I ask why?" Mnemosyne settled into the chair across from me, her gaze direct but not intrusive.

I hesitated. How much should I reveal? The memory mage was a stranger, and in the Spire, information was currency. But I needed her help, and some level of honesty might be necessary to obtain it.

"They may have important bearing on my future," I said carefully. "On decisions I need to make."

Mnemosyne nodded, seemingly satisfied with my partial answer. "And these memories—do you have any sense of what they contain? Any fragments or impressions that remain?"

I closed my eyes, trying to reach for the elusive shadows that had haunted me since my father's confession. "I believe they involve my mother's death and the events leading up to it. I was told she died of illness when I was eight, but recently I learned that she died protecting me when I was fourteen, and that I witnessed it."

When I opened my eyes, Mnemosyne was watching me with a mixture of compassion and concern. "Such memories would be deeply traumatic for a child," she said. "If they were indeed suppressed by magic rather than your own mind's protective mechanisms, the process of retrieving them will not be simple or painless."

"I don't care about pain," I said, perhaps too quickly. At her raised eyebrow, I amended, "I mean, I'm not afraid of it. These memories are important."

"Important enough to risk madness?" she asked, her tone gentle but serious.

A chill ran down my spine. "Madness?"

Mnemosyne set down her cup with a soft clink. "Lady Blackrose, magic cannot simply be 'snapped' to restore your memories, especially if they were deliberately locked by a complicated mind-suppression spell. Assuming the sorcerer was powerful—and given what you've told me, I must assume they were—the cost of forcibly ripping those blocks from your mind is high. Madness is a common side effect, though not because of the spell itself."

"Then why?" I asked, though I suspected I already knew the answer.

"Because the rush of possibly traumatic memories can be devastating to the psyche," she explained. "Imagine experiencing the most horrific moment of your life with the full emotional impact of your child self, but with none of the protective distance that time normally provides. It can shatter the mind."

I reached out with my truth-sense. She wasn't lying or exaggerating. She genuinely believed what she was saying.

But I also sensed a certain reservation, as if she wasn't telling me everything.

"There are other methods, though, aren't there?" I pressed. "Less catastrophic ones."

A flicker of surprise crossed her features. "You have a keen perception, Lady Blackrose." Mnemosyne sighed, leaning back in her chair. "There are gentler approaches, yes. Ways to coax the memories back rather than tearing down the walls that contain them. But they require time, patience, and a willingness to face what you might find piece by piece, rather than all at once."

Time was something I didn't have in abundance. Not with the Shadow King spreading through the ley lines, Auremar hunting those of heroic bloodline, and the fragile state of my marriage to a man who couldn't say three simple words.

"How long would this gentler approach take?" I asked.

"Weeks, at minimum. Possibly months."

I shook my head. "Too long. I need these memories now."

"May I ask why the urgency?" Mnemosyne's gaze was penetrating, as if she could see through my carefully constructed facade to the turmoil beneath.

I chose my words with care. "As I said before, there are events unfolding that may be connected to what happened that night. Understanding my past may be crucial to navigating my future."

After studying me a long moment, she nodded. "Very well. There is a middle path—a potion that will lower the barriers between your conscious mind and the suppressed memories, allowing them to surface gradually over the course of a few days rather than in a single, overwhelming rush. It's still risky, but less so than a sudden breaking of the spell."

Hope flared in my chest. "And this potion—you can make it?"

"I can," she confirmed. "But I must warn you, Lady Blackrose—even with this method, you'll be vulnerable while the memories surface. Disoriented, possibly experiencing both past and present simultaneously. It would be wise to have someone you trust nearby, someone who can ground you if the memories become too overwhelming."

Kazimir's face flashed in my mind, but I quickly pushed the thought away. No. Not him. Not when things between us were so strained.

"I'll manage," I said firmly.

Mnemosyne looked skeptical but didn't argue. "The potion will take time to prepare—until tomorrow, at least. And I'll need something from you to attune it properly."

"What kind of something?" I asked, wariness creeping back into my voice.

"A lock of hair is traditional," she said with a small smile. "Though a drop of blood would work better, given the nature of the spell we're trying to counteract."

Blood magic. Of course. It often came back to blood with the truly powerful spells. I hesitated only briefly before extending my hand. "Blood, then."

Mnemosyne produced a small silver knife from within her sash. The blade gleamed in the sunlight as she carefully pricked my finger, catching the welling drop of blood in a tiny crystal vial. The moment the blood touched the crystal, it began to glow with a soft golden light—the signature of my heroic bloodline.

Mnemosyne's eyes widened slightly. "Fascinating," she murmured. "Your blood is unusually potent."

"So I've been told," I said drily, thinking of Kazimir's experiments with my blood that had revealed the fortyfold amplification effect. "Will that be a problem?"

"No," she said, sealing the vial with a cork. "If anything, it will make the potion more effective. Return tomorrow morning, and it will be ready."

I rose to leave, but Mnemosyne caught my wrist gently. "Lady Blackrose," she said, her voice low and serious. "Whatever you discover in these memories—be prepared for it to change how you see not just your past, but your present as well. The truth has a way of reshaping everything it touches."

A shiver ran down my spine, but I nodded. How could anyone truly prepare for the unveiling of a past they didn't remember? "You're not what I expected to find in the God Spire."

Mnemosyne laughed lightly. "The Spire attracts all sorts, Lady Blackrose. Not everyone here deals in souls and shadows. Some of us simply provide services that might be frowned upon elsewhere."

As I turned to go, Mnemosyne called after me. "Lady Blackrose."

I paused at the door, looking back over my shoulder.

She hesitated, as if weighing her next words carefully. "Remember what I said about having someone you trust nearby. The mind can play tricks when confronted with long-buried truths."

I nodded in acknowledgment but made no promises. Trust was in short supply these days, especially after Kazimir's betrayal at the Gilded Gallows. And the last thing I needed was him hovering over me, trying to protect me from my own memories.

No, this was something I would face alone. Whatever horrors awaited me in the locked chambers of my mind, I would confront them on my own terms. After all, I was Arabella Blackrose, Dark Lady of Skyspire, wife to the most feared villain in the Western Realms.

And I was done letting others decide what truths I was allowed to know.

32

Realize You're in Love

(at the Exact Moment You Become Her Greatest Threat)

Kazimir

The skull of a dead god made for an interesting conversation piece.

Even for me—a man who has witnessed demons tear themselves apart and watched a necromancer puppeteer an entire village with nothing but a flute and some creative finger movements—the sight was impressive.

"Do you think it can still hear us?" Arabella asked, tilting her head for a better look. We'd arrived early to the ritual chamber so I could assess the space without the Alchemist's watchful presence.

"If it can, I imagine it's thoroughly bored by now." The massive cranium hung inverted from the ceiling of the chamber, its eye sockets large enough to sail a ship through. Teeth the size of pillars formed a jagged crown around the top of the room. Whatever this entity had been in life, death had not diminished its grandeur. More importantly, it was the closest we could get to the metaphysical ley line nexus without actually swimming through solid rock. "Centuries of villain monologues and dark rituals. We're probably just background noise at this point."

Arabella didn't laugh, but I caught the slight twitch at the corner of her mouth.

She hadn't told me where she'd disappeared to after breakfast, and I hadn't asked. Now, I sensed a strange calm in her—not the brittle peace of suppressed anger, but something more settled. Whatever she'd needed—air, space, or just time away from my spectacular failure at emotional intelligence—it seemed to have helped.

I caught her glancing at me from the corner of her eye, her gaze lingering on my jaw. I'd forgotten to shave and hadn't remembered until we were halfway here. I never forgot. My appearance was as much a weapon as my magic, carefully cultivated to project power and control. The Dark Lord didn't have stubble unless he chose to have stubble.

But after a night wrestling with those damned whispers in my head, with the memory of trying to compel my own wife, personal grooming had been the last thing on my mind.

When Arabella's eyes traced the line of my stubble again, I allowed myself an arrogant smirk. At least she'd never minded the rougher look. If anything, the way her pupils dilated slightly suggested she more than didn't mind it.

Small victories.

"I didn't ask," I said quietly. "Are you up for this?"

She arched one perfect eyebrow. "Are you?"

Classic Arabella. Never backing down, never admitting weakness. Whatever else lay broken between us, her competitive nature remained intact. She'd focus on the task at hand because failing wasn't in her vocabulary any more than it was in mine.

"I'll take that as a yes," I murmured.

"The Alchemist is late," Arabella observed, examining the runes we'd prepared yesterday. Her fingers traced the edges of a particularly complex sigil.

"Dramatic timing," I said. "Can't have the mysterious advisor arriving early like some eager apprentice."

The temperature dropped suddenly, and the Alchemist materialized from the shadows as if they'd been there all along.

"Shall we begin?" they asked without preamble. "The corruption spreads even as we speak."

I bit back a sarcastic response about their tardiness. We needed this to work, to buy time to gather the other heroic bloodlines. As much as it galled me to follow someone else's plan, the alternative was watching the Shadow King's essence poison all magic in the realm.

And I didn't need any competition for world domination.

The ritual itself was straightforward enough, though not something I'd ever attempted before. It was an ancient ritual that the Alchemist insisted the Weavers had guarded for centuries. Because of its simplicity and elegance, I had hope that Arabella and I could master it even with our problems with the Heirloom.

We'd spent yesterday preparing the runes and enchanting the chamber. Today was about execution. I gestured to the runic circle we'd carved into the bone floor. "I still say we could have used more conventional binding symbols in the third quadrant."

"Conventional thinking is what allowed this problem to fester," the Alchemist replied smoothly. "Sometimes one must think like a god to fix what gods have broken."

Arabella moved to her position across from me, the circle between us.

"Remember," the Alchemist said, taking their place at the edge of the circle, "you're not trying to destroy or redirect the ley lines permanently. Simply convince them to take a detour. The nexus beneath us connects to all major confluences in the realm. If you can shift the connection between here and Solandris, the corruption will be isolated."

"Convince them," I repeated drily. "Because ley lines are known for being reasonable."

"Would you prefer I said 'wrestle them into submission through sheer magical dominance'?" the Alchemist asked. "I thought that went without saying, given present company."

Arabella snorted.

I shot her a look, but there was amusement dancing in her eyes.

"Whenever you're ready," the Alchemist prompted. If they wondered how we were going to perform this ritual without the Heirloom present, they didn't ask. Arabella had been correct—they already knew it was fused to her in some way. Perhaps, if all went well later, they would have ideas about removing it.

I placed my hands on the carved symbols, feeling the familiar burn of my runes responding to the magical current. Across the circle, Arabella mirrored my position. The Heirloom pulsed once, twice, syncing with our heartbeats.

The incantation was older than most kingdoms, pulled from texts that predated even the First Hero. The Alchemist had told us that the Weavers had been schooled in ancient magic from the time they could walk. As the words spilled from our lips in unison, the air in the chamber thickened. Reality grew soft around the edges, malleable.

I closed my eyes and *reached*.

The ley lines appeared in my mind's eye like rivers of sunlight, flowing beneath the surface of everything. The nexus directly below us was a massive confluence, streams of power converging from every direction. Most were thin like spider silk, but here, beneath the God Spire, they converged into a massive lake of raw magical potential. I could feel them all—threads stretching to Skyspire, to the Golden Rose Fields, to a thousand other places of power.

Through our shared bond, I felt Arabella's consciousness alongside mine, her presence a warm, golden light in the darkness. Together, we traced the flow of energy, searching for the main artery that led toward Solandris, beneath the Eastern Sea.

A pulsing channel of power, thicker than the others, stretched away from the nexus toward the distant kingdom.

There, I thought, pouring my will into the working. Arabella's power joined mine, bright where mine was dark, healing where mine sought to dominate. Together, we grasped that line.

Moving a ley line was like trying to redirect a river with your bare hands. It wanted to flow where it had always flowed, following grooves carved by centuries of use. But we were nothing if not stubborn. Inch by inch, we pulled. The line resisted, thrashing like a living thing. Sweat beaded on my forehead as I poured more power into the working, my runes screaming in protest.

And then—

It *moved.*

The ley line snapped away from its original path, curving back toward the Spire in a loop that bypassed the corrupted nexus entirely. The shift was so sudden I nearly lost my grip on the magic, but Arabella's presence steadied me.

We did it.

I felt her elation, fierce and bright. The sheer headiness of it—the power we'd just wielded, the fundamental force we'd just altered—made my blood sing. This was what we were meant for. This was—

The magic curdled in my stomach.

One moment I was riding high on our success, the next I felt like I'd swallowed acid. Rage, sudden and inexplicable, flooded my system. Not the cold, calculated anger I typically wielded, but something primal and destructive.

MINE.

The thought wasn't mine—or at least, it didn't feel like mine. It carried an ancient weight, a possessiveness that went beyond mere territorial instinct. I clenched my jaw, forcing my expression to remain neutral even as my runes began to burn like brands. Arabella's eyes found mine across the circle, a question in their depths. She'd felt the shift.

I gave her the slightest shake of my head. *Not now.*

The Alchemist was saying something about the successful separation, about how we'd bought ourselves time, but their words seemed to come from very far away.

The world tilted. The ley lines' power still sang through my bones, and with it came something else—something that had been sleeping.

One moment I was standing in the ritual chamber, the next I was on a battlefield littered with the dead. The sky above was the color of old blood, and the air tasted of iron and ash.

I stood atop a mountain of corpses, shadow stretching around me. Below, armies fled in terror from my approach. This was before Soriven, before the golden rose, when I was whole and terrible and—

"Kazimir?"

Arabella's voice snapped me back to the present. I blinked, finding myself still in the ritual chamber. Both she and the Alchemist were staring at me with concern.

"I'm fine," I said automatically, though my hands were trembling slightly. "Just aftereffects from moving the ley line."

But even as I spoke, more images flooded my mind. Not visions this time, but memories.

A woman with eyes like stars, carving runes into a child's bones.

Skyspire, but different. Built with my power when the world knelt at my feet and I was—

The golden rose, burning against my essence. Soriven's face, implacable as he spoke the binding. The prison weaving around me, then century after century of trying to break free—

I gasped and staggered back a step.

I remembered.

Not just the vision from the Heirloom chamber, but *something deeper*. Echoes of sensation that weren't mine but felt intimately familiar—the weight of ancient armor, the taste of absolute dominion. And more. Strategies I'd never learned, rage at imprisonment I'd never suffered, the inexplicable certainty that I'd built Skyspire with my own hands centuries before I was born. The Shadow King wasn't some ancient evil lurking in the ley lines beneath Solandris.

A piece of him lived *inside* me.

Had been shaping me my entire life.

My mother's runes hadn't just enhanced my magic—they'd cracked open something that had been sleeping inside me since birth. Each cut had been a key, awakening instincts and hungers that felt both foreign and inevitable. And now, with the Heirloom activated, with my connection to Arabella—Soriven's own descendant—with the ley lines still singing against my palms, whatever had been dreaming inside me was finally waking up.

And it recognized what I'd just touched.

It wanted to go *home.*

I was the monster in the fairy tales. The darkness that had once threatened to devour the world. The enemy of everything Arabella's bloodline represented.

Triumph surged through me—vicious and ancient. *Finally. Soriven's descendant, right here, vulnerable. Destroy her. Consume her bloodline's power and—*

No.

That wasn't *me.*

I forced my eyes open, forced myself to look at her across the circle. Arabella stood with her chin raised, power still crackling around her fingers, watching me with those sharp hazel eyes that had never once looked away from what I was. She'd seen me at my worst—manipulative, cruel, ruthless—and she'd chosen to stand beside me anyway. Not because she was compelled or coerced, but because she'd decided I was worth the risk.

The fragment inside me screamed for her destruction.

But I looked at her and felt something the Shadow King had never known in centuries of existence.

Fear.

Not of her power, though she was formidable. Not of her bloodline, though it had bound the Shadow King once before. I was terrified of losing *her.* Of watching that fierce intelligence dim. Of never again hearing her sarcastic commentary on my villain monologues or feeling her magic twine with mine in perfect, chaotic harmony. Of a world where Arabella Blackrose didn't exist to challenge me, infuriate me, match me step for step.

The ancient consciousness inside me wanted vengeance.

I wanted her safe.

The fragment saw an enemy.

I saw the woman who'd performed a ritual that could have killed her just to save my life. Who'd stood in front of the Hero's Guild and claimed me as hers. Who'd looked at the darkness in me and instead of running, had smiled and asked what we were going to break next.

My mother's voice echoed in my memory: *I love you, my son. This will make you strong.*

Love, in her mouth, had been a prelude to pain. A justification. The last time someone had claimed to love me, it had left scars I still carried.

But Arabella had never said those words to me. She'd simply *shown* me. With every defiant glare, every moment she chose to stay when she could have run, every time she'd matched my darkness with her own and made it something we could wield together instead of something that would destroy us both.

And I realized, with the kind of clarity that only comes when you're staring into the abyss of losing everything that matters—

I was in love with her.

Had been, probably, since the moment she'd set fire to my carefully laid plans and forced me to see her as more than a tool. Since she'd made me *want* to be seen, not as the Dark Lord or the monster, but as *Kazimir*. The man who could be vulnerable with her and not find a knife in his back.

We'd danced around those words for weeks now, both too proud or too afraid to say them first. And now I understood why the silence had felt so heavy. Because love wasn't just a feeling—it was a choice. A vulnerability. The ultimate surrender of control.

The memory surfaced then—hazy and dreamlike, but undeniably real. The vision in the Heirloom chamber. I'd been drowning in the Shadow King's consciousness, ancient and terrible and *hungry*, and something had pulled me back. Not duty. Not ambition. Not even self-preservation.

Her.

I'd chosen Arabella over the Shadow King's power once before. Some part of me, buried beneath the fragment's influence, had recognized what mattered. Had chosen love over vengeance without even understanding what I was doing.

Without knowing it, she'd been saving me all along.

And the terrifying truth was this: If I'd somehow activated the Heirloom alone, if she hadn't been there at my side in that chamber, the fragment would have already consumed me. I'd be nothing but a shell, a puppet for an ancient evil to wear like a favorite coat.

The Alchemist was saying something about the other bloodlines and their true reason for delay after we arrived. I heard none of it. Sensing my distraction, Arabella linked her hand with mine, her fingers warm and solid and real.

The fragment inside me thrashed like a caged animal, furious at being denied. Images slammed through my mind: Arabella's throat beneath my hands, her blood feeding the ley lines, her power consumed and added to mine. The Heirloom pulsed in response, amplifying the fragment's rage until my runes felt like they were tearing through my skin from the inside.

MINE. SHE IS MINE TO USE. MINE TO DESTROY.

I yanked my hand away from Arabella's before I could hurt her.

"Kazimir?" Her voice was sharp with concern.

"Aftereffects from the working," I said, as if that explained the cold sweat on my brow and the ancient rage clawing at my thoughts.

I clamped down on that voice with every ounce of will I possessed. I was Kazimir Blackrose. I had built my own empire, forged my own identity through pain and conquest. Whatever ancient consciousness lurked within me, it didn't define me completely.

The fragment was screaming now. It had been whispering suggestions before. Now it was *demanding.* Now it knew I was fighting back.

And it was fighting harder.

33

Dine with Villains

(and Try Not to Get Murdered over Dessert)

Kazimir

It's called a restaurant. Fancier than inn or pub food."

Griffin's voice carried the particular brand of condescension reserved for explaining basic concepts to barbarians. The lift descended through the God Spire's innards with a grinding mechanical whir that set my already frayed nerves on edge.

"I know what a restaurant is," I said, leaning against the lift's railing. My runes still throbbed from the ritual, a dull ache that matched the pounding in my skull. "I've conquered several kingdoms that had them."

"Yes, but have you actually eaten in one?" Griffin adjusted his spectacles—a nervous habit that intensified whenever he thought he might be pushing his luck. "Without, um . . . executing the chef afterward?"

"That was one time." I caught Arabella's lips twitching in my peripheral vision. She looked equally exhausted, though she hid it better. Only I could see the slight tremor in her hands, feel the bone-deep weariness through our bond. "And there was a hair in my soufflé."

Weak. Pathetic. In my time we would have razed the entire establishment and salted the—

I gritted my teeth, forcing the voice back down. It had been screaming at me since we'd left the god's skull a couple of hours ago, a relentless torrent of rage and hunger that made my own thoughts feel like whispers. Every moment was a battle to keep it contained, to maintain the facade that everything was fine.

Everything was decidedly not fine.

Reality had reasserted itself, but the revelations kept coming. Not visions now—*understanding.* Like puzzle pieces clicking into place, showing me a picture I'd been too blind to see.

Skyspire had never been mine. Not really.

I'd thought I'd claimed it through conquest, through sheer force of will when I was barely more than a boy playing at being a warlord. But now I could feel the truth thrumming through the ley lines beneath my feet: The citadel had been *waiting* for me. The fragment inside me had recognized its ancient seat of power and pulled me there like a lodestone.

Every strategic decision I'd made, every seemingly brilliant tactical move—how much of that had actually been *me*? How much had been the Shadow King's consciousness, dormant but not dead, guiding me toward reclaiming what it had lost?

The thought made my stomach churn.

I'd always prided myself on my cunning, my ability to see three moves ahead of my enemies. But what if I'd never been the mastermind I thought I was? What if I'd been a puppet dancing on strings I couldn't see, congratulating myself on my own cleverness while something ancient pulled me exactly where it wanted me to go?

Skyspire. The obsession with Solandris that went beyond mere ambition. The way I'd pursued the Heirloom with single-minded determination that bordered on madness. Even my mother—gods, had she known? Is that why she'd carved those runes into my bones, trying to wake something she sensed sleeping inside me?

The Shadow King had tried before. I could feel echoes of other attempts, other lives. Warlords and sorcerers throughout history, all touched by his essence, all drawn to Skyspire. All failing to fully manifest his power because they lacked what I had—the Heirloom, activated by a marriage bond to Soriven's own bloodline.

I was the closest it had come in centuries to breaking free completely.

And the worst part? I couldn't even be certain which ambitions were mine and which were his. Did I want to conquer the Western Realms because of my own drive for power, or because the Shadow King wanted to reclaim his former dominion?

My hands clenched into fists. No. I refused to accept that everything I was could be reduced to some ancient evil's machinations. I was Kazimir Blackrose. I had built my empire with these hands, carved my legend with my own will. I'd made my own choices. Killed my own father. The fragment might have influenced me, might have amplified certain tendencies, but the core of who I was—that was *mine.* The fact that some primordial essence lurked in my soul didn't negate thirty-three years of being *me.*

The lift shuddered to a halt, and we spilled out into the Spire's lower levels. The corridors here were narrower, lit by enchanted sconces that cast dancing shadows on the walls. That wasn't a metaphor—the shadows were in the middle of performing a complicated and lively jig with daggers. The place was perfect for ambushes, my mind noted automatically. Also perfect for hiding if you were, say, a traitorous former servant with a talent for disappearing.

I'd wanted to be alone after the ritual. Needed time to process the catastrophic revelation that something ancient and murderous had apparently been living inside me this whole time. But being alone meant being trapped with my thoughts, and my thoughts were currently a war zone between what I knew to be true and what that *thing* kept insisting was real.

So instead, I'd agreed to Griffin's suggestion of dinner near the Academia of Malice. Anything to avoid another confrontation with Arabella in the confines of our apartment. We'd managed civility during the ritual, even worked together seamlessly, but that was business. Personal was complicated.

Personal was dangerous when I couldn't trust my own mind.

I focused on keeping my expression neutral, my breathing even. No one could know. Not about the voice, not about what I'd felt when we touched those ley lines, not about the memories that kept trying to surface.

I caught Arabella glancing at me, probably wondering why I'd insisted on dinner out when we were both dead on our feet.

I looked away before she could read too much in my expression.

She suspects. She knows. Destroy her before she—

No. Absolutely fucking not.

But gods, I was tired. Every second was a battle to shove that voice down, to keep it from bleeding through into my actions. The fragment—or shard of consciousness or whatever—wanted control. Wanted to use my power for purposes I could only glimpse in flashes of ancient memory.

"The Writhing Tentacle," Griffin announced as we rounded a corner. "Best experimental cuisine near the Academia. They do things with transmutation magic that would make your average hedge wizard weep."

"Experimental cuisine," Sebastian repeated, his violet eyes widening slightly. "That sounds . . ."

"Potentially lethal?" Thorne suggested. My security chief had been in a foul mood all day, his search for Pip yielding nothing but dead ends and increasingly creative profanity.

"Exciting," Sebastian finished firmly. Then, more quietly: "Though I did offer to cook."

"Your cooking is fine," I said, pushing through the door. My shoulders ached with tension I couldn't release, muscles locked tight from hours of fighting my own mind. "But I needed—"

To get out. To move. To not be trapped in close quarters with her where the voice keeps screaming to either destroy her or claim her or both and I can't tell which impulse is mine anymore—

"—a change of scenery."

The interior was exactly what one would expect from a restaurant catering to villains with experimental tastes. The walls were lined with preserved specimens in jars—some recognizable, most decidedly not, each labeled with helpful descriptions like "Last Thought of a Dying God" and "Weekend's

Regrets, Pickled." Tables floated at various heights, requiring patrons to either levitate or use the provided rope ladders. The ceiling showed a view of a deep-sea trench, complete with tentacles occasionally pressing against the magical barrier.

A hostess with scales instead of skin and too many teeth smiled at us. "Table for five? Might I recommend the mezzanine level? Excellent view of the transmutation kitchen."

We were seated at a table that hovered ten feet off the ground, accessible by a rope ladder that Sebastian climbed with surprising grace. I simply levitated, as did Arabella—though I noticed she gripped the table's edge tightly once seated. The exhaustion from the ritual was hitting us both harder than we'd admitted.

At least focusing on mundane concerns gave me something to concentrate on besides the increasingly creative threats the fragment kept whispering about what it wanted to do to everyone in this room.

"So," Griffin said, spreading his napkin with a flourish, "shall I order for everyone? I've studied the menu extensively."

"No," four voices said in unison.

The menu itself was a work of art. The text shifted and rearranged itself as you read, descriptions morphing from appetizing to alarming and back again. All I wanted was some godsdamned food, but I had no one to blame for this little excursion but myself.

"The appetizer sampler includes pickled demon eyes and something called 'void-touched calamari,'" Griffin read excitedly.

I sighed, forcing my hands to remain steady on the table instead of clenching into fists. "Just order something that won't actively try to escape the plate."

"Oh, they have roasted phoenix! I've always wanted to try that."

"It resurrects in your stomach," Sebastian said quietly, reading over his shoulder. "Says so right there in the fine print."

Griffin's face fell. "Oh."

I found myself watching Arabella as she studied her own menu, noting the tiny furrow between her brows. She'd pulled her hair back into a simple side braid after the ritual, baring one side of her neck.

Mine. She's mine. Take her. Make her understand she belongs to—

I dug my nails into my palm hard enough to draw blood, using the pain to anchor myself. The voice was finding new and creative ways to twist every thought about Arabella into something possessive and dangerous.

The irony wasn't lost on me. I'd finally figured out what I felt for her—this terrifying, all-consuming thing that had to be love because nothing else explained the way my chest constricted when she looked at me—and it was the worst possible timing. How could I tell her when I couldn't trust that the words wouldn't come out wrong? When every protective instinct was being amplified and corrupted by something that wanted to own her like a possession?

"'Essence of Forgotten Dreams, lightly seared,'" Sebastian read aloud. "Is that meat?"

"Best not to ask," Thorne advised, flagging down a server. "Just order something that was definitely dead before it got to the kitchen."

We ordered—a process that took far longer than necessary thanks to Griffin's need to understand the magical properties of every ingredient. And Sebastian spent five minutes interrogating the waitress about whether the vegetables in his salad were ethically sourced from willing plants.

"You know," Griffin said, leaning back in his chair with a grin that made him look almost impish, "Sebastian and I have become quite the investigative team since that night at the Gallows."

"Have you now?" I asked, grateful for the distraction from my own thoughts.

"Oh yes. We've been comparing notes on the various magical anomalies around the Spire. Sebastian has this fascinating theory about how the ley lines here interact with organic matter, and I've been developing a detection matrix that could—"

"Please don't tell me you two are planning to experiment on the Spire's infrastructure," I interrupted.

"Not planning," Sebastian said quickly. "Just . . . observing. Academically."

"The same way you 'academically observed' the Bone Witches before inviting them to a ball?"

Sebastian's cheeks colored. "That was different."

"Speaking of academic pursuits," Griffin said, his excitement bubbling over, "you'll never guess who I ran into this afternoon!"

"The Bone Witches?" I suggested drily.

"No! Though that would have been fascinating. No, it was Emissary Pyrrha from the Ashen Wastes delegation. She's an alumna of the Academia and apparently has quite a bit of influence there." Griffin was practically vibrating in his seat. "She was at your wedding, saw my lightning bridges in action, and was so impressed that she wants me to give a lecture tomorrow! An actual lecture at the Academia of Malice!"

"Congratulations," Arabella said warmly. "That's quite an honor."

"It is, isn't it?" Griffin beamed. "I mean, the Academia is the most prestigious institution for advanced magical theory in the known world. To be invited to speak there—even just as a guest lecturer—it's the kind of opportunity most enchanters only dream about."

I watched Griffin's enthusiasm with a mixture of amusement and concern. On one hand, it was good to see him recognized for his talents instead of his disasters. On the other hand, this was Griffin. Giving him a platform to demonstrate his innovations was like handing a pyromaniac a torch in a fireworks warehouse.

"What will you be lecturing on?" I asked carefully.

"The stabilization matrices I developed for the lightning bridges, of course! Emissary Pyrrha was particularly interested in how I managed to create a dynamic, self-adjusting network that responds to both physical and magical variables. She thinks it could have applications for—"

"Please tell me this lecture won't involve live demonstrations," Thorne interjected.

"Well, I was planning to bring a small-scale model . . ."

"No explosions," I said firmly. "Charts only."

"The bridges don't explode!"

"Not intentionally," Sebastian added helpfully.

Griffin shot him a betrayed look. "I thought we were friends."

"We are. That's why I'm trying to help you survive your own lecture."

Their easy banter was distracting in a calming sort of way, if a reminder of how easily Sebastian fit in with our little family.

The fragment chose that moment to surge forward with a wave of paranoia so intense I had to grip the table edge to keep from lashing out. *Traitors. They're all traitors. The smiling ones are always the first. Remember what happened with—*

I shoved it down again, but my hands were shaking now. I hid them in my lap, forcing my breathing to stay even.

"My lord?" Thorne's voice was careful. "You all right?"

"Fine," I lied, using the same excuse from earlier. "Just tired from the ritual."

It was a convenient excuse, one that explained the tension in my shoulders, the slight tremor I couldn't quite hide, the way I kept glancing at Arabella as if to reassure myself she was still there. Everyone accepted it because it made sense.

No one needed to know I was fighting a war in my own head.

Sebastian absently waved his hand, and tiny flowers began sprouting from the wooden chair legs.

"Must you?" I asked.

"Sorry. Nervous habit." But he didn't stop the growth, and soon delicate white blossoms covered half his chair.

What the fuck was he nervous about now?

While we waited for our food—I'd ordered something called "Temporal Beef" that supposedly aged backward and if you didn't eat it fast enough became a live cow—Sebastian kept fidgeting. The white blooms released a sweet fragrance.

"It helps me think," he said defensively when he caught me glaring.

I found myself struggling to focus on the mundane chatter. The memories kept intruding, flashes of a life that felt both mine and foreign.

The first time I'd seen Skyspire, it had been new. I'd raised it from the bones of the earth with will alone, each stone sung into place with power that made the world tremble. My citadel. My throne. My—

A bee buzzed past my ear.

Then another.

Within seconds, a small swarm had materialized, drawn by Sebastian's impromptu garden. They settled on the flowers with enthusiasm, and one particularly ambitious specimen made a beeline—pun intended—for Arabella's wineglass.

"Quit showing off," I snapped, my patience fraying as I batted away a bee investigating my collar. "This isn't a bloody greenhouse."

Sebastian's flowers withered instantly, sending the bees into confused spirals. "I wasn't—I mean, I didn't think—"

"That's the problem with you hero types," I snapped. "Never thinking about consequences."

"Kaz." Arabella's voice was carefully neutral, but I felt her concern. A gentle probe, asking without asking if I was all right.

I wasn't. Perhaps dinner had been a bad idea, after all.

Griffin launched into a detailed account of his day exploring the Spire after they left the Academia, dragging Sebastian to various magical supply shops and one memorable incident involving a cursed mirror that showed your worst fear.

"Mine was apparently running out of ink during an important experiment," Griffin said cheerfully. "Sebastian's was—"

"Private," Sebastian cut in quickly, color rising in his cheeks.

Probably something to do with disappointing people or causing harm through good intentions.

"Any trouble?" I asked, though I already knew the answer.

"None," Sebastian confirmed. "Actually, people seemed to actively avoid us. One merchant practically threw his goods at Griffin rather than haggle."

Good. Word of what I'd done to those thugs had spread. The God Spire respected few things, but decisive violence was one of them.

Our food arrived. My Temporal Beef appeared to be de-aging before my eyes, cycling through various states of doneness. Arabella had ordered something that might have been fish if fish had evolved the ability to photosynthesize. Griffin's plate contained what looked like edible mathematics.

"So," Griffin said, dissecting his geometric meal, "dare I ask how your meeting with the Alchemist went? You both look rather depleted."

"It went," I said curtly.

"We accomplished what we set out to do," Arabella added, more diplomatically.

That was our agreed upon story, which was too sensitive for public conversation. Though after what I'd felt in that ritual, after touching those ley lines and feeling something dark and familiar stir in response, I wondered if we'd contained anything at all.

Maybe we'd just given it a clearer path.

"Does that mean we can go home, my lord?" Thorne asked. "I could send word to the *Sky Serpent* tonight."

"No. We don't leave until we find him."

Thorne knew who "him" was. He lowered his voice so that neighboring tables couldn't overhear. "I've scoured every corner of this place with your shadow warriors. No sign."

My jaw tightened. Pip was here somewhere—I could feel it like an itch between my shoulder blades.

"It's a vast place," Thorne grumbled. "Lots of comings and goings. Dark corners everywhere. A rat could hide here for years if it knew what it was doing."

"Keep looking," I said quietly. "I want every shadow, every crevice checked again. We'll start fresh in the morning, cover every inch of this place."

I wanted to start now, tonight, but my bones ached and my magic felt like I'd run it through a cheese grater. The ritual had taken more out of me than I'd anticipated, and I'd be useless stumbling around in the dark. Especially when I couldn't trust my own judgment or be certain which impulses were mine and which belonged to the thing sharing my skull.

"About tomorrow," Griffin said, "I'm expected at the Academia for the lecture. Emissary Pyrrha specifically requested an early afternoon time slot so the students could attend."

"Fine," I conceded.

"Thank you, my lord!"

Dessert arrived in a flourish of unnecessary pyrotechnics. My

"Deconstructed Concept of Sweetness" looked like someone had taken the idea of cake and tortured it until it confessed its deepest secrets—a geometric arrangement of crystallized sugar, essence of vanilla suspended in temporal bubbles, and the theoretical essence of frosting. Arabella's "Frozen Moment of Joy" actually giggled when she poked it with her spoon.

I was just raising my fork, hoping that focusing on the absurdity of my dessert would quiet the screaming in my head, when every instinct I'd honed through decades of paranoia fired at once.

The attack came from three directions simultaneously.

I moved without thinking, shoving Arabella down and to the side as a sickly green curse sizzled through the air where her head had been. My shadows erupted outward, forming a dome of protection around our table just as two more spells slammed into them. The magic made my defensive barrier spark and writhe. Through the translucent darkness, I spotted three figures in nondescript robes, already moving to flank us with magic building in their hands, aimed directly at my wife.

Professional assassins, judging by their coordinated movements. The kind that cost more than small kingdoms.

Something inside me snapped.

Not the cold, calculated anger I typically wielded. This was the fragment surging forward, no longer content to whisper and scream from the depths of my mind. It rose like a tidal wave, and this time, I didn't fight it.

Because they'd tried to hurt her. Tried to kill what was *mine.*

I dropped the shield and let the fury take me.

The first assassin tried to dodge, but I had already reached him. My hand closed around his throat, and I *pulled*—not just at his flesh but at his very essence, the way the fragment remembered doing a thousand times before. He had enough time to scream before he simply ceased, reduced to component atoms that scattered like dust.

The second had better reflexes, managing to get off another curse that caught me in the shoulder. Pain flared, but it only fed the rage—both mine and the thing that shared my bones. I gestured sharply, and every piece of cutlery in the restaurant responded, turning into a whirlwind of sharp metal that pursued him across the room. He made it three steps before being reduced to confetti.

The third tried to run.

Coward.

I didn't chase him. Instead, I reached out with my magic, grasping the very air in his lungs. He stopped mid-stride, clawing at his throat as I slowly, methodically increased the pressure. Part of me—the part that was still Kazimir Blackrose and not dancing on the edge of something ancient and terrible—whispered that I should keep him alive, interrogate him, find out who sent them.

But he'd tried to hurt what was mine. Tried to take my—

The assassin imploded. I may have gotten a bit carried away.

The restaurant was in ruins. Tables overturned, that fascinating ceiling view cracked and leaking sea water. Other diners cowered behind whatever cover they could find, staring at me with the kind of terror I usually welcomed.

I stood in the center of the devastation, breathing hard, my runes burning so hot I could smell charred fabric. The fragment was still there, still screaming, but now it was screaming in triumph.

The display of power was exactly what we'd been trying to avoid. Every Syndicate member with half a brain would know something had changed, would know I'd accessed power levels that should have been impossible. So much for hiding whatever changes the Heirloom had wrought.

But as I turned to check on Arabella—found her unharmed if wide-eyed, Sebastian's vines having provided additional protection—I found I didn't care.

They'd tried to kill her. In front of me. That was unforgivable.

The fragment and I were in complete agreement on that point.

I might have something ancient and murderous sharing space in my skull, but I was still Kazimir Blackrose. And the sheer audacity of attacking my wife in my presence made my vision blur red.

I could feel power thrumming beneath my skin, and my runes began to feel like they were writhing instead of burning, as if they were trying to shape themselves into something new. I flexed my hands, half expecting to see blood pouring from the old scars. But nothing was different except my magic felt sharper and hungrier.

For once, the voice in my head was silent. Not because it had gone away, but because we finally wanted the same thing.

Who the fuck tried to kill what's mine?

34

Ask Your Wife to Trust You

(When You Don't Trust Yourself)

Kazimir

I was halfway to the door when Arabella's voice cut through the apartment.

"Where exactly do you think you're going?"

I didn't turn around. Couldn't. The fragment had been screaming since we'd left the restaurant an hour ago, a relentless assault of violent impulses that made my skull feel like it was splitting. Every second in her presence was a battle between wanting to protect her and the ancient thing inside me that wanted to either destroy her or claim her so completely she'd never escape.

Both options were unacceptable.

"Hunting," I said curtly, reaching for my coat. "Someone tried to kill my wife. I intend to find out who and introduce them to creative applications of pain."

"Without me?"

I finally glanced back. Arabella stood in the common area, dressed in her new black leathers. The sight of her sent the fragment into a possessive frenzy.

Mine. She's mine. Make her submit. Make her—

I gritted my teeth. "Yes, without you. You're the target. The safest place for you is here, behind wards."

Her eyes flashed. "The safest place for me is wherever I can see the threats coming. Or have you forgotten what happened the last time you tried to keep me 'safe' by leaving me behind?"

"This is different," I snapped, shadows curling around my body in agitated spirals. "Professional assassins just tried to kill you in a public restaurant. Whoever sent them will try again."

"Exactly." She crossed her arms, and the movement drew my attention to the twin daggers strapped to her thighs. "It was *my* life they threatened. I have every right to hunt the bastards who tried to take it."

Logically, she was right. But logic had nothing to do with the war raging in my head.

Keep her close. Never let her out of your sight. She's yours to protect, yours to control, yours to—

"Fine," I bit out, the word tasting bitter. "But you stay behind me. You don't engage unless I give the order. And if I tell you to run, you fucking run."

Her lips curved into something that wasn't quite a smile. "I don't take orders well. You should know that by now."

"Arabella—"

"I'll be careful," she interrupted, moving past me to the door. "But I won't be left behind. Not again."

The fragment screamed its approval and its rage simultaneously, a cacophony of contradictory impulses that made my vision blur. Part of me desperately wanted Arabella where I could see her, protect her, ensure nothing could touch her. The other part—the ancient, terrible part—wanted to lock her away where she'd be safe and *his* and unable to defy him ever again.

I was going to lose my fucking mind before this night was over.

Thorne entered from the hallway leading from his room, armed and alert. "My lord. I heard you were planning a hunt."

"Word travels fast."

"It does when you destroy a restaurant and leave three corpses in your wake." His eyes flicked to Arabella, then back to me. "No one threatens Lady Blackrose and gets away with it as long as I'm head of your security. I'm coming with you."

It wasn't a request. Thorne had been with me long enough to know when to push and when to back off. This was apparently a pushing moment.

"Fine," I said again, the word coming easier this time. Having Thorne along meant another set of eyes on Arabella, another layer of protection between her and whatever threats lurked in the Spire's depths. And in me.

You don't need help protecting what's yours.

I shoved the voice down with enough force to make my runes flare hot beneath my skin. The pain helped.

A shadow near the window began to ripple and distort, reality itself seeming to fold inward like fabric being pulled through a too-small opening. The air grew thick with the scent of thunderstorms and burnt sugar as darkness peeled away from the wall in layers.

Then Nyx's head emerged.

It wasn't a smooth transition. The dragon's snout appeared first, followed by her neck at an angle that suggested she'd miscalculated the exit point by about three feet. Her front legs came through next, scrambling for purchase on thin air before she realized she was upside down. With an indignant squawk, she tumbled out of the shadow space in a tangle of pink-shimmering limbs and leathery wings.

She landed on the floor with all the grace of a drunk falling down stairs.

The pink blaze on her snout had spread since last night, bleeding across her cheeks in rosy streaks that made her look like she'd face-planted into a bowl of crushed raspberries. Her scales shimmered with that same sunset-through-storm-clouds iridescence, and even her wing membranes had taken on a faint blush.

She shook herself off, sneezed a puff of purple smoke, and fixed Arabella with a look of pure devotion.

Then she noticed me watching and her liquid silver eyes narrowed to slits.

"Absolutely not," I said before anyone could suggest it. "The dragon stays here."

Nyx's answering hiss made her opinion of that plan abundantly clear. She positioned herself between Arabella and me, her tail lashing in agitation.

"She can help," Arabella said, moving to stroke Nyx's snout. The dragon immediately softened under her touch, though she kept one wary eye on me. "Her shadow-walking is getting better."

"'Better' is a generous term for what I just witnessed." I gestured at the dragon, who was still slightly off-balance from her graceless entrance. "She looks like she's been dipped in pink paint."

Nyx made an offended chirping sound and deliberately turned her back on me, pressing her head against Arabella's chest.

"She's still learning," Arabella said, scratching behind the dragon's horns. "And she'll be useful. You know she will."

I wanted to refuse. But the truth was, Nyx's developing abilities *would* be useful. And having the dragon focused on protecting Arabella was even better than Thorne.

Besides, Nyx clearly didn't trust me right now. The feeling was mutual—I didn't trust myself either.

"Fine," I said for the third—fourth?—time, wondering if I'd lost all authority in my own domain.

I pulled shadows around us like a cloak, darker and denser than I typically bothered with. No half measures tonight. If I was going to hunt through the God Spire's underbelly, I'd do it properly—as the predator I'd spent my life becoming, not the man trying desperately to hold on to his humanity.

The fragment purred its approval.

We left the apartment in silence, descending through levels that grew progressively darker and more dangerous. The Spire's lower reaches catered to the kind of clientele who preferred their business conducted in shadows, where questions weren't asked and bodies disappeared without fuss.

My kind of people, usually.

I'd started the search for Pip at the Gilded Gallows two nights ago, following the same cold trail that had led nowhere. No magical signature, no physical trace, nothing but Arabella's certainty that she'd seen him. And her truth-sense didn't lie. Which meant someone was using magic powerful enough to fool even my detection spells. The Pip I'd known had possessed no magic of his own—he'd been a servant, nothing more. If he'd suddenly acquired the ability to hide from me, someone had given it to him.

The question was who.

The timing bothered me. Arabella spots Pip at the Gallows, and two days later, professional assassins try to kill her in a restaurant? I had enemies everywhere, though, many of whom had tried to assassinate me on multiple occasions. Could the two events be unrelated?

Sure. And I could sprout wings and start shitting rainbows.

We moved through the corridors like ghosts. Arabella stayed close by my side—not quite touching, but near enough that I could feel the heat of her presence. The distance between us felt both necessary and unbearable.

Thorne brought up the rear, his hand never straying far from his weapon.

And Nyx . . . Nyx continued her erratic phasing practice, leaving a trail of minor destruction and confused residents in her wake.

"She's getting better at it," Arabella murmured as Nyx extracted herself from a wall sconce. "The phasing, I mean."

"She's also developing an impressive talent for property damage," I said, watching the dragon shake plaster dust from her wings.

Despite everything, Arabella's lips twitched. "She hasn't exploded anything yet."

"The night is young." At least the dragon's antics were helping distract me from the roaring in my head.

We reached the lower market levels. The shops were mostly closed at this hour, their wares locked behind warded gates and protective spells. A few establishments catered to the nocturnal crowd—a poison dealer, an information broker, a shop that sold curses by the dozen.

I spread my senses wide, searching for any trace of unusual magic.

Nothing. Just the usual background hum of a thousand competing enchantments, layered protections, and illusions designed to hide everything from contraband to murder.

Nyx phased into a narrow alley, and this time she actually managed a clean entry and exit. She solidified near a dark stain on the cobblestones and began sniffing at the ground, her tail swishing.

Arabella moved toward her, and I followed automatically, unable to help myself.

"Anything?" I asked roughly.

Arabella shook her head. "Just old blood. Days old, at least."

I crouched beside the stain. A quick test confirmed it was human, but beyond that, nothing useful. The Spire saw violence daily. This could be from a simple mugging or a complex assassination. No way to tell.

We continued the search, moving through the levels methodically. Thorne checked doorways and alcoves. Nyx phased in and out of shadows, investigating spaces too small or too warded for us to access easily. Arabella used her magic to sense for recent disturbances, her truth-sense alert for any hint of deception or concealment.

And I fought a losing battle with the thing in my head.

Every time Arabella moved too far away, the fragment screamed. Every time she came too close, it screamed louder. When she used her magic, the ancient presence surged with a hunger that made my runes burn. When she looked at me with concern—because of course she could sense something was wrong—it twisted that concern into a weapon.

She knows. She suspects. Destroy her before she can act against you. Or claim her so completely she'll never dare—

This was why I'd wanted to hunt alone.

"Kazimir."

Her voice cut through my spiraling thoughts. I looked up to find her watching me with Nyx pressed protectively against her side. The dragon's silver eyes tracked my every movement.

"What?"

"You're bleeding." She nodded at my clenched fists.

I uncurled my fingers, noting the crescent-shaped wounds where my nails had broken open the wounds from earlier in the evening. "It's nothing."

She took a step closer, and the fragment roared. "Something's wrong. Is it your runes?"

"Not here," I rasped, unable to meet her eyes. Gods, I loved her. And gods, I needed her to listen. Whatever rift was between us right now was a good thing. I needed her to keep her distance.

She stepped back, her expression shuttering. "Of course. Forgive me for caring."

Fuck. I was making things worse. I opened my mouth—to apologize, to explain, to push her further away—

Thorne's low whistle cut through the moment. He stood at the end of the corridor, gesturing for us to join him.

I moved toward him, grateful for the interruption. Arabella followed. Nyx materialized ahead of her in another burst of pink-tinged shadow. This time the dragon managed a relatively clean entrance, though she still came out facing the wrong direction and had to turn around with an embarrassed huff.

"Found something?" I asked Thorne.

"Someone." He jerked his head toward a side passage. "Lady Zaraiah. Heading this way." He cracked his knuckles. "Funny how she shows up right after assassins try to kill Lady Blackrose."

My shadows snuffed out the closest sconces. "Indeed."

"No other chairs were supposed to be at the Spire," Arabella said quietly.

"They weren't." I forced myself to breathe, to think past the rage and paranoia. The fragment screamed for blood and violence and an end to all threats. I shoved it down with brutal force, focusing on strategy instead of slaughter.

Thorne's scowl turned his scarred face into something feral. "I'd be happy to accidentally stab her, my lord."

"Let's see what she has to say first, then go from there."

Thorne muttered his displeasure just as Zaraiah appeared around the corner, that crimson dress she favored a slash of color against the Spire's dark stone. She moved with that predatory grace I remembered too well, her eyes lighting up when she spotted us.

She opened her mouth to speak—

And froze.

Nyx had phased directly behind Arabella, rising to her full height with her wings spread wide. The dragon loomed over my wife's shoulder, a pink-shimmered nightmare of scales and teeth, her liquid silver eyes fixed on Zaraiah.

A low rumble built in the dragon's chest.

All the color drained from Zaraiah's face. The Chair of Whispers, who'd faced down armies and kings and survived Syndicate politics, took an involuntary step backward.

"Is that—" Her voice cracked slightly. "Is that a *shadow dragon*?"

Shadows coiled around Arabella's hands. "Yes. Wedding gift from my husband. Thoughtful, wasn't he?"

Nyx's rumble grew louder, her wings spreading wider until they touched the walls on either side. The pink shimmer of her scales made her look even more otherworldly, like some fever dream given flesh and fury.

Arabella moved before I could stop her, shadows coiling around her hands. She stepped forward, placing herself between Zaraiah and me—a reversal that clearly caught the Chair of Whispers off guard.

"You have exactly ten seconds to explain why you're here," Arabella said, her voice cold enough to frost the stone, "before I test whether my healing magic works in reverse on Syndicate chairs."

Zaraiah's gaze darted between Arabella and the very large, very pink, very angry dragon currently looming over my wife. She'd expected me to be the threat, not my wife and a dragon. "My, my," she managed. "Marriage has given you teeth, hasn't it, little hero?"

"Six seconds."

Nyx chose that moment to bare her own teeth and release a puff of purple smoke that smelled of brimstone.

Zaraiah flinched.

I should have stopped this. Should have stepped in, taken control of the situation. But the fragment was howling for blood, and watching Arabella defend me from a woman who'd tried to weaponize my worst trauma sent something fierce and possessive surging through my chest.

And Nyx . . . Nyx was magnificent. The ridiculous pink dragon who'd spent the last hour getting stuck in walls was now every inch the apex predator, radiating menace with a competence she'd been thoroughly lacking all evening.

For a moment—just a moment—the fragment's screaming dimmed to background noise. *This is real. She is real. We are real.*

"I'm here," Zaraiah said, her eyes never leaving the dragon, "meeting with a contact about the eastern trade routes. Your lockdown is interfering with my schedule."

"Bullshit," Arabella said flatly. Nyx's rumble intensified.

Zaraiah's eyebrows rose. "Excuse me?"

"You're lying." Arabella took another step forward. Nyx moved with her, perfectly synchronized, a pink-scaled extension of my wife's will. The dragon's maw was mere inches from Zaraiah's face. "Try again."

The Chair of Whispers swallowed hard.

"Nyx," Arabella said calmly, not looking at the dragon. "Sit."

For once—for the *first time all evening*—Nyx obeyed instantly.

The dragon kept her gaze locked on Zaraiah as she sat, but the immediate threat of violence shifted to something more controlled.

Zaraiah's throat worked as she swallowed again.

"Answer the question," I said, finally stepping up beside Arabella. Shadows gathered around us, responding to the barely controlled fury radiating from both of us. "Why are you really here?"

Zaraiah's gaze flicked between us, calculating. Her eyes kept returning to Nyx, who sat perfectly still except for the slow lash of her tail and the occasional wisp of smoke curling from her nostrils.

"Fine," she said finally. "I'll admit, I'm curious. Someone made a move against you"—she nodded at Arabella, carefully avoiding any sudden movements—"in the heart of the God Spire. Any luck with that? Or are you just wandering the halls, hoping inspiration strikes?"

Arabella's shadows solidified into twin blades, dark and wicked and lethal. She held them loosely at her sides, but the threat was unmistakable. "I don't care about Syndicate politics or your precious games," she said. "You tried to humiliate my husband in our own home, in front of witnesses."

Zaraiah's smile had vanished completely now. "That was business."

"And now someone's tried to kill me"—Arabella's voice dropped to something deadly as she continued, as if Zaraiah hadn't even spoken—"and you show up, skulking around in the dark, claiming you're just 'curious'?"

She raised her blades. Behind her, Nyx's tail lashed in agitation. "Give me one reason I shouldn't skin you and feed you to my dragon."

The fragment screamed its approval. *Yes. Yes. Let her do it. Let her—*

And that's when I realized.

The Shadow King wanted this. Wanted me to stand back and let Arabella commit murder. Wanted us to isolate ourselves, to make enemies of the Syndicate, to burn every bridge until there was nothing left but rage and paranoia and violence.

Wanted me to become exactly what he had been—alone, powerful, and utterly mad.

And we couldn't afford to kill a Syndicate chair in the God Spire—it would guarantee that the rest of them would try to stab me in the back as soon as I turned toward Solandris, if they weren't already planning it.

So I did the hardest thing possible.

"Arabella," I said quietly. "Stand down."

She didn't look at me, her eyes still fixed on Zaraiah. "Why?"

I moved closer, carefully, until I stood beside her. Our shoulders barely touched, but I felt her tense at the contact. "Because I'm asking you to."

That made her glance at me. Just for a second. But it was enough for her to see whatever was written across my face—the barely controlled rage, the calculation, the *please trust me* that I couldn't voice aloud.

Her jaw clenched. The shadow blades trembled in her grip. "Kaz—"

"I *know*." The words came out rough, layered with everything I couldn't say in front of our audience. *I know she deserves it. I know you want blood. Gods, so do I.*

The fragment pulsed with vicious satisfaction but it was no longer dominating my mind.

Arabella held my gaze for a heartbeat longer. I saw the war playing out behind her eyes—fury versus trust, vengeance versus whatever she was reading in my expression. Her fingers flexed on the hilts of her shadow blades.

Then, slowly, deliberately, she let them dissolve back into formless darkness. Nyx made a disappointed sound in her throat.

"This time," she said, her voice still carrying an edge. The words were for Zaraiah, but her eyes stayed on mine a moment longer. *I'm trusting you. Don't make me regret it.* "But if I find out you're involved in this, Zaraiah? If I discover you had anything to do with those assassins?" Arabella smiled, and it was the most dangerous expression I'd ever seen on her face. "Then I'll find you. And when I do, you'll discover exactly what kind of monster the Dark Lord married."

Zaraiah smoothed her dress with hands that weren't quite steady.

"Tell us why you're really here," I said. "Everything. And maybe—*maybe*—we'll forget this conversation happened."

"I don't know who hired the assassins, if that's what you're asking." Zaraiah's smile returned, sharper now, though it didn't quite reach her eyes. Not while a shadow dragon was staring at her like she was dinner. "I heard you'd shut down all transportation out of the Spire—that kind of dramatic gesture gets attention even across the sea. So I came to see what chaos you were stirring up this time. That's when I heard about the attempt on Lady Blackrose's life." Her expression shifted, the mask of the information broker sliding into place. "I've been asking questions since I arrived. They were hired *here*. In the Spire. Within the last two days."

My fury sharpened into cold calculation. "So it was an impromptu attempt."

"Yes. They were looking for an opportunity, and one presented itself." She glanced between us. "Whoever hired them had to know you were in the God Spire, had to have access to the kind of networks that can arrange an assassination on short notice, and had to be confident enough in their anonymity to risk making a move in neutral territory."

"That could be every member of the Syndicate," Arabella said flatly. Apparently, her truth-sense wasn't pinging.

"Could be," Zaraiah agreed, sliding farther away while keeping her gaze on Nyx. "Or it could be someone with Syndicate connections who isn't a chair. The God Spire attracts all sorts."

"Who would have that kind of information except a chair?" Arabella asked.

"That's what I'm trying to find out." When no one stopped her, Zaraiah eased toward the end of the corridor, clearly eager to put distance between herself and us. "But whoever it is, they either have resources or friends in the right places."

She paused at the corner, looking back. Her gaze lingered on Nyx one more time before returning to us. The dragon huffed uncertainly, looking between Arabella and Zaraiah like she was trying to decide whether to eat the Chair of Whispers anyway.

"For what it's worth, Kazimir," Zaraiah said. "I prefer my enemies alive and suffering, not dead and beyond my reach. I didn't hire them."

Then she was gone, crimson dress disappearing into the shadows.

I stood there, breathing hard, my entire body trembling with the effort of not pursuing her. Of not giving the fragment what it wanted.

"Kaz."

Arabella's hand found mine, her fingers threading through my clenched fist. The touch was gentle, grounding, and it cut through the fragment's screaming. I forced myself to breathe, to focus on the warmth of her hand instead of the cold rage trying to consume me.

"You were right to stop me," she continued. "I wanted to kill her. Still do, honestly. But you were right—we don't need to fight a war on multiple fronts. Solandris first."

Despite everything, my lips twitched. "Bloodthirsty, aren't we?"

"She hurt you." Arabella's voice went soft and fierce simultaneously. "I don't forgive that."

The fragment purred its approval, twisting her protectiveness into something possessive and dark. *She's yours. She defends what's yours.*

"We should head back," I said abruptly, needing to get away from this corridor, from the lingering scent of Zaraiah's perfume, from the memory of how close I'd come to losing control. "We're not finding anything else tonight."

The walk back was tense and silent. Thorne kept his professional distance, pretending not to notice the way my shadows kept reaching toward Arabella without my conscious direction.

Nyx kept phasing in and out, completely oblivious to the human drama unfolding around her. At one point she emerged from a wall with someone's boot, looked confused, and phased back in to return it.

We heard a distant yelp of surprise.

When we reached the apartment, I headed straight for the library, intending to lock myself away until I had this thing under control. But Arabella and Nyx followed.

"Kazimir, please. Talk to me."

I stopped at the doorway, my hand gripping the frame hard enough to make the wood creak. "I can't be near you right now."

"What?"

At the pain in her voice, I forced myself to turn, to look at her.

Nyx had positioned herself protectively beside Arabella. The dragon's silver eyes fixed on me with unmistakable wariness, her tail lashing once in warning. I didn't know how much the dragon understood, but she knew Arabella was upset and I was the cause.

I couldn't even be angry about it. The dragon's instincts were better than mine right now.

Arabella was quiet for a long moment. Then: "What happened during the ritual with the Alchemist?"

Everything. Nothing. The end of the world as I knew it.

I released the doorframe. "We need sleep." I adopted my best irritating smirk, though it felt like a mask that didn't quite fit anymore. "Unless you'd like to kick the dragon out of our bed, I'm sleeping in here, so if you don't mind . . ."

The words were meant to be final, though not cruel. Arabella narrowed her eyes at me before turning toward the bedroom with Nyx squeezing down the hallway after her.

I closed the library door and leaned against it, letting my head fall back with a dull thud.

Soon, the fragment whispered. *Soon you'll understand. Soon you'll accept what you are. What you've always been.*

Mine.

I slid down to the floor, wrapped my arms around my knees, and prepared for a very long night.

35

Make Reckless Decisions Alone

(Because Communication Is for Heroes)

Arabella

The vial was lighter than it should have been.

I turned it over in my fingers, watching the opalescent liquid shift like trapped moonlight. Mnemosyne's warning echoed in my head: *Wait until you have someone you trust with you.* Sound advice, really. The kind any sensible person would follow.

Too bad I'd never been accused of being sensible.

"What do you think?" I asked Nyx, who had somehow managed to wedge herself into the narrow alley between two shops. Her silver eyes tracked the vial with unnerving intensity. "You count as someone I trust, right? You're here for moral support. And to stop me from doing anything too catastrophically stupid."

She huffed, a puff of smoke curling from her nostrils. She knew me too well.

The morning had started badly and gotten worse. I'd given up on sleep around dawn. The attack itself hadn't kept me awake—that had been over so fast I'd barely registered the danger before Kaz shoved me aside. No, it was what came after.

The look in his eyes as he'd torn through those assassins hadn't been entirely human.

I'd seen Kaz angry before. Seen him possessive, violent, utterly ruthless. But last night had been different. For a moment, just a heartbeat, I could have sworn I'd seen someone else looking out through his eyes. Someone older. Angrier.

Someone who'd worn a crown of shadows and made the world kneel.

The same presence I'd glimpsed in that vision weeks ago, when the Heirloom had shown me the truth about what—who—my husband really was.

And then, his struggle last night during our hunt through the Spire. He tried to hide it, but couldn't completely. Not from Thorne, and definitely not from me. The crack in his usual control was alarming.

My fingers tightened around the vial. I knew I should have told him about the Shadow King. Should have told him weeks ago. But how exactly did one bring up that particular conversation? *"Darling, remember that time you had a vision and forgot about it? Well, funny story—you're actually history's greatest monster. Pass the wine?"*

No. He had enough to deal with. Adding an existential crisis about being the Shadow King would only make things worse.

Besides, if the ritual with the Alchemist had weakened him enough for the Shadow King to start bleeding through . . . well, knowledge might not be power in this case. It might be the final push that let the ancient bastard take control completely.

Nyx bumped her head against my shoulder, nearly knocking me into the wall. She'd been like this all morning—my scaly, overprotective shadow. Even during last night's hunt, she'd positioned herself between Kaz and me whenever his control seemed to slip, her silver eyes tracking his every move ment with wary suspicion.

She'd seen it too. Whatever was happening to him.

"I'm fine," I told her for the hundredth time. "And you're here to make sure I stay that way, right? That's what Mnemosyne meant by having some-one trustworthy. Someone to ground me."

She preened slightly at being called trustworthy, her scales shimmering with pride. Never mind that she was still a juvenile, still learning to control her own abilities. She was *my* dragon, and that made her infinitely more reliable than, say, telling Kaz what I was about to do.

Because that conversation would go over *wonderfully*.

No, Nyx was the perfect solution. Present, protective, and unlikely to ask uncomfortable questions about ancient evils or marital honesty.

The confrontation with Kaz this morning had been a masterclass in barely controlled tension. When dawn came, I'd found Kaz still in the library, shadows pooling around him like he'd forgotten how to dismiss them.

"Did you sleep at all?" I'd asked.

"No." The word had been clipped, exhausted. "But I will find him. I will find whoever's behind this."

"You need rest."

"I need answers."

"You need—" I'd bitten off the rest. *You need to stop letting the thing inside you drive you to exhaustion.* "Fine. Do what you want."

His laugh had been bitter. "Since when do I need your permission?"

And there it was. The heart of our problem, laid bare in seven words. We'd gone from forced proximity to genuine partnership to this careful dance around each other's feelings. Too proud to apologize. Too connected to truly separate.

Nyx had chosen that moment to squeeze through the doorway, plant herself between us, and growl at Kaz. Just like last night, I'd expected him to be furious. And, just like last night, he'd surprised me.

"Keep her with you," he'd said. "At all times."

"I don't need a babysitter."

"You need protec—" He'd cut himself off, jaw clenching. I'd felt the effort it took not to lock me somewhere safe until he'd eliminated every possible threat. "Just . . . keep the dragon close."

And then he'd left to go back to his hunt.

I'd left right after. Obviously, he hadn't wanted me with him during the day any more than he'd wanted me there last night—not really. But that didn't mean I had to sit around and twiddle my thumbs all day in the apartment.

Now, standing in this alley with my possibly catastrophic decision in a bottle, I wondered if I was making things worse. I'd been wandering the market levels for the better part of an hour, the vial burning a hole in my pocket, until I'd ducked into this narrow space between shops and thought: *Screw it.*

I needed to know. Needed to understand what had been taken from me, what memories Auremar's mages had locked away. Maybe they'd help me understand why I was drawn to dangerous men with ancient souls. Maybe they'd show me how to help Kaz without destroying what was left of him.

Or maybe they'd drive me mad. Only one way to find out.

"If this goes badly," I told Nyx, "don't let me jump out a window. Or set anything important on fire. Or marry any more Dark Lords."

She rumbled agreement, though I caught a hint of amusement at that last part. Her attention sharpened, silver eyes fixed on me with an intensity that suggested she understood the gravity of what I was about to do.

I uncorked the vial. The scent hit me immediately—roses and copper and something that made my heroic bloodline sing with recognition. My mother's magic, maybe. Or just the echo of what had been stolen.

"Bottoms up," I muttered, and downed it in one go.

For a moment, nothing happened. The potion tasted of summer rain and old books, sliding down my throat smoothly. I had enough time to think maybe Mnemosyne had given me a dud, some overpriced placebo for desperate nobles.

Then the world exploded into fragments of the past, and I understood why she'd wanted someone trustworthy nearby.

The alley tilted sideways. Nyx's concerned rumble seemed to come from very far away as the first memory crashed into me.

Mother's hands, gentle on my hair. "Remember, little rose, power isn't in the magic itself. It's in choosing when to bloom and when to show your thorns."

Another memory, sharper now. *A dark-haired man with stern eyes kneeling beside my bed. "Your mother is sick, Arabella, and the tower helps her feel better."*

The memories came faster now, each one a shard of glass cutting through the fog of forgetfulness. My mother teaching me to channel light into my palms. My father—and it was strange to see him young, almost caring—warning me to hide my gifts. "The king has uses for girls like you," he'd said. "Best he never knows what you can do."

But I'd been young. Proud. Stupid.

The memory that came next made me gasp. I was eleven, standing in the great hall of Solandris's Sunspire Palace, facing a man in royal robes. King Auremar, though younger, his golden crown catching the light. He'd wanted to see my magic, and I'd been so eager to impress.

The light I'd conjured had been beautiful. Pure. Everything the heroic bloodline was meant to be.

His smile had been worse than any sneer. "Magnificent," he'd said. "She'll do nicely."

Do for what? I had remembered that event very differently—that the king had sent me home with barely a word. Then I realized the original memory had been altered. The image fragmented before I could find out anything more, but the next one provided context. My mother, pale and shaking, arguing with my father in hushed tones. "You can't let him take her. You know what he does to girls with the bloodline—"

"The king has made his decision."

"Then I'll make mine."

Light burst from my hands, and I was jerked back to the alley.

I stared at my palms, horrified, as golden radiance spilled between my fingers. Not the controlled magic I'd learned to wield, but something raw and primal, responding to the emotions flooding through me with each recovered memory.

Nyx's head snapped toward me, her silver eyes widening. She moved quickly, wrapping herself around me, her wings folding over us both like a protective blanket.

My magic surged, wild and uncontrolled. This was bad. This was very, very bad. If anyone saw—if the Syndicate realized what power I wielded—

Then something extraordinary happened.

Nyx began to *glow*.

Not with reflected light, but with her own luminescence. The rosy tint that had been spreading across her scales brightened to a brilliant pink, and I felt our bond flare with sudden intensity. She was *absorbing* the magic, pulling it into herself.

"Nyx—" I tried to warn her, but another memory crashed over me and more power erupted in response.

The potion was working too well now, memories cascading over one another in a nauseating rush. But Nyx held firm, her body a barrier between my uncontrolled magic and the rest of the Spire. I felt her strain, felt her juvenile abilities stretched to their limit as she absorbed wave after wave of wild energy.

But I couldn't stop watching the show in my head, couldn't look away from the truth I'd been denied for so long.

Auremar's mages arriving at our estate in the dead of night, led by a sorceress in gray robes and hood pulled low over her face. My mother breaking the suppression spells placed on her. The surge of power that followed was wild and uncontrolled. My mother standing between them and my bed, magic crackling around her.

"You want her power?" she'd said, and even in memory her voice made me shiver. "Then take mine first."

They had.

The battle that followed was brief and brutal. My mother had been strong, but she'd been one against six. I'd watched from a corner, frozen in terror, as they'd worn her down spell by spell. Watched as she'd fallen. Watched as the leader had raised her hand for the killing blow—

And I'd screamed. Not just with my voice, but with my magic. The light that erupted from me had been nothing like the pretty sparkles I'd shown the king. This was raw, primal, the fury of a child watching her mother die.

The memory of that power called to my magic now, and I felt it answer. Golden light exploded around us, so bright it should have been visible to everyone in the market. But Nyx absorbed it all, her entire body shuddering with the effort.

I'm sorry, I tried to tell her. *I'm so sorry.*

She sent back something that felt like stubborn determination mixed with fierce protectiveness. She'd chosen to be here and shield me from the consequences of my impulsive decision.

At my attack, one mage had been instantly vaporized. Another had clawed at his eyes, screaming about the burning light. The rest had fled, but not before their leader had pointed at me and spoken a word that made everything go dark.

When I'd woken, my mother was gone. My memories were gone. And my father had a story about illness and tragedy that everyone believed because the alternative was too terrible to consider.

The king had killed my mother. My father had let him. And I'd been locked in a tower not just to hide my growing power, but to keep me from remembering what I'd done to those mages. What I was capable of when pushed.

More memories flooded in—fragments of defiance quickly suppressed, moments of clarity stolen away, a childhood rewritten to suit the narrative of a danger-prone daughter who needed a firm hand. But underneath it all, one truth remained constant:

I had always been dangerous. The tower hadn't been to protect me from the world, but to protect the world from me.

The potion's effects were reaching their peak now, and I was drowning in years of stolen moments. Nyx's presence was the only anchor keeping me grounded as memory after memory crashed over me, each one triggering another involuntary surge of magic that she absorbed with increasingly labored breaths.

My mother's lessons in controlling light—because she'd known, even then, that the heroic bloodline was more complex than the stories claimed.

My father's transformation from protector to jailer as the king's gold filled his coffers. The night I'd first manifested destructive magic and the panic in everyone's eyes.

But there was something else. Something darker woven through the memories. In every interaction with Auremar, in every meeting with his mages, I could sense something wrong. A hunger that went beyond political ambition. A darkness that felt familiar in the worst possible way.

Because it felt like the thing I'd seen looking out through Kaz's eyes last night.

The realization hit me just as the potion's effects began to fade, leaving me gasping against Nyx with her labored rumbles filling my ears. The light finally stopped pouring from my hands, and she slowly unwrapped herself from around me.

I stared at her in horror. Her scales, once gleaming obsidian with just a hint of pink, now blazed with rosy luminescence. She looked like she'd been carved from pink tourmaline, every scale shimmering with absorbed magic. Even her wing membranes had taken on the hue, giving her the appearance of some exotic jewel.

"Oh gods, Nyx. What did I do to you?"

She huffed. Through our bond, I felt her exhaustion, but also satisfaction. She'd done what she'd set out to do—kept me safe, kept my uncontrolled magic from alerting every power-hungry bastard in the Spire to my presence.

I wrapped my arms around her neck, burying my face in her scales.

"You brilliant dragon," I whispered. "Thank you."

She rumbled softly, already half-asleep from the exertion. At least the glow was starting to fade.

The memories were settling now, finding their places in my mind like books being reshelved. Not comfortable—they ached like wounds exposed to air—but bearable. I was myself again. Just . . . more myself than I'd been an hour ago.

I needed to tell Kaz. Not about his true nature—that revelation could wait until we weren't surrounded by enemies in the heart of the Syndicate's power. But about Auremar, about what he'd been planning even then. Because I realized that Auremar had his eye on me all along. My mother had fought it, and my father had gone along with it, knowing what Auremar was up to. I was starting to see the connection between the king's obsession with bloodlines and the ancient evil my husband carried in his soul. I still felt like a few pieces were missing, but Mnemosyne had said they would be remembered over a short time.

But first, I needed to stop sitting in an alley like a vagrant with a glowing dragon.

"Come on," I told Nyx, hauling myself to my feet. She wobbled slightly, still drained from her magical feast. "Let's get you back to the apartment and find you some food. I'd say we need to be discreet but everyone is going to see you looking like a giant gemstone."

As we made our way back, I couldn't shake the feeling that I was missing something. Some crucial piece that would make all the other pieces fall into place.

The memories had shown me the what. Auremar's cruelty, my father's betrayal, my mother's sacrifice. We knew the king had been desperate to collect those of heroic bloodline, and what he'd planned to do with us. He'd already accomplished part of his task.

After all, what better way to control an ancient evil than with the blood of those created to oppose it?

But had he ordered my memories erased simply because of my mother's death and the power I'd shown? I'd had the impression the mages were there to alter my memories anyway, and my mother had intervened.

What had they wanted me to forget?

36

Resist Ancient Whispers
(That Make Excellent Points About Murder)

Kazimir

Wind clawed at my face, desperate to tear me from the Spire's landing platform. I welcomed it. After a night and morning of fruitless searching, the physical discomfort was almost a relief from the chaos in my head. Even Griffin's experimental, exceptional—and nonexplosive—tracking runes had failed to find Pip's trail.

And there wasn't much of a trail left to follow from the assassins. They'd hidden their movements with magic, and since I had so thoroughly dispatched the bodies, I didn't have much to work with.

The Alchemist stood at the platform's edge, their shifting robes creating a hypnotic display of color against the gray sky. They didn't turn when I approached, though I knew they'd sensed me coming.

"Your display at the restaurant was . . . excessive," they said, their musical voice carrying perfectly despite the wind. "The Writhing Tentacle has been a neutral meeting ground for three centuries. Now it's rubble and viscera. The kraken will have to be relocated."

"They attacked my wife," I snapped. Everything came out sharper these days, like there were thorns growing in my throat. "What would you have had me do? Politely ask them to stop?"

"I would have had you show restraint." The Alchemist finally turned, and though their mask hid their upper face, disapproval radiated from every line of their body. "The power you wielded—that wasn't just dominion magic. The Heirloom's influence?"

Mostly, I thought. The Heirloom had certainly amplified things, but there'd been something else.

"You summoned me," I said, changing the subject. "I assume it wasn't to critique my combat techniques."

The Alchemist's face twitched. "No. I summoned you to deliver a warning. The other chairs are concerned."

"Concerned." I let the word hang between us.

"They're asking for your resignation."

Ah. There it was. The real reason for this meeting. I stepped closer to the edge, close enough that one good shove would send the Alchemist plummeting into the abyss below. The thought was tempting. So tempting that I had to clench my fists to keep from acting on it.

Do it. One less complication.

I forced myself to step back. "There's only one way a chair resigns. They planning to come collect?"

"Not while you're here, certainly. None of them are that foolish." The Alchemist tilted their head, studying me. "But they don't need to face you directly to make your life difficult. What will you do when Lord Gilt decides to fund Auremar's campaign? When Lady Zaraiah's spy network turns against you? When Baron Revek's cursed artifacts find their way into your enemies' hands?"

"They wouldn't dare." But even as I said it, I knew better. The Syndicate had survived this long by being pragmatic above all else. If they saw me as a threat to their profits . . .

The Alchemist began to pace, their robes swirling. "Your mercenaries have given us victories, yes. But mercenaries can be hired from other places. Your territories can be isolated, your trade routes strangled. Are you prepared to fight a war on multiple fronts?"

Ultimately, yes. With the ley lines under my control—both here and eventually in Solandris—I'd have power the Syndicate couldn't imagine. But there was another complication.

The voice in my head had been just as loud this morning as it had been all night—a constant, insidious hiss that I couldn't silence no matter how hard I tried. I'd attempted meditation, fury, even channeling power through my runes until pain should have drowned it out. Nothing worked.

"You're quiet," the Alchemist observed. "Calculating odds? Or perhaps thinking of your wife? What makes you so certain you would win?"

My jaw clenched. "Get to the point."

"The point is that you're becoming everything the Syndicate was created to prevent—a singular power that threatens the balance. But I didn't call you here to threaten you."

I laughed harshly. "Could have fooled me."

"I called you here because I voted for you to join our ranks, and I feel a certain responsibility for what you've become."

That caught my attention. "You voted for me because you owed me a debt."

"True. But not the whole truth." They stopped pacing, facing me fully. "Do you know why I really supported your membership?"

"Enlighten me." The words dripped sarcasm, but I was genuinely curious.

"Because I saw your hunger for power and recognized it. As a guardian of the ley lines, I should have opposed you. Should have died rather than allow another villainous overlord to rise." They paused, and when they spoke again, their voice carried an odd note of respect. "But I also saw someone strong enough to eventually oppose Auremar. Someone whose honest tyranny might be preferable to the hypocritical 'good' that lets children starve while kings feast. And most importantly, to stop the destruction that was weakening the Shadow King's prison every time Auremar performed a ritual."

I processed this in silence, too tired to fully mask my surprise. The Alchemist admired me? That was unexpected.

"Of course," they continued, "I didn't anticipate you'd acquire the Heirloom and a wife capable of wielding it. That does complicate things."

"Life's full of surprises." I rubbed my eyes, feeling every hour of my fruitless hunt. "Speaking of surprises—did you know my former servant Pip would be at the Gilded Gallows?"

The Alchemist's mask tilted slightly. "I'd heard rumors the boy had been seen there, yes. Consider it a freely given favor. I cannot abide traitors either."

"And the assassins?" I pressed. "Do you know who sent them?"

"No." The word was flat, unadorned. Truth, or at least partial truth. Without Arabella's truth-sense, I had to rely on instinct, but the Alchemist had no reason to lie about this. They needed Arabella alive for their plans to restore the ley lines. Killing her would be counterproductive. "Though I have my suspicions."

"Share them."

The Alchemist moved back to the platform's edge, staring out at the roiling clouds. "Consider the timing. Pip appears and then mysteriously disappears so thoroughly that no amount of your considerable resources—or your shadows—can find him. I've done my own searching, with the same lack of results. Then assassins strike where collateral damage would cause maximum chaos."

I nodded. "You believe they're connected. I agree. Was it a Syndicate member?"

"If it was, I have not heard. Did Pip know of the Heirloom?"

I rubbed a hand on the back of my neck. "Not intentionally, but I believe that somehow he found out, and then used that information to barter or even give it to the Hero's Guild."

"To what end?" The Alchemist turned back to me, their ever-present smile somehow sharper.

"That, I don't know," I ground out. But it'd crossed my mind that Pip was working for someone. Which brought me to another problem. "Lady Zaraiah is at the Spire."

The Alchemist's smile widened. "Yes. She's been quite busy." Their fingers drummed that maddening rhythm. "She wants you gone, Lord Blackrose. Permanently, I suspect. Do watch your back."

"So you won't tell me anything I don't already know."

"Because I have no new information to give you," the Alchemist said. "Perhaps you should focus on what you do know. You cannot remain here indefinitely, hunting assassins and chasing ghosts through the halls. The fate of our world—quite literally—depends on your return to your task."

Rage flared hot in my chest. How dare they dismiss this threat to Arabella as mere distraction? The voice surged forward. *Kill them. One gesture, one thought, and they cease to exist. No more debts. No more obligations.*

My hand twitched toward the shadows, magic crackling along my bones. It would be so easy. The Alchemist stood at the platform's edge, perfectly positioned for a fall that would look like an accident. Or I could simply tear them apart, let the wind scatter the pieces across the Lawless Expanse.

Do it, the voice urged.

No. I forced my hand still. If I broke my word to the Alchemist, if I failed to repay this debt, the magical consequences wouldn't fall on me alone. The magic would rebound onto Arabella, who owed the debt. And we needed the Alchemist's knowledge.

"I'm not abandoning the search," I said instead, each word carefully controlled. "I'll be sending my most elite guards to continue the investigation. They'll arrive within the week. I'll be leaving shadow warriors as well. They'll patrol the Spire, hunt for our missing traitor, and report back anything suspicious."

For the first time since I'd known them, the Alchemist went completely still. "Shadow warriors that can operate independently at such a distance? That's . . . that level of power shouldn't be possible. Not even with your bone-carved runes."

I smiled coldly. "I do have the Heirloom of Dominion, after all." I let shadows curl around my fingers. "And thanks to our little ritual yesterday, I now have a rather convenient connection to the ley lines here. The nexus makes an excellent anchor point, don't you think?"

The Alchemist was silent for a long moment, and I could practically feel them reassessing the threat I posed. Finally, they nodded slowly, as if they'd expected nothing less than my immediate exploitation of the power they'd helped me access.

"Very well. Your shadows may remain, though I expect them to follow the Spire's rules of engagement. No killing without cause."

"They'll be perfect guests," I assured them, the lie rolling off my tongue. My shadows would follow my rules, no one else's.

37

Fail at Everything

(Except Wanting Her Forgiveness)

Kazimir

When I entered the kitchen a few minutes later, Thorne looked up from where he'd been sharpening one of his many blades. Wind battered the God Spire with relentless fury, and the ancient structure responded with a slow, stomach-turning sway.

Arabella stood by the window, cradling a cup of coffee. Nyx sprawled at my wife's feet, her bulk consuming half the kitchen. Her tail coiled around a table leg, and those liquid silver eyes tracked my every movement. I was so tired that it took me a full two seconds to realize she was brilliantly pink now.

"Summon the *Sky Serpent*," I ordered, tearing my eyes away from the dragon. "We're leaving."

"Any luck?" Thorne asked, though his tone suggested he already knew the answer.

"None." I stalked to the counter and poured myself coffee. "It's like Pip vanished into the void itself. Even my shadows can't find a trace."

Arabella didn't turn from the window when she added, "Same here. I checked every gambling den and questionable establishment I could find. No one's seen him."

Her casual admittance that she'd gone searching by herself came as no surprise, but I had to quell the anger rising in me once more. I took a long drink before speaking again. "And the assassins?"

"Ghosts." Thorne set down his knife. "Every contact, every informant—willing or otherwise—claims complete ignorance. Either they're all lying with remarkable consistency, or—"

"Or whoever's behind this has resources we haven't accounted for." I rubbed my temples. "Just like Zaraiah said."

Arabella finally turned, and I caught the exhaustion etched in the lines around her eyes. She looked as tired as I felt, but still breathtakingly beautiful. The morning light caught in her hair, turning it to spun gold, and for a moment I forgot about assassins and missing spies and the voice in my head that whispered terrible things.

I wanted to cross the room, pull her against me, breathe in the scent of her hair. I wanted to apologize for the night at the Gilded Gallows, for trying to compel her, for being the kind of man who would even think to do such a thing. I wanted—

I scanned the room, noting the conspicuous absence of two members of our party. "Where are Griffin and the Scone Lord?"

Thorne cleared his throat. "The Academia of Malice, sir. Griffin's lecture. Sebastian accompanied him."

"Go retrieve them," I said, then caught myself. Griffin's lecture was probably the highlight of his year. Dragging him away early would result in weeks of sulking and "accidentally" explosive experiments. Despite the voice in my head urging anger and violence, I took a calming breath. "How much longer?"

"Another hour, perhaps two." Thorne checked the elaborate timepiece on the wall—a grotesque thing made of bones. "The Academia's afternoon sessions run long."

Two hours. The voice in my head whispered that I should just leave Griffin and Sebastian behind, let them find their own way—

"I'll go with Thorne." Arabella moved toward the door, and Nyx rose to follow. "I'd like to see the Academia before we leave."

I opened my mouth to object, then caught the look in her eyes. Not quite a challenge, but close. And really, what right did I have to tell her where she could or couldn't go? I'd lost that particular privilege when I'd tried to compel her to stay in that booth, if I'd ever had it at all.

I turned back to my coffee, not trusting myself to say anything. But when I didn't feel her leave, I faced her again.

"Kaz—" she began, then stopped herself. Something in her tone made me study her more closely. She seemed . . . quiet wasn't quite the right word. Subdued, maybe.

"Yes?" I prompted, and my heart squeezed, hoping.

Finally, she shook her head and left with Nyx forcing herself impossibly through the kitchen door. As the dragon's tail slipped out of view, I let out a breath.

Maybe Arabella was just relieved to be going home. Gods knew I was, even with the monumental task ahead of us. Gathering heroic bloodlines, performing another ritual to force the Shadow King out of the ley lines, preventing him from consuming all magic in existence—just another typical week in the life of a Dark Lord.

Thorne grabbed his weapons and followed, pausing only to give me a look that clearly said, *Try not to destroy anything while we're gone.*

The door closed behind them with a soft click, leaving me alone with my thoughts. Dangerous company these days.

I moved to the window that Arabella had vacated, watching the writhing chaos of the Spire's lower levels. Somewhere out there, Pip was hiding. Whoever had sent those assassins was planning their next move. And here I was, about to leave it all behind to play hero-wrangler.

I huffed out a laugh. Kidnapping heroes. Under different circumstances, it might have been fun. The kind of dark adventure Arabella and I would have enjoyed together, trading quips and stolen kisses between acts of villainy.

There was something darkly amusing about the reversal—instead of heroes coming to rescue innocents from my clutches, I'd be the one doing the collecting.

I just hoped they weren't all like Sebastian. One perpetually cheerful hero was more than enough for any self-respecting villain to handle.

38

Defend Your Friends

(with Extreme Prejudice and Broken Windows)

Arabella

The Academia of Malice lived up to its reputation as the premier (and only) institution for aspiring villains, teaching everything from demon summoning to tax evasion.

I looked up at the twisted spires and floating staircases that defied both logic and gravity. Signs pointed toward things like: Necromantic Studies—Third Spiral; Applied Torture Theory—Basement Level 7; and my personal favorite, Ethics of Unethical Magic—Location Variable.

"'Lecture Hall of Catastrophic Consequences—Third Floor,'" Thorne read from a floating sign that helpfully pointed the way with a skeletal finger: Stabilization Matrices and Their Applications in Controlled Chaos.

"Sounds about right for Griffin." I stepped over a puddle of ink that was attempting to spell out obscenities on the floor. Nyx padded beside me, her massive form somehow managing to avoid the various magical hazards littering the corridors. Students pressed themselves against walls as we passed, though whether from fear of the pink dragon or recognition of who I was, I couldn't tell.

The doors to the lecture hall were carved from dark wood. I pushed them open as quietly as possible, not wanting to interrupt Griffin's moment of academic glory.

The scene inside was not what I'd expected.

Griffin stood at the podium, his impossibly long frame hunched as he dodged a flying textbook. Then another. Then an enchanted scroll that was attempting to beat him over the head.

"—and that's why the tertiary stabilization matrix must be calibrated to—" He ducked as a bottle of ink sailed past his head. "To account for the inherent chaos coefficient!"

The audience was a mixed bag of villains, apprentices, and students. Some took notes with genuine interest. Others seemed more invested in using Griffin for target practice. In the front row, the demon-adjacent delegation with horned features and flaky, charcoal-colored skin sat with their heads in their hands, looking mortified. They must have been the diplomats from the Ashen Wastes.

"Is this normal?" I whispered to Thorne.

"Academia can be brutal," he replied, though his hand had moved to one of his many weapons.

"Poor Griffin." The voice at my elbow made me jump. Sebastian had materialized beside us, and I noticed writhing vines kept sprouting from the floor at his feet. He tamped them down with frustration. "I've been keeping to the shadows. Some of the students were giving me . . . interested looks."

I could imagine. Sebastian, even in his subdued colors, stood out like a beacon of wholesomeness in this den of villainy.

"He doesn't deserve this," he continued, and there was an edge to his voice I rarely heard. "Griffin's brilliant. These idiots just can't appreciate genuine innovation when they see it."

The anger in his tone—the protective fury on behalf of someone he cared about—triggered something in my mind. A memory, rising like a bubble through dark water.

A garden at night. Sunspire Palace, years ago. I'm arguing with my father, my chin raised in defiance as he grabs my arm. His fingers dig in hard enough to bruise.

"Your behavior is unacceptable," he snarls. "No daughter of mine will—"

"Let her go!" A younger Sebastian, thirteen, wearing a ridiculous golden tunic that makes him look like a canary. He steps between us, violet eyes blazing with righteous fury.

My father's hand cracks across Sebastian's face. The sound echoes through the garden.

I gasped. Sebastian had tried to defend me. Had taken a blow meant for me. And I'd forgotten. How could I have forgotten?

But there was more. The memory kept unfolding, reaching further back to earlier that same night.

The garden again. Pixies flutter through the topiaries, playing and teasing each other. Sebastian and I sit beneath a flowering tree, and he's wearing that same golden tunic.

"You're beautiful," he says, with all the earnest awkwardness of a boy experiencing his first real crush.

I laugh, but it's gentle. "You're ridiculous in that tunic."

"My mother picked it out." He's blushing now, visible even in the moonlight. "She said it brings out my eyes."

"It does." And then, because I'm thirteen and brave and a little bit in love with my best friend, I lean in and kiss him.

It's sweet and clumsy and perfect, tasting of the honey cakes we'd stolen from the kitchen. His hand comes up to cup my cheek, gentle as butterfly wings.

When we pull apart, we're both breathless and grinning like fools.

The memory slammed into me with the force of a lightning strike. That's why Father had been so angry. He'd caught his daughter kissing the son of a minor lord, and his plans for my advantageous marriage had been threatened even though I was so, so young.

Shame and fury warred in my chest. I'd kissed Sebastian. We'd been . . . something. And they'd stolen it from me. Erased it like it never mattered.

Another book flew at Griffin's head, and I snapped.

The shadows responded before I'd fully formed the thought. Dark tendrils erupted from every corner of the room, but this time they were laced with golden light—my heroic bloodline and my chosen darkness working in perfect harmony.

The hecklers found themselves yanked from their seats by constructs of pure shadow wrapped in aureate fire. Their surprised shouts turned to screams as I hurled them through the high windows of the lecture hall. Glass shattered with the sweet sound of destruction.

The room erupted in panic. Students dove under desks. The Ashen Wastes diplomats looked ready to faint. And every eye in the room found me standing in the doorway, shadows and light still swirling around me. A living, breathing storm in their midst. Nyx loomed behind me, wings spread.

So much for not revealing the extent of my power. I wasn't any better than my husband. But I found I didn't care. They'd hurt my friend. They'd disrespected someone under my protection.

I was Lady Blackrose, and I was done playing nice.

Griffin stood frozen at the podium, his amber eyes wide behind his glasses. Then a slow smile spread across his face. He raised one impossibly long arm, gave the audience a gesture that was decidedly not academic, and announced, "Class dismissed."

The lecture hall emptied in record time. Students trampled one another in their rush to escape, leaving behind scattered notes and overturned chairs. Only the Ashen Wastes delegates remained, approaching us with the careful steps of people who were calculating their odds of survival.

"Lady Blackrose!" The lead delegate, a woman whose skin looked like cooled lava, bowed so low her ornate headdress nearly touched the floor. "I'm Emissary Pyrrha. We are mortified by this display! Such disrespect toward your companion—well, the students were protesting the mandatory attendance requirement, but that is no excuse for such behavior!" She wrung her hands, and sparks flew from her fingers. "We deeply apologize for any offense—"

"Perhaps next time," I said coolly, "you'll ensure your audience has proper manners before subjecting my friends to their company."

I kept my gaze fixed on the delegates, carefully avoiding looking at Sebastian. The memory of that kiss was so fresh, so vivid, it might as well have happened yesterday. For me, it had. Meanwhile, he'd been sitting across from me at dinner, helping Griffin with experiments, making himself at home at Skyspire, all while carefully pretending that kiss had never existed.

It was years ago, I told myself. *We were children.*

But the shame still burned, not because of the kiss—that had been innocent enough—but because he had to remember. And I'd forgotten.

"Of course, of course!" Pyrrha said. The delegates continued their frantic apologies, bowing and scraping like their lives depended on it. Which, given what I'd just done, they might have thought they did.

A man in elaborate robes approached, and I recognized the ostentatious display of skulls and dark crystals that marked him as Academy faculty. He was trembling slightly, though trying to hide it behind an air of authority.

"I am Dean Mortifax of Theoretical Villainy." His voice quavered only slightly. "And I must insist—that is, I demand—well, I strongly suggest that you pay for the damages to our windows."

I tilted my head, letting a small smile play at my lips. "Since when do villains pay for damages?"

"Well, there are certain protocols—"

"Besides," I continued, my voice dropping to something more dangerous, "such treatment of my friends will not be tolerated. Tell me, Dean, how far is the drop from those windows?"

He paled further, if that was possible. "Not . . . not too far. The students are likely revivable. With effort."

"Pity."

There was something familiar about him, something nagging at the edge of my memory. "Have we met before? Were you at my wedding, perhaps?"

His entire demeanor changed, the fear melting into eager delight. "Yes! Yes, I was! Such a magnificent ceremony. The shadow binding, the bone rings—truly inspirational! I'm so honored you remember!"

I didn't, actually, but I nodded as if I did. The wedding had been a blur of faces and veiled threats. Half the villain community had been there to size up Kazimir's new bride.

Griffin finally managed to push through the crowd, his face glowing with excitement—though I noticed Pyrrha and her companion positioned themselves on either side of him, close enough that wisps of smoke from Pyrrha's increasingly heated skin were drifting across his robes.

"Lady Blackrose! That was magnificent!" Griffin seemed oblivious to the sultry looks being directed at him from both sides. "Did you see how they scattered? Like roaches when you light a lamp! And the way you combined shadow and light—it was magnificent!"

"Griffin," I said gently, trying to stem the tide of his enthusiasm while also trying not to laugh at the way Pyrrha's cracks were glowing brighter with each word he spoke.

"—and the best part is, some of the smarter attendees actually paid attention to my lecture!" He gestured wildly, nearly elbowing the male delegate in the face. "Ten of them want to apply as my apprentice! Though I don't really need another apprentice, I have so many already." His face fell slightly. "They do tend to die rather frequently, though. Occupational hazard of experimental enchantment, I suppose—"

"We remember your demonstrations at the wedding," Pyrrha purred, and actual flames flickered in the cracks of her skin. "The lightning bridges were *exhilarating.*"

Her companion nodded with equal fervor. "We've been hoping for a repeat performance."

And then I remembered a tale about Griffin being drunk at the wedding and disappearing across a lightning bridge with these very delegates. That memory hadn't been stolen, simply buried under a mountain of others during that chaotic time.

Griffin blinked at them both, utterly befuddled. "Oh! Well, I could certainly arrange another lecture on dynamic magical architecture if you're interested in the technical specifications—"

I caught Sebastian's eye and saw him fighting a smile.

"Griffin," I said more firmly, placing a hand on his arm and gently steering him away from his admirers. "We're going home."

"Oh." He blinked. "Right. Of course. Let me just gather my notes—"

I felt Sebastian's gaze on me. He hadn't said anything since my display of power, but I could sense his concern, his questions. I knew that if I looked at him now, I'd see that earnest worry in his violet eyes. The same look he'd had when he stepped between me and my father all those years ago.

I couldn't deal with that. Not now. Not with the memory of honey cakes and pixies still fresh in my mind.

"Thorne," I said, proud of how steady my voice sounded. "Please help Griffin with his materials. We leave as soon as the *Sky Serpent* arrives."

I turned and walked out of the lecture hall, Nyx padding silently beside me. I had bigger problems to worry about. Like the fact that I'd just revealed my hybrid magic to an entire lecture hall of villains. Or that we were about to embark on a quest to gather heroic bloodlines with my husband, who was slowly being consumed by an ancient evil.

Or that I could still taste honey cakes when I pressed my lips together.

Or that in his current state, Kazimir could never, *ever* find out about that kiss.

39

Replace Emotional Honesty with Orgasms

(a Tried-and-True Method)

Kazimir

The *Sky Serpent* flew low enough over the dark sea that I could taste salt spray when the wind shifted. We'd left the God Spire later than planned—something about Griffin needing to "properly catalog his new apprentice applications" while Sebastian fussed over him like a mother hen.

I checked with Captain Brecca one more time. "Two days to Skyspire if the winds hold, Lord Blackrose."

"They'll hold." I made sure of that with a touch of dominion magic, binding the air currents to our will. The effort sent a familiar ache through my bones, but nothing like the agony from before.

No sky krakens, no rival airships, no heroic interceptors trying to play savior. Just the endless dark of the ocean below and the promise of Skyspire in two days' time.

Two more days trapped on a ship with this suffocating tension between my wife and me.

The whispers had been quieter since we'd left the Spire, but only marginally. They lurked at the edges of my consciousness like shadows at noon—always there, just harder to see. I needed something to stop this restless energy that had been building since our argument.

Take what's yours. Make her submit.

I pushed the thoughts aside and made my way to our cabin. Sleep. I needed sleep. Or a fight. Or at least a bottle of something strong enough to knock me unconscious. Then I remembered my private stores contained potions strong enough to knock out a mountain troll. And if those failed, there was always the option of having Thorne hit me over the head.

I wouldn't dare ask Arabella—she'd probably crack my skull.

I pushed open the door to our cabin, prepared to find it empty. Arabella had been avoiding me with impressive dedication, and I'd expected her to be elsewhere—perhaps with Sebastian and his insufferable flowers, or watching Griffin tinker.

Instead, I found her sitting at the vanity, brushing her hair.

The sight made me suck in a breath. She wore one of her silk nightgowns, the deep blue one that made her skin glow in the lamplight. Each stroke of the brush through her golden hair was methodical, almost meditative. She didn't look up when I entered, but I saw her shoulders tense.

"Where's Nyx?" I asked, closing the door behind me. Safe topic. Neutral ground.

"Hunting." She set the brush down but still didn't turn. "It's the first chance she's had in days. She was getting restless."

I understood the feeling.

I pulled off my coat. The cabin was small but well-appointed—rich fabrics, polished wood, a bed that would be comfortable if we weren't both pretending the other didn't exist. The vanity where Arabella sat dominated one wall, its mirror reflecting the entire space.

"Griffin told me about the Academia." I kept my tone conversational, testing the waters. "Said you threw half the lecture hall out the windows."

I moved closer, drawn despite myself, and stopped just behind her chair, close enough to smell the lightly scented oil she used in her hair.

A small smile tugged at her lips. "They were being disrespectful."

The fierce protectiveness in her voice made pride well in my chest. This was my Arabella—loyal, dangerous, magnificent. I picked up the brush and began working it through her golden strands. She stiffened for a moment, then relaxed, letting me continue. The whispers agreed with my assessment of her, though their appreciation was darker. *Such power. Such potential. Wasted on protecting that fool Griffin.*

"I wish I'd seen it." And I meant it. Arabella unleashing her power, shadow and light working in harmony, would have been magnificent.

"Speaking of the Spire," she said, turning on the stool to face me properly. I let go of her hair. "I should tell you something."

Every muscle in my body went rigid. "Yes?"

"I visited a memory mage. Mnemosyne's Memories, in the lower markets." She lifted her chin, as if daring me to challenge her. "I took a potion to restore what was stolen from me."

"You did *what*?"

"I'm getting my memories back. I didn't want you to think something else was wrong when—"

"A memory mage?" Alarm bells rang in my mind. The God Spire housed countless dangers, many disguised as legitimate businesses, but I'd never heard of such a shop there. "Did you even verify the proprietor's credentials? Do you have any idea what unregulated memory magic can do to a person?"

"Of course I do." Her eyes flashed. "I'm not an idiot, Kazimir."

"Then you're being deliberately reckless." I loomed over her, shadows gathering at my feet. "Memory magic is volatile under the best circumstances. The mind isn't meant to have pieces carved out and shoved back in. People go mad. They lose themselves entirely. They—"

"They what?" She stood abruptly, the stool scraping against the floor. "They die? Like I almost died performing the Lifeweave Ritual? Like I could die any day being married to you?"

Her words took the breath from my lungs. "That's different," I growled.

"How, exactly? Because from where I'm standing, our entire relationship is built on risks you decided I should take."

"I never—"

"Never what? Never lied to me? Never manipulated me? Never kept secrets that could destroy us both?" Her voice cracked slightly, and I saw her swallow hard. "You have no right to be angry about this. None."

The Shadow King roared in my mind, urging me to show her exactly how much right I had, to demonstrate who held the power here. I gritted my teeth against the surge of foreign rage, focusing on the woman before me—flushed with anger, magnificent in her fury, so achingly beautiful it made my chest tight.

Part of me wanted to deny it, to deflect, to turn this into another verbal sparring match. But the fear clawing at my chest—the bone-deep terror at the thought of losing her to some back-alley magical mishap—wouldn't let me.

I moved without thinking, crowding her against the vanity. My hands braced on either side of her, caging her in.

"You're right." The words came out rough, barely controlled. "Our relationship may have started on a lie. But tell me"—power radiated from me until it rattled the bottles on the table— "tell me if it still is."

Her breath hitched. Her pupils swallowed the hazel of her eyes. The air between us crackled with magic.

"No," she whispered.

That single word shattered what little control I had left.

I crushed my mouth to hers, pouring all my frustration and fear and need into the kiss. She responded instantly, her fingers tangling in my hair, pulling hard enough to hurt. I felt a sharp pain as she bit my lower lip. Good. I wanted it to hurt. Wanted something real to cut through the voice in my head.

I lifted her onto the vanity, bottles and brushes scattering. She wrapped her legs around my waist, grinding into me, and fuck, I'd missed this. Missed her. Even when she was right there, I'd missed her like a severed limb.

This wasn't about making up. This wasn't about forgiveness or understanding or any of that emotional nonsense we'd been dancing around. This was about need, pure and simple. The need to claim and be claimed, to lose ourselves in something that made sense when nothing else did.

"This doesn't fix anything," she gasped against my mouth.

"I know." I bit down on her lower lip, soothing it with my tongue when she hissed. "Don't care. Just want you." I moved lower, nipping at the tender skin of her throat. "I hate when you put yourself in danger."

Yes. Mark her. Claim her. Make it hurt.

Once again, the whispers were getting harder to distinguish from my own thoughts.

"And I hate watching you fight battles I can't help with," she gasped, her head falling back to give me better access.

I stilled, my hands on her thighs. She wasn't talking about external enemies. She'd seen the war raging in my head these past days, the way I'd been pulling away, fighting something she couldn't name but clearly sensed.

"Arabella—"

Her hand slid between us, finding me hard through my trousers. "Whatever it is, whatever you're not telling me"—she squeezed, making me hiss—"stop trying to protect me from it."

I captured her wrist, but gently this time, pressing it against my chest where my heart hammered. "Some battles"—I struggled for words that wouldn't be lies—"some battles have to be fought alone."

"No." Her eyes met mine, fierce and knowing. "They don't. Not anymore."

The fragment roared at her defiance, at her presumption, but beneath that foreign rage was my own stunned realization that as she'd been watching me struggle, she was worrying about *me* the way I worried about her.

"I never thought—" I started, then stopped. Never thought she'd care the same way? Never thought I was worth worrying about?

"I know," she said simply, and pulled me down for another kiss.

I released her wrist to free my cock. "Hurry," she demanded, and who was I to deny my wife? The vanity creaked ominously as I pressed her back against the mirror and shoved her nightgown farther up her thighs. I needed her. Needed to lose myself in her body, to drown out the whispers with her gasps and moans.

When I slid into her, we both groaned. She was soaking wet, as desperate for this as I was. I set a punishing pace that had the vanity slamming against the wall with each thrust. She met each thrust with her own, her legs locked around me like she was trying to climb inside my skin. I hooked an arm under her knee to spread her wider.

There was another ominous cracking sound from the mirror.

Before she could respond, I pulled out and spun us, pressing her against the wall.

"Watch." One hand tangled in her hair to make her face the now cracked mirror, and we both watched our reflection as I pushed her nightgown up around her waist with the other.

What I saw in that reflection should have disturbed me. My eyes held too much darkness, runes glowing across my skin in patterns that weren't entirely normal. But Arabella was radiant. Light danced along her skin where my shadows touched it, creating something beautiful and terrible. I held her gaze in the mirror as I thrust into her from behind, burying myself deep.

"Harder," she demanded, pushing back against me.

I obliged, driving into her with enough force to make her cry out. I needed skin, needed to feel her, needed to remind myself that she was here and real and mine. Her nightgown tore under my hands. I only left a bit draped around her front to protect her breasts from the wooden wall.

Then I lost myself in our torrid connection. The familiar pressure was building, that sweet oblivion just within reach. Magic leaked from both of us, shadow and light swirling through the cabin like a localized storm.

I felt her getting close, the way her breath hitched and her inner walls began to flutter around me. I released her hair to grip her hips, pulling her back from the wall to change the angle. The new position made her cry out a string of creative profanities.

"Look at us," I commanded, and she turned her face toward the mirror again. "Watch what I do to you."

Each thrust drove deep, lifting her onto her toes. Her palms braced against the wall for support as I held her suspended between my body and the wood, caught in that perfect space where she could push back to meet me.

"Kaz"—she gasped, her body starting to tense—"I'm going to—"

"Do it." I leaned forward, my chest against her back, never breaking eye contact in the mirror. "Let me see you fall apart."

She came with a scream that probably woke half the ship. The feel of her clenching around my cock, the sight of her—head thrown back, mouth open, completely undone—pushed me over the edge. I followed her down, my vision going white as I emptied myself inside her.

Our magic erupted in a barely controlled explosion of shadow and light, rattling the porthole windows. Sparks of gold and tendrils of darkness danced across the ceiling before dissipating into the air.

For a moment, we stayed pressed against the wall, connected and panting, trying to control our magic. When I finally looked at Arabella's reflection in the mirror, there were tears on her cheeks. "Hey." But when I straightened to see her face, she turned it toward the wall. "Did I hurt you?"

She shook her head and righted herself.

I hesitated, torn between concern and wanting to respect her wish for privacy. I opted for holding her tightly in confusion.

The vanity chose that moment to give up entirely, the mirror shattering into a thousand glittering pieces. I buried my face into her shoulder to stifle a laugh.

"If the others hadn't heard us before," Arabella said with an amused, if muffled, snort, "they definitely heard that."

"They're used to it." I ran my hands up her hips, feeling her smooth skin and wondering how I'd managed three days without this closeness to her.

She turned in my embrace. Her eyes were red-rimmed but clear, the storm passed. Though her freckles stood out on her nose more than ever. We still hadn't made up, not really. The anger was still there, simmering beneath the surface. But at least we were talking again.

The cabin looked like a hurricane had hit it—furniture overturned, belongings scattered, glass on the floor. I scooped her up and carried her to the bed without even trying to fix anything. We collapsed onto the sheets in a tangle of exhausted limbs, but I resisted the urge to fall immediately into sleep. Instead, I pulled Arabella toward me, her breasts pressed against my chest, my erection still proudly straining between us.

I brushed her drying tears with my thumb. The words rose in my throat—three simple syllables that normal people said every day. *I love you.* I took a breath.

The instant the thought formed, the Shadow King's presence surged through my mind.

WEAK. PATHETIC. You would bare your throat to her blade?

The violence of the response made me want to destroy more than a vanity, but I forced myself to remain calm so Arabella didn't know. The voice had been strong for days, but this felt like claws raking across the inside of my skull.

But Arabella was here, warm and real in my arms, still catching her breath from how thoroughly I'd just claimed her—

Claimed. Possessed. Owned. These are words of power. "Love" is surrender.

The fragment was right about one thing: Saying those words would be surrender. Complete, irrevocable surrender of the last walls protecting my mind. I could feel it—how thin those defenses had become, how desperately the thing inside me wanted me to lower them completely.

Every time I looked at her, every moment of tenderness, every wall I let down for her—the Shadow King grew stronger. And if I said those words now, gave voice to the truth that was already carving itself into whatever remained of my soul . . .

Say it, the voice suddenly purred, shifting tactics with dizzying speed. *Tell her. Open yourself completely. Let her see all of you.*

The sudden reversal made my blood run cold. If the Shadow King *wanted* me to say it—

No. I couldn't. Not yet. Not when I didn't know if the man saying those words would still be me tomorrow, or something ancient and terrible wearing my face. Not when declaring my love might be the very key the Shadow King needed to finally break free.

"I hope," I said finally, the words a poor substitute for what I really wanted to say, "that someday you'll share some of those memories with me."

Coward, whispered both the Shadow King and my own heart.

Arabella sighed contentedly. "I will. Someday soon."

I kissed her forehead, but I was already making plans. This Mnemosyne person—whoever they were—had given my wife a potion that could destroy her mind. That required investigation. A memory mage powerful enough to undo deliberate suppression, operating right under the Syndicate's nose? That didn't happen by accident. Someone was protecting them. Someone with significant power.

I needed to know who. And more importantly, I needed to know what else they might have done to Arabella's mind while they were in there.

The whispers agreed. *Find them. Question them. Make them tell you everything.*

I didn't argue.

40

Face the Past
(Even When It Destroys You)

Arabella

The gentle sway of the *Sky Serpent* told me we were still airborne, though the quality of light filtering through the porthole suggested dawn wasn't far off. We'd dock at Skyspire today. No stopping at Azroth's Claw, but Kaz had already promised we'd return there for a real visit.

I'd woken with my arm draped across his chiseled chest, my body spooning his in a reversal of our usual position. He was still deeply asleep, his breathing steady and even, one hand loosely holding mine where it rested over his heart.

It was rare—so wonderfully rare—to wake up with him still beside me. Usually, he was up before dawn, already three schemes deep into his day while I was still trying to remember my own name. But these past two days on the ship, he'd stayed in bed with me.

We still hadn't fully reconciled after our fight, dancing around each other with careful politeness interspersed with bouts of desperate sex. The words that needed saying remained lodged in our throats—those three little words neither of us seemed capable of uttering. But we'd found a kind of truce in the physical—in tangled limbs and shared breath and the way our magic sang when we touched.

I studied him in the pale light. Dark hair spilled across the pillow, longer than I was used to seeing it. It matched the short beard he'd grown during our journey, making him look more like a pirate king than a Dark Lord.

What goes on in that gorgeous, complicated head of yours? Unable to resist, I ran my fingers through his soft hair. My gaze traveled lower, tracing the curve of his shoulder and the muscles that corded beneath his skin.

I pressed a kiss to one of the runes on his back, feeling the slight raised texture against my lips. His skin was warm, almost feverish, but that was normal for him. The bone-deep magic that powered him ran hot.

Pressing my forehead against his back, I breathed him in—winter storms and steel, with that underlying note of clove that was uniquely his. For a moment, I let myself pretend this was simple. That we were just a married couple waking up together, with nothing more complicated than breakfast to worry about.

The Heirloom had other ideas.

A sharp pulse of energy shot through my skull, making me wince. It didn't like when I got too close to him now, as if it sensed something dangerous in our connection.

Fuck off, I thought.

I carefully extracted myself from the bed, and he made a soft sound of protest.

The last two days on the *Sky Serpent* had been nice. Not the tense, silent affair I'd feared. Our friends had stopped tiptoeing around us, though I'd caught Thorne giving us the side-eye when Kaz and I emerged from our cabin looking thoroughly disheveled.

At least Captain Brecca hadn't started a betting pool this time.

I dressed quietly, choosing practical leather trousers and a tunic rather than one of my gowns. Griffin had asked me to review his apprentice applications this morning, and knowing him, that would involve at least three explosions and possibly some light maiming. Best to dress accordingly.

As I pulled on my boots, I glanced back at Kazimir one more time. Part of me wanted to crawl back into bed and steal a few more moments of this fragile peace. He'd sprawled across our bed, one arm now flung over the warm spot I'd vacated. A ray of morning sunshine was shining across his torso.

The sight triggered a flutter at the edge of my consciousness like a moth against glass.

Then the world tilted, and I was—

Elsewhere.

The memory potion was working its magic again, dragging me back into the past whether I was ready or not.

Colors bled and re-formed until I stood in a familiar corridor of golden-veined marble and soaring arches.

Sunspire Palace.

I was fourteen. A pretty golden ring on my finger caught the light as I passed tall windows, and I twisted it absently. Mother had given it to me just this morning, pressing it into my palm with one of her sad smiles.

"For my brave girl. It was your grandmother's."

I'd promised I would be careful with it, thrilled to have something so beautiful and grown-up. Now I wore it as I wandered the palace halls, supposedly heading for the royal library while Father conducted whatever boring business had brought us here.

But the palace was vast and full of secrets. Of course, I'd gotten distracted. When had I ever been able to resist exploring where I shouldn't? I'd already discovered three hidden passages and a courtyard where the fountains ran with wine instead of water. If only Sebastian were here—he loved exploring with me. But he'd gone back to the Academy after his summer break.

I took a turn down a corridor I'd never seen before, drawn by the elaborate tapestries and that particular brand of recklessness that had always gotten me into trouble. The corridor grew darker as I ventured deeper into the palace's heart. Fewer windows here, more shadows. The air here felt charged with a kind of energy that made the hair on my arms stand up.

I rounded a corner and collided with a woman.

"Watch where you're going," she snapped, steadying herself against the wall.

The sorceress wasn't dressed like Auremar's other mages in their gaudy gold and white. Her robes were gray, shot through with strange red stitching like veins of blood. Her dark hair was pulled back severely from her face, revealing sharp cheekbones and gray eyes.

There was something familiar about her, something I couldn't quite place. A scent, perhaps, or the cadence of her voice.

"I'm sorry," I said, dipping into a curtsy as I'd been taught. "I was looking for the library."

"You're far from the library, girl." Her voice was silk over steel, beautiful and terrifying in equal measure.

"I got lost," I lied, lifting my chin. Even at fourteen, I'd never been good at playing the helpless noble girl.

Her eyes narrowed, and I felt magic probe at the edges of my mind. Not the gentle touch of a healer, but something invasive and wrong. I tried to step back, but my feet wouldn't move.

"Interesting." She moved closer, and I noticed how the shadows seemed to bend toward her. I caught a whiff of her scent—bitter herbs and something metallic, like old blood. "Lord Evenfall's daughter, aren't you? Yes, I can smell the heroic blood on you. Very interesting indeed. I wonder if—"

The memory shattered.

I came back to myself with a cry, my knees buckling. The cabin wall was the only thing keeping me upright as the full horror of recognition crashed over me.

That face. Those robes. I'd seen them again, only days later, on the worst night of my life.

That sorceress was the one who'd killed my mother.

Strong arms wrapped around me before I could fall, and then Kazimir was there, naked and warm from the bed, cradling me against his chest. His dominion magic crackled against my skin, ready to obliterate whatever threat had made me cry out.

"What is it?" His voice was rough with sleep but alert, ready for violence. "Are you hurt?"

I couldn't speak past the sob building in my throat. This time, I didn't try to hide the tears that spilled down my cheeks. I pressed my face against his chest and let them come, ugly and raw and unstoppable.

Kazimir didn't demand answers or try to fix it. He just held me, one hand stroking my hair while the other kept me anchored against him. His shadows wrapped around us both, creating a cocoon of darkness that felt safer than any fortress.

"Memory?" he asked quietly when the worst of the storm had passed.

I nodded against his chest, not trusting my voice yet.

"Your mother?"

Another nod. He made a low sound of understanding, his arms tightening. We stayed like that for long minutes, my tears soaking his chest while he offered the kind of quiet support I'd never expected from the Dark Lord of Skyspire.

Finally, when I could breathe without hitching, I pulled back enough to meet his eyes. "I saw her before. The sorceress who killed my mother. I saw her days earlier, at the palace."

His expression darkened, shadows literally gathering in his eyes. "Tell me."

So I did. I told him about wandering where I shouldn't have, about the strange corridor and the woman in gray robes with red stitching. About the way she'd looked at me like I was a particularly interesting specimen.

Kazimir's arms tightened around me. "Gray and red," he repeated, his voice carefully neutral. "Are you certain?"

"Yes. And I was wearing a ring," I whispered, touching my bare finger where the ring had once sat. "The night she died, I was wearing my mother's ring. The one she'd just given me."

Kazimir's jaw clenched, and I felt his magic pulse with barely controlled fury. But his touch remained gentle as he wiped the tears from my cheeks.

"It's connected, isn't it?" My voice cracked on the words I'd been afraid to voice. "The sorceress saw me that day, and then a few days later she came for me and . . . my mother tried to stop her. What if"—I had to stop, swallow hard before I could continue—"what if my mother died because I went wandering where I shouldn't? Because I drew that woman's attention?"

The question hung between us, heavy with guilt and grief. I searched Kazimir's face, desperate for him to tell me I was wrong, that it was just coincidence, that a fourteen-year-old girl's curiosity hadn't signed her mother's death warrant.

But Kazimir had never lied to make me feel better, and he didn't start now.

His silence was answer enough.

41

Accept Help from Heroes

(Even When It Physically Pains You)

Kazimir

Pass the jam, would you?" Sebastian asked Vex, who was seated across from him at the war room table.

The massive obsidian surface—the one Arabella and I had destroyed and subsequently replaced—was currently covered in an incongruous spread of breakfast foods. Scones (Sebastian's contribution that I refused to eat on principle), bacon, eggs, and Griffin's very first attempt at pancakes that had somehow achieved sentience and were trying to escape their plate.

"Raspberry or blackberry?" Vex asked.

"Raspberry, please. Though they're both excellent. Who made these?"

"—and then," Griffin continued, gesticulating wildly with a piece of bacon, "this apprentice applicant writes that his greatest magical achievement was 'successfully animating his grandmother's dentures to bite his uncle at a family dinner.' Can you imagine?" He turned to Sebastian with a grin. "I mean, points for creativity, but that's not exactly what we're looking for in a citadel enchanter."

Sebastian laughed, nearly dropping jam onto his shirt. "Are you going to accept him?"

"Of course not." Griffin paused with his bite of wriggling pancake halfway to his mouth, then added sheepishly, "Though I did ask for details on that spell matrix. Purely for academic purposes."

I listened to this exchange while pretending to study the maps spread between the food. Griffin had clearly overcome his hero worship somewhere on our journey and was now treating Sebastian like an old friend rather than a deity to be revered from afar.

"The kitchen staff made them," Vex replied to Sebastian's earlier question. "Though I did suggest adding cardamom to the blackberry. It pairs well with the fruit's natural tartness."

"Brilliant!" Sebastian beamed. "There's this little bakery in—"

"For fuck's sake," Thorne interrupted, stabbing a sausage. "We get it. You like jam. Some of us are trying to eat without a side of courtship rituals."

"No one's forcing you to listen," Vex said mildly, though I caught the slight twitch at the corner of her mouth. "You could always take your breakfast elsewhere."

"And miss whatever chaos is about to unfold?" Thorne gestured at the room with his fork. "Not a chance. Besides, someone needs to make sure the pretty lord doesn't accidentally seduce half the citadel with his earnest appreciation of preserves."

Sebastian flushed slightly but lifted his chin. "I hardly think discussing jam constitutes—"

"You made three separate varieties of flowers bloom just from Vex acknowledging your existence," Thorne pointed out. "There's an entire garden sprouting under your chair."

I glanced down. He wasn't wrong. Delicate white flowers were indeed pushing up through the cracks in the stone floor, their petals unfurling in Sebastian's direction. Maybe there *was* something to Arabella's theory about Vex and Sebastian. I resisted the urge to roll my eyes.

"That's unintentional," Sebastian muttered, and the flowers immediately wilted. "I'm just happy to be on solid ground again. Or rather, at least *feel* like I'm not floating in the sky. Thank the gods that the seasickness wasn't as bad the second time around. Though I could have done without the captain barking 'Over the side!' every time she saw me."

Thorne jerked his thumb at me. "Take it up with management."

Arabella, who had been unusually quiet throughout this exchange, finally looked up from the tea she'd been nursing. "I'm glad to be home too." She smiled softly, and some of the tension I'd been carrying since yesterday eased.

Unsurprisingly, she'd been subdued since the memory incident, and I'd been watching her closely, noting the shadows under her eyes and the way she kept touching her temple when she thought no one was looking.

She saw her mother's killer, the voice said darkly. *She has a score to settle.*

So did I. Thanks to Arabella's description of the sorceress, I knew exactly who to hunt, though I'd long assumed—hoped—that particular woman was dead. Gray robes with red stitching like veins of blood. Sharp cheekbones and gray eyes. The scent of bitter herbs and old blood. Every detail Arabella had shared yesterday matched perfectly with memories I'd spent years trying to bury. The description had been rattling around in my skull ever since, a venomous snake coiling tighter with each passing hour.

I shoved the thought away, along with the intrusive thoughts. One crisis at a time. Today was about preventing an apocalypse, not settling old scores. That particular reckoning could wait until after we'd secured the heroic bloodlines.

The Shadow King's essence might be bleeding through, but I'd be damned if I'd let it use my old wounds to control me.

"Right," I said, pushing back from the table. "As delightful as this domestic scene is, we have an apocalypse to prevent. Vex, the map."

She cleared a space while I activated the tracking spells etched into the war table's surface. The map shimmered to life, showing the Western Realms in exquisite detail.

"The situation," I began, "is thus: Auremar has been systematically hunting down those with heroic bloodlines, using them for sacrifices to obtain power from the Shadow King's prison. But he's weakening it to the point of no return. We need to find the heroes he hasn't grabbed yet and secure them before he can perform another ritual."

"Secure them," Arabella repeated, raising an eyebrow. "That's a very polite way of saying 'kidnap.'"

"It sounds more likely to result in criminal charges," Sebastian muttered, then seemed to realize he'd spoken aloud. "Not that I'm—I mean, obviously you don't care about—"

"No, I don't," I agreed. "Though I appreciate your concern for my reputation. Now, the question is where to find these would-be sacrifices. Auremar's been thorough in Solandris, but he can't have reached everyone yet. Sebastian, you're ostensibly familiar with noble bloodlines, which is why I've asked you to be at this meeting."

Sebastian had been briefed on the essentials: Auremar was hunting those with heroic blood for some catastrophic ritual, the Shadow King's prison was failing, and time was running out. He didn't know—and I hadn't told him—about the Heirloom of Dominion or exactly how we planned to stop the apocalypse. But he knew enough to understand that every person with heroic blood Auremar captured was one step closer to the end of the world.

That had been sufficient motivation. Sebastian might be a pacifist, but he wasn't an idiot. When faced with the choice between helping the Dark Lord kidnap people or letting them be sacrificed to free an ancient evil, even he could do the math.

Sebastian straightened, clearly pleased to be consulted despite the circumstances. "The obvious choices would be the allied kingdoms. Valmont to the northwest, and Meridian Isle to the south. Both have intermarried with Solandrian nobility for generations. The bloodlines would be diluted but still present."

"Vex?" I prompted.

"Lord Bela Varga of Valmont married a Solandrian duke's daughter, Lady Pennyweather, forty years ago," Vex said without hesitation. "They had three children, all of whom married locally. At least seven grandchildren of confirmable heroic descent. Similarly, Meridian Isle's royal family has two cadet branches with heroic blood through the maternal line."

Arabella leaned in to me. "How does she do that? Did you brief her last night?"

"No," I murmured back, watching Vex continue her impromptu genealogy lesson. She was spectacular when she had data to work with.

"—which means Auremar likely hasn't moved on them yet," Vex was saying. "Both kingdoms have defense treaties with Solandris. If Auremar's called in those treaties for the war effort, their militaries will be mobilizing. Perfect chaos for us to slip in and extract our targets."

Thorne cleared his throat and pulled a folded report from his jacket. "Speaking of chaos in Solandris, this report came in this morning. Three more spontaneous magical fires in the merchant quarter of Sunspire yesterday. And the King's Bridge—you know, that massive enchanted bridge that handles all the trade from the western provinces—collapsed at dawn. No warning, just"—he made a crumbling gesture with his hands—"gone. The magical supports apparently started eating themselves."

"Eating themselves?" Griffin asked, fascinated despite the grim implications.

"That's what it says." Thorne tossed the parchment onto the table between the jam pots. "Everything heading to Sunspire from the west is now stuck on the wrong side of the Silverrun Gorge. Food, supplies, reinforcements—all of it. They're trying to reroute through the mountain passes, but that adds weeks to the journey."

Griffin began muttering about not having enough time to watch everything that came across the Doom Scroll. He was positively addicted to that thing. While he was distracted, one of the pancakes slid off his plate and bounced toward the door. Then another followed, dripping syrup all over the stones.

"It's all caused by the Shadow King spreading through the ley lines," I said, ignoring them. "The magical infrastructure of Solandris is starting to fail."

Arabella picked up the report, scanning it quickly. "This is going to make Auremar desperate."

I nodded and turned back to the map. "Two kingdoms to target," I mused.

"One ringed by mountains, the other an island. Both allied with our enemy. Both probably mobilizing their forces as we speak."

"It's a logistical nightmare," Thorne said cheerfully. "I love it. How many teams are we talking?"

"That's the problem." I traced the distance between the two kingdoms with one finger. "Time and distance. We can't hit both sequentially—by the time we finish with one, Auremar might have moved on the other. Or worse, they might have marched to reinforce Solandris."

"So we split up," Arabella said, as if it were obvious. "Two teams, simultaneous extraction. Kaz and I will each lead a team, since we're the most powerful. It's the only logical solution."

Every instinct I had screamed against it. Splitting up meant vulnerability. It meant I couldn't protect her if something went wrong. It meant—

It means she could act without you watching, the voice whispered. *Without you controlling. Without you claiming what is yours by right of conquest.*

I gritted my teeth. Between our unresolved fight, my status as a potential vessel for an ancient evil, and the way the Heirloom pulsed whenever we were too close, perhaps distance wasn't the worst idea.

"Agreed," I said, and watched shock ripple around the table.

Arabella stared at me. "Just like that? No argument? No declaration that I'm too precious to risk or too important to the mission?"

"Would you listen if I did?"

"No."

"Then why waste the breath?" I turned back to the map, ignoring the way Thorne was grinning. "We'll each take a scrying crystal so we can communicate. You'll take Meridian Isle, which should be straightforward. Take Nyx and Vex with you. Both have proven capable of keeping you alive, which is a full-time occupation." Arabella shot me a flat look. "I'll handle Valmont with Thorne—"

"Actually," Sebastian interrupted, then seemed surprised by his own boldness. "Has anyone considered looking for heroic bloodlines outside the nobility?"

The room went quiet. Even Griffin stopped trying to corral his escaped pancakes, which had led him on a chase around the room.

"Explain," I said.

Sebastian fidgeted, and a small vine began creeping up the table leg. "Well, nobles aren't exactly known for their fidelity. Bastards exist. Plenty of them, both acknowledged and not. The bloodline doesn't care about legitimacy."

"You're suggesting we hunt for bastards," Arabella said slowly. "Noble by-blows scattered across the kingdoms."

"Not hunt." Sebastian's jaw firmed. "Find. Help. Before Auremar remembers they exist and starts expanding his search parameters. He's arrogant enough to focus on 'pure' noble blood first."

It was, annoyingly, an excellent point. I'd been thinking too narrowly. Of course there would be bastards. Nobles rutted like rabbits and had the morals of honey badgers.

"And you know how to find them?" I asked as Griffin returned to his seat with the escaped pancakes speared on his fork.

"I have connections." Sebastian met my eyes. "People who trust me. People who definitely wouldn't trust the Dark Lord of Skyspire showing up at their door."

I scoffed. "It's not about trust. They'll be coming with me whether they want to or not."

"That's why it's called a kidnapping," Griffin said helpfully, spraying pancake crumbs over his plate in his haste. I glared at him.

I felt Arabella's subtle shift beside me, the slight tilt of her head that meant she was using her truth-sense. After a moment, she gave me an almost imperceptible nod. Sebastian was being honest.

Which left me at a crossroads. Trust the man who'd been sprouting flowers at breakfast, or throw him in the dungeons for safekeeping?

Kill him, the Shadow King suggested helpfully. *He knows too much. He wants what's yours. End the threat before—*

I cut off the thought.

"Interested in joining our merry band of kidnappers?" I asked Sebastian. "Fair warning: The hours are terrible, the moral compromises are constant, and there's a significant chance of death or dismemberment."

Sebastian considered this for longer than most would have. I could see the war in his expression—everything he'd been taught about right and wrong battling against the reality of what needed to be done. Small flowers bloomed and died around his feet as his nervousness peaked.

Finally, he straightened. "I'd be honored to help stop Auremar's atrocities. Beyond that . . ." He shrugged. "I suppose we'll see."

"Good," I said, allowing myself a sharp smile. "Because that's all I was offering—a trial basis."

"So how many heroes are we talking about?" Vex asked. "And what exactly are we going to do with them once we've acquired them? Should families be placed together in the guest quarters or given their own rooms?"

"Guest quarters?" I scoffed. "They'll go in the dungeons, obviously."

"Absolutely not," Arabella said immediately. "They're not enemies."

Vex nodded in agreement. "The Dark Lady is right. The dungeons would be entirely inappropriate."

I stared at them both, feeling distinctly ganged up on. "Of course they're enemies. They're *heroes*. I'm the Dark Lord. It's the very definition of enemies."

"Are we going to sacrifice the remaining heroic bloodlines in our own ritual?" Thorne asked, perking up with disturbing interest. "Because I've been working on some new blade designs that would be perfect for ceremonial bloodletting."

Griffin's eyes widened, and the last pancake wiggled feebly on his fork. "Oh! If we're conducting sacrifices, I should prepare the proper equipment! The great hall has excellent acoustics for ritual chanting, and I've been experimenting with a new incense blend that amplifies magical resonance during—"

"No!" Sebastian and Arabella shouted in unison.

I pinched the bridge of my nose. This conversation was spiraling rapidly out of my control. The Shadow King's whispers grew louder, suggesting increasingly creative ways to silence everyone and reassert dominance.

"We are not," I said through gritted teeth, "sacrificing anyone. That's Auremar's approach, not mine."

"But you just said they were enemies," Thorne rumbled.

“They are,” I insisted. “But that doesn’t mean I’m going to kill them for a ritual, as appealing as that would be. This time, I prefer my enemies alive and thoroughly inconvenienced.”

“Then what *are* we going to do with them?” Vex pressed.

I sighed. “To answer your first question, we need as many heroes as possible. Every heroic bloodline we secure is one Auremar can’t use. As for what happens after . . .” I trailed off, not wanting to admit I hadn’t thought that far ahead. I’d been a bit busy.

“The Alchemist mentioned a ritual,” Arabella supplied, watching me carefully. “Something to get the Shadow King out of the ley lines without sacrificing anyone.”

“Yes,” I said, seizing on this. “The Alchemist has a ritual in mind.” I didn’t mention my suspicion that whatever this ritual entailed, it would likely involve considerable pain for all participants. No need to scare off our new recruit before he’d even started.

Sebastian narrowed his eyes. “So we’re just . . . collecting them? For safekeeping?”

“Think of it as preventative custody,” I suggested. “We’re preventing worse kidnapping.”

“That’s not a thing,” Arabella muttered.

“I’m the Dark Lord. I decide what’s a thing.”

“And they definitely won’t be sacrificed?” Griffin asked.

“No sacrifices,” I said firmly.

Griffin and Thorne exchanged a look of profound disappointment.

“We haven’t done a proper sacrifice in ages,” Griffin added wistfully. “The last one was when we tried to summon that weather spirit for the solstice celebration, and that hardly counts since it was just a goat.”

I caught Arabella’s horrified expression and Sebastian’s growing pallor, and decided this particular conversation had gone far enough. We had heroes to kidnap and a world to save—preferably without anyone fainting in the war room.

42

Keep It Professional

(for Approximately Twelve Minutes)

Arabella

"Try again," Kaz commanded, his voice carrying that particular edge that meant his patience was wearing thin.

I stood in the center of the training room, sweat beading on my forehead. We'd spent the last two days preparing for our respective missions. Portal magic had been Kazimir's nonnegotiable addition to my training before we separated. His version of a goodbye gift—an impossible spell and a morning to learn it.

"I am trying," I shot back, attempting the portal incantation for what felt like the hundredth time. My hands traced the required runes in the air, shadow magic gathering at my fingertips. "Maybe if you explained it better instead of just barking 'wrong' every time—"

"Your wrist angle is off by three degrees." He demonstrated the gesture. "And you're rushing the third syllable. Portal magic requires exactitude, not enthusiasm."

"Exactitude," I muttered, mimicking his tone. "Right. Because that's definitely my strong suit."

A ghost of a smile touched his lips before he caught himself. We'd been dancing around each other like this for the past hour—him trying to maintain professional distance, me trying to pretend I didn't notice the way his eyes kept drifting to where my leathers hugged my curves. It felt like old times.

"This is emergency magic only," he reminded me for the fifth time. "Short distances. A last resort if you're cornered."

"I understand."

"Do you?" He stepped closer, and I caught his scent—more steel today than winter storm. "Because portal magic isn't like shadow constructs or healing. One miscalculation and you could scatter yourself across three dimensions."

I took a deep, centering breath. Portal magic was notoriously difficult—not only because it required immense power, but because it demanded precise control. According to Kazimir, it was all about understanding the space between places, the thin membrane of reality that could be pierced and reshaped with the right application of will.

For the tenth time that morning, I gathered my magic, focusing on a spot across the training room. I imagined the air thinning, becoming permeable. With a sharp gesture, I slashed at the invisible barrier.

Nothing happened.

"Fuck," I muttered, wiping sweat from my brow.

"You're forcing it," Kazimir said, stepping closer. "It's not about brute strength. Think of it like picking a lock, not kicking down a door."

"Easy for you to say. You've been doing this for years."

"And I'm trying to compress years of learning into a single morning," he replied, his tone softening slightly. "If you're cornered on Meridian Isle with no other options, a short-distance portal might save your life. But it's not reliable, and you won't be able to take anyone with you."

I frowned at that last part. "So I'd have to leave Vex behind?"

"Yes."

The thought made me uneasy. I would never abandon a companion in danger. The very idea made my stomach turn, but I didn't voice it.

Kaz would probably accuse me of heroic tendencies.

"I wish Nyx was big enough to carry both Vex and me," I said instead, changing the subject. "It would make the Meridian Isle extraction much simpler."

"That day is rapidly approaching." Kaz moved behind me, adjusting my stance. "Though mastering flight on a dragon is just as difficult as portal magic. Different skills, same learning curve."

"You always ruin my best fantasies."

He chuckled, and his voice dipped low. "Pretty sure I'm terrific at making your fantasies come true."

Kaz's chest pressed against my back, and his arms encircled me. His hands hovered over mine, not quite touching. Even through the leather, I could feel the heat of him, the controlled power in his frame. My body responded immediately, a flush spreading across my skin.

I turned to face him, bringing us chest to chest, watching his pupils dilate. "Are you going to teach me this portal magic properly or are we going to keep pretending you're not staring at my ass?"

"Your stance is crucial for—" He broke off as I deliberately shifted my hips against his. He spun me around, pressing my back against his chest again.

"Attempting to distract your instructor is poor classroom etiquette," he murmured against my neck.

"Good thing this isn't a classroom." I leaned into the hard planes of his body. "And you're hardly a traditional teacher."

"I should hope not." His hand splayed across my stomach, holding me in place.

I tilted my head back against his shoulder. "You're distractingly attractive when you're being all intense and broody."

"I don't brood."

"You're literally brooding right now."

"This is concentration." But I could hear the smile in his voice. It made me ache to run my hands over his body and show him just how distracting he was.

"Show me again," I said, surprising us both with the request. "The portal gesture."

He slowly guided my hands through the motion. His beard tickled my ear as he spoke. "Feel the space. The air isn't empty—it's filled with potential. You're not creating something from nothing; you're reshaping what's already there."

I closed my eyes, trying to sense what he described. With his proximity, my magic responded more readily, rising to meet his. I could feel the edges of his dominion magic brushing against my own power. I concentrated, letting his power blend with mine.

And then—it clicked.

Reality tore open in front of me with a sound like silk ripping. A portal, no bigger than my fist, shimmered in the air in front of my face. Through it, I could see the other side of the training room, distorted and wavering but unmistakably *there*.

"I did it!" I gasped, triumph surging through me.

But the moment the words left my mouth, pain lanced through our connection. Kaz's breath hitched, his hand spasming against my stomach. The portal winked out of existence.

"Your runes," I said immediately, turning in his arms. The Heirloom pulsed against my skin, trying to sync with him—its rightful conduit for dominion magic. But something was fighting it, and that resistance was burning through his bones.

"It's nothing." He stepped back, creating distance between us. He ran a hand through his hair, and I caught the slight tremor in his fingers. "The runes are reactive today."

"Let me help," I offered, my healing magic already gathering at my fingertips.

"No," he said brusquely. "It's fine. Let's continue."

I dropped my hand, stung by his rejection but not surprised. Kazimir had always been stubbornly self-reliant when it came to his pain, refusing assistance even when it was clearly needed. Usually, I attributed this to pride, but lately, something else seemed to be driving his reluctance. He'd been pulling away more and more, ever since the ritual with the Alchemist.

I studied him, noting the tight lines around his eyes, the careful way he held himself.

"Is that why you agreed so quickly?" I asked suddenly. "To splitting up? To sending me to Meridian Isle?"

His expression shuttered. "You wanted autonomy. I'm giving it to you."

"Bullshit." My truth-sense tingled, not quite indicating a lie but definitely suggesting an omission.

"I beg your pardon?"

"You heard me." I crossed my arms. "You never agree to anything that easily. Especially not when it involves me being out of your sight for more than five minutes."

"Perhaps I'm evolving. It's what you wanted, right?"

I stepped closer and reached for him. He caught my wrists, holding me at bay. "Why are your runes getting worse?"

His gaze searched mine. "My runes have always caused me pain. You know this."

"Yes." I looked between us at my trapped hands. "But what about this distance you keep putting between us? This wall you're building?"

"Protection," he said quietly.

"From what?"

His grip on my wrists tightened. "From me." I could see the war in his eyes—the desire to pull me close battling with the need to push me away.

"I can handle myself, Kazimir. And I can handle you."

"Can you?" His eyes darkened, and for a split second, I thought I saw something ancient and hungry looking back at me. "You have no idea what I'm capable of."

"I have a pretty good idea," I said, refusing to back down. "I've seen you at your worst."

"No," he rasped. "You haven't."

His tone sent a chill down my spine, but I pushed the feeling aside. Whatever demons Kazimir was wrestling with, I wasn't about to let him face them alone—even if he was determined to push me away. "You're an idiot."

His eyebrows shot up. "Excuse me?"

"You. Are. An. Idiot." I punctuated each word by trying to free my wrists, without success. "I didn't pour my life force into a magical artifact to save someone who's afraid of their own shadow."

"Arabella," he growled.

I pressed into his hold now, bringing our faces inches apart. "You think I don't know something's wrong? You think I can't feel the darkness that's been growing in you since the Spire?"

He went very still.

"But here's the thing," I continued, my voice dropping to match his. "I don't care."

"You should."

I smiled, sharp and challenging. "I married the Dark Lord. I learned shadow magic. I merged with an ancient artifact. I think we're well past what I 'should' do at this point."

"Arabel—"

"Shut up." I surged forward, catching his mouth with mine.

For a moment, he resisted. I could feel the tension in him, the desperate need to maintain control. Then he spun us around, pressing me against a pillar hard enough to steal my breath. His mouth was hungry on mine, all that careful control shattered into desperate need. I gasped, and he took advantage, deepening the kiss until I could taste his darkness, his desire, his fear.

My hands were still trapped between us, but I didn't need them. I nipped at his lower lip, satisfaction surging through me when he groaned.

"This is a terrible idea," he muttered against my mouth. "We have too many things to do."

"Most of our ideas are terrible." I arched against him, feeling his body's immediate response. I rolled my hips deliberately. "Unless you'd prefer to send me off to Meridian Isle all hot and bothered? I'm sure that'll help my concentration."

He pulled back just enough to meet my eyes, and the heat in his gaze made my knees weak. "How terribly inappropriate, Lady Blackrose. I thought I was your teacher?"

"Fuck propriety."

"Language," he murmured, before tasting the salty skin of my neck.

"And fuck you," I gasped, my nails digging into his shoulders.

"That does appear to be where this is heading."

His hands found the buckles of my leather vest, working them loose. "These were a mistake," he muttered.

I laughed, the sound breathless. "You chose them."

"A decision I'm deeply regretting." He finally managed to loosen the top enough to expose my collarbone, which he immediately traced with his tongue.

"Kaz—" Whatever I'd been about to say dissolved into a moan as he found that spot where my neck met my shoulder, the one that always made me melt.

"You were saying?" His voice was dark with satisfaction.

"I hate you."

"Liar." He lifted me, my legs wrapping around his waist automatically, and carried me to the center of the room. I tugged at his shirt, frustrated by the fabric between us. "Less talking, more—oh."

He'd set me on my feet only to drop to his knees in front of me, looking up through dark lashes. "More what?" His hands skimmed up my thighs, finding the laces of my leather pants. "Tell me what you want, Arabella. I want to hear you say it."

I grinned with my lower lip between my teeth. "Teach me something new."

His eyes flashed silver—possession, satisfaction, and underneath it all, that fear he couldn't quite hide. But then his mouth was on me through the leather, and I forgot how to think.

Afterward, we lay on the floor, clothes still mostly on but askew, both of us breathing hard. Kazimir's head rested on my stomach.

My new leathers would definitely need reconditioning after this.

I ran my fingers through his hair. "That . . . was new."

"The runes feel better now," he said after a while, voice muffled against my skin.

I tugged lightly on his hair, forcing him to look up at me. "Are you saying all you needed was sex?"

The corner of his mouth lifted in a half smile. "It does seem to have a calming effect."

"On your magic or your mood?"

"Both." He shifted, moving to lie beside me and propping himself up on one elbow. I studied his face, noting the lingering shadows in his eyes despite his relaxed posture. Whatever was troubling him hadn't been fully exorcised by our encounter.

I could practically feel his walls being erected once again. I sat up, ignoring the protest of muscles that had been pressed against stone.

"You better not die while we're separated," I said abruptly.

He raised an eyebrow. "Planning to kill me yourself when you return?"

"No." I began adjusting my clothing. "I still have a lot of things to say to you, once you get your head out of your ass."

Instead of the sharp retort I expected, Kazimir laughed. "I'll do my best to stay alive, then," he said, reaching out to tuck a strand of hair behind my ear. "We'll go to our respective kingdoms, kidnap some heroes, save the world. Standard Tuesday."

I stood and attempted to restore some dignity to my appearance. "When has anything about us been standard?"

He watched me rebuckle my vest, his expression unreadable. "You'll be careful on Meridian Isle."

"I thought I'd announce myself at the gates and challenge the entire royal guard to single combat."

"Arabella—"

"I'll be careful." I softened my tone. "I have Vex and Nyx, and can contact you via the scrying crystals. We'll be fine."

"And if something goes wrong?"

"Then I'll use that portal magic you barely taught me and probably scatter myself across three dimensions." I grinned at his expression. "Kidding. Mostly."

He stood quickly, catching me around the waist. "This isn't a joke."

"I know." I met his gaze steadily. "But if we don't laugh, we'll go insane. And you're already halfway there with all this brooding. Besides, I'm not quite ready to call it a day, and since we've worked out some of our . . . distractions, I want to try that portal again."

43

Try Diplomacy First

(Just Kidding, Kill Everyone Who Saw You)

Kazimir

The portal deposited us in a back alley of Kheldvar's merchant quarter, between a bakery that smelled of burnt bread and a taxidermy shop specializing in two-headed creatures. I'd visited Valmont's capital twice before—once to negotiate trade routes, once to assassinate a particularly annoying diplomat. The city hadn't improved. Thorne emerged behind me, somehow managing to look like he'd just stepped out of a tavern brawl.

"Remind me again of our target?" he asked, brushing imaginary dust from his leather armor.

"Lord Matthias Brightwater." I pulled out the list Vex had provided, cross-referenced with Sebastian's more eclectic additions. The flower lord had proven surprisingly useful, providing names of merchants, healers, and even a street performer who apparently juggled while accidentally channeling heroic light. "Owns a shipping company. Heroic bloodline through his grandmother. Should be at his warehouse office this time of day."

"And we're just going to walk in and kidnap him in broad daylight?"

"Preventative custody," I corrected. "We're saving his life. No time for stealth today. There are too many on the list here."

Thorne's expression suggested he found the distinction academic at best. "And he has confirmed heroic blood?"

"Trace bloodline," I repeated, stepping over what appeared to be a taxidermic badger that had fallen from a shop display. "We're reduced to kidnapping people whose great-aunt's cousin once sneezed near the First Hero."

"I prefer the old days when we just conquered things."

"Where's your sense of adventure, Thorne? Our other kidnappings went smoothly, and that one this summer worked out very well." I suppressed a grin, remembering the way Arabella's portals had only gotten better each time she tried. And her parting "gift" to me before we separated. "At least it did for me."

Thorne grunted, which could have been acknowledgment or his version of an eye roll.

This was day three of what had become a grinding campaign across the kingdom. Kheldvar was just the latest city on our list. We'd already swept through the borderlands and the town of Goldmar, collected scattered bloodlines from minor holdings in Ironholt, and left a trail of confused nobility in our wake. The portal magic made it possible—I could deposit our rescued targets at Skyspire, grab a few hours of sleep, and be back before dawn—but it was taking its toll. The runes in my bones ached from constant use, and Thorne and I had consumed enough coffee to keep a small army awake.

Kheldvar was everything Solandris wasn't—cramped, practical, and refreshingly lacking in Golden Roses. The mountain city had built itself into every available crevice, creating a vertical maze of stone bridges and precarious walkways. Perfect for hiding. Terrible for large-scale invasions.

Which was probably why no one had bothered with it yet. For me, Solandris was the bigger prize, but Valmont was on the list.

We kept to the shadows, hoods pulled low. The last thing I needed was some eager guard recognizing the Terror of the Western Realms and raising an alarm. Not because I couldn't handle them—I could turn the entire city watch into decorative ice sculptures if needed—but because discretion was key. The moment word spread that I was collecting people with heroic bloodlines, Auremar would accelerate whatever he was planning.

We found Brightwater's warehouse easily enough. The man himself was harder to locate, buried under shipping manifests in a cluttered office that reeked of pipe tobacco and disappointment.

"Lord Brightwater?" I didn't bother knocking.

He looked up, squinting through wire spectacles. "Who the blazes—oh." His face went pale as recognition dawned. "You're him. The Dark Lord."

"Guilty as charged." I smiled, showing perhaps too many teeth. "I need you to come with us."

"I . . . what? No! I have shipments due in—"

A knock at the door interrupted him. "Everything all right in there, Lord Brightwater?" A guard's voice, concerned and professional.

Thorne and I exchanged glances.

"Fine, Terrance!" Brightwater called, his voice cracking. "Just discussing contracts!"

The door opened anyway. A young guard peered in, took one look at us, and reached for his sword. "Intrud—!"

My shadow spear took him through the throat before he could finish. He gurgled, slumping against the doorframe.

"Was that necessary?" Brightwater squeaked.

"He saw my face." I stepped over the body, already weaving a disposal spell. The corpse dissolved into shadow mist that would dissipate within minutes. No evidence. "Where were we? Ah yes, your impending rescue."

"Rescue? You just murdered Terrance!"

"To be fair, Terrance was about to complicate my day significantly." I let shadows curl around my fingers, a not-so-subtle reminder of who he was dealing with. "King Auremar has developed an unhealthy interest in heroic bloodlines. Yours, specifically."

"That's preposterous. I'm nobody. I ship grain and occasional exotic birds."

"Your grandmother was Lady Pennyweather," Thorne said, consulting our list. "Third cousin to the First Hero's line. It's distant, but apparently close enough for Auremar's purposes."

Brightwater's face went from pale to ashen. "How do you know about—"

"Because I make it my business to know." I stepped closer, noting how he shrank back. Good. Fear made this easier.

"This is kidnapping!"

"Preventative custody," Thorne and I said in unison.

Brightwater looked between us, clearly searching for options. Finding none, he deflated. "Can I at least leave a note for my secretary?"

"No." I was already weaving the sleep spell, subtle threads of shadow magic designed to induce unconsciousness. No point in having him cause a scene. "Take a deep breath, Lord Brightwater. This will be much easier if you don't fight it."

His eyes widened as the magic took hold. "You can't just—"

He slumped forward. I caught him before he could brain himself on the desk.

"One down," Thorne said, already pulling out a pre-prepared sack. We'd learned after the third rescue at the border town of Goldmar that unconscious nobles were much easier to transport when properly packaged. "Where next?"

"The Fekete twins. They run a healing clinic in the lower district." I glanced at Sebastian's additions to the list. "Apparently, they also make excellent jam. Sebastian was very specific about that detail."

I opened another portal, this one leading to an abandoned warehouse we'd designated as our collection point. No sense in dragging unconscious bodies all over Kheldvar. Thorne hoisted Brightwater over his shoulder and deposited him inside.

The route to the healing clinic took us through Kheldvar's notorious Crow's Nest district—a vertical slum where buildings clung to the cliff face in defiance of gravity and common sense. Unfortunately, it was also heavily patrolled.

"City watch ahead." Thorne nodded toward a pair of guards checking papers at a bridge checkpoint.

We could turn back, find another route through the Crow's Nest. But that would add an hour to our timeline, and I had a dozen more targets to collect before nightfall. I sighed. "I don't suppose they'd accept a bribe?"

"You could try."

We approached casually, keeping our hoods low. The guards—one veteran with a scarred face, one fresh-faced youth who couldn't be more than eighteen—barely glanced up.

"Papers," the veteran grunted.

"We don't have any."

The veteran's hand moved to his sword hilt—a trained response, nothing personal. But the young one made a fatal mistake. His eyes widened as he caught sight of my face beneath the hood.

"By the First Hero, you're—"

No choice now. The moment my name left his lips, every guard in a three-block radius would converge.

Two shadow spears, two bodies. I was getting quite efficient at this.

"You know," Thorne observed as I dissolved the corpses, "at this rate, Kheldvar's going to have a significant guard shortage."

"They should invest in better training. Specifically, a 'Don't Stare at Dangerous Villains' course."

"You could have tried the bribe," Thorne pointed out mildly.

"And when they inevitably refused and recognized me anyway?" We crossed the bridge. "This was always going to end one way. How many is that now?"

"Seven, including the warehouse guard."

"Still better than that time in Drakenhold when I had to kill the entire palace guard because one of them recognized my boots."

"To be fair, those were very distinctive boots."

The Fekete twins were, predictably, in the middle of treating a patient when we arrived. A young boy with scales covering his body lay on their examination table, his mother wringing her hands next to him.

I strode into the clinic with an announcement. "This establishment is temporarily closed."

The twins—identical women in their thirties with prematurely gray hair—looked up in perfect synchronization. It was creepy as hell.

"Lord Blackrose," they said together. Also creepy.

"You know who I am. Excellent. That saves time." I gestured to Thorne, who was already moving toward them with sacks in hand. "I need you both to come with me."

"We're in the middle of—"

"Treating a curse, yes. Dragon pox, if I'm not mistaken." I examined the boy briefly. "Third stage. You were going to use moonwort and silver-blessed water."

The twins exchanged glances. "How did you—"

"I'm not completely ignorant of healing magic." Thanks to Arabella's influence, I'd been forced to expand my knowledge beyond mere destruction. "The treatment will work. The mother can administer it." I turned to the terrified woman. "Three drops in warm water, once every six hours. The scales will start flaking off by tomorrow night."

"But—"

"Ladies." I let my patience fray, allowing a bit of dominion magic to enter my voice. "This is not a debate. King Auremar wants your blood for a ritual that will, and I cannot stress this enough, end very badly for everyone involved."

They did that creepy synchronized head tilt again.

"Our blood?"

"For what purpose?"

"Nothing good." The mother was still here, frozen in terror. No point in elaborating while she listened, even if I had been inclined to answer questions. "Suffice to say, you're safer with me than here."

"We can't just abandon our patients—"

The door burst open. Three city guards rushed in, swords drawn. "We had reports of—"

I didn't let them finish. Shadow tendrils erupted from the floor, wrapping around their throats. They had just enough time to look surprised before I tightened my grip.

"Honestly," I said conversationally as the guards dropped, "doesn't anyone knock anymore?"

The mother screamed. The twins stared. The boy with dragon pox whimpered.

"Right." I turned back to the twins, who were now backing toward the rear exit. "Let's skip the negotiations."

The sleep spell took them both simultaneously. They crumpled in perfect unison. Still creepy.

"The mother?" Thorne asked, already bagging the twins with admirable efficiency.

I considered the terrified woman. "She didn't see my face clearly. Leave her." I placed a small bag of gold on the counter. "For your silence and your son's treatment. If anyone asks, bandits took the healers."

She nodded frantically, clutching her son.

By the time we'd collected our sixth target—a baker who made "exceptional" croissants and happened to have heroic blood—I was beginning to feel like a demented fairy-tale villain. There was something particularly absurd about kidnapping people for their own good.

"This is taking too long," Thorne observed, dumping the unconscious baker next to the others. Our collection point was starting to look like the world's most eclectic morgue. "At this rate, we'll be here all week."

"Agreed." I consulted the list again. Two dozen names in Kheldvar alone, and we'd barely made a dent. Plus, I'd already killed—I did a quick count—thirteen guards. "We need a more efficient method."

"Mass sleeping spell?"

"Too broad. We'd knock out half the district and someone would definitely notice." I paused, an idea forming. "But what if we lured them somewhere first?"

Thorne's expression grew calculating. "What did you have in mind?"

Twenty minutes later, we'd set up in Kheldvar's town square. Thorne had procured a small platform from somewhere—I didn't ask where—and I'd conjured enough banners to make it look official. The message was simple: Free Heroic Bloodline Testing. Generous Compensation for Qualified Individuals.

"This is ridiculous," Thorne muttered, watching people pass. "No one's going to believe—"

"Sir?" A young woman approached, clutching a worn shawl. "Is it true? You're paying for heroic bloodline verification?"

I kept my hood low and put on my most trustworthy smile. Which, admittedly, wasn't very trustworthy. "Indeed. The political situation has made such bloodlines valuable. I'm offering protected employment to those who qualify."

"Employment?" An older man pushed forward. "What kind of employment?"

"Protected positions within my organization." It wasn't technically a lie. They would be protected. From everything. Including freedom of movement. "The testing is simple and painless."

More people gathered. Word spread quickly in a small city like Kheldvar. Within an hour, we had a crowd of nearly one hundred fifty hopefuls, all eager to discover if they had magical heritage worth monetizing.

Of course, that's when the city watch decided to investigate.

"What's all this, then?" A guard captain pushed through the crowd, flanked by six men. "No one cleared this gathering with—" He squinted at us suspiciously. "Let's see some identification."

"Of course," I said smoothly, keeping my face carefully angled away. "My associate has our permits."

Thorne, bless him, actually started patting his pockets as if searching for documents we definitely didn't have.

"Actually," I said, "I just remembered. We don't have any."

Both guards stepped closer, hands moving to their swords. The captain's eyes narrowed. "Then you'll need to come with—"

"Just a moment, sir!" One of the guards—a thin, nervous-looking fellow—pulled out a thick leather-bound tome from his belt pouch.

He frantically flipped through pages. "There must be regulations for this. Unlicensed merchants—no, that's a fine. Operating without permits . . . ah! Here we go—'Procedures for Undocumented Individuals Conducting Public Business.' Let's see . . . subsection twelve, paragraph four . . ." He looked up triumphantly. "You're entitled to a three-day grace period to obtain proper documentation!"

"A grace period," I repeated flatly.

"Yes! You just need to fill out form 23-A for temporary merchant status." He was still reading. "In triplicate. During normal business hours. Which are . . . oh dear, the office closed an hour ago."

The guard captain groaned. "Jenkins, they're clearly suspicious—"

"But sir, regulations clearly state—"

I unleashed a wave of shadow spears. The guards dropped like wheat before a scythe, Jenkins still clutching his book of regulations as he fell. The crowd screamed, some fleeing, others frozen in shock.

"NOBODY MOVE!" I amplified my voice with magic, adding just enough dominion power to make compliance seem like an excellent idea. "I am here to offer legitimate employment opportunities. The guards were simply overcome with enthusiasm."

"They're dead!" someone shrieked.

"Yes, well, they were very enthusiastic." I gestured, and the bodies dissolved like the others. "Now then, shall we proceed with the testing? I assure you, it's perfectly safe for those who qualify."

Amazingly, about two-thirds of the crowd stayed. People would overlook anything—even fresh corpses—if you convinced them they were chosen.

"What's the test?" someone called out.

I produced a vial of what looked like ordinary water but was actually a diluted solution infused with my own blood. Arabella's heroic bloodline had reacted violently to my essence during our early experiments. Diluted enough, it would only cause a mild warming sensation in those with the bloodline.

"A single drop on your wrist," I announced. "If you have heroic heritage, you'll feel warmth spreading up your arm."

They lined up with varying degrees of reluctance. Most felt nothing—disappointed civilians who shuffled away muttering about charlatans. But every seventh or eighth person gasped as the solution reacted to their blood.

"Congratulations," I told each successful candidate. "Please stand to the side. We'll discuss terms once everyone's been tested."

Thorne kept a careful count. By the time the crowd thinned, we had fifteen confirmed bloodlines of varying potency. Not all were on Vex's list—Sebastian's theory about distant lineages had been more accurate than expected.

"Now then," I addressed our gathered heroes, noting how they preened. "If you'll all gather close, we can discuss your new positions."

They crowded in, eager and unsuspecting.

The mass sleep spell took them all at once. Bodies crumpled. A few remaining bystanders screamed, but I was already opening the portal.

"Efficient," Thorne commented, beginning to drag bodies through. I levitated five at once. "Morally questionable, but efficient."

"Story of my life." I paused, hearing more guards approaching. "How many city guards do you think that is now? Twenty?"

"Twenty-three, my lord."

"Excellent. Let's see if we can make it an even thirty before we leave." I cracked my knuckles, shadows already gathering. "After all, Kheldvar's guard could use some downsizing. I'm practically doing them a favor, weeding out the ones too slow to run from a Dark Lord."

The guards rounded the corner, saw me standing amid unconscious bodies, and actually had the audacity to charge.

"Points for bravery," I admitted, right before the shadows took them. "Negative points for intelligence."

Dozens of guards dead, and the voice that usually screamed for more carnage when Arabella witnessed my violence was barely a murmur. Distance from her made everything clearer—my thoughts, my control, even my shadows moved with less resistance. I filed that observation away, disturbed by its implications.

As we hauled the last of our kidnapped heroes through the portal, I couldn't help but reflect on the absurdity of it all. Here I was, the Terror of the Western Realms, reduced to running a recruitment fair and playing hide-and-seek with city guards.

"Next time," I told Thorne as we prepared to return for another batch, "we're just conquering the kingdom first. This heroic restraint is exhausting."

"Sounds good, my lord."

"And Thorne? Remind me to send Kheldvar a donation for their guards' widow fund."

"The one you just created?"

"The very same."

The last hero of the day—a silversmith who crafted blessed jewelry and apparently descended from some obscure saint—went through the portal without much fuss. Unconscious people were remarkably compliant.

"That's the last on the list for today," Thorne said, hefting the man through the swirling darkness. "Shall we return to Skyspire, my lord?"

The alley was particularly narrow, wedged between a tannery and an apothecary. The competing scents of leather and medicinal herbs made my nose burn. I held out my hand, and Thorne handed me the list.

I scanned it, pausing on a name halfway down. I glanced through the portal, where our unconscious recruits waited in their magically induced slumber, and then closed it. "They're not going anywhere. There's one more we should investigate tonight."

44

Feel Something Genuine
(and Immediately Regret It)

Kazimir

The Black Eagle squatted in Kheldvar's merchant quarter like a stubborn old soldier refusing to retire. Three stories of weathered stone and timber, windows that glowed amber against the evening dark, and a sign depicting an eagle so faded it looked more like an angry chicken. But the moment Thorne and I approached the entrance, I felt a peculiar tingle of old magic—the kind that predated most kingdoms and gave exactly zero fucks about Dark Lords or their ambitions.

"This is the place?" Thorne asked, eyeing the door.

"According to the list." I consulted Vex's notes again. "Istvan. Proprietor. Heroic bloodline through his great-grandfather." I paused, rereading Sebastian's addition. "Also makes exceptional goulash and has 'a laugh like summer thunder,' whatever that means."

"Are we taking him now?"

"After a drink." Arabella wouldn't be at Skyspire tonight anyway. She was probably off charming Meridian Isle with her aggressive compassion.

I pushed open the door, and the scent hit me immediately—ale and pipe smoke, yes, but also hearth fire and something indefinable that made me think of my mother's kitchen before everything went to shit. Which was to say, I had no actual memory of such a thing, but the smell convinced me I should.

The interior was exactly what you'd expect from a establishment frequented by mercenaries, smugglers, and the occasional assassin between contracts. Rough wooden tables, benches scarred by knife fights and spilled drinks, walls decorated with weapons that had definitely seen use. But despite the rough clientele—I spotted at least three I recognized from wanted posters and a demon who was supposed to be banned from this plane—everyone unconsciously wiped their feet at the threshold.

Including me.

I paused, staring down at my boots on the worn mat, irritated that I'd done it without thinking.

Hearth-spirit magic. Subtle, insidious, and apparently very concerned with muddy boots.

I nodded toward a corner table that gave us clear sight lines to both exits and the bar.

The man behind the bar had to be Istvan. Broad-shouldered, with the kind of weathered face that suggested he'd seen violence and chosen hospitality instead. Salt-and-pepper hair pulled back, and hands that moved with the efficiency of someone who'd poured ten thousand ales and could probably do it blindfolded. He caught my eye, nodded once in acknowledgment, and went back to serving a table of mercenaries who were arguing about the best way to poison a rival.

A bard occupied a small cleared space near the fireplace—a woman in her forties with laugh lines around her eyes and a lute in her hands. Her voice carried through the tavern without effort, something about a sailor and a selkie and a bargain that ended poorly for everyone involved.

"Two ales," I told the serving girl who appeared at our elbow. She was maybe sixteen, with the kind of sharp awareness that suggested she'd grown up in places where being oblivious got you killed.

"Dark or light?"

"Dark. And whatever your kitchen's serving tonight."

She nodded and disappeared, weaving through the crowd.

I settled back, letting my shoulders relax for the first time since leaving Skyspire. The building's magic hummed around us—not threatening, just present. Watchful. Like having a very polite but very large dog observe you from across the room.

"Kazimir Blackrose." The voice came from my left, amused and wary in equal measure. "Didn't expect to see you in my territory."

Keld Marton slid into view, all wiry muscle and calculated menace. Valmont's minor villain. We'd met briefly years ago when I'd done business in Kheldvar. I left his operations alone; he didn't interfere with my supply lines. He'd been smart enough not to challenge my presence then, and apparently smart enough to recognize me now despite my hood and the distance of many years.

"Keld." I nodded to the empty chair. "Just passing through. No territorial ambitions tonight."

"That's what you said about Azroth." But he was smiling as he said it, the kind of smile that suggested he knew exactly how dangerous this conversation was and found it entertaining. "Mind if I join you? The bard's ignoring my attempts at flirtation, and watching her pretend not to notice is getting depressing."

"By all means." I gestured to the chair. "Though I'd think a man of your reputation could manage better than longing glances."

"You'd think." He settled in, flagging down the serving girl for his own ale. "But Elowen's got standards. Apparently, 'local crime lord' doesn't meet them."

After his drink arrived, Keld studied me over his mug. "Speaking of standards going to shit—you hear about all the chaos in Solandris? Even Valmont's starting to see problems. Had a merchant's preservation charms fail mid-transport last week. Lost an entire shipment of goods."

"Solandris has always had unstable magic," I said, keeping my tone neutral. "Too much power concentrated in one place."

"Maybe." Keld's eyes narrowed slightly. "But this feels different. Like something's eating at the foundations." He paused. "You wouldn't know anything about that, would you?"

"If I was causing magical chaos in Solandris, would I be sitting in a Valmont tavern drinking ale?"

Thorne grunted into his mug—a sound that could have meant anything.

Keld let it drop, but I could see him filing the information away.

The bard—Elowen—finished her song about the selkie to applause and a few coins tossed into her hat. She took a long drink from a mug beside her instrument, then straightened, a gleam entering her eye that made several regulars groan.

"Right, then!" Her voice carried authority despite its warmth. "It's been too long since we've had a proper gift night. What do you say, loves? Shall we honor the house? It's been generous—warmth, good ale, better company. Time to give something back."

The groans intensified, mixed with a few enthusiastic cheers. I glanced at Keld, who was suddenly very interested in his ale.

"Gift night?" Thorne asked.

"You'll see." Keld's smile had gone slightly pained. "And you'll participate, whether you want to or not. The building gets cranky otherwise."

Elowen launched into a traditional opening verse, something in Old Valmontian that I only half understood. But the magic responded immediately—settling over the room like an expectant presence, warm and insistent and oddly playful.

The first volunteer was a merchant with more enthusiasm than talent, who murdered a sea shanty so thoroughly it should have been considered a crime. Elowen encouraged him anyway, leading the room in applause that was only slightly mocking.

A mercenary followed with a joke so filthy it made even Thorne blush. Then a smuggler recited poetry that was surprisingly good, and a pickpocket demonstrated a card trick that ended with Istvan's pocket watch somehow appearing in the fireplace.

"Your turn," Elowen called to a nervous-looking clerk. "Come on, love. The house won't bite."

"Much," someone added, to general laughter.

Thorne was on his fourth ale—not drunk, he never got truly drunk, but definitely relaxed. When Elowen's gaze swept past our table, he stood before I could stop him.

"Thorne—" I started.

"I have something." He moved to the performance space with the deliberate care of a man who knew exactly how steady he was and wanted everyone else to know it too.

Keld leaned over. "Your lieutenant about to embarrass himself?"

"Probably." Though I'd never actually heard Thorne sing. For all I knew, he sounded like a dying cat.

Thorne cleared his throat, and the room quieted. When he spoke, his voice rumbled as usual, roughened by years of shouting orders across battlefields.

"This is a soldier's song," he said simply.

Then he began to sing. The ballad was old, something about a soldier's last night before battle. Simple words, but delivered with genuine emotion that caught me completely off guard.

"The fire burns low, the wine runs red,
Tomorrow's dawn brings steel and dread,
But tonight we're warm, tonight we're whole,
Tomorrow can't touch a soldier's soul."

The tavern went absolutely silent. Even the demon stopped mid-drink.

Thorne continued through three more verses, each one building on the last. His deep voice transformed the simple ballad into something that made my heart ache. I'd heard this song before, years ago, sung by men who knew they were marching to their deaths. Thorne sang it like he'd been one of them.

When he finished, the silence stretched for three heartbeats before the room erupted. Elowen was beaming, her eyes bright with appreciation. Keld looked like someone had just stolen his favorite knife.

"Well," Elowen said as Thorne returned to our table, "I think we have a new favorite."

Thorne sat down, looking pleased with himself in that subtle way that suggested he knew exactly what he'd done. "The bard seems charmed." He winked at her, and she smiled.

"Bastard," Keld muttered into his ale.

I was about to comment when I felt the building's attention turning toward me like a massive, invisible eye. My ale suddenly tasted flat. My chair developed an uncomfortable ridge that definitely hadn't been there before. And despite sitting close to the fire, the warmth seemed to stop just short of reaching me.

Keld followed my gaze toward Elowen, who was looking at me expectantly. "You're next."

"I don't perform."

"The building doesn't care." He gestured around the room, where patrons were starting to glance my way without quite meaning to. "Istvan's grandmother was a proper hearth-spirit. Wouldn't let anyone leave her table until they'd eaten thirds and shared a story. The building has the same attitude about participation."

I could destroy the building. Turn it to rubble with a thought. But the petty hearth-spirit magic would probably just attach itself to the debris and follow me for weeks, making my life incrementally more annoying. Plus—and this disturbed me—I was curious what would happen if I participated.

"Fine." I stood, ignoring Thorne's surprised expression. "But I'm not singing."

The room went completely quiet as I moved to the performance space. Recognition rippled through the crowd—the Dark Lord, Terror of the Western Realms, standing in their tavern like any other patron. The tension was thick enough to cut.

I chose an old war chant from my mercenary days, something my first company used to recite before particularly brutal battles. The words were rhythmic, describing the calm before violence with honesty.

"Steel weighs heavy in the hand,
Heavier still in another man,
The calm before the storm's first break,
Is sweeter than the blood we'll take."

My voice was controlled, commanding, turning what could have been a simple soldier's song into something genuinely menacing. The temperature in the room seemed to drop as I continued, describing the certainty of blood, the emptying of the soul, the moment when violence became inevitable.

"We know the cost, we pay it still,
The battlefield demands its fill,
But in this breath before we fight,
We're gods of war in mortal night."

When I finished, the silence was absolute. I returned to my seat, and the building's magic settled around me like a satisfied cat. The warmth returned. My ale tasted right again.

Elowen launched into another song, something cheerful and bawdy that pulled the room back from whatever edge I'd pushed it toward. Gradually, the normal tavern atmosphere returned.

I should have felt satisfaction at a reputation maintained.

Instead, I felt . . . strange.

The hearth-spirit had looked at my darkness—really looked at it—and simply accepted it. Not tried to change it. Not recoiled. Just incorporated it into the evening like it was as valid as Thorne's soldier's ballad.

This is what it feels like to be seen and not destroyed.

The thought came unbidden, and immediately, something else stirred.

That ancient presence that lived in the spaces between my thoughts. It *noticed* the crack—the moment of genuine feeling, of lowered defenses—and pressed against it like testing a weak point in armor.

I slammed the walls back up. My runes burned cold as I forced everything back into its box.

Fuck.

I'd been vulnerable before. Stripped down, broken apart, someone else's hands on every piece of me—body, mind, will. I'd survived by holding on to one truth: No matter what was done to my body, to my mind, *I* was still in here somewhere.

The voice that plagued me was different.

Malphas had wanted to *own* me, but the fragment wanted to *consume* me.

And the warmth in my chest wouldn't fully dissipate, no matter how hard I tried to smother it. Something about the offering to the hearth-spirit had cracked me open, and the fragment was already slithering through the gap.

I watched the room, forcing my breathing to steady. Villains and criminals, all of them. Content. Present. Participating in something that wasn't about power or survival, just about being human together for a few hours.

When did I stop knowing how to do that?

I knew exactly when. The first time I'd shown genuine emotion during one of my mother's carvings and she'd had to start over because her hand had slipped.

"Emotion makes you sloppy, Kazimir. Sloppy gets you killed."

She'd been right. Just not in the way she'd meant.

Emotion didn't make me sloppy. It made me *accessible*. Every genuine feeling was a doorway the fragment could exploit. Every moment of vulnerability gave it more room to work.

"You all right, boss?" Thorne's voice cut through my thoughts.

"Fine," I said automatically.

Thorne jerked his chin toward Istvan at the bar. "If we're going to grab him, now's the time."

Right. The mission.

I stood, and the fragment pressed again—curious, hungry. I could feel it trying to twist the feeling, use it as leverage.

This is why, I thought viciously, shoving it back. *This is why I can't afford to feel anything real.*

Not when every genuine emotion gave the Shadow King another foothold in my mind. Not when vulnerability didn't just risk my heart—it risked my entire fucking consciousness.

I approached the bar, my walls firmly back in place, the warmth buried under layers of control.

The hearth-spirit's magic had shown me something I'd forgotten: that being seen didn't always lead to destruction.

But it had also reminded the fragment that I was still in here. Still capable of feeling. Still vulnerable.

And that was far more dangerous than any comfort was worth.

Istvan was wiping down mugs, still humming along with Elowen's songs. He looked up as I approached, his expression shifting from jovial tavern keeper to the hard look of an ex-soldier recognizing a threat.

"Lord Blackrose." He set down the mug deliberately. "What can I get you?"

"A moment of your time." I kept my voice low. "Somewhere private."

"I don't think so." His hand moved under the bar—toward a weapon, probably. "I'm quite happy where I am."

"You have heroic blood. King Auremar is collecting people like you for a ritual that will end in your death." I sent shadows to curl behind the bar. "I'm here to prevent that."

His jaw set. "Then I'll handle it here. The Eagle needs me."

But the sleep spell was already forming, shadows weaving through the air between us. Istvan fought it longer than most—his hearth-spirit heritage giving him resistance against my dominion—but eventually his eyes glazed and his shoulders slumped.

Thorne caught him before he fell, supporting him like a drunk friend.

As we moved Istvan from behind the bar, the building itself seemed to notice. The fire dimmed. The warmth pulled back. The cheerful atmosphere became subdued, like a house realizing its family had left. Glasses rattled on tables. A few drops of ale wept from the tap.

"The Eagle will be fine," Istvan murmured, still fighting the spell even as it dragged him under. "Was here before me. Will be here when I return."

But I could feel the magic already fading, the hearth-spirit presence dissipating without its anchor. Within weeks, this would just be another rough tavern. No more gift nights. No more unconscious respect for the rules. No more neutral ground that even killers honored.

For a moment, I hesitated. Places like the Black Eagle were rare pockets of strange magic that existed outside the usual power structures. I was destroying something unique. The kind of small, beautiful thing that made the world worth conquering.

But then I thought of Auremar's mages, of what they'd do to Istvan, and my resolve hardened. Better the tavern lose its magic than Istvan lose his life.

Thorne supported him as we moved toward the door. To onlookers, we were just helping a drunk friend home. Elowen watched us leave, curiosity in her eyes but smart enough not to interfere. Keld raised his mug in a mock salute, understanding exactly what was happening but too practical to get involved.

As we stepped outside, the cold mountain air sucked the tavern's warmth from my body. Kheldvar's narrow streets were mostly empty at this hour, just a few late-night stragglers and the occasional patrol.

I was already opening a portal in the alley when I saw her.

A figure in gray robes with red stitching like veins of blood, walking down the dark street. Dark hair pulled severely back from sharp cheekbones. A presence that made my bones ache with recognition even before my mind caught up.

It'd been sixteen years since she'd abandoned me after I killed my father. Sixteen years of silence. I'd hoped she was dead, but when Arabella had told me about the sorceress who killed her mother, I realized it was a fantasy.

There was no mistaking the woman now. The way she moved, the tilt of her head, the particular quality of menace she radiated.

Amaryska.

My mother.

45

Avoid the Rooster

(Spoiler: You Cannot)

Arabella

Land ho!" Captain Brecca called from the helm of the *Sky Serpent*. Her face creased into a crooked smile, accentuating the thin scar along her jaw. "Meridian Isle, dead ahead. Made exceptional time. That husband of yours knows his wind magic."

I leaned against the rail, watching the island emerge from the afternoon haze like something out of a dream. Even in autumn, Meridian Isle looked like summer had decided to take up permanent residence. Golden beaches curved around turquoise water so clear I could see schools of fish from here. Palm trees swayed in a breeze that carried the scent of jasmine and sea salt.

Ten hours of flying south over land and now sea, and we'd finally arrived. While Kazimir could portal back and forth to Skyspire between his targets in Valmont, the sheer distance to Meridian Isle meant the *Sky Serpent* would be my base of operations for the next week or so. Vex and I would be camping on the ship between kidnappings, keeping our new guests as comfortable as possible without allowing them to leave.

Not exactly how I'd imagined my first major solo operation as Lady Blackrose, but at least the weather was nice.

"It's beautiful," Vex said, coming up beside me. Her long hair whipped in the wind. "Much nicer than that frozen rock we call home."

"Kaz won't like you disparaging his architectural choices."

"Oh, I'd tell him to his face. Skyspire is magnificent, but it's also perpetually cold, damp, and trying to kill people with lightning bridges." She tilted her face toward the sun. "This, however, is paradise."

A memory hit me just then—sudden and sharp, courtesy of that damned potion. My mother, brushing my hair before bed, telling me stories of an island where flowers bloomed year-round and the water was warm enough to swim in even during winter.

"Can we go there, Mama?" Seven-year-old me, already planning adventures.

"Perhaps when you're older, darling. Meridian Isle is far from here, but I have cousins there who would love to meet you."

"Father says islands are for pirates and wastrels."

My mother's hands had stilled in my hair. "Your father says many things."

The memory faded, leaving me gripping the rail hard enough to leave marks. Another thing he'd stolen from me—the chance to see this place with *her*.

"Are you all right?" Vex touched my shoulder, her relaxed demeanor shifting to concern.

"Fine." I forced my hands to relax. "Just remembering something."

"The memory potion?"

I'd told her about it on the way here, needing someone to confide in who wasn't currently having an identity crisis about being an ancient evil. Vex had listened without judgment, occasionally making dry observations that somehow made the whole thing less overwhelming.

"My mother wanted to bring me here. Father forbade it." I watched the harbor grow closer. "I'm starting to think 'because Father forbade it' should be my new life motto. If Atticus Evenfall hated something, it's probably wonderful."

"A sound philosophy." Vex's expression turned calculating. "You know, there's nothing stopping you from moving Skyspire here. The floating fortress is mobile, after all."

"Kaz would have a fit."

"Lord Blackrose would adapt. Especially if you asked nicely." She waggled her eyebrows. "Or not nicely. I've seen how he looks at you when you're being demanding."

"Vex!"

"What? I'm simply observing that our Dark Lord has very specific preferences when it comes to—"

"We're about to kidnap people," I interrupted, face burning. "Can we focus on that?"

Vex grinned. "I can multitask. Discussing your husband's kinks while planning abductions is practically a Thursday at Skyspire."

I pressed my hands to my burning cheeks. "How often do people have these 'Thursday' discussions?"

"Oh, constantly." Vex's eyes sparkled with mischief. "Though I shut them down when I'm around. Still, everyone knows that our fearsome Dark Lord is utterly besotted." She watched me with a gentle expression. "It's rather sweet, actually."

The silence stretched between us, comfortable despite the chaos of the ship as we prepared to land. I found myself studying Vex's profile—the sharp line of her jaw, the way her silver hair caught the light. Today the ends faded to black, like ink bleeding into moonlight.

"How long have you known him?" I asked suddenly.

Vex turned back to look over the rail. Warm sea air blasted us from below, lifting her hair. "Sometimes it feels like I've always known him."

"That's not an answer."

"No," she agreed, a small smile playing at her lips. "It's not."

I waited. One thing I'd learned about Vex—she'd answer questions, but in her own time, in her own way.

"We met when he was in a low place," she said finally, her gaze distant.

"Lower than most people know. He needed someone who could see him clearly, without judgment or expectation." Her smile turned wry. "Or fear, for that matter."

My chest tightened. "Was it . . . was it after the demon?"

Her head turned sharply toward me, strange silver eyes widening slightly. "He told you about Malphas?"

The name sent a chill down my spine even though I'd only heard pieces of that story. "A little," I said quietly. "Enough to know it was bad."

"Bad." Vex huffed. "That's certainly one word for it." She was quiet for a moment, studying my face as if weighing how much to say. Then her expression shifted—a decision made. "If he told you about Malphas, then . . ." She took a breath. "When I found him, he was barely holding himself together. The demon had kept him for almost a year. A year of—" Her voice caught, and for the first time since I'd known her, Vex looked genuinely distraught. "Malphas specialized in breaking people from the inside out. Not just physical torture, though there was plenty of that. It was the mental games, the way he would wear different faces, make Lord Blackrose think he'd escaped only to reveal it was another illusion. And it would . . . take things. Make him do things. Use his own body against him in ways that—" Vex's jaw clenched. "Demons don't see boundaries the way we do. They see shame as a tool, intimacy as a weapon. Malphas was particularly creative in that regard."

She reached out and squeezed my hand, her grip almost painful. I squeezed it back, too overcome with emotion to be able to do anything else.

"By the time he actually did escape, he didn't trust his own senses anymore. Couldn't tell what was real. He'd killed Malphas, yes, but the thing about demons is they leave marks that don't show on skin." Vex's silver eyes were distant, lost in memory. "For weeks after, he'd wake up screaming, convinced he was still in that place. Still trapped. He'd test everything—pain, mostly, because pain was the only thing he could trust to be real."

My stomach twisted. I'd seen the scars, of course. The ones that weren't from his mother's runes. Some were battle scars. But hearing this . . .

"That's when you met him?"

"Yes. He needed someone who could be near him without triggering those memories. Someone who didn't want anything from him, who wouldn't try to use what had happened as leverage." Vex's smile was sad. "I'm glad he told you. Even a little. He doesn't talk about that time. With anyone. The fact that he trusts you enough to share even a piece of it . . ." She squeezed my hand again, gentler this time. "That's everything, my lady. That's him saying you're safe in a way no one else has ever been."

I had to look away, blinking hard against the sudden burn in my eyes.

"Gods," I whispered. "No wonder he—" I broke off, thinking of his need for control, his careful distance from everyone except me. And now, even with me, something was pulling him away. And I didn't know how to help him.

"I'm glad he had you, Vex," I said once I could trust my voice again. "Obviously he felt safe with you, too."

Vex's expression shifted, concern replacing the distant look. "I know something's wrong," she said, her voice dropping so low I could barely hear her over the wind. "With him. I've known for a while now, but it's getting worse, isn't it?"

My throat felt tight. I wanted to tell her everything—about the Shadow King, about the visions, about the way Kaz sometimes looked at me with anger and violence that wasn't his. But Captain Brecca was only a few feet away, and sailors were everywhere, and some truths were too dangerous to speak aloud even among allies.

"Do you know what it is?" I asked carefully.

Vex's jaw tightened. "I have an idea."

We looked at each other, a whole conversation happening in the space between words. She knew. Maybe not the details, but she knew something ancient and terrible had its hooks in him.

Her hand was still on mine, warm and solid. "When we get back home, we'll figure it out."

I nodded, grateful beyond words. Then, because I needed to shift to safer ground before I started crying on deck, I asked something I'd been wondering about for months.

"Why does your hair change color with his moods?"

Vex blinked, clearly not expecting the question. "What?"

"Your hair. It changes." I gestured to the black ends. "It's been black or deep red more often than not lately. And I've noticed it seems to correspond to . . . to how he's feeling." I paused. "Is that your magic? I realized I don't even know what your magic is."

For a moment, Vex looked uncomfortable—a rare expression on her usually composed face. Her free hand went to her hair, fingers catching in the silver-and-black strands.

"It's complicated," she said finally.

"That's also not an answer."

She smiled. "Let's just say my magic is tied to his in ways that are difficult to explain. The hair thing is a side effect. Mostly harmless."

"Mostly?"

"Well, it does mean I can't hide it when he's in a particularly foul mood. Bit inconvenient when trying to maintain an air of mystery." She was deflecting with humor now, and we both knew it.

I opened my mouth to press further—because "tied to his magic" raised about a dozen new questions—but Nyx chose that moment to land on the deck with a thud that shook the entire ship. She'd been circling above us for the past hour, hunting seabirds. Judging by the feathers stuck to her snout, she'd been successful.

She burped a small cloud of smoke that smelled distinctly of roasted pelican.

Vex wrinkled her nose. "I'm glad Nyx is with us. It'll make getting out of trouble really simple—she can simply roast anyone who stands in our way."

Before I could respond, Captain Brecca called out again. "Best ready yourselves, ladies. We'll be making anchor in that cove there—nice and hidden-like."

The sun was painting the sky in shades of amber and rose by the time we made it ashore. Our landing party consisted of me, Vex, and a dozen shadow warriors that Kaz had bound to my command. They flickered in and out of visibility, perfect for stealth work.

"First target?" I asked.

Vex consulted the list Sebastian had helped compile. "Lady Elena Clearwater. Minor noble, age nineteen. Lives in the village of Coral Bay with her mother, stepfather—Lord and Lady Coralven—and younger half-siblings."

"Any defenses?"

"Two family guards and a very aggressive rooster, according to our intelligence."

I stared at her. "A rooster?"

"Apparently, it's won several local fighting competitions against a barnacle-encrusted sea sprite. The notes are very specific about avoiding the rooster."

"Sebastian?"

"Sebastian."

We made our way through the tropical forest that bordered the beach. Everything here was so different from Solandris—bright birds instead of crows, fruit trees instead of oaks, the constant sound of waves instead of mountain wind. Even the magic felt different, lighter somehow, like champagne bubbles instead of wine.

Coral Bay turned out to be exactly what you'd expect from a fishing village that happened to have a minor noble family in residence. Neat little houses with thatched roofs, nets drying in the evening air, and the Coralven manor sitting slightly apart on a small hill. If you could call it a manor. It was more like a large house with delusions of grandeur.

"That's it?" Vex sounded almost offended. "My closet is bigger than that."

"Not everyone can live in a floating death fortress," I reminded her. "Besides, it's quaint."

"It's tragic. Look, they've painted shutters on the house instead of having actual shutters."

We crept closer, shadow warriors fanning out to surround the property. Through a window, I could see the family gathered for dinner—Lord and Lady Coralven, Elena, and three younger children ranging from maybe ten to fourteen.

My stomach twisted. These weren't soldiers or mages. They were just a family having dinner.

Auremar won't be kind, I reminded myself. *He'll drain them dry and leave nothing but husks.*

"Second thoughts?" Vex murmured.

"No." I squared my shoulders. "But we're taking them all."

"All?"

"You think Auremar will stop at just Elena? If he can't find her, he'll take the siblings just to check if they have a trace of the bloodline too." I made my decision. "We take the whole family. Kaz won't mind."

Vex's smile was full of glee—I'd never seen such a look on her. "Now you're thinking like a Dark Lady."

I knocked politely on the front door.

"Good evening," I said pleasantly when Lord Coralven answered himself. "I'm terribly sorry to disturb you, but I need your family to come with me immediately."

He blinked, taking in my dark traveling clothes and the pair of shadow warriors visible behind me. "Excuse me?"

"Your stepdaughter Elena has heroic bloodline. King Auremar plans to use her in a ritual that will, to use technical terminology, be very bad for everyone involved." I kept my tone conversational, as if discussing the weather. "So we're relocating your family to somewhere safe."

Lord Coralven puffed up like an angry fish. "You can't just—"

Another shadow warrior materialized directly behind him.

"Actually," I said, "I can. I'm Lady Arabella Blackrose, by the way. You might have heard of my husband?"

His face went from red to white so fast I worried he might faint. "The Dark Lord's wife?"

"The very same. Now, would you prefer to pack a few things, or shall we just—"

A blur of feathers and fury exploded from somewhere behind the house. The rooster—and it was definitely The Rooster, deserving of capital letters—came at us like a feathered missile. It was massive, with spurs that looked capable of taking out an eye and an attitude that suggested it had never lost a fight in its life.

It went straight for the nearest shadow warrior, which was a mistake. Being made of shadow, they are notably difficult to peck. The Rooster passed right through, squawking in outrage.

Then it spotted me.

"Oh, fuck—"

I dove sideways as The Rooster launched itself at my face. Vex shrieked. Lord Coralven shouted something about Ferdinand. Shadow warriors milled about in confusion, unsure how to handle a poultry-based threat.

The Rooster came at me again, wings spread wide and spurs aimed at my throat. This time, I was ready. A quick burst of shadow magic created a cage around the demonic bird, trapping it mid-leap.

It did not take this well.

"BRAWWWK!" The Rooster slammed against the shadow bars, feathers flying. "BRAWWWWWK!"

"Ferdinand!" A young boy—one of the Coralven children—came running out. "Don't hurt Ferdinand!"

"I'm not hurting him," I said, watching The Rooster attempt to murder the shadow cage. "I'm saving everyone else from him."

"He's just protective," the boy insisted. "He doesn't like strangers."

"I noticed."

By now, the entire family had crowded into the doorway, staring at the scene in their front garden—shadow warriors, a caged rooster, and two women in dark clothes trying to look official.

"Perhaps," Lady Coralven said faintly, "we should discuss this inside?"

Twenty minutes later, we'd explained the situation, weathered Lord

Coralven's blustering, comforted crying children, and negotiated a temporary truce with Ferdinand. The family would come with us, but they needed an hour to pack essentials.

"Ferdinand comes too," the youngest boy insisted, clutching The Rooster's new cage.

I looked at the bird. It looked back. Hatred burned in its beady eyes.

I sighed. "Only if he stays caged."

"This is ridiculous," Vex muttered as we supervised the packing. "We're supposed to be villains kidnapping people in the night, not helping them decide which toys to bring."

"Would you rather traumatize the children?"

"No, but there's got to be a middle ground between trauma and whatever this is." She gestured at the controlled chaos of a family packing for unexpected relocation. "That one's trying to bring a potted plant."

"Let her. It'll make her feel better."

"You're too soft."

"I'm practical. Willing hostages are easier to manage than unwilling ones. I should know."

By the time we got the family settled on the *Sky Serpent*—with Ferdinand in a reinforced cage that Nyx kept eyeing speculatively—full dark had fallen.

"One down," Vex said, checking our list. "Seven more to go on this island alone."

I was already calculating logistics. The *Sky Serpent* was big, but not that big. "We might need to make multiple trips."

"Or," Vex suggested, "we could try being actual villains and just take the ones we need."

I thought about Auremar, about what he'd done to those he deemed useful. About my mother, murdered for trying to protect me. About all the families who'd be torn apart if we only took some members.

"No," I decided. "We take them all. Every last one."

Vex studied me for a long moment. "You know what? You are an excellent Dark Lady. Different from Kaz, but excellent nonetheless."

"Different how?"

"He rules through fear. You're going to rule through aggressive compassion." She grinned. "It's somehow more terrifying."

I pulled out the scrying crystal Kaz had given me, turning it over in my palm. I could contact him. Tell him about Ferdinand the Rooster and the families who'd organized their own kidnapping. Maybe hear his dry commentary about my "aggressive compassion."

Instead, I tucked it back into my pocket. He was in the middle of his own operation in Valmont. The last thing he needed was a distraction.

Besides, I wasn't ready to hear his voice yet. Not with Vex's story still echoing in my head—a year of breaking, the demon wearing different faces, making him think he'd escaped. My throat tightened. If I saw him now, I'd want to ask questions he'd never answer. Questions I wasn't sure I had any right to ask.

Or if he'd ever trust me enough to answer them even if I did earn that right.

46

Face Your Creator
(Easier Said Than Done)

Kazimir

I waited for Thorne to go through the portal with Istvan before closing it behind them.

Except my hand wouldn't move.

Close it, I commanded myself. The portal hung open, a tear in reality that any passing mage could sense. *Close the fucking portal.*

My fingers twitched. Stayed frozen.

She was already disappearing around the corner—gray robes with red stitching that looked like veins of blood. Two of Auremar's mages in gold and white followed her like obedient dogs.

Amaryska.

The shadows responded before I did, coiling around me protectively. My hand finally obeyed, collapsing the portal with a whisper of dying magic. I stood alone in the narrow alley, every muscle locked in place.

The last time I'd seen her, she'd been standing over my father's headless corpse with an expression of such profound satisfaction it had chilled even me. She'd disappeared right after, her revenge complete after using me to destroy Vargus.

Now here she was, working for the very king I'd sworn to destroy.

Move. Follow her. Don't let her—

My feet carried me forward. Of course they did. I'd always followed her, hadn't I? Even when following meant the knife, the runes, the—

Focus.

I melted into the shadows, trailing at a distance. My mother had taught me this particular trick when I was seven, right after she'd carved the concealment rune into my left shoulder blade. *Shadows recognize their own, my son.* The memory came with phantom pain—the exact pressure of her blade against bone, the smell of my own burning flesh as she sealed the magic.

Soon after, I'd learned to hide from the sound of her footsteps on the stairs, though it had never worked for long.

She moved through Kheldvar's vertical maze with confidence. The two mages flanking her kept a respectful distance—not equals, then. Subordinates.

Which meant my dear mother had climbed high in Auremar's service.

Of course she had. Amaryska never did anything by halves.

The walk felt endless. Time moved strangely, stretching and compressing as I noticed everything and nothing—the exact rhythm of her footsteps (the same rhythm that used to echo up the stairs), the way other pedestrians unconsciously moved aside for her (sensing the predator among them, just as I had), the precise shade of gray in her robes (storm cloud gray, the color of her eyes, my eyes).

They turned into the merchant quarter.

She was heading directly for the street we'd left earlier. Toward the houses we'd already emptied of their heroic-blooded occupants.

I kept pace, moving to the rooftops now. Shadow-walking between buildings. Part of me—the Dark Lord part—cataloged exit routes, noted potential ambush points, calculated the exact angle needed to drop down and snap her neck before her mages could react.

The other part couldn't stop counting her footsteps.

I'd counted them as a child too, listening from my room, trying to predict if she was coming for me or going to her workroom without me. Forty-seven steps meant workroom. Twelve meant my door.

Stop it. You're thirty-three years old. Count something useful.

She paused outside Brightwater's warehouse, studying the entrance with that particular tilt of her head I'd learned to read before I could read books. Considering. Calculating. Deciding which bone to break first.

No. Which *door* to break first.

"The records indicate Lord Brightwater often sleeps in his office, Lady Amaryska." The eager young mage stepped forward, practically vibrating with the need to please her.

Lady Amaryska. She'd come far from the island sorceress who'd traded her soul for power.

"The door is ajar." Her voice carried despite the distance—silk over steel, beautiful and terrifying. The same tone she'd used when she'd said, *"Hold still, darling, this will only hurt for a moment."* A lie. "Check inside."

The mage disappeared into the warehouse. The smell of bitter herbs drifted up to my rooftop perch. Old blood. The scent of her workroom. I could taste copper on my tongue.

You're not there. You're here. On a rooftop in Kheldvar. Thirty-three years old. Dark Lord. Not—

The mage emerged, face pale. "The office is empty, my lady. There are signs of dissolution magic. Shadow residue."

My mother's stillness was absolute.

The stillness before the storm that I'd learned to fear as a child. Before her hand moved and the world became pain.

My left shoulder blade burned. Not real pain. Memory pain. Except my body didn't know the difference.

"He was here," she said finally.

"Who, my lady?"

She didn't answer, already moving toward the next address. The Fekete twins' clinic. Where they'd find more emptiness, more shadow residue, more evidence of my efficiency.

I followed.

They reached the clinic. Found it empty. Moved to the next location. And the next.

Each empty house seemed to tighten something in her posture. I watched her shoulders, reading the tension there. She was getting angry.

"Seven locations," the second mage reported nervously. "All empty."

Amaryska turned in a slow circle.

My shadows deepened instinctively, wrapping tighter around my form until I was less a person and more an absence of light. For one heart-stopping moment, I thought she'd spotted me. But her gaze passed over my hiding spot without pause.

"Send word to His Majesty," she commanded. "Someone is collecting bloodlines. Someone with significant shadow magic capabilities."

Someone. Not *my son.* Did she know? Of course she knew. Amaryska was never a fool.

"The Dark Lord?" the eager mage suggested.

"Possibly." She tilted her head—that same gesture she'd made while deciding which bone to carve next. "Double the collection teams," she ordered. "And send scouts to check the other kingdoms. If someone is collecting them . . ."

"They're planning something," the second mage finished.

"Or preventing something." Uncertainty flickered in her voice. "We will return to the capital. I need to consult the old texts."

They left, my mother's gray robes disappearing into the darkness.

I released my hold on the shadows and remained on the rooftop. My hands were shaking.

She was hunting the same bloodlines. Which meant Auremar was planning another ritual sooner than we thought. We'd been right to act quickly.

The runes in my bones burned hotter. All of them now, not just the shoulder blade. A symphony of remembered agony.

You're not seven. You're not twelve. You're not seventeen and bleeding in a demon's lair.

I was thirty-three. The Dark Lord of Skyspire. I'd killed my father at his own dinner table. I'd escaped a demon that should have broken me.

My mother was just another enemy. Another obstacle to remove.

Except my hands wouldn't stop shaking.

A clock tower chimed somewhere in the distance. Time to return to Skyspire. To sort our rescued bloodlines and plan the next move. To hold my wife and tell her that her mother's killer was my mother.

I couldn't keep that from Arabella any longer.

I raised my hand to tear open a portal back to Thorne—

"I knew it was you."

The voice slithered from the darkness behind me, and every muscle in my body locked.

Not metaphorically. Not *feeling* frozen. Actually, physically unable to move.

Turn around. Face her. Kill her.

Nothing happened.

I heard her footsteps. Soft. Measured. Twelve steps to my door.

Move. MOVE.

"Still so dramatic." The footsteps stopped. She was close enough that I could smell her, and it made me feel sick. "Though I suppose I taught you that."

My body finally obeyed, turning slowly.

Amaryska stood at the rooftop's edge, gray robes rippling in the evening breeze. The red stitching looked like fresh wounds in the moonlight.

"Amaryska." The Dark Lord spoke through my mouth, cold and controlled. (The child underneath was screaming.) "I thought you were dead."

"Hoped, you mean." Her gray eyes studied me with clinical interest. The same look she'd given me before each carving session, assessing which rune would fit where. "You've grown powerful. More than I anticipated when I left you to that demon."

Her casual admission struck with brutal force.

When I left you—

Time fractured.

I blinked and I was seventeen, waking up in chains in a demon's lair, my supposed allies' laughter still echoing. They'd known exactly when to strike. Exactly where I'd be vulnerable.

I blinked and I was thirty-three again, standing on a rooftop, staring at my mother.

Left you to that demon.

"When you *left* me?" The words came from somewhere deep and raw.

"Oh, don't look so surprised." She tilted her head. That gesture. That fucking gesture. "You were always too clever not to figure it out eventually. Though I'd thought the demon would take care of you. Imagine my surprise when you turned up a year later, even more powerful than before."

"It was your idea all along." My voice was still steady. Still controlled. (The child was howling now, clawing at the inside of my skull.) "You helped them sell me to that thing."

"I orchestrated it." No shame. No regret. Just that same matter-of-fact tone she'd used when explaining why she needed to break my fingers before carving the strength runes.

The Shadow King whispered of similar betrayals across centuries. I shoved him down viciously. This was my rage, my pain. Not his.

"You were becoming too powerful, too quickly. I was afraid of what you'd become." She paused. "And I was right to be afraid."

The rage exploded.

My shadows erupted outward in a wave of darkness, racing across the rooftop toward her. (*Tighter,* the child begged. *Make her stop breathing. Make her stop talking. Make her STOP.*) She sidestepped with infuriating grace, her own magic flaring to life—essence magic, the brutal foundation from which my dominion had evolved.

Crimson threads erupted from her palms, seeking to bind rather than command.

I lunged forward, channeling raw power through the combat runes in my arms. She deflected with a gesture, more threads whipping from her fingers to intercept my strike.

I was already moving. Using the momentum to spin and strike from a different angle. My shadows formed into blades, slicing through the space where she'd been a heartbeat before.

The air reeked of copper and the metallic tang of essence magic.

"You sold your own son!" The words tore from my throat—not the Dark Lord's controlled fury, but younger.

"I tried to contain a weapon that had grown beyond its purpose." She danced backward, weaving defensive spells with the same precision she'd used to carve runes. "You were meant to kill your father, nothing more."

Nothing more.

I was seventeen again, watching my father's head roll across the floor, looking to her for approval and finding only cold satisfaction.

And now my mother was still talking about me like I was a tool that had outlived its usefulness.

I caught her wrist as she tried to cast something particularly nasty, her essence magic already coiling around my bones, trying to bind me from the inside out. The contact sent shock waves of pain through us both—her magic recognizing the runes she'd carved, trying to turn them against me.

Her eyes widened. She hadn't expected me to be strong enough to resist.

"And Arabella's mother?" I yanked her closer, shadows wrapping around her throat. "Was murdering her part of your grand plan too?"

Surprise flickered in Amaryska's expression. "How did you—"

My shadows tightened, cutting off her words. But she hissed a single syllable through clenched teeth—a command that burned through my shadows. I recoiled as she twisted free, but not before I sent more shadows flying toward her chest.

She twisted at the last second, taking the blow to her shoulder instead. Blood splattered across the rooftop.

Real blood. Red and hot and—

It was my blood on the floor and she was saying, *"Hold still, darling."*

I realized she was moving, speaking words in a language that predated the kingdoms. A portal began to tear open, reeking of sulfur and old magic.

No. NO.

"No!" I lunged forward, shadows racing to seal the portal, to trap her here where I could finish this—

She stumbled backward through the tear in reality, clutching her wounded shoulder. Our eyes met for one frozen moment—mother and son, creator and creation, betrayer and betrayed.

I blinked and she was gone.

The portal snapped shut, leaving me alone on the rooftop with nothing but the echo of my rage and the scent of her blood on the stones.

I stood there, chest heaving, shadows in chaos. My hands were shaking again. My whole body was shaking.

The shame of letting her go was worse than the rage. Worse than the pain in my bones.

The scrying crystal burned against my ribs where I'd tucked it into an inner pocket. I could contact Arabella. Tell her . . . what? That I'd found my mother? That she'd orchestrated my betrayal to a demon? That I'd had her and let her escape because I couldn't stop being seven years old?

That my mother had killed hers?

No. That conversation required me to look my wife in the eye. To be present enough to handle whatever came after.

Not while I was still bleeding emotion all over a Kheldvar rooftop.

Pathetic.

Let Amaryska hide behind Solandris's walls and think herself safe. Let her believe the portal had saved her. Because when I finally got my hands on her again, there would be no portals. No escape. No blinking between ages while she slipped away.

Only the reckoning she'd earned with every scar she'd carved into my bones.

I raised my hand—still shaking, fuck—and tore open a portal back to where Thorne waited. Then we'd go to Skyspire.

Time to stop being seven years old and start being the Dark Lord who would burn the world to ash if that's what it took to get revenge.

The portal swallowed me, and I left my mother's blood drying on the rooftop behind me.

A promise. A threat. A preview of what was coming.

47

Achieve Maximum Capacity

(in Chaos and Cargo)

Arabella

The next few days blurred together in a series of increasingly absurd kidnappings. We'd rescue a family, get them settled on the *Sky Serpent*, then sail off to our next target. Each "rescue" came with its own unique challenges.

There was the merchant family where we had to wait twenty minutes for their elderly grandmother to finish her bedtime prayers. The healer who insisted on bringing her entire herb garden. The blacksmith's apprentice who turned out to have six siblings, three dogs, and a pregnant cat.

"This is getting out of hand," Vex observed as we watched the apprentice's family board the ship. "Lord Blackrose is going to have thoughts about this."

"Kaz can cope." I was tired, sandy, and somehow had feathers in my hair from an earlier altercation with another aggressive bird. "Besides, he's probably having similar issues."

"You think the Terror of the Western Realms is negotiating with roosters and helping pack toys?"

"No," I admitted. "He's probably just knocking everyone unconscious and sorting it out later."

"You say that like it's a bad thing."

I thought about it as we approached our next target. "It's just . . . not me."

"And that's why you two work," Vex said. "He's the iron fist, you're the velvet glove. Together, you're a complete tyrant."

The kidnapping that night proved more challenging. The Marenti family had actual guards—not many, but enough to notice our approach.

"Finally," Vex whispered as we crouched in the bushes outside their villa. "A proper challenge."

"You sound disappointed by the lack of violence so far."

"I'm Steward of Skyspire. I have a reputation to maintain." She studied the house. "Two at the front, probably more inside."

"Shadow warriors can handle them."

We struck fast and hard. Shadow warriors materialized behind each guard, rendering them unconscious before they could raise an alarm. We were inside the villa before anyone knew we were there.

The Marenti family was larger than expected—parents, four children, and an elderly aunt who immediately started hitting me with her cane.

"Ow! My lady, please—ow! I'm trying to save your life!"

"Burglar! Ruffian! Scoundrel!" Each word came with another whack.

"Actually, I'm a Dark Lady," I said, catching the cane mid-swing. "Which is much worse than any of those things."

That gave her pause. "You're the Blackrose woman? The one who married that villain?"

"Guilty."

"Hmph." She looked me up and down. "You're shorter than I expected."

I narrowed my eyes.

"And prettier. The rumor mill makes you sound like some sort of succubus."

"Only on weekends."

That startled a laugh out of her. "Well then. I suppose if we're being kidnapped, at least it's by someone with a sense of humor. I'm Cordelia Marenti, by the way. You may call me Aunt Cordelia—everyone does. Children! Pack your things. We're being relocated."

The efficiency with which she organized the family was impressive. Within minutes, she had everyone moving with military precision.

"You're taking this very well," I observed.

"My dear girl, I'm eighty-three years old. I've survived two wars, four kings, and seven marriage proposals. A kidnapping by the Dark Lord's wife barely registers." She paused. "Though I do hope you have comfortable accommodations. My arthritis doesn't care for cold."

"Skyspire has excellent heating," Vex assured her—not even a guilty glance at me. "Magical climate control in every room."

"How modern. Very well, I'm convinced." Aunt Cordelia turned to her family. "Stop dawdling! The nice villainesses are waiting."

By the time we finished our final kidnapping for the evening—a family of pearl divers named Delacroix who were remarkably chill about the whole thing—the *Sky Serpent* looked less like a fearsome vessel and more like a refugee ship. Children ran around the deck, dogs barked, Aunt Cordelia had started a card game with some of the older teens, and Ferdinand the Rooster crowed every few minutes just to remind everyone he existed.

"This is chaos," Vex said, but she was smiling. "Absolute chaos."

I watched a little girl offer Nyx a piece of candy. The dragon accepted it delicately. "They're safe. That's what matters."

Captain Brecca approached. "Begging your pardon, Lady Blackrose, but we're at capacity. Any more and we'll be stuck on the ground."

I checked the list. We'd gotten everyone from the main Meridian Isle, but there were outlying islands with one or two. "Can we make multiple trips?"

"Aye, but it'll take time. These aren't exactly short journeys."

I made a decision. "Then we take these families back to Skyspire first. Make sure they're settled safely." I glanced at Vex. "Think you can handle the intake process?"

"I'll have them sorted and housed within an hour of arriving." She paused. "What about you?"

"I'll stay here with the shadow warriors." I was already planning. "By the time you return, I'll have everyone gathered and ready to go."

"Lord Blackrose won't like you staying alone."

"Kaz isn't here." I softened the words with a smile. "Besides, I'm hardly alone. I've got shadow warriors and a pink dragon who's developed a taste for candy."

Indeed, Nyx was now surrounded by children, all of whom seemed to have decided she was the world's largest, scaliest dog. She was preening under the attention.

"If you're sure," Vex said doubtfully.

A few minutes later, I stood on an island beach, watching as the *Sky Serpent* prepared to depart. Maybe Vex was right. Maybe I was too soft.

But as I watched the ship disappear into the darkness, carrying dozens of people to safety, I decided I was okay with that. Kaz could be the iron fist. I'd be the velvet glove.

Together, we'd save the world.

Whether it wanted to be saved or not.

48

Survive an Abduction Attempt

(by Becoming the Scarier Villain)

Arabella

The last kidnappings went as expected, and a day later I made my way along a moonlit beach, waiting for the *Sky Serpent*. Assuming it had dropped off its passengers and turned right back, it would arrive any minute. The Moonbay family had been surprisingly cooperative once I'd mentioned the word "plague." Nothing motivated nobility quite like the threat of pustules. Now I just needed a moment to myself.

Above, Nyx's shadow blotted out stars as she circled, her wingspan casting moving patches of darkness across the silver-touched waves. She was making sure no one left the beach, though all of them were too petrified to wander far. The shadow warriors flanked me as I explored, their forms rippling at the edges where moonlight tried to define them.

Magic slammed into me from seemingly nowhere.

The impact sent me staggering, and before I could regain my footing, a spell wrapped around me, so heavy that the air compressed until it made it hard to breathe. I spun toward the tree line, magic crackling around my hands, ready to strike at whoever dared—

"Lady Blackrose." Zaraiah stepped out from behind a cluster of palms. She wore dark traveling leathers instead of her usual provocative gowns, her short-cropped hair accentuating the classic beauty of her face. "How delightful to find you here. And alone, it seems."

Fuck.

She'd sworn she wasn't involved in the assassination attempt, that she preferred her enemies "alive and suffering." Kaz had stopped me from killing her.

Apparently, we should have gone with my instincts.

A forgettable man emerged beside her—average height, brown hair, the kind of face your eyes wanted to skip over. Every instinct screamed danger.

"Shadow warriors!" I commanded, but nothing happened. They flickered at the edges of my vision, still visible but suddenly unreachable through what felt like an invisible wall. I tried again, pulling at the bindings Kaz had placed, but it was like grasping smoke.

Fine. I'd handle this myself.

I launched a spear of shadow at Zaraiah's smirking face, but it shattered against something I couldn't see. A follow-up blast of light magic met the same fate.

"What the—" Then I saw it. Barely visible in the moonlight, a shimmer in the air. A perfect dome surrounding me, cutting me off from everything outside.

"Impressive," I admitted, testing the magic. It was elegant work, clearly designed specifically for me. "How long did it take you to craft it?"

"Weeks." She preened. "I had my mages start working on it as soon as I left Skyspire. I knew eventually I'd get you alone, away from his protection. Men like Kazimir always think they can shield their toys forever."

"I'm not his toy."

Her laugh was harsh. "Don't be naive, darling. Kazimir doesn't do partnerships. He does ownership."

The man behind her shifted, and I caught something familiar in the movement. Something that made my blood run cold even before my brain processed why.

"Did you send the assassins, after all?" I asked, buying time while Nyx circled closer overhead. She'd sensed something was wrong and was assessing. "At the God Spire?"

Zaraiah's perfect nose wrinkled. "That? No. That was Garrick's idiotic attempt. I could have told him it wouldn't work, if he'd only asked."

The Chair of Death. I would have thought he was better at his job. "Then why—"

"Because I have a better plan." She stepped closer, and I fought the urge to retreat. "I'm turning you over to Auremar."

My heart stuttered. "What?"

"Oh yes. His Majesty is very interested in acquiring Arabella Blackrose, and the rewards for delivering you will be substantial."

"The Syndicate—"

"—is done with your husband." She examined her nails with affected casualness. "The other chairs decided Kazimir has become too much of a wild card. Too powerful. Too unpredictable. And far too obsessed with you to think clearly. Shutting down the Spire proved that."

And what about the Alchemist? What part did they play in this?

"The Syndicate won't dare move against him directly," I said.

"Not yet. But when Kazimir realizes his precious wife is in enemy hands?" She tilted her head. "He'll come for you. Recklessly. Emotionally. Right into whatever trap Auremar sets. The Syndicate will watch from the sidelines as the Dark Lord destroys himself trying to save you. Then they'll divide up his territories like civilized villains should."

"You're betting everything on him caring that much."

Her smile turned vicious. "I've seen the way he looks at you. Like you're the only real thing in his world. Men like Kazimir don't love often, but when they do?" She laughed. "It destroys them. The Syndicate knows this. So why fight him directly when his weakness is standing right here?"

I probed the dome again with my magic. "What makes you think I'll let you use me in that way?"

"Because I know exactly what you are." She moved closer, until she stood just outside the barrier. "A sheltered girl playing at darkness. A healer pretending to be a killer. You might fool others with your dramatic displays, but I see through you."

The forgettable man behind her stepped into the moonlight, and his features rippled. For a moment, he wore the face of Dean Mortifax from the Academia. I barely felt surprised before that face melted away, revealing freckled cheeks, tousled brown hair, and wide, darting eyes.

"Pip," I said, shocked.

"Not Pip," he said, and even his voice was different—deeper, with an accent I couldn't place. "Never was Pip. That boy died on the road to Skyspire over two years ago. Barely worth the effort to consume, but his invitation to serve the Dark Lord?" He smiled, and too many teeth showed. "That was worth everything."

My stomach turned. A doppelganger. A fucking doppelganger had been living at Skyspire.

Parasitic demons, the lowest and most reviled of their kind—creatures that survived by literally consuming their victims from the inside out. They didn't just steal faces; they devoured memories, mannerisms, even opinions, wearing the digested remains of a person's entire existence like an outer shell. The real Pip's thoughts, his nervousness, his memories of his carpenter master—all of it had been absorbed and puppeteered by this thing for two years.

No wonder my truth-sense had never caught him. The demon wasn't lying about being Pip—it *was* Pip, in the most grotesque way possible.

"Kazimir was right." The pieces clicked together with sickening clarity. "You let the Hero's Guild in."

"Among other things." He studied me. "You have no idea how tedious it was, playing the nervous servant. Watching. Waiting. Learning every secret passage, every weakness." His form rippled again. "Then you arrived, and suddenly the Dark Lord had much more interesting vulnerabilities."

"Why?" My voice came out raw. "Why go to all that trouble?"

His face went hard as stone. "Because fifteen years ago, Kazimir Blackrose seduced and murdered my liege. My creator. The demon prince Malphas."

Oh.

Oh fuck.

The demon's words hit me like ice water, then immediately boiled into rage. Magic crackled around my hands.

"Your *liege*?" The word tasted like poison. "The demon who *bought* him? Who enslaved a seventeen-year-old?" My voice rose to a near shriek. "Who did gods-know-what to him while he was chained and powerless?"

The doppelganger's form flickered with rage. "He tore Malphas apart from the inside out. Then burned half the demon realm on his way out." His hands clenched. "I spent years rebuilding what he destroyed. Years plotting the perfect revenge."

I laughed, sharp and bitter. "Your precious Malphas got exactly what he deserved. Actually, no—he got off easy. If I'd been there, I would have made it last *weeks*."

"You dare—" The doppelganger's features twisted, cycling through faces I didn't recognize, each one contorted with fury. "Malphas was royalty! A prince of the demon realm! And your husband *seduced* him, made him believe—" He choked on his own rage. "Then ripped him apart while he was vulnerable, while he thought they were—"

"Good!" I snarled, my magic flaring brighter. "I hope it hurt. I hope he died knowing exactly how it felt to be powerless and used. Just like he did to Kaz."

The doppelganger took a step forward, his form rippling with barely contained violence. "You weren't there. You didn't see what he became. The thing that walked out of that realm wasn't human anymore. Your precious Dark Lord is more than man."

"And every twisted, broken piece of him belongs to me now," I spat back. "Every scar, every shadow, every bit of darkness your master carved into him—they're *mine* to protect. Mine to defend. And I'll destroy anyone who thinks they have a claim on him."

Zaraiah stepped closer to the barrier as if unwilling to be left out of the equation. "Such passion." Her voice dripped false sweetness. "And how convenient for me. You see, after Kazimir spurned me, I went digging for information about our dear Dark Lord. Imagine my delight when I found someone"—she gestured to the doppelganger—"with both the means and motivation to help bring him down."

I remembered that conversation with Pip—or what I'd thought was Pip—about the "Incident That Shall Not Be Named." He'd mentioned a demon. It was hardly outside the realm of kitchen gossip, so I hadn't thought much about it. But it hadn't been gossip, had it? It was inside information.

"You were trying to drive a wedge between us," I said to him.

The doppelganger's lips pulled back in half snarl, half smile. "It should have worked. Most women would run screaming if they knew the details of what he did to Malphas. The way he laughed as my master died." His fingers twitched, as if imagining wrapping them around my throat. "I figured you'd ask the Dark Lord about it and stir up trouble."

"Yeah, well." I flexed my fingers, light magic sparking. And I realized that when I moved, the magical barrier didn't move with me. Interesting. "I'm not most women."

"No," Zaraiah agreed. "You're the key to something much greater. Auremar is building a new world order. One where creatures like Kazimir—and you—will be properly leashed. We've chosen the winning side."

I laughed. I couldn't help it. The irony was just too perfect.

"What?" Zaraiah demanded.

"You think Auremar is the power you're aligning with?" I shook my head. "You have no idea what's really happening, do you? What's actually pulling his strings?"

"Enlighten us," she said coldly.

I could have told them about the Shadow King. About him spreading through the ley lines. About how their grand alliance was really just feeding an ancient evil that would devour them all.

Instead, I smiled. "No. I don't think I will."

Zaraiah's face flushed. "Fine. Your secrets won't matter once Auremar has you."

A shadow fell across us.

She didn't even look up. "I was wondering when your pet would arrive."

Nyx dropped from the sky like vengeance incarnate, all teeth and claws and fury.

Zaraiah raised her hand, and a shimmer erupted around the dragon—another barrier, similar to mine but crackling with different energy. Nyx slammed into the barrier. She rebounded, wings flailing, then dove again—claws raking uselessly against the shimmer. A keening wail tore from her throat as she thrashed, her massive body contorting in midair. Then she crashed into the ground.

"No!" I yelled.

"Did you think I wouldn't prepare for her after seeing her at the Spire? A shadow dragon will fetch an excellent price from the black market."

Zaraiah turned back to Nyx, gesturing with both hands. The barrier around the dragon contracted, shimmering walls closing in like a fist. The doppelganger circled closer, watching with clinical interest as Nyx's struggles grew more frantic.

"Careful," he warned. "Shadow dragons can phase when cornered."

"Not through *this* spell." Zaraiah's smile was vicious. "I accounted for that. She's locked in both this realm and the shadow—"

Rage burned through me, hot and bright. They were going to cage her. Sell her. *My* dragon.

Over my dead body.

I reached out my hand to test the barrier. It sparked and gave me an unpleasant jolt, but there had to be some way . . . something desperate and probably stupid.

The magical barrier contained me within this dome. They hadn't bothered to block anything else—why would they? Everyone knew portal magic took years to master. Even Kaz had said it was emergency only, a last resort if I was cornered.

Well, I was definitely cornered.

I'd managed it twice more in training after that first success—each one a little larger, a little more stable. But never under pressure. Never with my life on the line.

My hands moved before my brain could catch up, tracing the gesture Kaz had drilled into me just days ago. *Three degrees off and I scatter myself across dimensions.*

No time to worry about wrist angles now.

I slashed at the air. The space between here and *there* shimmered, reality bending in a way that made my stomach lurch. For a terrifying moment, nothing happened. Just like in training. Just like every failed attempt where Kaz had sighed and corrected my stance.

Then I felt that thin membrane between spaces that he'd described. Without his steadying presence, without his power amplifying mine, it felt like trying to thread a needle during an earthquake. The portal flickered into existence, barely large enough for me to squeeze through, its edges crackling with unstable energy.

Fuck it.

I dove through before I could second-guess myself, praying I'd calculated the exit correctly.

The world twisted, compressed, then snapped back into focus. I stumbled out behind Zaraiah and Pip as they were still watching the dragon. My knees hit sand, and every nerve screamed in protest. But I was whole. I was *here*, and the magical barrier they'd conjured was over *there*.

I'd actually done it.

Power crackled around my hands as I pushed myself up, riding the high of not having accidentally dismembered myself across three dimensions. They didn't know how powerful I really was—hell, *I* hadn't known I could pull off emergency portal magic until five seconds ago.

The shadow warriors suddenly snapped back into focus, responding to my will. They rose from every shadow, surrounding us in a ring of darkness.

Nyx's thrashing suddenly stilled. For a heartbeat, she sagged to the sand, her scales shimmering that strange rosy pink. Then her form flickered—solid, translucent, solid again—like she couldn't quite decide which realm to exist in.

"No," Zaraiah breathed. "That's not—"

With a sound like tearing silk, Nyx *shifted*. Not quite phasing into shadow, not quite staying corporeal. The barrier, designed to trap a being in one state or the other, couldn't hold something that was neither and both.

It shattered in a puff of smoke, sending Zaraiah flying backward into the sand.

Nyx shrieked her fury and took to the air. She spread her wings, teeth bared, silver eyes flashing.

"The spell should have worked!" Zaraiah scrambled backward. "I modified it perfectly for—"

Nyx, wait!

My dragon pulled up inches from taking Zaraiah's head off, hovering with slow wingbeats that sent sand swirling.

"Here's the thing about being underestimated," I said conversationally. "It means you're always surprising people."

Zaraiah spun to face me. I didn't give her the chance to use a spell or weapon. A spear of condensed shadow took her in the shoulder, spinning her around. She hit the sand hard.

The doppelganger moved, but I was ready. Light and shadow wove together in my hands—that hybrid magic that was mine alone. It slammed into him like a wall, sending him tumbling across the beach.

"You want to talk about Kazimir's cruelty?" I stalked toward them, power crackling around me like a violent storm. "Let me tell you what I'm capable of. I killed Hero's Guild members without blinking. I threw Academia students out of windows for disrespecting my friend."

Zaraiah tried to push herself up, hand pressed to her bleeding shoulder. "You're nothing but—"

"I'm the woman who chose the Dark Lord." I crouched beside her, voice dropping to something intimate and terrible. "Not because he seduced me.

Not because he forced me. Because I looked at all that darkness, all that violence, all that magnificent villainy, and thought, 'Yes, that's what I want.'"

Her eyes widened.

"You made one mistake, Zaraiah." I straightened. "You thought I needed protection from him. But really?" I smiled, and it felt like one of Kaz's smiles—all teeth and promise. "He needs protection from me."

The doppelganger laughed, harsh and bitter. "Pretty words. But you're still just a healer playing dress-up."

"Am I?"

I reached for that place inside where light and shadow met. Where my mother's legacy tangled with everything Kaz had taught me. Power erupted outward—not an attack, but a display. The beach itself seemed to dim as shadows rose like wings behind me. But threaded through the darkness were veins of pure light.

Both Zaraiah and the doppelganger flinched.

"I'm going to kill you both," I said matter-of-factly. "Then I'm going to tell my husband exactly how you died. How you plotted against him. How you tried to sell me to his enemy. How you failed."

"Wait—" Zaraiah started.

"No." I raised my hand. "You had your monologue. You revealed your master plan. Gloated about your cleverness." Shadows sharpened into blades in my hands. "But you forgot the most important rule of villainy."

"What's that?" the doppelganger asked.

"Never give your opponent time to counter-monologue."

Zaraiah tried to shield herself, but she was already wounded and slow. My shadow blade drove toward her heart, punching through the first layer of her magical protections—

And hit something solid.

A figure materialized between us—the doppelganger, his form already shifting, taking the blade meant for her. He didn't even scream, just locked eyes with me as my shadow magic tore through his chest.

"Go," he rasped to Zaraiah.

She was already scrambling, pulling something small from her belt that she crushed between her fingers.

"Nyx!" I commanded, but too late.

A crystal shattered in a burst of acrid smoke. It made reality itself *hiccup*. The air around Zaraiah rippled, and suddenly there were *three* of her, all running in different directions.

Nyx's jaws snapped shut on empty air where the middle one had been. The illusion dissolved into wisps.

"Fuck!" I yanked my blade free from the doppelganger and spun toward the other two Zaraiahs, but they were already dissolving too. Decoys. All of them.

Her voice drifted from somewhere in the darkness beyond the beach, already distant: "Tell Kazimir I'll be seeing him soon, darling."

I sent a spear of light magic toward the voice, but it hit nothing. She was gone. Nyx was circling back, furious at having been fooled.

I turned back to the doppelganger. "Your betrayal killed Sims." The words tore from my throat, raw and vicious. "My friend."

Nyx landed beside me with a ground-shaking thud, her silver eyes fixed on the doppelganger. A low growl rumbled from her chest.

The doppelganger laughed wetly. "Fifteen years of planning. You think . . . killing me changes anything?" Blood—or whatever passed for blood in his kind—bubbled at his lips. "Others will come. The demon realm remembers. We *always* remember."

I looked at Nyx. Her scales shimmered with that strange pink-black iridescence as shadows rippled across her hide.

"Kill him," I said coldly.

Her jaws snapped shut around the doppelganger's throat. For a moment, nothing happened—demon flesh was notoriously resilient, able to heal even from grievous wounds. I doubted if we'd actually kill him but merely send him back to his realm. Then Nyx's peculiar magic flared, purple-tinged shadow fire igniting along her teeth.

The doppelganger's form rippled one last time, cycling through faces in what looked like panic—the dean, strangers I didn't recognize, and then . . . Pip. Those wide, anxious eyes staring up at me. Those freckles. That nervous, earnest expression I'd seen a hundred times bringing me tea or hovering in doorways.

His scream cut off as something fundamental inside him was severed—not just his physical form, but the demonic essence that animated it.

Nyx released him, and he dropped to the sand with Pip's face still frozen in place, truly dead this time. No regeneration. No resurrection. Whatever Nyx's pink-shifted magic had done, it had destroyed the part of him that made him immortal.

I stared down at that familiar face, at the boy who'd never existed to me, who'd been dead on a road somewhere for two years while this *thing* wore his skin and served me breakfast. The real Pip had probably been kind. Nervous. Genuine. Everything this creature had mimicked so perfectly that even my truth-sense couldn't detect the lie.

I stood there shaking, power still crackling around me in violent spurts. The doppelganger's blood soaked into the pristine beach, black in the moonlight. My hands wouldn't stop trembling—not from fear, but from the need to destroy something else. To chase Zaraiah down and tear her apart with my bare hands. To resurrect the doppelganger just so I could kill him again, but slower.

A sound ripped from my chest, half scream, half sob. Magic exploded outward, carving deep gouges in the sand.

Even as the rage slowly banked to something colder, I felt cheated. Zaraiah's escape burned hotter than any victory. The Syndicate had threatened Kaz. They'd threatened our people. They'd chosen their side.

They'd chosen wrong.

Nyx was batting the doppelganger's body around like the world's most macabre cat toy, complete with enthusiastic pouncing.

"We need to get back to the captives and be ready to leave as soon as the *Sky Serpent* arrives." I had to tell Kaz the Syndicate would be coming for us. The last thing we needed was to fight a war on multiple fronts, but it seemed that was going to be the case. Zaraiah had fucked up my abduction, but she would recover quickly.

Nyx made a questioning sound, gesturing at the doppelganger's body with her tail.

"You want to . . ." I stared at her. "Really?"

She licked her lips.

It wasn't Pip, I knew, but still I hesitated. Then I thought about Sims, about this *thing* serving me breakfast while plotting our destruction. Nyx made that questioning sound again, almost hopeful. She'd skipped dinner in our rush to get the last families. And the doppelganger had plotted against Kaz and tried to kill me. The least he could do was be useful in death. "You know what? Fine. We don't have time to clean up anyway."

I turned away as she began her grisly meal. My hands were still shaking when I pulled out the scrying crystal. It pulsed once in my palm, responding to my touch, then flared with light.

Kaz's face materialized in the crystal's depths, sharp and focused. He was somewhere dark—a portal space, maybe, or a shadow-shrouded alley.

"Arabella." His eyes scanned what he could see of me, cataloging the blood, the wild look I probably wore. "What happened?"

"Zaraiah." I kept my voice steady through sheer force of will. "She tried to kidnap me. Had Pip with her, but he was a doppelganger the whole time. They were going to deliver me to Auremar."

Kaz's face went absolutely still in that way that meant he was calculating exactly how to murder someone. "Are you hurt?"

"No. Nyx killed the doppelganger. Zaraiah escaped." I swallowed. "Kaz, she said the Syndicate is moving against you. That they were going to use me as bait to make you reckless."

For a moment, he struggled to rein in his temper. When he spoke, his voice was cold and commanding. "Where are you now?"

"Still at Meridian Isle but leaving soon." I watched his expression carefully. "I'm safe. But I wanted you to know."

The weight of everything unsaid pressed between us. I wanted to ask if he was okay. Wanted to tell him I'd been thinking about him constantly. Wanted to hear him say my name in that particular way he did when we were alone.

Instead, I said, "I'll be home soon."

He paused. "Be careful, Arabella."

The crystal went dark.

"Arabella!"

I spun to find Sebastian of all people running down the beach toward me. Behind him was the silhouette of the *Sky Serpent*, hovering above the water. He skidded to a halt, taking in the scene—me splattered in blood, Nyx enthusiastically dismembering a corpse, shadow warriors standing sentinel.

"Sebastian? What are you—"

"Vex sent me with the ship." He was breathing hard. "She said you'd be alone and might need—" His gaze landed on what was left of the doppelganger. "Protection."

Despite everything, I laughed. "As you can see, I handled it."

"I . . . yes." He swallowed hard, looking faintly green. "That's certainly . . . handled."

49

Unpack Emotional Baggage

(So You Have Room for More Daggers)

Arabella

"No, no, the pustules won't appear until the third day." I patted Lady Moonbay's trembling hand as she clutched her youngest daughter. "And that's only if you were exposed. Which you weren't. Because we got you out in time."

The *Sky Serpent* creaked in the wind, and half the rescued families whimpered. They'd been doing that for the past three hours.

"But the lesions—" Lord Tidehaven started.

"Also third day. Sometimes fourth." I forced a bright smile. "Really, you're all perfectly safe now."

Note to self: Next time, skip the plague excuse. Pirates would have been simpler. Or dragons. Everyone understood dragons. I even had one to use, if they didn't believe me.

I escaped to the upper deck, leaving the families to their hypochondriac panic. The salt wind whipped my hair around, still stiff in places from dried blood I hadn't quite managed to wash out. Nyx circled lazily above, occasionally diving to snatch fish from the waves. At least someone was having a good time.

My fingers found the Heirloom beneath my skin, that constant presence that had become as familiar as my own heartbeat. Through our bond, I could feel Kazimir—distant, his emotions a muted hum of satisfaction tinged with something darker. Whatever had happened in Valmont, he'd handled it.

But Zaraiah's words kept echoing: *The Syndicate is done with him.*

"Lord Pearlbridge is convinced he has early-stage boils."

I didn't turn at Sebastian's voice. I'd been avoiding him since we left the God Spire, finding excuses to be elsewhere whenever he appeared. The ship wasn't that big, but I'd managed it through sheer determination and creative hiding spots.

"They're mosquito bites," I said.

"I told him that." He moved to stand beside me at the rail, careful to keep a respectful distance. "He asked for a second opinion from someone who'd actually seen plague boils."

I smirked. "Turns out 'the king wants to sacrifice you' doesn't motivate people quite like 'your face might melt off.'"

Sebastian laughed—that same warm sound I'd heard in my recovered memory. The one from when we were children, before everything went to hell.

I finally turned to look at him properly—really look at him for the first time since we'd left the Spire.

The wind caught his long blond hair, pulling strands loose from where he'd tied it back. In the fading light, he looked like something out of a storybook—the kind of handsome that made court ladies fawn and write terrible poetry. Sharp jawline, violet eyes that seemed to glow in certain light, the sort of aristocratic features that belonged on coins or tapestries.

Objectively, I could acknowledge he was beautiful. The same way I could acknowledge a sunset was beautiful, or a well-crafted blade. It was a fact that existed independent of any personal feeling.

But when I looked at him, all I felt was . . . fond. The way you might feel about a favorite book from childhood, or a particularly comfortable pair of shoes. Warm, but utterly uncomplicated.

Nothing like the electric charge that ran through me when Kazimir so much as glanced my way.

"Sebastian." I leaned on the railing. "We need to talk."

His eyebrows rose. "That sounds ominous."

"About the kiss."

His face went through several interesting color changes before settling on a pink that clashed with his violet eyes.

"Ah." He cleared his throat. "You remember that."

"Recently, yes. Along with you defending me from my father. And the time we tried to teach ourselves levitation and ended up stuck on the conservatory roof for six hours."

A smile tugged at his lips. "Your governess was furious."

"She thought we'd been kidnapped." I matched his smile despite myself. "We could hear her screaming about ransom notes while we were trying not to fall off."

The memory was warm, untainted by what came after. "We were idiots."

"We were twelve."

"Same thing." I sobered, meeting his eyes. "Sebastian, I'm sorry. About forgetting. About . . . all of it."

His expression shifted to something more serious. "Arabella—"

"My father had mages alter my memories." The words tumbled out quickly. "After my mother died. After I started showing power. They took years from me, scrambled things, made me forget anyone who might have . . ." I swallowed. "Anyone who might have cared. And I remembered you, but not everything."

Sebastian's hands clenched on the rail, knuckles white. For a moment, I saw something in his gentle features that reminded me of Kazimir—a flash of genuine rage.

"I knew something was wrong." He spoke roughly. "When you came back from that 'illness,' you looked right through me. Like we'd never spent every summer together. Like we hadn't—"

He stopped abruptly, his jaw working as he visibly fought to control his anger. When he spoke again, his voice was low and bitter in a way I'd never heard from him.

"Someone had to have known." The words came out clipped. "The court physicians. The servants who saw you locked in that tower. The nobles who watched a vibrant girl turn into a shadow of herself. They all just . . . pretended not to see."

I felt my chest tighten. "I'm still working through that myself," I admitted quietly. "The idea that people I smiled at, danced with, drank tea with . . . they might have known what was happening to me and just . . ." I trailed off, unable to finish.

"Decided it wasn't their problem." Sebastian's laugh was harsh. "The great nobility of Solandris. So concerned with propriety and honor, unless it means actually doing something difficult."

The bitterness in his voice surprised me. This wasn't the gentle, diplomatic Sebastian I remembered.

"You sound like Kazimir," I said without thinking.

He turned to look at me, and for a moment, I saw why he'd been willing to invite Bone Witches to a ball, why he'd fled rather than turn himself over to Auremar. There was steel under all that kindness.

"Maybe the Dark Lord has a point about some things," he said quietly. "At least he's honest about what he is."

We stood in weighted silence for a moment before Sebastian seemed to shake himself, the anger draining from his features.

"I'm sorry," he said, running a hand through his hair. "That's not—I shouldn't be angry at ghosts. It doesn't help you now."

"It helps to know someone else sees it," I admitted. "That I'm not just being dramatic about how wrong it all was."

He studied me for a long moment. "Do you remember everything now? From before?"

The question hung between us, loaded with meaning we both understood.

"Most of it, I think." I turned back to the sea, needing the distance. "The important parts, anyway."

"The Palace Garden?" His voice was carefully neutral.

I closed my eyes. "Near the topiaries with the pixies. You'd just had honey cakes."

"You said you loved me." The words were quiet, almost lost in the wind.

"I remember."

"I said it back."

"I remember that, too."

We stood in silence for a moment, the past and present tangling uncomfortably between us.

I'd told Sebastian I loved him when we were children, when the word came as easily as breathing. Back then, I'd known what love was—my mother's gentle hands braiding my hair, her soft songs at bedtime, the warmth of being cherished. I'd been loved, so loving in return felt natural.

But Kazimir? I wasn't sure he'd ever experienced love—in any form. Not from his mother who carved runes into his bones. Certainly not from his father who saw him as a threat. Not from anyone, really. The thought made my heart ache for him. How could I expect him to say words he'd never heard? How could I blame him for not knowing the language of something he'd never received?

"For what it's worth," Sebastian said, pulling me away from my guilty thoughts, "you were my first kiss."

I opened my eyes to find him studying the horizon, a self-deprecating smile on his face.

"At the time, I thought we'd get married." He laughed, but it sounded forced. "Stupid, really. Even then, I should have known you were destined for bigger things than a life of agricultural reform and trade negotiations."

"Sebastian—"

"Oh, I'm not that boy anymore." He held up a hand quickly. "I grew up. Saw the world. Learned that first loves rarely survive reality." His smile turned more genuine. "Especially when said first love becomes a terrifying dark sorceress who throws people out of windows."

My mouth twitched. "Just the one time."

"Still." He turned to look at me properly. "I'm glad you're happy, Arabella. After everything you've been through, you deserve it more than anyone I know."

The sincerity in his voice sent warmth through me. "Don't let Kazimir hear you say that. He already thinks you're trying to steal me away."

"Wouldn't dream of it." He shuddered theatrically. "I don't want to end up like those assassins."

We fell into easier conversation after that, trading memories. The time we convinced the stable boys we'd seen a dragon and caused a panic. The summer we decided to map every secret passage in the palace and got hopelessly lost and missed the summer solstice festival. The way he'd always brought me books from his family's library, the ones about magic theory that proper ladies weren't supposed to read.

It felt nice. Like finding a favorite toy from childhood and discovering it still brought joy.

"Your father," I said eventually. "Is he safe?"

Sebastian's expression darkened. "I got word from him a few days ago. He's been holding Auremar off, claiming I'm on urgent family business in the Eastern Realms. But the king's getting impatient." Sebastian watched Nyx dive under the ship. "And it didn't help that the entire company of soldiers chasing me were found slaughtered, though Auremar rightly believes that's the Dark Lord's doing, for daring to get too close to the border." Sebastian picked at a splinter on the rail. "Father's considering formally disowning me just to make me useless for Auremar's purposes. I didn't have the heart to tell him that Auremar wants to literally sacrifice me, and my status as the heir to the Northern Peaks won't change anything."

"That's—"

He shrugged. "Better than my father being in danger of knowing too much about Auremar's plans."

I thought about Lord Evenfall, rotting in Skyspire's dungeons. Our families were so different. "What will you do? After all this is over?"

"Honestly? I don't know." He was quiet for a moment. "I'd be lying if I said I didn't want to make sure you were safe first."

"Sebastian—"

"I know you don't need protection." He held up a hand. "That's not what I meant. It's just . . ." He frowned, choosing his words carefully. "Something's not quite right with the Dark Lord."

My spine stiffened. "Excuse me?"

"I'm not questioning your choice." His tone was gentle but firm. "Or your happiness. But there's something in his eyes sometimes. Something that has nothing to do with being a villain and everything to do with—" He shook his head. "I don't know. It's probably nothing."

It wasn't nothing. If he was picking up on the Shadow King's influence bleeding through, it was worse than I thought.

"I don't need you to save me from my husband," I said carefully.

"I know." He smiled sadly. "You never needed saving. Not really. You just needed people to stop trying to cage you."

The truth of that struck me with unexpected force, settling somewhere deep in my chest where all the complicated feelings about my father and my past lived in a tangled knot I still hadn't quite unraveled.

"So," I said, desperately needing to change the subject. "What's going on with you and Vex?"

Sebastian blinked at the shift. "Sorry?"

"Oh, come on. She seemed very interested in your scone recipe."

"Well, the scones are exceptional," he said with a crooked grin. "Can't blame anyone for that."

"Right." I studied his face, finding only good-natured amusement. Nothing hidden, nothing deflected. "What about Griffin?"

The change was immediate. Sebastian's ears turned pink, and he suddenly found the horizon fascinating.

"Griffin is . . ." He cleared his throat. "He's brilliant."

"And?"

"And nothing." But his voice pitched slightly higher, and my truth-sense gave the faintest tingle—not a lie, but definitely not the whole truth.

I leaned closer, delighted. "What happened at the God Spire?"

His ears turned pink. "He got hurt trying to find me after I left the Gilded Gallows. I just—I wanted to make sure he was all right. Anyone would have done the same."

"Mmm-hmm. And the fact that he looks at you like you hung the moon?"

"He looks at everyone like that when they're kind to him." Sebastian's voice went soft, almost sad. "Which says more about how he's been treated than anything else."

The gentle observation was so perfectly Sebastian—seeing the loneliness in Griffin's hero worship instead of just being flattered by it.

"He's lucky to have you as a friend," I said quietly.

Sebastian met my eyes, something complicated flickering in his expression. "I'm not sure I'm what he needs."

"What do you mean?"

Sebastian opened his mouth, closed it, then shook his head with a rueful grin. "You have surrounded yourself with an interesting group of people, Lady Blackrose."

And that, apparently, was all he would say on the matter. He pointed dramatically at the darkness below the *Sky Serpent*. "Look, dolphins!"

"We're over land."

"Must have just missed them. Shame." He was already backing away with a grin. "I should go check on our guests. Make sure their mosquito bites haven't evolved into certain death."

"Sebastian!"

But he was gone, leaving me alone with the wind and unanswered questions.

"Interesting group of people," I muttered. "That's one way to put it."

50

Cage Your Problems
(Before They Cage You)

Kazimir

The portal snapped shut behind us, and we deposited our final batch of unconscious charges near the guest quarters. Five more heroic bloodlines from Valmont sprawled across the stone, their gentle snoring a stark contrast to the chaos of their collection. Thorne lifted the sack with Viktor Moorhazi—a bastard with the right bloodline and wrong luck—over his shoulder.

I scanned the courtyard, searching for a particular flash of golden hair.

The scrying crystal was silent in my pocket. Arabella hadn't contacted me again since her warning about Zaraiah, and I hadn't reached out either. Better to wait until she was here. Until I could touch her and remember why I was fighting so hard to stay myself.

"Lady Blackrose is on her way." Vex materialized from the shadows near the guest quarters, her black hair catching the afternoon light. "Should arrive within the hour. Lord Sebastian is with her."

My jaw tightened. "Why aren't *you* with her?"

"Because someone needed to handle the twenty-two families currently trying to murder each other in the guest quarters." She stepped over an unconscious juggler. "Did you know the Shellfords and Moonbays have a three-generation blood feud over fishing rights?"

"I don't care if they have a thousand-year war over who invented the wheel." Shadows coiled at my feet. "Zaraiah attacked Arabella. The Chair of Whispers ambushed my wife while you were here playing referee."

Vex's eyes widened. "I didn't know—"

"She's fine." I forced my voice level. "But you should have—"

A surge of power rippled through the air, dark and familiar. A single magical signature pulsed from the forest below, just beyond the swamp's edge. The wards chimed—not the bone-deep shriek of an attack, but the insistent warning of someone deliberately triggering them.

Someone powerful wanted to be noticed.

As one, the lightning bridges all shut down as a precaution. The new wards might overreact to a squirrel's sneeze, but I'd rather that than miss a genuine threat.

Vex grimaced. "I hope no one important was on the bridges. Who would be dumb enough to trigger the defenses after what we did to the Hero's Guild?"

"It's the Alchemist." I flexed my fingers, feeling the runes beneath my skin pulse with interest. "This should be enlightening."

Vex's expression tightened. "The Alchemist doesn't make social calls."

"No, they don't." I was already drawing the portal sigils in the air. Whatever they wanted, it was important enough to risk approaching Skyspire alone. "Have Griffin prepare that doppelganger kit of his. And Vex? We're not finished discussing this."

Before she could ask any questions, I ripped open a portal to the forest edge.

I stepped through darkness onto soft forest loam, the portal snapping shut silently behind me. Twenty feet away, the Alchemist stood with their hands raised in a gesture of peace, their robes shifting through hypnotic shades of green and violet. No army. No backup. Just them and the humid air of the swamp.

"Let me guess," I said conversationally. "You're here to tell me the Syndicate is tired of me."

"So you know, then." The Alchemist lowered their hands slowly.

I let shadows pool at my feet, a casual display. "Zaraiah attacked my wife."

The Alchemist's visible features beneath the mask shifted—eyes widening, mouth parting slightly. Their fingers twitched in that nervous pattern. "Is she harmed?"

"She survived." I let ice creep into my tone. "No thanks to the task you set her on. Zaraiah got away, though."

Their hands fluttered upward, then dropped. The robes flickered through a rapid sequence of colors—gold to crimson to deep purple—before settling on an uneasy amber. They made an irritated huff. "That explains why Zaraiah didn't contact me directly. But she's voting with the others—Revek, Gilt, Vespera, and Garrick are invoking Protocol Nine." Their voice held none of its usual musical quality. "They want you removed from the Syndicate. Permanently."

"And you came all this way to warn me?" I tilted my head. "What do you want in return?"

"Nothing." They paused. "Consider this an investment in future cooperation."

The air between us crackled with unspoken tension. The Alchemist had always been the most pragmatic of the chairs, the one most likely to see beyond immediate gain to long-term advantage. But there was something else in their posture now. Something careful. Calculated.

"There's more," I said. It wasn't a question.

The Alchemist's masked face tilted, studying me with an intensity that made the runes beneath my skin itch. "Yes. Though this next part is . . . delicate."

They took a step closer, and I felt their magic probe at mine—not attacking, but analyzing. Reading. "Your magical signature is layered," they said quietly. "Two consciousnesses occupying one vessel."

Every muscle in my body tensed. "Careful."

"The Shadow King." They said it like a diagnosis, clinical and certain. "You have a piece of him inside you."

"How long have you known?" My voice was deadly quiet.

"I suspected after the restaurant incident, and then again during our ritual at the God Spire. When you and Lady Blackrose redirected the ley lines, I felt two distinct magical signatures flowing through you—one was your dominion magic, but the other . . ." They paused. "The other was the same corrupted resonance I've been tracking through Solandris's ley lines."

Shadows erupted around us, a cage forming before I'd consciously commanded it. The Alchemist didn't even flinch.

"And then there's the Heirloom itself," they continued calmly. "The artifact was designed to contain the Shadow King's power—forged from his essence, bound by Soriven's magic. It resists you because it recognizes what's inside you. It's trying to protect itself from being corrupted by the very entity it was created to imprison."

"How do you know it's been resisting me?"

The Alchemist tsked. "Would you have made such a conventional move against Solandris's northern outpost if you had the full might of the Heirloom at your disposal?" They spread their hands. "I came here to give you a chance to explain. To tell me I'm wrong. Or to confirm what I already know and discuss what happens next."

"And if I don't feel like explaining myself?"

"Then you'll do exactly what you're doing now." The Alchemist gestured to the cage surrounding them, but their tone held a note of approval. "I expected you to be pragmatic. You can't afford to let this information spread. Not yet. Not until you've consolidated your power base and dealt with whatever's happening inside your head."

The Shadow King's essence stirred within me. *Interesting. They know what we are and came anyway.*

I shoved the thought aside. "Here's what's going to happen. You're going to be my guest for a while. A very comfortable, very secure guest."

"I assumed as much." The Alchemist's shoulders relaxed slightly. "I have conditions."

"You're in no position to negotiate."

"On the contrary. I'm in the perfect position." They nodded to the forest around us. "I came alone, yes. But I'm not foolish. My creations are extensions of my magic, Kazimir. There's a vial sitting in every chair's quarters right now, and in the courts of a dozen kingdoms besides—a vial that is perfectly invisible and inert, so long as I remain comfortable and connected to my craft. Sever that connection—kill me, suppress my magic, or neglect me long enough for my focus to slip—and those vials open themselves." Their half smile sharpened. "You can imagine what a detailed account of your *condition* would do in the wrong hands."

Another threat for the collection.

"What conditions?"

"You hold up your end of our agreement regarding the ley lines. We finish what we started at the God Spire—stop the Shadow King from spreading. And when you're ready to deal with your situation, you allow me to help." They paused. "I'm one of the Weavers, Kazimir. If anyone can help you separate yourself from the Shadow King without destroying you, it's me."

"Why help me at all?"

"Because the alternative is watching the Shadow King fully possess you and destroy everything I've worked to build." Their voice held genuine concern. "And because despite everything, you're the most interesting thing to happen to the Western Realms in centuries. It would be a shame to waste that potential."

I stared at them for a long moment, weighing options, calculating risks. The Alchemist knew too much. But they were also offering something I desperately needed—expertise in the very magic that bound me to this ancient evil.

"Fine." The shadows around them darkened and compressed until the Alchemist was bound with their hands at their sides. "But you'll forgive me if I take precautions."

"Of course. I'd be disappointed if you didn't. Though I should warn you," they continued, "the other chairs are coming. When they move against you, it won't be just a vote. It'll be an execution."

"I look forward to watching them try. Now then." I conjured a portal back to Skyspire, and for good measure, gagged the Alchemist in case they decided to blurt out any inconvenient truths. "Let's get you settled. I'm thinking one of our well-appointed dungeon suites."

We emerged on the platform outside the Dungeons Complex just as Arabella appeared at the far end of the lightning bridge, which had just been restored.

Everything else ceased to matter.

She crossed to me immediately, her hands finding mine. The contact sent warmth through me, chasing back the cold that had been settling deeper into my bones over the past few days. I caught her face between my palms, needing the contact more than I wanted to admit. For just a heartbeat, I pressed my forehead to hers—a brief surrender before the mask had to go back on.

She placed her hands on my chest and breathed deeply, her fingers curling into the fabric of my coat. When I pulled back enough to see her face, her eyes were too bright, tears threatening to spill over lashes that trembled with the effort of holding them back.

Her gaze traced over my features with an intensity that made my chest tighten, as if she was trying to memorize every detail. Or perhaps seeing me differently than she had before.

One of her hands moved from my chest to my jaw, her thumb brushing across my beard with devastating gentleness. The touch carried weight I couldn't quite name—not pity, thank the gods, but something that made the Shadow King's presence recoil slightly, as if even that ancient evil recognized it had no place in this moment.

Her breath hitched, and a single tear escaped, tracking down her cheek. She didn't wipe it away. Neither did I. We just stood there, her hands on me like she could hold me together through sheer will, my forehead still pressed to hers while the world continued its chaos around us.

Whatever she was feeling, it was there in the trembling of her fingers, in the fierce protectiveness radiating from every line of her body. In the way she looked at me like I was precious and breakable, even as I held her face between palms that had killed more people than I could count.

She opened her mouth as if to speak, then closed it again. Finally, she glanced between me and the bound Alchemist and cleared her throat.

"Why is the Alchemist here?" she whispered.

"A lot's happened." I brushed my thumb across her cheekbone, catching that stray tear. "Are you hurt?"

"No, but—" She frowned, clearly reading my emotional state. "We need to talk."

"We do. After I get our guest settled." I forced myself to step back, to remember we had an audience.

The Alchemist's attention had sharpened, their masked gaze studying us with careful interest. But they remained silent, just watching.

Sebastian came up behind Arabella, as if he'd made it his goal to follow her around like a puppy.

"Lord Sebastian." I inclined my head. "Thank you for accompanying my wife."

He blinked. "I . . . of course. Though she didn't really need—"

"Yes, I'm aware she's perfectly capable." I cut him off. "But intention matters. You went after her when it counted. That's worth acknowledging."

Sebastian stared at me like I'd grown a second head. Which, given recent events, wasn't entirely outside the realm of possibility.

I considered him. Sebastian was annoying as hell, but he wasn't a coward. He was just . . . good, and I found it weird that Sebastian would even want to be associated with the Dark Lord. Unlike when Arabella came to me and indulged her darker tendencies, Sebastian wasn't remotely swayed by my darkness or seeking it for himself at all.

Perhaps we needed a different perspective at Skyspire, from someone who'd proven himself trustworthy. Our allies were becoming scarce.

"You're welcome to extend your stay," I continued somewhat reluctantly. "Your assistance with gathering the bloodlines has been . . . valuable."

"I . . ." He glanced at Arabella, then back at me. "Thank you?"

It came out as a question, which was fair. Good people always seemed confused when I didn't immediately murder them.

"Kaz." Arabella's voice held amusement. "Are you formally inviting Sebastian to join your inner circle?"

The Alchemist made a muffled sound that might have been a laugh.

"Right. Dungeons." I grabbed their shoulder. "Vex!"

Vex materialized from inside the dungeons with her usual impeccable timing. I had no idea how she'd ended up there. Her gaze flicked to Arabella, lingering a fraction too long. Her shoulders dropped—barely perceptible, but I'd known her long enough to recognize the release of tension.

I'd thrown Zaraiah's attack at her like a blade, sharp and meant to cut. A rebuke for not being there. But Vex cared for Arabella too, and I'd just told her the woman she'd sworn to protect had been ambushed while she played referee to feuding nobles.

"Ensure Lord Sebastian gets appropriate quarters within the Inner Sanctum. Near Griffin's laboratory, perhaps."

Vex straightened. "Of course, my lord. I'm sure Griffin will be delighted to have a neighbor."

Sebastian's face flushed. "That's really not—"

"And congratulations, Lord Sebastian," Vex said. "It seems you're now part of the family business."

"Family business?"

"Chaos, destruction, and the occasional world-altering magical event." Vex's joke came out forced, but she managed a grin.

Sebastian looked between all of us, probably wondering what he'd gotten himself into.

"Don't worry," Arabella said, patting his shoulder. "You get used to it. Eventually."

The Alchemist shifted their weight and made another muffled comment.

“Yes, yes, we’re all very impressed by your patience.” I gave them a nudge toward the dungeon entrance. “Now come along. We have a cell with your name on it.”

As we moved toward the entrance, I felt Arabella’s gaze on my back. Soon, I’d tell her everything. But first, I needed to secure the Alchemist and ensure this particular secret stayed contained.

I never tired of bringing a new prisoner to the dungeons. Some joys were timeless.

51

Receive Therapy from Your Minions

(Rock Bottom Looks like This)

Kazimir

"Tell me again," I said to Vex, who stood with her clipboard, "*why* they brought livestock?"

I stood in the Great Hall, watching with growing horror as yet another family of twelve unpacked their belongings. The Moonbays had brought their entire household staff. The Tidehavens had arrived with seventeen trunks of "essentials." And somewhere in the chaos, a rooster crowed.

"That would be Ferdinand." Vex made a note. "Lady Elena Clearwater's half brother insisted he was family."

"It's a rooster."

"Yes, my lord." Another note. "Marna is threatening to serve coq au vin for dinner."

I watched as two children raced past, shrieking with laughter. One of them knocked over a suit of armor.

"The dungeons," I said, not for the first time today. "We could put them all in the dungeons. They'd be much easier to manage."

"Lady Blackrose would object."

I rubbed my temples. "Lady Blackrose is in our chambers, avoiding this chaos like the clever woman she is."

Sebastian appeared at my elbow, looking harried. "Actually, she's in the training room. Said something about needing to hit things."

Of course. She was just as keyed up as I was. I'd barely had a chance to tell her how proud I was of how she'd handled Zaraiah and Pip, though I had many reasons for wishing I'd been there myself.

For the fun, obviously.

The Syndicate's betrayal gnawed at me—Zaraiah's attack on my wife, and Pip's treachery finally explained. My shadows had twitched restlessly since Arabella's recounting, eager for vengeance I couldn't yet claim.

But rage without strategy was just noise. The Syndicate would answer for their games, but first we had to survive long enough to make them regret it.

"Speaking of chaos," Sebastian continued, "I've done a full accounting. Auremar got to more bloodlines than we thought. At least thirty in Valmont alone."

"How many did you manage to save in Solandris?"

"Forty-three of the lesser bloodlines." He shifted uncomfortably. "I brought them all when I came back two days ago. Before I went after Arabella."

"Forty-three." I stared at him. "By yourself?"

Sebastian nodded to a far table near the back of the hall. The entire cluster of them—bastards and forgotten branches, the kind of people who'd never seen the inside of a proper keep—pressed together at the far end of the hall like rabbits cornered by wolves. Their wide eyes tracked every shout, every clash of silverware, every burst of indignant squawking from the demon rooster.

They looked exactly how I felt.

A crash echoed from somewhere. Vex sighed and made another note.

"I'm still not sure why they're all gathered here instead of being silent as the grave in their rooms."

She looked at me with an arched brow. "There's nowhere else safe for them to congregate, my lord, and locking them in their rooms would be the equivalent of putting them in the dungeons."

"Exactly. It's perfectly harmless."

"Anyway, Griffin's supervising." Vex paused. "Well, attempting to supervise. Last I saw, they'd convinced him to demonstrate his self-writing poetry quills."

Griffin was scrambling between tables, lunging for animated quills that darted just out of reach. Teenagers shrieked with laughter as the quills scrawled across napkins. Lady Coralia Montaven pressed one hand to her chest, her mouth forming a perfect O of horror. Meanwhile, someone Vex had called "Aunt Cordy" held a completed sonnet at arm's length, cackling like a woman half her age.

"The quills that only write erotic sonnets about tentacles?" I asked.

"Those would be the ones."

I was going to need a stiff drink. "How many heroic *guests* are currently in my fortress?"

Vex consulted her clipboard. "Seventy-eight of heroic bloodlines with their family members equals two hundred thirty-one total."

"Two hundred thirty—" I cut myself off. Deep breaths. "And they're all getting along?"

"Oh, absolutely not." She smiled brightly. "The Shellfords and Moonbays have a three-generation blood feud, as I mentioned. Lord Brightwater thinks the Fekete twins are beneath him. The rooster has declared war on the kitchen cats. And someone started a rumor that you eat babies for breakfast."

"I haven't eaten a baby in years," I said drily.

"I'll be sure to clarify that at dinner." She made another note. "Oh, and three marriage proposals have arrived for you this morning."

"I'm already married."

"Yes, but apparently some of our guests think you might be open to alternatives." She pulled out a perfumed letter. "Lady Moonbay's eldest daughter was quite creative in her suggestions."

I incinerated the letter without reading it. "Where's Thorne?"

"Hiding in the armory. He said, and I quote, 'I didn't sign up to babysit nobility.'" Vex paused and finally looked up at me from her notes. "My lord," she began carefully, "perhaps you should speak with Lady Blackrose."

"Perhaps I should turn this entire hall into a mass portal and dump everyone in the swamp."

"The environmental impact—"

"I don't care about the fucking environmental impact!"

Vex and Sebastian exchanged looks.

"Fine. I'll go check on Arabella," I said, desperate to escape. "Try not to let anyone burn down my fortress while I'm gone."

"We'll do our best," Vex said. "Though I make no promises about Ferdinand."

As if summoned, the rooster strutted into view, his red crest gleaming. He fixed me with one beady eye and crowed.

"I'm the Dark Lord," I told him. "I've conquered kingdoms. I've broken demons. I am not going to be intimidated by poultry."

The rooster regarded me for a moment, then squawked loudly before turning and running off.

"At least someone around here has some sense," I muttered. Then I suddenly remembered why I'd even entered this chaos in the first place. "Vex, a word."

I led Vex to a small alcove off the Great Hall, where the noise from the impromptu refugee camp was only slightly muffled. The sounds of children shrieking, nobles arguing, and that damned rooster crowing created a cacophony worse than any solstice party I'd ever attended.

"This is worse than the time the Syndicate hosted that orgy-slash–book club," I muttered, leaning against the stone wall. "At least there, the participants knew when to use their inside voices."

Vex's lips twitched. "I believe Lady Blackrose would call this 'hospitality.'"

"Speaking of my wife." I fixed Vex with a hard stare. "You left her alone."

Vex's expression didn't change, but she glanced at the shadows darkening the alcove. "She wasn't alone. She had Nyx and the shadow warriors."

"You were supposed to stay with her." Heat built beneath my skin, the runes responding to my rising anger. I forced my voice level, but it took effort. "That was the entire point of sending you."

Vex met my gaze, and I saw genuine regret flash across her features. "Lady Blackrose ordered me to return with the first group of families. Who was I supposed to obey?"

"Me," I snapped. "Obviously me."

Yes, the voice whispered. *They should all obey. They should all kneel.*

My hands were trembling. I pressed them flat against the wall behind me.

"Because from where I stand," Vex continued as if I hadn't spoken, "Lady Blackrose is perfectly capable of knowing her own mind and issuing her own orders." She paused meaningfully. "And enforcing said orders."

I exhaled through my nose. Then took a deep breath. Vex was right, damn it.

She studied me for a moment, her silver eyes unreadable. "Speaking of which—you and Lady Blackrose seem different lately."

The strain in our relationship since the God Spire was obvious to anyone who knew us well, and Vex knew us better than most.

"What did she tell you?" I asked, my voice low.

"Nothing specific. But I've served you for almost fifteen years, my lord. I notice things."

The reminder of our history only intensified my discomfort. Vex had been there through some of my darkest moments. She'd seen me at my worst and stayed anyway. But this—this was different. This wasn't about conquest or power or even vengeance.

This was about how I'd attempted to use my dominion magic on the one person I'd sworn never to control.

The one person who mattered more than anything.

A hairline crack appeared in the stone where my hand pressed against the wall. I pulled back, flexing my fingers. The runes pulsed with heat, then cold, then heat again. My body couldn't decide if it wanted to burn or freeze.

"I may have fucked everything up," I admitted. The words scraped my throat raw, and saying them aloud made my chest constrict.

Vex leaned against the opposite wall. "If it was truly unsalvageable, she would have already killed you."

I snorted. "Is that supposed to be comforting?"

"It's perspective." She folded her arms. "Lady Blackrose isn't exactly known for her restraint when crossed. The fact that you're still breathing suggests she believes there's something worth saving."

"Or she's planning something particularly creative for my demise." My voice cracked on the last word. Shit. I was falling apart, piece by piece, and Vex was watching it happen.

The shadows coiled tighter around my ankles, climbing up my legs like chains.

"Always a possibility." Vex's tone softened slightly. "What happened at the Spire?"

I looked away, studying the tapestry on the alcove wall. Telling Vex would mean admitting my weakness, my failure. It would mean speaking aloud the fear that had been gnawing at me since that night.

That I was becoming something I couldn't control.

That I was losing myself.

That I was going to hurt Arabella, and I wouldn't be able to stop it.

You were always meant for this, whispered a voice that wasn't quite mine. *Dominion is your birthright.*

The runes flared hot enough to make me gasp. I pressed my hand against my chest, feeling them burn beneath skin and bone.

"I tried to control her," I forced out. Each word felt like pulling thorns from my throat.

Vex didn't respond immediately. The silence stretched, broken only by the distant sounds of chaos from the Great Hall and my own ragged breathing.

"Physically?" she asked finally, her voice carefully neutral.

"Magically." I grimaced. "We were at the Gilded Gallows. She saw Pip—or who we thought was Pip—and I wanted to go after him. She wanted to come with me. I—"

I couldn't finish.

"Ah." Just that single syllable, loaded with understanding.

"It didn't work," I added quickly, desperately. The shadows were climbing higher now, wrapping around my ribs. "She broke through it immediately. But I still did it. I still tried."

"And now? How do you feel about what you did?"

I turned back to face Vex, and I knew my eyes were too bright. Knew she could see the cracks in my armor, the way I was barely holding on to my magic. The Shadow King's essence coiled inside me like a hungry serpent, and I knew he would use this vulnerability against me.

"How do you think I feel?" My voice broke. "I betrayed her trust. I became exactly what she feared I would be."

The shadows reached my throat. Squeezed.

No, I told them. They reluctantly retreated.

"Did you?" Vex tilted her head. "Or did you make a mistake? There's a difference, you know."

"Not to Arabella."

"Have you asked her?"

I hadn't. We'd barely spoken since returning from the Spire, both of us too busy with the preparations for the ritual, the gathering of bloodlines, the constant threats from all sides.

Or at least, that's what I told myself. The truth was simpler and more terrifying: I was afraid of what she'd say.

"This reminds me of something," Vex said, her voice distant. "Do you remember the first time I called you by your name? Not 'my lord' or 'Dark Lord' or any of your other titles. Just Kazimir."

I frowned, searching my memory through the fog of emotion. "After the demon. When I was still . . ." I trailed off, unwilling to name the broken thing I'd been then.

Unwilling to acknowledge how close I was to becoming that broken thing again.

She nodded. "Almost fifteen years ago now. You were drowning yourself in rage. Using it as a shield against everything else you were feeling."

The memories surfaced, sharp and jagged. The pain had been too intense then, the humiliation too complete. I'd been eighteen, betrayed by my allies, sold to a demon prince who'd seen me as nothing more than a toy to break.

And break me he had, in ways I still couldn't fully recall.

The runes burned hotter. My vision swam.

"You brought me out of it," I said quietly.

"I reminded you that you were still human," Vex corrected. "That feeling pain didn't make you weak. It made you alive."

Alive, the voice mocked. *You're so much more than alive. You're eternal. Powerful. Why cling to humanity when divinity awaits?*

Frost formed on the tapestry, creeping down the wall. My breath misted in the air.

I'd found Skyspire not long after, guided by instincts I couldn't explain and dreams I couldn't remember upon waking. It had been abandoned then, a ruin of a fortress that had once belonged to a forgotten mage. I'd claimed it, rebuilt it, turned it into the seat of my power.

"Why are you bringing this up now?" I managed.

"Because I see the same thing happening again." She stepped closer, and I had to force myself not to retreat. "You're using anger to avoid pain. You're so afraid of what you might have lost that you're not even trying to find out if it's still there."

"That's not—"

"Isn't it?" She cut me off, a liberty few would dare take. "You're the Dark Lord. You've conquered kingdoms, broken demons, intimidated poultry. But you can't bring yourself to have an honest conversation with your wife?"

"What if she can't forgive me?" The question escaped before I could stop it.

Once again, the shadows surged up my body, responding to my loss of control. They wrapped around my chest, my throat, my face—

I shoved them back with effort that left me gasping.

"What if she can?" Vex countered, her voice gentle but relentless. "What if she's waiting for you to show her that you understand what went wrong? That you're willing to do the work to make sure it never happens again?"

"I don't know how." The admission came out barely above a whisper. "I've never . . . this isn't something I've had to do before."

I'd never cared enough to try. Never let anyone close enough to hurt me like this. Never opened myself up to the kind of vulnerability that could destroy me more completely than any demon or battlefield ever had.

And now I was paying the price for that ignorance. Drowning in emotions I didn't have the tools to process, while an ancient evil whispered encouragement in my ear, and my body tried to tear itself apart from the inside.

"I know." Vex's voice gentled further. "But you're learning. That's what matters. Remember, Kazimir, that though the heart and mind are seemingly at odds, it takes both of them to control the man you want to be—the man you have become."

I looked up sharply, my vision clearing for a moment. What did Vex know?

Her expression was unreadable, but there was something in her eyes. Understanding. Concern. And maybe—just maybe—a hint of fear.

She knew something was wrong, beyond the obvious strain between Arabella and me.

A crash from the Great Hall interrupted us, followed by several shouts and what sounded like a table being overturned.

"I should probably—" Vex began.

"Go." I waved her off, my hand still trembling. "Before they destroy anything irreplaceable."

She hesitated. "Will you talk to her?"

"Yes." The word came out clear. I meant it. I had to mean it, because the alternative was losing her. "I will."

Vex nodded, satisfied, and turned to leave. She'd taken only a few steps when Griffin appeared in the alcove entrance, his face flushed.

"My lord!" he gasped. "The Shellfords and the Moonbays are having a duel in the main hall! With serving platters!"

"Handle it," I said wearily.

“Also,” Griffin continued, shifting awkwardly from foot to foot, “I couldn’t help but overhear some of your . . . conversation.”

I fixed him with a glare that should have sent him running. The shadows coiled at my feet, ready to strike.

He paled but held his ground. “It’s just that—I might have some scrolls that could help. From the Enchanted Isles. They’re about, um, relationships. And communication. And, er, other things.”

“Are you suggesting I read relationship advice scrolls,” I said flatly.

“Not advice, exactly.” His face reddened further. “More like . . . illustrated guides? To, um, reconnecting. Physically. And emotionally. But mostly physically.”

Vex made a strangled sound that might have been suppressed laughter.

“Get out,” I told Griffin.

“Right! Yes! Going!” He scurried away, nearly tripping over his own feet in his haste.

When he was gone, I turned back to Vex, who was visibly struggling to maintain her composure.

“Not a word,” I warned.

“Wouldn’t dream of it, my lord.” Her eyes danced with amusement. “Though I do wonder what sort of illustrations—”

“Vex.”

She paused. “Before I go make sure our heroes don’t kill each other, there’s one more thing we need to discuss. Some very sensitive information has come to my attention.”

I straightened, forcing the emotions back down, the shadows to retreat. Rebuilding the armor piece by piece, even though every crack still showed. “What is it?”

52

Share Your Trauma

(It's Called Emotional Availability, Apparently)

Kazimir

I could breathe again. Barely. The shadows retreated as I descended to the training room, responding to my will instead of fighting it. Vex had given me clarity, at least. A direction.

Now I just had to not fuck it up.

"This is your fault." I stormed in to find Arabella in the center of the space, magic crackling between her hands.

Perhaps it wasn't the best opening, but I was still feeling raw and irritated.

She whirled on me, and the look in her eyes could have melted steel. "Excuse me?"

"We agreed to collect the bloodlines." I gestured wildly back toward the chaos I'd escaped. "Just the bloodlines. Not their entire extended families, household staff, and rooster."

"Oh, I'm sorry." Light and shadow swirled around her fingers in a display that was both beautiful and terrifying. Her hair was pulled back in a messy braid, sweat glistening on her skin. "Should I have left the children behind? Maybe with a nice note for Auremar explaining where their parents or aunts and uncles went?"

The magic between her hands pulsed brighter, and I realized this might not be the ideal moment to discuss our houseguest situation. I'd save that particular argument for when my wife wasn't actively channeling enough power to drop Skyspire into the swamp.

"What are you doing?" I asked instead, moving closer despite the danger.

"Practicing." She turned back to the far wall, where a portal shimmered. The edges were ragged, unstable, but that she was creating them at all was impressive. "I barely formed that portal that saved me from Zaraiah."

"And yet you did." My voice was hoarse. Part pride, part fury that she'd been in that position at all.

I wanted to delay the moment I'd come down here for, so I leaned against the wall, content to watch Arabella work. Each failed attempt brought a furrow to her brow that I wanted to smooth away with my thumb. Each success made her eyes light up in a way that sent heat straight to my cock. Soon, most of the tightness in my chest had eased.

The air around her rippled as she gathered her magic. Light and shadow twined around her arms. She thrust her hands forward, tearing a hole in the fabric of space. The portal stabilized, edges smoothing into a perfect circle that revealed the gardens outside.

"Fuck me," I breathed.

She glanced over her shoulder, a smirk playing at the corner of her mouth. "Maybe later, if you ask nicely."

Look at her, the Shadow King whispered, his presence sliding through my mind. *All that power, just begging to be claimed. We could take her right here, bend her over that table and—*

I slammed mental walls between us so hard my vision blacked out for a moment. When it cleared, Arabella was watching me with concern.

"Are you all right?"

"Fine." I took a deep breath. "Just . . . the runes are acting up."

She studied me for a long moment, and I wondered if she could sense the darkness coiling through my thoughts. If she knew how hard I fought every day to keep the Shadow King's influence at bay. How much harder it had become since learning the truth.

"Take a break," I said, grabbing a water flask from the supply shelf. "We need to talk."

The concern in her eyes deepened, but she nodded, dismissing the magic with a gesture. We settled on a bench along the wall.

"What is it?" she asked, accepting the water I offered.

I'd rehearsed this conversation a dozen times—first on the *Sky Serpent* when she'd described those robes, then every day since. None of the versions had gone well. I chose my words carefully, but there was no gentle way to deliver this particular blow.

"When you told me about the sorceress you remembered," I began, "the one in gray robes with red stitching—I recognized the description."

Arabella went very still. "You did? Who?"

"My mother," I rasped. "Amaryska wore robes like that. It's her signature—gray with red stitching that looks like veins of blood. I should have told you then, but I . . ." I trailed off.

I could see her mind working, processing. "I thought your mother disappeared after you killed your father."

"So did I."

"Then that means—" The flask slipped from Arabella's fingers, clattering to the floor. Water spilled across the stone. Her face had gone pale, eyes wide with shock.

"Yes." I reached for her hand, half expecting her to pull away. She didn't. "I believe my mother killed yours. I should have told you."

Arabella's grip tightened painfully on mine, her nails digging into my skin. I welcomed the pain. It was infinitely preferable to the hollow look in her eyes. "Why didn't you?"

"Because I'm a fucking coward when it comes to you." The admission burned. "Because telling you would make it real, and I wasn't ready to face what that meant. For us. For everything."

The silence stretched between us, heavy with all the things I still wasn't saying. The Shadow King whispered encouragement to take control of the conversation, to make her understand, to force her compliance—

I forced the voice down. "I saw her."

Arabella's gaze found mine.

The words tumbled out. "In Valmont, when I was collecting the bloodlines. Amaryska was there, wearing those exact robes. Working with Auremar's mages. Has been for who knows how long."

I waited for the explosion. For the rage, the accusations, the perfectly justified fury. Instead, Arabella turned on the bench to face me fully, her eyes searching mine. "How do you feel about seeing her?"

The question caught me completely off guard. "What?"

"Your mother." She loosened her hold on my hand but didn't let go completely. "How do you feel?"

I stared at our joined hands, trying to process her reaction. She should be screaming at me, demanding to know why I hadn't already told her, why I hadn't killed Amaryska on sight. Instead, Arabella was worried about me?

"I don't understand," I admitted.

"What's not to understand?" She put her other hand on my arm, over my runes. "You just found out your mother is alive. That can't be easy."

"She murdered your mother."

"Yes." Her voice hardened slightly. "And I want her dead for it. But that doesn't mean I can't also care about what this means for you."

Something cracked inside my chest. This woman, this impossible, infuriating, magnificent woman, was putting my feelings above her own need for vengeance. I didn't deserve her. The Shadow King whispered a protest, but I shoved him down even further.

"I don't know how I feel," I said honestly. "Angry. Betrayed. Not surprised, which might be the worst part."

She leaned against my shoulder, and I breathed in the scent of her magic and sweat. "Tell me everything."

I did. I told her about following Amaryska through Valmont, watching as she discovered the empty houses where heroic bloodlines had lived. About her appearance on the rooftop.

"I tried to kill her," I said quietly. "She escaped through a portal before I could finish it."

"Is she very powerful?" Arabella asked quietly.

I understood what she was really asking. How did the Dark Lord let his own mother escape?

The old me would have deflected. Made a joke about tactical retreats or blamed the portal's speed. But something about the way Arabella looked at me, without judgment or accusation, made the walls crumble.

"Yes," I said. "But that's not why she got away."

Arabella waited, her hand still warm in mine. Not pushing. Just present.

"When I saw her, I—" The words stuck in my throat. I forced them out anyway. "My body stopped working the way it should. My hands were shaking. The shadows wouldn't obey properly. I kept—"

I cut myself off, but Arabella squeezed my hand. Encouraging without demanding.

"I kept seeing myself as a child," I admitted, the confession scraping my throat raw. "Hearing her footsteps on the stairs. I was thirty-three years old, standing on that rooftop, and all I could think about was being seven and trying to be quiet enough that she'd forget I existed."

The shame burned hot, and I couldn't even look at Arabella. I waited for her to pull away. To see me as weak and broken.

Instead, she shifted closer, her free hand coming up to rest against my chest. Right over my heart.

"That's not weakness," she said firmly. "That's trauma."

"I'm the Dark Lord. I shouldn't—"

"You're also human, Kaz." Her eyes met mine, fierce and unwavering. "Your mother abused you when you were a child. Of course your body remembered. Of course you froze."

The knot in my chest unraveled, leaving something raw but strangely lighter in its wake. "It felt pathetic," I continued quietly. "Standing there, shaking like a child while she escaped."

Arabella's thumb traced small circles over my sternum. "You're allowed to be human with me, you know. You don't have to be the Dark Lord every second."

The relief that washed through me was so intense it was almost painful. Like lancing a wound I hadn't known was infected.

"I've never told anyone that before," I admitted. "About being afraid."

"Thank you." She leaned her forehead against my shoulder. "For telling me now."

And somehow, impossibly, it did feel good to say it aloud. To let someone see the parts of me I'd kept locked away. To trust that Arabella wouldn't use my vulnerability as a weapon.

The Shadow King whispered warnings, but for once, I barely heard them over the sound of my own heartbeat slowing to match Arabella's.

"This is new territory for me," I said, my voice rough. "Being this . . . open. I'm not sure I'm doing it right."

"There's no 'right' way." Arabella pulled back just enough to meet my eyes. "Just honest. And you're being honest with me. That's enough."

She was quiet for a moment, then let her hand drop from my chest to my thigh, not in a sensual way, just reassuring. "Where is she now?"

"Likely back at Sunspire Palace, with Auremar."

Arabella huffed in frustration. "Of course. Because why wouldn't the woman who murdered my mother be hiding in the one place we can't easily reach?"

I could have pointed out the irony—her own father still rotted in our dungeons because she couldn't decide what to do with him. Of the two of us, I was the one who'd killed a parent. I understood the weight of that decision in ways she couldn't yet comprehend.

"There's more," I said instead. "When we fought, she admitted to orchestrating my betrayal. The demon, all of it—it was her plan."

Arabella's hand tightened on mine hard enough to hurt. "Oh Kaz."

"She said I'd grown too powerful. That I'd exceeded my purpose." The words tasted bitter.

"Fucking bitch." The vehemence in her voice made more warmth bloom in my chest.

"I believe she's helping him directly with the Shadow King's prison. The ley lines, the bloodline sacrifices—it all points to the prison. Amaryska's been obsessed with ancient magic since before I was born. If anyone could help Auremar tap into the Shadow King's power, it would be her."

"But why?" Arabella shook her head. "What does she gain from it?"

I scowled. "It's always been about power with her. She traded her soul for it once before. This would just be another bargain."

Arabella leaned into me again. I wrapped my arms around her, holding her close as she processed everything I'd told her. Her body was tense, coiled like a spring ready to release. "Do you think that's why she came after me? Because I'd seen her in the palace?"

I sighed. "That's my theory, yes."

We were silent awhile, sitting with our own thoughts.

"I want her dead," Arabella said finally, her voice muffled against my shirt.

So bloodthirsty, the voice purred. *She'll make a perfect queen for us.*

I tightened my grip on her, as much to ground myself as to comfort her. "Amaryska will pay for what she's done. To both of us."

Arabella nodded. She sat up, straightening her shoulders. "What's our next move?"

"We need to speak with the Alchemist," I said. "To figure out exactly what to do with the bloodlines we've gathered."

A corner of her mouth lifted. "I guess it's a good thing you kept them as an overnight guest. I only hope they'll feel like cooperating after this."

My runes began burning beneath Arabella's hand. "They want the Shadow King contained as much as we do. But if not, I'll make them see reason." I hesitated, then added, "There's something else you should know. About the prison."

Arabella's expression tightened. "What about it?"

I opened my mouth to tell her the truth—that I was part Shadow King, that the ancient darkness Auremar sought to harness was a part of me. That I'd been fighting it since the ritual at the Spire, trying to keep it contained.

She'll never understand. She'll turn against you.

I sighed heavily. Arabella had just learned that my mother murdered hers.

Adding the revelation that I was harboring an ancient evil might be more than even our tenuous relationship could bear.

"They got to as many heroes as we did," I said instead. "Auremar and my mother could be sacrificing them right now, weakening what little hold the prison has on the Shadow King."

She nodded, resolution hardening her features. "Then we'd better get moving."

I watched her, this woman who had entered my life as a pawn and become something I couldn't bear to lose. Despite everything—the betrayals, the secrets, the darkness that threatened to consume us both—she was still here. Still fighting.

She'll be magnificent when she breaks, the voice whispered.

I silenced it with a thought. Arabella wouldn't break. Neither would I.

53

Balance Warfare and Spite

(The Dark Lord's Guide to Time Management)

Kazimir

The dungeons of Skyspire had a particular smell—damp stone, old fear, and the lingering traces of necromantic experiments that even Griffin's cleaning enchantments couldn't quite erase.

I'd left Arabella in the Great Hall, where she was attempting to mediate a dispute between Lord Brightwater and Lady Marenti over whose ancestral claim to some insignificant valley was more legitimate. The irony of "heroes" behaving like petty nobles wasn't lost on me. At least it kept her occupied while I dealt with this.

I'd handed Griffin's detection kit to Thorne with orders to test everyone at Skyspire for doppelgangers—no exceptions. Nyx had killed the one infiltrator, but I wasn't fool enough to assume there weren't others.

The tests came back clean, and there were plans to adapt the same principles to the fortress wards. Until then, everyone—including our heroic guests—would submit to weekly testing.

The spiral staircase descended into the Undercroft Gaols, each step worn smooth to the point of being treacherously slippery. I needed answers from the Alchemist about what to do with our collection of heroic bloodlines, and I needed them before Auremar sacrificed his own captives and weakened the Shadow King's prison even further.

But first, I had to pass through Griffin's previous punishment.

I found him exactly where I'd ordered him to be—on his hands and knees in the corridor outside the holding cells, painstakingly inscribing containment runes into the stone floor. His robes were hiked up around his knees, and his gangly frame was bent at an awkward angle as he traced the intricate patterns with a piece of enchanted chalk before carving it.

A cart sat nearby, loaded with supplies and the Doom Scroll propped against a stack of reference books.

"My lord," Griffin said without looking up, his voice tight with concentration. "I'm making excellent progress. Only seventy-three more runes to go."

I stopped beside him, examining his work. The runes were precise, each line exactly the correct width and depth. No shortcuts, no magical assistance—just hours of mind-numbing manual labor.

"I'm surprised you didn't try to delegate this to one of your apprentices again," I observed.

Griffin's hand jerked, smudging a line. He cursed under his breath and reached for a correction cloth. "You specifically said I was to do it myself, my lord. As penance for the, ah, incident with the prisoners."

"I did say that." I crouched down, inspecting the rune he'd just smudged. "And yet I'm surprised you're actually following instructions for once."

"I learned my lesson." Griffin's voice was miserable. "No more unsupervised demonstrations of necromantic theory. No more showing off to Sebastian. No more accidentally releasing prisoners who then float away in magical cages."

The idea of Sir Darian Lightbringer and Lord Evenfall drifting across the sky in a Tempest Cage would have been hilarious if it hadn't been such a massive security breach.

"At least you're learning," I said, straightening. "Continue."

I moved toward the cart to retrieve a report I'd asked Griffin to compile on the heroic bloodlines' magical signatures. My gaze snagged on the

Doom Scroll instead, its surface rippling with fresh updates.

I picked it up, scanning the latest headlines and passing over fresh reports of magical catastrophes.

SOLANDRIAN FORCES MOBILIZE TO RETAKE NORTHERN OUTPOST

KING AUREMAR RALLIES ALLIES FOR DECISIVE BATTLE

BLACKROSE INVASION STALLS AS DEFENDERS REGROUP

My jaw clenched. I scrolled through the details, each one worse than the last. Auremar had summoned his scattered forces and was marching them toward the northern outpost we'd taken.

He was preparing for a full-scale counterattack.

Ten thousand soldiers, the Scroll reported. *Allied reinforcements from Valmont and the coastal kingdoms. Mage battalions specializing in offensive magic.*

I'd lost the element of surprise. The quick, brutal conquest I'd planned—sweeping through Solandris's defenses and taking the capital before Auremar could organize—was no longer possible. Now it would be a grinding, bloody siege where I was outnumbered at least two to one.

Perfect, the Shadow King purred in my mind. *A proper battlefield. Rivers of blood to consecrate our victory.*

The thought sent a thrill through me—anticipation mixed with hunger. I could already see my shadow warriors tearing through enemy ranks, hear the screams of the dying, feel the satisfying crunch of bones beneath my magic—

I slammed the mental walls down so hard I saw stars.

When they cleared, my hands were shaking.

How much of that bloodlust was mine? How much had always been the Shadow King's influence, whispering in the back of my mind since I was a child? I'd built my entire reputation on ruthless conquest, on the thrill of warfare. But was any of it real?

Does it matter? the voice laughed. *We are the same now. Your desires, my desires—there's no difference.*

"Shut up," I muttered.

"My lord?" Griffin looked up from his rune work, confused.

"Not you." I forced my breathing to steady. I tossed the Doom Scroll back onto the cart. The damned thing had delivered news about my enemy before my own intelligence network. "Go find Thorne. Tell him to send scouts to confirm this report about Auremar's army. I want numbers, positions, and an assessment of their defenses."

Griffin scrambled to his feet, nearly tripping over his robes. "Right now, my lord? But the runes—"

"Can wait." I turned toward the deeper cells where the Alchemist was being held. "This takes priority."

"Of course, my lord."

I needed to deal with the Alchemist first. Then I'd tell Arabella that our invasion had just become exponentially more complicated. That instead of a quick strike at the capital, we were looking at a prolonged campaign.

You're going soft, the Shadow King whispered. *Weak. All because of her.*

I ignored him and continued down the corridor. The cells here were older. Reserved for prisoners who required special attention.

"Blackrose!" a voice roared from one of the cells. "You bastard! You can't leave me down here to rot!"

Evenfall.

I paused outside his cell, considering. The man pressed against the bars in the door, his once-fine clothes filthy and torn. His eyes were wild, desperate.

"I'm a lord of Solandris." His voice cracked. "I can—"

I leaned closer to the bars, forming shadows into wolves with glowing silver eyes. Evenfall backed into the wall of his cell. "I think about your death often. Every day, I imagine how creatively I can kill you—and how long I can make it last."

Evenfall's face went pale.

I let my dominion magic fill the corridor with the scent of ozone and winter storms. My eyes flared silver as more shadows writhed along the walls of his cell, responding to the raw power I was channeling. I wanted him to see a figure of terror, one who would deliver on each promise of violence.

"As soon as Lady Blackrose gives the word," I said in a soft, dangerous voice. "I'll come for you, Evenfall. Mine will be the last face you ever see."

One of the shadow wolves drifted through the door of the cell and became solid. It looked real, with its hair and gleaming teeth. The smell of a predator filled the space, and it snarled silently. Evenfall was about to piss his pants—pity I couldn't wait around to watch.

I turned away from the cell. I'd leave the construct there for a while. Evenfall's desperate sob echoed off the stone as I descended deeper into the dungeons. The Alchemist waited in the most secure cell we had, and I needed answers more than I needed to torment Arabella's pathetic excuse for a father.

Though I had to admit, it had been satisfying.

See? the Shadow King murmured. *You enjoy the cruelty. We're not so different.*

I rebuilt my mental walls in preparation for the conversation with the Alchemist. As a bonus, it also cut off the Shadow King's laughter.

54

Consult the Expert

(Who Definitely Knows You're Possessed)

Kazimir

The Alchemist's cell was in the secure wing, behind three sets of wards and a door that could only be opened by my blood. I'd been generous, with a proper cot, a desk, even some books. They'd been here less than a day, but I hoped it was enough time for reflection.

I pressed my palm to the door, feeling the familiar sting as the ward tasted my blood. The locks clicked open.

The Alchemist sat cross-legged on the floor, their robes pooled around them in shifting colors. They didn't look up. "Lord Blackrose." Their voice held that same musical quality that had always set my teeth on edge. "Come to gloat? Or perhaps to threaten more creatively than yesterday?"

"Neither." I conjured a chair and sat facing them. "I need your knowledge, as we discussed. Unless you'd like to release my wife and me from your task."

"Ah." They finally looked up. "The mighty Dark Lord needs something from his prisoner."

I resisted the urge to wrap shadows around their throat. Barely. "Are you being deliberately difficult? You know what's happening to the ley lines. You know about the Shadow King's prison."

"I know many things." They tilted their head, studying me. "Including what you are."

I kept my expression neutral, but inside, the Shadow King stirred, sensing danger.

I slammed mental walls between us, focusing on the Alchemist's masked face. "And what exactly do you think I am?"

"A man fighting a war on two fronts." They rose gracefully, robes shifting from green to purple to gold. "One against Auremar and his machinations. The other . . ." They tapped their temple. "Against yourself."

I said nothing. Denial would be pointless; confirmation could be equally dangerous.

"The question," the Alchemist continued, beginning to pace the small cell, "is whether you're winning either battle."

"I'm managing."

"Are you?" They stopped directly in front of me. "Tell me, Lord Blackrose—can you learn sensitive information without making certain aspects of yourself aware?"

The question was so precisely targeted I nearly flinched.

"Yes," I said carefully. "I've been practicing. I can compartmentalize when needed."

"Fascinating." They resumed pacing. "And when is it most difficult?"

I thought of Arabella, of how the whispers grew louder whenever she was near. How the Shadow King's hunger sharpened into something almost painful when she smiled at me, touched me, challenged me.

"When I'm having . . . feelings," I admitted through gritted teeth.

The Alchemist laughed—a sound like wind chimes in a graveyard. "Feelings. How delightfully mortal of you."

My shadows darkened the cell. "Don't mock me."

"I'm not mocking." They settled back onto the floor, arranging their robes carefully. "I'm observing. You believe your feelings make you vulnerable."

"They do." The words tasted bitter. "The thoughts are more intrusive when I'm around my wife or remembering certain events."

"Then you're thinking about it wrong." The Alchemist stood again as if they couldn't bear to be still, moving to the small window that looked out over the swirling mists below. "The Shadow King was defeated once before. Do you know how?"

"The First Hero bound him with blood magic and Golden Roses." Though there were few texts on the subject, I'd barely slept for days, and I'd had time to think about everything we'd learned.

"Partially correct." The Alchemist turned back to me. "But Soriven didn't defeat the Shadow King through power alone. He won because he had something the Shadow King didn't."

"Which was?"

"Love." The word hung in the air between us, sickeningly sweet. "Soriven loved his people, his land, his family. That love gave him the strength to do what was necessary, no matter how terrible."

I thought of Arabella again, of the way she'd looked at me in the training room. How she'd put aside her own pain to ask about mine.

"Love makes me vulnerable," I insisted. "It gives the Shadow King leverage."

"Does it?" The Alchemist tilted their head. "Or does it give you a reason to fight?"

I had no answer for that.

"You must keep your loved ones close," they continued. "Not despite the danger, but because of it. They remind you who you are. Who you choose to be."

The words echoed Vex's advice from earlier in the day so intimately that for a moment I wondered if she'd been to see the Alchemist. But I realized she couldn't have, and wouldn't. "And if I fail? If the Shadow King uses my feelings against them?"

"Then you'll have failed trying to be human." They shrugged. "There are worse ways to fall."

I stood abruptly. "If I fall," I growled, "so does your chance of stopping the Shadow King."

Before they could respond, footsteps echoed down the corridor. Light, confident, familiar. Arabella. The Alchemist heard her too.

"Does your charming wife know about your . . . condition?"

Frost spread across the stones as my magic responded to the threat. "No."

"I see." They didn't seem bothered by the sudden cold. "And you'd prefer it stays that way?"

I lowered my voice. "If you tell her—anyone—about this, I'll make what I did to those assassins look like mercy. I might even give in to the Shadow King out of spite."

I wouldn't. I'd die before I let that ancient darkness have Arabella. But the Alchemist didn't need to know that.

"Understood." They inclined their head. "Your secret is safe with me."

"Kazimir?" Arabella's voice carried a note of irritation. "Why didn't you tell me you were coming down here?"

She appeared in the doorway, hands on her hips, looking beautifully annoyed. Her hair was slightly mussed from dealing with our houseguests, and there was a smudge of something—ink or soot?—on her cheek. I wondered if she'd set anyone on fire—that hadn't happened lately and she was overdue.

"I haven't been here long," I said, moving to her side. "Good news, though. The Alchemist has agreed to continue helping us."

Her eyes narrowed slightly—she knew I was deflecting—but she let it go. Instead, she conjured her own chair and sat down with the air of someone settling in for a long conversation. "Then let's hear what they have to say."

The Alchemist watched our interaction with obvious interest. I could practically see them cataloging every glance, every small gesture. "Very well," they said finally. "Let's ensure we're all on the same page, shall we?"

They began pacing again, robes shifting through a spectrum of dark colors. "King Auremar has been manipulating the Golden Rose Fields for years, using them to enhance his own power while maintaining the fiction of their sacred nature. The roses aren't just magical plants. They're channels between our world and the dimension where the Shadow King is—or was—bound."

A piece clicked into place in my mind. "He's been poisoning the Hero's Guild with that power."

The Alchemist's eyes glittered with what looked like pride, as though I were a particularly apt student who'd finally grasped a complex theorem. "Auremar has been feeding his most loyal followers diluted essence from the prison. It grants them power, creates addiction, and—most importantly for his purposes—marks them as servants of the Shadow King."

They continued. "Every improper harvest weakens the anchor points. Every ritual Auremar performs to extract their essence frays the web holding the prison together. He believes he's siphoning power safely, but he's actually—"

"Letting the Shadow King bleed through," I cut in. "Yes, we remember."

The Alchemist nodded gravely. "Before I was so graciously invited to stay at Skyspire, I was monitoring the situation through my various channels. The magical collapses are accelerating exponentially. What took decades to degrade is now happening in months, even weeks."

They moved to the window, gazing out at the mists. "The Golden Rose Fields themselves are showing signs of rapid deterioration. Entire sections that bloomed just last month have withered to ash. The farmers are panicking, though Auremar keeps it quiet. He's been sending mages to cast illusions over the dead patches for any visiting dignitaries."

"How long do we have?" I asked.

"At the current rate of acceleration?" The Alchemist turned back to us, their mask catching the light. "Perhaps three months before the degradation becomes irreversible. Maybe less if Auremar continues his extraction rituals."

Arabella and I exchanged a look.

"So what do we do?" Arabella leaned forward. "We have over seventy heroic bloodlines here. How do we use them to stop this?"

"That," the Alchemist said slowly, "is where things become complicated."

They moved to the narrow window, staring out at the mists. "The prison must be resealed. The ley lines must be cleansed. These are facts. The question is method."

"A ritual circle," I said slowly. "Using the bloodlines as anchor points."

"Precisely. Though it will be far more complex than that." They settled back onto the floor. "Soriven was many things, but compassionate wasn't one of them. He loved—yes, loved—his people, his legacy, his vision of order. But that love was cold, strategic. He bound the Shadow King through blood and suffering. The roses were planted in soil enriched with the blood of hundreds. That's why they maintain their power and connection with the ley lines."

Arabella went very still. I reached for her hand, but she pulled away.

"You're lying."

"I never lie," the Alchemist said simply. "I merely present truth in its most useful form. And the truth is this: Your beloved ancestor built his prison on a foundation of corpses." They stood again, as if unable to remain still for more than a minute. "Which brings us back to our current dilemma. We need those bloodlines to repair what Auremar has broken. The question is whether we follow Soriven's example . . ."

"Or find another way," I finished, glancing at Arabella, who was glaring at the Alchemist, and no doubt remembering the discussion in the war room about sacrifices. "Which is what we aim to do."

"There is another way." The Alchemist moved closer, voice dropping to barely above a whisper. "But it requires something far more difficult than death."

"Which is?"

"Cooperation." The mask turned between us. "Willing participation from every bloodline. A ritual circle, yes, but one powered by choice rather than force. It's never been done before on that scale."

"Because it's harder to convince people to bleed for you than to simply take what you need," I said.

"Precisely!" They clapped their hands. "As you perhaps know better than anyone here, Lord Blackrose: Why negotiate when you can simply conquer?"

I thought of the hundreds of people currently crowding my citadel. Heroes and their families, children playing in halls meant for darker purposes. The chaos of it all.

"We'll find a way," Arabella said firmly. "We'll explain the situation, make them understand—"

"Will you tell them their sacred bloodline exists solely to maintain a prison built on murder?" the Alchemist interrupted. "That their choice is to bleed willingly or watch the world burn?"

"If that's what it takes."

They studied her for a long moment. "You might actually do it. How fascinating."

"Is that everything?" I asked, suddenly exhausted. The weight of secrets—mine and history's—were making my runes burn.

"For now." The Alchemist waved a hand dismissively. "Though I'll need access to your library to refine the ritual specifics."

"You'll stay in the dungeons," I said flatly. "But I'll have books brought to you."

"Acceptable." They settled back onto their cot.

I turned and left before I could do something we'd all regret. Arabella followed, her silence damning.

We climbed the stairs without speaking, the only sound our footsteps and the distant echo of a few remaining prisoners making their protests known. It wasn't until we reached the main level that she finally spoke.

"You're keeping something from me."

I stopped walking. "Arabella—"

She held up a hand. "I know you have secrets. I know there are things about your past, about your magic, that you haven't told me. And that's fine. We all have darkness we'd rather keep hidden."

"Then what—"

"Just promise me something." She turned to face me fully, and the vulnerability in her eyes nearly broke my resolve. "When you're ready—if you're ever ready—you'll tell me yourself. Not because you have to, not because someone forces your hand, but because you choose to trust me."

The Shadow King laughed in my mind, cruel and knowing.

"I promise," I said, and meant it.

She studied my face for a moment, then nodded. "Good. Now come on. Lord Torok is threatening to duel Lady Marenti's eight-year-old son, and I need backup."

I raised an eyebrow. "The heroes are trying to duel *children*?"

"Apparently, the boy called his ancestor a 'pompous windbag.'"

I followed, muttering, "And I thought *we* were the villains."

55

Dance Without Music

(Because Your Villain Is Secretly Sentimental)

Arabella

I slammed another tome onto the growing pile, earning a withering look from Magister Vellum.

"Lady Blackrose." His voice scraped like parchment being torn. "The books are not your enemies."

"They're not being particularly helpful, either." I glared at the stack of texts on ritual magic, blood ceremonies, and theoretical ley line manipulation. Two days of research, and I was no closer to understanding how to convince seventy-eight people to willingly bleed for us.

Vellum's enormous spectacles caught the library's orblight as he turned away. "Perhaps if you specified your exact needs—"

"I need a miracle." I rubbed my temples, feeling a headache building behind my eyes. "Or at least a compelling argument for why our houseguests should trust us with their blood when half of them are still demanding to know why they woke up in our guest quarters."

That was Kazimir's fault. His brilliant plan to enchant half of Valmont into unconsciousness had worked perfectly—right up until they'd woken up separated from their families and extremely pissed off. Janos Torok had tried to challenge three different people to duels in the last hour alone.

"The section on persuasive magics is in aisle seventeen," Vellum offered, already gliding away between the shelves.

I gathered more relevant texts—carefully, because Vellum was still watching—and made my way toward the lightning bridge. On the other side, the corridors were chaos. Children raced past, chasing one of Nyx's shed scales that an unnatural wind was blowing around the room. Lady Delacroix's son had discovered the echo in the west hall and was testing its limits with increasingly creative profanity. And somewhere in the distance, I could hear Griffin explaining to someone why they absolutely could not borrow the explosive devices from his laboratory.

"Lady Blackrose!" A harried-looking woman intercepted me—Lady Clearwater, I thought, though keeping track of everyone was becoming impossible. "My sister is allergic to the sheets in our quarters, and that dragon of yours ate Ferdinand!"

"Ferdinand?"

"Our rooster!"

Right. The demon rooster from Meridian Isle. Oh no . . . How terrible of Nyx. I'd need to give her an extra treat tonight before bed. "I'll look into it."

She huffed off, and I continued toward the Great Hall, where Vex had promised to help me sort through accommodation complaints before I met with Kazimir to take the books to the dungeons.

The hall was suspiciously empty when I arrived. No arguing nobles, no children attempting to climb the columns to reach the chandelier, no sign of the usual chaos that had defined the last two days.

"Vex?" I called, setting the books on a side table. "If you've finally snapped and murdered them all, I need to know where you've hidden the bodies."

Movement in the shadows by the main doors. I reached for my magic, ready to defend myself—

"SURPRISE!"

The lights blazed to life, revealing Vex, Griffin, Thorne, Sebastian, and—impossibly—Kazimir, all grinning at me like idiots. Well, Thorne was doing his version of grinning, which looked more like mild constipation. A banner hung across the far wall reading "HAPPY BIRTHDAY" in Griffin's handwriting, complete with small explosions drawn around the edges.

And there, curled beside the feast table, was Nyx. A ridiculously large bow—bright pink to match her scales—had been tied around her neck. She lifted her head, silver eyes gleaming with what I could swear was amusement.

I stood frozen, trying to process what I was seeing. "What—"

"It's your birthday!" Sebastian bounced forward. "Your twenty-fifth! Did you really think we'd let that pass without celebration?"

"Um." I'd honestly forgotten. Between the invasion, the kidnappings, the Syndicate coup, and everything else, the date had completely slipped my mind. "How did you even know?"

"I told them." Sebastian looked pleased with himself. "Well, I told Vex and Griffin, and they told everyone else. We've been planning this for weeks, since before leaving for the God Spire!"

Nyx rumbled a low, contented sound like distant thunder, and I felt her presence brush against my mind. *Surprise,* the feeling seemed to say, tinged with satisfaction.

"Weeks," I repeated, looking at Kazimir. "You knew about this?"

He shrugged, but I caught the slight smile tugging at his lips. "Vex presented it as an urgent matter. Threatened me with creative dismemberment if I ruined the surprise, actually."

"We thought you could use a break," Vex added, moving to guide me toward the table they'd set up. "An hour or two where we pretend the world isn't ending and celebrate the fact that you've survived a year of spectacular danger."

"Even Nyx helped," Griffin added proudly. "She only ate two of the decorative arrangements! And she let us put the bow on her without setting anything on fire."

The dragon snorted, a puff of smoke escaping her nostrils as if to say she'd been extraordinarily patient with their nonsense.

The table was laden with food—not the formal feast fare we'd been serving our guests, but comfort foods. Roasted meats, fresh bread, potatoes, fruits that weren't in season but Griffin had grown in the greenhouses under magical conditions, and in the center . . .

"A cake?" I stared at the magnificent creation—three tiers of chocolate, decorated with sugar flowers that bloomed and withered in an endless cycle.

"I made it!" Sebastian beamed. "Each layer tastes like your favorite dessert from a different period of your life."

"Childhood, adolescence, and now," Griffin added helpfully. "I helped with the temporal taste enchantments!"

"You helped by nearly setting the kitchen on fire," Thorne rumbled. "Twice."

"The second time was intentional! For the flambé!"

Nyx snorted, her tail swishing across the floor.

I sank into a chair, overwhelmed. After days of being Lady Blackrose, the Dark Lord's wife, the mediator, the researcher, the woman trying to save the world—they'd given me this. A moment to just be Arabella. "I don't know what to say."

"'Thank you' is traditional," Kazimir murmured, taking the seat beside me and draping his arm over the back of my chair. "Though 'you're all insane' would also be appropriate."

"Thank you," I said, meaning it. "You're all insane."

Nyx came over to rest her massive head on my lap. The pink bow was even more ridiculous up close, and I couldn't help but laugh as I stroked her snout.

"Now that's settled," Vex said, producing a bottle of wine from Kazimir's private collection, "let's eat before some crisis drags us away."

The next hour was perfect. No one mentioned bloodlines, ley lines, or impending doom. Instead, Griffin regaled us with stories of his explosive failures before he came to Skyspire. Thorne demonstrated his party trick of bending spoons with his literally steel spine—it required odd contortionist movements that I was still doubting hours later. Sebastian made flowers bloom along the table's edge every time he laughed.

Nyx contributed by stealing entire roasted chickens when she thought no one was looking, though we all pretended not to notice. At one point, she and Griffin engaged in what could only be described as a staring contest over the last honey-glazed ham. Griffin lost.

Even Kazimir relaxed, the tension that had been riding him for days easing as he watched me open presents. Vex gave me a set of throwing knives ("For when magic just won't do"). Griffin presented me with a self-warming cloak that definitely wouldn't explode ("I'm seventy percent certain!"). Thorne's gift was practical—a leather journal warded against magical interference, perfect for keeping notes on our research.

Nyx, not to be outdone, disappeared briefly and returned dragging something that clinked. She deposited it at my feet with obvious pride—a small chest filled with various shiny objects she'd been hoarding. Coins, jeweled buttons, what looked suspiciously like Lord Saltieri's missing cufflinks, and . . .

"Is that my hairpin?" Vex asked, reaching for a silver piece.

Nyx's tail swept it back into the pile, her eyes narrowing. Apparently, once gifted to me, there were no take-backs no matter their origin.

Sebastian gave me a pressed flower in a crystal frame. "From your mother's garden," he said quietly. "I saved it years ago and had my father send it. Thought you might want something to remember the good times."

I had to blink away tears at that one.

"And this," Kazimir said, producing a small black box, "is from me."

Inside was a ring—not strange and macabre like our wedding bands, but a simple band of dark metal set with a black moonstone. The stone appeared nearly opaque at first glance, dark as a starless night. But when I tilted it, flashes of blue fire and silver streaks suddenly flared across its surface. The effect was subtle, intimate—beauty that only revealed itself to those paying close attention.

His signet—black roses wrapped around a bleeding sword—was etched into the band. But it had been altered. The roses alternated between gold and black when I tilted it back and forth. Black for Kaz, gold for me.

"I figured the family crest could use an update. It's connected to mine." He showed me an identical band on his right hand. "When you're feeling something strongly about me, mine warms. When I'm feeling something about you, yours does the same. Sentiment rings." A wry smile. "Fair warning—I have no idea how to turn it off."

"Kaz." I slipped it onto my finger, feeling the magic settle against my skin. "It's beautiful."

"Useful," he corrected, but his eyes were soft. "Beautiful is just a bonus."

"Like you, then," I said without thinking, then felt heat flood my cheeks as everyone laughed.

Nyx rumbled her amusement, nudging me with her snout.

"Smooth, my lady," Sebastian teased. "Very smooth."

"Shut up and cut the cake." I wiped a stray tear from my face and kissed Kaz, my lips lingering on his. When I pulled back, I held his gaze. "I love it—thank you."

He smiled and took my hand to look at the ring on it. "I enchanted it myself. No chance of anyone else tampering with it or causing accidental explosions." He said the last with a pointed glare at Griffin, who was oblivious as he whooped at the way the icing sparkled when the cake was cut.

Kaz leaned in to whisper seductively in my ear. "And you'll have another birthday present *coming* later. I hope you'll love it just as much."

I whispered back. "Is your ring telling you how I feel about that?"

His lips brushed my ear. "The ring's telling me you're already imagining it."

More heat bloomed across my cheeks as my own ring pulsed warm against my finger.

The cake was, as promised, magical. The first bite tasted like the honey cakes our cook used to make, before my mother died—they reminded me a bit too strongly of Sebastian, but I let it slide. The second layer was pure nostalgia—the strawberry tarts from the summer festival, when I was a child and still believed in happy endings. The final layer . . .

"Spiced pear and . . ." I looked at Sebastian in surprise. "Mulled wine?"

He grinned. "Lord Blackrose suggested the flavor, but he wouldn't say why. Just insisted it had to be this one." His eyes sparkled with curiosity. "I assume there's a story?"

I glanced at my husband, who was very deliberately studying his wineglass. Heat crept up my neck as I remembered that night—the kitchen, the blankets, his confession that he had no interest in trifles because he was "sufficiently occupied with one infuriating woman."

"There might be," I said softly.

Kazimir leaned close, his voice low enough that only I could hear. "It was one of the first times I knew I was falling for you."

My breath caught. The memory sharpened—his hands braced on either side of me on the counter, the possessive heat in his eyes when he'd said, "What's mine stays mine," the way he'd left me alone in his bed rather than push for more.

"You left that night," I whispered back. "Walked away."

"Gods knew I wanted to stay." His fingers found mine under the table. "And that terrified me."

The ring on my finger pulsed warm, echoing the heat spreading through my chest.

Around us, I became dimly aware of the others pointedly not listening. Griffin had launched into an enthusiastic explanation of his latest explosive compound to Thorne, who was nodding with the patience of a man who'd heard this speech before. Vex was trying to coax her hairpin away from Nyx, who was growling. Sebastian had suddenly become very interested in making the sugar flowers on the cake bloom and wither in increasingly complex patterns.

"It's perfect," I said in a voice everyone could hear. "All of it. Thank you."

We were debating whether Griffin should be allowed to demonstrate his "completely safe" indoor fireworks when a knock interrupted. One of the servants entered, looking apologetic.

"Forgive the interruption, but Lord Sebastian has an urgent message."

Sebastian frowned, taking the sealed paper. His face went pale as he read. "I need to go. My contact in Solandris—" He looked up at us, clearly torn. "I'm sorry. This can't wait."

"Go," I said. "We'll save you some cake."

"Happy birthday, Arabella. Try not to save the world for at least another hour." He squeezed my shoulder as he passed. Kaz scowled, and Sebastian snatched back his hand as if he was afraid to lose it. Apparently, my husband's limits were still in place despite the warm atmosphere.

After he left, the mood shifted. Griffin yawned dramatically. "Well, I should probably check on my familiars. Make sure Nyx hasn't eaten any more of them."

The dragon gave him an innocent look that fooled no one.

"And I need to patrol," Thorne added, though I noticed him pocket an extra slice of cake first.

Vex was smiling contentedly. "I suppose I should make sure Lord Torok hasn't challenged any more children to combat. I threatened him with the actual dungeon, and he said he'd behave." She stood. "Though I don't quite trust these hero types."

They filed out, each pausing to wish me happy birthday again. Nyx lingered, her silver eyes moving between Kazimir and me with an intelligence that was sometimes unsettling. Then she too padded toward the small side door, somehow managing to squeeze her large frame through without breaking it. The pink bow, I noticed, had mysteriously vanished.

And then it was just Kaz and me, alone in the Great Hall with the remains of my surprise party.

"You knew," I said. "This whole time, you knew it was my birthday and didn't say anything."

"Vex was very specific about the dismemberment." He poured himself another glass of wine. "Besides, you needed a moment of normalcy."

"Nothing about our life is normal."

He smirked. "But that's what makes it fun."

I studied him in the candlelight. The sharp angles of his face, the way his dark hair fell across his forehead—it was longer than ever.

"Dance with me," I said suddenly.

He raised an eyebrow. "There's no music."

"So?" I stood, holding out my hand. "It's my birthday. I want to dance with my husband."

He took my hand and stood, pulling me close. We swayed in the empty hall, no music but the sound of our breathing and the distant chaos of our overcrowded citadel. His hand was warm on my waist, his other holding mine like something precious.

"I need to tell you something," he said quietly.

My heart stuttered. Was this it? Was he finally going to share about the Shadow King? I hoped he would, and also hoped he wouldn't. I didn't want to confront that tonight.

"I'm terrible at birthdays," he continued. I let out a relieved breath. "Never celebrated my own, never understood the point. But seeing you tonight—" He spun me gently, then pulled me back. My breasts brushed against the hard muscles of his chest. "Maybe I understand a little better."

"Oh?" I looked up at him. "And what do you understand?"

"That it's not just about marking another year survived." His voice dropped. "It's about having people who care that you survived it."

The words hit deeper than he probably intended. I thought of the years after my mother's death, when the date passed unmarked and unmourned except for whatever meager gift my lady's maid Agnes could smuggle to me in the tower. After my kidnapping, my father had dismissed her—as if she'd been the one to fail him. But Vex's recent inquiries had turned up something better: Agnes had found employment with a gentler household, helping two young girls who probably adored her. I'd sent her a note, just to let her know she wasn't forgotten and all was well.

The warmth of Kazimir's palm against my lower back pulled me back to the present—to this man who'd become my everything. I leaned into him, drawing on the power radiating from his frame even while he was dancing.

"Kaz—"

"You have people now," he said firmly, as if he'd known where my mind had wandered. "A family, dysfunctional as it is. Griffin might blow things up and Thorne communicates primarily in grunts, but they're yours. We're yours."

"And I'm yours," I said softly.

His expression shifted. "I know."

The moment stretched between us. Then I rose on my toes and kissed him, tasting mulled wine and spiced pear.

When we broke apart, I took his hand, feeling that his ring was as warm as mine. "Come on."

"Where are we going?"

"To our chambers." I pulled him toward the door. "You promised me another present."

56

Get Dragged Out of Bed

(for Apocalyptic News and Dead Flowers)

Arabella

The pounding on our chamber door could have woken the dead. Which, given Griffin's recent experiments, wasn't entirely hyperbole.

"Go away," Kazimir growled into my hair, his arm tightening around my waist.

The pounding intensified. "Lady Blackrose! Lord Blackrose! It's urgent!"

Sebastian. Of course it was Sebastian. I groaned, burying my face deeper into my pillow. "What time is it?"

"Too fucking early. It's not even light yet." Kazimir's voice rumbled through his chest, the vibration doing interesting things to my already oversensitive body. Last night's birthday celebrations had extended well past midnight, and I was deliciously sore in all the best ways.

His shadows began to stir, responding to his irritation. I reluctantly extracted myself from my husband's embrace, ignoring his sound of protest. "Five minutes!" I called through the door.

I fumbled for a robe, trying to make myself presentable while Kazimir remained sprawled naked across our bed. "You're not getting up?" I asked, hunting for something to tie my hair back with.

"I'm contemplating murder. It requires focus."

"Kazimir."

"Fine." He rolled out of bed, yanking on pants but not bothering with a shirt.

I opened the door to find Sebastian looking haggard, his usually perfect hair messy and sticking out in interesting directions. Flowers—wilted and gray—were blooming along his collar. "If this is about Torok challenging another child to combat—"

"It's not!" Sebastian's voice cracked. His eyes widened as he took in Kazimir's state of undress, then immediately snapped back to my face. "I—sorry. I'm so sorry. But we have a problem."

"When don't we?" Kazimir leaned against the door, radiating menace despite—or perhaps because of—his lack of shirt. "Speak quickly, before I remember how much I enjoy throwing people off lightning bridges."

Sebastian swallowed hard. "Auremar's accelerated his timeline. My contact in Solandris just sent word that he's taken more people."

The last vestiges of sleep evaporated. "How many?"

"At least thirty individuals with confirmed heroic bloodlines. Including . . ." He thrust a crumpled paper at me. "Including multiple Princess Violets who'd gone into hiding when they heard Auremar was collecting people. He found them anyway."

Kazimir read over my shoulder, his body radiating heat and barely contained violence. "When?"

"Two nights ago." Sebastian's hands shook as more flowers bloomed and immediately withered at his feet. "My contact only just managed to get word out. The captives are being held in the lower levels of Sunspire Palace, and"—Sebastian's voice cracked—"he's already started preparations for some kind of mass ritual. Something about the moon phases being optimal in five days."

"Five days." I felt the blood drain from my face. "The ritual the Alchemist described—"

"Will be worthless if Auremar completes his first." Kazimir's voice had gone deadly quiet, which was always more terrifying than when he shouted. "How many families does that give him?"

Sebastian swallowed again. "Combined with the ones we couldn't reach in time? Between seventy and one hundred individuals with heroic blood. Maybe more."

"War room, twenty minutes," Kazimir ordered Sebastian. "Bring Vex, Griffin, and Thorne."

Sebastian fled, leaving a trail of dead petals in his wake.

I turned to find Kazimir already grabbing clothes with sharp, economical movements. The playful husband from moments ago had been replaced by the Dark Lord, all business and barely contained violence.

"We can't let him complete that ritual," I said.

"We won't." He yanked on a shirt, then paused to cup my face in his hands. "But this changes our timeline. We need those bloodlines to agree to help us now, not after lengthy negotiations."

"They're terrified nobility who think we kidnapped them." Which, to be fair, we had. "How exactly do we convince them to willingly bleed for us in the next few hours?"

"That's your department." He pressed a quick kiss to my forehead. "I'll handle the military logistics. You handle the people things."

"And what are those?"

"You know." He waved a hand vaguely. "Emotions. Empathy. Not threatening to eviscerate them if they don't comply."

Twenty minutes later, we assembled in the war room. The massive table was already covered in maps, troop deployments, and what looked like Griffin's calculations for portal stability. Kazimir stood at the head.

"Report," he commanded as Sebastian entered, still trailing dead flowers.

Sebastian pointed to Sunspire on the map. "The prisoners are being held in the old wine cellars—stone walls, limited access points, and heavy magical wards. The kind that prevent portals."

Kazimir's fingers drummed against the table.

"Can we break the wards?" I asked, thinking of the Heirloom's power thrumming beneath my skin.

"Not without alerting every mage in the palace," Griffin said, pushing his glasses up his nose. "Wards that strong are tied to alarm systems."

Vex leaned forward, her newly black hair catching the light. "So we need a distraction. Something big enough to pull the guards away from the palace."

Kazimir nodded toward the map. "I'll take our main force and hit their eastern garrisons."

I frowned. "But our army is at the northern outpost. It would take days to march them into position."

Thorne scratched the side of his scarred face. "And their forces are between us and the capital. Already marching to meet us."

A dangerous smile curved Kazimir's lips. "We're going to save them the trip. We portal our forces inside their defensive line—just outside Sunspire itself. Let them scramble to defend their own capital while their army is marching in the wrong direction."

"Why not just move Skyspire itself?" I asked. "Position the entire citadel over Sunspire."

"Takes too long." Kazimir's response was immediate. "The citadel's movement enchantments require days of preparation for a journey that distance. We don't have days."

It made sense tactically, but something in his tone felt off. "Besides," he added, "I don't want Skyspire anywhere near the Shadow King's prison. Not until we understand the full extent of the corruption."

I wondered why, but he changed the subject.

His shadows spread across the map, marking positions. "Griffin, can you create a stable portal large enough for five thousand troops?"

Griffin's eyes went wide. "That's . . . theoretically possible. But the power requirements—"

"I'll handle the power." Kazimir's voice brooked no argument. "You handle the calculations."

I watched my husband carefully. The casual way he dismissed the massive magical expenditure, the slight tremor in his left hand that he was trying to hide—something was different. The struggle within him, whatever it was, was growing worse as the conversation continued.

"Even with the distraction," Thorne said, "extracting seventy prisoners from a warded location won't be simple. We need an exit strategy that doesn't involve fighting our way through the entire palace."

"What if we prepare an extraction point outside the ward boundaries?" I suggested. "Somewhere close enough to move the prisoners quickly, but far enough that we can portal out?"

Sebastian nodded slowly. "Just outside the Palace Garden. They'll be beyond the ward perimeter, and there's a service entrance near the cellars that's usually only guarded by two men."

"Usually," Vex emphasized. "With prisoners this valuable—"

"They'll have sufficient guard," Kazimir finished. He studied the palace layout Griffin had produced. "We'll need to be surgical about this. In and out before they realize what's happening."

"I'll lead the infiltration team," I said.

"No." Kazimir's response was immediate, shadows darkening the room. "Auremar wants you specifically. Walking into his stronghold is exactly what he's hoping for."

I recognized the possessiveness for what it was—fear. Real, bone-deep terror at the thought of me in Auremar's hands. But it wasn't going to change the facts. I folded my arms. "Would you prefer I lead the military distraction? Because I will, but I think my magic would be more useful freeing prisoners than playing general. Other than Sebastian, I know Sunspire Palace better than anyone here."

Kazimir's hands gripped the table hard. My new ring flared cold on my finger. For a moment, I thought he'd forbid it outright, Dark Lord commands and all, and then we'd have a repeat of the Gilded Gallows. But then he surprised me. "Fine. But you're not going alone."

"I'll accompany her," Sebastian offered. "My magic might help with distractions. Plus, I know some of the prisoners. They'll trust me."

"And I'll be there," Thorne added, in a tone that suggested arguing would be pointless.

"Shadow warriors," Kazimir said. "At least a dozen. And if things go bad—"

"We handle it," I interrupted.

Kazimir nodded sharply. "The moment you have the prisoners, you get out. No heroics, no side missions."

"Agreed," I said, though we both knew I'd do whatever was necessary in the moment.

"The primary objective is the rescue," Kazimir said, his shadows spreading across the map. "But I'm not wasting this opportunity. While their forces are scrambling to respond to our 'invasion,' we take the capital."

Thorne's eyebrows rose. "You're planning to hold Sunspire?"

"I'm planning to make Auremar understand he's already lost." Kazimir's smile was sharp. "When he crawls out of whatever hole he's hiding in—and he will hide, the coward—he'll find his capital under new management."

"What about the Hero's Guild?" Sebastian asked, his flowers wilting faster. "They've been different lately. More aggressive. Less coordinated."

"The Shadow King's corruption," I said quietly. "They're addicted to his magic now."

Kazimir's expression darkened. "I have plans for the Guild."

"What plans?" Vex asked.

"The kind that work better as a surprise." The casual menace in his voice suggested those plans were decidedly unpleasant.

"But Auremar himself?" I pressed. "We can't kill him. Not until we understand his connection to the Shadow King's prison."

"Capture, not kill," Kazimir agreed, though he looked pained by the concession.

Griffin held up a hand. "I'll need at least six hours to prepare extraction portals. They'll need to be keyed to specific locations to avoid the ward interference, and stable enough to transport seventy-plus panicked nobles."

Kazimir nodded. "Vex, I need you coordinating from here. Someone needs to keep our current guests from rioting while we're gone."

"Oh good," Vex said drily. "Babysitting duty. My favorite."

"About that," Sebastian said hesitantly. "How exactly do we convince so many nobles to participate in a blood ritual? My father always said appealing to their sense of honor and duty to the kingdom—"

"Won't work," I interrupted. "These people have been kidnapped, held against their will, and now we're asking them to bleed for us? Honor and duty are abstract concepts when you're terrified for your life."

"Then what do you suggest?" Kazimir asked, though his attention seemed split, his gaze occasionally going distant.

"We make it personal." I stood, pacing around the table. "We show them exactly what happens if the Shadow King rises. Not to their kingdom or their honor—to them. Their families. Their children. Make them understand that this isn't about saving Solandris. It's about saving themselves."

"Fear as motivation." Kazimir smiled approvingly.

"Self-preservation," I corrected.

His shadows curled possessively around my ankles. "Fear, self-preservation, survival—they're all just different words for the same instinct."

I studied him again. The intensity in his gaze, the way his shadows moved with unusual agitation—whatever was happening inside his head was getting worse.

"We'll need the Alchemist's help with the actual ritual," Thorne said, bringing us back to practical matters. "Have they provided the specifics?"

"I'll meet with them after this," Kazimir said. "Finalize the requirements. Griffin, I want you there as well. I'll bring the Alchemist to the North Tower for the meeting."

"You're letting them out of the dungeon?" Griffin's eyes widened.

"The apocalypse really is upon us," Vex murmured.

"What about Nyx?" I asked. "She could be useful for reconnaissance."

"Or she could eat their scouts and alert them to our presence." Kazimir shook his head. "She stays here. We'll need her for the actual assault if things go wrong."

"When," Vex corrected. "When things go wrong. They always do."

"Your optimism is noted," Kazimir deadpanned.

As if summoned by her name, Nyx's massive head appeared in the window, silver eyes gleaming with interest. She'd been perched on the scaffolding clinging to the outside wall, apparently eavesdropping.

"Don't look at me like that," I told her. "You ate Ferdinand. You're grounded."

She snorted, sending a puff of smoke into the room before disappearing again.

Kazimir straightened, shadows pulling tight around him. "Everyone knows their tasks. We reconvene in four hours to finalize the rescue plan."

As the others filed out, Kazimir caught my arm. "A word?"

I waited until we were alone, then turned to face him. "What aren't you telling me?"

His mask slipped for just a moment, and I saw exhaustion beneath. "What makes you think—"

"Kazimir." I stepped closer, placing my hand over his heart. His pulse was too fast, his skin too warm. "I know you. Something's wrong."

He covered my hand with his, and I felt the tremor he was trying to hide. "The magical expenditure for moving the army will be significant."

"You've done massive magic before."

"Not like this." He pulled me closer. "Not with the ley lines still partially corrupted. Not with—" He cut himself off.

"Not with what?" I pressed.

For a moment, I thought he'd tell me. His shadows swirled around us, forming into wolves and other beasts that I wasn't certain were entirely under his control. Then he kissed me, fierce and possessive.

"Not with you in danger," he finished when we broke apart. "I need you to promise me something."

"What?"

"If the extraction goes bad, you run. You take the portal and you run."

"Kazimir—"

"Promise me." His hands cupped my face. "I can't lead the distraction if I'm worried about you."

I saw the fear beneath the command. Whatever was happening to him, his terror of losing me was overriding everything else.

"I promise to make smart choices," I said carefully. "But I won't abandon the prisoners. Or Sebastian. Or Thorne."

His jaw clenched. "Arabella—"

"That's the best you're getting." I kissed him again, softer this time.

“Trust me to handle my part. I’ll trust you to handle yours.”

He exhaled slowly. “You’re infuriating.”

“You love it.”

“I do.” The admission seemed to surprise him. “Be careful with the heroic bloodlines. Some of them might have opinions about helping the Dark Lord save the world.”

“I’ll emphasize the ‘save the world’ part and downplay the ‘Dark Lord’ part.”

“Lying by omission. I’m so proud.” He pulled me in for another quick, fierce kiss. “Don’t let Torok challenge you to a duel.”

“Please. I’d destroy him.”

57

Convince Heroes to Bleed for the Greater Good

(It's Surprisingly Difficult)

Arabella

I found Sebastian waiting in the corridor. More flowers—these a sickly yellow—were already sprouting from the stone floor around him.

"Ready to convince a bunch of terrified nobles that bleeding for us is actually a good idea?" I asked.

"Nothing I enjoy more than public speaking to hostile audiences while the world ends." He fell into step beside me. "How do we even start? 'Hello, we kidnapped you for your own good, now please donate your blood to stop an ancient evil'?"

"I was thinking more along the lines of 'Congratulations on not being ritually sacrificed by King Auremar, would you like to help ensure that continues?'"

We made our way to the Great Hall, where Vex had gathered most of our "guests" for what she'd called an "informational meeting about your temporary accommodations." The noise hit us before we even opened the doors—dozens of voices raised in complaint, confusion, and in Lord Janos Torok's case, challenges to single combat.

"Deep breath," I told Sebastian. "We're about to walk into a room full of people who have every reason to distrust us and ask them to voluntarily participate in blood magic."

Another flower—this one black—bloomed and immediately crumbled to ash on his shoulder. He brushed away the remains as I pushed open the doors.

The Great Hall fell silent as we entered. Seventy-eight pairs of eyes turned to us with expressions ranging from suspicious to openly hostile. Torok, predictably, had his hand on where his sword would be if we hadn't confiscated all weapons.

"Lady Blackrose," Lady Kovacs spoke first, her voice carefully neutral. "We've been gathered here for days with no explanation beyond 'for your protection.' I think we deserve answers."

"You're right," I said, moving to the front of the room. Sebastian took position slightly behind me, flowers now growing in a nervous rainbow at his feet. "You all deserve the truth."

"Which is?" Lord Brightwater demanded.

I took a breath. Here went nothing. "If you haven't already heard, King Auremar has been systematically hunting down and capturing everyone with heroic bloodlines. What you might not know is that it isn't for political marriages or alliances, but for a ritual that will free an ancient evil called the Shadow King from his prison beneath Solandris."

After a beat of silence, the room erupted. Denials, gasps, accusations of madness. The Fekete twins laughed in sync, which was creepy.

"Preposterous!" Lord Brightwater's face had gone an alarming shade of purple. "King Auremar is—"

"A fraud who's been siphoning power from a magical prison to fuel his kingdom's prosperity," I interrupted. "The Golden Rose Fields? They're not just pretty flowers. They're anchor points that Auremar has been systematically weakening by sacrificing people like you."

"You expect us to believe—" someone started.

"I expect you to use your brains," I snapped, my patience already fraying.

"Why else would the Dark Lord and the last free scion of House Evenfall bother collecting random nobles and their families? For fun? We have better things to do with our time."

"Like conquering kingdoms," someone muttered.

"Yes, actually." I let a bit of irritation creep into my voice. "My husband was in the middle of invading Solandris when we discovered Auremar's plan. Do you think he abandoned a military campaign to play innkeeper out of the goodness of his heart?"

That gave them pause. Even Lord Brightwater looked thoughtful.

Sebastian stepped forward, and immediately half the room relaxed. Say what you would about his political effectiveness, but people instinctively trusted him.

"It's true," he said quietly. "All of it. I've seen the evidence. Auremar tried to capture me for the same reason. My bloodline, your bloodlines—we're all keys to a lock that should never be opened."

"But why should we help you?" Lady Goldmary asked. "You kidnapped us!"

"Because the alternative is letting Auremar complete his ritual and unleash something that makes my husband look like a children's birthday entertainer. The Shadow King doesn't just want to rule," I continued, letting real fear color my voice. "He wants revenge. More than seventeen hundred years of imprisonment, and guess whose bloodline put him there? Ours. Every person in this room carries Soriven's legacy in their veins."

I paused, meeting their eyes one by one. "When he rises—and he will if we don't act—he won't just kill us. He'll make examples of us. Our children, our families, anyone who shares even a drop of heroic blood will be hunted down and destroyed in ways that would make the worst stories seem like mercy."

Sera Marenti-Cross pulled her son closer. Even Lord Brightwater had gone pale.

One of the Fekete twins leaned forward. "What exactly are you asking of us?"

This was the tricky part. "There's a cleansing ritual. One that can cast the

Shadow King out of the ley lines and strengthen his prison. But it requires the willing participation of those with heroic blood."

"Blood magic." Lord Brightwater's voice was flat. "You're asking us to participate in blood magic."

"A few drops," I said. "Willingly given. No one's being sacrificed, no one's being drained. Think of it as donating to a cause."

"The cause being saving the world," Sebastian added helpfully. A small garden was now growing around his feet.

"And if we refuse?" someone called from the back.

I met their gaze steadily. "Then we all die when the Shadow King breaks free. But hey, at least you'll have maintained your moral high ground."

"That's not helpful," Sebastian murmured.

"Neither is stubborn refusal to see reason," I shot back.

The room dissolved into arguments. Some people seemed convinced, others violently opposed. Lord Brightwater was loudly declaring that he'd rather die than participate in dark magic, which several people pointed out was exactly what would happen.

"ENOUGH!" I let power roll through my voice, shadows dancing at the edges of the room. Everyone fell silent. "King Auremar has captured more families. People just like you, with children just like yours. In five days, he plans to sacrifice them, and he'll break the prison completely."

Gasps echoed through the hall.

"We're mounting a rescue," I continued. "But even if we succeed, we need your help to perform the cleansing ritual. This isn't about politics or power plays. This is about survival. And if you can't see past your prejudices long enough to save your own lives, then you're not the heroes your bloodline suggests you should be."

"How do we know this isn't all an elaborate trick?" Lady Clearwater asked.

"You don't," I admitted. "But consider this—if we wanted to use your blood for nefarious purposes, would we be asking permission? We have you all here, defenseless. If we were the villains you think we are, we'd have taken what we needed already."

That uncomfortable truth settled over the room.

"I'll do it," a small voice said.

Everyone turned to see Lady Moonbay's daughter, barely thirteen, standing with her chin raised. "If it saves people, I'll do it."

"Absolutely not—" her mother started.

"Mom, they saved us." The girl's voice was steady. "Lord Blackrose's soldiers got us out before King Auremar's people arrived. I heard the servants talking. We'd be prisoners—or worse—if they hadn't acted."

"I'll participate," one of the Fekete twins said. "If it's truly voluntary and only a few drops."

"As will I," her sister added. They nodded together, and I suppressed a shudder.

Slowly, others began to voice their agreement. Not all—Lord Brightwater looked like he'd swallowed a lemon—but enough. More than enough.

"Thank you," I said, meaning it. "We'll perform the ritual once we've rescued the others."

"What about our families?" Lord James Pearlbridge asked. "The ones without heroic blood?"

"They'll remain here, safe and protected," I promised. "This isn't a punishment or a prison sentence. Once the threat is dealt with, you're free to go wherever you wish."

"Assuming we survive," Lord Brightwater muttered.

"Yes, well, that's rather the point of all this. Survival." I fixed him with a hard stare, and he shrank back.

As the crowd began to disperse, Sebastian and I shared a look of exhausted triumph. One crisis managed, approximately seven hundred more to go.

"That went better than expected," he said.

I watched Lord Janos Torok storm off, probably to challenge a suit of armor to combat. "We have enough volunteers. It'll have to do."

"The children helping shamed some of the adults into it," Sebastian observed. "Funny how that works."

"Children usually have more sense than adults," I agreed. "Less time to learn stupid prejudices."

Vex appeared at my elbow, having materialized from whatever shadow she'd been lurking in. "Well done. Only three threatened to riot, and Torok only challenged two people to duels during your speech. I call that a win."

"We'll need to move them," I said. "The volunteers, I mean. Once we rescue the others, we'll need to perform the ritual quickly."

"The *Sky Serpent* can handle it," Vex assured me. "I'll coordinate with Captain Brecca."

"Just the ones with heroic blood this time," I emphasized. "Their families stay here where it's safe."

"Understood." She vanished again, off to handle logistics with her usual terrifying efficiency.

Sebastian and I stood in the emptying hall, surrounded by the detritus of his stress flowers.

"Five days," he said quietly.

"Think we can pull off a rescue, an invasion, a ritual, and save the world in that time?"

"Honestly? No." He smiled wryly. "But we'll do it anyway, won't we?"

"Of course we will." I clapped him on the shoulder. "We're heroes, remember? Impossibly stupid plans are kind of our thing."

"I thought you were the Dark Lady now."

"I'm whatever I need to be to keep the people I care about safe. Even if one of them is an impossibly stubborn Dark Lord with a martyr complex."

"He loves you, you know," Sebastian said quietly. "I've seen how he looks at you. Like you're his entire world."

"I know." I slowly exhaled. "That's what scares me."

Because love could make people do terrible things. And if Kazimir ever had to choose between me and the world . . .

I wasn't entirely sure which he'd pick.

58

Pretend You're Fine

(Everything's Fine)

Kazimir

The Alchemist's fingers twitched like a puppeteer testing strings as they examined Griffin's latest contraption—a crystal matrix that hummed with unstable energy. The Alchemist had been delighted by Griffin's laboratory, though they kept eyeing his "experimental mistakes" shelf with professional concern.

"Fascinating," they murmured. "The resonance frequency is entirely wrong, of course, but the underlying theory . . ."

"Focus," I said, massaging the bridge of my nose.

The voice in my head—the one that wasn't mine—had been growing louder all morning. A constant, seductive tirade that promised power beyond imagination if I'd just let go.

They're all traitors. The Alchemist will betray you. Arabella will abandon you. Kill them all and take what's yours.

The Shadow King continued to alternate between urging me to murder my wife or assert my control over her so we could use her. I'd decided it was easier to ignore the why and focus on the what—which was that

I'd do neither, no matter how loud the voice screamed.

I tightened my mental grip, forcing the voice back into its cage.

"The ritual preparations are nearly complete," I said, deliberately focusing on the Alchemist. "Other than the site—which we won't have access to until we defeat Auremar—we're as ready as we can be. Griffin has managed to stabilize the crystal array for channeling the energy."

Griffin, who'd been nervously hovering nearby, bobbed his head. "Mostly stable. Eighty-three percent stable. Which is really quite good considering the temporal fluctuations in the—"

"Griffin."

He flinched. "Right. Yes. Stable enough. Probably won't explode."

The Alchemist's eyebrows rose. "Probably?"

"Definitely," Griffin amended, then immediately undermined himself by adding, "Unless someone sneezes too hard near the northwestern crystal. But what are the chances of that?"

I resisted the urge to throw something at him. "Lady Blackrose is speaking with the captives now. Attempting to secure their willing participation."

"And if she fails?" the Alchemist asked, their tone deceptively casual.

I gritted my teeth. "If she fails, we'll find another way."

"Another way meaning . . . ?" The Alchemist's eyes fixed on mine, probing.

"Meaning whatever is necessary to stop Auremar and seal the prison." I met their gaze unflinchingly. "I won't pretend I'm above sacrificing a few nobles if it means saving the world. Or more importantly, saving my wife."

Griffin made a small, distressed sound. "Lady Blackrose will convince them. She's quite persuasive."

"It's not her abilities I doubt," I said, turning away to examine a row of bubbling potions. "It's the nobility of Solandris. Self-important, shortsighted fools who'd rather die with their principles intact than live pragmatically."

The Alchemist's gaze lingered on me a moment too long. "You should know, Lord Blackrose, that for some types of magic—particularly purification rituals like the one we're planning—willing blood is significantly more powerful than unwilling."

“I’m perfectly aware of that.”

“It’s a matter of magical resonance,” they continued, as if I hadn’t spoken. “Unwilling sacrifices create discordant energy. If you’re summoning a demon, for instance, that demon will want unwilling blood. Fear. Pain. These are the currencies of darker realms. But for restoring corrupted ley lines? You need harmony. Alignment. Willingness.”

I turned back to face them. “And yet, you told me the First Hero sacrificed his victims to seal the Shadow King the first time. Why wouldn’t that be the best approach now?”

The Alchemist went very still. “Did I say that?”

“You did.” My eyes narrowed. “In fact, you specifically mentioned that Soriven’s victory was built on ‘blood and suffering.’ Your exact words.”

The Alchemist’s fingers twitched again, but this time I recognized it as nervousness, not enthusiasm. “Times change. Methods evolve. Perhaps you should consider your wife’s preferences in this matter.”

My hand slammed down on the workbench, rattling vials and sending Griffin scurrying backward with a yelp. “I AM considering her!” The shadows in the room darkened, and a cold wind whistled through the tower. Something on a shelf whimpered. “She may not forgive me if I make the sacrifices, but at least she’ll be alive. At least we won’t have the fucking Shadow King to contend with.”

But you do. I’m already here. Inside you. Part of you.

“Shut up,” I hissed.

The Alchemist took a careful step back. “Lord Blackrose?”

I forced myself to breathe. In. Out. The shadows receded. “Do you have an answer or not? Or have you been guessing about this ritual the whole time? Now is not the time to hedge.”

They studied me. “I’m as sure as anyone can be, more than you. And yes, I believe willing participants will mean we need fewer heroes in the end because they’ll be more powerful. But perhaps we should continue this discussion later. After Lady Blackrose has spoken with the nobles.”

“Perhaps.” I straightened my jacket, regaining composure. “I’ll personally escort you to new quarters. We've prepared more suitable accommodations than the dungeons, near the base of this tower."

The Alchemist glanced around Griffin's laboratory, taking in the bubbling potions, the half-assembled contraptions, and what appeared to be a miniature tornado contained in a glass jar. "I believe I'll remain in the dungeons, if it's all the same to you."

"You prefer prison?"

"After seeing this tower?" They gestured to a shelf where a cloth seemed to be moving on its own. "The dungeons seem safer."

I couldn't help the small smile that tugged at my lips. "Only marginally. We've had a problem with them expelling prisoners into the swamp recently."

"I'll take my chances with the swamp creatures over whatever that is." They pointed to a corner where one of Griffin's experiments was emitting an ominous hum.

"That's just Herbert," Griffin said defensively. "He's harmless unless you feed him after midnight."

The Alchemist stared at him.

"As you wish." I gestured toward the door. "Griffin, continue the preparations. I want everything ready to test by tomorrow morning."

"Yes, my lord." He was already distracted again, poking at something that sparked.

As the Alchemist and I descended the tower's spiral staircase, they spoke quietly. "We're running out of time. I can feel it, even here."

"All the more reason to act quickly."

"And the voice? The one you were telling to shut up? Is that accelerating too?"

I stopped mid-step, turning to face them. "I don't know what you mean."

Their expression remained neutral. "Of course, Lord Blackrose. My mistake."

We continued down in silence, the only sound the tap of our footsteps on stone. When we reached the main corridor, I paused.

“If willing blood truly is more effective,” I said carefully, “then I hope my wife succeeds in her persuasion. But understand this—I will not risk Arabella or this world on the moral qualms of a few entitled nobles. If they won’t willingly give what’s needed, I’ll take it.”

“Even if it means becoming what you’re fighting against?”

I smiled, and there must have been something of the Shadow King in it, because the Alchemist took another step back. “I’ve never pretended to be anything other than what I am. A villain. A conqueror. A Dark Lord. The difference between Auremar and myself is that I’m honest about it.”

Yes. Embrace what you are. What WE are.

“And what about Lady Blackrose?” they asked. “Is she a villain too?”

The question caught me off guard. “Arabella is complicated.”

“Most people are.” They studied me with those unnerving eyes. “The Shadow King wasn’t always a monster, you know. Once, he was just a being with too much power and too little restraint.”

A chill ran down my spine. “What are you implying?”

“Nothing at all, Lord Blackrose.” They bowed slightly. “Merely an observation on the nature of power.”

I marched the Alchemist to the dungeons, fighting the urge to demand answers the whole way—but I didn’t want to give them the satisfaction. The surges of anger had weakened my defenses once more. Just thinking about Arabella allowed—

I forced myself to breathe again. In. Out.

You’re weak. Pathetic. You could rule everything if you’d just accept me.

“I already rule everything I care about,” I muttered once I was back out under the open sky.

Liar. You don’t even rule yourself.

I clamped down on that insult and turned away, heading toward the Great Hall. I needed to find Arabella, to see if she’d succeeded with the nobles. To reassure myself that she was still safe, still mine.

The Shadow King’s laughter echoed behind the walls I determinedly built once more.

Instead of taking a lightning bridge, I ripped open a portal and stepped into it. They were as simple as breathing now.

If all went according to plan, in a few days I would finally silence the Shadow King for good.

If not . . . well. I'd always been good at contingency plans.

59

Practice Your Aim

(and Avoid Saying What You're Really Feeling)

Arabella

I threw another knife, watching with satisfaction as it embedded itself into the center of the target with a solid thunk.

The Southeast Tower armory was nothing like the massive forge on the outer isle. That place was all fire and chaos, with the constant ringing of hammers and shouting of smiths. This space was intimate and precise, a carefully curated collection meant for the elite guards who protected the Inner Sanctum. Thorne's domain.

Rows of gleaming weapons hung on the walls, organized by type and lethality. Blades of every length and shape, from delicate stilettos to two-handed broadswords. A glass-fronted cabinet displayed daggers emitting a faint glow of different colors. The room smelled of metal and leather and the faint tang of magic—the scent of power.

Kazimir had spent more than a decade scheming his way toward Solandris. The final push had come together in four breathless days of organized pandemonium—Griffin's matrices exploding twice before stabilizing, nobles bickering over blood magic, and my husband reducing a quartermaster to tears over supply chain inefficiencies. But somehow, we were ready.

Tomorrow, we marched on Solandris.

I picked up another of the throwing knives Vex had given me for my birthday. The weight felt perfect in my hand, the blade balanced for someone of my size and strength. I'd been practicing for the past hour, and my aim was improving. The knives weren't just beautiful; they were deadly efficient.

I felt a familiar shift in the air, like the atmosphere itself recognized his dominion.

"Not bad."

I turned to see Kazimir leaning against the frame, arms crossed, watching me with that intensity that still made my stomach flip. His dark hair was slightly disheveled, as if he'd been running his hands through it—a habit when he was troubled. Now that it was longer, it looked even more chaotic.

"But my stance could use work, right?" I asked, twirling the knife between my fingers and expecting a critique.

"Your stance is perfect. You must have studied under the best." He stepped into the room, his gaze sweeping over my battle leathers, which I'd laid out on a nearby table for inspection. "Planning for tomorrow?"

"Just making sure everything's ready." I threw the last knife—hitting dead center—and walked to retrieve the blades. Kaz leaned against the table behind me.

"I paid a visit to your father the other day."

My hand stilled on one of the knives. "Oh?"

"He's looking well-fed and miserable, as expected." Kazimir's tone was casual, but his eyes were watchful. "We should decide what to do with him before we leave."

I yanked the last knife free. "I've been avoiding that particular decision."

"I noticed."

I returned to the table, laying the knives out in a neat row. Kazimir had been giving me space to make a decision about my father, and I appreciated that more than I could say. But he was right—it was time. Part of me wanted to storm down to the dungeons and force my father to look me in the eye while I demanded answers for every betrayal, every lie. But another part—a growing part—just felt tired of giving him space in my head, in my heart.

"I think," I started slowly, "I'm ready to move on from him. From what he represents." I met Kazimir's gaze. "But that doesn't mean we can't make use of him."

A slow, appreciative smile spread across Kazimir's face. "I was hoping you'd say that."

"You have an idea."

"I always have ideas. It's part of my villainous charm." He moved closer, his voice dropping to that conspiratorial tone that never failed to send a shiver down my spine. Kazimir picked up one of my knives, testing its weight. "We could let him escape."

I stared at him. "Um."

He threw the knife without even looking at the target, landing a perfect shot in what would have been its left eye. Show-off.

"A carefully orchestrated escape this time," he continued. "Or rather, make him believe he's escaped because there's no time for a real one. Feed him just enough information to make him valuable to Auremar—specifically, that I'll be attacking east of the capital."

Understanding dawned. "To make sure Auremar sends his remaining forces out to meet you before we get there."

"Precisely." Kazimir's smile was all predator now. "Your father is desperate enough to curry favor with Auremar that he'll deliver the information immediately, and prideful enough to believe he escaped on his own."

I considered it, running a finger along the edge of one of the knives. I liked the idea of turning my father into nothing more than a pawn. "It could work. But what if he doesn't go to Auremar?"

"Where else would he go? His estate is seized, his reputation in tatters. Auremar is his only potential ally now." Kazimir moved closer, his fingers brushing mine as he picked up another knife. "Besides, we'll have him followed."

"By whom? Everyone's coming with us."

"Shadow warriors." He threw the knife, hitting the target's other eye.

I nodded slowly. "It's a good plan. Better than letting him rot, which is what I was leaning toward."

"Really? I thought you might want one last confrontation. To make him answer for your mother."

A memory flickered through my mind—my mother's laugh as she braided my hair. The sound was so clear, so real, I could almost believe she was in the room with us.

These fragments had been returning steadily since I took the potion, filling in gaps I hadn't even known existed. Not the dramatic, painful memories of her death, but the quiet moments that had shaped me—her kindness, her strength, the way she'd loved me unconditionally.

The knowledge that I was loved, that I was worthy of love, had helped me understand my own heart better, including the feelings I'd been wrestling with regarding Kazimir. The hesitation I'd felt about loving him—really loving him, not just desiring or needing him—had begun to dissolve as I remembered what real love looked like through my mother's example.

The words I'd been struggling to say to Kazimir felt less terrifying now.

"No," I said finally. "I don't need anything more from my father. I know what happened now, and no explanation he could offer would change it or make it better."

Kazimir studied me, his expression unreadable. "You've changed."

"Is that a complaint?"

"An observation." He moved closer, his hand coming up to brush a strand of hair from my face. "You seem lighter. Despite everything."

I leaned into his touch. "The memories help. Not just the terrible ones, but the good ones too. Remembering who she was, who I was with her."

"And who was that?"

I smiled. "Someone who wasn't afraid to love."

Something flickered in his eyes—uncertainty, perhaps, or longing. Then it was gone, replaced by his usual intensity.

"So we use Evenfall as bait," he said, returning to the safer topic of strategy. "Let him think he's escaped on his own, but make sure he overhears just enough to make him valuable to Auremar."

"And then what? Once he's served his purpose?"

Kazimir shrugged. "He stays with Auremar and goes down with that sinking ship, or he tries to run and gets caught in the cross fire. Auremar is likely to kill him once he gets the information, anyway."

I nodded, turning back to my battle leathers. The jerkin was reinforced with thin plates of enchanted metal between layers of supple leather, offering protection without sacrificing mobility. The pants were similarly constructed, with additional padding at the knees and thighs. All of it was dyed black to blend with shadows.

Kazimir ran his fingers over the intricate stitching. "I'd prefer you didn't need these at all."

I should tell him. The words burned in my throat. Three simple words that had become so complicated. My mother had loved freely, openly, and look where it had gotten her. But she'd also lived fully, without the regrets that came from silence.

We both spoke at the same time.

"Kaz, I—"

"If anything happens tomorrow—"

"Don't." I pressed my fingers to his lips. "We're not doing deathbed confessions before the battle even starts. It's bad luck."

He caught my hand, pressing a kiss to my palm. "Since when are you superstitious?"

"Since I married the Dark Lord and started fighting ancient evils." I tried to keep my tone light, but my heart was pounding. Part of me wanted to tell him everything—that I loved him, that I'd never felt this way about anyone, that the thought of losing him terrified me more than any battle.

But maybe it wasn't the time. Kazimir had been struggling with something these past few days. I'd seen it in the tension around his eyes, heard it in the way he sometimes muttered to himself when he thought I wasn't listening. Whatever war he was fighting inside his head, I wasn't sure if my declaration would help or hinder him.

And tomorrow, we needed him focused. We needed the ruthless, calculating Dark Lord who could outmaneuver Auremar and lead an army. My feelings could wait.

"Big day of villainy tomorrow," I said instead.

Kazimir nodded, but his eyes lingered on my face as if searching for something. "Right. I'll arrange for Evenfall's 'escape'—"

"—and then let's go scandalize the staff one more time before we save the world."

As we left the armory, I cast one last look at the throwing knives arranged on the table. Tomorrow, I'd be using them for real. And maybe, if we survived, I'd find the courage to tell Kazimir what he meant to me.

60

Make It Look Convincing
(with Fists and Blood Magic)

Kazimir

I'd always found the smell of stone, iron, and despair in the dungeons comforting. Tonight, however, I was in no mood to savor it.

"You're certain you want to be here for this?" I asked Arabella as we descended the spiral staircase.

"I'm not letting you have all the fun," she replied, her voice steady despite the shadows playing across her face. The orbs floating above us cast her features in sharp relief, highlighting the determined set of her jaw. "Besides, he's my father. I should be involved in his release."

The way she said "release" made it clear she understood exactly what we were doing. This wasn't mercy. This was strategy wrapped in cruelty—my favorite kind.

We reached the bottom of the stairs and navigated the narrow corridor that led to the isolation cells. I felt the shadow wolf still pacing just inside Evenfall's door, its forms rippling slightly in the dim light. It bowed its head as we approached, then melted into the walls, returning to the shadows from which I'd summoned them.

I placed my hand on the heavy iron door, feeling the wards hum against my palm. "Last chance to change your mind."

Arabella's eyes met mine. "Open it."

The wards recognized my magic and dissolved with a faint sizzle. The door swung open on well-oiled hinges, revealing the man who had imprisoned his own daughter.

I hadn't forgotten my earlier threat to her father. I figured I'd still get my chance. He was a sniveling whiny bastard, and those types often ended up living through some scheme or other.

Lord Atticus Evenfall sat huddled on his cot, eyes filled with terror. His hair, which had been meticulously styled when we first brought him in, hung in greasy strands around his gaunt face.

"Come to gloat?" he asked.

I smiled, letting my dominion magic curl around me. "Actually, we've come to release you."

Confusion flickered across his face. "What?"

"You heard me." I stepped farther into the cell, enjoying the way he pressed himself against the wall. "We're letting you go."

Evenfall's gaze darted between Arabella and me, searching for the trap. "Why?"

"Because you're no longer useful to us," Arabella said, her voice cold. "And keeping you fed is becoming tedious."

I had to admire her performance. The casual cruelty in her tone was perfectly calibrated—believable enough to convince her father, yet still a performance. My little villain was learning.

"Stand up," I ordered, infusing my voice with just enough dominion magic to make his muscles twitch in response. He rose shakily to his feet, still pressing himself against the wall as if he could melt through it.

"What's the catch?" he asked, his eyes narrowing with suspicion.

"The catch," I said, moving closer until I could smell the fear on him, "is that if you ever return to Skyspire, I'll skin you alive and use your hide to bind my grimoires." I let my magic flare, the runes carved into my bones heating beneath my skin. "Is that clear?"

He nodded rapidly, his throat bobbing as he swallowed.

"Good." I turned to Arabella. "Shall we?"

She nodded, her expression impassive. I opened a portal in the center of the cell, the darkness swirling like ink in water. Through it, I could see a stretch of forest at the edge of Solandris—nearly at the capital city gates and close enough that he'd reach Auremar in time to deliver our false intelligence.

Evenfall stared at the portal, then back at us. "Just like that? You're letting me walk out?"

"Would you prefer to stay?" Arabella asked, arching an eyebrow.

He shook his head quickly.

"Then go," I said, gesturing to the portal. "Before I change my mind."

Evenfall took a hesitant step toward the portal, then another. As he passed me, I grabbed his arm, my fingers digging into the thin flesh. "One more thing."

Fear flashed in his eyes. "What?"

"We need to make this convincing." Without warning, I slammed my fist into his face. The crack of cartilage breaking was immensely satisfying, as was his howl of pain. Blood spurted from his nose, spattering across his already filthy shirt.

Before he could recover, I hit him again, this time in the stomach. He doubled over, gasping. I followed with a blow to his ribs that sent him sprawling to the floor.

"Kaz," Arabella said, her voice soft but firm. "He won't make our deadline if you injure him too badly."

I stepped back, flexing my fingers. The runes beneath my skin were thrumming with pleasure. "Just making it look like he had a difficult journey."

Evenfall pushed himself up onto his hands and knees, blood dripping from his nose onto the stone floor. He looked pathetic, broken—how a man might look after escaping a villain's dungeon and traveling for days through hostile territory. I was tempted to make it even more convincing, but we didn't have time.

"Get up," I ordered, drawing a knife from my belt.

He struggled to his feet, swaying slightly. His right eye was already swelling shut, and his breathing came in ragged gasps that suggested at least one broken rib.

I glanced at Arabella, silently asking if she wanted a turn. She considered her father for a moment, then shook her head. Her restraint impressed me—I wouldn't have shown the same in her position.

"Now," I said, turning back to Evenfall, "there's one more detail to address."

I raised the knife and slid it across my forearm, following the path of an old scar that had been reopened countless times. Blood welled in the shallow cut. Evenfall tried to back away, but there was nowhere to go. He sagged against the wall, and I held him there with shadows and let three drops of my blood fall onto his forehead. They soaked into his pale skin, leaving no trace behind. His eyes were wide with fear, the whites showing all around his irises as he strained against the shadow bindings.

"This will hurt," I said, not bothering to hide the satisfaction in my voice. "I'd apologize, but we both know I wouldn't mean it."

The rune at my throat warmed as I activated it, feeding power into the incantation I spoke. Blood magic was crude—effective, but inelegant compared to my dominion magic. Still, it had its uses. I wanted Evenfall to eventually remember what he'd done, to know he'd been merely a pawn in the villain's game.

Evenfall screamed as the magic took hold, his back arching unnaturally. The shadows binding him tightened, keeping him from thrashing too violently. Then more shadows shot forward, wrapping around his head and sinking into his eyes, nose, and mouth. He made a choked sound, his body going rigid.

This was the delicate part. Memory alteration was complex magic, requiring precision and control. I couldn't simply erase his memories—that would make him useless as a carrier of false information. Instead, I had to modify them, creating a convincing narrative of escape and hardship that would explain his condition when he reached Auremar.

I sifted through his recent memories, finding the ones of his imprisonment. I left those intact but added new ones: picking the lock on his cell door with a piece of metal stolen from his food tray, sneaking past guards, fighting his way out of the citadel. I created memories of days spent hiding in forests, stealing food from villages, narrowly avoiding patrols of shadow warriors.

And then, most importantly, I planted the false intelligence: overhearing me discussing plans with my generals to stage a diversion outside Sunspire—something flashy and threatening enough to force Auremar to recall his army from the north and avoid a battle. The memory needed to be convincing but not too obvious. Auremar had to believe it was real intelligence, even if he suspected it might be a trick.

The magic was invasive, violating—and I enjoyed every second of it. Making him believe he'd fought his way to freedom when in reality he was nothing but our puppet felt like poetic justice.

When I finished, I withdrew the shadows. Evenfall collapsed to his knees, gasping and clutching his head. His eyes were unfocused, his expression dazed as his mind struggled to integrate the false memories with the real ones.

He mumbled something unintelligible, but his eyes were glassy, already somewhere else—stumbling through forests, picking locks, running for his life. The new memories were taking root.

I grabbed him by the collar and shoved him toward the portal. He stumbled through, disappearing into the forest beyond. The portal remained open, allowing us to watch as he looked around in confusion, then began limping in the direction of the palace.

"Shadow warriors?" Arabella asked.

I nodded, summoning two of my shadowy servants and speaking to them in the harsh language of my youth. "Follow him. Make sure he reaches Auremar."

The shadow warriors bowed and slipped through the portal, their forms immediately blending with the darkness of the forest. I closed the portal with a flick of my wrist, the darkness collapsing in on itself until it vanished completely.

Arabella and I stood in silence for a moment.

"How do you feel?" I asked, studying her face.

She considered the question, her expression thoughtful. "Relieved, I think."

"Not upset about the memory alteration?"

She shook her head. "He allowed mages to alter my memories for years. There's a certain justice in it."

I couldn't help but smile at that. My little villain indeed.

"Besides," she continued, "it serves a greater purpose than mere revenge. Though I won't pretend I didn't enjoy watching you rough him up a bit."

I leaned in, offering her my arm. "I was holding back."

She took my arm, her fingers warm against my skin. "I noticed. I was expecting something more creative from the Dark Lord."

"Believe me, I had ideas." We left the cell, making our way back up the staircase. "But this plan serves our needs better than indulging my more elaborate fantasies."

"Such as?"

I glanced at her, noting the genuine curiosity in her eyes. "Are you sure you want to know?"

"I wouldn't ask if I didn't."

I considered for a moment, then decided honesty was the best approach. "I thought about turning him into one of my shadow warriors—binding his soul to my service for eternity. Or perhaps feeding him to Nyx, piece by piece, keeping him alive to feel every bite."

Arabella's expression remained neutral, but I felt her grip tighten slightly on my arm. Not in fear or disgust, I realized, but in consideration.

"Those do have a certain appeal," she admitted as we reached the top of the stairs. "But I think I prefer this. Using him as a tool, then discarding him. It's fitting. Do you think it will work? The false intelligence?"

"Auremar is desperate and paranoid. He'll believe Evenfall because he wants to believe he's caught us planning something to take his ten thousand soldiers away from the northern outpost." I opened the door to our chambers, ushering her inside. "And even if he suspects a trap, he can't afford to ignore the information. He won't recall his entire army, but he'll have to commit his remaining forces to defend Sunspire, where he thinks I'll be staging some sort of villainous trick."

“The irony is that even if he were to recall the army, it wouldn’t be there in time to defend him. I like the way you think, Lord Blackrose.”

I smirked. “Among other things about me.”

Our chambers were warm and inviting, the fire in the hearth casting an inviting glow. It struck me, not for the first time, how different this space had become since Arabella arrived. What had once been a utilitarian retreat was now a safe space.

Somewhere in the back of my mind, a voice that was both mine and not mine whispered that I should tell her the truth before it was too late. That I should confess everything.

But as I pulled her into my arms, I pushed the thought away. Tomorrow would bring enough challenges without adding that particular confession to the list.

Besides, there would be time after our victory.

Time to figure out what to do about the darkness inside me.

I pulled off her clothes and made good on my promise to scandalize the servants one more time with her. My magic mingled with Arabella’s as I brought her to release, and we didn’t try to contain it as we usually did. Our mingled light and dark tangled and lit up the chamber brighter than any sun. Anyone looking toward Skyspire would see the exact moment when I shuddered inside her and she screamed my name. It would be seen as a bright star all to the way to Azroth’s Claw and the sea to the east. To the northern wastes and the southern reaches. Solandris. Valmont. Maybe even Meridian Isle far to the southwest.

All the places I had conquered and would conquer. The tower rumbled with the force of our joining, with what was to come. I sagged down beside her and pulled her close.

Time to find the right words to tell Arabella.

Sleep took me before I could complete the thought, dragging me down into dreams of ancient battles and a power that hungered for release.

61

Achieve Your Life's Ambition

(It's Everything You Dreamed)

Kazimir

The morning of battle arrived with a chill that had nothing to do with the weather.

I stood at the edge of the northern outpost, watching the sun rise over the rolling hills of Solandris. The golden light painted everything in warm hues, a stark contrast to the cold purpose running through my veins. My shadow warriors moved among the troops, their forms flickering between solid and vapor as they carried my orders across the camp.

Five thousand soldiers—my finest, most loyal fighters—were preparing for the largest magical transportation in the history of warfare. The air hummed with tension and anticipation, the scent of steel and leather and sweat mingling with the earthy aroma of dew-damp grass.

"Quite the view," Arabella said, appearing at my side. She wore the battle leathers I'd commissioned for her, the dark material hugging her curves in ways that would have distracted me under different circumstances. Her hair was pulled back in a severe braid, and the Heirloom—still fused to her and hidden with a glamor—called to me.

"It will be more impressive when we're looking at it from the steps of Auremar's palace," I replied, allowing myself a small smile.

She returned the smile, though it didn't quite reach her eyes. "Nervous?"

"The Dark Lord doesn't get nervous," I said, the lie rolling easily off my tongue. The truth was more complicated. What I felt wasn't exactly nervousness—it was something more primal. The voice in my head had grown stronger over the past days, a constant whisper urging me toward destruction. And no matter how many times I slammed down my mental walls, he kept finding cracks.

Take what's yours. Burn it all. Make them kneel.

I pushed the thoughts away, focusing instead on Arabella's face. There was so much I wanted to tell her—needed to tell her—but the words stuck in my throat. Last night, after we'd sent Evenfall to Auremar with false intelligence, I'd meant to confess everything. To tell her about the darkness growing inside me, about the ancient entity whose memories sometimes flooded my mind. To tell her that despite everything, despite who and what I was, I loved her.

But I'd hesitated, and the moment had passed. Now, with battle looming, it wasn't the time for such revelations. We needed clarity, focus. The confession would have to wait.

"Where's Griffin?" I asked, changing the subject.

"Finishing the calculations for the portal," she said. "He says it'll be ready when you are."

I nodded, my gaze sweeping over the assembled troops one last time. "And you? Are you ready?"

Her hand found mine, squeezing briefly. "As I'll ever be."

The gesture was intimate—a moment of connection before the chaos that was to come. I wanted to pull her into my arms. Instead, I simply squeezed her hand in return.

"Let's go, then," I said, releasing her and turning toward the center of the camp where Griffin waited.

Griffin stood in a cleared space, surrounded by an intricate pattern of runes drawn in what looked like crushed obsidian mixed with blood. Probably his own. The fool was nothing if not committed to his craft.

"Ah, there you are!" he called, waving frantically. His hair stood up in all directions, and dark circles shadowed his eyes. He'd been working through the night ever since I'd proposed this crazy plan. "I've just finished the final calculations. It's going to be magnificent. Or catastrophic. Possibly both!"

"That's not as reassuring as you seem to think it is," Arabella muttered.

I stepped closer, examining the runic array. It was complex, far beyond anything I'd seen Griffin attempt before. The pattern spiraled outward from a central point, each line and curve precisely placed to channel and amplify magical energy.

"You're certain this will work?" I asked.

Griffin pushed his spectacles up his nose, his expression growing serious. "Theoretically, yes. The math checks out." He hesitated.

"But?" I prompted.

"Well, no one's ever attempted a portal of this magnitude before," he admitted. "The energy requirements are substantial."

I smiled, feeling the Heirloom's power thrumming through my connection with Arabella, fed by the nexus at the God Spire. "Energy won't be a problem."

"Right, yes, of course." Griffin fidgeted with the edge of his sleeve. "There is one other small concern."

"Which is?"

"The stability of the portal depends on your concentration. If your focus wavers, even for a moment"—he made an explosive gesture with his hands—"poof."

"Poof," I repeated flatly.

"More like a catastrophic collapse of space-time that could potentially tear a hole in reality," Griffin clarified, "but yes, essentially—poof."

Arabella looked at me with a mix of concern and amusement. "No pressure."

I rolled my eyes. "Your confidence is overwhelming."

"You'll be fine," she said, her tone softening. "Just don't get distracted."

The way she said it made it clear what kind of distraction she meant. I arched an eyebrow at her. "I'm a professional, Lady Blackrose."

"Of course you are, Lord Blackrose." Her smile was teasing, but there was a warmth in her eyes that made my chest tighten.

Tell her now, a part of me urged. *Before it's too late.*

But Griffin was already moving into position, gesturing for me to take my place at the center of the runic array. The moment passed, slipping away like sand through fingers.

"Thorne," I called, and my security chief materialized at my side, seemingly from nowhere. "Are the troops ready?"

Thorne nodded grimly. "In position and awaiting your command, my lord."

"Good." I turned to Arabella. "You know what to do?"

She nodded. "You create a distraction big enough that Auremar won't notice a small team infiltrating his palace."

"And?"

"And I stay alive," she added, rolling her eyes. "Yes, I remember the plan."

I simply nodded. "Then let's begin."

I stepped into the center of the runic array, feeling the magic immediately respond to my presence. The runes began to heat, a familiar pain that I welcomed. Pain meant power, and I would need every ounce of it for what was to come.

Griffin took up position at the edge of the array, his hands hovering over specific runes. "Ready when you are, Lord Blackrose."

I closed my eyes, reaching for the well of dominion magic that resided within me. It rose eagerly to my call, dark and hungry. Through my connection with Arabella, I could feel the Heirloom's power joining with mine, amplifying it to levels I'd never experienced before.

The voice in my head grew more insistent.

Yes. Show them what true dominion can do.

I opened my eyes, directing my gaze to the empty space before me. "Begin."

Griffin pressed his hands to the runes, and they flared to life, glowing with an eerie purple light. The magic surged through the pattern, following the paths he'd laid out, gathering and focusing at the center where I stood.

I raised my hands, channeling the power through my body. The runes beneath my skin burned white-hot, and I could feel sweat beading on my forehead from the effort. The air around me began to distort, reality bending to my will.

A small tear appeared in the fabric of space, no larger than my hand. I pushed more power into it, forcing it to expand. The tear widened, edges fraying as it struggled against the natural order of things. It was like trying to rip open a steel door with my bare hands—possible, with enough strength, but requiring a level of effort that bordered on agony.

The voice grew louder still, almost drowning out my own thoughts.

More. Take more. Break through.

I reached deeper, drawing on reserves of power I hadn't known I possessed, and finally . . . drawing on the power of the ley lines beneath the God Spire. The Heirloom's energy flowed through our connection, a torrent of ancient magic that made my blood sing. The tear in reality expanded rapidly, growing until it was the size of a doorway, then a carriage, then larger still.

Through the portal, I could see the outskirts of Sunspire, Solandris's capital city just beyond the famous Golden Rose Fields. Except the fields, which should have been a sea of shimmering gold, were black—the roses withered and dead, their once vibrant petals now charred husks.

"The roses," Arabella gasped, stepping closer to the portal. "They're—"

"Dead," I bit out. "Auremar's work, no doubt."

The implications were clear and disturbing. The Golden Roses were more than just Solandris's most precious export—they were conduits to the Shadow King's prison. If they were dead, the prison's integrity was compromised far more than we'd realized.

Yes, the voice hissed. *The prison weakens. Soon, I will be free.*

I gritted my teeth, pushing the voice aside and focusing on maintaining the portal. It had reached its full size now, a massive tear in reality large enough for an army to march through. The strain of holding it open was like trying to hold back an ocean with my bare hands.

"Now!" I shouted to Thorne, who relayed the command down the line.

The troops began to move, marching through the portal in ordered formations. First the vanguard with the banners snapping in the wind, then the main force, followed by supply wagons and support units. Finally, three larger wagons rumbled past, their wheels groaning under the weight of wooden crates—each one filled with bones harvested from the outpost's fallen.

Sweat poured down my face, and my muscles trembled with the effort of maintaining the portal. The runes beneath my skin felt like they were trying to burn their way out, the pain a constant, screaming presence.

"Kaz?" Arabella's voice cut through the haze of pain and concentration.

"I'm fine," I managed.

Before I could protest, she placed her hand on my arm. Immediately, I felt her magic flowing into me, cool and soothing against the burning heat of my own. The Heirloom glowed brighter, and the strain of holding the portal eased slightly.

"Better?" she asked.

I nodded, not trusting myself to speak.

The last of the troops passed through the portal, and they were forming up on the other side, preparing for battle. Through the magical gateway, I could make out movement on the horizon—Auremar's forces, already mobilizing to meet us. But not the main force of ten thousand. We'd done it.

"He took the bait," I said, satisfaction coloring my voice despite the strain. "Evenfall delivered our false intelligence."

"Let's hope he's still alive for you to thank personally," Arabella said dryly.

I laughed hoarsely. "I'd rather thank him with the edge of my blade, but I take your point."

As the last of my ground forces passed through, the *Sky Serpent* emerged from behind our rear lines, its dark sails billowing as it sailed through the massive portal. Captain Brecca stood at the helm, with the volunteers—those with heroic bloodlines who'd agreed to our counter-ritual—safely aboard. The ship would keep its distance from both the capital and the fighting, hovering just close enough that we could summon them when needed. I watched it glide through the tear in reality, a dark silhouette against the morning sky, carrying our best hope for sealing the Shadow King's prison. Then it banked west, away from the battlefield, disappearing behind a line of hills.

Sebastian and Thorne were the last of our forces to go through. Now it was our turn. I looked at Arabella, suddenly reluctant to let her go. I wanted to say more—to make her promise to return to me, to tell her what she meant to me. But the portal was growing unstable, the edges flickering as my concentration wavered.

"Go," I said instead. "I'll see you when it's done."

She hesitated, then stepped forward and kissed me—fierce and quick, a promise and a goodbye all at once. "Once again, try not to die, Dark Lord."

"I wouldn't dream of it, my lady."

With one last smile, she stepped through the portal, finding Sebastian and Thorne and disappearing into the chaos beyond. I followed a moment later, the portal collapsing behind me as I released the magic holding it open.

The sudden absence of that crushing magical weight left me momentarily hollow, my legs threatening to buckle. But the runes beneath my skin were already cooling, the pain receding to a manageable burn. My body replenished itself faster than it used to, before the Heirloom's power became mine to draw upon. Within moments, the trembling in my muscles eased, replaced by the familiar hum of ready magic.

The scene that greeted me was one of organized chaos. My troops had formed battle lines, facing Auremar's forces across a stretch of open ground. The dead rose fields lay to our right, a stark reminder of what was at stake.

Solandris's capital city rose in the distance, its white stone walls gleaming in the morning sun. Auremar's palace dominated the skyline, its towers reaching toward the heavens like spindly fingers.

I could see confusion and fear rippling through the enemy ranks. They'd expected us to attack from the east, where Evenfall had told them our forces were gathering. Instead, we'd appeared on their doorstep, an army materializing from thin air.

Relief and anxiety warred within me. Arabella was beyond my reach now, facing dangers I couldn't protect her from. But she was capable and powerful. I had to trust that she would succeed—that we both would.

One of my generals awaited orders.

I turned my attention back to the battle. "Let's give King Auremar a proper greeting, shall we?"

I reached for my magic again, feeling it respond eagerly. The voice in my head surged forward, hungry for blood and destruction.

Make them kneel or die.

For once, I didn't fight it. In battle, at least, our purposes aligned. I wanted Auremar's forces broken, his kingdom conquered. If the darkness within me helped achieve that goal, so be it.

I raised my hands, and the shadows responded. With a gesture, I sent them racing across the battlefield, forming into massive, wolflike constructs that tore into the enemy's flanks. Screams rose from Auremar's lines as my shadow warriors ripped through flesh and armor alike.

My own troops surged forward, meeting the enemy head-on. Steel clashed against steel, magic flared in brilliant bursts of light and darkness. The battle was joined, a chaotic dance of death and power.

I had no intention of wasting this opportunity. If we could take the capital while rescuing the prisoners, all the better. Auremar's fall would be complete, his kingdom mine for the taking.

I moved through the battlefield like a living shadow, my dominion magic cutting down any who stood in my path. Soldiers fell before me, their wills crushed by my power, their bodies broken by my shadows. It was exhilarating, intoxicating—the kind of raw, unfettered power I'd always craved.

The voice in my head grew louder with each kill, each display of dominance.

It whispered promises of even greater power, of a throne that was rightfully mine, of a world remade in my image.

This is just the beginning. When I am free, when we are whole, none will stand against us.

The words should have disturbed me, but in the heat of battle, they felt right—a truth I'd always known but never fully acknowledged. I was meant for more than just conquering a kingdom. I was meant to rule, to dominate, to reshape the world according to my will.

A contingent of Auremar's elite guards formed up before me, their armor gleaming with protective enchantments. Their captain, a burly man with a scar running down his face, pointed his sword at me.

"In the name of King Auremar, surrender or die, villain!"

I laughed, the sound dark and cold.

The captain's face reddened with anger. "Attack!"

They charged as one, their enchanted weapons raised. I stood my ground, gathering my power. As they reached me, I released it in a wave of pure dominion magic that slammed into them. Half of them crumpled instantly, their wills shattered. The others staggered but remained standing, protected by their enchanted armor, but barely.

The captain swung his sword at my head. I sidestepped, then caught his wrist in a grip enhanced by magic. I could feel the bones grinding together beneath my fingers.

"Is this truly the best Auremar has to offer?" I asked, my voice low and dangerous. "Pathetic."

With a twist, I snapped his wrist. Bone splintered beneath my grip—a wet crunch that cut through the din of steel and screaming. Before he could even cry out, I released a pulse of dominion magic directly into his mind. His eyes went wide, then vacant.

"Kneel," I commanded.

He dropped to his knees, broken wrist forgotten, his will completely subjugated. The remaining guards watched in horror as their captain—their *leader*—became nothing more than my thrall.

"Now," I said, still holding the captain's vacant stare, "draw your dagger and kill the man to your left."

The captain's good hand moved mechanically, fumbling the dagger from his belt. The guard beside him—a younger man with fear-bright eyes—raised his sword in trembling defense. "Captain, no! Fight it!"

But there was nothing left to fight. The captain batted the younger man's sword away and drove the blade up under his chin with the cold efficiency of a butcher. Blood sprayed across enchanted armor as the young guard crumpled.

The remaining soldiers stumbled back. One of them made a choking sound of horror.

I released the compulsion, and the captain collapsed over his victim's body, his broken wrist cradled against his chest, comprehension and horror flooding back into his eyes.

"Tell your king," I said, my voice carrying over his ragged breathing, "that Kazimir Blackrose has come to claim what is his. And that his strongest warriors are nothing but playthings to me."

I shoved him toward his men. "Go. Run back to your master like the dogs you are."

They retreated, dragging their injured captain with them.

The battle raged around me, but it was clear we had the upper hand. My troops were better trained, better equipped, and bolstered by my shadow warriors. Auremar's forces were already falling back, their lines breaking under the relentless pressure.

But it wasn't enough. I wanted more—needed more. A display of power so overwhelming that resistance would become unthinkable. Something to cement my victory in the minds of all who witnessed it.

And something to command the attention of every enemy on the field, for any reserves to be called in.

Thorne had diligently collected the bones from the outpost—the remains of Auremar's soldiers who had fallen to our initial assault. It was time to use them.

The Bone Behemoth. A creation I'd been working toward for months, a fusion of necromancy and dominion magic that would create a monster of unprecedented power. I'd attempted it once before, at Skyspire, but the strain had been too great. Now, with the Heirloom's power flowing through me, I could finally bring it to life.

I found a relatively clear space on the battlefield and knelt, placing my hands on the ground. The earth responded to my touch, a tremor running through it as my magic sank deep. I called to the bones buried in the supply wagons at the rear of our lines, feeling them respond to my summons.

They came in a macabre rain, femurs and skulls and rib cages arcing through the air to land in a growing pile before me. Auremar's soldiers watched in horror, some breaking ranks and fleeing at the sight. Even my own troops gave the area a wide berth, their expressions a mix of awe and fear.

The voice in my head grew to a roar, drowning out all other thought.

Create! Destroy! Show them the true meaning of power!

I began the incantation, ancient words flowing from my lips as if I'd known them all my life. The runes carved into my bones flared with pain, but I welcomed it, channeling it into the spell. The bones before me began to shift and merge, joining together in unnatural configurations.

A skull the size of a wagon wheel formed from many, surrounded by a crown of individual skulls. Rib cages fused into a massive torso, while femurs and tibias created limbs as thick as tree trunks. Smaller bones filled in the gaps, creating a skeletal monstrosity that towered over the battlefield.

The magic required was immense, draining me even with the Heirloom's power to draw upon. Sweat poured down my face, and my vision blurred with the effort. But I pushed on, driven by a need that transcended mere strategy. This wasn't just about winning a battle—it was about proving something to myself, to Auremar, to the world.

That I, Kazimir Blackrose, was unstoppable.

The final words of the spell left my lips, and for a moment, nothing happened. The massive skeleton remained motionless, a grotesque monument to death.

Then, slowly, it began to move. First a finger, then a hand, then an arm. The skull swiveled, empty eye sockets somehow fixing on me with an attentive gaze. It rose to its full height, easily twenty feet tall, a behemoth of bone and dark magic.

"Serve," I commanded, my voice hoarse from the strain of the spell.

The Bone Behemoth inclined its massive head in acknowledgment, then turned toward the enemy lines. With a roar that seemed to come from the depths of the earth itself, it charged, each step shaking the ground.

Auremar's lines broke, their discipline shattering at the sight of the monstrous creation bearing down on them. Some stood their ground, firing arrows or hurling spells that bounced harmlessly off the behemoth's skeletal frame. Others fled, throwing down their weapons in their haste to escape.

The behemoth tore through their ranks, massive hands sweeping soldiers aside like toys. It was a scene from a nightmare, a display of power and horror that would be remembered for generations.

And at the center of it all, directing the chaos, stood me—Kazimir Blackrose, Dark Lord, conqueror of Solandris.

The voice in my head laughed, a sound of pure, malevolent joy.

This is your destiny.

This felt right—this unleashing of power, this conquest. As if I were reclaiming something that had always been mine.

I watched as my forces surged forward, following in the behemoth's wake. The path to the capital lay open, Auremar's army in disarray. Victory was within my grasp.

But even as I reveled in the triumph, a part of me remained focused on the true objective. Arabella, Thorne, and Sebastian would be in the palace by now, searching for the prisoners. Their success or failure would determine the fate of the ley lines, of the Shadow King's prison—of the world itself.

I hoped Arabella was faring better than the soldiers facing my behemoth. I hoped she was safe, that Sebastian was proving his worth as an ally. I hoped that when this was over, I would have the chance to tell her everything I'd been holding back.

That despite the darkness within me and the voice that whispered of destruction, I loved her. And that love was the one thing the Shadow King couldn't claim.

I raised my hand, signaling the advance. My troops surged forward, and I moved with them, shadows forming giant leathery wings behind me.

The Bone Behemoth roared again, a sound of triumph and hunger. I echoed it with a laugh of my own, embracing the darkness that had always been part of me.

Kazimir Blackrose had come to claim his throne.

62

Storm the Palace

(with a Flower Lord)

Arabella

The palace wards hit me like a wall of bricks, stopping us cold before we even reached the manicured gardens.

"Fuck," I muttered, rubbing my forehead where I'd smacked into the invisible barrier. "That's new."

Sebastian winced beside me, shaking out his hand where he'd touched the magical boundary. "Auremar must have upgraded the defenses after your . . . departure."

"You mean after I was kidnapped by my now-husband?" I shot him a wry smile. "Seems a bit like closing the stable door after the horse has already been stolen and married to a villain, doesn't it?"

Thorne, ever the pragmatist, drew a knife and tested the edge of the barrier. The blade sparked violently against the invisible wall, leaving a brief shimmer of golden light in its wake.

"Can you break it, Lady Blackrose?" he asked, his gravelly voice low.

I studied the barrier, feeling the texture of the magic with my senses. It was stronger than I would have expected from Auremar's mages. The magic had a familiar signature, though, something that tickled at the edges of my memory.

Through our bond, I could feel Kazimir's battle rage like distant thunder, a storm of power and darkness that both thrilled and terrified me. Triumph surged through the connection, and I knew his attack was going well. I forced my fear for him aside, keeping just enough awareness to monitor his status.

"Lady Blackrose?" Thorne prompted again.

"I'm thinking," I replied, my eyes tracing the golden shimmer of the ward.

The Palace Garden stretched before us, a riot of color and scent in the morning light. Topiaries shaped like mythical beasts stood sentinel among beds of exotic flowers, their forms casting long shadows across the perfectly manicured lawns. Beyond them rose Sunspire Palace itself, its white stone towers gleaming in the light, windows glittering like jewels.

I'd spent countless hours in these gardens as a child, before my father decided I was better off locked in a tower. The memory of those happier times hit me with unexpected force—running through the maze with Sebastian, hiding from our tutors, watching the pixies that made their homes in the hollow centers of the topiaries.

Sebastian had kissed me under that oak tree, the one with the swing. It had been awkward and sweet and nothing like the consuming fire I felt with Kazimir. But it had been a moment of innocence before everything went to hell.

The palace, the gardens, the memories—they belonged to a different Arabella. A girl who believed in heroes and happy endings, who wanted to believe her father loved her, who didn't know the taste of blood or the feel of shadow magic curling through her veins.

That girl was gone, burned away by betrayal and darkness and the love of a villain.

I was Lady Arabella Blackrose now. And I'd never felt more in control of my destiny.

"Stand back," I said, my voice hardening as I stepped forward to face the barrier again.

Sebastian's eyes widened. "What are you—"

"Just trust me."

I closed my eyes, reaching for my magic. The light came first, as it always did—the healing power of my bloodline, bright and pure. But I pushed past it, diving deeper, searching for the darkness I'd discovered with Kazimir's help.

There it was, waiting for me. Shadow and dominion, twisted together like lovers. I wrapped my will around it, drawing it up and out.

The Heirloom on my head grew warm, then hot, responding to my call. Power surged through me, far more than I'd expected, and I gasped at the intensity of it.

Show them what you're capable of, a voice whispered in my mind. It wasn't Kazimir's voice, but it wasn't entirely foreign, either. *Break their pathetic defenses. Take what's yours.*

I opened my eyes, raising my hands toward the barrier. Shadow magic coiled around me, darker than night, shot through with veins of gold.

"Lady Arabella Evenfall," I said, my voice echoing strangely in the still air, "daughter of this house, demands entry."

The barrier shimmered, recognizing my bloodline, but held firm.

I smiled, a cold expression that would have shocked the girl I once was. "I thought not. Very well."

I pushed, not with my hands but with my will, sending a surge of shadow magic against the barrier. It struck with the force of a battering ram, causing the entire ward to flare golden in response. For a moment, the two magics warred against each other, light against dark, creation against destruction.

Then I reached deeper, drawing on the Heirloom's connection to the ley lines themselves. Power flooded through me, raw and ancient, and I shaped it with the techniques I'd learned watching Kazimir. Not brute force, but precision—finding the weak points in the ward's structure and exploiting them, using dominion magic to command rather than destroy.

"Dissipate," I whispered, my voice carrying the weight of absolute authority.

The barrier hesitated, as if the magic itself was considering rebellion. Then it unraveled, threads of golden light dissolving silently into the morning air like mist under sunlight. No alarms. No shattering. Just a ward that decided—or was convinced—it had never existed in the first place.

I staggered, suddenly lightheaded from the effort. Sebastian caught my elbow, steadying me.

"That was—" he began, then shook his head, apparently at a loss for words.

"Impressive," Thorne finished for him, a rare note of approval in his voice. "Lord Blackrose has taught you well."

"Let's not stand around congratulating ourselves." But as we hurried forward, I allowed myself to feel a moment of pride anyway.

We slipped through the gardens, keeping to the shadows. The palace grounds were eerily empty—most of the guards had likely been called to defend against Kazimir's attack. Still, we moved with caution, aware that even a single alarm could doom our mission.

The service entrance was just where I remembered it, a modest door set into the base of the east wing, partially hidden by a trellis of climbing roses. Two guards stood watch, looking nervous and jumpy.

Only two—that didn't bode well. I'd expected many more to guard the captive heroes.

"I'll handle this," Thorne murmured, drawing a pair of wickedly curved daggers.

"Wait," Sebastian said, his voice barely audible. He gestured subtly, and I watched as tiny seedpods fell from his sleeve, landing silently near the guards' feet.

Within seconds, the pods burst open, releasing a cloud of pollen that the guards inhaled before they could react. Their eyes rolled back, and they slumped to the ground, unconscious.

I raised an eyebrow at Sebastian. "Sleep pollen? That's new."

He shrugged, a faint blush coloring his cheeks. "I've been experimenting."

"Experimenting is Griffin's job," I said with a small smile. "But I'm not complaining."

Thorne moved forward, checking the guards to ensure they were truly out. With a practiced motion, he slit their throats quickly and silently.

Sebastian winced but said nothing.

"Sorry," I said, not really meaning it. "But we can't afford to leave enemies at our backs."

"I know," he replied quietly. "I just . . . never mind. Let's keep moving."

We slipped through the service door and into the palace. The corridors were dimly lit and deserted. I led the way, navigating the familiar passages with ease despite the years since I'd last walked them. My newly restored memories made it easier, and if I didn't remember a turn, Sebastian did.

The wine cellar was located deep beneath the palace, accessible via a narrow staircase that wound down from the kitchens. We encountered two more guards on our way, dispatching them as quietly as we had the first pair.

The cellar door was locked. I placed my palm against it, feeling for the mechanism with tendrils of shadow magic. A moment later, the lock clicked open.

"Useful trick," Thorne murmured.

I shrugged. "Kazimir taught me. Apparently, Dark Lords have strong opinions about locks being suggestions rather than obstacles."

We descended into shadows thick with dust and the musty sweetness of centuries-old vintages. As we entered the main cellar, magical sconces along the wall flared to life with bright flames, sputtered, and then almost died. When they stabilized, they were dimmer than I'd hoped, creating deep pockets of shadow throughout the large space. Even the magic of Sunspire was struggling in the wake of the ley lines' corruption.

Row upon row of bottles stretched into darkness. Ancient oak barrels lined the walls, some large enough to hide a body—or several. I ran my fingers along the cold stone walls, searching for hidden catches while Thorne tested each barrel with soft taps. Sebastian moved between the towering wine racks, his violet eyes scanning for anything of interest, occasionally pressing his palm against a rack as if feeling for a hidden lever.

No sign of the prisoners.

We searched methodically, moving deeper into the vast cellar. The air was cool and damp, heavy with the scent of aged wine and earth. But as we reached the far end of the chamber, it became clear that there were no captives.

"They're not here," Sebastian said, stating the obvious.

"I can see that," I snapped. "The question is, where are they?"

A noise at the entrance made us all freeze. At the sound of several pairs of boots clunking down the stairs, I slipped into a dark alcove and pulled shadows around myself like a cloak. Thorne and Sebastian were silent as they hid, as well.

Four guards entered at the far end of the cellar, carrying torches that brightened up the area better than the sconces.

"I swear I heard something," one of them said, his hand on the hilt of his sword.

"Probably just rats," another replied. "This place is infested with them."

"And I suppose rats turned the lights on themselves, did they?" a third guard snarled. "Get busy and make sure we don't have a prisoner hiding down here. His Majesty would have our heads if anything interfered with tonight's ceremony."

They spread out, moving between the wine racks with weapons drawn. One of them was heading straight for Sebastian's hiding place.

I caught his eye across the cellar and nodded slightly. He understood, his fingers moving in a subtle gesture. Vines erupted from between the stones of the floor, wrapping around the guards' ankles and rapidly climbing up their bodies. Within seconds, all four were bound tightly, unable to move or cry out as the plants covered their mouths.

I stepped out from among the shadows that trailed after me. The guards' eyes widened in recognition and fear.

"Hello, boys," I said, my voice deceptively light. "I seem to have misplaced some prisoners. Perhaps you could help me find them?"

One of the guards made a muffled sound behind his gag of leaves. I approached him.

"I'm going to remove this," I said, gesturing to the plant covering his mouth, "and you're going to tell me where Auremar is keeping the people with heroic bloodlines. If you lie to me . . ." I let the shadows around my hand darken and twist. "Well, let's just say I've learned some interesting techniques from my husband."

Sebastian loosened the vine enough for the guard to speak. The man gasped for air, his eyes darting frantically between us.

"I don't know what you're talking about," he stammered. "What prisoners?"

I sighed dramatically. "They never listen the first time." It was practically cliche at this point.

I placed my palm against his chest and inverted my healing magic, sending a pulse of energy that attacked rather than mended. The guard screamed as blood vessels burst beneath his skin, creating a spiderweb of red that spread across his torso. I didn't have to see it to feel the damage beneath his armor.

"Let's try again," I said, leaning in close. "Where are the prisoners?"

"They were moved!" he gasped, tears streaming down his face.

"Where?"

"To the ritual chamber beneath the Golden Rose Fields. Last night. That's all I know, I swear!"

My truth-sense confirmed the guard was telling the truth. "How do we get there?"

"A tunnel," the guard whimpered. "From the old temple ruins on the north side of the fields. But it's heavily guarded, and the entrance is warded."

Sebastian stepped forward, his expression grim. "The Chamber of Petals. It's an ancient site used for ceremonies involving the Golden Roses since the time of the First Hero."

I raised an eyebrow at him. "You know about this?"

He nodded.

I turned to Thorne and jerked my head toward the guards. He moved swiftly among the bound guards, slitting their throats one by one. The last one, the one who had spoken, stared at me with wide, betrayed eyes as Thorne approached.

Sebastian made a small noise of protest, but it was half-hearted at best. I glanced at him, surprised by his lack of resistance.

"What?" I asked as Thorne finished his work. "No lecture about mercy or the sanctity of life?"

Sebastian's expression was troubled, but there was a hardness in his eyes I hadn't seen before. "We're at war," he said simply. "And I've seen what Auremar is willing to do. Some lines can't be uncrossed."

I studied him for a moment, wondering what exactly had happened to change the gentle boy I'd known into this grimly practical man. But there was no time to dwell on it. "If they've moved the prisoners to the ritual chamber, they must be planning to use them sooner than we thought."

"The temple ruins are at least a mile north of here," Sebastian said. "And if the guard was telling the truth, the entrance will be heavily defended."

"Then we'll fight our way through," I replied, shadows coiling around my hands in anticipation. "The time for stealth is over."

Through our bond, I felt a surge of dark triumph from Kazimir, followed by a wave of something wilder. He was fully in his element now, reveling in the battle. The sensation was both thrilling and concerning—there was an edge to his emotions that felt almost foreign.

I pushed the worry aside. Kazimir could handle himself.

"Let's go," I said, heading for the cellar stairs.

We moved through the palace with less caution now, our pace quickening. The few guards we encountered were dealt with swiftly—Sebastian's plant magic or my shadows binding them, Thorne's blades finishing them off.

I felt a strange exhilaration as we fought our way forward. The power of the Heirloom hummed through me, amplifying my magic to levels that would have terrified me just months ago.

The feeling of power from the ley lines all the way from beneath the God Spire was intoxicating, and I wondered what it would feel like to draw on the ones beneath Solandris.

We burst through a side door and into the palace grounds. The north temple ruins were visible in the distance, a crumbling structure of white stone set at the edge of what had once been the Golden Rose Fields. Now the fields were a blackened wasteland.

Once again, the sight of the devastation hit me harder than I expected. The Golden Roses had been the pride of Solandris, their beauty legendary throughout the realms. To see them reduced to this . . .

"Auremar has much to answer for," I murmured. Beside me, Sebastian let out a long exhale.

"Tell me about this Chamber of Petals," I said as we moved quickly across the scorched earth.

"All those with heroic bloodlines learn of it eventually," he said, his voice tight. "It's where the traditional harvesting rituals are performed—where those of us with the First Hero's blood feed drops of our life force into the roses during harvest to ensure they bloom again and their essence remains potent. The ceremony's supposed to follow the ancient forms exactly, renewing the magic with each generation. I remember going with my mother when I turned sixteen."

I glanced at Sebastian, who gave me an apologetic look. I'd never had the same opportunity with my mother.

His expression darkened. "Though looking back, Auremar had already started changing things—drawing more blood than tradition called for, harvesting out of season, pushing for higher yields."

I noticed he wasn't rhyming. Whatever was running through his head, it wasn't panic.

As we neared the ruins, the true scale of the defenses became clear. We dropped into a crouch behind the blackened remains of what had once been an ornamental hedge, using it for cover.

A contingent of guards stood at the temple entrance, at least twenty of them, along with what appeared to be three mages in the distinctive gold-trimmed robes of the Royal Arcanum.

"That's a lot of security for some ruins," Thorne observed drily.

"Obviously our captives are there," I said.

"What's the plan?" Sebastian asked, eyeing the guards.

I considered our options. We were outnumbered, but not outmatched. With my power combined with the Heirloom's, Sebastian's surprisingly effective combat magic, and Thorne's steel, the guards would quickly fall.

"Sebastian, can you create a distraction? Something to draw their attention while Thorne and I rush them?"

Sebastian nodded. "I think I can manage that."

He closed his eyes, concentrating. For a moment, nothing happened. Then the ground around the temple began to tremble. Vines burst from the earth, thick as a man's arm and covered in wicked thorns. They writhed and twisted, forming a living wall that surged toward the guards.

Chaos erupted as the guards tried to fight off the attacking plants. The mages began casting, balls of fire materializing in their hands to burn away the vines. While they were fighting off enemy plants, Thorne and I charged forward.

I summoned shadows as I ran, forming them into blades that extended from my hands. The first guard who turned to face me died before he could raise his sword, my shadow blade slicing through his throat. The second managed to parry my first strike, but my training with Kazimir paid off as I ducked under the man's counter and drove my blade up through his chin and into his brain.

Across the courtyard, Thorne moved like a whirlwind of death, his daggers finding gaps in armor with uncanny precision. Three guards fell to him in quick succession, their bodies crumpling to the ground before they fully registered the threat.

One of the mages spotted me and turned, abandoning the vines to face this new threat. He hurled a fireball at me, the heat of it searing the air as it passed. I dodged, rolling to the side and coming up with my shadow blades at the ready.

The mage began another incantation, his hands weaving complex patterns in the air. I didn't give him time to finish. Drawing on the Heirloom's power, I sent a wave of shadow magic toward him.

The shadows engulfed him, wrapping around his body like a cocoon. I clenched my fist, and the shadows constricted. The mage's scream was cut short as his rib cage collapsed, blood spurting from his mouth.

I turned to find my next target, only to see Sebastian engaged with the remaining two mages. His plant magic was holding its own against their fire, vines sprouting faster than they could be burned away. But he was on the defensive, unable to press his advantage.

I moved to help him. The mages saw me coming, one of them turning to face me while the other continued to battle Sebastian.

The mage facing me was older, his face lined with experience. He smiled coldly as I approached, clearly confident in his abilities.

"Lady Arabella," he said, his voice carrying easily across the battlefield. "Your father will be so disappointed."

I faltered for a moment, recognizing him from a newly emerging memory. I knew him. "Magister Caine. You were at the tower that night, with Amaryska."

The night my mother died. The night they took my memories.

Rage surged through me, hot and fierce. The shadows around me darkened, responding to my emotions. Through my bond with Kazimir, I felt an answering surge of darkness, as if my anger had called to his.

"You remember," Caine said, sounding surprised.

"I had help," I snarled, advancing on him.

He gestured sharply, and the air around me suddenly thickened, becoming heavy as lead. I struggled to move, my limbs fighting against the magical weight pressing down on me.

"A simple gravity manipulation," Caine explained, as if lecturing a student. "Effective against most opponents."

I gritted my teeth, pushing against the spell with my own magic. The Heirloom flared hot against my skin, and I felt its power surge through me, breaking Caine's hold.

His eyes widened as I straightened, shadows swirling around me unhindered. "Impossible," he breathed.

I struck, not with shadow blades this time but with pure dominion magic, the kind Kazimir had been teaching me. It hit Caine in the chest and sent him staggering back. Before he could recover, I was on him, my hand at his throat.

"For my mother," I whispered, and inverted my healing magic, sending it coursing through him in a wave of destruction.

Caine's scream echoed across the courtyard as his body withered from the inside out, blood vessels bursting, organs failing, skin shriveling against bone. In seconds, he was reduced to a desiccated husk, his eyes wide with shock and pain.

I let the corpse fall, turning to find Sebastian and Thorne finishing off the last of the guards. The remaining mage lay dead at Sebastian's feet, his body wrapped in vines that had pierced him through in a dozen places. "The entrance to the tunnel should be inside the temple," he said.

I nodded, stepping over Caine's remains without a backward glance.

The temple had once been a grand structure, dedicated to Solandra, the goddess of light and healing. Now it was little more than a shell, its roof long gone, its walls crumbling.

In the center of what had once been the main sanctuary, a large stone altar remained intact. Sebastian approached it, running his hands over the ancient symbols carved into its surface. After a moment, he paused and pressed a sequence of glyphs. The altar slid aside with a grinding noise, revealing a dark stairway leading down into the earth. "This is one of the last places I visited with my mother before she became sick," he said. "Now I wonder if what Auremar was doing caused her death."

I placed a hand on his arm, feeling a surge of sympathy. "We were both lied to, Sebastian. But we're going to make it right."

He nodded, his jaw set.

Thorne moved to the entrance, peering down into the darkness with daggers drawn. "I'll take point. Stay close."

63

Lose Control of Your Monster

(Both of Them)

Kazimir

The Bone Behemoth's roar shattered what remained of Auremar's eastern line, and I felt a surge of dark satisfaction as soldiers scattered like ants under a boot. Each swing of its massive arms sent soldiers flying, their screams cut short by the sickening crunch of bone against bone.

But they regrouped faster than I'd expected.

Golden light erupted from their rear guard, and I watched with narrowed eyes as mages in white robes stepped forward, their hands weaving complex patterns in the air. The light coalesced into barriers, slowing my behemoth's advance.

"Interesting," I murmured, shadows coiling around my fingers. "They've learned some new tricks."

The voice in my head hissed its displeasure. *Crush them. Break their pathetic defenses.*

I was already moving, summoning shadow wings to fly above the battlefield. From this vantage, I could see the full scope of Auremar's response. The mages weren't just creating barriers, though. They were channeling something different that made the air taste of copper and old magic.

Then I saw the Hero's Guild, or what remained of it after our last encounter. They emerged from concealed positions, their burnished silver armor dulled to gray, their movements too fluid and synchronized to be natural. The corrupted substance Auremar had been feeding them had changed them, made them faster, stronger.

More dangerous.

"Finally," I said, a cold smile spreading across my face. "A real challenge."

I'd prepared for this possibility. The false intelligence we'd fed Evenfall hadn't just included troop movements—it had contained specific weaknesses in our formation, bait for the Guild to exploit. They thought they were springing a trap.

They had no idea they were walking into mine.

I descended, landing hard enough to crack the earth beneath my feet. The nearest Guild members turned toward me, their eyes glazed with that telltale sheen of addiction. Whatever Auremar had done to them, it had stripped away their humanity, leaving only weapons.

It would make killing them so much easier.

"Shadow Formation Seven," I commanded, my voice carrying across the battlefield through magical amplification.

My troops responded instantly, shifting their positions with precision. What had appeared to be a standard assault formation revealed itself as something far more complex—a magical array drawn with living soldiers, each one a focal point for the spell I was about to unleash.

The Guild charged, their enhanced speed turning them into blurs of motion. The first one reached me in seconds, his sword wreathed in corrupted golden fire. I caught the blade with my bare hand, shadows hardening around my skin to protect me from the flames.

"Too slow," I said, and twisted.

The sword shattered, fragments of enchanted steel spinning through the air. Before the knight could react, I drove my other hand through his chest, shadows extending from my fingers to pierce armor and flesh alike.

He died with a gurgle, black blood pouring from the wound.

More, the voice urged. *Kill them all.*

I obliged.

The battle became a dance of death. Each strike was calculated for maximum carnage, each spell designed to inspire terror. I wasn't just fighting—I was performing, creating a spectacle that would be seared into the minds of every survivor.

A group of Guild members tried to flank me, moving with that unnatural synchronization. I spun, shadows exploding outward in a wave of cutting darkness. They fell in pieces, their enhanced bodies no match for raw power.

But more kept coming. Dozens of them pouring from hidden positions across the battlefield. Auremar had held them in reserve, waiting for the perfect moment to strike.

They dare challenge us? Show them their folly.

My vision began to blur at the edges, darkness creeping in. Not the darkness of my magic, but something older, hungrier. Memories that weren't quite mine flickered through my mind—images of battles long past, of armies kneeling before a figure wreathed in shadow.

I shook my head. This wasn't the time to lose focus. Arabella needed me to maintain the distraction, to keep Auremar's forces occupied while she completed her mission.

Arabella.

The thought of her anchored me, pushing back the encroaching darkness. I could feel her through our bond, distant but safe, her determination a bright flame against the shadows trying to consume me.

"My lord!" One of my commanders approached, his armor splattered with blood. "The array is ready."

I nodded, raising my hand. "Activate it."

The soldiers in position began to chant, their voices rising in unison. The ground beneath us started to glow with purple light, runes appearing as if burned into the earth itself. The spell I'd designed was simple in concept but devastating in execution—it would turn the corrupted magic in the Guild members' blood against them.

The first screams started within seconds. Guild members clutched their heads, falling to their knees as the substance that gave them strength became poison. Some tried to flee, but the array's influence extended across the entire battlefield.

"Did you think I wouldn't prepare for you?" I called out, my voice carrying over the sounds of agony. "Did you think Auremar's pet project would save you?"

The Bone Behemoth continued its rampage, now facing less resistance as the Guild members writhed in pain. It grabbed one of the white-robed mages, crushing him in its massive fist before hurling the body into a cluster of soldiers.

Victory was close. I could taste it.

Then she appeared.

I'd been waiting for her. Of course she would come—Amaryska never could resist watching while other people did her work. The moment she materialized from a fold in space, every muscle in my body tensed, but this time I was ready. This time, I wouldn't freeze like a child counting footsteps on the stairs.

Her gray and red robes remained pristine despite the carnage, the red stitching like veins of blood against storm-cloud fabric. My mother looked exactly as she had in Kheldvar—sharp cheekbones, dark hair pulled back severely, those gray eyes that had watched impassively as she carved runes into my bones.

The vertebrae in my spine burned. Phantom pain. Memory. I pushed it down.

Not this time.

"Hello, my son," she said, her voice silk over steel.

The rage I'd been holding back since Kheldvar erupted, but controlled now—channeled into purpose rather than paralysis. The voice in my head roared its approval.

Kill her. Make her suffer as she made us suffer.

My hands weren't shaking. I'd made sure of that, practicing the encounter in my mind a hundred times since that rooftop. I'd prepared words, strategies, contingencies. But seeing her again still made something foul curl in my chest—not fear this time, but a darker cocktail of fury and old pain that the Shadow King's whispers eagerly fed upon.

"Mother." The word tasted sour on my tongue. I kept my voice steady, the Dark Lord's mask firmly in place even as that seven-year-old child inside me wanted to scream. "Come to watch your creation in action?"

She tilted her head, studying me with that clinical detachment I remembered so well. "You've grown strong."

"No thanks to you." I stalked toward her, shadows writhing around me. "Tell me, was selling me to that demon part of your grand plan? Or just a happy accident?"

"Everything I did was necessary," she replied, not moving as I approached. "You needed to be forged in darkness to fulfill your purpose."

I barked a laugh. "The only purpose I have is the one I chose. And right now, that purpose involves removing your head from your shoulders."

I struck without warning, shadows lashing out with lethal intent. But Amaryska was already moving, her form blurring as she dodged. She reappeared twenty feet away, a small smile playing at her lips.

"Still so direct," she said. "I taught you better than that."

"You taught me pain," I snarled, pursuing her. "Let me return the lesson."

We clashed in a fury of magic and malice. She was skilled, I'd give her that—her spells were elegant, efficient, designed to kill with minimal effort. But I was stronger, had been for years. Each of her attacks I batted aside, each defense I shattered with raw power.

The battlefield around us became collateral damage. Soldiers from both armies fled our vicinity as spells meant to kill missed their targets and devastated the landscape instead. The ground cracked and split, reality groaning under the strain of our conflict.

"Your wife should be meeting Auremar about now," Amaryska said as she narrowly avoided a spear of shadow. "Such a lovely girl. It would be a shame if something happened to her."

The voice in my head screamed for blood, but I forced myself to remain calm. Through the bond, I could feel Arabella—tense but unharmed, focused on her mission. If she were in real danger, I would know.

I sent a wave of dominion magic at my mother. "Did you really think such an obvious ploy would work?"

She twisted away, but not quite fast enough. The magic clipped her shoulder, sending her spinning. When she regained her footing, blood stained her robes.

"First blood to me," I observed coldly.

Amaryska's eyes narrowed. "You always were an ungrateful child."

The words shattered something inside me. "I was your weapon! You carved me into shape, pointed me at your enemies, and I *delivered*. I killed Vargus for you—gave you the revenge you couldn't take yourself. And the moment I succeeded, you sold me to a demon because I'd grown too powerful for your comfort!"

The admission burned coming out—that I'd known all along I was nothing more than her tool for revenge. But saying it aloud, here on this battlefield, made the old wound fresh again. My connection with Arabella slipped. And the voice in my head seized on that old pain, twisted it, fed it back to me amplified.

Amaryska used you. Discarded you. Make her pay.

I attacked with renewed fury. The voice in my head merged with my own thoughts until I couldn't tell where one ended and the other began. All that mattered was making her suffer as I had suffered.

But Amaryska was nothing if not a survivor. Every time I thought I had her, she slipped away—a teleportation here, an illusion there. She didn't fight to win; she fought to frustrate, to delay, to escape.

And it was working. Each near miss, each failed killing blow, fed the rage building inside me. The careful control I maintained over my power began to crack, darkness seeping through the fissures.

Let go, the voice whispered. *Embrace what you are. Show her true power.*

"Stand and fight!" I roared, shadows exploding outward in all directions.

Amaryska appeared atop a pile of corpses, looking down at me with those cold gray eyes. "You're losing control, Kazimir. Just as you always do when emotions run high."

"Shut up!"

I reached for more power, pulling from reserves I didn't know I had. The Bone Behemoth responded to my rage, its attacks becoming wilder, less discriminating. It no longer distinguished between friend and foe, crushing anyone in its path.

Screams rose from my own troops as the behemoth's massive fists came down on their formations. I heard them, distantly, but couldn't bring myself to care. All that mattered was catching Amaryska, making her pay.

Yes, the voice purred. *This is who you are. Who you've always been.*

Ancient memories flooded my mind—not my own, but familiar nonetheless. Images of battles that spanned centuries, of kingdoms rising and falling at my command. Of a name that echoed through history: Shadow King.

I stumbled under the weight of the memories. Amaryska used the distraction to put more distance between us, her form flickering as she prepared another spell.

"No!" I snarled, reaching out with dominion magic to hold her in place.

But the spell went wide, my control shattered by the chaos in my mind. She vanished, reappearing at the edge of the battlefield.

"Until next time, my son," she called, already fading into another portal.

She was gone, leaving me standing among the carnage, rage and ancient memories warring for control of my mind. The Bone Behemoth continued its rampage, no longer responding to my commands. It attacked indiscriminately, a monument to my loss of control.

Why do you fight it? the voice asked, no longer whispering but speaking with terrible clarity. *You know who you are. Who you've always been.*

More memories crashed over me—the confrontation with Soriven, the Golden Roses that bound me, centuries of imprisonment. Not metaphorical imprisonment, but literal, my consciousness doomed to roam in pieces, looking for hosts while my power remained sealed.

I was the Shadow King.

I had always been the Shadow King.

Welcome back, the voice said, and I realized it had never been separate from me at all. It was me—the part of myself I'd been denying, fighting, trying to forget.

The Bone Behemoth roared, and I roared with it, the sound shaking the very foundations of the earth. Power, true power, flooded through me. Not just the magic I'd cultivated as Kazimir Blackrose, but the ancient strength of the Shadow King himself.

I could feel it all—every ley line in the realm, every pulse of magic, every living thing connected by threads of power I could manipulate with a thought. The Heirloom on Arabella's head sang to me, recognizing its true master.

Take it all, I thought. *Reclaim what was stolen.*

The battlefield transformed as my power manifested fully. Shadows rose from the earth itself, taking shape as warriors, beasts, monstrosities beyond mortal comprehension. The sky darkened, stars vanishing as if consumed by an endless hunger.

This was what I was meant to be. Not just a Dark Lord playing at conquest, but a force of nature, inevitable and unstoppable.

Through it all, one small part of me—the part that was still Kazimir, still the man who loved Arabella—screamed in horror. But that voice grew fainter with each passing second, drowned out by the roar of ancient power reclaiming its throne.

The Shadow King had returned.

And the world would tremble.

64

Stop a King's Madness

(While Your Husband Embraces His Own)

Arabella

The tunnel smelled like death and old magic, a combination that made my nose wrinkle as we descended into darkness.

"I'm starting to think Auremar has a thing for underground chambers," I muttered, conjuring a ball of light to hover above my palm. "First the wine cellar, now this. What's wrong with a nice, well-ventilated throne room?"

Thorne's gravelly chuckle echoed off the stone walls. "Easier to hide the screams underground, my lady."

I sent the light ahead, illuminating rough-hewn walls that glistened with moisture. The stairs seemed to go on forever, spiraling down into the earth like a stone throat ready to swallow us whole.

Through my bond with Kazimir, I felt another surge of triumph, fierce and wild. Whatever he was doing up there, it was working. But there was also darkness threading through our connection, more than usual. I pushed the worry aside. One crisis at a time.

The tunnel curved sharply, and Thorne raised a fist. I extinguished my light, plunging us into darkness. Ahead, I could hear voices—guards, from the sound of it.

"—that chanting is just fuckin' eerie," one was saying.

"Shut up and do your job," another snapped. "We can't afford for the ritual to be interrupted, or Amaryska will have our heads."

I felt cold at the mention of Kaz's mother, wishing she were here for me to confront her. But the way the guards continued talking suggested she wasn't present. That would make our mission easier, but I wondered why she wasn't overseeing the ritual herself.

Then I felt a surge of anger and complex emotional pain from Kaz, and knew. She was on the battlefield. His distraction had drawn her away from the Chamber of Petals. I hoped he killed her even as I wished I was there to help him.

But the ritual had already started, and that left no time for further distraction. I touched Thorne's shoulder in a silent question. *How many?*

He held up four fingers. I nodded, shadows already gathering around my hands.

Thorne moved first, melting into the darkness. I heard a soft gurgle, then the sound of a body hitting stone. The second guard had just enough time to turn before my shadow blade took him in the throat.

We rounded the corner to find the other two guards already reaching for their weapons. Sebastian reacted faster than I'd ever seen him move, vines erupting from cracks in the floor to wrap around their legs. They toppled forward, and Thorne was on them before they could cry out.

"Getting good at this," I said to Sebastian as we stepped over the bodies.

He grimaced. "Not sure that's something to be proud of."

"It is when it keeps us alive."

We reached the bottom of the stairs, emerging into a narrow corridor lit by torches that burned with an unnatural blue flame. The air was thick with magic, making my skin prickle and the Heirloom grow warm against my scalp.

The chanting hit us before we even saw the chamber—dozens of voices speaking in perfect unison, the sound reverberating through stone and bone alike.

"That's a lot of mages," Sebastian whispered.

We crept forward until we could see into the Chamber of Petals, and for a moment, I forgot how to breathe.

The room was massive, carved from the rock in a perfect circle. Ancient murals depicting the First Hero's victory over the Shadow King covered the walls, though age and moisture had faded them to ghostly impressions. But it wasn't the architecture that stole my breath.

It was the scene before us.

At least sixty prisoners were arranged in concentric circles around a raised dais, each one bound and gagged, with glowing runes carved into the stone beneath them. Men, women, even children.

But worse were the mages. Two dozen of them stood in ritual positions, wearing masks of beaten gold that hid their faces. They chanted in perfect synchronization, their hands weaving complex patterns that left trails of purple light in the air. The magic they were building made my teeth ache.

And defending them were at least six battle mages in crimson robes, their hands already crackling with offensive spells. A dozen guards stood at strategic points, weapons drawn.

"Shit," I breathed.

Through my bond with Kazimir, I felt his rage spike suddenly, followed by something ancient stirring. The Heirloom pulsed hot.

"We need that portal open," I whispered to Thorne. "Now."

He pulled out the crystal Griffin had prepared. "I need thirty seconds and clear space."

"Sebastian, can you handle the guards and start freeing prisoners?"

He nodded, jaw set.

"Good. Because I'm about to make a lot of noise." I stood, shadows coiling around me. "When I move, you move."

I didn't wait for confirmation. I burst into the chamber like an avenging storm, heading straight for the battle mages.

The first one spun toward me, fire already forming between his hands. I didn't give him the chance to release it. My shadow blade took his hand off at the wrist, and his scream disrupted the perfect harmony of the chanting for just a moment.

"The Dark Lady!" someone shouted. "Stop her!"

The battle mages converged on me, and suddenly I was dodging fire, lightning, and shards of ice. I wove between the attacks, my shadows forming shields when I couldn't dodge. Behind me, I heard Sebastian's vines erupting from the floor, the shouts of guards being entangled.

A bolt of lightning grazed my shoulder, sending me spinning. I used the momentum to launch myself at another battle mage, driving both shadow blades through his chest. He fell, blood pooling beneath him.

The masked mages never stopped chanting. Their voices rose higher, more urgent, as if they were racing to complete the ritual before we could stop them.

Through our bond, I felt Kazimir's consciousness flicker, something vast and dark pressing against his mind. My worry spiked even higher, and I used it to drive me forward.

Two battle mages attacked in tandem, one high, one low. I jumped, using shadows to propel myself over their attacks, then came down hard on the first one's shoulders. The crack of his neck breaking was audible even over the chanting.

"Ready, my lady!" Thorne called.

"Sebastian, start moving them through!"

I could see him cutting prisoners free, Thorne helping guide them toward the shimmering doorway that led directly onto the deck of the *Sky Serpent*. But we'd only freed a handful. The ritual was building to crescendo. Any second, the killings would begin.

I needed to disrupt those masked mages.

Drawing on the Heirloom's power, I sent tendrils of shadow toward the nearest group of chanters. The shadows wrapped around their throats, cutting off their voices. Three of them fell, clawing at the darkness.

The remaining battle mages pressed their attack, forcing me back. One of them, a woman with silver hair, was particularly skilled. Her spells came faster than I could fully deflect, each one designed to kill.

"You cannot stop this," she hissed.

I snarled back something unintelligible because at the same time, I felt Kazimir's mind fracture. Something terrible was happening to him, and for the first time that day, I was truly afraid.

The Heirloom burned against my scalp, sending visions flashing through my mind—darkness spreading across a battlefield, shadows rising from the earth, and Kazimir at the center of it all, but not Kazimir. Something wearing his face.

The distraction nearly killed me. The silver-haired mage's spell caught me in the chest, sending me flying into the wall. I hit hard, tasting blood.

"Arabella!" Sebastian called out, starting toward me.

"No!" I forced out, pushing myself up. Every captive saved weakened the ritual.

The chanting reached a fever pitch. Purple light began to emanate from the runes beneath the prisoners, and I realized with horror that the ritual was about to complete.

That's when Auremar arrived.

He didn't enter through the doorway. He simply appeared, materializing from shadow itself in the center of the dais. And he was wrong. Oh so wrong.

His golden hair had streaks of black running through it, his skin had taken on a grayish pallor shot through with veins of darkness. But it was his eyes that made my blood run cold—they glowed with sickly yellow light, and when he smiled, his teeth had grown sharp.

"Lady Arabella," he said, his voice carrying harmonics that shouldn't exist in a human throat. "How good of you to join us. And Lord Sebastian, too. Perfect. Two more bloodlines for the harvest."

"The only thing being harvested here is your head from your shoulders," I spat, shadows coiling around me despite my exhaustion.

Auremar laughed, the sound echoing strangely. "Such fire. I can see why Blackrose wanted you. But you're too late. The ritual is nearly complete. In minutes, the prison will crack, and I will claim the Shadow King's power for myself."

"You're insane," Sebastian said, horror clear in his voice. "You can't control something like that!"

Auremar gestured, and Sebastian suddenly convulsed, purple energy crackling over his skin. "I've been feeding on his power for years, learning his secrets, his techniques. I am no longer merely human."

Sebastian dropped to one knee, face contorted in pain. Without thinking, I sent a wave of shadow toward Auremar. He deflected it with ease, but it forced him to release Sebastian.

"Continue the ritual!" Auremar commanded the masked mages. "I'll deal with our guests."

He moved faster than any human should be able to, suddenly right in front of me. His hand closed around my throat, lifting me off the ground. His corrupted face was inches from mine.

"You were always meant to be mine, Arabella. Your bloodline, your power—wasted on that upstart Blackrose."

"I was never meant to be anyone's," I croaked. My hands were wrapped around his, holding on. I forced golden magic into his fingers, but his grip only tightened. Every breath and word was a struggle. "I . . . chose Kaz. I choose him every day."

As stars swam through my vision, I let go of Auremar's hands and formed shadow blades. In the same motion, I drove those blades into his sides. He dropped me with a roar of pain, and I gasped for breath.

Through our bond, I felt Kazimir's desperate struggle. He was losing, drowning in memories and power that threatened to erase everything he was.

Everything we were.

"No!" The word tore from my throat, and I attacked Auremar with everything I had left.

Shadow and light merged in my assault. It struck Auremar in the chest, sending him crashing onto the dais.

"My lady!" Thorne called. "We've got half of them through!"

Only half. The masked mages were still chanting, the ritual still building. I had to choose—stop the ritual or save the prisoners.

Through our bond, I felt the moment Kazimir's defenses shattered completely.

Auremar rose, laughing despite the blood running from his mouth.

Through our bond, I felt Kazimir scream.

A cry of rage and pain and recognition? The Heirloom flared so hot I cried out, and for a moment I saw Kazimir on the battlefield above, shadow creatures rising from the earth.

"You did this," I said to Auremar, my voice deadly quiet. "You awakened something that should have stayed buried."

"I awakened power!" he roared. "Power that will be mine once the prison breaks!"

He attacked again, purple fire streaming from his hands. I deflected it, but barely. The fight with the battle mages had drained me, and Auremar was drawing on corrupted power I couldn't match.

But I had something he didn't.

Drawing on the Heirloom and the ley lines from the faraway God Spire, I shaped my magic into chains of shadow and light. They erupted from the floor around Auremar, binding his limbs.

He struggled against them, but they held.

The power flowing through me was intoxicating, addictive. I could feel the corrupted ley lines pulsing beneath my feet, could sense every thread of magic in the chamber. I felt like I could unravel it all with a thought.

"Sebastian! Thorne! Get everyone out now!"

The masked mages suddenly stopped chanting, turning toward me in perfect unison. As one, they reached up and removed their golden masks.

I recognized some of the faces—minor nobles, court mages, even members of the Hero's Guild. All of them had been part of Auremar's conspiracy.

“The king has fallen,” one of them said, voice hollow. “The ritual fails. The Shadow King rises anyway.”

They began to dissolve, their bodies crumbling to ash as whatever dark bargain they’d made claimed its price. Within seconds, nothing remained but golden masks clattering to the stone floor.

The walls shook violently, cracks spreading across the ancient murals. The ritual’s failure was destabilizing everything. Or something more was happening above.

“The last of them are through!” Sebastian called from the portal.

I looked at Auremar, still bound in my chains, then at the portal. The smart thing would be to leave him here, let the collapsing chamber deal with him.

But the Alchemist’s warning echoed in my mind. Auremar was tied to the prison somehow. His death might make things worse. But I didn’t dare bring him onto the *Sky Serpent*. His power was too unpredictable.

“Damn it,” I muttered, then knocked the king unconscious with a pulse of magic.

With a grunt of effort, I opened a small portal—not far, just outside the temple entrance—and unceremoniously shoved his limp body through. He landed in an ungraceful heap on the grass, still wrapped in my shadow chains.

“Someone else’s problem now,” I said. If he survived what was coming, we could retrieve him. If not . . . well, at least I’d tried.

“Arabella!” Sebastian shouted as larger chunks of ceiling began to fall.

“Go,” I told him. “Tell the Alchemist what happened. Tell them to begin the cleansing ritual immediately.”

“What about you?”

Through our bond, I felt Kazimir—or the thing wearing his face—turn its attention toward Sunspire Palace. Toward me. The ancient consciousness recognized the Heirloom, recognized the blood of its enemy.

It was coming.

“I have to save my husband,” I said, and threw myself through the portal, leaving Sebastian and Thorne to protect the prisoners as I ran to face whatever Kazimir had become.

I landed near the temple ruins to find hell itself had come to Solandris.

The sky was black with dark clouds and unnatural shadows. On the battlefield, chaos reigned. The Bone Behemoth was stomping madly through friend and foe alike. Shadow creatures tore through both armies with equal hunger, and at the center of it all—

My breath caught.

Darkness poured from Kazimir in waves, his eyes solid black, power beyond comprehension radiating from his form. When he smiled, it was the smile of something ancient and terrible finally free.

"Kaz," I whispered, and started running again.

I had to reach him. Had to pull him back from whatever edge he was balanced on.

Had to save him, even if it meant damning myself in the process.

Even if I wasn't sure there was anything left to save.

65

Say It Out Loud

(While Standing Over His Body)

Arabella

The sky above churned with darkness so thick it seemed to swallow light itself. I ran toward Kazimir, dodging the shadow creatures, the panicked soldiers, and even a swipe of the Bone Behemoth. Through our bond, I felt nothing but vast, ancient hunger. The man I loved was drowning.

"Kaz!" I screamed, but my voice was lost in the cacophony of battle.

A shadow creature lunged at me from the left. I barely had time to raise a shield before its claws raked across the magical barrier. The impact sent me stumbling, but I kept moving. Nothing mattered except reaching him.

Bodies littered the ground—Solandrian soldiers, our own forces, all equal prey to the darkness Kazimir had unleashed.

Another creature attacked, this one more solid than shadow. I drove a blade of light through its center, watching it dissolve with an inhuman shriek. The Heirloom burned against my scalp, feeding me power I'd never felt before. It was intoxicating, terrifying, and absolutely necessary.

Because the thing wearing Kazimir's face had finally noticed me.

He turned slowly, and my steps faltered. His eyes were pools of absolute darkness, no trace of the storm gray I loved. When he smiled, it was the smile of something that had waited centuries for this moment.

"The heir of Soriven," he said, but it wasn't Kazimir's voice. It carried the weight of ages, the echo of tombs. "How fitting that you should witness my triumph."

"Give him back," I demanded, closing the distance between us. "I know you're in there, Kaz. Fight him!"

The Shadow King laughed, a sound that made my bones ache. "He is nothing. A vessel worn by time. He served his purpose."

"That's fucking bullshit." I was close enough to touch him now, close enough to see the familiar scars on his hands, the way his hair fell across his forehead. "Kazimir Blackrose bows to no one, especially not some ancient parasite. And he's *mine*."

What's mine, stays mine.

I reached for him, but faster than thought, a hand closed around my throat for the second time in a few minutes.

The touch burned cold as frost spread from his fingers. I gasped, clawing at his grip, but it was like trying to move stone. My already bruised neck felt ready to break.

"Your ancestor bound me," the Shadow King hissed through Kazimir's lips. "Trapped me in darkness for centuries. It seems fitting that I should start my revenge with you."

Black spots danced at the edges of my vision. Through our bond, I searched desperately for any trace of Kazimir, any spark of the man who'd taught me to embrace my darkness, who'd held me through the return of my memories, who'd—

There. Buried deep beneath the ancient presence, I felt a flicker of recognition. A flash of horror at what his hands were doing.

"Kaz," I wheezed, pouring everything into that single word. "I know you're in there. You"—I clutched his wrist and squeezed, pouring my magic into him—"*promised*."

The grip tightened. The Shadow King's smile widened.

And then, because I might never get another chance, because if I was going to die it would be with truth on my lips. I had no air, no voice, but I formed the words anyway:

I love you.

The Shadow King froze. Even the battle seemed to pause.

For a heartbeat, then two, three, nothing moved. Then those bottomless eyes shifted. A crack in the darkness.

"Arabella?" It was barely a whisper, but it was Kazimir's voice. His real voice.

The ancient presence surged back, trying to reassert control. I saw the battle play out across his features—my husband fighting a god for control of his own body.

Fight him, Kaz. You're stronger than him. You've always been stronger.

His hand loosened slightly, trembling. The darkness in his eyes flickered between solid black and familiar gray.

"No," the Shadow King snarled, but there was fear in it now. "You are mine. You have always been mine!"

"Wrong," I rasped, pressing my hand over his where it gripped my throat. "He's mine. And I'm not letting go."

I poured my magic into him through that touch—not an attack, but the same sharing of power Kaz and I had done dozens of times before. Light and shadow twisted together, our magics recognizing each other, yearning to merge.

The Shadow King recoiled from the intimacy of it. This wasn't how power worked in his age. This was a give and take that he couldn't understand or counter.

Kazimir's entire body went rigid. His eyes rolled back, showing only white, and then he collapsed.

I barely caught him as he fell, lowering us both to the blood-soaked ground. His breathing was shallow, erratic, but he was breathing. The titanic struggle happening in his mind shuddered through me—Kazimir fighting to reclaim himself.

Distantly, I registered a halt to the Bone Behemoth's rampage and the armies suddenly more confused than ever as the shadow creatures faltered.

"That's it," I murmured, cradling his head in my lap. My throat was raw and barely formed sound. "Fight for me. Fight for us."

I began channeling power into him, the same way I'd done after battles, after nightmares, after that first terrifying fusion with the Heirloom. Our magics knew each other, trusted each other. Where the Shadow King brought only hunger and darkness, I offered something else.

A future. A choice. A reason to fight.

The humming thread that connected us, the one that had become as natural as breathing, was gone—snuffed out by the entity wearing his face. But then, a fierce, defiant heat bloomed from the birthday ring on my finger. Since the sentiment rings connected us through Kaz's magic, and his alone, they didn't depend on the Heirloom to keep us connected.

He was still in there, fighting.

A blast of red magic slammed into the ground near us, sending up a spray of earth and stone. I looked up to see Amaryska hovering above the battlefield, her gray robes billowing with power.

"Meddling whore!" she shouted. "I will kill you just like I did your mother."

My mother's face flashed before my eyes—those final moments I'd only recently recovered, her desperate attempt to protect me before Amaryska's magic tore through her. Grief twisted in my chest, sharp and immediate, but it was quickly consumed by something far more powerful.

Rage.

Pure, incandescent rage that made my earlier fury look like a candle flame. This bitch had murdered my mother.

My magic erupted outward in shadow entwined with golden light. The ground cracked beneath my feet. My vision tinged red at the edges, and I felt my lips pull back in a feral snarl.

She gestured, and the shadow creatures that had been dissipating suddenly solidified again, turning their attention to our position. To Kazimir's unconscious form.

I couldn't move him while he was fighting his internal battle. But I could protect him.

Standing over his body, I reached out with my magic. The Heirloom pulsed, and suddenly I was aware of everything—every thread of power on the battlefield, every creature, every spell.

Including the Bone Behemoth.

It stood motionless where it had stopped, awaiting commands. I'd never controlled something so massive or complex. But my blood was singing with the combined power of the Heirloom and Kazimir's dominion magic flowing through our bond.

What was the worst that could happen? I'd fail? We were already surrounded by enemies with my husband unconscious at my feet. Might as well go big.

I reached out with my will, touching the behemoth's consciousness. It was like trying to grasp smoke at first—the construct was attuned to Kazimir, not me. But our magics were intertwined now.

Move, I commanded.

The behemoth's massive skull turned toward us.

Protect him, I ordered, pouring more power into the command. *Protect us.*

The ground shook as the behemoth took its first step under my control. Then another. Bones the size of tree trunks swept aside shadow creatures like they were gnats. Its roar—if a creature without lungs could roar—sent our enemies scattering.

"Impossible," Amaryska hissed. "You shouldn't be able to—"

I cut her off by sending the behemoth's massive fist toward her. She barely dodged, her hover faltering.

"Fuck you!" I shouted hoarsely.

Shadow creatures converged on us from all sides. I split my focus—maintaining the flow of power to Kazimir, controlling the behemoth, and conjuring shields when enemies got too close.

Through our bond, I felt Kazimir's struggle intensifying. Flashes of memory that weren't mine flickered through my consciousness—ancient battles, civilizations rising and falling, the moment of binding beneath fields that would one day bloom with Golden Roses.

"Come back to me," I whispered, even as I sent the behemoth crashing through a wave of shadows. "I know you can hear me, Kaz. You're not him. You're not the Shadow King. You're the man who kidnapped me and then got upset when I didn't appreciate the accommodations. You're the one who taught me to make weapons from darkness and light. You're mine, and I'm not letting some ancient asshole take you away."

A shadow creature slipped past the behemoth's defense. I barely got a shield up in time, the impact driving me to one knee. The position left me vulnerable, and three more creatures rushed in.

That's when Nyx arrived.

My dragon materialized from nothing, fully phased between dimensions in a way I'd never seen her achieve before. One moment empty air, the next a fury of shimmering pink scales and purple fire. She grabbed the nearest shadow creature in her jaws and shook it like a dog with a toy.

"About time," I gasped, using her distraction to regain my footing.

Nyx's roar shook the entire battlefield. More importantly, spells that should have torn through her scales simply slid off, unable to find purchase on something that existed partially in another dimension. She was untouchable, unstoppable, and extremely pissed off.

Together, we held the line. The behemoth's massive fists crushed any enemy that got too close. Nyx danced between dimensions, striking and vanishing before retaliation could come. And I stood over Kazimir's body, channeling power and defiance in equal measure.

Our army, seeing the tide turn, rallied. Thorne's voice rose above the chaos, organizing our forces. I wondered where the *Sky Serpent* was and why he wasn't on it, but the captives weren't as important as this battle right now. Without the Shadow King's will directing them, the shadow creatures became less coordinated. More beast than soldier. Enemy forces were scattering, their will broken.

We were winning.

"My lady!" one of our soldiers called out, pointing.

Amaryska was fleeing too. I would find her eventually, but not now.

I looked down at Kazimir, still unconscious but breathing steadier. I felt the battle raging in his mind reach a crescendo. He was so close to breaking free, so close to coming back to me.

I dropped back to my knees beside him. "You've got this. Show that ancient bastard who really owns this body."

Nyx landed beside us, her wings unfurling to create a protective barrier. The behemoth stood sentinel on our other side. Around us, our forces were mopping up the last resistance, but I barely noticed.

All my attention was on Kazimir, on the flutter of his eyelids, the way his fingers twitched as if reaching for something.

Victory was within reach.

If only Kaz could defeat the Shadow King.

If only he could find his way back to me.

"I love you," I whispered again, pressing my forehead to his. "Do you hear me? I love you, and you don't get to leave me now. Not ever."

The Heirloom pulsed with warmth, and through our bond, I felt a shift. A wall crumbling. A chain breaking.

Soon. Soon he'd open those storm-gray eyes and smirk at me like the arrogant bastard he was. Soon we'd argue about whose fault this mess was while planning our next move.

Soon.

I just had to keep fighting for him the way he'd always fought for me.

Because that's what you did when you loved someone. You stood over their body on a battlefield and commanded an undead monstrosity while your dragon ate your enemies.

66

Reject Godhood

(for the Woman Who Set Your Shirt on Fire)

Kazimir

I was drowning in memories that were mine and not mine.

I stood in a throne room of volcanic glass, watching myself—no, the Shadow King—accept tribute from terrified subjects. I felt the satisfaction of their fear, the intoxication of absolute power.

This is what you were meant to be, the voice whispered, no longer separate from my thoughts but woven through them like poison through blood. *This is what we can be again.*

The scene shifted. Now I commanded armies that darkened the horizon, each soldier bound to my will through chains of shadow. Cities fell before me like wheat before the scythe. The world reshaped itself according to my desires, every ley line singing my name.

Everything you've ever wanted, the Shadow King purred. *The power to remake reality itself. No more games with petty nobles. No more bargaining with syndicates. Just pure, absolute dominion.*

It was beautiful. It was everything I'd dreamed of when I first claimed Skyspire, when I'd carved my father's empire from his cooling corpse. The

Western and Eastern Realms unified under my banner. Magic itself bending to my will. Even death would bow before me.

Another memory—binding the first bone runes into a follower's flesh, watching them scream as power rewrote their very existence. The technique my mother had used on me, but perfected. Refined. I could make anyone into a weapon. Everyone into an extension of my will.

Yes, the Shadow King breathed. *You understand. You've always understood. We are the same, you and I.*

The visions continued, each more intoxicating than the last. I saw myself standing where Auremar had fallen, but instead of his pathetic attempts to siphon power, I would crack the prison wide and absorb it all. Every drop of magic the First Hero had stolen would return to me. The ley lines would burn with my essence.

Accept what you are, the Shadow King urged. *Stop fighting your nature. You were born to rule, bred for conquest. Every scar on your body, every betrayal you've suffered—it all led to this moment.*

He was right. Gods help me, he was right. This was what I'd always wanted. What I'd spent years building toward. Why else had I searched for the Heirloom? Why else had I kidnapped—

Arabella.

Her name cut through the visions. For a moment, I saw her as the Shadow King did—another descendant of that bastard Soriven, key to my revenge, a tool to be used and discarded. First, her blood would open every lock. Then, her death would—

No.

The word came from somewhere deeper than thought. The visions flickered.

She betrays you, he hissed. *Even now she stands with your enemies, ready to bind you as her ancestor did. She is the heir of your ancient enemy. She will destroy us.*

Another vision—Arabella standing over my corpse, the Heirloom glowing on her brow as she commanded my own shadow warriors. Her face cold, beautiful, terrible. The Golden Roses blooming again from soil watered with my blood.

This is her destiny, the Shadow King insisted. *To complete what Soriven began. She has made you weak, clouded your judgment with sentiment. Without her, you would already rule. With her, you will fall.*

But even as he painted her as my doom, I remembered other things. Arabella in my training room, setting my shirt on fire and trying not to laugh. Wielding her power for the first time unfettered by her father's machinations. Her eyes practically glowing as she demanded I teach her dark magic. Arabella standing beside me against the Syndicate, her chin raised in defiance. Fighting the Hero's Guild and defending our home.

Arabella beneath me, around me, her magic twining with mine until I couldn't tell where I ended and she began.

Sentiment, the Shadow King spat. *Weakness. I offer you the world, and you're choosing chains.*

"They're not chains," I said, or thought I said. In this place between minds, speech and thought were the same. "They're—"

She's using you. His voice turned sly, knowing. *Think, boy. Why did she stay after you kidnapped her? Why did she bind herself to you? The heroic bloodline knows its purpose. She's been guiding you to this moment, to make you vulnerable. To make you love her so she could—*

"Shut up."

The Shadow King recoiled at the venom in my voice. The visions wavered.

"You want to know why she stayed?" I snarled. "Because she's magnificent. Because she saw what I was and chose it anyway. Because she's *mine*, and I'm hers, and you can't comprehend that, can you? You can't understand choosing connection over control."

Love is *control,* he sneered. *The ultimate dominion. She controls you even now, makes you weak, makes you—*

"Makes me more than you ever were." I was finding my footing now, remembering who I was beyond these ancient memories. Even as I begrudged the thought, I realized what Soriven had known all along. "You had power.

You had fear. You had everything except the one thing that mattered."

And what's that?

"Someone worth fighting for."

The words clanged through the mindscape like a badly shaped bell. The Shadow King's beautiful visions cracked, showing the truth beneath—empty halls, silent kingdoms, the loneliness of absolute power.

You would choose her over godhood?

"Every. Fucking. Time."

Fool!

The attack came without warning. Not visions now but pure force, the weight of centuries pressing down on my consciousness. I felt myself fragmenting, pieces of Kazimir Blackrose scattering like leaves in a storm.

But through it all, I heard her voice.

"I love you."

The Shadow King screamed. Those three words burned through his assault. Because he couldn't understand them. In all his centuries, he'd never felt what they meant, not even through the pieces of his consciousness that had lingered outside of the prison.

But I had. Gods help me, I had.

I thought of Arabella standing in my war room, covered in blood and defiant. I thought of her performing the Lifeweave Ritual, pouring her life into an artifact to save me. I thought of every moment she'd chosen to stay, chosen to fight beside me, chosen to see past the villain to the man.

"I love her," I said, and the words were armor and weapon both. "I love her more than power. More than conquest. More than your promises of godhood."

Then you deserve your fate! the Shadow King raged. *You could have been eternal! You could have—*

"I could have been you." I gathered every fragment of myself, every memory that was truly mine. "Alone. Hungry. Reduced to a parasite wearing other men's faces because you never learned the one truth that matters."

What truth?

"Power shared is power multiplied." *By fortyfold, in my case.* I smiled, feeling Arabella's magic flowing into me, light and shadow twisted together in a way the ancient being could never replicate. "She's not my weakness. She's my strength. And you? You're nothing but a ghost screaming in the dark."

The Shadow King lunged one final time, trying to overwhelm me through sheer force. But I wasn't fighting alone. I felt Arabella's presence, her absolute faith that I would find my way back to her. I felt our bond, stronger than any chain, warmer than any throne.

I wrapped that feeling around myself and pushed.

The Shadow King screamed. His presence, vast and ancient and terrible, compressed down to a single point of absolute rage. For a moment, I thought he might take me with him into whatever abyss awaited.

Then he was gone. Not destroyed—I could feel him somewhere deep, a whisper in the darkest corners of my mind. But no longer in control. No longer me.

I was Kazimir Blackrose. Dark Lord of Skyspire. Husband to Arabella.

And I was myself again.

Consciousness returned swiftly. Every nerve ending screamed as I reconnected with my body. I was lying on the hard ground. My throat felt raw, as if I'd been screaming. The smell of blood and ozone filled my nostrils.

But beneath it all, I felt her. Arabella's magic still flowing into me, her presence in our bond.

I forced my eyes open.

The first thing I saw was my Bone Behemoth towering above, its massive form swatting shadow creatures from the air like gnats. The second was Nyx, circling overhead with purple fire dripping from her jaws.

The third was Arabella.

She stood over me like an avenging angel, power crackling around her more intense than I'd ever seen before. The glamor had fallen from the Heirloom, and it blazed on her brow. But it was her eyes that caught me—fierce, protective, magnificent. She was commanding my behemoth. She was holding an entire battlefield at bay.

For me.

I tried to speak, to tell her I was back, but my body wouldn't cooperate. Everything felt distant, disconnected, as if I was puppeteering my own flesh from a great height.

But she must have felt the change, because she looked down. Our eyes met.

Relief crashed across her features, followed immediately by that smirk I loved so much.

"There you are," she said, sinking to her knees beside me. A shadow creature tried to flank us; she destroyed it without looking. "Don't worry, I've got you."

And despite everything—despite the battle raging around us, despite my body's refusal to move, despite the whisper of ancient hatred still echoing in my skull—I believed her.

She had me. She always had.

67

Defend What's Yours

(Better Known as "Oops")

Arabella

The tears wouldn't stop coming.

I knelt in the blood-soaked earth, cradling Kazimir's head in my lap once again as relief loosened all the tension in my body. He was back. The darkness that had consumed him, that ancient thing wearing his face—it was gone. I could feel him again through our bond, not the Shadow King's cold hunger but Kazimir's familiar presence, sharp and warm and *mine*.

"You absolute bastard," I whispered, running my fingers through his hair. "You scared me."

His lips twitched, trying for his trademark smirk but not quite managing it. His body was still recovering from whatever internal battle he'd fought. I kept one hand on his chest, feeling his heartbeat steady under my palm.

The Bone Behemoth swayed above us, awaiting new commands. Around us, the battlefield had gone eerily quiet. Solandrian forces were scattered or dead. Our own soldiers held their positions, uncertain what to do now that their Dark Lord lay unconscious.

"Can you stand?" I asked, already knowing the answer from the way his muscles trembled with each breath.

He made a sound that might have been a laugh. "Give me . . . a moment."

"Take all the time you need." I shifted so his head rested more comfortably against my thigh. "I've got things handled."

And I did. The Heirloom thrummed with power on my brow, connecting me to every shadow warrior on the field. The Bone Behemoth responded to my will as easily as my own limbs. Even Nyx circled overhead in perfect synchronization with my commands.

For the first time in my life, I felt truly powerful. Not just magically gifted or tactically clever, but *powerful* in the way Kazimir had always been. The kind of power that reshaped battlefields and—

Movement at the edge of my vision.

I turned, expecting another wave of soldiers or perhaps one of our generals approaching for orders. Instead, I saw two figures stumbling across the corpse-strewn ground.

Auremar.

The golden king looked like death walking. His robes were bloodied and torn, his crown askew, dark veins spreading across his skin. But he was *alive*, and the chains of light and shadow I'd wrapped around him were gone.

Behind him, barely visible in the smoke, a familiar figure in gray and red robes disappeared through a portal.

Amaryska.

That bitch had freed him but was now running.

"Kazimir Blackrose!" Auremar's voice cracked as he stumbled closer, mad eyes fixed on my husband's prone form. He raised his hands, corrupt magic gathering between his fingers—the Shadow King's power in a vessel that couldn't properly contain it.

Time slowed.

I saw Auremar's intent written in every line of his body. He wasn't trying to reclaim his kingdom or salvage his ritual. He just wanted Kazimir dead. A rival eliminated while vulnerable.

My hands moved without conscious thought.

The throwing knives Vex had given me for my birthday were perfectly balanced, their weight familiar from practice in the armory. I'd gotten quite good, actually. Good enough that I didn't need to aim, didn't need to think.

I just threw.

The first knife took Auremar through his left eye, punching through with enough force to crack the orbital bone. The second found his throat, severing his windpipe with a wet sound. He dropped to his knees, hands clutching at the blade in his neck. Blood poured between his fingers, mixing with the corruption already eating at his flesh.

"What's mine stays mine," I said.

Auremar's remaining eye found mine. I saw confusion there, maybe even betrayal. Had he really thought I'd let him hurt Kazimir? That I'd hesitate?

The king toppled sideways, convulsing once before going still.

For a heartbeat, nothing happened.

Then I felt a vibration through the ley lines, like a too-tight string suddenly released. Auremar had been connected to the Shadow King's prison, I realized with dawning horror. Not just siphoning power from the cocoon but tapping directly into it, a parasitic strand feeding on the web itself.

And when he died, that strand didn't dissolve.

It *snapped back.*

The recoil blasted me off my feet. Through the Heirloom, I felt the ley lines beneath Solandris shudder as Auremar's connection whipped back toward its source. Except he had no source—he'd had no First People heritage, no natural resonance with the ancient magic. He'd forced his way in through blood and sacrifice and stolen power.

When the strand snapped back, it had nowhere to go.

Except I was standing right there. Connected to the ley lines through my magic, wearing the Heirloom, my hybrid power still singing in the air from trying to save Kazimir.

The Heirloom blazed on my brow.

Not the golden warmth it usually produced but a terrifying cold fire of recognition. The artifact was made from the same essence as the web itself, First People magic wound around Shadow King power. It knew what was coming through the ley lines. It knew what was flowing toward us.

And it *opened*.

I tried to sever my connection, but it wouldn't close. The Lifeweave Ritual had bound it to me, and now that binding became a trap. The artifact held me in place as it transformed from crown to gateway, creating a doorway between the metaphysical plane of the ley lines and my physical body.

There you are, a voice whispered through the opening. Not spoken aloud but felt through every nerve. *I've been watching you, little hero.*

The Shadow King didn't crash into me. He flowed, deliberate and controlled, moving through the ley line network with the patience of something that had waited centuries for an opportunity. I could feel him in the web—not imprisoned anymore but distributed throughout it, his consciousness spread across the magical infrastructure of the world.

And now he was coming *here*. Into *me*.

Distantly, I registered Nyx's roar split the air as she desperately dove toward me.

"Arabella?"

Kazimir's voice, weak but urgent. He'd felt the change, was trying to sit up despite his body's protests.

I wanted to answer him. Wanted to tell him to run, to get away, to—

My vision fractured. I saw the battlefield as it was—corpses and mud and dying light. But I also saw it as it could be, *would* be, *should* be under his dominion. A kingdom of shadow where the sun never rose, where the very air obeyed his will, where—

Perfect, the voice purred as his consciousness flooded into every corner of my mind. *Strong enough to hold me. Clever enough to be useful. Bound to my fragment through that delicious little marriage bond. And the artifact remembers who it was made from. You're everything I needed, Arabella Blackrose.*

I distantly registered what was happening even as more images were forced into my mind. Of course. The Heirloom of Dominion had been forged from the Shadow King's own essence, bound by Soriven's magic. And now it was connecting with its source, opening pathways that should never have existed.

I felt myself changing. Not physically—not yet—but metaphysically. The Heirloom wasn't just channeling the Shadow King's power into me. It was transforming me into something new. An anchor point, like the Golden Roses had been, but mobile. Alive.

A doorway that walked and breathed and could act in the physical world while remaining connected to the ley lines.

The failing anchors beneath the blackened Golden Rose Fields shuddered as the magical balance shifted. I could sense them through the web—seven ancient points of power, weakened by centuries of misuse. They'd been designed to hold the Shadow King's prison stable, to keep the cocoon of ley lines tight around his essence.

But I was something different. Something he'd never had before.

A way to be in *both* places at once.

His consciousness settled into my body like a hand sliding into a glove. Not fighting my defenses but flowing through them, around them, *becoming* them. The Shadow King had been scattered for so long—main essence in the cocoon prison and then the ley lines, and what I saw as fragments lost across the centuries. Now he was consolidating, pulling himself together.

And I was the missing piece that made it all work.

My body stood without my permission. My hand released Kazimir's head, letting it fall back to the blood-soaked ground. When I looked down at him, I knew my eyes were no longer my own.

"Hello again, old friend," my voice said, though the words weren't mine. "Did you miss me?"

I tried to fight, to push back against the consciousness drowning mine, but the Shadow King had been planning this, *watching* me for weeks through the ley lines. He'd been waiting for his opportunity. Auremar's death had given it to him.

And then when the opening came, the Shadow King seized it.

My will shattered against his. Every mental barrier I threw up crumbled to dust.

Don't fight, he whispered inside my skull. *You're not being destroyed, little hero. You're being elevated. Together, we'll reshape this world into something glorious.*

The last thing I saw before the Shadow King's will enveloped mine was Kazimir's face—the moment of recognition, of horror, of understanding that in trying to save him, I'd doomed myself.

Then the ancient consciousness wrapped around mine like chains, and the woman called Arabella Blackrose drowned in shadow.

68

Win the Battle, Lose Your Wife

(Classic Villain Move)

Kazimir

"Hello again, old friend. Did you miss me?"

The words came from Arabella's mouth, but they weren't hers. The inflection was wrong, the cadence ancient, and her eyes—fuck, her eyes were pools of living darkness that reflected nothing.

Nyx landed hard beside us, her wings spread wide and trembling. The dragon's liquid silver eyes were wild with distress, and she let out a keening wail that made my bones ache. She stretched toward Arabella, then recoiled.

Arabella's head jerked to the side in an unnatural angle, then snapped back, her limbs moving in stuttering, puppetlike motions as if invisible strings controlled her body and she was fighting against them.

I tried to push myself up, but my body betrayed me. Every muscle screamed from the internal battle I'd just fought. The runes throbbed with a dull, persistent ache that made thinking difficult.

Our bond was silent. No warmth from the Heirloom's power, no electric current of connection between us—just a hollow void inside my chest where Arabella's presence should have been.

Nyx circled us in agitation, her claws scoring deep grooves in the earth. Every few seconds she'd dart forward, trying to reach Arabella, only to pull back with a distressed rumble.

"What's wrong?" Arabella's voice continued, though it was the Shadow King speaking. Her arm twitched before extending toward me in a grotesque parody of concern. "No witty retort? No villainous monologue? You've changed, Kazimir. Or should I say that you've forgotten who you really are."

My gaze flicked to Auremar's corpse. The golden king lay in a spreading pool of blood, Arabella's throwing knives still protruding from his eye and throat. Part of me—a dark, vicious part—wanted to crawl over there and mutilate the body. To tear it apart with my bare hands for what his death had caused.

But that impulse passed as quickly as it had come. Revenge on a corpse wouldn't save Arabella.

"Get out of her," I growled, finally managing to sit up properly. The battlefield spun around me, but I forced myself to focus.

The Shadow King laughed with Arabella's voice, and it was wrong, so fucking wrong. Her body convulsed with the laughter, shoulders jerking backward before her spine arched at an impossible angle. And I guessed that the Shadow King was purposefully allowing the strange movements to torture me. "But she basically invited me in when she killed that pathetic excuse for a king. All that power, all that hybrid magic singing through her veins. She's a much better vessel than you ever were."

I searched her face for any flicker of recognition, any hint of my wife beneath those hazel eyes. But where I'd built walls against the Shadow King's whispers over weeks of constant battle, she'd had no warning, no defenses—just raw power singing through her veins when that ancient darkness came calling.

The only inkling I had that she was still in there somewhere was the steady warmth from the ring on my finger.

I should have told her about the Shadow King. I'd kept it from her out of fear, but if I'd just shared my struggle with her, she might know how I'd been fighting him. To make matters worse, she'd told me she loved me. It's what saved me, and yet I hadn't said those words back as soon as I opened my eyes.

For the first time in my villainous life, I wanted to weep with regret.

"My lord!"

Thorne's voice cut through the fog in my head. My security chief emerged from the smoke, his armor splattered with blood and worse. His eyes went wide when he saw Arabella standing over me, the Heirloom visible and blazing with dark power on her brow.

"Stay back," I warned, but Thorne was already moving closer. His sense of loyalty wouldn't let him leave me on the ground.

"We've secured the captives," he reported, his voice carefully neutral as he assessed the situation. "Lord Sebastian is preparing for the cleansing ritual to reseal the prison, to free the ley lines from—"

"It won't work," I interrupted.

Thorne's scarred face hardened. "What do you mean?"

"Oh, do tell him," the Shadow King purred through Arabella's lips. Her head cocked to the side in that gesture that was so reminiscent of my mother it nearly made me sick. But of course the evil that had been living in my head would know that. "Explain how the Heirloom of Dominion is central to your plans. But you no longer have control of it."

I ignored the taunting, focusing on Thorne. "The Heirloom is bound to Arabella. Without her . . ."

Thorne's gaze tracked from the circlet blazing on Arabella's brow to my face, then back again. His jaw worked silently as the pieces clicked together—the artifact we'd hidden, the malevolent power radiating from her, the implications of what I'd just admitted. He didn't need to hear the whole story to know that something was very, very wrong with Lady Blackrose.

His hand clenched around his sword hilt until his knuckles went white. "Fuck."

The Shadow King tsked. "Is this the quality of minion you're keeping these days? Standards have really slipped since my time."

Rage boiled through me, hot and useless. I wanted to tear the Shadow King apart, to rip him from Arabella's body with my bare hands. But that wasn't how possession worked, if that's indeed what this was. Violence would only hurt her.

"There has to be a way," Thorne said, his hand moving to his sword before he caught himself. "Some way to extract—"

"There isn't," I said, cutting him off. Not through any method we had access to here, not with my magic depleted and Arabella's will being systematically crushed.

But there was one option. One person who might know something, anything, that could help. I forced myself to stand. My legs shook but sheer will kept me upright.

The Shadow King watched with Arabella's face, amused by my struggle. "I suppose I should thank you for the assist. All those years of building your mental defenses, keeping me locked away, only to tear them down for love. How beautifully ironic."

I stepped closer to Arabella—to the thing wearing her face. The Shadow King didn't retreat, confident in his control. Her arm reached for me in stuttering movements, fingers alternating between clawed and relaxed.

"I'm sorry," I whispered.

The Shadow King's laugh was cruel. "For which part? Letting me possess your wife? Failing to protect—"

I slammed my dominion magic into Arabella's mind.

Not gently. There was no time for finesse or room for careful extraction. I drove my power deep, past the Shadow King's presence, searching for Arabella's consciousness. When I found it—that flickering flame—I wrapped it in layers of magical sleep.

Nyx's roar split the air, but she didn't interfere.

The Shadow King snarled and Arabella's body convulsed as I forced her into unconsciousness. It wasn't elegant. It wasn't kind. But it might, *might*, preserve some part of her mind while I found a real solution.

Her body went limp. I caught her before she hit the ground, cradling her against my chest. The Heirloom still blazed on her brow, but at least the Shadow King couldn't use her voice anymore.

Nyx spread her wings, bristling with threat. But when I cradled Arabella closer, the dragon's aggression crumbled into a low, mournful crooning as she pressed her massive head against Arabella's unconscious form.

"My lord," Thorne began, "what are you—"

I didn't let him finish. Didn't explain, didn't leave instructions, didn't do any of the things a responsible leader should do. I just gathered Arabella in my arms, called on every scrap of power left in my bones, and tore open a portal.

The last thing I heard before stepping through was Thorne shouting my name and the whoosh of Nyx's wings as she took flight.

Then I was in Skyspire's dungeons, standing before a cell.

The Alchemist looked up from their meditation, those shifting eyes taking in everything—my haggard appearance, Arabella unconscious in my arms, the dark power radiating from the Heirloom.

"Well," they said, their shifting eyes softening with sympathy. "This is unfortunate."

69

Make the Worst Deal Ever

(But She's Worth It)

Kazimir

I kicked open the training room door. The sound echoed through the chamber like a thunderclap, but I didn't care about subtlety. Not with Arabella unconscious in my arms and the Shadow King wearing her like a second skin.

"Fascinating," the Alchemist murmured, following me inside. Their eyes swept across the space with obvious interest. "So this is where the great Dark Lord hones his craft. I'd always wondered."

"Save the tourism for later," I snapped, carrying Arabella to the center of the room. The protective circles etched into the stone floor glowed faintly at our approach, recognizing my magical signature.

The Alchemist circled the perimeter, running their fingers along the walls. "These wards are exquisite. Old Dominion design, if I'm not mistaken. Modified, of course, but the foundation work . . ." They paused, tilting their head. "You didn't create these. You found them."

"Does it matter?" I laid Arabella gently within the largest circle. Even unconscious, her face was wrong—too still, too empty of the spark that made her *her*.

"Everything matters when dealing with entities like the Shadow King." The Alchemist crouched beside us, studying the Heirloom that still blazed on Arabella's brow. "The question is whether they'll hold what's inside her now."

When I'd first found Skyspire, I'd assumed the original foundation and wards were built by some forgotten warlord. Now I knew better. The Shadow King's architecture, bone-deep and familiar in a way that made my skin crawl. But I shoved the thought aside.

I wanted to grab the Alchemist by their shifting robes and shake answers out of them. Instead, I forced myself to breathe. To think. Violence wouldn't save Arabella any more than panic would.

"Can you extract him?"

The Alchemist's laugh was slightly maniacal. "Extract the Shadow King? One does not simply pluck out an entity that predates the ley lines themselves. He's not some parasite to be removed with a clever potion."

"Then what do you suggest?"

"Wake her."

I stared at them. "Are you insane? The Shadow King—"

"Is already in control whether she's conscious or not," the Alchemist interrupted. "At least awake, we might learn something useful. Unless you prefer to sit here and watch her sleep while he consolidates his hold on her mind?"

They had a point. I hated it, but they had a point.

I placed my hand on Arabella's forehead, feeling the unnatural cold radiating from her skin. My dominion magic was depleted, but I had enough left for this. I found the layers of sleep I'd wrapped around her consciousness and carefully began peeling them away.

Her eyes snapped open.

"Well, well." The voice was Arabella's, but the inflection was ancient, amused. "The would-be tyrant and his pet Weaver. How delightful."

I kept my hand on her forehead, ready to force her back under if necessary. "Let her go."

The Shadow King sat up. Arabella's body moved in a stilted fashion, as if the entity inside her wasn't quite sure how everything worked. There was a tremor in her left hand, and her right shoulder hitched half a second too late. But I didn't think the Shadow King wasn't an accomplished puppet master.

No. Arabella was fighting.

"But we're having such fun together," he said. "Her mind is fascinating—all those delicious memories of you. The things you've done to this body . . ." He ran Arabella's hands down her sides in a gesture that made my stomach turn. "She's quite fond of your particular brand of brutality."

"Don't." The word came out as a growl.

"Don't what? Touch what's mine?" The Shadow King stood, and the protective circle flared brighter, trying to contain him. He glanced down at it with mild interest. "Ah, the old containment matrices. I remember when these were first designed. Cute, but hardly sufficient."

The Alchemist stepped forward, and something in their bearing changed. For a moment, their form seemed to flicker, showing something vast and incomprehensible beneath the mundane exterior. For a moment, I wondered if the Alchemist was more than they appeared. But then the flickering disappeared, leaving me to question if I'd simply been seeing a trick of their robes.

"Weaver," the Shadow King acknowledged with Arabella's lips. Another twitch in Arabella's left eye. "I wondered when one of you would crawl out of hiding. Still playing keeper of the ley lines, I see."

"Someone has to clean up the messes," the Alchemist replied mildly. "You've made quite a spectacular one this time."

"Have I?" The Shadow King examined Arabella's hands as if seeing them for the first time. He flexed her fingers, testing each joint like he was learning the controls. Her pinky finger spasmed. Definitely fighting. "I'd say young Auremar deserves most of the credit. All that blood, all those sacrifices, weakening my prison year by year. I merely took advantage of an opportunity."

"An opportunity that required possessing an innocent woman," I said.

The Shadow King laughed, and it was wrong, so wrong coming from Arabella's throat. "Your wife is many things, Kazimir, but innocent isn't one of them. She has blood on her hands, doesn't she? Ask her. Oh wait—you can't. Because she's rather preoccupied fighting a losing battle for control of her own mind."

Her left hand clenched suddenly, fingernails digging into her palm. Blood welled.

I took a step forward, but the Alchemist caught my arm. "He's baiting you."

"Of course I am," the Shadow King agreed too cheerfully. Arabella's natural sarcasm had a different cadence. "It's so easy with you. All that love, all that desperate need to protect her. It's almost touching, but it makes me want to gag."

"What do you want?" I forced the words out through gritted teeth.

The Shadow King tilted Arabella's head, considering. "What does any prisoner want after centuries of confinement? Freedom, of course. Complete, unrestricted freedom."

"The prison—"

"Is failing anyway." Her right shoulder jerked—Arabella again. The Shadow King smoothed the motion into a dismissive gesture, but I saw it. "Thanks to Auremar's meddling, the anchors are already breaking down. It's only a matter of time before I'm free regardless. But time is something your dear wife doesn't have much of."

I felt ice form in my chest. "Explain."

"Possession is such a violent process." He was turning in a circle now, using Arabella's body like a marionette. Every third step came a fraction too late—her resistance throwing off his rhythm. He stilled. "Two consciousnesses battling for control of one body. Eventually, something has to give. Usually, it's the weaker mind that shatters. Would you like to know how long Arabella has? Hours? Days? It's hard to say. She's surprisingly strong, but strength only delays the inevitable."

"You're lying."

He smiled with Arabella's face, stretching her lips into the wide, painted smile of a jester. The muscles in her cheeks spasmed violently—not a twitch this time, but a full revolt against the expression. "Feel free to wait and find out. Watch as she slowly loses herself, piece by piece. Watch as I consume everything that makes her who she is."

I held back my anger, but shadows still writhed in the corners of the room. "Or?"

"Or you could release me properly. Break the remaining anchors, open my prison completely. Once I'm free, I'll have no need for this vessel. I'll leave her body and reclaim my true form. Everyone wins."

The Alchemist's grip on my arm tightened. "You can't seriously be considering—"

"The fuck I can't!" I shook them off, my eyes never leaving Arabella's possessed form as I said, "Tell me another way, Alchemist. Tell me how to save her without releasing him."

Silence.

"That's what I thought." I took a deep breath, feeling the weight of the decision settling on my shoulders. The world with Arabella versus the world without her. Not even a contest. "Fine. Tell me how to open the prison."

"Kazimir, no," the Alchemist protested. "You don't understand what you're agreeing to. The Shadow King free in the world again—"

"I understand perfectly." The words came out flat, final. My gaze was still fixed on the evil that was shining through Arabella's eyes. "I don't care if the world burns. I don't care if he drowns the realm in darkness. *None of it matters without her.*"

The Shadow King clapped Arabella's hands together. The movement was violent enough that I heard her knuckles crack. "Oh, how romantic! The Dark Lord choosing love over the fate of the world. It's almost poetic."

"Tell me how," I repeated.

"Patience," the Shadow King chided. "First, we need to discuss terms. After all, I am nothing if not a creature of contracts and agreements. It's only civilized."

Creatures of contract had rules. Rules could be exploited. I forced myself to nod. "What terms?"

“Simple ones. You release me from my prison—completely and without tricks. In exchange, I leave your wife’s body intact and relatively unharmed. Everyone gets what they want.”

“Define ‘relatively unharmed.’”

“Well, possession does leave its marks.” Her left eye twitched violently. “She might have a few lingering effects. Nothing fatal, I assure you. Probably.”

The Alchemist made a sound of disgust. “You’re making a deal with the architect of suffering itself. This won’t end well.”

“It’s already not ending well,” I barked. “At least this way, she lives.”

“If he keeps his word.”

“I always keep my word,” the Shadow King said, and for a moment, genuine offense flickered across Arabella’s features. “I’m not some common villain who breaks bargains for sport. I have standards.”

Her fingers clenched again, drawing more blood.

I looked at her face, cataloging every micro-expression. The way her jaw clenched between words. The rapid eye movements that didn’t match the Shadow King’s speech patterns. The slight tremor in her left hand that came in waves—fighting to surface, being pushed down, fighting again.

She was still in there. Still fighting. Still mine.

For a moment—just a moment—I thought I saw a bit of *her* flicker in those hazel eyes. A plea. A warning. Or maybe just my own desperate hope.

“I’ll do it,” I said.

The Alchemist sighed, a sound like wind through empty halls. “Then we’re all damned.”

“We were damned the moment Auremar started his rituals,” I corrected. “This is just choosing which hell we burn in.”

The Shadow King smiled with Arabella’s lips, but her eyes—I took a shuddering breath.

Her eyes screamed a warning I was already choosing to ignore.

70

Confess Your Feelings
(Then Put Her in a Coma)

Kazimir

The weight of what I'd just agreed to crashed over me. Free the Shadow King. Save Arabella. Doom the world.

Simple math, really.

"Excellent choice," the Shadow King said through Arabella's lips, but her left eye twitched violently mid-word. "Now, shall we discuss the specifics? The anchors are already weakened, but—"

"Shut the fuck up." I needed to think. How exactly does one free an ancient entity from a prison designed by the First Hero? Destroy the Heirloom? No—we'd need it to fight him later. Besides, the damned thing was still fused to Arabella's head, pulsing with that sickening dark light.

The Alchemist watched me with disapproval radiating from every inch of their body. "You're actually considering this madness."

"I'm not considering anything. I've decided." I studied Arabella's possessed form, watching the micro-rebellions of her body against the Shadow King's control. A finger spasm here, a shoulder jerk there. She was still fighting. "But I need somewhere secure to keep her while I figure out the logistics."

"Keep me?" The Shadow King laughed, and Arabella's throat convulsed mid-sound. "I'm not a pet to be kenneled, boy."

Boy. The condescension in that single word made my teeth grind. But I had bigger problems than my pride.

Where could I put her that would be secure enough? The dungeons were out of the question—the dark magic there might strengthen the Shadow King and hinder Arabella. The war room was too central and not secure enough. Our private chambers held too many memories, too many ways for the Shadow King to twist our intimacy into weapons.

Then it hit me. The one place in Skyspire even I rarely ventured. The structure that had resisted every attempt at renovation when I first conquered the citadel, where workers experienced strange accidents and tools broke inexplicably. I'd tested whether that resistance could be useful and discovered it was exceptional at containing dangerous magical items. I'd repurposed it as a vault for things too dangerous to destroy—cursed artifacts, failed experiments, unstable magical items.

Now I thought I understood why it had such potent containment properties.

"What keep?" The Shadow King's interest sharpened, but Arabella's fingers clenched involuntarily. Still fighting. Still mine.

I ignored him. I had a choice to make. Put her back to sleep, silence the Shadow King, and remove her ability to resist? Or keep her conscious, let her continue fighting even though it meant enduring his mockery and manipulation?

I'd tried to strip her of her agency once before, at the Gilded Gallows. The memory of her fury, her sense of betrayal, still burned. If she could speak now—really speak, not through the Shadow King's puppet strings—I knew what she'd say.

Let me fight, you controlling bastard.

"You stay awake," I decided. "Fight."

"How touching," the Shadow King drawled, but there was something calculating in the way he tilted Arabella's head. "Though I wonder if you're keeping me conscious for her benefit or because you enjoy hearing her voice, even corrupted as it is."

I ignored him, turning to the Alchemist. "Will you help me free him?"

"Absolutely not." Their response was immediate, vehement. "I've spent my life maintaining the balance of the ley lines. I won't be party to unleashing that kind of chaos."

I resisted the urge to threaten them. The Alchemist would rather die a horrible death or live in misery than go against their purpose. "Then will you at least help contain him now?"

The Alchemist was quiet for a long moment. "That I can do. Someone needs to minimize the damage of your romantic stupidity."

Good enough. I wrapped shadows around Arabella's wrists and ankles—not tight enough to hurt, but firm enough to restrict movement. She—the Shadow King—tested the bonds with an amused expression.

"Kinky," he commented. "She has such interesting memories of your shadow play. Would you like me to share the details?"

I pressed my hand to Arabella's shoulder and tore open a portal. The destination was clear in my mind: the one place in Skyspire that might contain what she'd become.

We emerged on a small island separated from the main citadel. The Old Keep rose before us, half-crumbled walls and narrow windows giving it the appearance of an ancient ruin. I'd deliberately kept it looking abandoned—better that people thought it forgotten than knew what I stored here.

The Shadow King turned Arabella's head to survey the structure. Her neck moved in stuttering jerks—still fighting.

A shimmer of pink-tinged shadow rippled through the air, and Nyx materialized in a graceless tumble of wings and claws. She collapsed onto the stone floor, sides heaving, her scales flickering between obsidian and rose like a dying ember. The dragon's liquid silver eyes rolled wildly before fixing on Arabella's bound form.

Nyx's keening cry pierced the air. She dragged herself forward, wings trembling from the strain of phasing across half the Western Realms.

"Guard the keep," I commanded. "I'll take care of Arabella."

The dragon's head swayed, a low rumble building in her chest. For a moment, I thought she might try to tear through me to reach Arabella. Instead, Nyx spread her wings and launched herself upward. Stone crumbled beneath her claws as she found purchase on the keep's highest remaining wall, positioning herself where her silver gaze could track every movement below.

I set Arabella down just inside the dusty entrance, checking the shadow bonds. After unlocking the heavy wards at the door, I summoned Vex through the scrying crystal in my pocket.

Old Keep. Now. Bring Griffin.

Her response was immediate. *On our way.*

It would take a few minutes. Griffin would need to create a lightning bridge to get here. I always portaled when I came, and no one else was ever allowed. Arabella had never even been here.

While we waited, I studied the chamber with fresh eyes. The exterior might look like a ruin, but inside, the ancient magic remained potent. The space was functional if austere, and the floor was already marked with containment circles I'd discovered when I first claimed Skyspire—circles I'd been using to store my most dangerous acquisitions. They'd proved more effective than any wards I could create myself.

Now I knew why. They were his work. The Shadow King's original containment circles, and the layers were obviously his previous attempts to retake the citadel.

The walls bore scorch marks from experiments gone wrong, and if I looked closely, I could see where blood had been scrubbed from the stones but never quite erased.

Arabella's left hand spasmed so hard her fingernails drew more blood from her palm.

The door opened before I could respond. Vex stepped through first, her expression shifting subtly as she took in the scene. Griffin followed, his gangly frame hunched with curiosity that died the moment he saw Arabella. "My lord?"

"The Shadow King," I said. "He's possessing Arabella."

Griffin's eyes widened. "But . . . how?"

"There's something I haven't told either of you," I said, flatly. "I am the Shadow King. Or rather, I'm his vessel. I've carried a fragment of his consciousness inside me since birth. When the Heirloom activated, I had a vision of what I was, of him. . . ." My failure to protect Arabella made my voice crack. "I defeated him, but when Arabella killed Auremar to protect me on the battlefield, the Shadow King transferred to Arabella through our connection, possibly because the Heirloom is bound to her. Possibly because of what Auremar was doing with the magic."

Griffin staggered back a step, his face draining of color. "That's—that's not possible. You can't be—" His eyes darted between me and Arabella, scientific mind clearly struggling to reconcile this revelation with everything he thought he knew.

Vex had gone utterly still. I'd seen her in countless situations, facing every crisis Skyspire could offer, but I'd never seen that look on her face. What struck me most wasn't just the fear in her eyes—it was the lack of surprise at my revelation. As if she'd already known, or at least suspected. But how? When I myself had only learned the truth weeks ago?

"The Old Keep," she said slowly. Her gaze swept the chamber—the containment circles, the cursed artifacts stored in shadowed alcoves, the ancient magic thrumming through the stones. Then her eyes found Arabella's possessed form, and genuine anguish crossed her features. "You brought us to the Old Keep."

"Desperate times," I said.

"Vex!" The Shadow King's delight was nauseating coming from Arabella's throat. "Oh, this is delicious. Should I tell him what you really are? The truth might break his little mind."

Vex's face twisted into a snarl. "You know nothing about me."

"Don't I?" The Shadow King leaned forward as much as the shadow bonds allowed. "Mirror, mirror, on the wall . . . who's the most fragmented of them all?"

Griffin looked between them, confused and frightened. "What's he talking about?"

"Nothing," Vex said. "He's trying to divide us."

The Shadow King turned those dark-pooled eyes on Griffin. "Speaking of divisions, how's that weather manipulation experiment going? Still having nightmares about the Frost incident? All those frozen corpses because you couldn't control the thermal dynamics?"

Griffin went white. "That was—how do you—"

"I know everything she knows," the Shadow King said simply. "Every memory, every secret, every shameful little moment she's witnessed or been told. For instance, Kazimir, would you like to know what she really thinks when you—"

"Enough." I cut him off, but not before catching the malicious glint in those possessed eyes. "Griffin, I need a containment matrix. The strongest you can create. Layer it with everything you have."

Griffin nodded rapidly, eager for something to focus on besides the Shadow King's taunts. "Yes, yes, I can do that. The foundation's already here, I just need to—" He was already pulling components from his robes, hands shaking slightly.

"Vex," I continued, "recall the *Sky Serpent*. Get everyone back to Skyspire immediately."

She hesitated. "And the ritual?"

"Won't work without her." I gestured to Arabella. "She needs to help channel it through the Heirloom, and as you can see . . ."

"She's indisposed," the Shadow King finished cheerfully. "Though I do love what she's done with her hair. The blood really brings out her eyes."

Vex's jaw tightened, but she nodded. "I'll handle it."

As she left, Griffin worked frantically, chalking symbols around Arabella while muttering calculations under his breath. The Alchemist observed from the corner, occasionally offering corrections that made Griffin's eyes widen.

The Shadow King settled onto the floor like someone relaxing into a favorite chair. "Don't you want to know how I did it?"

I ignored him and fed more power into the shadows binding him.

"Oh, don't be petulant. I'm about to give you the history lesson you so desperately need." He settled Arabella's body more comfortably on the floor, despite the restraints. "Let me tell you a story about prisons, and fragments, and the slow, agonizing death of a god."

"You're no god," I said flatly.

The Shadow King's smile was terrible on Arabella's face. "Perhaps not anymore. But I was close enough that it took the First Hero's blood magic and the power of the First People themselves to bind me in that prison made from the ley lines themselves."

He paused, and Arabella's fingers twitched. "Soriven, that half-breed bastard, made a mistake. Actually, several mistakes, though he never knew about the first one. When he imprisoned me, the trauma of that binding—the agony of being torn from the physical world and wrapped in pure magical essence—it shattered me. Seven pieces broke away during those first moments, fragments of my main consciousness that slipped through the forming weave before it could fully seal. Each one carried pieces of me—my drives, my instincts, my hunger for dominion. Fragments of memory, magical affinity, strategic brilliance. Not enough to be truly conscious, but enough to recognize power when they found it. They couldn't escape entirely, of course. They were caught in the spaces between, neither free nor imprisoned."

My runes began to ache, but I folded my arms over my chest. "And you're telling me this because why? You've been lonely?"

Arabella's body hitched in a weird chuckle. "The story's very interesting, actually. I've only just myself pieced everything together since flowing into the ley lines. Before that, I didn't even know about the fragments, only a vague sense of being incomplete."

Griffin's chalk snapped. He fumbled for another piece, not looking up from his work.

"For centuries, those fragments drifted in that liminal space. But prisons decay. Magic weakens. And as your precious heroic bloodlines grew corrupt, siphoning power from my prison for their own petty ambitions, the ley lines around me began to fray." The Shadow King's voice took on a quality of satisfaction. "One strand at a time, the web unraveled. And each time a strand broke, a fragment slipped through."

"You had no control over it," the Alchemist observed quietly.

"None whatsoever," the Shadow King agreed. "Pure cosmic accident. The fragments sought hosts on their own, drawn to certain conditions. Children with natural darkness, ambition, magical talent. The fragment would integrate during those early, formative years. The child would grow up thinking those impulses—that hunger for power, that strategic brilliance, that need to dominate—were entirely their own."

Griffin's hands stilled for a moment before resuming their work with renewed urgency.

"Each one showed such promise," the Shadow King continued. "Before being killed by heroes, by their own recklessness, by pure chance. And each time a fragment died, that piece of me died with it." The Shadow King hurried on, as if even he sensed his time was running out. "And then along came you, Kazimir. Born under the darkest star in three centuries, to a mother who understood power and a father who embodied brutality. You were perfect."

"But I didn't awaken," I said slowly. "Not naturally."

"No," he agreed. "You might have lived your entire life with that fragment dormant, just another brutal warlord in a world full of them. But then dear Amaryska carved those runes into your bones." He gestured at my scarred arms with Arabella's hand. "She thought she was creating a weapon. She had no idea she was creating a resonance. Those runes vibrated at the same frequency as my prison, because all dominion magic originates with me. Every spell she carved was like striking a tuning fork against my cage."

The aching in my bones intensified. Everything made horrible sense.

Griffin made a strangled sound. "The runes . . . unlocked the fragment."

"Broke the lock keeping it dormant," the Shadow King confirmed. "Created a channel between you and my prison. Weak at first, barely a whisper. But it grew stronger as you grew stronger." He paused, and when he spoke again, there was something almost wistful in his tone. "I've been with you your entire life, Kazimir. Every strategic insight that came to you like breathing. Every inexplicable draw toward conquest. Your obsession with Skyspire, with Solandris. That wasn't just ambition. That was me, recognizing what was mine."

"And the Heirloom?" I asked. If the Shadow King was offering information, I'd let him talk.

"Ah yes, Soriven's great mistake." The Shadow King's glee was palpable. "He forged it from my own essence, bound with his First People magic. It was meant to control the ley lines, to maintain my prison. But he couldn't bear to destroy it afterward—the power was too intoxicating. And when you and your lovely wife activated it with your combined magics, it touched the ley lines directly. My fragment woke and recognized what it was."

The containment circle Griffin was working on flared suddenly, making him yelp and scramble backward.

I forced myself to speak. "Why didn't you take control before today?"

"Because you were too well defended." Arabella's shoulders lifted in a shrug, but her left arm jerked violently mid-motion. "All that emotional detachment, that cynical armor you built around yourself. You thought it made you strong, made you safe from betrayal. But it also made you a fortress I couldn't breach. Your refusal to feel, to connect, to love—it kept me locked away as surely as Soriven's prison kept my body bound."

The Alchemist's expression shifted to something like understanding. "Lady Blackrose."

"Arabella Blackrose," the Shadow King said. "My fragment watched her for weeks after the activation. Watched every wall you'd built start to crumble. All those feelings you'd suppressed for decades came flooding back. And with them came cracks in your mental fortress. Cracks I could slip through. And then, when Auremar's meddling allowed me to flow into the ley lines, I saw what the fragment was seeing. That's when I truly woke. Not just the fragment in you, but my main consciousness in the prison. For the first time in seventeen centuries, I was aware. I could see through the fragment's eyes, feel through your senses. And I could sense both you and your wife through the Heirloom."

My hands clenched into fists.

"But I wasn't truly free." His frustration bled through Arabella's voice. "I can inhabit the ley lines, yes. Move through them, influence them. But I can't leave them. I can't create a physical form from pure magical energy. I'm a consciousness without a body."

He smiled with Arabella's cracked lips. "I felt her power every time she touched the Heirloom. This beautiful, powerful creature, bonded to an artifact forged from my own essence. Heroic bloodline strong enough to contain me. Magic potent enough to channel me. And so deliciously connected to you—my last fragment, my final piece. She was perfect, and since you kept rejecting me, I kept looking for an opportunity."

Arabella's body convulsed, fighting against his words. I was breathing hard, and needed a moment to control myself. Griffin was working faster now, his movements frantic as he layered symbol over symbol.

Arabella's lips curved into a cruel smile. "Did you know she's known the truth since that day you activated the Heirloom? She's been carrying that knowledge ever since, watching you hide it from her, wondering if you'd ever trust her enough to tell her."

My blood went cold. "You're lying."

"Ask yourself—why do you think she's been so careful around you lately?" The Shadow King laughed. "She saw everything in that vision, Kazimir. She knows exactly what monster sleeps inside you. Watching. Waiting. Planning her escape routes in case you lost control."

"No." The word came out flat, certain. Arabella didn't plan escape routes. She planned attacks.

"No?" The Shadow King's eyebrows rose. "You think she stayed out of love? She stayed because—"

"She stayed because she was waiting for me to trust her." The realization hit like a physical blow. Arabella had known. Had chosen to bear that weight rather than add to mine.

"And here you were," the Shadow King continued, "trying so desperately to keep the truth from her. All that guilt, all that secrecy, and she already knew."

My throat tightened. She hadn't told me because she couldn't know if the knowledge would make my fight harder. If knowing the Shadow King was inside me would give him more power over me. So she'd stayed silent, watching, waiting to see which would help me more—truth or ignorance.

The Shadow King's lie had revealed more than he'd intended—he could mimic love's cruelty but not its sacrifices. For all his centuries of existence, he still didn't understand that love wasn't about watching for weakness.

But I was beginning to understand.

Love was about guarding someone's blind spots while they fought their demons.

"As I was saying," he continued. "On the battlefield, I showed you what we could be together. The power we could wield. But you chose her. Again." Arabella's face twisted into something between admiration and disgust. "You actually rejected godhood for a woman."

"So you took her instead," I growled.

"I took the next best option." The Shadow King's smile was predatory. "Auremar's death created the perfect opening. He'd made himself into a strand of the prison, you see, a parasite feeding on it. When he died, that connection snapped back like a broken strand. And there she was, standing at the nexus with the Heirloom fused to her head. A perfect anchor point. A perfect vessel. I simply . . . flowed through. Through the Heirloom, into her. Not a possession from outside, but an extension from within the very network of magic itself." He spread Arabella's arms wide. "I'm reaching through the ley lines, using her as my anchor in physical reality. My main consciousness remains distributed through the network, but now I can act. I can touch. I can destroy."

"She's stronger than you expected, though," the Alchemist observed.

"Frustratingly so," the Shadow King admitted. "I thought I could simply overwhelm her consciousness, but her will is remarkable. She keeps pushing back. It's almost annoying." Arabella's entire body convulsed again before he regained control. "But it doesn't matter. Time is on my side. Eventually, she'll exhaust herself and break."

"No, she won't," I said. "Because I'm going to free you."

The Shadow King looked down at their bonds and laughed. "Then why bother with containment?"

The Alchemist snorted. "I suppose if we just let you wander Skyspire, you'll sip tea harmlessly in front of a fire while we work?"

"I suppose I could behave. But then again, Arabella has such interesting muscle memory. Her hands know exactly how to hold a blade, where to strike for maximum damage. And so many people here trust her. They'd never see it coming until it was far too late."

Arabella's right hand jerked hard enough to crack her wrist against the floor.

"She didn't like that—thinking about what I might do with her body. All the people she loves that I could hurt. You, obviously. But also that charming Lord Sebastian. Such a gentle soul. I bet he'd trust her right until the moment I slid a knife between his ribs."

"Griffin," I said, my voice flat and emotionless, "how much longer?"

"Almost done, my lord. Just need to—"

"Ignoring me won't make me go away." The Shadow King smiled with Arabella's lips, which had cracked. "And once I'm loose in the world, who knows what mischief I might cause? Though I suppose you don't care about that. The great Dark Lord, choosing love over the fate of millions. It's pathetically human."

Griffin's array suddenly blazed to life, lines of power connecting in a complex geometric pattern. "Done," he gasped.

The Shadow King glanced down at the glowing symbols with mild interest. "Impressive work. Won't hold me, of course, but impressive nonetheless."

"It'll hold you long enough," I said.

The Shadow King's expression shifted to something unreadable. Then Arabella's body went rigid, every muscle locking as she fought against his control with renewed fury. For a moment—just a moment—I saw her break through. Her eyes cleared, focused on mine with terrified urgency.

"Kaz—" she started.

Then the Shadow King slammed back into control, but not before Arabella's right hand tore free from its shadow binding with sheer, furious will.

It happened in seconds. A bolt of raw magic erupted from her palm—that amazing hybrid of golden light and shadow that marked her unique power. It struck the wall near Griffin's head. The explosion shook the entire keep. Stone shattered, dust and debris raining down as a section of ceiling groaned ominously. Griffin yelped and scrambled backward as chunks of masonry crashed where he'd been kneeling.

When the dust settled, we all stared at the devastation. A hole the size of a merchant's cart had been blown in the wall, revealing the swirling clouds beyond.

"Oops," the Shadow King said mildly.

But I understood what had just happened with perfect, horrible clarity. Arabella's will was a weapon, yes. But the Shadow King could hijack it, turn her own power against us. She wasn't just possessed—she was a tactical liability of world-ending proportions.

The Alchemist sighed heavily. "Do you understand now? Every moment she stays conscious, she's a danger. To herself, to us, to everyone."

I looked at Arabella—really looked at her. Past the Shadow King's mockery, past the possessed puppet show, to the faint, terrified flicker I could still sense underneath. My wife. My equal. My everything.

And I made the hardest decision of my life.

I knelt before her, ignoring the Shadow King's smirk. My hands cupped her face, and I spoke not to the entity wearing her skin, but to the woman trapped beneath.

"You're a fighter, Arabella. The fiercest I have ever known." My thumbs traced her cheekbones, feeling the unnatural cold of her skin. "But I won't ask you to fight a battle that will tear your mind to shreds. I will not watch you break."

The Shadow King opened Arabella's mouth to speak, but I wasn't done.

"I will end this," I promised, my voice rough with everything I couldn't say. "I will find a way to save you. But I need you to trust me now, even when I'm taking away your choice. Again."

Her gaze shifted to hold mine, and for just a heartbeat, I saw her. Really saw her. And in that moment, I gave her the words I should have said on the battlefield.

"I love you."

Before the Shadow King could twist those words into mockery, I pressed my palms to Arabella's temples and released everything I had left.

Not a jolt this time. Not a crude slam of power. This was deeper, more precise—a wave of dominion magic crafted to induce not just sleep, but complete stasis. A magical coma so profound that nothing could reach her, not even dreams.

The Shadow King snarled as I wrapped layer after layer of compulsion around Arabella's consciousness. He fought me, but I had one advantage: This was my magic, my specialty. And I was fighting for her.

For a moment, I felt resistance—not from the Shadow King, but from Arabella herself. She was the only person who'd ever been able to resist my compulsion magic, and even now her will pushed back against mine. Not in panic or anger, but with deliberate, measured force. In that resistance, I understood what she'd been trying to tell me. She didn't want to be used as a weapon against those she loved. Not against me, not against Griffin, not against anyone at Skyspire.

Then, like a tide retreating from shore, her resistance faded. She understood this was the only way. Her surrender was a choice—her last act of agency before the Shadow King could strip it away completely. I felt her acceptance like a brush of fingers against my mind, and knew with absolute certainty that beneath her sarcasm and fire, Arabella loved all of us at Skyspire, whether she would ever admit it aloud or not.

Arabella's body went limp. I caught her before she could fall, cradling her against my chest. The malevolent light in the Heirloom dimmed to a sullen glow, like banked coals waiting to reignite. The Shadow King was still there—I could feel his presence—but he was trapped now. Blind, deaf, and mute.

She looked peaceful, finally. Like she was just sleeping.

The Alchemist exhaled slowly. “That was the correct choice. Painful, but correct.”

I sat holding Arabella. The lover in me wanted to stay here, to hold her until I found a solution. But that man was a luxury I couldn’t afford right now.

The Dark Lord had work to do.

I turned to Vex, who had returned during the chaos. “You’re in command of Skyspire. Full authority in my absence.”

Her eyes widened slightly. “Your absence?”

“Thorne guards this tower,” I continued, ignoring her question. “No one enters except the Alchemist. No one. If anyone other than the Alchemist tries, Thorne has permission to kill first and ask questions never.”

Vex put a hand on my arm. “Where are you going?”

I looked down at Arabella’s sleeping face, then back at my most trusted advisors. The answer was obvious, really. There was only one person who might know how to free the Shadow King. One person who had studied his prison, who had worked with Auremar to weaken it.

One person I should have hunted down and killed years ago.

“I’m going to find my mother.”

71

Face Your Nightmare

(to Doom the World)

Kazimir

The portal snapped shut behind me, leaving me standing before the gates of Sunspire Palace. Smoke rose from the eastern horizon where my army still fought—or more likely, stood around wondering where the hell their commander had gone. Once more, I'd left them just as victory was ours, but I couldn't bring myself to care about it just now.

I recalled my shadow warriors with a thought that sent spikes of pain through my skull. One hundred tendrils of darkness raced back across the battlefield, abandoning their posts. The effort nearly dropped me to my knees. Without the Heirloom's amplification, without Arabella's power feeding into mine, I was just a man with some impressive bone carvings and a talent for dramatic entrances.

Well. That and a fragment of an ancient evil rattling around in my subconscious. But I had locked him away on the battlefield. My internal battle with him was won, and now Arabella was paying the price.

The palace gates hung open, one twisted off its hinges. Bodies littered the courtyard—guards, mages, a few of my own soldiers who'd pushed too far.

The Golden Roses that had once climbed every wall were dead, their metallic petals scattered like coins across blood-soaked stone.

Movement caught my eye—a figure emerging from behind an overturned fountain. I had a shadow blade forming before I recognized the ridiculous amount of flowers sprouting from cracks in the paving stones.

"Sebastian?" I let the blade dissolve. "What the hell are you doing here?"

He straightened, brushing marble dust from his formerly pristine jacket. Now it was torn at the shoulder, splattered with blood. But he didn't look injured that I could see. "I could ask you the same question, Lord Blackrose. Aren't you supposed to be commanding an army?"

"Aren't you supposed to be on the *Sky Serpent* heading back to Skyspire?"

He stepped carefully around a particularly aggressive patch of thorny vines that had erupted near the fountain. "When you recalled the ship, I . . . disembarked."

"You jumped off a flying ship."

"I created a rather impressive cushion of moss." He gestured vaguely at the palace. "I couldn't leave without checking on something."

I didn't have time for whatever sentimental mission had drawn him back here. But I needed to find Amaryska, and Sebastian knew this palace better than I did.

"I'm looking for someone," I said. "A sorceress. Gray robes with red stitching, dark hair, about this tall." I held my hand at shoulder height. "Probably wherever Auremar kept his mages."

Sebastian's expression shifted, flowers wilting slightly around his feet. "Why would you—"

"It's important." I started toward the palace entrance. "Can you show me where the royal mages work or not?"

He fell into step beside me, careful not to slip on the blood-slicked stones. "I know where the arcanum is. Arabella and I used to sneak in there when we were children."

"Lead the way," I said.

The palace interior was chaos. Servants ran past carrying everything from silver candlesticks to rolled tapestries, looting what they could before order returned. Most fled at the sight of me—the Dark Lord himself, walking their halls like he owned them. Which, technically, I might. Did killing a king automatically transfer property ownership? I'd have to ask Vex about the legal precedents.

Nah. My army was at the doorstep. I'd say that was an automatic transfer of power via conquering.

Sebastian navigated the corridors with easy familiarity, occasionally pointing out hidden passages or shortcuts. "Arabella knew all the secret ways," he said as we climbed a servants' stair. "She had this game where she'd hide and see how long it took the guards to find her. Once she stayed hidden for three days. They thought she'd been kidnapped."

We'd entered a long hall covered with paintings on the wall—all portraits, hundreds of them. "Sounds like her."

"The king and her father were furious. That was a year before—" Sebastian stopped abruptly, staring at one of the portraits near the end. A young woman with golden hair and kind eyes, holding a book of pressed flowers. "That's her mother, Lady Iona Evenfall."

I'd never seen a portrait of Arabella's mother. The resemblance was striking, though Arabella had a sharpness her mother lacked.

"She was kind to me," Sebastian said quietly. "When my grandmother died, she'd invite me to tea and let me talk about her. She never told me to stop crying or 'be strong' like everyone else did. My own mother was ill by that time, so—"

"Amaryska killed her." The words came out flat, matter-of-fact. Easier to say it like that—like a tactical briefing—than to think about what it meant. That I was about to ask my mother for help. That I needed her. "The woman I'm looking for. She's the one who murdered Arabella's mother."

Sebastian turned to stare at me. "And you're seeking her out? Why?"

Because she might know how to free the Shadow King. Because I'd promised to save Arabella, even if it meant dooming everyone else. Because I was a selfish bastard who'd choose his wife over the world every single time.

"It's important," I repeated.

He studied my face, and I saw the moment he understood something was terribly wrong. Not the specifics—he couldn't know about the Shadow King possessing Arabella—but he recognized the desperation I was trying to hide.

"This way," he said simply, and continued down the corridor.

The Royal Arcanum occupied an entire wing of the palace, though most of it appeared abandoned. Doors hung open on empty workshops and libraries, their contents either looted or carried away by their fleeing owners. Only one section showed signs of recent use—a suite of rooms at the far end, where the smell of bitter herbs and old blood grew stronger.

"Wait here," I told Sebastian.

"I'm coming with you."

"No." I put enough command in my voice to make lesser men soil themselves. Sebastian was not a lesser man, much as I'd wanted him to be. "This is between me and her."

Sebastian crossed his arms, and a ring of protective thorns sprouted around his feet. "With all due respect, Lord Blackrose, you look like you're about to collapse. Whatever you're planning, you might need help."

"I don't need—"

"Arabella," he interrupted, looking worried. "That's what this is about, isn't it? Something's happened to her."

Damn him and his emotional intelligence. I missed the days when my problems could be solved by threatening to feed people to void beasts.

"Stay here," I growled, and pushed through the door before he could argue further.

The workshop beyond was exactly what I'd expected from someone who'd carved runes into her own child's bones. Tables covered in anatomical diagrams, jars of preserved organs, and tools that belonged in a torture chamber more than a mage's laboratory. And at the center of it all, sitting calmly at a desk as if she'd been expecting me, was my mother.

The sight of Amaryska in a workshop should have triggered more memories and feelings of pain, but I only had one reason for being here. I had no strategies. I wasn't here to kill her.

I was here to beg.

"Kazimir." She didn't look up from the book she was reading. "You always did have dramatic timing."

"You were waiting for me."

"I hoped you would come." She closed the book carefully, marking her place with a ribbon. When she finally looked at me, I saw no fear in her eyes. Only a strange sort of satisfaction. "You look terrible. The burden of power, I suppose. Or is it the burden of love?"

"Don't." My voice held an edge I couldn't quite control. My hands clenched into fists, and I felt the runes in my bones pulse with heat—not the Shadow King's influence, just my own barely contained rage. Hours ago, she'd reduced me to a child counting footsteps. Now I needed her help. The humiliation burned almost as hot as the fury. "You don't get to talk about her. Not after what you did."

"What I did?" She stood, moving with the same coiled grace I remembered from childhood. "You mean freeing her from a life of heartache? Her mother was weak, clinging to fairy tales about redemption and hope. Arabella was better off remembering her mother as she was when the girl was younger, not as being the reason she died."

"You murdered her."

"I did what was necessary." She circled me slowly, studying me like I was one of her experiments. "Just as I opened a door for you when I carved those runes into your bones. Pain is such an excellent teacher, don't you think?"

"Is that what you told yourself when you sold me to a demon?" The words came easier each time I said them aloud.

She laughed—actually laughed. "Oh, my darling boy. You still don't understand, do you? I didn't sell you to just any demon. I sold you to Malphas, Prince of Ambition. I knew you'd either die or become something magnificent. And look at you now—the Dark Lord himself, Terror of the Western Realms."

"I killed him," I said flatly. "Tore him apart with his own shadows and used his bones to reinforce my rune carvings."

"I know." Her smile was proud, fond, even. "I've been following your career with great interest. Every conquest, every cruelty, every step closer to your true destiny. Though I'll admit, I didn't understand the full scope of it until recently."

The thought of her cataloging my conquests like a proud parent made my skin crawl. But I didn't have time for disgust. I needed answers, and she was the only one who had them.

She moved to a shelf, pulling down a black leather journal. "After you killed your father, I went looking for answers. How had my son become so powerful? What was the source of this incredible dominion magic that couldn't be explained by runes? That's when I found them."

"Them?"

"The Cult of the Eternal Shadow." She opened the journal, showing me pages covered in symbols I recognized from my own bones. "They've been preparing for the Shadow King's return for centuries. Keeping the old knowledge alive, maintaining the weaknesses in his prison, waiting for the right vessel to be born."

My blood ran cold. "You knew. You knew what I was."

"I suspected." She traced one of the symbols with her finger. "The signs were all there—born under a black star, natural affinity for dominion magic, the way shadows bent toward you even as an infant. But I couldn't be certain until you survived Malphas. Only someone carrying the Shadow King's essence could have consumed a demon prince and lived. It explained everything about you."

"So you joined Auremar." The pieces were falling into place, forming a picture I didn't want to see. "Not to help him, but to help the Shadow King."

"Auremar was a fool," she said dismissively. "He thought he could control that kind of power, bind it to his will with blood and roses. But I knew better. The Shadow King cannot be controlled, only unleashed. So yes, I helped weaken the prison. I guided the rituals, selected the sacrifices, all to hasten his return."

"Why?" The word came out raw, desperate. "What could you possibly gain from releasing that monster?"

Her eyes hardened. "Your father took everything from me. My freedom, my dignity, my soul. I traded it all for power—power I used to create you, to give you the tools for revenge. But it wasn't enough. Watching you kill him wasn't enough." She closed the journal with a snap. "I want to watch the world that allowed him to exist burn. I want to see kingdoms fall and heroes weep. I want chaos and darkness and the complete unmaking of everything that let a man like him thrive."

"You're insane."

The words came out flat, but underneath was something more complicated—a twisted understanding I didn't want to acknowledge. She'd been violated, broken, remade into something monstrous. And in response, she'd made me into a weapon. We were both products of violence, both shaped by men who took what they wanted without asking. The difference was, I'd chosen to build something with my rage. She'd chosen to burn everything down.

She set the journal aside. "And now you're here, which means something has gone wrong with your little wife. Let me guess—the Shadow King found a new vessel?"

I didn't answer, but she read it in my face.

A cold light shined in her eyes. "The First Hero's descendant, possessed by the very evil her bloodline was meant to contain. The irony is delicious."

"Tell me how to free him." The words tasted like ash. "What will it take to release the Shadow King from his prison?"

Her eyebrows rose. "Well, this is an unexpected development. I assumed you'd come here to kill me in some misguided attempt to save your bride."

"Can you do it or not?"

Asking her for anything made me want to vomit. Every instinct screamed to wrap shadows around her throat and squeeze until she stopped breathing.

But Arabella was running out of time, and my pride—my rage, my need for revenge—none of it mattered compared to saving her. So I swallowed the bile and waited for her answer.

Amaryska studied me for a long moment, then smiled. It was the same smile she'd worn when she'd heated the carving tools all those years ago. "Of course I can. The prison is already crumbling—Auremar's ham-fisted attempts saw to that. One more sacrifice should do it. One more drop of heroic blood, willingly given, and the seals will shatter completely."

"One more—*willingly* given?"

"Oh yes. That's the trick, isn't it? The First Hero built his prison on sacrifice and will. It can only be unmade the same way. But you and I both know certain types of sacrifices are more potent with willing victims. Auremar never asked any of his sacrifices, and it took a great deal more of them than it should have since we didn't have your wife. What I could have done with a few misguided but *willing* nobles or their brats—well." She sniffed and moved close enough that I could smell the bitter herbs and old blood that clung to her robes. "Lucky for you, I know exactly where to find a willing sacrifice."

"Where?"

She looked past me, toward the door. "Why don't you ask him yourself?"

I turned to find Sebastian standing in the doorway, his face pale. He'd heard everything. Of course he'd disobeyed a direct order. He was infected with a sense of righteousness that I'd forgotten the last few days, with all the plans and emergencies.

"Sebastian," I growled.

"I'll do it," he said simply.

72

Doom the World

(in the Name of True Love, Obviously)

Kazimir

The Chamber of Petals stank of death and failed magic.

Golden masks littered the floor like discarded party favors. Piles of ash dotted the floor around the dais. The chamber walls, partially covered in murals depicting the First Hero's triumph, were cracked and bleeding some kind of black ichor. I hadn't had a chance to ask Arabella or Sebastian what had happened down here. I only knew they had completed their mission and rescued the captives.

Sebastian had followed us down, his face showing little emotion, for once, but flowers sprouted from cracks in the stone steps, then immediately withered and died. I wasn't going to stop him if it would save Arabella. Even if she hated me for it later.

But then I'd have to . . . owe him? Fucking heroes.

I stepped over a battle mage's corpse, his face frozen in an expression of shock. Six of them scattered across the floor, throats slit or hearts pierced by shadow blades. Arabella's work, judging by the precision. My wife didn't do things by halves. The regular guards had fared no better—at least a dozen bodies cooling in their own blood, but some of them were killed with vines and thorns rather than blades.

Sebastian had taken my advice to heart, apparently.

"The door is directly beneath us." Amaryska moved to the center of the chamber, where a raised dais still showed scorch marks from whatever Auremar had attempted. "Not a physical door, you understand. The prison exists in its own realm, a pocket of reality the First Hero carved out specifically to contain the Shadow King. This chamber is simply the closest point of contact."

I felt it the moment I stepped onto the dais—a thrumming in my bones that had nothing to do with my carved runes. Something vast and ancient pressed against the boundaries of reality, testing for weaknesses. The part of me that had once entertained the Shadow King stirred, recognizing its missing piece.

No. I slammed mental walls around that recognition. I'd beaten him back once. I wouldn't let him in again.

"How much blood?" I asked, voice flat.

Amaryska produced a silver bowl from her robes. "Not much. A few drops should suffice, given how weakened the seals already are. The important part is that it's freely given."

Sebastian stepped forward without hesitation. "Let's get this over with."

"So eager to die for love," Amaryska mused, producing a ritual blade. "How disappointingly heroic."

"I'm not dying for love." Sebastian rolled up his sleeve, exposing his forearm, and I noticed he wasn't rhyming. "I'm giving so Arabella can live. It's a simple enough choice."

She grabbed his wrist, positioning the blade over his vein. "Even if the fate of the world hangs in the balance?"

Sebastian's perfect face hardened, and I recognized something in his expression. Something that only recently I'd allowed myself to experience—*love.* A muscle flexed in my jaw. *Sebastian loved my wife,* and I wasn't sure how platonic his feelings ran. For a heartbeat—or three, maybe—I thought about telling Amaryska to drain him dry. But I kept my peace. There'd be time to assess the depths of his *feelings* later.

The cut was quick. Blood welled up, dropping into the silver bowl with soft metallic pings. One drop. Two. Three.

"That should be—" Sebastian started.

Amaryska's grip tightened. The blade cut deeper.

"Mother," I warned. I may have just contemplated Sebastian's death, but if anyone was going to kill him eventually, it would be me.

"Just ensuring we have enough." More blood flowed, far more than necessary. Sebastian's face went pale. "The prison threads are quite stubborn, you know. Better to be thorough."

"That's enough."

She ignored me, watching Sebastian's blood fill the bowl with avid fascination. His knees buckled. Still she held on, blade pressing deeper while she whispered a spell. His blood poured out of the wound.

I grabbed her wrist, shadow-wrapped fingers crushing until she released him. Sebastian collapsed, clutching his arm. Blood seeped between his fingers.

"You said a few drops."

"I said it *should* suffice." She pulled free of my grip, cradling the bowl like a precious child. "But why take chances? The boy volunteered. I simply ensured his sacrifice would count."

I knelt beside Sebastian, stripping out of my leather jerkin and tearing a strip from my shirt to bind his wound. His breathing was shallow, skin clammy. He'd lost too much blood, too fast. The wound's edges had already turned black. Poison.

Rage flooded through me, but I shoved it down. Deal with her after. First, free the Shadow King. Then make her pay.

"Can you stand?"

He tried, legs shaking. "I'm . . . I'm fine. Do the ritual."

He wasn't fine. He was dying. But I had no healing magic to give, and Arabella—Arabella needed this to work.

I helped him to the edge of the dais, propping him against a fallen pillar. "Stay conscious. I'll get you help after."

"Sure." His laugh was weak. "After you free an ancient evil. No pressure."

Amaryska had already begun setting up the ritual circle, using the conspirators' ash to draw symbols I recognized from the journal she'd shown me. The silver bowl sat at the center, Sebastian's blood dark and still.

"Stand there." She pointed to a position across from her. "When I begin the incantation, channel your dominion magic into the circle. The blood will do the rest."

I took my position, feeling the weight of what I was about to do. Somewhere above us, my army was probably mopping up the last resistance.

"Ready?" Amaryska asked.

I nodded.

She began to chant in a language that predated human speech, each word scraping against reality, the words she had beaten into me as a child. The blood in the bowl began to bubble. I fed magic into the circle, watching the ash symbols flare with sickly light.

The chamber groaned. Dust rained from the ceiling as something fundamental shifted. The black ichor on the walls flowed faster, forming patterns that mimicked the symbols.

Yes, a voice whispered. Not in my head—in the air itself. *Yes, finally, YES.*

The Shadow King's presence slammed into me once again. Not trying to possess me—he had a better vessel now—but recognizing me, acknowledging what I'd been. What I'd rejected.

You could have been a god, the voice said. *We could have remade the world together.*

I gritted my teeth and pushed more magic into the circle. I didn't want to remake the world. I just wanted my wife back.

The bowl cracked. Sebastian's blood rose in a crimson spiral, suspended in midair. Amaryska's chanting grew louder. The chamber shook violently.

Then, between one heartbeat and the next, something gave way.

The dais split down the middle. Not just the stone—reality itself tore open, revealing a yawning void that swallowed light and sound and sanity. From that void came laughter, ancient and terrible and free.

"He rises!" Amaryska threw her arms wide, tears streaming down her face. "The Shadow King rises! The world will burn, and from its ashes—"

The ceiling chose that moment to collapse.

A chunk of stone above the dais broke free, plummeting toward the tear in reality. Amaryska looked up, still smiling, still welcoming her precious chaos.

The stone crushed her instantly.

I was already moving, grabbing Sebastian and hauling him away from the widening fissure. More of the ceiling fell, the entire chamber coming apart as something vast and terrible pulled itself through the gap between worlds.

No time to process my mother's death. No time to consider what I'd just unleashed. I wrapped shadows around Sebastian and myself, tearing open a portal with the last of my strength.

The Chamber of Petals disappeared in a rush of falling stone and eldritch laughter. We tumbled through darkness, my portal unstable, uncontrolled. I held tight to Sebastian, feeling his blood soak through my shirt, and focused on the only destination that mattered.

Skyspire. Arabella.

I just needed to know if my wife was herself again.

73

Make Heartfelt Declarations

(Now That the Apocalypse Is Underway)

Kazimir

The portal spat us out in the Old Keep like the universe itself was rejecting what I'd done.

I hit the floor hard, Sebastian's weight dragging me down. He collapsed beside me, clutching his bandaged arm. His breathing was shallow, and his skin had taken on a waxy, gray pallor. Blood had soaked through the makeshift binding, spreading across my torn shirt. The metallic scent filled my nostrils, mixing with the dust and old magic of the tower.

But I barely noticed any of it.

Because I could feel Arabella again.

She floated in the center of Griffin's containment matrix, suspended in a web of golden light. Her eyes were closed, body perfectly still in the magical stasis I'd forced on her. But the connection between us, that bond forged by blood and magic and love, sang with life. It thrummed with her fierce presence—no foreign consciousness, no ancient evil wearing her skin. Just Arabella. Exhausted, battered by her internal battle, but *her*.

The Shadow King was gone.

I scrambled to my feet, nearly tripping over the Alchemist's unconscious form. They'd fallen asleep propped in a chair, a half-empty vial of something glowing faintly blue clutched in their hand. Probably exhausted from maintaining whatever wards they'd added to Griffin's work.

I crossed to the matrix in three strides and began dismantling Griffin's handiwork. The enchanter had outdone himself—layers upon layers of protective circles, stabilization runes, and power dampeners. But I knew every symbol Griffin had ever learned, every configuration he favored. The matrix unraveled at my touch, dissolving into motes of fading light.

Arabella hung suspended in midair for a heartbeat before I caught her, her body limp but warm in my arms as we sank to the floor. The Heirloom still crowned her head, but its energy was clean now—pure without a trace of corruption. Just as it had been before Auremar's death had torn everything apart.

My hands trembled as I pressed them to her temples, feeding dominion magic into the stasis I'd created. Layer by layer, I peeled back the compulsions, the forced sleep, the magical chains I'd wrapped around her mind.

Come back to me.

Arabella gasped, her whole body convulsing as consciousness returned. Her eyelids fluttered. Once. Twice. Then those hazel eyes opened, focused, and locked onto mine.

"Kaz?" Her voice was hoarse, weak, but utterly *her*.

"You're safe." The relief that crashed through me was almost painful. "He's gone. The Shadow King is—"

A cough from behind made me turn. Sebastian had managed to prop himself against the wall, but fresh blood was spreading across the stones beneath him. Too much blood. Far too much.

"Shit." I started to rise, but Arabella's hand caught my wrist.

"What happened to him?" She struggled to sit up, gaze sharpening as she took in Sebastian's condition. "Why is he—"

"Amaryska." I helped Arabella to her feet, steadying her when she swayed. "She poisoned the blade she used on him for the blood sacrifice. I was so focused on—I didn't check for her tricks."

Arabella stumbled over, dropping to her knees beside Sebastian. I tore open his shirtsleeve. The wound was worse than I'd thought—not just deep, but already showing signs of corruption. Black veins spider-webbed from the cut, creeping up Sebastian's arm.

"Tell me what happened," she said without looking up. Golden light sputtered from her palms, then flared as she pulled power through the Heirloom. Her magic poured into him, battling the spreading poison. Sebastian's back arched, a strangled sound escaping his throat. Flowers burst from every crack in the floor—morning glories, their blue petals unfurling in defiance of the chamber's darkness. "I remember the Shadow King wanting freedom, but after you put me in that stasis—"

"I found Amaryska at Sunspire." The words tasted bitter. "She knew about the Shadow King for a long time. She'd been working with Auremar to weaken the prison, but for her own reasons. She wanted chaos, destruction, the unmaking of the world that had wronged her."

Arabella's hands stilled for just a moment before resuming their work. "And Sebastian?"

"He volunteered." The black veins retreated slowly, grudgingly. I watched the color slowly return to Sebastian's face as Arabella's magic neutralized the poison. "The ritual to free the Shadow King required willing heroic blood. He didn't even hesitate."

"Of course he didn't." Something in her voice made me look closer. Not surprise—resignation. As if she'd expected nothing less from him. "He never could stand by when someone needed help."

"He loves you." The words escaped before I could stop them.

Arabella's hands paused again, longer this time. "Kaz—"

"I'm not blind. Or stupid. Usually." I crouched beside her, close enough to feel the warmth of her magic. "He sacrificed himself to save you. That's not something you do for casual friendship."

She finally looked at me. "That's not—he doesn't—"

"He does."

She was quiet for a long moment, studying Sebastian's unconscious face.

I watched emotions flicker across her features—surprise, confusion, a touch of sadness.

"I don't love him," she said finally. The wound began to close, flesh knitting together under her touch. "Not like that. He's my friend, my childhood companion, but I—" She shook her head and looked up at me, her gaze sweeping over my face and then down to the blood on my torn shirt.

"You're alive," Sebastian said.

Arabella and I looked down.

His eyes were open, looking at Arabella. "You're you."

"Thanks to you, apparently." She sealed the cut with a final pulse of magic, then leaned back on her heels. "That was incredibly stupid, Sebastian. Noble, but stupid."

He managed a weak smile, then noticed me watching. "The ritual worked, I take it?"

"Spectacularly." I helped him sit up against the wall. "The Shadow King is free, Amaryska is dead—crushed by the ceiling when the chamber collapsed—and we're all probably doomed."

"Ah." Sebastian closed his eyes again. "At least Arabella's safe."

There it was again—that note in his voice that spoke of feelings deeper than friendship. But before I could address it, Arabella's expression shifted, the full weight of our situation crashing down on her.

"The Shadow King is free." She said it slowly, as if testing the words. "Actually free. Not bound, not contained, just . . . out there."

"Yes."

She finally looked at me. Really looked at me, those hazel eyes seeing straight through to the guilty, desperate core of me. "And you didn't hesitate."

I met her gaze steadily. "Not for a second."

I braced for anger. For recriminations about the choice I'd made, the evil I'd unleashed to save her. Instead, she met my eyes with perfect understanding.

"I would have done the same thing," she said quietly.

A pleasant ache began in my chest, and I sank to my knees on the stone floor. "Arabella—"

"No, listen." She moved closer, leaving Sebastian propped against the wall. Morning glories were still blooming around him, which probably meant he was fine. "I know what you did. I know what it cost. If our positions were reversed, I'd have torn the world apart to free you. I'd have made any bargain, freed any evil, burned any bridge. So I can't—I *won't* blame you for doing the same."

My throat tightened. We were terrible people, selfish and shortsighted and willing to damn everyone else for each other. I guess that's what made us villains.

"There's more." I ran a hand through my sweaty hair. "Something I should have told you weeks ago."

She waited.

"The Shadow King—he's not just some external threat. He's been inside me all along. A piece of him, anyway. I'm his vessel, his reincarnation. Whatever you want to call it, I've been carrying his consciousness since birth."

The Shadow King had already told me Arabella knew, but it was my responsibility to tell her myself. I still half expected anger at another secret kept.

Instead, she smiled. It was tired and sad and knowing all at once. "I know."

I blinked, certain I hadn't heard correctly. "And you weren't terrified? Angry that I didn't tell you?"

"No." She took my hands. "The Shadow King wasn't lying. I did see the vision, Kaz. All of it. Your connection to him, the way he's been trying to claw his way into your thoughts.

I couldn't do anything but stare in shock as she touched my beard.

"All these weeks, I've watched you choose to be better than him. Choose to be *you*, not the monster he wanted you to become." She shook her head. "Even at the Gilded Gallows, when his influence was strongest, you fought against it."

The Gilded Gallows. That disaster felt like a lifetime ago. "I tried to compel you. Take away your choice."

She shifted closer, and I could feel our bond humming between us, stronger than ever. "I knew the way your control slipped that the rage wasn't quite yours. And I knew you'd hate yourself for it later, so I let you believe I was just angry about the compulsion itself. I mean, I was, but . . ."

"This whole time, you knew what I was, and you stayed."

"Of course I stayed." She smiled. "You're not him, Kaz. You're not some ancient evil wearing human skin. You're the man who kidnapped me and then let me negotiate terms. The man who gave me a shadow dragon and taught me to embrace my power. The man who just unleashed hell itself to save me."

"So why didn't you—"

"Because you weren't ready to hear it. You were barely holding yourself together, fighting a battle I couldn't help you win. If I'd confronted you about it, you'd have pulled away. Hidden it deeper."

I looked down at our linked hands. "I didn't know until we redirected the ley lines at the God Spire, but I think I was fighting him before that. I should have told you." I looked up at her, the words spilling out in a rush. "If I'd just talked to you about it, maybe you would have been better equipped to fight him yourself."

Her thumb traced my cheekbone. "You couldn't have known what would happen."

"I'm sorry." The words felt inadequate, but they were all I had. "For the compulsion at the Gallows. For putting you in stasis without your permission."

"The stasis was the right choice." She leaned into me, exhausted. I pulled her closer, burying my face in her hair as she continued. "I could feel myself losing control. The Shadow King was getting stronger, and I was—" She took a deep, shuddering breath. "I *was* terrified that I'd hurt you. Or Griffin. Or Vex. When you put me under, it was a relief." Another deep breath. "Anyway, you hated taking my choice away—I could feel it when you did it."

Sebastian stirred again, mumbling something about proper yeast ratios before his breathing evened out as he drifted off into slumber.

And then, because I was done with missed opportunities, the words I'd been choking on for weeks finally broke free. "I love you."

Arabella pulled back enough to look at me, eyes widened slightly. Not in surprise—more like she'd been waiting to hear it while conscious.

"I've been trying to find the right moment to tell you," I hurried to say, "but I'm a coward when it comes to feelings . . . and then the world kept ending."

"Technically, it's still ending."

"Details." I pulled her close again, savoring the simple pleasure of holding her without ancient entities between us.

"I love you too." She wrapped her arms around my neck. A feeling of great . . . joy? . . . washed over me. "I *love* you, Kaz. I love your arrogance and your dark sense of humor. I love that you cheat at eyeball golf and get jealous of my childhood friends. I love—"

I kissed her, cutting off her rambling with all the fierce possessiveness I'd been holding back. She melted against me, fingers tangling in my hair, and for a moment the world narrowed to just us. No ancient evils, no magical catastrophes, no bleeding pacifists on my floor.

When we finally broke apart, I noticed the ley lines beneath Solandris felt different. Cleaner. The corruption that had tainted them was gone, washed away by the Shadow King's departure from them, just like the Alchemist had predicted.

"The ley lines," Arabella murmured, sensing it too. "They're free."

"One problem solved, another created." I tucked a strand of hair behind her ear. "The Shadow King is loose in the world, and we have no idea where he went or what he's planning for his world domination."

"He did monologue for a long time, though. I wonder why he gave us all that history?"

I snorted. "Because he's arrogant. He doesn't believe there's anything we can truly do to him."

"We'll figure out something." She glanced at Sebastian, who was now muttering about the proper temperature for proofing dough. "After we get Lord Disaster here to the infirmary."

Sebastian's eyes fluttered open to reveal that distinctive violet color. He looked at us still clasped in each other's arms, then at the explosion of blue flowers surrounding him, and groaned. "Did I miss the heartfelt declarations of love?"

"Yes," I said flatly.

"Vex said that would happen any day now . . ." He winced. "Did we save the world or doom it? I'm a bit fuzzy on the details."

"Both," Arabella and I said together.

"Ah. One of *those* days." He struggled to his feet, still yet more flowers blooming where his hands touched the floor. "I appear to be stress-flowering again. Morning glories are an interesting choice, though."

"You nearly died," I said. "You're entitled to some botanical displays."

"I should go bake something. It helps with near-death experiences." He edged toward the door, clearly desperate to escape whatever was about to happen between Arabella and me.

"Sebastian," Arabella called, stopping him at the threshold. "Thank you."

He smiled—genuine, warm, and only a little bit heartbroken. "What are friends for?" Then he left in a flurry of blue petals.

The Alchemist stirred in their chair and rubbed their eyes, knocking their mask askew. I noticed deep pink scarring before they adjusted it back into place. "What did I miss?" Their gaze moved to Arabella and paused, recognizing the change in her and what that meant. "So it's done, then."

I gave the Alchemist a curt nod.

They rose from their chair and stumbled wearily to the door. "I'll see myself back to my cell."

"Make sure Sebastian doesn't fall off the lightning bridge first," I said. *Though it* would *take care of that problem*—no. Sigh. I owed him for what he did for Arabella. I didn't think I could ever repay that debt.

The Alchemist nodded, and the door closed behind them with a decisive click.

"Sebastian's taking this remarkably well," Arabella observed.

"He's in shock. It'll hit him later."

Arabella looked around for the first time. "Where are we exactly?"

"The Old Keep." I gestured at the ancient stone walls. "I think the Shadow King built it first, before expanding outward." I let out a dark laugh. "Now I know why it resisted all attempts to renovate or tear down. His essence is woven into every block, every beam. The magic's rooted too deep to extract."

Arabella's eyes swept the chamber, taking in the containment circles carved into the floor—circles I'd discovered but never created. "So you've been using the Shadow King's own fortress as his prison." Her lips curved into that sharp smile I loved. "There's something beautifully twisted about that."

"Even if it was only temporary." I pulled her closer, needing the reassurance of her body against mine.

Arabella tilted her head to give me better access to her neck. "The world is ending."

"The world is always ending." My teeth scraped against her throat, making her shiver. "Right now, I just want to celebrate the fact that you're alive, you're you, and you love me."

She hummed in agreement. "And then we should probably go check on the army."

"Have I ever told you how the stench of battle on you makes my cock hard?"

"You've mentioned it once or twice."

74

Make Love First, Save the World Later

(Priorities, People)

Kazimir

I scooped Arabella into my arms, ignoring her half-hearted protest about being perfectly capable of walking.

"Humor me," I said, heading for the door. "I just got you back. I'm not letting go for at least the next decade."

She rolled her eyes but settled against my chest, one hand playing with the torn fabric of my shirt. "You realize we're both covered in blood, sweat, and battlefield grime?"

"All the better." I kicked the door open. "I plan to get us significantly dirtier before we clean up."

The path outside the Old Keep was empty except for Thorne, who stood guard with the patient stillness of a man who'd been at his post for hours. His shoulders sagged with relief when he saw Arabella conscious and whole in my arms.

"My lord." He straightened, professional mask sliding back into place. "My lady."

"How long have you been standing there?" Arabella asked.

"Since Lord Blackrose departed for Sunspire." No reproach in his voice, just fact.

Nyx dropped from the wall above in a rush of wings. Her eyes fixed on Arabella, checking her over. Seemingly satisfied, Nyx pressed her snout against Arabella's arm, nostrils flaring. Her wings mantled wide, creating a protective canopy around us both while she gave a rumbling purr.

"I'm fine," Arabella assured her, freeing one hand to stroke the pink blaze on Nyx's snout. "Just tired."

I shifted Arabella's weight, noting how Thorne's gaze tracked the movement—checking for injuries, cataloging our condition with the efficiency of a man who'd spent years keeping me alive despite my best efforts to the contrary.

"Send word to the generals," I said. "They're to hold position outside the city walls. No looting, no unnecessary violence. Just maintain the perimeter and continue treating the wounded."

"And tomorrow?"

"Tomorrow we march in and take Solandris officially." The words should have filled me with triumph. I'd been working toward this moment for over a decade. But all I felt was exhaustion and the pressing need to get Arabella somewhere private where I could verify every inch of her was intact. With my tongue. "After that's done, get some sleep, Thorne. You've more than earned it."

He inclined his head. "Shall I send food to your chambers?"

"No." Arabella's fingers traced patterns on my chest that made the runes beneath my skin hum. "We'll manage."

Thorne's expression didn't change, but I caught the slight twitch at the corner of his mouth. "Very good, my lady."

I carried Arabella over the lightning bridges and through the winding corridors of Skyspire, taking the long route to avoid the main halls where our heroic "guests" might be lingering. The fortress felt different now—less like a bastion of dark power and more like . . . home. Our home.

Nyx had followed, her massive form pressing so close that she was practically attached to my hip. When we reached the final lightning bridge, she nearly sent Arabella and me tumbling into the void below.

"Tower," Arabella commanded once I'd recovered my feet. "Perch there."

The dragon's silver eyes narrowed to slits. A defiant puff of purple flame escaped her nostrils, but she launched herself skyward, her wings beating hard enough to whip Arabella's hair across my face.

We made to the main courtyard with no further mishaps.

"What are you thinking?" Arabella murmured against my neck. Her hot breath made my magic stir.

"Just realizing I conquered the wrong kingdom." I turned down the final corridor to our chambers. "All those years obsessing over Solandris when I should have been conquering you."

"You did conquer me." She nipped at my throat. "Repeatedly. Enthusiastically. In many different positions."

"And yet you conquered me right back." I shouldered open our door. "Seems we're at an impasse."

"Mutual conquest, then." She slid from my arms the moment we crossed the threshold, already pulling at the leather of her armor. "Though right now I'd settle for conquering a bath."

"No." I caught her wrist, spinning her back against me. "Bath later."

"Kaz, we're filthy—"

"Good." I backed her toward the bed, my hands already working at her remaining clothes. "I want you exactly like this. Covered in the evidence of what we survived. What we won."

Her pupils dilated, and I felt the spike of heat through our bond. "That's . . . unexpectedly romantic."

I tore through the last of her armor, baring her to my hungry gaze. Dark purple bruises were forming over her ribs. I traced each one reverently. "Romance is clearly a tool for men who are catastrophically in love with their wives."

She laughed, the sound bright and alive and everything I'd been terrified I'd never hear again. "Catastrophically?"

"Utterly. Completely. Catastrophically." I shed my own ruined clothes, not caring where they landed. My runes pulsed in anticipation. "I tried to resist it. Failed spectacularly."

"Your first failure in years, I'd imagine."

I pressed her back onto the bed, covering her body with mine. "I've been failing at resisting you since the day we met."

Her legs wrapped around my waist, pulling me closer. "The day you kidnapped me, you mean."

"Best decision I ever made." I caught her wrists, pinning them above her head. "Even if you did ruin all my careful plans."

"Your plans were terrible." She arched beneath me, testing my grip.

"But they worked out okay in the end." I leaned down to bite the junction of her neck and shoulder, marking her. "Instead, I fell in love with you. Gave you my power, my fortress, my entire fucking heart. Completely destroyed my reputation as a proper villain."

"You freed an ancient evil to save me." Her breath hitched as I moved lower, my lips and tongue trailing over her breastbone, my tongue tasting the salt on her skin. "I think your villain credentials are intact."

I released her wrists to grip her thighs, spreading her wider. "I love you."

She tangled her fingers in my hair, tugging hard enough to make the runes along my spine flare with delicious pain. "I love your methods. I love your darkness. I love—oh fuck, *Kaz*—"

I cut off her words with my mouth on her, determined to worship every part of her properly. She was wet and wanting, her body responding to my touch like we were made for this—made for each other. I'd had her countless times since our wedding, but this felt different.

No secrets. No ancient evils. No unspoken feelings. Just us.

I licked her slit from one end to the other, tasting her before plunging my tongue inside her. My shadows wrapped around her thighs, holding her open for me.

She gasped, hips rolling against my mouth, her grip on my hair tightening. I replaced my tongue with my fingers and began working her, curling them to hit that spot that made her see stars. She shattered with my name on her lips, her release flooding through our bond and nearly undoing me. But I wasn't done. Not even close.

I kissed my way back up her body, savoring the salt of her sweat, the rapid beat of her pulse. When I reached her mouth, she kissed me while wrapping one hand around my erection.

"Inside me," she demanded against my lips. "Now."

"I've created a monster." I positioned myself at her entrance, rubbing up and down with the head of my cock. "A beautiful, deadly monster."

She wrapped her legs around me again, using the leverage to pull me closer. "A monster that can match your darkness. That has killed for you and would do it again."

I slid inside her, her walls stretching around me, forcing me to pause as I adjusted. "We fit together so perfectly." I caught her throat in a light grip—not squeezing, just holding. Claiming. "The way you've carved out a place in my chest and filled it so completely, I can't imagine existing without you."

"Good." Her nails raked down my back, leaving marks I'd wear proudly. "Because you're stuck with me. Forever."

"Forever isn't long enough." I pulled out and slowly slid back in, angling so that I stimulated her clit and made her squirm. I was so hard that the sensations were overwhelming, my dominion magic leaking out to wrap us both in shadows. I increased my pace, driven by the need to get closer, deeper, to merge with her completely. "I want eternity. Every lifetime."

"You have them." She clenched around me, already close again.

I made love to her with all the pent-up emotion of the last horrible hours. The fear when the Shadow King took her. The rage at my mother's betrayal. The desperate relief when Arabella opened her eyes and said my name.

"Mine," I growled, feeling my control finally snap. My shadows darkened the room until there was nothing but us, nothing but this bed and our bodies moving together. "My wife. My Dark Lady. My everything."

"Yours," she agreed, then bit my shoulder hard enough to draw blood. "And you're mine. My villain."

The words sent me over the edge. I came with a roar that probably echoed through half the fortress, spilling inside her as she found her own release again. The bond between us flared white-hot, our magic intertwining until I couldn't tell where I ended and she began.

We collapsed together, a tangle of sweat-slicked limbs and racing hearts. I rolled to the side, pulling her with me so she sprawled across my chest. Neither of us spoke for long moments, content to simply breathe and exist in this perfect bubble of postcoital bliss.

"So," Arabella finally said, tracing the glowing scars on my chest, "we conquered Solandris, freed an ancient evil, and declared our undying love for each other. What do we do for an encore?"

"Bath," I decided. "Then food. Then I'm going to fuck you again. After that, we'll figure out how to track down the Shadow King and put him back in his box."

"Solid plan." She yawned. "Though maybe we could sleep at some point? I did just fight off possession by an eldritch horror."

"Fine. Bath, food, sleep, *then* more fucking."

"You're such a romantic."

"I know. It's disgusting." I pressed a kiss to her forehead. "Next thing you know, I'll be writing poetry about your eyes glowing golden in battle."

She snuggled closer, boneless and content. "I love you, Kazimir Blackrose. Even if you did ruin my life."

"I love you too, Arabella Blackrose." I tightened my arms around her. "Thank you for ruining mine right back."

She laughed, and I felt that pleasant ache in my chest expand until it threatened to crack my ribs. This woman had destroyed everything I thought I knew about myself, torn down every wall I'd built, and made me into someone I didn't recognize.

Someone who loved. Someone who was loved in return.

I should have been terrified. Instead, I was planning all the ways I could make her laugh like that again. All the ways I could worship her body and challenge her mind and feed her darkness until we were both glutted on it.

The Shadow King was free. Solandris was in chaos. The world was probably ending.

But Arabella was in my arms, alive and whole and *mine*, and that was the only victory that mattered.

The rest we'd figure out tomorrow. After all, what kind of villain would I be if I didn't start at least one apocalypse?

75

Savor the Calm

(Because Storms Are Definitely Coming)

Arabella

The sheets still smelled like sex and battlefield grime when I slipped out of bed, leaving Kazimir sprawled across the mattress.

His hair stuck up at odd angles, and a line of drool connected his mouth to the pillow. The most feared villain in the realm, reduced to this. I bit back a laugh and grabbed one of his shirts from the floor, pulling it over my head. It fell to mid-thigh and smelled like smoke and shadow magic.

My stomach growled, reminding me that we'd skipped the "food" part of our post-battle plans in favor of more pressing activities. Three times, to be exact. My thighs still trembled slightly as I padded toward the door.

The Inner Sanctum's small kitchen was tucked away inside the main fortress, a private space reserved for family. The fact that I thought of it that way—family—should have been more jarring. Instead, it felt right. Natural. Like everything else about this insane life I'd chosen.

The smell hit me before I rounded the corner. Cinnamon. Vanilla. Fresh bread. And underneath it all, the green, earthy scent of Sebastian's magic.

I found him at the wooden table, surrounded by what looked like a bakery's worth of goods. Tarts lined up in perfect rows. Loaves of bread still steaming. Cookies stacked in precarious towers. His hands moved mechanically, kneading dough that probably didn't need any more attention.

"Still stress-baking?" I asked from the doorway.

He didn't startle. Just kept working the dough. "Couldn't sleep."

The kitchen was warm, almost stifling with the ovens running. I counted at least six different types of pastries cooling on the counters. How long had he been at this?

"Sebastian—"

"There's fresh coffee." He nodded toward a pot on the stove, still not meeting my eyes. "And those almond croissants you like. Third tray from the left."

I wanted to push, to ask about the ritual, about his sacrifice, about what Kazimir had said. But Sebastian's shoulders were rigid with tension, his movements too controlled. He wasn't ready.

Instead, I poured myself coffee and selected a croissant, biting into it with probably indecent enthusiasm. "Oh, fuck. This is incredible."

A ghost of a smile touched his lips. "Try the lemon tarts. I think I finally got the curd ratio right."

I obliged, sampling my way through his stress-fueled production. Each bite was perfection, but I could taste the anxiety baked into every layer. Sebastian's emotions were completely scrambled.

"You know," I said carefully, licking custard from my thumb, "we probably have enough food here to feed half the fortress."

"Good thing we have half the kingdom's nobility as houseguests, then." His voice was too light.

I set down the tart. "Sebastian—"

"How is he?" The question came out rushed. "Lord Blackrose. After everything."

"He's fine. Sleeping." I studied Sebastian's profile, noting the dark circles under his eyes, the slight tremor in his hands. "How are you?"

"Spectacular. Never better. Did you try the chocolate soufflé? I'm particularly proud of—"

"You gave your blood to free an ancient evil." The warmth of the kitchen seemed to absorb those words and throw them back at me. "That's not nothing."

His hands stilled on the dough. For a moment, I thought he might actually talk to me. Then he resumed kneading with renewed vigor. "It worked, didn't it? You're free. The Shadow King is . . . wherever he is. Mission accomplished."

My truth-sense didn't ping exactly, but it rippled with the weight of things unsaid. Sebastian was very carefully not lying while also not telling the truth.

"Kaz said—" I stopped myself. Did I really want to open this door?

"Said what?" Now he did look at me, and the raw vulnerability in his eyes made my chest tight.

"Nothing. Just . . . thank you, Sebastian. For what you did. For being willing to—"

"Don't." The word came out sharper than I'd ever heard from him. He took a breath, visibly pulling himself together. "I mean, you're welcome. But let's not make it into something more than it was. A necessary sacrifice to save a lady. Very heroic. I'll probably get a ballad out of it."

The kitchen door burst open before I could respond, saving us both from a conversation neither of us was ready for.

"Can't sleep," Vex announced, shuffling in wearing black silk pajamas. "Too much adrenaline. Too many feelings. Need sugar."

She stopped short at the sight of Sebastian's bakery explosion. "Holy shit. Did you rob a pastry shop?"

"Help yourself," Sebastian said, already pulling another ball of dough from somewhere. Where was he even getting all these ingredients?

Griffin appeared next, his hair sticking up in twelve different directions and his striped nightshirt inside out. It only fell to just above his knobby knees. "I smelled cinnamon rolls. Please tell me there are cinnamon rolls. I've been up all night trying to figure out how to track magical signatures through dimensional barriers and my brain needs sugar."

"Second shelf, left side," Sebastian directed without looking up.

Thorne was the last to arrive, somehow looking perfectly put together despite wearing simple sleep clothes. He surveyed the scene with his usual calm assessment.

He stared at Sebastian with a question on his scarred face.

"Productive insomnia," Sebastian offered in answer.

Thorne selected a simple butter cookie and rumbled something about "pretty lords and their quirks."

We fell into easy companionship, the five of us scattered around the kitchen like this was normal. Like we hadn't just survived a battle, freed an ancient evil, and fundamentally altered the balance of power in the realm.

Vex was in the middle of an elaborate story about a merchant who'd already tried to sell her "genuine Shadow King artifacts" when footsteps echoed down the corridor.

Kazimir appeared in the doorway, and my brain short-circuited.

He'd shaved. And cut his hair. The wild mane I'd gripped during our earlier activities was now cropped short, emphasizing the sharp angles of his face. The beard I'd felt between my thighs was gone, revealing the strong line of his jaw.

He looked every inch the man I'd first met—sharp, dangerous. Absolutely edible.

"You cut your hair," I said stupidly.

"Magic," he said, running a hand through the short strands. "Figured I should look presentable for claiming Solandris tomorrow. Can't have the artists drawing me for the history books looking like a wild hermit."

"I liked the hermit look," Vex said, then made a face. "Actually, no. This is better. Less 'crazy goblin living in a cave' and more 'ruthlessly efficient conqueror.'"

Kazimir moved to the wine cabinet, pulling out bottles. "Since we're all awake and Sebastian has apparently opened a bakery in our kitchen, we might as well celebrate properly."

"Celebrate what?" Griffin asked through a mouthful of cinnamon roll.

"My wife is alive and unpossessed. We conquered Solandris. The world hasn't ended yet." He uncorked a bottle. "Pick one."

Soon we all had drinks—wine for most of us, though Griffin had found some kind of fluorescent blue liqueur that I didn't know the origin of. Kazimir raised his glass.

"To survival," he said simply.

"To family," Vex added.

Warmth bloomed in my chest.

We drank, and the alcohol mixed pleasantly with the sugar from Sebastian's stress-baking. Conversation flowed easier now, jumping from topic to topic with the loose association of the slightly drunk and very exhausted.

I found myself next to Vex as the others debated whether Griffin's blue liqueur was actually safe for human consumption.

"Can I ask you something?" I kept my voice low.

She tilted her head, reading something in my expression. "About Lord Blackrose?"

"You suspected what he was."

Vex was quiet for a long moment, swirling wine in her glass. "I did. When he started struggling with those episodes, when his control began slipping. I'd seen enough of his past to recognize the signs of something trying to claw its way out."

"But you stayed."

"Of course I did." She looked at me like I was insane for suggesting otherwise. "He gave me purpose. Became my family when I had nothing. A little thing like being possessed by an ancient evil wasn't going to change that."

I thought about what the Shadow King had said to her, the taunts about her past, the wounds he'd so casually reopened. "In the tower, when the Shadow King was speaking through me . . . what he said to you."

Vex went very still.

"I heard it," I said quietly. "If you ever want to talk—"

"I don't." The words were sharp, final. Then, softer: "But thank you. For offering."

We stood in comfortable silence, watching our strange little family. Griffin was now trying to convince Sebastian to bake something with his questionable liqueur. Thorne was methodically sorting the baked goods into storage containers. Kazimir leaned against the counter, looking more relaxed than I'd seen him in weeks.

"You haven't tried the scones," Vex observed, her sharp eyes tracking Kazimir's careful avoidance of a particular tray.

"I've had scones before," he said dismissively.

"Not Sebastian's scones." Griffin had unwound a second cinnamon roll and was whirling it around. "They're legendary. Sebastian, didn't you tell me about an incident where a minor lord challenged someone to a duel over the last scone at a banquet?"

Sebastian looked up from his dough, alarmed. "That's not—I mean, they're just scones."

"Just scones," Vex repeated flatly. "My lady, tell your husband he's being ridiculous."

I watched Kazimir's jaw tighten, recognizing the stubborn set of his shoulders. He was avoiding them on principle. Because Sebastian made them. Because they were probably annoyingly perfect.

"They are really good," I offered, taking another bite of my croissant to hide my smile.

Kazimir's eyes narrowed at me. *Traitor,* that look said.

"The Dark Lord of Skyspire," Thorne rumbled from his position by the storage containers, "afraid of baked goods."

That did it. Kazimir's pride wouldn't allow that particular jab to stand. He stalked to the tray, selected a scone with all the gravity of choosing a weapon, and bit into it.

His expression went carefully, dangerously blank.

We all watched in silence as he chewed. Swallowed. Stared at the remaining scone in his hand like it had personally betrayed him.

"Well?" Vex prompted.

"It's adequate," Kazimir said, his voice tight.

Sebastian beamed. "Oh, thank you! I wasn't sure about the butter ratio this time—"

My truth-sense practically vibrated. "That's the biggest lie you've told all week."

Kazimir shot me a look that promised retribution later. Then, with visible reluctance, he took another bite. And another. The scone disappeared in record time.

I heard him mutter something under his breath as he reached for a second one, trying to make it look casual.

"What was that?" I asked sweetly.

"Nothing."

But I'd heard it. Caught the words even as he'd tried to swallow them along with his wounded pride.

Fucking heroes.

He took an aggressive bite of the second scone, his expression suggesting he was imagining it was something far less delicious and far more deserving of his teeth. Like maybe a political enemy.

Sebastian, oblivious to—or perhaps because of—the internal crisis he'd caused, simply smiled and went back to his dough.

"What's the plan for hunting him down?" Vex asked quietly. "The Shadow King."

"We don't have one yet." I took another sip of wine.

I caught Kazimir's eye, and he smiled—a real smile, not his usual smirk or villainous grin. Just pure, uncomplicated happiness despite just being forced to eat the best scone in his life.

Then Griffin accidentally set his sleeve on fire with whatever was in that blue liqueur, and the moment dissolved into chaos and laughter and Sebastian's exasperated attempts to extinguish flaming clothing.

Tomorrow would bring new challenges. But tonight, we were just a family, slightly singed and covered in flour, celebrating the simple fact that we were all still alive.

It was enough. More than enough.

It was everything.

76

Survey Your Conquest

(While Planning Your Exit Strategy)

Kazimir

I stood in the highest tower of Sunspire Palace, watching my forces secure the city gates glittering in the bright morning sun.

No resistance. No dramatic last stands. Just silent streets and frightened faces peering from behind curtains. The mighty kingdom that had defied me for years had fallen with barely a whimper. It should have felt like victory.

Instead, it felt like inheriting a house infested with termites.

"The eastern quarter is secure," Thorne reported from behind me. "No sign of remaining nobility. Most fled when word spread of Auremar's death."

I turned from the view, finding my council assembled in what had been Auremar's private study. Arabella perched on the edge of the massive oak desk, one leg swinging idly. Vex stood by the window, cataloging the palace's assets on a scroll that magically grew longer by the minute. Griffin hunched over a map, muttering about ley line convergences.

And Sebastian sat in one of the plush chairs, looking entirely too comfortable for someone in the conquered palace of his former king. Morning glories had sprouted along the chair's carved arms, their delicate blue petals opening toward the sunlight. I noticed with irritation that they were all morning glories now—no more random wildflowers or nervous weeds. Just those damned morning glories, everywhere he went.

I had too much to worry about to puzzle out why his stress flowers had suddenly become so consistent.

"And the western districts?" I asked, dragging my attention away from the way Sebastian's fingers absently traced the petals.

"Also secure." Thorne hesitated, then added, "There's the matter of Auremar's northern army."

I raised an eyebrow. "The ten thousand he was marching to meet us at the northern outpost?"

"They're still marching," Thorne confirmed. "Last reports had them three days out from the northern border. If word of Sunspire's fall hasn't reached them yet—"

"It will soon," Vex interrupted, looking up from her scroll. "Merchants talk. Refugees talk. Someone will get word to the commanders within hours if they haven't already."

Griffin tapped the map nervously. "Ten thousand soldiers is a significant force."

"It was before we had direct access to Solandris's ley lines," I corrected, flexing my fingers and feeling them hum beneath Sunspire like living veins of power. I moved to the map, tracing the paths of power I could now sense threading through the conquered kingdom. "Auremar kept his army enhanced with corrupted magic from the Golden Rose Fields. Now those fields are dead, and I control the ley lines they were drawing from."

"Which means?" Sebastian asked.

"Which means their mages are starving for power," I said. "And I could crush half that army before they realized what was happening."

Thorne's expression shifted to something like satisfaction. "The Heirloom changes the equation."

"Just as it was always meant to do." I felt Arabella's presence through our bond, felt the way the Heirloom resonated between us. "What would have been a grueling siege a month ago is now barely an inconvenience."

Sebastian's eyes went wide. "You could use the ley line convergence to cut off their magical support entirely. Just redirect the flows away from their position."

"I could do that," I agreed. "Or I could do something more dramatic. The Bone Behemoth was just a taste of what's possible now."

Griffin shifted uncomfortably. "Even without Auremar's magic backing them, they could cause considerable damage if they decide to—"

"Avenge their fallen king?" I finished. "Or they could surrender the moment they realize their cause is lost."

"Or splinter," Sebastian offered quietly. "When the Northern Peaks fell to internal conflict decades ago, the army broke into three factions. Some went home. Some turned to banditry. Some tried to prop up a new leader."

"The ones from Valmont and Meridian Isle are only there because of their alliance with Solandris. They might not even care—well, except for the ones with something to lose, like the merchants and nobility."

Arabella folded her arms. "We can't leave ten thousand armed soldiers wandering around making their own decisions."

"No," I agreed. "We can't."

Arabella leaned forward. "What do you have in mind?"

"We send an envoy and offer terms." My runes burned at the thought of not crushing every last one of my enemies, but strategic restraint had built my empire, not mindless slaughter. "Most soldiers aren't interested in dying for a corpse's honor. They want to go home." I tapped the map where the army's position would be. "We give them that option—lay down arms, swear not to take up rebellion, and they can walk away."

"And if they refuse?" Thorne asked.

"Then we remind them that the Dark Lord who conquered their kingdom in a single day is not someone they want as an enemy. One way or another, that army ceases to be a problem." I flexed my fingers, feeling the ley lines pulse beneath Sunspire like living veins of power. "But ten thousand corpses would destabilize three kingdoms and won't help us at all when the Syndicate moves against me. Worse, it would leave ten thousand angry, desperate souls wandering Solandris—exactly the kind of chaos the Shadow King could exploit."

I met Arabella's gaze. "Half that army isn't even professional soldiers. Minor lords called up for feudal service. Farmers who know more about wheat than warfare. The kind of people who'd follow anyone who promised them safety or revenge."

"You think he'd try to claim them," she said quietly.

"I think we don't know the full extent of his powers yet." The admission tasted bitter. "Better to send them home grateful to be alive than leave them vulnerable to whatever he's planning. Dead, they're a problem. Dominated by an ancient evil, they're a catastrophe."

"The officers and mages will be the problem," Arabella noted. "The ones with enough rank to organize resistance."

"Those, we'll need to have a more personal conversation with. But I have a feeling that as soon as the mages are dealt with decisively, everyone else will fall in line."

Thorne nodded, making notes. "I'll see to it. This will be much easier than I anticipated."

"Everything's easier now," I said, though the words tasted strange. We had the power to reshape kingdoms, to crush armies, to bend the very earth to our will. And somewhere out there, the Shadow King was free, with his own plans for that same power.

"What about my father?" Arabella asked quietly.

Everyone turned to look at her. She was gazing steadily at me.

"We never found him after the battle," Thorne reported. "No body. No trace. But he could have died and been tossed somewhere. We'll still be weeks putting things to order."

"Or he ran like the coward he is," Arabella said. Her voice was flat, but I felt the complicated tangle of emotions through our bond. "The false memories Kaz planted would make him useless to anyone he tried to sell information to."

"He's not a threat," I confirmed. "Even if he survived, he has nothing left. No power, no allies, no kingdom to return to."

She nodded once.

Thorne's expression turned carefully neutral. "There's the matter of our houseguests. We're overflowing with them."

Right. The two hundred or so nobles we'd "preventively relocated" to Skyspire. They'd served their purpose—or rather, hadn't needed to, since the Shadow King had found his own way out. Now they were just mouths to feed and potential problems to manage.

"Send them home," I said. "We don't need—"

"They'll be targets." Arabella's voice cut through my dismissal. "The Shadow King knows who they are. If we send them back unprotected . . ."

She didn't need to finish. I could picture it clearly enough—the Shadow King systematically hunting down every drop of heroic blood, either to eliminate threats or to fuel whatever scheme he was hatching.

"So what do you suggest?" I kept my tone even, though the idea of playing protector to a bunch of entitled nobles made my teeth ache. "We can't keep them at Skyspire indefinitely."

"Why not?" Vex looked up from her scroll. "Half of them have already offered to pay rent. Kata Goldmary's son has ideas about establishing new trade routes through our territories. The Fekete twins want to set up a healing practice alongside our Skyspire healers."

"Because Skyspire isn't a fucking boardinghouse!" I pressed my fingers to my temples. "Besides, we can't stay there."

That got everyone's attention.

Arabella hopped off the desk. "What do you mean?"

I moved to the map Griffin had spread across the table, tracing the floating islands that made up my fortress. "Everyone knows where Skyspire is now. Hell, we've been advertising our location with magical signatures visible from three kingdoms away."

"You want to move it." Griffin's eyes lit up with manic enthusiasm. "Oh, that's brilliant! We haven't done that in ages. The amount of power required would be staggering depending on where we go, but now that we can harness the ley lines—"

"Not over Solandris," I cut him off before he could launch into a full technical dissertation. "I'd always planned to park it here eventually, symbol of conquest and all that. But now . . ."

Now the Shadow King was free. Now everything had changed.

"You think he'll come for it," Arabella said quietly. It wasn't a question.

"Skyspire was his seat of power once." I stared at the map. "The original fortress, before I rebuilt it. There's something about that place, something beyond just strategic advantage."

"The bones," Griffin whispered suddenly. We all turned to look at him. His face had gone pale. "When I was researching the citadel's history, I found references to 'the bones of the first darkness.' I thought it was metaphorical, but what if—"

"What if there's something buried in the floating rock beneath Skyspire?" Vex finished. She looked at me. "You raised your five-pointed star fortress over the old ruins. Do you think it's connected?"

I nodded. Why else would I have been so drawn to that particular floating rock? Why else would the restoration have come so easily, like the stones remembered their proper shape?

"We move it," I decided. "Keep it mobile. Make ourselves harder to track while we figure out what he wants."

"And the nobles?" Arabella prompted.

I met her gaze, seeing the challenge there. She knew I hated this. Knew it went against every instinct to shelter potential enemies. But she also knew I'd do it anyway, because she was right. They were targets now, whether they'd asked for it or not. And we couldn't afford to let our enemy get his hands on them. Not now. Not ever.

"They can stay," I ground out. "Temporarily. With conditions."

"I'll draw up contracts," Vex said immediately, her quill already moving. "Loyalty oaths, behavior agreements, payment schedules—"

"And I can set up monitoring systems," Griffin added. "Make sure no one's sending messages to enemies or planning revolts."

"Some of them might revolt," Sebastian said from his chair. He was gazing out the window again.

I countered. "Then we make them see *reason*. I'm still the Dark Lord. They don't have a choice."

"Some of them might actually be useful," Thorne pointed out. "Lord Janos Torok has a military background and knows siege engineering. He could help with fortress modifications if we can keep him from challenging people to duels."

They were already planning, already organizing, already turning my reluctant agreement into actionable strategy. This was why I kept them around—they took my grand pronouncements and made them actually work.

"What about Solandris itself?" Arabella asked. "We can't just leave it to fall apart."

She was right about that, too. The kingdom's infrastructure was already failing without Auremar's magic to maintain the illusion of prosperity. The Golden Rose Fields were dead, their primary export gone. We'd also discovered that the treasury was nearly empty, drained by Auremar's obsession with the Shadow King.

"Install a regent," I said with effort. The drastic change of my lifelong plans was costing me. "Someone competent enough to keep things running but not ambitious enough to cause problems."

"Oh!" Sebastian straightened in his chair, causing a fresh cascade of morning glories to bloom along the armrests. "My father, Lord Peregrine, would be perfect for that."

I turned to glare at him, my possessive instincts flaring. He was trustworthy—I knew that, had proven it—but something about the way he just . . . existed in spaces that should be mine made my dominion magic itch. And now he was suggesting his father run Solandris *in my stead*.

"Father's an excellent administrator," Sebastian continued, either oblivious to or ignoring my territorial display. "He's been managing the Northern Peaks beautifully. Very practical, not at all interested in power for its own sake. Just likes making sure people have food and the roads stay clear."

"He's already sent word about wanting to help," Vex added carefully, "after what we did for Sebastian. His letter reached us right after I told the merchants selling 'relics' to fuck off."

"Father also mentioned he's concerned about the trade disruptions." Sebastian absently plucked a morning glory and twirled it between his fingers. "He'd probably jump at the chance to stabilize things. Plus, he's very good at boring paperwork. Loves it, actually. Says it's soothing."

Arabella smiled. "He would be excellent at the job."

"And he'd keep an ear out for your father," Sebastian offered. "If Evenfall surfaces here or tries to seek refuge anywhere in Solandris, we'll know. Of course, he'd do that whether he was regent or not."

Arabella's expression didn't change, but I felt her gratitude through our bond—for Sebastian's practical approach, for not making it emotional, for simply treating her father as the strategic problem he was.

I watched Sebastian for a long moment. "Fine. Have Lord Peregrine start immediately. I want basic services restored within the week. For now, we focus on stability. Keep people fed, keep order maintained, keep them from forming angry mobs."

"The bare minimum of tyranny," Arabella said drily.

I shot her a look. "Would you prefer I raze the city and salt the earth?"

"Would you?" She tilted her head, genuinely curious.

"No," I admitted. "Destroying Solandris serves no purpose. Better to let it limp along as a cautionary tale about trusting golden kings with golden promises."

"How unexpectedly merciful." But she was smiling—that small, private smile that made my chest tight.

"Father will be thrilled," Sebastian said brightly. "Well, as thrilled as he gets about anything. He'll probably say something like 'adequate' and then immediately start reorganizing the tax system."

The morning sun had climbed higher, casting the room in harsh light that made the gilt decorations look tawdry rather than grand. Sunspire was long overdue for less pomposity and more substance, but redecorating would have to wait until we eliminated the Shadow King's threat.

"He's out there somewhere." I couldn't quite keep the growl from my voice. "Free to do whatever he wants."

"Then we'll stop him." Arabella said it like it was simple. Like we hadn't just barely survived our first encounter with him. "We have the Heirloom. We have each other. And now we know what we're fighting."

I wanted to argue. Wanted to point out that we'd had all those things before and still nearly lost. But she was looking at me with such fierce certainty, such absolute faith in us, that the words died unspoken.

"I love you," I said again, because now that I'd started, I couldn't seem to stop.

Vex made a gagging noise. "If you two are going to be disgusting, at least wait until Griffin and I leave."

"Please don't," Griffin added. "I'm still digesting breakfast."

Sebastian just smiled serenely, though I noticed a few more morning glories bloomed along the windowsill. "It's rather sweet, actually."

I glowered at him, but Arabella just smiled, crossing the space between us to press a quick kiss to my jaw. "I love you too." She patted my chest. "Come on, Dark Lord. Let's go take a look at your new kingdom before we have to abandon it."

Behind us, Vex, Griffin, and Thorne fell into step, already bickering about the logistics of moving an entire floating fortress. Sebastian trailed after, leaving a scattered path of blue flowers in his wake.

77

Chase Answers

(That Lead to More Dangerous Questions)

Arabella

A bitter wind whipped across Skyspire's battlements, carrying with it the promise of early snow and the faint scent of woodsmoke from the main kitchens.

I pulled my heavy cloak tighter, grateful for the fur lining Vex had insisted on adding. Three days of organizing chaos had left me exhausted, but there was still so much to do before we moved the entire floating fortress north. To my surprise, most of the families staying with us were now happy for the Dark Lord's protection, though a few grumbled about our failure to put the Shadow King back in his prison. I hadn't given them the details, however. They didn't need to know that we'd been the ones to actually free the Shadow King.

The battlements were mercifully empty except for the shadow sentries that rippled along the walls. I found my husband exactly where Thorne had said he'd be—standing at the eastern edge, staring out at the horizon where storm clouds gathered.

Kazimir wore only a thin silk shirt and dark pants, the fabric rippling in the wind. No cloak. No jacket. Just him and the elements, as if the bitter cold couldn't touch him.

But I could see the truth in the rigid line of his shoulders, the way his fingers gripped the stone parapet. His runes were burning again.

"You're going to freeze," I said, coming up beside him.

"I run hot." His voice was flat, distracted. "How goes the herding of entitled sheep?"

"About as well as you'd expect." I leaned against the parapet, studying his profile. "Lord Brightwater is convinced his room is haunted. I didn't know Skyspire had ghosts."

Kazimir's laugh was dark, humorless. "How can it not be? Every stone in this place has witnessed death. The dungeons just happen to concentrate the screaming in one convenient location, but that's not the extent by a long shot. But Griffin's probably been experimenting with spectral resonance again . . . or trying more hand gestures. He's probably angered all the ghosts, though I can't say I'm sorry that Lord Brightwater has been inconvenienced."

I huffed a laugh. "The real problem is the families."

Kaz turned to look at me, and I caught the flash of pain in his eyes before he masked it. "What families?"

I pinned him with a look. "The hostages from the Chamber of Petals want their loved ones brought to Skyspire. Same with the ones from Valmont. They're worried about retaliation, about the Shadow King targeting anyone with even a drop of heroic blood." I sighed. "We're looking at potentially doubling our . . . population."

"Absolutely not." The words came out as a growl. "I agreed to temporary shelter for those already here. I'm not running a refugee camp for every nervous noble in the Western Realms."

"They have a point, though. If the Shadow King—"

"Can track heroic bloodlines, yes, I'm aware." He turned back to the horizon. "Fine. But they work. Everyone works. No freeloaders in my fortress."

"Already ahead of you. I've been assigning jobs based on skills." I paused.

"We're going to need more supplies, though. And more space. Griffin's already drawing up expansion plans—"

"Of course he is." But there was fondness beneath the exasperation. "Anything else I should know about? Any other ways my perfectly good fortress of doom is being transformed into a small city?"

"Well, Lord Peregrine arrived this morning to officially take over as regent of Solandris."

Kazimir's hands tightened on the stone. "And?"

"And he brought a gift. Apparently, the Northern Peaks' wool is excellent for winter clothing, so he sent several crates." I smiled. "He also said, and I quote, 'The administrative systems are adequate but will require significant restructuring.' Sebastian nearly died of embarrassment."

"Thrilling." Kazimir's voice was dry as dust. "I'm sure the wool will be very useful when we're fleeing for our lives from an ancient evil."

"You're in a mood."

"I'm always in a mood."

"This is a different one." I stepped closer, close enough to feel the unnatural heat radiating from his body. The runes were definitely active. "What's wrong?"

For a moment, I thought he wouldn't answer. Then he pulled a letter from his pocket, holding it out to me. "This arrived an hour ago."

I took the parchment from Marlowe. As I read, my stomach dropped.

> *There is no memory mage in the Spire. No Mnemosyne. No shop. The name belonged to a mage who died a century ago. I have been trying to track down more information for weeks, but with no results.*

"That's—" I stared at the words, trying to make sense of them. "Impossible. I was there. I spoke to her. My truth-sense didn't alert me to anything suspicious."

"I'm wondering if there are ways around that." Kazimir's eyes were sharp now, focused.

The wind howled around my ears, making my face raw and my eyes water. I squinted up at Kaz. "How so?"

"We had a spy at Skyspire. Your truth-sense never gave Pip—or rather, the doppelganger—away."

I gaped at Kaz. "True, but not everyone can be a doppelganger. They're incredibly rare in this realm."

He watched me intently. "My point is that we now know that your truth-sense isn't infallible. Perhaps there are other types of magic that could be impervious to yours."

"You think the Shadow King? He seems unlikely."

Kazimir shook his head and looked out at the lightning around Skyspire. Snow swirled in the flashes. "No, but there are other old types of magic that predate much of our current understanding of history, even Soriven himself. The Alchemist also thought your magic was different from other heroic blood, didn't they? So if not of Soriven, or only partly, it stands to reason it's something older."

"And just as I exist, so could other forms, as well," I mused.

He nodded.

I made a note to ask the Alchemist again, anyway. It'd be easy enough to find them still in a cell in the dungeons, which were darker but less crowded. Kaz had given him an upgrade, though, with a bigger window and their own fireplace and real furniture.

"Regardless, the restored memories are real," I insisted. "I saw your mother before you even knew she was alive. I remembered things Sebastian confirmed. The potion worked."

"That's not the question." He took the letter back, folding it carefully. "The question is who gave it to you and why."

I wanted to argue, but something cold was settling in my chest. The shop had been so convenient, so perfectly placed. And Mnemosyne herself had been so *helpful*. Understanding. Exactly what I'd needed in that moment. "You think someone was manipulating me."

"I think someone gave you exactly what you wanted when you were vulnerable and angry." His voice was gentle now. "Information is never free, Arabella. There's always a price."

"I paid her." But even as I said it, I knew how naive it sounded. "You're thinking of the Alchemist."

"The Alchemist's debt was clear." He gestured at the letter. "This is something else. Someone wanted you to have those memories. Someone with enough power to create an entire shop that doesn't exist, to pose as a century-dead mage, to brew a potion that actually worked."

The wind picked up, sending my hair whipping across my face. I pushed it back impatiently. "But why help me? What's the gain?"

"That's what worries me." Kazimir turned to face me fully, and I could see the genuine concern beneath his usual paranoia. "Every gift has strings. Every kindness has a cost. And we don't know what this one is yet."

I wanted to dismiss his fears. Wanted to believe that sometimes people just helped because it was right. But I'd learned too much about the world to be that naive.

"So what do we do?"

"We wait." He pulled me against him, and I could feel the heat of his runes through the thin silk. "We watch. And we prepare for whatever bill comes due."

I pressed my face against his chest, breathing in the scent of storms and dark magic that always clung to him. "I hate this."

"Which part? The mysterious benefactor with unknown motives? The fortress full of nobles we're apparently adopting? Or the ancient evil running loose in the world?"

"Yes." I felt him chuckle, the vibration running through his chest and into me. "All of it. Can't we just have five minutes of peace?"

"Where's the fun in that?" But his arms tightened around me. "Besides, you'd be bored within three."

He was probably right. Still . . .

"The memories helped," I said quietly. "Even if someone gave them to me for their own reasons, they helped. I understand things now that I didn't before."

"I know." He pressed a kiss to the top of my head.

We stood there as the wind howled around us, holding each other against the growing storm. Somewhere in the fortress below, nobles argued about accommodations, and Griffin probably set something on fire. Somewhere beyond our walls, the Shadow King plotted our destruction.

And somewhere, maybe, a mysterious benefactor waited to collect on a debt I didn't even know I owed.

The wind howled louder, and somewhere in the distance, thunder rolled through the clouds, shaking the foundations of the citadel.

78

Check Your Basement
(for Ancient Horrors, Probably)

Kazimir

The morning reports were already giving me a headache, and I hadn't even finished my second cup of coffee.

"—and Lord Brightwater insists the latrines near his quarters are inadequate," Vex continued, reading from her list. "He's threatening to write a formal complaint to 'the powers that be'—whatever that means—about 'substandard accommodations.'"

I set down my cup so hard it cracked the saucer beneath. "Tell him he's welcome to shit off the side of the fortress if he finds our facilities lacking."

"I'll phrase it more diplomatically." Vex made a note. "The kitchen staff also needs approval for expanded storage. With all the new residents our current supplies won't last through winter."

"Approved." I waved a hand. "What else?"

"Construction on the east wing is ahead of schedule. Griffin only set two things on fire yesterday, which is practically a record." She paused, frowning at her notes. "Though there is one issue."

I leaned back and arched an eyebrow. "Only one?"

“The workers repairing the wall near the Observation Tower found something.” Vex’s expression shifted to something between concern and curiosity. “An opening behind the stones.”

I straightened in my chair. Skyspire had been my fortress for over a decade. I knew every room, every passage, every secret corridor. Or so I’d thought. “An opening?”

“Leading down into the rock itself. The workers . . .” She hesitated. “They were terrified. Practically begged to be reassigned. Said they heard strange noises coming from below.”

“Strange noises.” I stood, already reaching for my coat. “Did they describe these noises?”

“Like whispers, they said. Or singing. Or screaming. They couldn’t seem to agree.” Vex closed her ledger. “I told them to seal it back up until you could investigate.”

“Good.” I pulled on my coat, checking that my daggers were in place. “Show me.”

We made our way through the fortress, and I again congratulated myself on sticking to the rule that there were to be no “guests” in the Inner Sanctum. At least here I could have some peace and quiet—

I leaped aside as two children—*children!*—ran past, chasing what looked like one of Griffin’s escaped experiments. Wait . . . why were they running through *my* courtyard?

“Vex,” I growled.

“It’s recess. They needed a more open area to let off some steam. Apparently, they haven’t been applying themselves to their studies since moving to Skyspire, and we thought—”

I turned to find the source of this chaos. The children had stopped their chase and were now staring at me with the unabashed curiosity only the young possessed, whispering behind cupped hands. And supervising this disaster? Thorne, my security chief, who was currently helping a small girl untangle a tentacled rabbit from her hair.

“Thorne?” I called out, my voice carrying that special edge that made grown men reconsider their life choices.

He looked up, his expression shifting from gentle patience to something approaching panic. "My lord! I was just—uh, the children needed—"

"Since when do you supervise recess?" I demanded.

His face reddened. "Lady Blackrose suggested someone trustworthy should watch them, and I—" He cleared his throat, trying to recover his usual gruff demeanor, but his consternation reminded me of Griffin. "Security protocols, my lord. Can't have unsupervised children running about."

One of the boys tugged on Thorne's sleeve. "Can you tell us that story about fighting three ogres at once?"

I raised an eyebrow. My terrifying security chief had been regaling children with *bedtime stories*?

"Later, lad," Thorne muttered, looking like he wanted the ground to swallow him whole.

"The Inner Sanctum is off-limits," I said firmly. "It's far too dangerous for children." Yes, that was it. Not because I didn't want sticky fingerprints on my walls or drawings of "Mean Mr. Dark Lord" appearing everywhere. Pure safety concerns.

"But my lord," Vex began, "the other courtyards are either under construction or—"

"What about the swamp?" I suggested. "Plenty of open space. Fresh air. Educational opportunities with the local wildlife."

Vex's eyes widened. "The swamp with the flesh-eating bog plants and mutant deer?"

"Character building," I said. "Besides, the plants are mostly dormant this time of year."

She opened her mouth to argue, then caught sight of my expression and thought better of it. "Of course, my lord. I'll, uh, arrange for swamp supervision immediately."

Behind her, I could hear one of the children asking Thorne if the Dark Lord really ate people for breakfast, and Thorne's fumbling response that I preferred toast.

I needed another coffee.

"My lord! My lord!"

The high-pitched squeaking could only belong to one person. I turned to see Griffin practically galloping across the courtyard, his too-short robes flapping around his spindly legs like demented wings attached to his ass. He skidded to a halt in front of us, nearly toppling over in his excitement.

"Griffin," I said wearily. "What's on fire now?"

"Nothing!" He beamed, then reconsidered. "Well, nothing important. Just a small incident with the—but that's not why I'm here!" His amber eyes were practically glowing behind his glasses. "I've made the most *fascinating* discovery about the ley line convergence patterns beneath the citadel!"

"Thrilling," I said flatly.

"No, no, you don't understand!" He pulled out Sims's Doom Scroll, now covered in his own incomprehensible notes and diagrams. He'd finally modified it, and judging by a few of the lines I saw scrolling past, had used Sebastian's suggestion of finding good news as well. "The harmonic resonance frequencies are completely unprecedented! If I can just calibrate the—"

"Griffin," Vex interrupted gently. "We're actually on our way to investigate something."

His eyes lit up even more, if that was possible. "Oh? What kind of something? Magical anomaly? Cursed artifact? Temporal distortion?"

"A hole," I said.

His face fell slightly. "Oh."

"A mysterious hole," Vex clarified. "Behind a wall. With strange noises."

Griffin's entire demeanor transformed. He practically vibrated with excitement. "What kind? Harmonic? Discordant? Are we talking spectral emanations or—"

"Whispers," I said. "Or singing. Or screaming. The workers couldn't decide."

"Oh, that's *magnificent*!" He clutched the Doom Scroll to his chest. "I must come with you! This could be exactly what I need to complete my calculations on the subsonic—"

"Absolutely not," I said.

His face crumpled. "But my lord, think of the scientific opportunities!"

"No."

"I promise I won't touch anything!" He held up one spindly hand. "Well, I won't touch anything without asking first. Or unless it seems really important. Or if it's making a particularly interesting sound—"

"Griffin."

"Right!" he squeaked. "Silent as a tomb! You won't even know I'm there!"

I highly doubted that, but the pleading look in his eyes was pathetic enough to give me pause. Plus, if there was something magical down there, having an enchanter along might actually be useful. Even if that enchanter had a tendency to accidentally animate inanimate objects.

"Fine," I said. "But if you so much as—"

"Thank you, my lord!" He practically bounced on his toes. "You won't regret this! Well, you probably will, but not immediately!"

The southwest wall was a hive of activity. Workers hauled stones and mixed mortar, repairing damage from our battle with the Hero's Guild. They scattered like mice when they saw me approaching, though a few lingered to stare at Griffin, who was already pulling out various magical instruments from the mysterious depths of his robes.

"Here." Vex led us to a section where fresh mortar showed recent work. "They covered it back up, but—"

I pressed my hand against the wall, sending out tendrils of shadow magic. There. A hollow space, just as she'd described. The stones below the new were different too—older, darker, not part of my original construction.

"Ooh!" Griffin had some sort of crystal pressed against the wall, and it was glowing faintly. "The thaumic density here is off the charts! This stone predates your fortress by *at least*"—he did some rapid calculations—"fifteen centuries! I can't believe we've never—"

"Stand back."

Vex retreated, dragging Griffin with her as he protested about needing more readings. I called my magic forward. The fresh mortar cracked and crumbled, stones shifting aside at my will. In moments, I'd opened a gap large enough to step through.

Cold air rushed out, carrying with it the scent of deep earth and a magic that made the runes on my bones ache with recognition.

"Fascinating!" Griffin had already darted forward, poking his head through the opening. "The temperature differential suggests a significant depth! And that smell—definitely Old Dominion construction. You can tell by the way it makes your teeth itch!"

"My teeth don't itch," I said.

"Give it a minute," he said cheerfully.

"My lord," Vex said quietly. "Perhaps we should bring backup."

"Where's the fun in that?" I conjured a ball of purple-black fire in my palm and held it out. The opening led to stairs carved directly into the rock. They spiraled down into darkness, worn smooth by countless feet over countless years. "Besides, it's my fortress. I should know all its secrets. And anyway, Arabella is the only person who could possibly get us out of trouble if we should find something I couldn't deal with. And she's busy catching up Lord Peregrine on pertinent information."

Neither Vex nor Griffin seemed comforted, as if they'd rather wait until Arabella was free. I grumbled and started down first. Vex followed despite her obvious reluctance. Griffin practically tumbled after us, his various instruments clanking and whirring.

"The acoustic properties are remarkable!" His voice echoed strangely. "I'm detecting at least three different types of stone in the construction, each with its own resonance frequency!"

"Griffin," I warned.

"Right, right, silent as a tomb!" He lasted approximately three seconds. "Though technically tombs aren't that silent. There's decomposition gases, settling stones, sometimes the occasional undead—"

"Griffin."

"Shutting up now!"

The temperature dropped with every step. My breath misted in the air, and frost began forming on the walls. The shadow fire in my hand flickered, fighting against some unseen pressure. We had passed the depth of the old foundation that housed the training room, and even the old storage space where Arabella trained with constructs.

Then I heard the sound the workers had described. Like whispers, yes, but also like singing. A chorus of voices just at the edge of hearing, but it wasn't a language I knew. The runes on my bones burned hotter, responding to those alien syllables.

"Oh my," Griffin whispered, all his manic energy suddenly subdued. "That's not good."

"What do you mean?" Vex asked.

"The frequency." He was fiddling with one of his crystals, which had gone from glowing to pulsing an alarming shade of red. "It's all wrong. Like something's trying to exist in two places at once."

"My lord—" Vex began.

"I hear it." I pressed forward.

The stairs ended abruptly, opening into a vast chamber that shouldn't exist in the floating rock below the citadel. My shadow fire expanded, trying to fill the space, but the darkness here was hungry. It ate at my flames, reducing them to a feeble glow that barely illuminated the entrance.

But what I could see made my blood run cold.

The walls were covered in carvings. Not just any carvings—runes that resembled the ones carved into my bones. Thousands of them, spiraling up into the darkness, telling a story I couldn't quite read but somehow understood.

"By the ancient texts," Griffin breathed, his voice barely audible. "These are . . . Primordial Binding Runes. The kind used to"—he swallowed audibly—"the kind used to imprison gods."

"How the hell do you know that?" Vex asked.

"I, um." He lowered his voice. "Ever since we learned of Lord Blackrose's alter ego, I've been doing some . . . reading."

"At least that's more helpful than illustrations from the Enchanted Isles," Vex muttered.

At the center of the chamber, barely visible in the dying light of my fire, something massive stirred.

"Lord Blackrose," Vex breathed, and I'd never heard that note in her voice before. "What is this place?"

I stepped forward, unable to stop myself. The whispers grew louder, more insistent, and for just a moment, I could have sworn they were calling my name.

Not Kazimir.

Something else.

"Um," Griffin squeaked, all his enthusiasm evaporating like morning mist. "I've changed my mind. I don't want to be here anymore."

The shadow fire died completely, plunging us into absolute darkness. But somehow, I could still see. The runes on the walls began to glow with a faint, sickly light, and in that illumination, I finally saw what waited in the heart of my fortress. My runes flared in recognition.

Griffin whimpered.

Vex's hand found my arm in the darkness, gripping it tight enough to bruise. "My lord, I think we should—"

But whatever she was about to say was lost as the thing in the chamber opened its eyes.

Griffin made a sound that could generously be called a squeak but was closer to the noise a stepped-on mouse might make. "Too late to run?" he asked hopefully.

The eyes—ancient, terrible, and familiar—fixed on us with interest.

"Far too late," I murmured.

The whispers rose to a crescendo, and the thing in the darkness began to move.

Acknowledgments

They say the second book is the hardest. They're right. But I've been blessed with people who made even the hardest parts feel possible.

To my husband, Eric: Thank you for not taking it personally every time you ask a simple question like "Do you want dinner?" and receive a hollow, unfocused stare from a woman whose brain is either complete mush or three chapters ahead of her fingers.

To Jeremy and Catie: Your enthusiasm continues to make me feel like the coolest person alive, which is a generous illusion I deeply appreciate.

To Nicole: Thank you for the continued late-night brainstorming and the unflinching feedback. You make every story better.

To my parents and the rest of my family: The formal request from book one still stands—do not read this one either. Just keep admiring the covers and telling people you're proud. I'm so grateful for your love and support.

To my incredible agent, Lauren: Thank you for your steadfast guidance. I remain astonished at my luck in having you in my corner.

To my brilliant editor, Sarah, and the entire team at Scarlett Press and Simon & Schuster: Thank you for giving Kaz and Arabella's continuing adventures such a wonderful home. Your editorial insight sharpened this book immeasurably, and your enthusiasm for these unhinged characters never fails to make my day.

To Nina and Brian: Thank you for once again lending your time and talent to this story. I'm endlessly grateful to you both.

And to every reader who followed these disasters-in-love from book one to book two: You're the reason this exists. Your reviews, messages, social media tags, and enthusiasm have been the greatest surprise of my life. Thank you for loving these villains as fiercely as I do. I hope the honeymoon was worth the wait.

TIFFANY HUNT writes all things fantasy romance with salty characters, action, kick-butt heroines, and spice. If it has castles, magic, and hunky, irresistible men (or elves, etc.), she's down for it. Her favorite tropes are enemies-to-lovers, one bed, fake dating, arranged marriages, and forbidden love.